GREEN WAVE

DAN KUESTER

Copyright © 2016 Dan Kuester
All rights reserved
First Edition

PAGE PUBLISHING, INC.
New York, NY

First originally published by Page Publishing, Inc. 2016

ISBN 978-1-68348-027-3 (pbk)
ISBN 978-1-68348-028-0 (digital)
ISBN 978-1-68348-029-7 (hardcover)

Printed in the United States of America

This book is dedicated to my lovely wife, Monique, and our two wonderful kids, Kalena and Ian. Without the support of these three people, this book would not have possible.

Also, to all my family members and dear friends who have tolerated my endless nattering about the work while in progress, thank you.

And to my mom and dad. Dad has recently raced on ahead without us. We will see you again.

PROLOGUE

The black-gloved hand reaches out to the slightly illuminated keypad that is adjacent to and controls the gray, metal, entry door. The tips of the leather-covered fingers touch down lightly on the pad numbers. Slowly, in the dim light, the nervous fingers press the sequence.

The man is dressed all in black on the dark night. He silently mouths the numbers and letters in English, a language foreign to him, as he presses them to make sure there was no mistake.

1…5…9…Alpha (A)…Lima (L)…Golf (G)…Alpha (A)…Echo (E).

With the press of each key, the pad emits a barely audible electronic beep.

The shadowy figure who is wearing the black gloves has a ski mask over his head, and a black sweatshirt and dark pants covering his athletic body.

In the roaring quiet of the evening, each slight beep is a shrill, ear-piercing screech that is certain to attract unwanted attention to him and his companion.

As the last (E) button in the sequence is depressed, the electric latch makes a slight click. The door unlocks and opens slightly. There is complete silence from the room on the other side of the door.

The figure breathes a thankful prayer that there is no alarm or buzz that signals that the door to the lab building is open at this late hour.

The gloved hand reaches out, and pushes the metal door open.

The intruder steps in.

The room is dark except for the safety lights near the floor, which give the lobby to the two-story building a soft glow.

"Perfect," thinks the man. The stocking cap on his head is warm for a May night in St. Louis.

For the first time all evening, the intruder has the courage to speak.

"The codes worked. Now, we just have to get the files and get out of here, Allah willing," he whispers.

Then, his partner follows him through the open door.

Even though they both are dressed identically, the two appear as different as night and day.

The first man is the taller of the two. He is also much heavier. Much thicker.

Not fat. Much more muscular. He's built like he lifts weights. The muscles showing through his lightweight sweatshirt reveal that he is a fitness fanatic, or, more likely, a military man, or even a mercenary. His broad shoulders and narrow waist give his silhouette a much more menacing outline.

The second man is about 5 five feet 7 seven inches tall, about 6 six inches shorter than the first, and he moves cautiously. He has an average-looking build, and probably doesn't need to be dressed in black to go unnoticed. His mannerisms and general demeanor don't look like someone who is comfortable breaking into the Danforth Laboratory on the campus of St. Louis University. He looks plenty spooked.

The two take another step inside. They let the heavy door close quietly behind them.

They don't take a moment to relax or celebrate.

The larger man puts his training to work right away. This is what he is built to do, and he goes about it effortlessly and efficiently.

His backpack slides easily off his back. He opens it silently and digs into its contents.

The smaller man also goes about his task quickly. He moves quickly because he doesn't want to spend any more time than he has to in this place.

He reaches clumsily into his backpack. He is neither as quick nor as efficient as his larger companion.

He retrieves from his pack an external hard drive to upload the information from the computer.

The glow from the safety lights is just enough to allow them to open their packs, and read the instructions on how to access the files they came for.

The small lobby area to the Danforth building is about ten feet by twenty feet. Near the back wall, there sits a modest admin desk. A couple government surplus guest chairs serve as the only stark furniture in this academic office space.

Sitting square in the middle of the top of the admin desk is the computer they are looking for.

The two are certain that they should be able to access all the files they need from this computer if their information is accurate.

Suddenly, a flash of light surprises the two. Someone from the far end of the hallway has turned on a light and the brightness spills into the lobby where the two are working.

It is only the semi-dull florescent light that is typical in these government buildings, but compared with the relative darkness, the light seems dazzling.

This is completely unexpected. The place is supposed to empty.

The two startled black figures look at each other.

The shorter one whispers, "There isn't supposed to be anyone here," in Arabic.

"I'll take care of this. You get those files," whispers back the larger, more confident man.

A voice calls from down the hallway. "Who is there?"

The larger man is quick to conceal himself behind the administrator's desk by the entrance to the hallway.

The smaller of the intruders is slower to react. He is forced to take cover in the only other place to hide and scurries behind one of the simple, metal chairs in the lobby.

His only hope of not being spotted is that the man walking down the hall is blind.

The voice from the approaching person calls out again, "Professor Hickson? Is that you? It's me, Xiang. What are you doing here?"

The two intruders are frozen as the voice grows closer. "I came in to put together some of the results to the work this week."

Into the lobby comes a 23-year-old grad student working late on the biofuel work headed by Dr. Elbert Hickson.

Xiang pauses. He looks around the lobby area.

The two men in black remain silent and motionless.

Xiang notices something odd behind the metal lobby chair and turns to examine it. His back is toward the desk.

Silently, and unnoticed by Xiang, the larger, black-clad intruder stands up behind the desk and raises his right foot onto the desktop.

The larger intruder silently lifts himself onto the desk while Xiang looks behind the chair and discovers the small man.

Xiang asks innocently, "Who are you…?"

At that moment, the dark intruder lets out a blood-curdling scream as he launches himself high into the air and comes down on his prey, the astonished Xiang, knocking him off his feet.

Xiang falls backward to the ground with the black-covered mass landing on top of him with a thud.

CHAPTER 1

"Crouch!"
"Bind!"
"Set!"

The rugby referee's calls were crisp, clear and had a rhythmic cadence.

On the command "Crouch," all sixteen men bent their knees and leaned toward their opposition. On the "Bind" command, props from both rugby packs reached out to one another and grabbed the shirt of the guy on the other team. On the "Set" order. The teams came together in a thick, solid thud. The ref nodded to the scrum half, indicating it was time to put the ball down the center of this man-made tunnel.

An audible grunt escaped from the two sets of goliaths as they pushed forward on each other's shoulders.

A rugby scrum looks a little like an American football play just before the ball is snapped when both teams are at the line of scrimmage. The largest and most powerful men are facing directly against the other team's strongest group.

In rugby, there are only three players in the front row. And instead of starting a play a yard apart as in American football, the rugby front row players in a scrum, are pushing against the other team with their heads and necks interlocked.

And unlike American football where these front row players are free to move their arms. In rugby, the front row players have their arms trapped behind the backs of players on their own team.

Paradoxically, as the two teams struggle to gain an advantage, they also must trust each one another to hold up the scrum.

The biggest difference between American football and rugby is the clothing.

Rugby players wear very few protective pads.

Some wear a small, leather or plastic cap to protect their ears. Others may wear a soft layer of padded protection inside their jerseys to absorb some of the contact during a match.

In addition to the slight protection, rugby players wear what is basically a pair of athletic shorts and cleats.

Their ball is a little bigger than an American football and is made to be a little easier to grip.

In a scrum, the three front rows are bound together. Then, two second row players are behind the front row. These men are crouched down and using their shoulders to push on the butts of the front row players. Behind them is another player bent over and pushing on the butts of the second row players.

Two flankers also help push the scrum forward by shoving on the outside butt cheek of the front row.

This time, as the scrum comes together, it collapsed between the two teams.

This is always a dangerous situation as the two front rows of the scrum fell down under the weight of their own inter-tangled strength.

In this formation, when the scrum collapsed, the players' hands were unable to break their fall. All six players in the front row—three from each team—had their heads driven hard into the ground. In addition to their own weight, which was ample, the entire weight of the eight men made for a dangerous situation.

In all, eight men from each team, sixteen in total, were pushing toward the center of the scrum.

That is nearly a ton of muscle and anger, driving the front rows together.

As the scum collapsed, the ref was quick to blow his whistle to alert everyone to stop the push.

Players from both teams' packs eased back. The front rows were at the bottom of the pile. They were the last get to their knees, and then their feet, and shake out the cobwebs and dust away the stars from their eyes.

Rugby is played with intensity, but not without humanity. Both teams were quick to help their own men up. And also help the men from the other team. They all knew that a collapsed scrum was a dangerous development in a rugby match. And since they were all amateurs, they equally understood that this game was nothing to get seriously injured over.

Just as quickly as the two sides untangled and helped each other to their feet, the accusations started about who was at fault for the collapse.

"Get him to bind right," shouted one of the large props wearing a black-and-white jersey at the ref.

He was talking to the ref, but there was no mistaking that he was shouting at the opposite player.

"BULLSHIT," the accused prop—wearing blue—responded. "He pulled it down."

The second prop emphasized his point with a sharp fist delivered to the underside of the jaw of the first player.

It was on.

All three front row players from each team were quick to follow suit. Each grabbing his opposite number and trying to deliver a few knuckles of understanding.

The ref blasted on his whistle and tried—not too hard—to get between the six fighting players. All of them were bigger than the ref who was desperately trying to get the players' attention. No luck.

"Blue, back away!" the ref shouted toward the blue team, with little result. Both sides continued to push and shove and grab the other players' shirt collars.

Another whistle and another order to stop.

"Black captain, get your players under control..."

After a few, quick punches between the props, aimed at each other's noses, the fight started to subside. The tense moment was over.

The ref stopped tooting his whistle, and the aggrieved players were subdued mostly by their own teammates.

There was scant more shouting. These moments can be common in a rugby match. And the referee doesn't mind them too much, because the referee knows that the players are engaged in a violent game. Sometimes that aggression comes out inappropriately, and that causes them to act poorly.

Off the rugby pitch, most of these men are businessmen and family men who dislike violence. The aggressiveness of the game seems to release their anger and allows them to become tame, almost docile off the field. But it is these short outbursts of temper that help the game continue without animosity. They can act like a pressure release valve that keeps the entire match from becoming a donnybrook.

"Captains, talk with your teams," scolded the ref, wearing a yellow, short-sleeved rugby jersey and white cotton shorts.

As much as the ref liked the players to shed their anger, Matty knew that he must keep control of the group. Once a match tips toward anarchy, the ref is almost powerless to regain control. Each captain marshalled his team into a small circle so he could calm his side down.

After addressing his team, the captain of the St. Louis Bombers—in the black—approached the ref from behind and put his hand on Matty's shoulder to get his attention.

The Bombers captain never got the chance.

When he put his hand on the back shoulder of the ref, the official nimbly took a quick half step forward and turned instinctively on his heel toward the captain. In the same pivot, he leaned back slightly and delivered a quick, smart blow of his own with the heel of his hand, jabbing firmly to the nose of the shocked captain. Matty had practiced this move hundreds of times in his military training and used it in the field on more than a few occasions. It was his favorite, and one of his most effective moves.

GREEN WAVE

The captain of the Bombers rugby club fell to the grass like a wet sack of potatoes.

He lay on the ground as though he had decided to take a nap.

Only, of course, the nap wasn't by choice.

The black captain had taken a hit, a hard punch, from one of the best, and toughest refs in rugby.

The referee of this Blues vs. Bombers match is Stuart Mateus, a.k.a. Matty, a former special-operations military man whose Navy training is never too far away. Matty even now still works for the government doing odd jobs. He spends his weekends trying to climb the ladder of international rugby refereeing.

Most players on the pitch know the rugby part of his résumé. A few know the military part.

The unfortunate Bombers captain just learned about it the hard way.

And because of his background, Mateus knows he had to be careful while he was reffing a match to ensure that he didn't get too worked up. He knew he needed to remain cool, especially when the players didn't.

And today, he was just starting to congratulate himself on keeping clear of the fight, when he felt that innocent hand on his shoulder that belonged to the Bombers captain.

Mateus was embarrassed that he got spooked and took down a player.

The captain lay motionless on the pitch. The Bombers coach came onto the field along with the team trainer. They poured water on the captain's forehead and tried to revive him.

"He'll be all right in a few minutes," said Matty to the trainer and coach.

While the captain recovered, Matty called both teams together and reminded them that there were strict sanctions against fighting in rugby. Any more of this and he would start sending players off.

"Any more of this nonsense and off you boys will go. No more of this shit. This is a good match and let's keep it going," Matty admonished them.

After seeing what the ref had done to the Bombers captain, both teams listened pretty intently and agreed heartily with the now highly respected referee.

"Yes, sir," members of both teams responded almost in unison.

After the chat with the teams, Matty knelt down on one knee over the captain. The captain was just opening his eyes.

"Sorry about that, Scotty," Matty said to the Bombers captain.

Matty had refereed Scotty's matches before, and the two were friendly.

"You know you shouldn't come up my backside and surprise me like that."

"Won't happen again," Scott Olring said as he came to his feet, a little wobbly in the knees for a second or two before he was steady enough to continue.

"Did you throw out that prick Blues prop for the cheap shot he gave our hooker?"

"I didn't because—"

"Well, tell them to keep up the scrum," Scotty interrupted. He knew he didn't have a chance to change Matty's mind, but was hoping to get a little sympathy for later in the match.

"Let's play some rugby," Matty interrupted him back.

The rugby game was ready for the restart.

The scrum was reset, the clock restarted and the ball was ready for play. Both sets of front row players, and all the members of both teams for that matter, were a little less eager to fight now, knowing that the ref could likely clean all their clocks.

"Crouch, bind, set," Matty repeated.

The scrum came together smoothly and cleanly.

The scrum half, with the number 9 on his back, put the ball into the mass. It was quickly heeled back through the two second-row players and without a single hand touching it on its journey, onto the feet of the man playing the position Number 8.

When the Number 8 had healed it out of the scrum, the scum half, who had now come around to the rear of the group, took the ball out of the back of the scrum and passed it out laterally to his standoff. And the game was off and running again.

Matty thought there was nothing as beautiful as rugby players passing the ball down the back line, one player catching the ball, handling it, and tossing to the next player. One after the other, after the next.

He loved the game, but not the fighting. He had gotten enough violence at his day job and while training as a field operative.

He loved the running around the rugby pitch, feeling the flow of the game. The great, green layout of the field. Watching the players showing off their skills and sometimes doing astonishing things during the matches.

The rugby pitch is just a little bigger than a football field. And on a cloudless day like today, it almost glowed with the intense green of the newly mowed grass.

CHAPTER
2

But today, Stuart "Matty" Mateus was distracted a little from the game right in front of him. And maybe that distraction caused him to lose focus and that might have led to the fight.

Matty was distracted because earlier in the match, he had seen Marty Bishop, his administrative contact from his federal agency Directed Discretionary Operations arrive at the sidelines to watch the game.

Whenever Matty saw Marty, he knew there wouldn't be time for postgame beers with the players. When Bishop arrived on the scene, is always meant Mateus was about to go to work.

In fact, whenever Bishop showed up at a game, or at Matty's house in St. Louis, or anywhere Matty happened to be, he knew his free time was over, usually for at least a few weeks.

Twenty minutes later, Matty blew his whistle to signal the end of the match.

The ref shared his customary handshakes with members of both teams accepting their congratulations on a game well officiated. In return, he always told them they had played well. It is a tradition in rugby to show good sportsmanship even after a match that produced some violence.

Matty had one more word with Scotty Olring about the punch he threw that knocked out the captain. Matty found, as he suspected, that there were no hard feelings.

Matty strode rather slowly to the end of the field, through the end zone, or try zone, as rugby players called it, and over the dead ball line.

A firm handshake from his co-worker of three years awaited Mateus.

"Good match," said Bishop.

Mateus disregarded the small talk.

"What is the mission?" asked Mateus, almost sounding annoyed. He was not trying to be short, but he didn't want to waste time.

"Algae," said Bishop.

"Huh?" asked a puzzled Mateus.

"Let's talk about it on the way to the Arsenal," said Bishop.

The two walked quietly and quickly to Bishop's government vehicle, a late-model dark-blue Chevy with four doors. It was very practical looking—trying its best not to look like an official government vehicle, which made it look exactly like a government vehicle.

The two pulled the doors shut and put the windows up. They were free to talk.

"What's this about algae?" asked Mateus.

"Well, we thought it was time to send you on an assignment that's in line with our latest directive from headquarters of being more 'green,'" said Bishop.

Bishop was pretty pleased with his little funny. After all, he had been working on the precise wording of this little joke since he had gotten into the car at the National Geospatial-Intelligence Agency Headquarters just south of downtown St. Louis and started his drive to pick up Mateus at the rugby pitch about an hour ago.

Mateus groaned to himself.

He didn't want to give Bishop the impression that his joke was even noticed. Matty knew that if Bishop sensed that someone was recognizing, or even enjoying his little efforts at comedy, the jokes would continue. And Stuart Locke Mateus did not want that.

Mateus knew that Bishop was a good guy at heart, and he didn't dislike him. It's just that Bishop was so different from himself.

For one, Bishop was still happily in the Navy. Mateus couldn't do it for more than the ten years he served on active duty, five at sea on board a destroyer, USS Neverdock he called it, and five more at an overseas billet in Naples, Italy.

Staying in the Navy was fine for guys like Bishop, figured Mateus. Bishop really knew how to play the game of office politics, and relationships, and meeting the right people, and having a sense of humor that would never offend, and therefore, in Mateus's mind, would never be funny.

Stuart Mateus ignored Bishop's joke and got down to business.

"What about the algae?" Mateus tried again.

"Well, here is what we know," Bishop handed Mateus a manila folder and started to walk him though the contents.

Giving debriefings is where Bishop earned his handsome U.S. Navy commander's salary. He could grasp the details of a government report, sift through what was important and was not, and give the boiled-down version to his colleagues and superiors quickly and efficiently. This skill always amazed Mateus.

"Item one," began Bishop, not knowing himself how good he was at this.

"The Danforth Plant Sciences Institute here in St. Louis does work on many different types of plants. They specialize in transgenic research. Do you know what that is?"

Mateus grunted.

It was clear to Bishop that Mateus didn't know anything about transgenics.

Bishop started into the backstory.

"Transgenic bio-research is taking a specific gene from one plant or animal and introducing it into another. For instance, say scientists have found a gene in a cactus that researchers believe makes that plant resistant to drought. Say, then, that scientists introduced that gene into a corn plant. Now, that would be very valuable to corn producers because they can plant that corn in areas that are traditionally drier. Even in the dry conditions they can still produce a good crop of corn. With me?" asked Bishop.

"Go on," said Mateus, genuinely interested but trying to stay cool in front of this guy who he regarded as sort of a dork.

"Now, where in the world would that be of good use?" asked Bishop.

"Africa, maybe?" Mateus said, genuinely unsure, he tried to make it sound as though he was being a smart-ass.

"Good, you are paying attention," said Bishop with a bit of sass that he got in his voice whenever he thought he had the advantage over Mateus.

Mateus understood the subtle dig from his superior and tried to show his interest a little more, but the comment by Bishop also allowed Mateus to return smart-ass fire with impunity whenever he felt like it.

The two continued the discussion of the transgenic research.

"What does that have to do with algae?"

"Getting to that," said Bishop. "Researchers at Danforth have been tinkering with the genes in algae plants, and found a way to make it grow and reproduce at an incredible rate. Now, that could upset the balance of power in the energy field."

"What?" Mateus was incredulous.

"I guess that's true. We're going to get a full briefing from the lab coats at Danforth in a few hours. Also, your buddy Steve Benson is flying in from Chicago to help with this one."

"How is his brother doing?" asked Mateus.

"Not good, I'm afraid. But he said he would like to get in on this. It might take his mind off the problem."

Mateus got a look of anxiety on his face thinking about the last time he and Steve talked. Steve's brother had been fighting through some lymphoma treatments and the outlook wasn't good.

While Matty was thinking about the situation with Steve's brother, Marty started the sedan and pulled it out of the parking lot and got on the road to the Arsenal, a government facility that housed a few agencies or portions of agencies over the years.

Mateus's look of concern for his friend soon turned to a sheepish grin as he started thinking about the seeing his old friend again.

The blue Chevy speed down Interstate 44 and headed for downtown St. Louis.

As usual, Mateus didn't know what he was in for, but so far, and as usual, he liked the idea that another adventure was ahead with his friend Steve.

CHAPTER 3

Steve Benson was seated in the small auditorium located in the central administration building of the St. Louis Arsenal.

Matty walked in and spotted him immediately.

The room was laid out like a small lecture hall on a college campus. Mateus had entered the auditorium though the door behind the lectern where the speaker was preparing his remarks. Mateus saw Steve and made a direct line for his old friend. On the way, Mateus ignored the military officers and civilians in the room who tried to make eye contact with him to give him a quick 'hello.' He walked past the speaker and brushed against him slightly and didn't even bother to apologize. He strode pell-mell to the bottom row of seats and up the stairs that led to the seating. He skipped up to the third row and slid into the empty seat beside his longtime friend.

"What is up, my friend?" Matty almost shouted above the murmuring of the ten or so people who were milling around waiting for the briefing to begin.

"Good. You?" Steve replied, equally glad to see his friend.

"How's Brett?" Mateus asked solemnly.

"Not good," Steve grimaced. "But I'm sure that he would feel better knowing that you were asking after him."

Mateus was a stocky man with broad shoulders. He stood 5 feet 10 inches tall and carried 212 pounds on his athletic frame. He was clean shaven today, because he was reffing a match, but usually wasn't bothered to rub against the razor more than two or three times a week, and only that often because waiting longer between shaves makes the process painful and long. He wore his dark brown hair short in a buzz cut. His face was well worn. He had a scar under his right eye brow and small bump in his nose where he had it broken when he was in a bar fight in Naples.

Other than the wounds, Matty's face was a fairly plain. Maybe it was a little more jowly than he deserved.

He wasn't overweight and only carried a few extra pounds, maybe fifteen, now that he was out of the service and getting close to thirty-three years old. But not enough extra to slow him down on the rugby pitch.

His hands were a little smaller than you would expect on a man of his size and his above-average strength. His physical appearance didn't give the visual impression that he was an emotional fellow. And for the most part, he wasn't. But for friends, especially lifelong friends, he was quite caring. He remembered birthdays, he asked about relatives, and he listened to the answers. Not many people that Steve knew still do the first two. Almost none do the last.

Benson knew that Matty's concern for Brett was sincere.

"Let's talk about it later," Matty said. "Do you know anything about this algae problem?" steering the talk to work, where he knew Steve would be comfortable.

"Dunno, sounds like something big though," said Steve. "Algae? Sounds like we are going back to biology class with this. Have you ever seen someone with a case of swimmer's itch? It's caused by this certain type of algae that gets onto your skin and can be itchy like crazy I guess. I've never had it, but I've seen guys who are scratching themselves raw with it. I bet that would drive me crazy…"

Just then, the lights dimmed and the presenter turned on his PowerPoint. On the first slide was the title "Algae and Geopolitical Implications."

Of the ten people in the room, most knew Mateus from his days in the Navy or his time at the Office of Directed Discretionary Operations—in the small auditorium that could hold around fifty.

At the flick of the lights the group moved quickly to their seats.

Marty Bishop had allowed the two old friends to talk and then he slid into an empty seat behind Matty.

"Where's The Admiral?" asked Steve. "He is never late to a briefing."

Admiral Guilbault-Johnson hadn't gotten to the lecture room yet, and he had earned a reputation of being punctual.

"Something must be wrong, or at least serious to keep the old man from an appointment," thought both Matty and Steve.

The Admiral, as he was known, always made sure that he arrived at all appointments from five to ten minutes early. He abhorred tardiness and incompetence. When The Admiral disapproved of something, he would often say that the offending behavior "betrays an untidy mind."

The speaker, Dr. Martin Spalding, hadn't started yet. He was dressed in a lab coat and appeared very professorial. He was maybe north of sixty and very much looked like you would think a biology professor should look. To get the attention of the group who were now all in their seats, he cleared his throat as a signal to his audience. He had never addressed a military audience and really didn't want to breach some unknown protocol.

His presentation was for the entire group, but everyone knew—including the speaker—that Stuart Mateus and Steve Benson were the two who most needed to get the facts. This presentation was aimed at them.

"Hello, I'm—"

Before he could even get out his name, the door behind the speaker flew open.

There was no door stop to slow the heavy metal, World War II-era door so when it swung all the way in and hit the brick wall, the contact made a metallic smashing sound that echoed through the hall.

The stunned speaker stopped his remarks.

Several military members of the audience instinctively reached for their side arms.

The Admiral came steaming through the door full speed ahead.

"MATEUS, BENSON, come here, now," said Guilbault-Johnson who quickly turned directly around 180 degrees and marched immediately back out the door and down the corridor to his office.

Both Mateus and Benson jumped from their seats, shuffled toward the aisle, walked down the steps and followed The Admiral, with Bishop, a few steps behind.

Bishop didn't have to be asked to go anywhere when The Admiral was concerned. He knew he was automatically invited along unless he was directly told to stay clear. He was The Admiral's right-hand man.

So much so that behind his back some people around the office called him Smithers—a reference to the sycophantic assistant on "The Simpsons" television show.

The Admiral was in his mid-sixties, six feet and one inch and had a full head of gray hair. He was a thin man with a very light complexion. He did have a ruddy red face when he was angry.

But he was a very temperate man, rarely raising his voice.

When he did shout, people noticed.

By the time the two men—three if you include Bishop—got to The Admiral's office, Guilbault-Johnson was already seated at his desk. Mateus and Benson immediately sat in the guest chairs closest to his desk. Bishop—who had the uncanny knack of finding a place in any room where he wasn't noticed and wouldn't be in the way—slid into the room and sat down in the hard, steel chair next to the door.

The Admiral's office was bare, almost Spartan. He never surrounded himself with memorabilia from travels or commands from his past. He preferred to emphasize his future. Walls were covered with his paintings, a hobby he was just starting. The different canvasses showed his remarkable growth in his hobby that he began at the age of sixty-two, just two years ago. The hobby really seemed to fit him and his meticulous nature. Always outwardly calm, The Admiral found the soothing effect of the brush strokes put his mind at ease. He was a commanding and composed presence.

On his walls were also several photos of his children. After forty years at sea, he had always felt guilty that he had not spent enough time with his kids.

His eldest daughter Trish, a beautiful short, blonde woman now in her thirties was a particular point of pride for him. More photos of her were on his wall and his desk than the other two children, who were also very attractive looking. Trish's petite build and sharp, blue eyes made her picture almost come alive. She was a beautiful girl.

There was not much else on the walls of his office. Not a wall hanging showing different types of knots. Nor a carved wooden ship from the golden age of sailing. Not even crest from any of the ships he had commanded.

The Admiral addressed his team.

The force and will in his voice often led those unfamiliar with The Admiral to believe that they were being shouted at, but both Steve and Matty knew different.

There was urgency in The Admiral's voice, but not a hint of anger or frustration.

"Your assignment just got clearer," said The Admiral, not wasting time on pleasantries even though he considered both Benson and Mateus to be dear friends. The Admiral hadn't had time to meet them before the briefing and thought he would have a chance to catch up with two of his favorite operatives before they were sent on assignment. Now it didn't look that way.

The Admiral knew about Benson's brother and his condition. The old man had tied himself in knots wondering if he should try to talk about the situation with Benson, or not. Or should he talk about it in private, since it was a personal matter. Or should The Admiral ask Benson about his brother with Mateus in the room, since the two both need to know if this would be a distraction and, more important, how it would affect the team.

He never really came to a clear idea of what he should do about it. So, The Admiral let it lay.

Sometimes, the best move is no move.

Right now, The Admiral also knew that Steve Benson's brother was not a situation to be mourned or pitied—it was a diversion to be minimized.

"Benson, your head clear?" the Admiral barked.

"Yes, sir," was the prompt response.

"Good, let's get down to it."

This was another of the Admiral's patent phrases.

This was the last time The Admiral would bring up Benson's brother unless Benson wanted to talk about it, or unless the situation was proving to be a hindrance to the mission.

"First, here is the briefing you were about to receive from Dr. Spalding from Danforth." The Admiral nodded to Bishop in the back of the room—who was almost forgotten about by the two operatives.

Bishop promptly handed Benson a computer thumb drive. Bishop knew that Benson was a practicing veterinarian. And even though he was distracted by his brother's illness, Benson would be the best one of the two to decipher the molecular biology in the presentation.

"We won't have time to go through it right now. We think we just found out who is behind this. But we still don't know why," said The Admiral.

"What is THIS?" asked Mateus, still confused about the mission.

"It is algae," said The Admiral calmly.

"So I gathered on the way down here—"

"I don't like to do this," said The Admiral, keeping on message and disregarding what he felt were interruptions. "But we will be sending you out blind. We don't have specific targets or motives or backgrounders. We will have to work fast and without a net."

"Second, two or more men broke into the Danforth Institute last night. We don't know anything about them. They killed a grad student. It appears to have been ancillary to their mission. One of the intruders was killed. Shot. We don't know how or by whom. By all first accounts, no one working in the building was armed and no security guards were near the incident. The escaped intruder has gone rabbit. But you boys will have to work just from that until we get a handle on the specifics. Right now I need you to go to Washington.

You will be looking for the person or persons who stole an algae file from Danforth."

Bishop broke his silence.

"Since there were no other known weapons in the building, is it possible that both people who were killed were the intruders?" he said.

"Good thought," responded The Admiral. "We think one of the bodies was an intruder, but the other is definitely a trusted grad student. He has been ID-ed by the professor. We are checking out all possibilities. Problem is, we just don't know yet."

"We don't know the names of the intruders or what they wanted with a file on algae research. Everything we do have—which isn't much—is in the file Bishop has for you," The Admiral continued.

Bishop efficiently handed Mateus a manila file.

"We have arranged for you, Mateus, to referee a PAC rugby match in Washington on their home pitch tomorrow at 1300 hours. Use the time between then and now to get smart about the case."

Refereeing a rugby match tomorrow, thought Mateus, was going to be difficult. He hadn't really had a chance to recover from the one he just finished.

It was only then that he realized that he was still wearing his gear from the match that he reffed at the Creve Coeur Park. And he had not filed a match report with the Missouri Rugby Union about the fight, or that he had leveled a player during the match.

Mateus couldn't think about that right now. He steered his mind back to the present. He had lots of questions for his boss, "What about—"

"Since you don't have any questions," The Admiral cut Mateus off abruptly. "Bishop is ready to take you to the airport. He has arranged the plane for a flight to Reagan Airport that leaves in about two hours. Since you are now on assignment, you'll be taking the usual precautions."

Benson asked, "So if we don't know who they are, why to D.C.? The situation happened here."

"Because if what we think happened, has happened, this may be a breach of energy security that has international implications," responded Admiral Guilbault-Johnson somberly. "This is not just a murder case about a couple poor saps in St. Louis. This could impact global energy policy, power, and national relations, and we will have to coordinate with lots of the D.C. groups…Homeland Security, Defense, State, and even the USDA."

"The Department of Ag?" Benson laughed.

"That's where they know about algae," answered The Admiral. "Now let's get down to it."

CHAPTER 4

The flight out of Lambert Field in St. Louis took off down the private runway with only the three operatives aboard—the pilot, Benson, and Mateus. The small jet was heading to D.C.

The plane reached speed on the runway and abruptly jerked skyward with the quick, sudden jump.

The pilot must have had gotten the word from The Admiral that time was critical.

Benson was sitting bolt upright in his seat and immediately began poring over the files about the algae heist on his laptop computer. He was looking at the PowerPoint presentation on the thumb drive that Dr. Spalding never got to show them.

"Too bad," thought Benson to himself, "it would have been an interesting presentation."

While Steve got to work looking over the file, Matty found a comfortable position in the chair across the aisle and tried to get some sleep. There were six seats in the private jet that was normally used to ferry high-ranking military and government officials to meetings around the country or the world.

From reading the files, Benson saw that Dr. Spalding worked as co-investigator with Dr. Hickson at the Danforth Institute. It was Hickson's assistant, Xiang, who was killed in the attack, or robbery gone wrong, or whatever it was. As best as Benson—a self-describer science nerd—could figure, the algae angle was an interesting one.

According to the Danforth's PowerPoint, algae, like most plants, never grows as large as it can because it is always struggling to get enough carbon dioxide. Biologists call this a limiting factor—limiting because lack of carbon dioxide (CO_2) is the reason that plants don't grow to their potential.

If the algae could get an unlimited amount of the so-called greenhouse gas, algae could grow and multiply at an incredible rate.

To facilitate the growth of cells, the researchers at the Danforth Institute isolated a gene in a rice plant that helps channel all the CO_2 that any plant can handle directly into the cells. Dr. Spalding had led a team of scientists that had taken that rice gene and introduced it into a certain type of algae. Once this was done, the altered algae can channel a virtually unlimited supply of CO_2 directly inside the algae cell. With the increase in CO_2, the algae grew at a rate that was almost unimaginable.

Benson was shocked. He checked the numbers again, but still couldn't believe it. He rubbed his eyes. Benson, who spent some time in a biology lab as a student, had known that noteworthy genetic improvements are measured in 1 or 2 percent "jumps." To increase the rate of any genetic change by 5 percent would put any researcher on the short list for a Noble Prize for science.

According to this file, the genetically "improved" Danforth algae saw an increase of 100 percent growth. "Twice as fast..." Benson muttered to himself. Now he understood.

Growth at that rate would allow for algae producers to make bio-oil at a rate faster than oil wells in the Middle East could pump it out of the ground.

But so what?

Steve read on as the plane buzzed on eastward over Indiana.

So, now we can grow algae faster than ever. Benson figured the worst that can happen is that the fast-growing algae will cover his farm pond twice as fast on his acreage back in Illinois with the slimy, green crud in July rather than August every summer.

Benson read on.

Algae is the target of researchers who want to turn it into biofuel ethanol. Algae has all the traits needed to become a solid and renewable source of fuel, just like corn does for ethanol. But better. For both corn and algae, the key to making ethanol is getting the starch of the plant separated from the protein. The starch is then converted into sugars and alcohols that are combustible as fuel.

The proteins and oils are either turned into feed for livestock or used in other agribusiness industries. Here is the kicker. Algae breaks down into the valuable starch easier than corn. That makes the conversion to fuel much easier.

Using either corn or algae or some other bio source, producers have to treat it with chemicals or heat or both to separate the protein and oil from the valuable starch.

But of all the fuels, algae can be separated the easiest. The starch separates from the plant's proteins with less intense treatment. That lowers production costs. Cheaper fuel from a more abundant source, algae was starting to look like a wonder fuel to Benson.

And best of all, it doesn't take corn out of the feed chain, so making algae-based ethanol would not increase food prices in the way that taking corn out of the agriculture chain does.

Some businesses have been working on this technology and have already made claims about how much ethanol their algae plants are going to produce in the next 5 to 10 years. These claims may be overly optimistic, according to the Spalding's PowerPoint from Danforth, but they were not impossible to conceive.

Steve squirmed in his roomy seat to get more comfortable.

The small plane's seats were spacious, and Steve's fit body nestled down into his, and it wrapped around his body.

The seat was more comfortable than he had originally thought, or maybe he was just more tired than he realized, but either way, sleep was coming, and he just realized how tired he was. He hadn't been getting much sleep at all lately with his brother Brett always in his thoughts. And today was worse than normal since he got the call from The Admiral's aide Marty Bishop that had woken him up in Illinois only about 16 hours ago. Since then, it had been calls and planes and government cars and meetings until he arrived at the St.

Louis Arsenal, and his friend Stuart Mateus had shown up at the lecture that never really got started.

Yes, it had been an exciting day.

Steve closed his eyes to rest for just a minute. He still had the boyish good looks of a man several years younger than his thirty-five years. In fact, he didn't look any older than the day he had allowed himself to be recruited into the office of Directed Discretionary Operations seven years ago as he was being released from the Army.

Steve had a pleasant, roundish face with straight, almost stringy blond hair that he rarely combed and was forever hanging into his eyes. He had the thinnish build of a man who spent much of his early years trying to lose weight for high school wrestling. His shoulders bent forward a little, typical of a man spending his life engaged in the physical labor of active farm veterinary work. His teeth were unusually white and straight, and a smile always seemed to be on his lips.

Still fit with deadly blue eyes and that full head of hair that still covered the top.

His face was friendly and Nordic. But when he was serious, a deep, almost cartoonish wrinkle would form on his brow. The 'Dorian Grey effect' Benson often called it. He always joked with his wife that the day he left his job at the DDO would be the day he would age quickly into an old man. So he just couldn't get out right now.

But he smiled less often in the past few years as the burden of his brother's illness weighed on him.

In all, he had spent less than two years on active duty in the Army. Mostly in Naples, Italy, where he met and befriended a Navy officer with whom he spent his time chasing girls. This new friend had an almost unpronounceable last name for the kid from the farm in Iowa. Ma-TAY-oos—what kind of name was that?

Steve was enjoying his time in the Army and serving overseas, even though he missed being back in the Midwest with his family. But after just 20 months on active duty, Steve got word that his brother Brett was ill. Steve asked for a compassionate release from the service to take care of things back home.

That was seven years ago. And his brother had so far survived the lymphoma that had taken so much of his strength. Now there was talk around Steve's family that Brett's condition had deteriorated to the point that he was ready to be put into a hospice. The doctors said there was really nothing more they, or modern medicine, could do for him. Since his condition was hopeless, they figured they might as well let him be comfortable. Steve knew there would be time to talk this over with Mateus during the course of the upcoming assignment, whatever it was.

About a week ago was the most recent time Steve saw his brother Brett. He was weak and weighed probably around 130 pounds. After his seven-year battle, the end looked close. Brett was no longer the 167 pounds he was in high school when he, also a wrestler—and secretly Steve's hero—wrestled his way to becoming a state champion in Iowa—one of the richest honors a person from the state can earn. He was also not near the 200 pounds he allowed himself to reach after his competitive days were through.

But Steve didn't want to think of his brother right now. He wanted to think about this new assignment with his friend Stuart. Steve didn't want to think about the Brett, but he couldn't help himself. He found himself thinking of their days growing up on the hobby farm outside of Cherokee, Iowa. They had a goat, named Billy of course. They had dogs and a few feral cats had made their home on the property. Steve's dad was a plumber who worked long hours and didn't have much time to spend with his kids. His mom took in laundry and earned what she could. Steve's best parent was his older brother Brett, and his best friends were Billy the Goat and the animals that shared the farm with his family.

He often thought that was why he became a veterinarian… because of the animals and the bond he formed with them while growing up.

With the plane engine buzzing, Steve's mind started to wander about the times when he and Brett would fight. Brett, four years older than Steve, was always careful not to hurt his brother. When Brett won the state wrestling championship, Brett shared the trophy with Steve. Brett let Steve wear the medal around his own neck. It made Steve feel like he had won it. Those were good memories for Steve. Maybe the best.

Steve lay back with his eyes closed. And reminisced on.

Like all brothers, they fought. Steve and Brett's fights were wild, but also tame. Brett was strong and, at the same time, gentle during those fights. There was never any danger of Steve getting hurt.

And sometimes, just by chance, Steve would get lucky and catch his older brother with a wild kick or wrestling hold and throw the older brother to the ground. Brett pretended to get angry and would chase his kid brother around the house. Brett wasn't really cross. He was just too proud to allow his little brother to win. When Brett chased Steve around the house, he always made certain not to catch him. Because if he did, he wasn't sure what he would do.

Learning to enjoy the physical contact helped Steve when he decided to join the Army right out of veterinary school.

When Steve was in officer training for the Army, he wasn't happy simply learning about military protocol and etiquette or "knife and fork" school as most veterinarian trainees did.

He wanted it all.

He wanted the full-contact drills with the infantry officers. He wanted the contact and punches. Benson was even on the boxing team for the six months he spent at officer training.

Maybe that was why he agreed to take this current mission. With life oozing out of his brother's body, maybe Steve was missing more than ever those days when the feel of a push or a shove, were the hidden feelings of the love of a caring older brother even as his life was leaving him at only 39 years old.

Whatever the reason, Steve was here, and he was ready. Maybe more so than he had been on any mission before as part of the DDO.

Steve was fiercely devoted to his wife of 6 years. Partly because Jeanne is very understanding about his odd hours at the veterinary practice. And also these spur-of-the-moment trips with his partner Matty. And partly because she could see right now that her tough guy husband, Steve, hurt inside whenever he saw, or even thought about his older brother in the hospice, waiting for that final phone call from the hospice staff. Forever waiting.

Steve was almost asleep now. His mind continued to drift. Back to a time when he was on a call to a farm to work with the cattle at his veterinary practice, Benson noticed the giggling farmers' daughters who were trying very hard to get his attention. The girls were shy, then loud. They didn't know to catch the eye of the handsome, young veterinarian.

Steve tried not to notice, but he did. He also tried not to become too flattered by it, but he was.

Not bad, he thought, for a man of his advanced age.

But thinking about it was all he ever did. He knew that there's nothing out there worth sacrificing what he had. And besides, it would be awfully bad for business if the farmers knew that the vet was doodling the local daughters.

Steve recently dropped some weight from a chiseled 150 pounds, to a still-respectable, but somewhat scrawny, 140. Those pounds still looked good on his athletic frame, but Steve could feel his trousers were looser than he liked. When he wore dress shirts, they were baggy and sloppy looking.

When he wore a shirt and tie to church on Sundays, the top button on his shirts drooped low around his neck and fasten about two inches below his Adam's apple.

He was getting puny.

He had been taking great care of himself for years. And not just because he liked the way the teenage farmers' daughters still looked.

A small bit of turbulence in the plane jarred Steve back to the present. He opened his eyes and immediately got back to the files.

After finishing the PowerPoint that The Admiral had given to him, Steve re-adjusted in his seat and opened the file folder that Bishop had given him.

The file picked up the story where the Danforth file had ended.

Cheap, available, and fast-growing fuels that can be produced in a lab would put a huge dent in Middle Eastern oil prices. If this were to happen, read the file, the world petroleum market would descend into chaos.

Steve didn't understand international markets, but it didn't take Charles Schwab to understand the concept. That must be the reason that the algae plans were stolen. What seemed to Steve like some silly cat and mouse over some odd algae technology was serious enough to get two people killed, so far.

CHAPTER 5

Steve looked over at his friend, Stuart Mateus, who was fast asleep. From a deep slumber, Stuart "Matty" Mateus started to awaken. He gave a shake of his head from side to side like a pitcher shakes off a sign from his catcher. His eyes cracked open.

When he was asleep, he was all the way asleep. No sound, no movement, no dreaming that he could ever remember.

He was a better sleeper than waker. It took him a few minutes to clear out the hold that sleep had on him.

There was a little corner of dry, white spittle residue on his mouth.

Matty was a big man and fit a little too snuggly into the airplane seat, even on this luxury airplane. His sleep wasn't very restful, but he was happy to get any down time after a match.

He finally woke up with the grace and demeanor of a bear from hibernation—with a growl and a snort and quick stretch.

"How you doing, twiggy?" he asked Steve when he opened his eyes. He immediately stuffed his hand into the pocket. He was looking for his whistle and referees book. Just an instinctive habit for a referee. His rugby shorts were no longer the crisp, white rugby shorts he put on this morning. They had gotten a little dirty and very sweaty during the match.

"Ah, I'm still wearing my kit," he said.

"Pretty good, tubby," replied Steve. "How about you? I bet you're good. At least it looks like you're eating well, huh? Geez, bubba, try to mix in a salad every now and then, OK? I'm a medical professional."

"Well, yeah, I mean you're a vet, you couldn't get into med school and now they don't let you treat real people," Mateus interrupted.

"That is still funny, even after, what? Six years of telling me that joke. Still…Still funny," said Steve. "Speaking of food, have you ever been to these organic places with the juice and the wheat grass and the whole thing. We got one in Palatine now. I think it's the Green Grasser, or something, anyway, me and Jeanne went in and had some wheat grass shots or something like that. You may not like it since they don't serve alcohol, Mr. Booze Bag, but it really wasn't bad. I don't think I could live on it. But maybe it would be a good idea for you and your little friend, there, Capt. Stomach."

The Captain Stomach that Benson was mocking about was the little paunch that Matty had let grow around his mid-section. He wasn't fat. He still wore a size thirty-four waist on his rugby shorts. He always told himself that that wasn't bad. But in truth, it was still 2 inches more than he liked. And getting a load of crap from his slender buddy, just reminded him of his ever-expanding girth.

Matty would like to get back to his weight in the military when he was a fitter 200 pounds. He was rock solid, strong, and intimidating. And that was how he liked it.

But if was ever going to return to 32 inch waist, he has needed to start turning things around.

Right now, he was going the wrong direction. Even as the current thirty-four-inch shorts were snugger than he would like. He knew that if he didn't get control of it, he could end up like his father at his death—almost four hundred pounds and barely able to get around the bedroom in his home.

For right now, the 212 pounds he carried on his frame was too much, but only a little too much. And he could lose it if he wanted. Right? Sure. Sure.

"You are always a delight to have around, Steve" Matty deadpanned.

"And around is just what you are getting, my friend," Steve countered.

"We've got to start thinking about work," Matty had had enough of being teased by his friend.

"What do you think about Guilbault-Johnson always with the 'usual precautions'? Sometimes that guy is just weird," Matty added.

"Yeah," agreed Steve. "Why doesn't he just say that you are going to referee a rugby match while you are in D.C. and leave it at that? 'The usual precautions'? I think he believes himself to be in a movie when he says crap like that," said Steve.

Matty started to giggle to himself about the ominous-sounding "the usual precautions" from The Admiral.

"Yeah," added Matty. "Guilbault-Johnson always makes it sound like he is going to get plastic surgery or wear a jet pack or have some James Bond-style meeting with 'Q' to outfit him with a laser beam gun."

Matty and Steve didn't really ever go undercover like actors do in the movies.

For one, they wouldn't be very good at it. For another, the missions they undertook for the DDO arose too fast to establish a cover, make connections, and carry out a well-planned action.

They relied on the half cover of being a rugby ref, or a couple of tourists, or whatever seems to fit the need.

"Have you had a chance to look through the file?" Matty asked finally, fully awake. He knew that the meticulous Steve would have already digested the facts.

"It is about the algae," Steve mocked in Bishop's voice.

They both laughed out loud.

After Steve explained the science and implications to the world of petro-dollars, Matty still didn't understand everything, and he knew he didn't really need to.

"So, this guy—" Matty began his recap of the job.

"Or these guys," Steve corrected him.

"…Or these guys," Matty picked up. "Have something—"

"Took something," Steve said.

"That we need to get back," said Matty. "Do I have the gist of it?"

"As always, you are right on top of it," said Steve.

"And this thing that we have to get back…it is in the form of some computer disc, or drive or file," continued Matty.

"Exactly," concluded Steve.

Matty wasn't finished feigning ignorance.

"And if we don't get it back, thaaaaat's…," Matty waited for Steve to jump in.

"That's bad," Steve finally took the bait.

"Very bad?" queried Matty mockingly.

"Yes, very bad," said Steve.

"Okey dokey. Then let's get it," said Matty.

It the end of their little silliness, Steve Benson and Stuart "Matty" Mateus opened and turned on their mobile phones to collect messages they knew that The Admiral had surely sent while the two were in transit.

The two had turned off their phones while traveling.

Steve turned his off because he didn't want to be interrupted while looking at the files and wanted to absorb the information.

Matty did it because he was tired.

Besides there was really nothing they could do while they were 10,000 feet in the air anyway.

As they turned on their devices, each had a message from The Admiral.

CHAPTER
6

As soon as Steve and Matty left The Admiral's office to make their way to the airport from the St. Louis Arsenal, the old man had gotten to work.

His staff of Intelligence officers were examining and re-examining satellite images from the previous night.

The National Geo-Spatial Intelligence Agency was the parent agency of the Office of Directed Discretionary Operations. The NGIA is co-located with offices in both Washington, D.C. and St. Louis. The St. Louis office was a smaller, satellite office that carried out some of the less official functions of the agency. The Admiral preferred to keep his office in the Midwest even though the agency would have liked him to move to the capital. He liked keeping a certain distance and anonymity that working in St. Louis afforded him. He also thought it was a better place than Washington to help his daughter Patricia recover from her issues.

The Admiral was especially careful to make sure that he could keep his office and title as the Director, Office of Directed Discretionary Operations headquartered out of St. Louis so the politics and prying eyes of congressional subcommittees would find it difficult to investigate the organization.

They were a squeaky clean organization. The Admiral saw to that.

But the investigation that the agency always feared was one that was driven by politics. The Admiral always believed that if the public knew what the office did, they would support him. What he feared was a budget-cutter telling half the story and trying to sway political opinion. Guilbault-Johnson knew his office could look like a real band of cowboys and therefore become a target for shut down if the right group tried to destroy them politically.

Republican budget cutters would love to find out about a semi-clandestine organization that had little oversight. That is always the perfect recipe for getting denied funding.

From the outside, the NGIA building that contained the offices of the DDO on the grounds of the St. Louis Arsenal looked just how a two-story government-contracted building from the 1950s should look. Simple brick, block-shaped with few windows.

Inside, however, the place was a high-tech menagerie.

The most impressive technological wonders are the six operational theatres in the building that had been retro-fitted with eighty-inch, ultra-high-definition television monitors. The screens were constantly updated with real-time satellite images from various "birds'" orbiting earth.

Each of the six 'ops' theater areas were staffed twenty-four -hours each day by military uniformed personnel, as well as civilian workers for the Department of Defense and civilian contractors who provided support for all the technical equipment in the building.

The map room—the area where all imminent situations are played out—was known as Room One and has a huge screen, more than 100 inches of high-def glow. It is mounted 10 feet off the ground with conference tables, work spaces, and viewing stations situated around the thirty-foot by thirty-foot space.

Whatever was on this biggest screen in this Room One was the highest priority of the mappers—the name used for the technicians who are constantly monitoring the images that were projected on the LED screen.

Room One was built somewhat like a theater. On one side of the room was the big screen—the civilian techies who worked on it called it Radiation King. The room also had several smaller, 4-foot by 6-foot screens on the side walls. These smaller screens usually had satellite images in support of the main screen, and also showed text readouts of communications.

Currently, The Admiral was watching Radiation King which was replaying scenes from the area around the Danforth Institute from last night. Some of the smaller screens were showing a section of Washington, D.C., around the Department of Agriculture building.

Along with the images taken by the satellites, there was other information displayed on the screens. Latitude and longitudes of the images. Time and date stamp. Likely subjects in the images. And other info as the staff thought would be helpful.

The screens also estimate the size, weight, dimensions, height, material, and density of the subjects on the screen. This was an experimental part of the computer diagnostic system. Sometimes it worked and agents could get critical information and vital elements of an event in real-time.

For instance, if the satellite sees a small object that moves slowly, it may guess that it is person. If the object is larger, heavier and moving more quickly, I will estimate that the object is a car.

But just as often the computer wasn't able to analyze what was on screen and the agents could get better information about the elements at an event by looking at Google Earth.

Over the past 12 hours, since the time directly after the murders were discovered at Danforth, Admiral Guilbault-Johnson had his best mappers reviewing the areas around the Danforth Institute looking for anything that might give them a clue to what had happened in the area.

The Admiral had his team checking on the images from last night analyzing anything the satellites could pick up.

Right now, he was not in a patient mood. He needed to find out any information that his two operatives could use.

"Well, what did we see?" he said to no one in particular while sitting in Room One looking at the Radiation King. He always used the first person plural when talking with or about his team. "We can't have that much image to review from midnight to 6:00 a.m., can we?"

No one in the room looked at the boss because they had nothing to tell him. Did the 'sats' get lucky enough to pick up any images of cars, equipment or people poking around the Danforth neighborhood? Did anyone over at the Department of Homeland Security know of anyone in the area who fit the profile of this crime? The Admiral looked around the room. He was nervous. Since no one was answering him, he knew that answers were not presenting themselves very quickly. He got up from his seat in the big ops room and walked down the hall to his office.

He got out of the big ops room because he liked to pretend that he was disgusted at the slow pace of the getting answers. But mostly he got out of there because he knew he was just making all thirteen of his agents working on the case very nervous. By getting out, the team could focus on the job and not on whether the boss was looking at them.

Guilbault-Johnson's office was as plain as white toast. Government chair. Government desk. Government file cabinets. All gray and as boring as an electric car.

He sat down and started to fidget in his chair He knew that he had sent his boys out flying blind as he put it with no real leads, only a direction.

A good Intel man would have provided his men both. He didn't. And it ate at him. So while he waited for images to come through from last night, he started to work the Intel from the human side.

He had to get something more for the team to use. If they know what to look for, there was a much bigger chance that they could find it. He needed some Intelligence on the killer and he didn't know how to find it other than get it the old fashioned way…looking for it, searching, reasoning, deducing what they knew. And then using facts and conjecture to figure out what they thought might be going on.

The Admiral laid out the facts to himself: two bodies found dead in the entry hallway of the Danforth Building on the campus of University of St. Louis.

Tap. Tap. Tap.

The Admiral hoped that the three smart knocks on his door would bring some good news for a change. "Come."

Lt. Jackson entered the office.

She was a perfect-looking Navy officer. More than 5 feet and 8 inches tall. She was perfectly shaped and fit into her uniform like someone right out of the Navy Exchange catalogue.

Her face was dark, almost like Africa dark. A perfect dark chocolate 80 percent cocoa. Her lips were full, but not big. Her face was thin. So thin that it seemed to pull her eyes back to the point she looked a little like she could be part Asian. At work, she wore her hair back in a tight bun under her garrison cap. She could have been a Victoria Secret model. But at work she was all business. Everything was by the book. And for her, that book was Official Navy Regulations, the guide to all things Navy.

She also led the best team of analysts at the National Geo-Spatial Intelligence Agency—in either St. Louis or Washington.

"Yes," demanded Guilbault-Johnson as Jackson walked in.

"Sir, we have some images on the set," said a confident Jackson.

"Go on, man," implored The Admiral.

The Admiral formerly prodded his charges onward with the expression "go on, boy."

But 10 years ago, one of the officers who worked at the DDO filed a formal complaint against him. The young officer was black and Guilbault-Johnson is white. The young officer, Lt. Herbert, who would later transfer to the D.C. office, thought that The Admiral was using racist language and didn't like it.

At the time, when Guilbault-Johnson was formally counseled, he didn't understand the problem. The Admiral actually met with a counselor who suggested that he try using other, less offending language. The Admiral actually invited the counselor to meet with him at his office across a very intimidating conference table at the DDO. The Admiral loved to get every advantage at every encounter.

At the meeting Guilbault-Johnson still didn't understand. "What offending language?" he asked at the meeting.

"The use of the word 'boy' when addressing fellow officers or even enlisted men, or even civilians is not acceptable," the counselor told Guilbault-Johnson. "Especially if they are black."

"But he is a boy!"

"What are you saying?" asked the astonished counselor. "I'm saying I'm sixty and Lt. Herbert is twenty-six! What else am I supposed to call him?" The Admiral asked.

"How about lieutenant? Or Mr. Herbert? Or any other dignified title," the counselor answered. "You know, people don't like to be called boy. The blacks have a little unpleasant history in this regard. I think you could make an effort."

Until this meeting, the counselor, a young black, female civilian Department of Defense employee had assumed that Guilbault-Johnson, who grew up in North Carolina, was being an obstinate old crank trying to stir up trouble for the young Herbert. Now she started to realize that he simply didn't understand that the 'boy' label can be a charged one.

"I call my own children 'boy'," Guilbault-Johnson explained. "It is a term of affection. A term of respect. And I won't be bullied into changing it."

"You may not be bullied," said the counselor, whose name Guilbault-Johnson had forgotten about 10 minutes after the meeting ended. "But you will change."

The counselor stood and stared at The Admiral defiantly.

The Admiral had not been talked to like that since he was a junior officer. And, you know, he sort of liked it.

The two public servants had both dug in pretty deep. They each stared firmly at the other. Not budging....5 seconds, no movement...10 seconds...the stare down continued.

Finally, Guilbault-Johnson started to soften and even managed a little smile.

When the counselor saw that the ice was melting in the room, she started to smile. She knew she was right and had won, but didn't want to leave the room as adversaries.

"So what do we do next?" asked Guilbault-Johnson.

"How about you just use 'man' instead of 'boy'?" she suggested.

"Damn fine idea," he said "Damn fine."

That was two years ago.

It took The Admiral years to discontinue using the word 'boy' and substituting the word 'man'. It would likely take him another 10 years to change from 'man' to 'woman' for Jackson. By that time he would be retired and out of the language-correct Navy that he was now part of.

To The Admiral's delight, Lt. Jackson didn't mind 'man.'

Lt. Jackson walked around The Admiral's desk and sat the chair next to her boss and took control of the desk computer.

"What do you have?" the Admiral asked.

Jackson touched the screen to bring it to life and entered the security codes to get into the system. All the computer monitors of the Office of Directed Discretionary Operations resembled huge tablet-style computers that could be operated by the keyboard or manipulating the screen.

Jackson talked while she got the old man's computer up and running.

CHAPTER 7

The screen on The Admiral's desk revealed the satellite images that were taken the night before as it flew over St. Louis.

Lt. Jackson explained the images, even though The Admiral could clearly see them himself.

The Admiral settled into a chair behind and to the right of the young lieutenant where he could see the computer but wasn't too close to be uncomfortable.

"Early last evening, at 1930 hours, one man entered the Danforth Building. We believe he may be Xiang. As you can see, his dark, straight hair and general appearance support the assumption that he is Asian. This is the man who would later become one of the victims," she reported matter-of-factly.

The Admiral jumped in, "What else to do we know about this Oriental…"

"Asian, sir," Jackson corrected. "Oriental is no longer the acceptable term. Remnant of Empire and all that, sir."

"Yes, we must keep it tidy," acquiesced The Admiral. "Any way, what do we know about him? Any connection to, well, any of this?"

"No, sir," replied Jackson. "He seems like he was just a wrong-place-at-the-wrong-time situation. We could look into him more, but I don't think— "

"Fuck him," said The Admiral. "If you don't like him as interesting, I don't either. Continue."

"Fuck him, aye, sir. Early the next day, 0030 hours, we can see that two figures here," she said.

Jackson pointed to the satellite images on the computer screen highlighting the blurry moving forms in the dark that are barely visible to untrained eyes. "The two approached the Danforth Building in an unusual, or possibly stealthy, manner."

"Mmm, good work, Jackson."

"As these two are next to the hatch trying to gain entry, it is easy to note that these two take a little longer than one would estimate would be the expected time to open the hatch." Jackson enjoyed using full-on Navy jargon when making her reports to superiors. "This indicates that they may not have been familiar with the opening mechanism of that hatch."

"What do they look like, man, these two?"

"Difficult to say, sir," replied Jackson. "One is larger and possibly an athlete or soldier. Moves like a pro. Other is smaller and moves awkwardly. Both have hair that is covered, so we don't have that bit of info. Maybe they are dark completed, Hispanic, or Middle Easterners. Again, hard to say. Since one dead is a Middle Easterner, we think, the other one may be as well."

"The little one get killed in some struggle? Is that your guess?" pushed Admiral Guilbault-Johnson.

This part of the chase always got his blood racing, even after four decades of being on the hunt. "Actually, it looks like it was the bigger, athletic one who was killed," said Jackson.

"Odd. Anyway, how is the hatch secured?" asked The Admiral.

"According to early reports from Danforth, it is a simple 10-key cipher lock triggered by an eight- or nine-digit entry code. Pretty simple to break by professionals."

"What was the code?" queried The Admiral.

"Already asked and awaiting a reply from Danforth. It may be a local code set by the user."

"Doubt it," snapped The Admiral. "This was a centralized system. This research was too important to be under the control of a graduate student who might put in his girlfriend's measurements as the code. Were the two figures at the door long enough to break the code? Or disable the alarm, or the lock?" asked Guilbault-Johnson.

"No, sir. They were at the entrance for less than a minute," Jackson was proud that she had already checked this and had the answer at the ready for The Admiral.

"Then why do you say that is longer than normal?"

"It took Xiang only five seconds to enter the proper code when he entered the building five hours prior to these two…er, is it too early to call them suspects?"

"Not too early. So, if these two took longer than the Oriental guy—"

"Asian, sir."

"Asian, but not long enough to break the code, what does that tell you, Jackson?"

Jackson paused…"I don't know."

"Were they drunk? This was late Friday night, you know," asked The Admiral. "If so, that would account for both the delay in getting the door open and for the unusual walking approach. Does the key pad have a light? The Asian entered while there was still plenty of sunlight. If you two suspects arrived at an unlit pad, they may have had trouble getting it open."

"I don't know," said the lieutenant.

The Admiral was never too busy to walk a junior officer through some logic exercises. He felt talking through a situation was often more important than the high-tech "gizmos" he called them that were supposed to aid in these types of Intel gathering. Logic was the key to all Intel work.

"Lieutenant, you've done some great work so far," praised The Admiral. "Now, let's keep it going. Do we know if the two figures took more than one try to enter the security code into the cipher lock?" asked Guilbault-Johnson.

"Why does that matter?" puzzled the junior officer.

"You tell me," prompted The Admiral.

"Because if they took two tries, or more, that would allow for your drunk or dark theory?" asked Jackson.

"It isn't my theory. We don't have time for any blasted theories yet. We are still getting facts," said Admiral Guilbault-Johnson. "Once we get more facts, we will have time for theories. But the answer is 'yes'. Drunk takes two tries to enter the code. While cautious and unfamiliar—and maybe foreign—takes one try to get the codes. But it can be a long and slow try to open the door."

Without prompting, Jackson, still at the Admiral's desk, cancelled out of the government secured maps-and-imagery program that she was using to brief The Admiral. She immediately logged onto the Web site for the Danforth Institute security department. Earlier she had gotten access and permissions from the security and IT people at Danforth.

Jackson was very adept at getting through unfamiliar computer systems and found no problem navigating into the information she was looking for on the Danforth site.

The entire process took about a full minute.

"Sir," said Jackson.

"Yes, man," replied Guilbault-Johnson. "…er, Jackson."

"The group of two men took only one try to open the cipher lock."

The Admiral frowned a little, thinking that he had lost a lead.

"But," said Jackson, "they pushed the keys very slowly. It took them almost a full minute to enter the pass code."

The Admiral became interested. "How long did you say…?"

"Less than 5 five seconds, sir," Jackson said, anticipating Admiral Guilbault-Johnson's next question of how long it took Xiang to enter his key code.

"They were not drunk then, right, Jackson?" said The Admiral. "And when they were approaching the building—"

Just then, Bishop knocked on the door to The Admiral's office. He was just returning from dropping Benson and Mateus at the airport, Lambert Field.

"Good man, Bishop," said The Admiral. "Jackson figured out who the murderers were. These two…"

Jackson hurriedly backed up the program showing the video on Guilbault-Johnson's computer screen just in time for Admiral Guilbault-Johnson to point out the figures to Bishop.

"…men here. Now, you can barely see them dressed in black and approaching the building from the south. We need to know who these men are. What they were doing. Why they were doing it. And where are they taking the algae information they got from Danforth. Get Homeland Security chief on the phone priority one. I will speak directly."

"Guilbault-Johnson here. How are you, Secretary?" said The Admiral into the phone.

"Great, great to hear it," The Admiral continued. "Say I have a problem with which I think you are uniquely situated to help. Got a minute?…Mmmm Hmmm. Fine, oh, busy my goodness, yes… Oh yes, that's long over. Turned out I'm just too old and set in my language….Well, I appreciate your helping out with that. And why didn't you ever say anything about it?…Well, it was a problem. I just didn't know it was. I'm not a China doll, you know. I won't break…. That's damn nice of you, Marcus, but I would feel better if you had brought it up. I mean, we've been friends for 30 years, well, I guess closer to 35 now…

"Anyway, we have two people, look like maybe Middle Eastern descent that may have caused us some problems here in St. Louis last night. One is dead and the other is a rabbit. Yep. Don't really know. They may have been here for months as far as we can tell. Maybe just days. Our first guess is more than 30 days, but that's all we have.

"Yes, it is the one that you've likely seen in some of the message traffic. Second body was collateral looks like…Mmmm Hmmm. Interesting. Is that right? Good. OK, thanks. Love to your wife."

The Admiral hung up.

"Jackson, Bishop, here is what we know, or what we think we know. The two men may be a couple from Iraq named Farooq Ali Jr. and Hussain Islam."

The Admiral explained that the two had been in the United States posing as tourists. Because of some of their connections back in the Middle East, they had been under the passive watch of the Department of Homeland Security. The two had come from Baghdad 32 days ago on a tourist visa. The tickets were purchased by a third man Qfar Mohammad.

"How do you know that?" asked Bishop, partly because he didn't know that answer, and partly because he knew The Admiral liked to talk about his progress when he was gathering information. It's not that Bishop was a suck-up to the boss. Bishop was a career administrator, and he looked and acted like it. He was 5 feet 10 inches tall with brown hair cut perfectly to Navy regulations. His khaki uniform was always neatly pressed, but not too neat as he was careful not show up his superiors. Bishop's face was a little white and doughy from lack of exercise and sometimes shows signs of rosacea—a red, puffy condition—when he drank coffee or got excited.

Bishop was so squared away that he may go unnoticeable entirely, except for the small scar running from the outside corner of his right eye two inches back toward his ear. No one knows how he got it, but it added an element of intrigue and mystery to an otherwise plain wrapper.

Behind the unimpressive exterior, Bishop had a sharp mind that could find relevance and importance to facts and figures that others miss. Five years ago, when Guilbault-Johnson needed an aide, he sought out Bishop who he had seen several years ago at an Intel officers' convention. The Admiral was never disappointed in his choice.

Bishop knows that drawing out his supervisors into speaking freely, even rambling, can be good at getting information from him that they may otherwise omit.

"The Department of Homeland Security has been keeping an eye on these two since they got here," said The Admiral. "They had been acting strangely, so they have had only had soft surveillance on them. Marcus is sending me the file on them now."

"One of the men," The Admiral explained, "was a member of the People's Freedom League in Iraq. It was one of several militant groups that Homeland Security was aware of. But beyond that, facts were hard to come by on this group. The only information they have is that they were an 'active' group."

While The Admiral was explaining the set up to his two most trusted aides, he received an e-mail from Marcus, at Homeland Security that contained the documents he had hoped for.

The Admiral asked the two to stand by while he turned his attention to his computer.

Opening the file, Guilbault-Johnson could see that Qfar's file was in interesting one. He pored over the electronic documents. Jackson and Bishop were preparing for a long, marathon session of silence as they often had to endure. Both were young and unmarried with little else to do, or so The Admiral always assumed.

They looked at each other and gave exasperated looks. They both thought "Another Saturday night down the crapper."

"Yes, here we are," said The Admiral to Jackson and Bishop after five minutes. "It seems that our two burglars—Ali and Islam—have been making quite a name for themselves around town over the past two months. They've gone out of their way to act as though they were terrorists or at least didn't conceal it if they were."

"How do you mean, sir?" asked Bishop. He knew The Admiral like to be prompted.

"Yes, good question, Bishop," he said. "Well, for instance, the DHS report says that these two have been under watch for almost the entire time they were here. About three weeks ago, the two were in a club near SLU and got into a scuffle with some local college kids. The two weren't arrested, but when police showed up and took a report, a couple of bar patrons said our boys, uhh, men, had been in a shouting match with some drunks. The boozers heard the visitors talking too loudly about Allah and confronted them. Same thing happened at a Cardinals game about two weeks ago."

"SLU? sir?"

"Sorry, St. Louis University. The fighting Billikens. College kids there often blow off a little steam by quaffing some brewskis at the local pub. Ali and Islam were trying to stir up some trouble, looks like," The Admiral explained. "Now, I ask you two. Why would two guys make themselves look like terrorists and extremists if they were not terrorists nor extremists? It would be counterproductive to give yourself away, to say the least…"

"But if your motive was not terrorism, then it would be a pretty believable cover story," jumped in Jackson. "Especially, for a couple Middle Easterners who were new in town with no local ties."

"Interesting theory. Seems strong enough to give to our boys on the hunt," said The Admiral.

Bishop immediately started to put the theory into a summation that he would forward to Stuart Mateus and Steve Benson who were still in the air on their way to Washington. It was about midnight Eastern Time and the two operatives would just be getting into Reagan National Airport.

The Admiral also sent several classified attachments to Bishop to forward to Benson and Mateus to explain the background on the burglars to include in the communication with the operatives.

CHAPTER
8

Matty was wide awake as the plane landed in Washington, D.C. When he and Steve got off the plane at Reagan National Airport, they knew a lot more than when they took off two hours before in St. Louis.

While the two were opening and reviewing the documents that Bishop sent, The Admiral phoned.

The operatives now knew almost everything that The Admiral knew. And that included Bishop's summary of what the St. Louis team knew and what they suspected. Here is where it stands for the two: Matty and Benson were looking for a specific person, who worked for a known group. He had killed one person, and was obviously dangerous. They also weren't certain if they were looking for the survivor of the Danforth killings or a murderer, or both—either Farooq Ali or Hussain Islam. Right now it didn't matter which one it was because they didn't have a photo of either of the two men yet.

And whoever it was had a twenty-hour head start.

The two operatives grabbed their weekend bags and went to the airplane exit, walked down the mobile staircase and onto the airport tarmac.

Rather than head for the secure military and government terminal that would require no proof or identification and would lead out onto the street and into a government supplied car, the two intentionally entered Reagan airport through the civilian section of the terminal.

They waved down a civilian cab and sped up US Highway 1 across the bridge bringing them into the city. As the two rode, they were stone silent in the back of the cab. They learned long ago that if you want to work in Intelligence, you didn't talk around strangers. And the cab driver was definitely a stranger.

The two had decided with The Admiral that they should not take official government transport right now in case either Ali or Islam were part of a larger group that might be looking for anyone flying into Reagan and using official vehicles and traveling in pairs, as agents often did.

The cab moved quickly across the lower side of D.C. past the Jefferson Memorial and the Tidal Basin. The car pulled off the exit and directly up to the front gate of the Washington Navy Yard, in an area of town called southeast.

They paid the cab quickly with a generous, but not flashy tip. The yellow cab pulled away leaving the two outside the gate after midnight in one of the worst areas of the murder capital of the nation. The Navy Yard is home to several of the Department of the Navy's most high-profile divisions and had twenty-four-hour security to gain access. The Yard is about 20 blocks square and surrounded by a ten-foot high brick wall with another five feet of barbed wired on top of that.

Marines guarded the Yard around the clock.

The Chief of Naval Operations (CNO), a four-star admiral and the man who is the leader of the sea service, had his official residence in the Yard. According to urban legend, sometime in the 1980s, the neighborhood was so crime-riddled that the CNO requested to live somewhere else around the capital city area. His residence on the Yard is now used as office space.

The two operatives approached the small guard shack where a Marine, smartly dressed in his khaki uniform, stood guard. It was an unusually bright night in May with the full moon almost making the street lights unnecessary. As the two showed the corporal their

IDs, the Marine waved them through and pointed them where they would find their quarters for the night.

Even though Matty and Steve had been on the Navy Yard a thousand times, they listened politely to the guard as if they didn't know their way and thanked him as they picked up their bags and headed toward the single officer's quarters down Isaac Hull Avenue and into the Dahlgren Building where they assumed billeting had been arranged by Bishop.

When they got to the Dahlgren Building, everything was arranged as they had expected. Bishop had never failed to handle his administrative duties perfectly and this was not the exception.

It had all been set up efficiently by Bishop after he had let them off at the St. Louis Airport. Matty and Benson checked in at the front desk and each went separately to their rooms. Benson immediately came over to Matty's room to set out their pursuit plan.

"What do we know?" asked Steve. "Have we heard from The Admiral yet? Say, do you think he likes it when we call him The Admiral? He hasn't ever said anything about it, but maybe he doesn't like to correct us now that he is trying to be so correct and unoffensive. Or is it nonoffensive? Or is it just not offensive. Whatever it is, The Admiral has never said anything about it to me. Does he just put up with it or does he dislike it? I don't dislike it when people call me by my nickname. You know what they called me when I was in the service? Huh? Do you?"

"Shut up?" said Matty.

"No, they don't call me that," said Steve. "Well, not so much anymore. In Italy they used to call me 'shut up.' Remember? You guys were real funny, you know. No, I mean the other nickname. Huh? Remember?"

"I don't remember," said Matty who clearly wanted to get down to work.

"Huh. You know. I don't remember either. But I bet it is very complimentary," Steve laughed at his own stupid joke.

"So, can we get to work," implored Matty. "It's past 1, and I hope to get some sleep tonight."

Matty and Benson sat down at the small table inside Matty's room and started formulating a plan to find and obtain the target as quickly as possible and without a body count if possible. From what they knew from training and from The Admiral's information, the two figured that the target would meet with a friendly contact at one of the embassies, probably Saudi Arabia as it was the most accessible and least monitored by U.S. forces of any of the Arab embassies. There, the target may try to acquire a new identity or even diplomatic papers.

Then, he would go immediately to a prearranged contact point, which could be anywhere in the world, to turn over the electronic documents and files taken from the Danforth Institute in St. Louis. Although he could be anywhere in the world, Matty and Steve decided that the contact point would most likely be here in D.C. If the target they are pursuing is smart, and at this point they were not sure if he was or was not or was being manipulated by handlers who were or were not very smart, they came to D.C. to make contact with someone.

After Matty and Steve had put together these few thoughts, they typed a memo and sent it to The Admiral's office so that he would see it first thing in the morning. They didn't think they had anything that was worth sending to The Admiral's home or mobile communicator. They knew that time at home was very important to the Old Man. He normally spent his nights calling his daughter on the telephone. He called her most every night to see how she was doing. He told the two very little about why he was so protective of her, and the two were respectful enough never to ask.

When he did feel like opening up, maybe after a glass of brandy in his office after a job was complete, he always called her Patty. And always added, "That her mother called her Trish, but I never did." He would talk about her grades as a young school girl and how she had limitless potential.

Never did he talk about the problems she seemed to develop as she got older. The stories of his little girl ended around the time she was in her mid twenties. And the two always did the math and figured she must be almost thirty-five by now.

Matty and Steve worked into the night figuring out how to go about locating the target. From the Navy Yard's secure offices area, the two could access all the information available.

They could link into the files from the Department of Homeland Security and all the security cameras that they have in all major airports around the country, and the world.

Matty and Benson figured that this may be the best way to solve this. They needed to look at all the tapes from planes coming into Reagan last night from St. Louis. If they could locate a man who appeared to be of Middles Eastern descent, they would find him on the manifest and get his name, which they assumed would be fake, but it would give the identity that the man was using, for now.

"Matty," said Steve. "Does anyone know why the Gulf Stream flows from the Caribbean northeast to England?"

"Ahhh, I'm sure someone has figured it out," replied Matty knowing he was in for the long haul. "Maybe tomorrow when we have time, we could Google it."

"There must be some reason, right?" pressed Steve. "Is it because the earth spins and causes the water to move? But I was thinking on the plane, the earth spins the wrong way for that to be the reason. Like if the earth was spinning sort of, right to left, as you look at a map, then you would figure that if the water was staying still, or at least not moving as fast as the earth, then the water would flow predominantly from east to west. Or from Europe to the east coast of the U.S., right? I was looking for a vacation spot in England or Scotland last week. Me and the wife are celebrating our anniversary and she wants to go to Great Britain and see the Queen. I mean not face to face, but see her palace. So I was looking at it on the web, and it stays pretty warm there all through winter. So we could go in February and it would still be pretty nice."

"Say, Benny," said Matty to Steve. "Why don't we call it a day for now? Huh?"

"Yeah, I guess we've been going at it all day," Steve replied.

For now, the two needed rest. The two knew there are limits to what they can do, and they had reached theirs.

Steve Benson, the veterinarian from Waukegan, Illinois, went next door to his room.

While Stuart Mateus got into his own bed in his own little room on the Washington Navy Yard. Sleep came quickly to them both.

CHAPTER 9

Matty's simple cover, or "usual precautions" as The Admiral called it, was to referee a rugby match at 1 o'clock at the home field of the Potomac Athletic Club, a Washington-based club that was one of the top tier rugby teams in the nation.

Most referees thought these were great games to work because the field was right in downtown Washington on the National Mall at the corner of Fourteenth and Constitution just a block away from the building that houses the Department of Agriculture. The pitch sits literally in the shadow of the Washington Monument.

On a beautiful May Sunday, the National Mall would be crawling with tourists. Some of them would be curious about the odd and vigorous game being played on the great green space in the heart of the capital of the Free World.

This audience, however small and uninformed, always gave the players a little extra motivation to play hard. Referees also got a boost from the crowds that gather around the games. Sometimes the crowds included international visitors who are familiar with the game. These guests were from rugby-playing nations, they would often feel free to express their enthusiasm at seeing a familiar site from their homeland.

Matty and The Admiral knew that the cover story they use isn't air tight. In fact, it is a little thin.

The cover story of being an international operative as a simple rugby referee wouldn't stand up to real scrutiny if they ran into a nosey target that had the resources and the energy to track them.

The advantages of the rugby referee cover story was that it was easy, cheap, and Matty liked doing it.

So what was the harm of arranging it with the USA Rugby Board in Colorado Springs, Colorado?

And besides, the subterfuge may bring Matty and Steve just a half-step advantage when they needed it.

It wasn't game time yet. And, as usual, Matty got up at around 6:00 a.m. back at the Yard. He struggled with what to wear. If he put on his rugby referee kit right now, he would be stuck in it for ten hours or more. If he didn't put it on, he may get caught in something and never get a chance to get changed and ready for the match.

He decided to go ahead and put his referee gear on now. That means by 2:30 or 3:00 p.m. when his game was done, he would have to slide out of some pretty smelly clothes.

Better safe than sorry, he thought, as he pulled on his tight, black, sport shorts, then his tight, black, sport shirt. Over his shorts, he pulled his white, cotton rugby shorts.

Matty then pulled on his long, polyester socks, or hose, as the rugby players called them. He wore a pair of dark blue hose today as he figured it was a good time to try out the new socks. For a shirt, he wore a plain, light blue, short-sleeved rugby shirt that almost looked like a golf polo, but was a little heavier fabric. Matty figured that if he ended up going straight from the match to, well, where ever, he may blend better in if he looked like a tourist.

The coffee that he had started to brew the instant he awoke was just starting to percolate. Matty didn't go in for many thrills, but he would always take the time to make, or buy, a nice cup of java in the morning, He loved the smell of it, the taste of it, and the entire sensation. He considered it one of his few vices.

The last part of his uniform were the cleats. He liked to carry them with him and wear flip-flops. His boots were a pair of low-top Adidas that were similar to the ones he wore when he played. They were black and well worn. He should get a new pair, but he loved these. Maybe next week he would spring for a new pair. After this caper was done, maybe he could expense a pair to the Navy. His referee flags were stuffed into his back pocket.

He carried a bag of standard game equipment that any referee would bring—some first aid equipment, athletic tape, a spare ball in case neither team had a useable one, and a spare whistle.

His game boots were tied together by the shoe lace a flung over a shoulder and now, with coffee in hand, he went next door to get Benson.

"Steve, time for work," said Matty through the door, but he knew that Steve would have been out of the room for at least at least a few hours.

As Matty suspected, no answer.

Matty left the barracks and made his way down Isaac Hull Avenue to the central headquarters of the yard in the Admiral Halsey Building. He showed his badge to security and got into the elevator, pressed 8, the top button on the column of numbers.

He took a sip of coffee. Paused, tipped his head back and enjoyed the flavor.

The elevator jolted up a few inches, then paused.

Matty was going to a protected floor, so he had to swipe his ID card through the scanner before the elevator would budge. He did, and it did.

After just a few moments, the elevator doors separated and Matty walked into a huge conference room. The elevator doors were facing west, so Matty had view across the conference room and through the room and out the eight-foot-high windows revealing a magnificent view of the city and the new ballpark for the Washington Nationals baseball team. The conference room occupied the entire top, eighth floor of the Halsey Building. And the windows went all around 360 degrees.

Matty stopped for a second to enjoy what he felt was the best view in the best room in the city.

To his right about two miles away is the breathtaking United States capitol dome. To his left was a view overlooking the Anacostia River. The river made a southward bend right at the Navy Yard.

He could see down river all the way until the Anacostia joined the Potomac near Fort McNair Army base.

Spectacular.

The Halsey Building was built in 1878 on the highest ground on the Navy Yard when there was still a threat that the capitol could be attacked by invading forces coming up the Potomac and the Anacostia. The eight-story structure was considered quite a marvel for its time.

The reason the building was erected was to give the Naval artillery officers a place to practice firing down the river. The long, unobstructed view allowed early sailors to fire away practicing aim at further targets with little risk of hitting anyone.

Long-range weaponry was in its infancy and many lessons learned at this very site would help the Navy in both World Wars and countless other conflicts and engagements.

The waters of the Anacostia River that were empty and used for target practice less than 150 years ago are now crammed with recreational boaters catching fish, pleasure cruising, enjoying the sun and puttering about in all types of watercraft. Even many rowers and scullers were out in the morning waters of the Anacostia today.

Seeing them all made Stuart smile thinking about how he would love to be aboard a little boat out on the water right now catching fish with them.

As Matty suspected, Steve Benson was sitting in the center control console of the room that controlled the windows, doors, screens and lights of this conference room.

The forty-foot by twenty-foot conference room that Steve Benson and Stuart Mateus had arranged for this morning's meeting had been transformed from its days as an artillery house. It is now a high-tech Intelligence center. Above the windows, encircling almost the entire room were television monitors. They were side by side and reached from just above the windows—about 8 feet above the deck—up to the top of the 12-foot ceilings.

"Hey, sleepy head," Steve said to Matty after he gave his friend a few seconds to enjoy the view. "I've got a few interesting things I want you look at."

"How'd you sleep?" asked Matty politely and trying to slow down his friend from getting too far ahead. Steve was always working at full speed at sunrise, while Matty needed a few cups of coffee and, hopefully, a little quiet time before he felt like he was functioning fully.

"Look at this," Steve said motioning to the screens that were above the north windows of the room. At the same time, Benson hit the button that electronically closed the blinds of all the windows.

When Steve has started work about two hours ago, the sun was down, so he could enjoy the nighttime views of the city all around. Now that the sun was coming up, the screens were easier to see with the black-out screens down.

Benson already had the video he wanted cued up to a section from the Lambert Field security cameras in St. Louis.

Steve had requested the video earlier that morning from the Department of Homeland Security's office at Lambert Field security office highest priority.

Steve now cued up the file to the point in the video that he thought gave them a clue to what they were looking for.

The video equipment in this conference room was always upgraded as soon as soon as new technology was available. From tape VTRs in the seventies, to cassettes and Beta in the eighties, to DVDs and now to a watching everything off the hard drive, this room was always equipped with the best technology.

Now, Steve hit the play arrow on the laptop that initiated the video on the huge screen in the room. The video showed a Middle Eastern-looking man boarding a Washington, D.C.-bound flight on Saturday, the day before. The suspect had a large carry-on bag and had no checked baggage. He was traveling under the name Anwar Chalabi.

Benson explained what he thought was going on.

"We don't have anyone named Chalabi in our alert system, but that doesn't mean anything. He could easily have two or three IDs with him from several different countries. This Chalabi has a United Kingdom passport. Meaningless," emphasized Benson. "Now on the

East screen I've got the tapes from Reagan National Airport from when that flight arrived."

Benson ran several tapes in succession, showing the suspect getting off the plane in one sequence; walking through the airport in another shot; and getting into the taxi cue in the final sequence. Then, Chalabi got into a cab and disappeared into the D.C. morning traffic.

"Why do you think it is this Chalabi?" asked Matty.

"Couple basic things," replied Steve. "He is one of only three men of Middle Eastern descent who took the plane from St. Louis to Reagan. I know it sounds impolitic, but that is the profile. And the two other men were travelling with families and looked like holiday makers. This guy travelled alone and without bags. Big indicators."

"OK, I'm sold. Any way to track down that cab?" asked Matty.

"We're checking on it already, but it doesn't look good," replied Benson. "With all GPS and tracking that cab companies do now, the cabs are more and more likely to do their work as independents not working for a company. The increase in monitoring of the cabs pushes the cabbies to work without monitoring. The markings on this cab looked like an independent worker. So that makes him very hard to trace. It also could be a taxi planted by Qfar Mohammad."

"Who?" asked Matty, still not 100 percent awake.

"The guy who may have organized this whole thing according the info The Admiral got from Homeland Security," said Steve.

"Right, don't give up on that one, that may be our best lead," said Matty.

"We'll stay on it. What's our next move?" Steve asked.

"Have you checked with the hotels in the city? Does anyone have a guest named Chalabi checking in yesterday?" asked Matty.

"Checking already. I've got a feeling that they will all be dead ends," said Steve.

"Probably. But get the D.C. cops on it anyway. We might get a break," said Matty.

"Now, what do you have here?" Matty asked as he pointed to the screens above the south side of the conference room.

"Oh, ah," Benson stammered. "That is some stuff I was checking on the Gulf Stream. It looks like the waters move from the south coast of the U.S. and moves across the Atlantic—"

"You were making vacation plans in the middle of an investigation?" Matty asked in mock astonishment.

"Well, I didn't know when you planned to join me, lieutenant sleepy head, so I thought I'd get some info for the wife," Benson shrugged his shoulders.

Matty replied softly, "You are a fucking idiot, you know that?"

"Have we heard from The Admiral?" asked Benson quick to turn the conversation to a different topic.

"Got a message on the walk up here," answered Matty.

"And?"

"And they are zeroing in on a few leads," said Benson. "Seems there are several Muslim cells that might be capable of pulling off this type of caper. Chalabi, or Ali, or whatever name he is using now is probably being outfitted with several new identities," said Benson.

"He will have several IDs to improve his chances to complete his mission," added Benson. "Or leave the country, or leave the country to complete his mission. Or complete his mission to leave the country. Or complete his mission to complete his mission. Wait, that one doesn't make sense."

"Hey, hotshot," said Benson. "It's getting close to ten. What time is your rugby match?"

"Oh crap," said Benson. I better get moving. Kick-off is at 1. Keep on this, will you?"

"Sure, as soon as I get my vacation plans sorted out. Ha just kidding, boss," said Benson.

Matty called the elevator and he took it down to the street where he got out of the Halsey Building, walked swiftly toward the North gate of the Yard and waved down a cab. The short cab ride took him onto Interstate 395/695 that runs across the southern edge of the city of Washington.

On calmer days, like this very May Sunday morning, Stuart Mateus liked that road. The Jefferson Memorial was his favorite monument in town and it is just off Interstate 395 and was always a great site for him.

Whenever he saw it, he thought about some of the times he visited it as a tourist. Inside the monument, as part of the exhibit, there are displays about the history of it. Among those displays, there are several of the alternative designs for the monument.

One of those designs was similar to the finished one that everyone now knows, but it didn't have the familiar domed roof. Stuart Mateus always fancied himself as a designer. And if he hadn't joined the Navy, he always thought he would have made a great designer. And he really liked the look of that Jefferson Memorial plan that didn't have a roof on it. He always wondered why they didn't pick that one.

He figured the reason was some typical Washington, D.C. political influence that made the choice instead of objectively picking the best memorial possible. Unions lobbied to get the dome put on to provide more jobs for their members. Maybe some congressman representing a state that has a lot of dome manufacturers greased a few palms. Yeah, Matty thought to himself, "This is the work of undue influence by the powerful lobbying group known collectively as 'Big Dome.'" Mateus giggled to himself thinking about that. Yeah, maybe some senator from North Dakota or even South Dakota made the difference when they made design decisions. Just then, the cab stopped near intersection of Fourteenth and Independence, just near the rugby pitch.

CHAPTER
10

Matty showed up at the rugby pitch and immediately took charge of the rugby field and the teams who were preparing to play—the Potomac Athletic Club and the Washington Renegades.

The skies were blue and the National Mall was packed with tourists. All up and down Independence Avenue were Americans of every description enjoying the warm spring day. Old, young, fat, thin, tall, short, light, dark and everything in between were meandering the streets and green spaces of the capital. They wandered in and out of the museums, up and down into the Metro train stops, to and from the monuments to Washington, Lincoln, Jefferson, World War II, Viet Nam, Korea and all the other highlights and serious memorials of the almost 250 years of the USA.

A few of the visitors were even taking a few minutes to line the sides of the rugby pitch to watch the match. Mostly they were wives and girlfriends and boyfriends and kids of the players. Among the crowd was a referee evaluator who was at the pitch to watch and evaluate the referee who was originally scheduled to work the match. Since The Admiral and the Office of Directed Discretionary Operations had substituted Matty as the ref for this match, the evaluator figured he may as well stay and evaluate Matty even though Matty ranked higher on the refereeing hierarchy than the evaluator.

So if anyone should have been evaluating anyone, Matty should have been the one checking up on the evaluator.

Some tourists wandered by the pitch during the weekend matches and gawked at the 30 men playing the very physical game that looked a little like football with the funny-shaped ball before wondering back to the real attractions in the area to buy their souvenirs and take their snapshots.

The day, combined with the tourists and the setting, right there off the mall, should have been a perfect situation for Matty to referee a great game.

The Renegades were a rugby club that everyone admired. The club was made up of mostly gay men from the D.C. area.

The presence of gay men on the rugby pitch always confounded the sparse crowds who watched the matches.

During almost all Renegades matches they have ever played, the whispers would start in the crowd.

"They are gay, you know."

"How could fags be involved in such a tough, physical, manly sport as rugby?"

Local television reporters would occasionally do stories on the 'macho' gay rugby players. The team was even featured in Time magazine once.

They were really quite an oddity.

Or so everyone thought.

The ruby players both on the Renegades, and those who matched up against them, knew better.

The game of rugby isn't about who a player sleeps with, or who shows the most bravado. It isn't even about who is the biggest or strongest. The game is really about working together for a common cause, and who among the players is ready to give everything for the team.

And the Renegades have those traits in spades. All the rugby teams who have ever faced the Renegades knew they were in for a game against a well-disciplined team that worked hard.

Maybe, Matty figured, it is because the Renegades felt like the rugby pitch was the place where they could all work together for a common cause. Or maybe it is because they could feel comfortable expressing their male, macho side without having to apologize. Or maybe it is because they are just good rugby players.

Whatever the reason, if there has to be a reason, they could play rugby.

It was one of the Renegade players who led the revolt on United Airlines flight 93 on 9-11 that was meant to crash into the Capitol building before the passenger uprising forced the radical Muslim hijackers to lay it into the ground outside Shanksville, Penn.

The Renegades had the respect of the other rugby teams and players. And they knew that. So they let the uninformed gawkers stare in amazement at what the gays could do.

The Potomac Athletic Club was no slouch either. They are a solid team that plays in the Premiership League against the best rugby sides in the country. PAC, as they are known, would be the favorites today, and they would be eager to show that they are the dominate side in the capital region.

Before all of his matches, especially high-profile ones like today, Matty liked to study the players before the match and get a feel for how the game should go. To prepare, Matty would talk with other refs who have worked these teams to see how they like to play—do they like to run more or do they prefer a kicking game? Do they like a defensive match or do they like to open it up with a more free-flowing style? Are they dominated by the pack forwards (the bigger, stronger players), of or do they like to have the ball in the hands of the backs (the faster, fleeter members of the team)?

In the game of rugby there is only one referee to watch thirty men play an in very physical contest.

It is not easy to see everything happening on the pitch and Matty liked to prepare by knowing the tendencies of the teams.

If Matty knew what to expect, he could get himself into position on the field faster and hopefully he could call a better match. Since he didn't have any time to prepare today, he was sort of working without a net, but he didn't mind too much.

Sometimes, being over-prepared, he thought, could make him anticipate too much. Maybe if he was too prepared, he may be overly eager to call a penalty on a player due only to that player's reputation as a rough player who plays on the fringes of the rules.

Over preparation was certainly not a problem for him today.

The PAC team had powerful forwards—the bigger, stronger players—for this Sunday match.

The weather was a little hot for rugby—which favors the visiting Renegades whose strength was their quick, well-skilled back line.

Washington, D.C., can be warm and humid in May. And today was typical. Although the match started fairly early in the day, it was already warming up pretty quickly.

The teams got onto the pitch as 1:00 p.m. approached. Matty counted to make certain there were fifteen men from each team on the field.

Matty asks the visiting team captain, "Ready, Renegades captain?"

The reply came, "Yes, sir."

"Ready, PAC captain?"

"Yes, sir."

A long, shrill tweet on Matty's whistle, a forward swing of his arm and the kicker raises the ball over his head to show his team that he is preparing to drop kick the ball and thereby start the match.

A swift strike at the ball with the kicker's right boot, and the game is underway.

In St. Louis, The Admiral was sending out text messages and receiving information on his mobile device and his computer at a remarkable clip. He had contacted most of the names on his considerable list of friends at various agencies around D.C., and asked what they know about the situation in St. Louis and if his contacts had any background.

There was no shortage of possibilities.

One friend in Homeland Security said the group El Sheiba could be connected to a larger terrorist cell operating out of Saudi Arabia. A contact at the Central Intelligence Agency thought the group could be a front group for the Al Qaeda cell in the United States that he was watching.

Another contact at the Pentagon had never heard of the group and so he thought they may not exist, or could be another higher-level terrorist group or even a group that is working for the CIA and secretly trying to permeate other terrorist groups and expose them.

None of these theories rang true to The Admiral. He thought he could smell a rat and this group smelled like a rat. Then the Admiral got a message that finally made some sense of the situation. He read it quickly and thoroughly.

After a deep breath, The Admiral muttered to himself, "Percy."

He sent messages to his boys in D.C., Matty and Benson letting them know that that he wasn't sure about anything, so beware for everything.

To show his uncertainty, the Admiral ended his message, "having a difficult case with no clear objective or target can be healthy for the players. It keeps one's mind tidy. TA."

About half way through the rugby match, Steve Benson arrived from the Navy Yard and found a spot on the touch line (side line) that he was certain made himself noticeable to Matty. During the match, when Matty had a moment during injuries or during substitutions, he would go over to Steve and see if the situation called for him to leave the match early.

The efforts made the crowd wonder, what was the interest between the referee and the spectator, who was holding the iPod-looking computer. Some assumed that Steve and Matty were a gay couple in keeping with the theme of the Renegades playing rugby.

As the game unfolded, Matty found himself distracted. And when it was finally over, he realized that he missed several crucial calls that may have decided the match.

"Inexcusable effort," he thought.

It was the first time in a long time that Matty felt that one of his objectives (working for the DDO) interfered with another of his goals (calling a solid match as part of his "usual precautions").

He started to wonder if he was taking his refereeing more seriously than he was taking his job. He did want to keep climbing the referee ladder and eventually get to call top-flight international matches. Or maybe, he was taking his DDO work more seriously than he should and he would be wise to give up the government job and really try to make an impact as a ref. When the match was over, Matty had a few minutes to reflect on his refereeing work today.

On one call he made during the match that he remembered distinctly, the ball had gone into touch (out of bounds) and the PAC fullback had thrown the ball back into play quickly, before the defense can get lined up and ready to defend. All perfectly legal, but in order to do it legitimately, PAC must use the same ball that went into touch and a fan cannot interfere with the ball. If the team gets a different ball, or a fan touches the ball, the PAC team is required to allow time for the Renegades to set up defensively and take a normal throw in.

At the time of the play, Matty was unsure if the ball was the same, but allowed the play to continue. PAC ended up scoring on that sequence, and that score put the PAC team firmly ahead to stay.

Directly after the match, the Renegades captain, asked about that play.

Matty sincerely didn't know what ball was used. And he told the Renegades captain that. It would certainly show up as a bad call on his match report from the referee evaluator, both because he wasn't sure about the call, and because he told the captain that he wasn't sure.

His call may have cost the Renegades the game. And that was a shame. No time to worry about that now, however.

The crowd dispersed and the two team captains thanked Matty for his work.

At the first chance he thought was appropriate, Steve walked over to meet Matty and filled him on the latest info from The Admiral. The Old Man would be expecting them to move on that info, or have a reason why they didn't.

The two, Matty still in his rugby refereeing gear and Steve in khaki pants and a polo shirt, walked eastward from the rugby pitch where Steve had parked the car he rented for the assignment. He tried to stay away from government vehicles. They found their car in a small employee parking lot at the back of the Holocaust Museum.

The museum faces busy Fourteenth Street. The small parking lot can seem like the only available parking spaces on high volume tourist days like this one.

The PAC rugby team always arranged with the museum for referees to park in this space when the PAC hosted matches.

The two strolled up to the car in relative silence not wanting any ears to hear anything they said.

When they got to the car, Matty turned to Steve and asked, "What do we know?"

Steve was all business.

"An unknown is here and the Old Man thinks the unknown is looking to move the information," said Steve.

"That's what you and I figured," Matty said.

"That's just half of it," Steve said. "He is meeting someone in the government…our government. A traitor."

"Who?" asked Matty.

"The Admiral wants us to check out someone named Percy at the Department of Agriculture. Just a block from here…says we can check out this guy Percy's office today since he won't be there. And tomorrow we can question him to see if he is involved in this. I'll tell you, something, my friend. If this guy is selling U.S. secrets, I'd love to nail him on it. So let's do it right," said Steve.

CHAPTER 11

Matty was still in his refereeing gear when he opened the trunk of the car that Steve had driven. It was dark blue.

It looked like the type of car a rugby referee approaching middle age would be driving.

"Nice car," Matty said with more than a little sarcasm.

"Yeah, well…" Steve didn't bother to muster a comment.

After realizing how close they were to the Agriculture building, they decided to go right away. A shower would have to wait.

Matty took his clothes out of his bag and quickly changed out of his rugby shorts and shirt and into a pair of white, loose-fitting walking trousers and pulled on a golf shirt while standing next to the car.

He now looked like a tourist visiting the capital.

But this tourist also shoved his Ruger SR45 into his waist band at the small of his back, and his other gun, his Ruger LCP, into his ankle holster.

He quickly pulled up his sock over the little Ruger and let his pant leg fall around the gun to help conceal it. He also pulled his striped Izod shirt down over his waist all around to hide his larger weapon.

The guns weren't concealed to a trained eye, but Matty was pretty sure that tourists wouldn't notice anything unusual. The two started walking quickly to the east toward the USDA building. There was a narrow driveway next to the Holocaust Museum and Steve and Matty walked quickly through the dark alley.

While alone for just a few seconds they talked quickly knowing that this may be the last chance they would get to talk openly.

"What is the level on this?" asked Matty.

"Black," said Steve.

Code Black means the two have a wide discretion on how to handle, how to detain, and how to capture, if possible, the suspect.

"What are we looking for?" Steve gets right to business, "Turns out, according to info that The Admiral got, the man we were looking at this morning—"

"Chalabi," interrupts Matty.

"Right Chalabi, is actually a man named Farooq Ali Jr. He is 30-35, Middle East features, 160 pounds, thin build."

Steve reached out his phone to show Matty the photo that The Admiral has sent of Ali. Matty glanced at the jpg. file photo of Ali.

"Not much to go on, and he probably shaved his beard and cut his hairs in the last twenty hours, but it is what it is," Steve said.

"Yes, we've worked on jobs with less..." said Matty. "Wait, did you say 'cut his hairs'?"

"Yeah, you know, that is a funny word. One hair is a hair, right?" queried Steve.

Matty declined to get into this discussion.

"Right?" pressed Steve. "Well, then, ten hairs are 'hairs,' right?"

Matty didn't respond as they walked on.

"But then," Steve reasoned, "When you get to a whole head of hair, it goes back to 'hair'. Why? You have one 'finger', and three 'fingers', but if you have a whole fistful, it stays as 'fingers'. Why does 'hair' go back to the singular when you have an entire group? I say enough. From now on, I am using the plural of hairs when I talk about a head full of hairs."

The two emerged from the Holocaust Museum parking lot and turned north to the intersection of Fourteenth Street and Independence Avenue. It was only then Matty realized that the mall was bustling with tourists on a beautiful Sunday afternoon. He had been so engrossed in his rugby match and later in getting dressed and the updates from Steve that he hadn't noticed all the people.

He didn't look at them as people, but as situational elements that could help the two operatives in some situations. They could also hinder them, if there was trouble.

The group could help conceal Matty and Steve if they found their mark. Or, all the people could cause confusion for Ali or the two agents if and that would allow the situation to devolved into a huge cluster fuck.

Matty always tried to keep in mind that the target was most important, but if he could achieve the target while avoiding any collateral damage, that would be best. But he knew civilian deaths were always a possibility.

As the two arrived at the intersection, they blended into the small group of ten to thirteen who had collected there to wait for the light to change.

When they got the green signal, the two moved slowly, matching the pace of the crowd of tourists.

As the group reached the south east corner of the intersection, the tourists started to dissipate. Some headed north towards the mall, while others, stopped to look at the sites. Steve and Matty continued eastward down Independence with the huge USDA building stretching out on their right side.

It was one of the biggest buildings in Washington. A remnant of the era when 95 percent of Americans worked and lived on farms.

Now only 5 percent make their living directly from agriculture, but the department still had one of the best locations in the city.

As Matty and Steve approached the entrance to the building that was closest to them, they saw a man exit the building. The sidewalk that Steve and Matty were on was parallel to the street. The man exiting the USDA building was on an entry sidewalk that connected to the street sidewalk.

If the two operatives kept up their speed and the other man kept his speed, the three would almost collide on the sidewalk.

Quickly, Matty sized up the man. He was dark-complexioned, and loosely fit the physical description of Chalabi, now known to both Matty and Steve as Ali. The man was about thirty feet from Matty and looking away from him, so it was hard for Matty to get a good look. The man was also carrying a briefcase that looked new.

That fits the profile, thought Matty.

The video surveillance they saw earlier today, showed Ali didn't have a brief case with him in St. Louis. And if Ali wanted to look like a local, he would have had to buy a few new things to complete his disguise in plain sight. A new briefcase would be part of the disguise.

Ali would have bought it the airport or a local shop during his head start.

Matty nudged Steve with his elbow as discretely as he could.

Steve glanced at Matty who motioned with his head toward the man.

Steve looked where Matty had indicated.

"Him?"

"Dunno."

The men were now about twenty feet apart and were still walking at a right angle towards each other.

It seemed that the man noticed the two coming towards him and started acting nervous. The man clearly thought that these two tourists didn't seem right.

The three men were now ten feet apart and still the Middle Eastern man looked hard at the two.

Just then, the man reached the sidewalk and turned to his right, eastward, and started walking more quickly down the sidewalk away from the pair.

Matty had a hard choice to make. And he had to make it right now.

If he decides to chase, and it isn't Ali, this could be an ugly international incident complete with diplomatic apologies and official sanctions.

And maybe the end of a career—Matty's.

And Matty didn't want that, at least not for a few more years.

Well, if he was this close to his target him and let him get away, that would be unforgivable. They may not get another shot at him.

"Let's get him, quietly," Matty said in a loud whisper.

The two started walking toward the man quickly. Trying to look that they were not doing exactly what they were obviously doing.

Within a few steps, Matty and Benson started to close the gap between themselves and the man they thought was Ali.

Already nervous, the man quickly noticed he was being followed and broke into a run.

Steve and Matty then give up all hope of surprise and subterfuge and started to run after him.

Ali was weaving through tourists and was carelessly bumping his briefcase into the tourists on the sidewalk. The effect was that he was slowed down considerably.

Steve moved quicker than Matty, who had just refereed an eighty-minute rugby match. Steve covered the ground between himself and the man right way, and was right on his tail in less than a block.

Steve jumped ahead to tackle the man around his head and shoulders. The two fell forward and hit hard on the sidewalk pavement. Ali struggled to get away, but it took just a second for the former wrestler to get control of the target.

Ali was face down on the cement walkway and Steve had his chest on the back of Ali using his weight to keep him prone. For good measure, Steve slipped a wrestling move known as turkey bar on Ali pinning his arms behind his back.

It wasn't a move the DDO approved when apprehending a suspect, but it was one of Steve's favorites.

As Steve lay on the man, Ali shouted out "STOP CALLING ME THAT."

Just then, Matty caught up to the two.

"WHAT THE FUCK ARE YOU DOING?" shouted a voice into Steve's ear.

It was the voice of a capitol policeman who had seen the whole thing and appeared out of nowhere.

"These two rednecks have been harassing me all day," said the man, in a very thick Middle Eastern accent.

When they heard the accent, Steve and Matty were now certain they had Ali.

"You two boys better get off that fellow right now," said the policeman, a thick, black man who must have weighed somewhere north of 250 pounds and would have stood 6 feet, and 6 inches if he had been standing straight up.

But he wasn't.

He was bent over with his head directly next to the ear of Steve who was still on top of Ali.

Ali's initial shout had confused Steve for a second.

But now he realized that it was going to be part of his defense, probably part of his training, as a simple tourist being persecuted by two evil Americans.

It gives them a quick bit of sympathy from crowds eager to denounce oppressors.

Ali's trick wouldn't last long, and he knew it.

"Officer, we are federal agents authorized to apprehend this man by whatever means needed," said Matty.

Matty leaned down to look the officer in the face and started to reach for his identification.

"Hold it there, cowboy," said the cop, trying to sort out the situation, but also not wanting to get himself in trouble if the two were actually who they said they were.

"Everyone get up," said the cop.

That is exactly what Ali was hoping for.

Three against one with him on the ground was an impossible situation. But on his feet Ali would have a chance at escape.

The three came to their feet as instructed. Steve wasn't going to let go of Ali though. He held Ali fast from behind with his arms around Ali's arms behind his back. He was pulling Ali's elbows together in that turkey bar.

Even though he was pretty helpless, Ali wasn't going to let go of that new, and now-scuffed, brief case.

"May I?" Matty asked as he reached into his pocket again to retrieve his ID.

"Slowly," instructed the cop.

"Here you go," said Matty getting his wallet out of his pocket.

Matty handed it over to Officer Davics, according to his shiny gold name plate on his well-pressed blue uniform.

"OK, give it here," said the officer.

Davics took Matty's badge and ID that were inside the official wallet that all agents are issued. It was black leather and Davics recognized the wallet as an official ID holder.

Davics leaned forward to look at the ID, but he was already realizing that the agents were telling the truth.

As a career man, Davics was glad he was respectful and thorough when he first encountered the group.

Just as Davics was pulling out his glasses and perched them on the tip of his nose to get a clearer view of the ID. He leaned forward and waited a second for his eyes to adjust to the glasses.

Farooq Ali saw his opening.

He was still gripping tightly the handle on the briefcase…his arms were bent and under much strain from the pressure Steve was putting on it, but he managed some wiggle room.

In a moment, Ali used all his force to swing the briefcase like a pendulum hard into Davics's face which was still looking directly at the ID. Davics didn't even see it coming.

With the cop still leaning slightly forward, the case hit square, and solid.

The corner of the new brief case connected with the cop square on the button, driving Davics's suddenly-bleeding nose, head and his shoulders up and backward. The cop's legs went weak. He dropped immediately to his knees.

The blood squirted hard from the Davic's's nose as he lost consciousness for just an instant. Instinctively he put his hand on his service revolver.

CHAPTER 12

As he sat in his chair back in St. Louis, The Admiral was getting some more information in the Command and Control Center at the National Geospatial Intelligence Agency. That additional information was on two men, Farooq Ali and Farooq Ali Jr.

The older Ali, the Intel said, was a civil servant in Baghdad who was cooperating and even friendly with the new, coalition-backed government.

"Not much radicalism there," thought the Admiral.

But then there was his son, Ali Jr.

Admiral Guilbault-Johnson had seen Ali Jr.'s name a few times over the last few years in other Intel reports but nothing seemed remarkable. Nothing much to worry about as he remembered.

He looked in his files and quickly pulled up what he had on the junior Ali.

"Ali Jr. Farooq" read the computer file that Guilbault-Johnson pulled up from a shared CIA/Navy Intel brief.

The Admiral scanned down all the details to the SUMMARY at the bottom of the doc.

"Ali Jr. maintains relationships with several Muslims who are known or suspected to have terrorist ties. Unclear if subject himself shares views of these elements. Unclear if subject is aware of activities of these elements.

"Current position by agency is that he does not share activities and is only tangentially involved. May not be involved at all."

Likely future adversary: low

Risk factor: low

"Interesting," The Admiral thought to himself as he scratched his chin and started to think about this…First step, he thought, was to find out who these friends are. He put in the order to monitor some of the Baghdad operatives who have historically been seen with Ali. That information would take weeks to accumulate and wouldn't be helpful for this investigation, but may be useful down the road.

The information that The Admiral currently has revealed that Ali Jr.'s friends were small timers, or even no timers.

Guilbault-Johnson didn't think that any of them were capable of involvement in an international piece of murder or espionage of this size.

But then, he thought, up until about thirty-six hours ago, he hadn't thought that this Farooq Ali Jr. was involved in anything like this.

"Best to always keep an open and tidy mind about these things."

Messages started to collect in The Admiral's secret Internet—called SIDR-NET. The Secure Internet Defense Resources Network is what the defense network used to transmit secure information. There are several networks around the world that are available to Intel officers, but The Admiral liked this one.

The several networks, required some very fancy IT work by the Department of Defense staff, but the DOD liked having separate networks to locate and stop Intelligence compromises more easily.

The Intel in those messages was coming in from the Navy and other military Intelligence resources that The Admiral knew. He started to scroll through them.

First, the Navy said that Farooq was not an operative that was of much concern. He didn't fit the profile of a radical Muslim.

Neither was the Ali family rich. It is the wealthy families living lives of leisure that give their children idle hours to percolate the hate. Idle time in affluent youth can plant the seed in young minds that all ills—real and perceived—in the world are the fault of the United States.

And these ills are hoisted specifically on the Muslim world by the USA. Ali Jr. had been involved in a few inconsequential activities, but nothing much. In fact, another message told The Admiral that Ali Jr. was considered so benign that the Navy had given some consideration to the idea that Farooq might be a good target for use as a counter-operative.

The Army email in The Admiral's inbox said pretty much the same with one small difference. They had some information suggesting that Farooq's family had experienced some financial difficulties recently.

According to these Army sources, it seems that his father, a mid-level bureaucrat in the government's department of water and sewage, had recently lost his job.

As things change so rapidly in a region that is undergoing such foundational changes so quickly, the older Farooq found himself displaced for no other reason than his department moved offices to another part of Baghdad, and his paperwork was lost.

The Admiral thought this was curious enough to pursue it. He read on...

It seems when Ali Sr. got to the new offices in another part of the city, there was no record of him working in the department. Even though he knew the front-desk receptionist when he arrived at the new offices—and she knew him. But without any records, she couldn't allow him to take his desk.

They had worked together for nearly a decade. His boss and co-workers had all made the move to the new office without incident, but because of some omission of some paperwork, he had become a non-person in this department.

The receptionist was a female who didn't wear the traditional hijab. She didn't conform to traditional Muslim dress for females. And she drove a car, even before the liberation.

"Exceptional woman," thought The Admiral. And now, she was telling a man, who was once her superior that he couldn't go to his new office.

According to the report, since Ali Sr. and the receptionist were always friendly, he didn't confront her, but instead waited to hear from his boss about why he wasn't able to take his new office.

When he did appeal to his boss, and to his boss's boss, and up the chain of command, he found that each was powerless to find the paperwork. And without that paperwork, so desperately vital in many developing countries, Ali Sr. was out of work.

Farooq Ali Sr. knew that losing his job would have some consequences.

The best case scenario meant that he would put in his paperwork and be eventually essentially be rehired to his old job. He would lose seniority; loose his vacation; loose his pay for the three months that it would take to get back on staff. But it was the way the system worked in Baghdad.

As The Admiral read on, he found out that the best case didn't happen this time. In fact, it could be said that what happened was the worst case.

At the time of Mr. Ali Sr.'s troubles, there was a hiring freeze that was in effect nationwide for all government jobs in Iraq. The Unites States' efforts to rebuild the country had come under some criticism at home. The Iraqi president needed some political cover. So he ordered that all civil service personnel that were on duty could stay there. In a culture that believed that working for the government was a lifelong right, the president couldn't take the drastic action to actually cut staff.

Those cuts in employment would have been a public relations nightmare and probably would have planted the seeds for domestic unrest, either through a coup or assassination attempt, or violent strikes. Instead of cutting staff, the president ordered government agencies to restrict hiring until further notice.

Ali Sr. understood the byzantine machinations of the world of government in his country. After all, he had been working in it for more than twenty-five years.

Farooq Ali Sr. also knew that no amount of forms and appeals were going to get himself back on the payroll of his water and sewage department anytime soon. As he read this, Guilbault-Johnson got quite interested.

"What an interesting little nugget this is," The Admiral said to himself.

The Army had done great work on gathering Intelligence, but The Admiral had a thought that hadn't previously occurred to the group of young guns down at Army Intel.

Guilbault-Johnson had a hunch, and started to sort through the facts to see if his hunch had some merit. He didn't like to play hunches, but he thought he was far enough into the case to start making deductions.

"Let's walk through this…The loss of the job of the number one earner in a family could, and most likely would lead to shortage of money and some hardship. The hardship could and probably would force the son, the second leader of the household, into trying to make some money quickly.

"And that doesn't always mean doing it legally or through ways that are approved by the military or whatever political group is now in power," The Admiral thought out loud.

The Admiral, who was still sitting in his office alone reached into his desk drawer. He glanced around the room to check for his staff.

Then, he pulled out a pack of cigarettes. Pulled one from pack and put it into his mouth. He lit it mechanically and took a long draw.

"This situation might, in fact, lead to a member of the family that had formerly been friendly, at least not unfriendly to the U.S. forces, to do things for money that are not quite according to Hoyle," The Admiral thought.

"After all, Farooq Ali Sr.'s was a big-ish family. Ali Jr. was living at home, and had few expenses. Ali Jr. had a mother and three little sisters, however, who depended on the elder Mr. Farooq's water plant job to keep them happy and thriving.

So, now Guilbault-Johnson thought he had a good explanation of how Farooq Ali Jr. may have been turned from a neutral to an enemy to a combatant.

Even deeper waded Guilbault-Johnson into the world of Intelligence and hypothesizing and guesswork.

It would be a very rare coincidence that found the son of a newly out-of-work civil servant collaborating with an enemy insurgent.

In fact, the odds of all this happening to one family seemed too wild to guess.

But the odds would be much better if the loss of the civil service job were manufactured by the members of the shady insurgent group, Al Queda.

"If Farooq Ali Sr.'s paperwork were intentionally lost, this would set up a scenario where the son, Farooq Ali Jr. would need lots of cash quickly to help support the family. Under this type of stress, the son may be a little more sympathetic to the rebel cause. It may even turn a non-ideologue from a middle class family with a record of only small, petty offenses into someone capable of espionage or murder for the cause."

A member of the group that wanted to get their hands on the algae formula could recruit a member of the personnel staff at the water plant to lose the records—probably with a bribe. The bribe probably wasn't a payment of money, but rather a promise not to cut off the hands of the civil servant. These types of bribes can be pretty effective. And the threats behind them are very real.

Any of several people who work with records and personnel files could have made Farooq Sr. a non-person and cost him his job.

"Clever devils," Guilbault-Johnson thought out loud.

He took another pull on his cigarette.

Then he quickly looked around his office to make sure that no one heard him talking to himself. Guilbault-Johnson was getting older, but he didn't want to give in to the natural aging of his body. He kept himself in tip-top shape for a man in his sixties, but there is only so much a person can do.

100 sit-ups and push-ups every morning kept him lean and ready. But still, his body wasn't what it was when he was a fit, young lieutenant forty years ago. And he knew it. And he accepted it, sort of.

But what he would not accept was that he was not as sharp mentally as he used to be. And the occasional reminder that he was getting older, like talking to himself, which he never used to do, made him feel older, and he didn't like it.

Guilbault-Johnson got his solo chatting under control and scolded himself for the moment of age-induced weakness. Then, just as quickly, he fidgeted in his desk chair for a moment, then he started to retrace the steps that Farooq Ali Jr. could have taken in the past months.

There are strong oil interests at work in the Middle East, of course. And as much as the rebels want to make the jihad and Al Qaeda about religious purity and oppression, the movement was also about getting claim to the rich, black crude that Jed Clampet called Texas Tea, which flows seemingly limitlessly from under the desert sands.

The Admiral then looked over the Intelligence report provided by the Department of Homeland Security. The report added little to the information from the Navy and Army Intel sources.

CHAPTER
13

When Farooq Ali Jr.'s briefcase smashed into Davic's's nose, both Matty and Steve froze for an instant.

Perhaps they were both too tired from chasing Farooq down a busy Washington street. Maybe they were astonished by the unexpected swiftness and violence of Farooq's nose-crushing move. Maybe they were shocked by the squirting blood.

It seems impossible to contemplate.

After all, these two men, Stuart Locke Mateus and Steven John Benson, had trained for much of their adult lives not to let the unexpected bother them. Not to allow themselves to be startled by acts of violence. They trained to be made of steel when other men around them turned to clay. To be giant oaks in a forest of lowly shrubs. To ride tall in the saddle when others are crawling on all fours.

But on this day in Washington, they both flinched.

Hey, it happens.

Whatever little thing or things caused that instant of hesitation, that little thing or things became Farooq's best friend for just a moment. And Farooq used it to his advantage. He ran.

Off he went down the sidewalk at top speed. He headed east, the direction that the three had been traveling before they met Officer Davics.

Steve went after him.

After his moment of shock, he turned toward the sprinting Ali and started to run. Slowly at first, then, as his head cleared, faster and faster. Ali had a big lead and Steve knew he had lots of ground to cover.

Matty was slower to his feet and reached for his mobile phone and quickly called Guilbault-Johnson to try to follow Farooq through the Intelligence agency's satellites.

If there was a satellite that was focused on the area—and since this is all happening in Washington, D.C., there was a pretty good chance that there was—Farooq would be fairly simple to track as a heat source through his infrared silhouette, and also by identification by visually following him on the screen.

In St. Louis, the phone ringing in Guilbault-Johnson's pocket made him start.

The Admiral was deep in thought about how to get Farooq Ali Jr. and do it in a way that didn't jeopardize any more lives, especially American ones. And if he was right about Ali Jr. and his family, Guilbault-Johnson would also like to save that family from anymore hardship if possible.

If Guilbault-Johnson's theory is correct and the Farooq's family isn't to blame for their situation, they may also be helpful in rounding up the maniac who had two people, including an innocent lab assistant, at the Danforth Center killed in cold blood. Ali's family could also still be in danger.

"Guilbault-Johnson," The Admiral identified himself out of habit as he punched the receive button on the government-issued mobile phone.

"Admiral, this is Matty, eh, Stuart Mateus. We found Farooq. He is currently transiting at high foot-speed eastward from my GPS position. Ali has gone rabbit."

Mateus used the Intel slang term for a target that is trying to escape on foot as a last resort. Matty hated rabbits.

"Be advised, target Farooq is believed to have algae formula with him," said The Admiral.

"Roger that. Can we get a location trailer for target," Matty barked. "Benson is in foot pursuit. Over."

Guilbault-Johnson instinctively reached forward and pushed a button on the desktop phone and communication system opening a communication line with a ranking petty officer who was stationed in the Admiral's outer office twenty-four hours a day.

Guilbault-Johnson's admin person at this moment was petty officer, yeoman third class (YN3) Caty Molina.

Molina responded to the intercom beep. She reached across her desk to activate the speaker and listened to The Admiral's instructions as the director repeated them to Mateus through his hand-held phone at the same time.

"Roger," said The Admiral, "will track high-velocity foot target east-bound from the coordinates of your mobile unit."

Then Guilbault-Johnson released the button on his desktop unit. He knew that those few words were all that was needed to set in motion a series of actions by Petty Officer Molina that would lead to the tracking of Farooq, who may or may not be a killer, who may or may not be personally responsible for two deaths that may or may not have been done at the direction of a person or persons that have yet to be identified.

Guilbault-Johnson said to Matty, "Anything more?"

Matty, "Not for now, over."

"And out," finished The Admiral.

On her side of the office wall, Molina quickly clicked on a joint NSA/Department of Defense, top secret computer program that mapped the Washington, D.C. area. She quickly located the coordinates of Stuart Mateus's phone signal. A simple [CTRL+L] command followed by the number of Matty's phone, and a virtual stickpin is placed at the location on her computer map electronically.

At the same time, Molina beeped into the main theater to get an officer and trained Intel specialist to come down to coordinate the pursuit.

Molina is not a trained Geospatial Intel specialist. She was, by training, an administrative assistant.

The young, thin, dark-haired Latina grew up in a rough part of Los Angeles and had a sense when there was trouble brewing. That sense, her "loco-detector" she called it, was valuable in getting her safely through some street violence in her hometown. That same sense serves her now when she gets messages from The Admiral when she can hear the tension in his voice.

As an admin person, Molina was not great. She sometimes put off work that Admiral Guilbault-Johnson wanted to done right away. She took long coffee breaks to go outside and smoke, even though smoking is against the Navy Operating Order for the building.

But she did most things right, and when the pressure was on, she could be relied on to keep her cool. After all, after you survive some gang violence in Southern California, what's a terrorist or two?

That coolness in pressure situations is why The Admiral trusted her completely.

Even though she was not an Intel specialist, she took extra training that was above her pay grade so she could access the tracking software. She applied for, and received, a top-secret clearance that her position as an admin didn't require. She figured if she was going to escape the LA slums for good, she better do all she can to get out and stay out of trouble.

The Admiral once asked her why she was so eager to take on extra duties and get extra training.

She said, "If they are going to give you free education, you may as well take all you can."

By listening to The Admiral's voice this time, she knew that this was top priority and not an exercise.

Molina knew that getting the first few steps done quickly for The Admiral could mean the difference between success and failure for this mission, and for her career.

She jumped at it.

Molina's computer screen map was really like a larger version of an iPad, only much bigger and faster with a better screen.

Her computer and The Admiral's were synchronized so that whatever he was seeing was what she was seeing in the outer office.

She saw the location of the stickpin and placed the stickpin that was synchronized to Stuart Mateus's location. It was just north of the USDA building in D.C.

By searching for a fast-moving heat source, she also saw the target—or what she assumed was the target—moving eastward down Independence Avenue.

Without direction, Molina attached a tracker to the person. A tracker is an electronic marker that monitors and follows the rabbit and will stay with the person on the big screen until removed or the situation gets too crowded for the computer to distinguish which person it is tracking.

She then took her iPad down the hall to a waiting Intelligence officer. The duty officer right now was Lt. She'Qlia Jackson.

Guilbault-Johnson always had the luxury of having one Intelligence specialist assigned only to him at all hours.

Whoever the Intel specialist was on duty, he or she knew they could have the easiest twelve hours in the history of the Navy, or it could be the craziest, and the most exciting.

For Lt. Jackson, it was about to become one of the most exciting. Jackson took the iPad from Molina.

While waiting for his Intel person to get to his office, Guilbault-Johnson had gotten back on the phone with Stuart and continued to talk through the situation.

"...so I think, and I have a confidence factor of 5 from ten, that Farooq may be the unwilling killer of those two in St. Louis and hijacker of the algae formula." Guilbault-Johnson concluded.

"Repeat the last," responded Matty. "Sounded like unwilling killer?"

"Roger that," said Guilbault-Johnson, "HQ has confidence factor of 5 from 10 that Farooq may be unwilling killer."

"Funny," said Mateus. "I had this weird feeling when we were arresting Farooq before he turned bunny, that he shouldn't be our target. It just didn't feel right. I've grabbed a couple of these radical guys before and they all seem to be very defiant, very ahh...angry. Something about them has some false bravado, some toughness that they try to show. Like no matter what happens, they know something that you don't.

"But this guy had a different feeling. More of desperation, maybe," said Matty. "Something different when I got my hands on him—Hey, there's my ID," Matty interrupted himself. He bent down to pick up the ID that Davics had dropped during the fight. The leather wallet was covered in blood and Matty tried to shake the blood off and then put it back into his pocket.

"Huh? Anyway, Correction," butted in Guilbault-Johnson. "You didn't get your hands on him."

Lt. Jackson looked over the information from Molena's oversized iPad and called up the information on the larger screen in front of her. Her computer was linked directly into the NGA mainframe computer bank.

She was able to pinpoint the exact spot on the south side of the national mall where Matty was standing. Jackson immediately identified Matty from the satellite image on his screen. It helped that Matty was still chatting with Guilbault-Johnson. The live signal emanating from the communicator device made the tracking easier.

Without pausing, Jackson started tracking eastward on the big screen looking for the high-foot-speed target that would be made by a person running. She easily found the tracker that Molina had applied to the suspect.

Jackson didn't know the name of the target, or even the reason they were tracking him. She didn't really care, either. These tracking events took up all her attention. She didn't have to know why, she only had to track, like a twentieth-century bloodhound. And Jackson was good at it. She didn't assume that it had to do with last shift's satellite images of St. Louis.

Guilbault-Johnson didn't intentionally keep Jackson in the dark about the reason the Office of Directed Discretionary Operation is seeking the blue dot on the computer screen.

If Guilbault-Johnson, or anyone else, had information that would help Jackson, they would pass it along. Information such as "intended destination," or "previous propensities," or "previous proclivities."

This last category of Intelligence that Admiral Guilbault-Johnson liked best because the information was usually a little naughty.

If ODDO had any information that would be helpful to Jackson, they would give it to her, but this was a rare time that they just did not have much on this target.

But, they didn't have nothing.

They knew there are several Middle Eastern cells in town that are not friendlies of the United States. A couple of these unfriendlies were right in D.C. while others were in the Maryland suburbs just north of the city.

But they didn't know if Ali was going to look up one of these cells, or had already arranged to meet a contact, or was leaving the country and would be going to an airport or train station, or even if Farooq had completed what he had come to town to do.

All the things that they didn't have were not important to Jackson.

Looking at the computer screen in front of her, Jackson saw a heat source moving at high foot speed eastward away from the location of Mateus.

"Gotcha," Jackson muttered to herself under her breath.

The small, iridescent figure on Jackson's computer screen was the target.

Jackson would not take any action against the heat source for two reasons.

First, Jackson could very quickly have the source picked up by local D.C. cops. But without any more proof than suspicion of being a high-velocity heat source on a crowded D.C. street, would never stick in court.

Second, Jackson wasn't told to pick up the suspect with D.C. cops of any other forces in the area. The Admiral might have something planned for the blue dot, so Jackson had better wait.

"Admiral, I've got him," said Jackson into her interoffice communicator with a direct line into Guilbault-Johnson's office. "Do you want to detain at this moment."

Guilbault-Johnson leaned forward in his chair and answered into his device, "Roger that, and negative. Do not detain, Jackson. Continue to monitor and report when status changes."

"Roger that, sir," said Jackson.

The heat source that Jackson was tracking was now slowing down in the afternoon heat. Either he was tiring, or was trying to blend in with surrounding tourists.

Jackson could continue to follow him as a heat source blip on his computer screen, or she could try to get Matty and Benson to obtain visual surveillance. But that would have to happen fast.

Jackson called Matty directly on her communicator.

"Matty, do you read me?" Jackson asked into her high-tech walkie-talkie.

"Matty, are you there?" she repeated.

"Jackson, is that you? What is up, my friend?" Matty responded. "Got a lead for me?"

"I do, looking at your GPS current, you are three blocks from target," said Jackson. "He is vectoring eastward toward Capitol Street. Request obtain confirmation visual."

Once he found his ID, Matty had started to chase in the direction of Steve and Ali. Even though he has started late, he was able to catch up to Benson.

Matty nudged Steve and indicated he could slow down now that the target was on computer and was being tracked.

They both paused for second to catch their breath.

After a few seconds, Matty was still on the phone with Jackson and he nodded to Benson and they both started to move eastward down Independence Avenue.

They didn't quite break into a run. They thought they attracted enough attention with blood stains on their clothes.

"Vectoring? Jackson, what kind of a word is that?"

Matty loved giving grief to his friend She'Qlia.

She was an academy girl and had the Navy pedigree that went back to her great-great-uncle Doris Miller, the first African-American to win the Navy Cross at Pearl Harbor. During the heart of the Japanese attack, when the Zeros were carving up the U.S. Pacific Fleet, Miller, a steward by training, manned a gun and was one of the few to actually fire back at the Japanese during the slaughter.

Jackson was all Navy, from the day she was born. She took pride in her work, her uniform, her demeanor and her service.

She was, really, all the things Matty was not. And Matty was always a little jealous of the purpose Jackson had, and that he himself lacked.

"Are we vectoring the right way?" continued Matty. "Or are we vectoring incorrectly? I hate incorrect vectoring, don't you Steve?"

Benson, walking quickly along Independence Avenue with Matty shook his head, "Don't get me in this," he said to Matty. He knew how Matty loved to harass coworkers even when the job got hot, especially when the job got busy, and right now Steve was most interested in finding the man who killed two in St, Louis, not giving shit to a Navy officer in St. Louis.

"Hey, Jackson, for the first time in since I've known him, Benson has decided not to talk. Could you please make a note in the log book?" said Matty.

By cracking jokes and being a smart-ass when the heat is on, it always made everyone think that Matty was the coolest of the cool. "This guy has it together," everyone always thought when Matty started with his shit talk. But the jokes and smart comments were not because Matty was cool, but they were the method he used to keep cool. And he figured they could afford to keep cool a little now that Jackson had Ali on her map.

"Roger that," said Jackson, ignoring the nonsense. "Continue eastward toward Capitol."

Jackson continued to monitor the foot traffic as best she could. The heat blip that she thought was Ali continued to weave in and out of all the tourists visiting D.C that day.

CHAPTER
14

Back in St. Louis, Marty Bishop arrived at Jackson's workstation just in time to see the heat blip that was designated Ali Jr. on Jackson's computer disappear into what showed up on the screen as an entrance into the Capitol South Metro Station on First Street Southeast.

The activity of the train station and the host of other people—heat sources—meant Ali was untraceable.

Ali was lost.

"Damn it. I lost him," Jackson said to herself. "Why had The Admiral not been keener on capturing him?" she wondered. "Is there still something I can learn from this old guy? Or he is losing it?"

Jackson looked at Bishop. Neither said anything.

They looked at each other in silence for a moment. A double murderer had slipped through the best-equipped, most high-tech tracking equipment in the world.

Heat trackers, motion sensors, outer-space cameras and humans on the ground, and the team still couldn't get him.

Suddenly, Jackson picked up the communicator that fed directly to Stuart Mateus. She pushed the button to include Steve Benson on the communication.

"Faster," Jackson barked into her receiver at Matty and Benson.

"C'mon, let's go. Are guys giving up?"

GREEN WAVE

Jackson looked at Bishop. Bishop was puzzled. Did Jackson pick up on something? Did she expect the pursuers to catch the train before it left the station? Or, did Jackson think that the two could meet the train at its next stop? What was the lieutenant up to?

Stuart Mateus and Steve Benson, on the streets in Washington broke into a sprint.

Just then, Jackson gave Bishop a wink.

Bishop laughed out loud. Luckily, the transmitter was off and Bishop's laughter didn't get broadcast to the two men running through the streets of our nation's capital.

If Matty had heard that laugh, it would have ruined all Jackson's fun.

"Are we getting closer?" asked Matty on the comm unit. He was huffing and puffing like a man completing a marathon.

"You're almost on him," replied Jackson. "Just a little faster. And don't worry about attracting attention. We need speed, sir. Get to the capitol as fast as you can. They are heading for the capitol. Target may be armed or wired with explosives."

Bishop couldn't take it. He was doubled over in laughter and trying not to let his howls become broadcast. Bishop had never seen anyone get the better of agent Mateus, and Bishop was enjoying this completely.

"Sir, urgent, please proceed with all possible speed," Jackson added once more.

Now Bishop was now on his knees in laughter.

Jackson was enjoying this, too, but she dare not break character.

She had to turn off her phone for fear of giggling and revealing her joke to the victims.

After 30 seconds of silence on the communicator, Matty asked "Jeez, where, did…this guy…go? Over." He gulped hard into the phone. "Are we (pant) close?"

"Aw, nuts, he just got away. Left the grid, likely into a Metro station. We will try to follow in closed circuit security cams provided by Wash police. Please stand by, Matty," said Jackson.

"Will reconnect with you as events dictate," added Jackson.

She and Bishop looked at each other and started to laugh all over again.

Farooq Ali stood on the edge of the platform in the Capitol South Metro station waiting for the next train. He strained his eyes down the tracks to the left and then right. He didn't want to miss the train, any train, to get out of the area. He wasn't a trained operative, but he knew that even in this bustling Metro station full of all kinds of locals from all over the city and tourists from everywhere on the planet, he now looked very out of place.

Sweat was pouring down his forehead. His heart was racing and he was nervous as fish in a bowl at a cat convention.

"Must think. Must get out of here. Get on the train. When is it coming? Is that man looking at me?" Ali's mind was going one hundred miles per hour.

The stress of being wanted for murder gets a man's brain ticking over pretty quickly.

"Is that man walking towards me?" "Does he have a gun?" "I must have been here thirty minutes by now. They've stopped the trains from running to find me…"

Finally, the 2-minute wait for the train was over. The Blue Line train came into the station.

Ali took his place on the platform waiting for the train's doors to open. Waiting. Waiting.

Swoosh. The doors slid open.

Ali took a deep breath and tried to steady himself. He made himself calm enough to allow those on the train to exit before stepping slowly onto the train. Finally, he thought, a moment of relief. He got onto the train.

He located the first open seat he could and collapsed into it without realizing he was sitting in a handicap space. Even if he had known, he wouldn't have cared.

His anxiety and nervousness now partially left him. He was suddenly aware of an overwhelming exhaustion taking him over. He was spent.

He could have fallen asleep right there on the train going, well, he didn't know where he was going. But he was glad to be sitting, glad to be out of sight of the police and glad to have a moment to run through the events of the past week.

Let's see…how did he get into this predicament.

It was a month ago when he got onto a plane in Baghdad with his Hussain Islam and eventually landed in St. Louis.

He hadn't wanted to be there, but events that were out of his control had taken him to St. Louis and on to the capital of the United States. This was a city that most everyone in the world loves to go to, Washington, D.C.

The cradle of the world's power. The seat of democracy. In other circumstances, he would have loved to be in this beautiful city, but right now, it was the last place in the world he wanted to be.

Everything was so strange to him. Nothing good to eat, people wore such odd clothes, like the ones he has seen so often on the television and the Internet back in his hometown in Iraq.

His father, the executive at the water utility back in Baghdad, had traveled to the West on conference visits a few times over the years, and had told Ali about the things he had seen, and brought back photos. But nothing is as exciting and as curious as the first trip to America for anyone who had spent their lives among the sights and sounds of the deserts of the Middle East.

Since arriving in the United States, Ali and his trainer Islam spent their days in the apartment that was arranged by a local Imam near the center of St. Louis. The two had spent much of their time studying the grounds of the Danforth Center. They spend many hours looking at maps of the area around the center and around the campus. They studied about algae so they could tell if they were getting the proper files when the night finally did arrive.

During the evening hours, they would take a bus to the Danforth Center and look around the grounds, getting familiar with the layout. They took notes of when and where people would come and go from the area.

"Hey, dude, what the fuck?"

A startled Ali was shocked back into the present. He jerked his head up.

Ali didn't understand the words, but he could tell that the man standing over him in the Metro train car was upset with something.

"This is a fucking handicap seat, man. My fucking grandma needs to sit there. Get your sweaty ass up and show a little fucking respect."

With that, the passenger gave Ali a gesture to move to another seat.

Of the entire encounter, the only part that Ali understood was that final gesture.

Ali did as he was asked and moved to the vacant seat.

After Ali got out of the seat, the outraged passenger caringly helped his elderly grandmother into the empty seat.

"You OK, Grams?" he asked the elderly woman. He then turned his head and offered a final "Fuck you" towards Ali.

Once re-seated, Ali again started thinking about the last few days.

The night finally arrived back in St. Louis. It was only yesterday, but seemed like a million years ago.

Ali and his boss, or overseer, or henchman or whatever you call it, the man named Islam, the hired muscle, who was in charge of the American side of the operation, were going to steal the algae files.

Ali didn't know why they were going to do it. What those files were. What they were going to be used for. Or who the two were going to give them to when they had them. Over the course of the month they were in St. Louis, Hussain Islam had not told Ali what the files were for and why they were spending all this time and expense getting them.

But the mission had to be successful. His family depended on it.

The two were dressed in black as they left the St. Louis apartment for the night. They carried with them a bag full of tools for the modern day burglar: blank DVDs, flash drives, computer codes, mobile phones, sensor detectors as well as knives and few small caliber guns. The two put everything into two small, student backpacks.

It was just last night, when they carried a duffle bag full of the clothes they had worn for the past few days, got into the rental car, which was also arranged by the local Imam, the skilled criminal Islam and the rank novice—Ali Jr.—placed the duffle, packed with their dirty clothes, into the dumpster at a nearby apartment complex. Not their own.

Ali figured that Hussain was being a sensible criminal. Throw out everything in case the police ever traced them back to the apartment. Tossing the clothes in the adjoining complex's garbage seemed like the smart move.

He was starting the think like a criminal, he thought.

He learned never to ask Hussain what his intentions were. Most times, Ali would get a normal answer, like "none of our business," or "shut up" from the larger Islam.

But over the month, Ali had seen Hussain occasionally fly into a rage over the simplest question or comment. Ali learned to hate Hussain and his anger and his instability.

CHAPTER
15

Farooq Ali Jr. didn't know anything about Mohammad's and Percy's history. And if he had, he wouldn't have cared.

Right now he was riding the Metro in a city he didn't know, and didn't want to be in, being chased by the police, or maybe even someone from Mohammad's group who somehow knew that he, Farooq, was the one who killed Hussain Islam at the Danforth Institute.

He had learned from Islam just less than forty-eight hours ago the name and address of the person he should contact if anything went wrong.

And did it ever go wrong.

That name was Percy Montgomery at Office 245 Alpha at the USDA building in Washington D.C.

Farooq got there easily enough with the help of the $50,000 cash that was part of the operational funds that Qfar Mohammad had sent with Hussain Islam and Farooq. Farooq had even planned ahead enough to buy himself a new set of clothes so when he met Percy, he would not look out of place.

On the train, Farooq closed his eyes and the scenes from the Danforth Institute came flooding into his brain.

Hussain Islam, the physically powerful man who had trained him for a month in preparation for the one night, had a defenseless, innocent, young man pinned to the ground. Then the beast, Islam, took an awful hunter's knife out of his pack and cut the throat of the young man.

It was an image Farooq would never get out of his head.

The bright, red blood shot out of the gash in the young man's neck with each beat of his heart.

It was then that Ali unconsciously reached his hand into his backpack. He felt his hand on the gun that Islam had put there.

He didn't really remember if he made a choice and decided to shoot Islam, or if the whole thing was just triggered when he saw Hussain Islam kill the innocent boy and Ali had the feeling of sickness pour over him during the gruesome slaying.

But his hand was on the cool metal handle of that pistol.

He had felt that handle a few times in the training sessions that led up to the night.

He had been practicing with Islam at a local shooting range. He mostly watched as Islam trained with the weapons. But Ali did shoot a few times, mostly fumbling with the weapon and never hitting the target he aimed for.

Last night he must have reacted instinctively when he saw the murder at the lab. Ali doubts that he could have made the choice to kill someone consciously.

He didn't remember putting his hand on the gun.

Perhaps Ali had first put his hand on the gun in his pack as a response to being surprised by the graduate student. It could have been a raw reaction of self-defense.

Whatever the reason, Ali had pulled his hand out of the backpack with the gun in it.

When Hussain Islam was leaning over the body of the student that he had killed, Ali came out from behind the desk, walked up behind the killer and pretended to lean over the body too. As he did, he stuck the revolver into the back of Islam's head and pulled the trigger.

In Ali's mind, Islam had become all the evil that was happening in Iraq. And Ali had killed it.

After watching and then taking part in such a gruesome act, Ali thought he would feel more frightened, or at least upset.

Actually, he had felt a remarkable calm come over him.

He stepped clear of the expanding pool of blood and quickly collected everything the pair brought with them stashed it all quickly into the two black pack packs they brought with them, and wiped down the 'crime scene' like he had seen them do on television.

Ali left the campus of the Danforth Institute undetected, and started walking towards downtown St. Louis. During the time he and Islam were in town, the two had plenty of free time during their month-long stay, and Ali gained an understanding of the general layout of the town. Using that as his orientation, he started to walk toward the city's core.

He recalled now that he was lucid on that horrible night, but suffering from a minor case of shock. He wandered down side streets that were unfamiliar, but he remained on a path, even if it was a circuitous one, towards the city center and the famous Arch.

After a few hours walking, still carrying both backpacks Ali's thoughts were jumping from subject to subject about as fast as he could blink.

He knew it was early Saturday because the heist was always on the schedule for a Friday night, which was bowling night for the laboratory crew. They knew that the lab was always empty on Friday nights. But why was student there? Why was he in the lab?

Ali didn't have any answers. It was bowling night for the whole group. Always they bowled on Fridays. He and Islam had watched them. They knew the movements of the laboratory group as a team and as individuals. They studied them. After Friday night bowling, every one of the group went home. No one had to cover the lab. No one had to work. The only person in the building, or even near it, should have been the security detail that comes through the area about once every two hours.

And the campus security guard wasn't in the area.

What had gone wrong with the plan they had prepared for over the previous thirty days?

At about 4:00 a.m., Ali wondered into an all-night adult dance bar on Delmar Blvd. in one of the St. Louis neighborhoods where someone who spoke little English, dressed in all black and carried two black back packs, but had handfuls of cash, would not attract too much attention.

As he entered the bar, the bouncer gave Ali an odd glance, but let him in when he saw Ali's wad of cash.

Ali sat down at a corner table and finally had a chance to think.

At his table with a drink, Ali started to sort out a few things quickly.

First, he went into the cramped bathroom to change out of his black clothes and into the set of casual clothes he had brought in case of a change of plans. He tossed into the bar's trash his black outfit and also the extra clothes Islam had brought. He also got rid of all the electronic gadgets they brought with them—iPod and two mobile phones and some electronic recording devices.

Ali figured that it would easier to get new electronics if he needed them rather than get caught with these and have all their information, e-mails and all the other personal information that could have been captured in the past month.

In the pack were a few notes of emergency numbers that Qfar had given them. Contacts in both St. Louis, and Washington, along with some flight information for planes going back to the Middle East. Ali quickly scribbled down the contact information on a pad of paper from the pack and tossed out everything else.

He kept the stack of bills that were there to help in an emergency, and this was certainly an emergency.

While having notes scribbled on a piece of paper was decidedly low-tech, Ali felt it would be easier to dispose of evidence if it were on a piece of paper than if it were on his phone and stored electronically.

Ali went back to his table and ordered another soda. He finally started to calm down. It had been a crazy few hours.

Ali sat in the bar for a few more hours, waiting. For what, he didn't know.

In accordance with his religion, he didn't drink alcohol. Not buying booze will usually get a person kicked out of place like this.

But the bartender didn't mind since Ali was tipping $5 for every Diet Coke he ordered.

While sitting at his table, Ali was going through some of the last papers from the pack and he found a note. It was a printout of an e-mail that was sent from Qfar Mohammad to Hussain Islam.

Islam must have kept this a secret from Ali because it ensured, or was intended to ensure that the project would not move to the next stage without himself. Well, the project was moving on, for better or worse, without Islam.

The message was simple: Huss-, take the info to DC to the USDA building and find Percy Montgomery at 202-555-1212. He will have info on where to go next. Right now, I think it will be Lissabon.

Qfar had used the German spelling for Lisbon, Portugal, as that was how he always referred to it and it more closely resembled how the city is pronounced in Arabic.

Ali paused and then decided he didn't like the idea of his back packs, clothes, personal items and other trash being the garbage in the crapper. It was too much evidence and too easy a place to find it.

He started to think that spending a month with Hussain Islam had turned him into a person who thought like a criminal.

So he went back to the bathroom and got his stuff out of the trash and made a trip outside to the dumpster behind the tattoo parlor that sat across the back alley from the Titalator, the skin joint where he was a guest.

He went back into the nudey bar and sat down again. His situation was getting better, he thought.

Now, he had shed his packs, cleared his head, and had discovered a name and number of where he needed to go.

Ali was ready to move. The Titalator had done him some good.

He was wearing a pair of khaki pants a green sweatshirt, and a pair of Adidas sneakers. He carried only a small string-style backpack with an Under Armor logo on it and a plain, blue ball cap.

He looked like he fit in. And more important, he felt like he fit in.

He had to get to the airport where he would do his best not to betray the fact that his pack was half full of American cash and he was a killer who was undoubtedly being hunted.

He finally poked his head out of the front door of the bar and looked up and down Delmar Blvd.

Nothing to see except a city starting to come to life in the early morning. He stepped boldly onto the sidewalk and continued his trek toward the arches of downtown St. Louis. It was another hour to the arches on foot and from there it was onto the bus to the airport.

The last hurdle to getting to D.C., as he saw it, was buying his ticket.

He knew that by paying cash he would be suspicious and the Department of Homeland Security crew would give him a close look. But he didn't have a choice. He just had to look as comfortable as he could, and maybe he could get through. After all, his father's livelihood and maybe life depended on it. Ali had already decided that he would buy a round trip ticket. A one-way ticket, by a Middle Eastern man paying with cash, would be too many red flags.

So, what is he doing with all that cash? What would his story be?

While on the bus to the airport, he pieced together a narrative that he hoped would pass muster if he were to be stopped.

He was a student at the Danforth institute, he would say. Through his months of studying the goings on at the institute, he thought he would be able to answer most any questions a security guard would pose. He was going to D.C. to meet with a diplomatic advisor from Iraq to extend his stay. He would explain the money by saying that he was going to have to bribe his advisor in Washington in order to get permission from his own government to stay in the U.S. to study.

Ali figured that Americans are eager to believe the worst about Iraqis. So, saying that he would have to bribe his government's own education liaison would give the Homeland Security team a perfect reason to believe him.

The story had a downside, because it tied him to the crime scene. But he hoped that the bodies had not been discovered yet.

Ali knew that this was a lot of stories and lies stacked atop one another. If one of the playing cards upon which he built this house of lies were to be pulled, the whole thing would collapse pretty quickly. So, he told himself to move around the airport with purpose, lie to security with sincerity, and if all else fails, ask to see someone from the Department of State to so he could tell the whole story and hope for salvation.

Farooq, still sitting in the train car in Washington, thought on about his Friday in St. Louis. He walked through it in his mind a second time.

He and Islam had gotten to the Danforth building just as they had planned. The pass code worked perfectly and the door to Ali's father's future opened.

He and Islam had started collecting the files from the computer just as Mohammad had shown them. They were easily accessing the computer at the work station just as Mohammad had described.

Then everything was disrupted by that young person walking in on them.

"Who was he?" "Where did he come from?" Ali kept asking himself.

There wasn't supposed to be anyone in the building, especially at that time of night. He didn't look like a security guard, thought Ali.

He and Islam had been trained to spot the campus police with their blue uniforms and radios. They didn't carry weapons, so they weren't considered a real threat and could be disposed of 'quickly and without incident' was the phrase that Mohammad and Islam had both used repeatedly when discussing the topic of any resistance.

'Weak westerners' was the phrase that Islam used when he talked of the campus police. He was a true believer in the cause of Jihad. He loved the use of force to solve conflicts and thought anyone who didn't think using force as the first, best option was weak. So weak, that killing them is doing them a favor.

Ali Jr. understood the mindset of the Jihadist. He had seen it is whole life in a few of his friends and some distant relatives growing up. A few of them had even contacted him about getting involved in the 'patriotic cause.' Ali always declined. And now, he was stuck in the middle of a murder and energy plot that he didn't understand because he didn't get involved in the Jihad.

Maybe it would have been easier to just to join and be done with it.

The mindset of jihadist was so rare though in his country, he never thought they would have the money or the energy or organization to pull off the worldwide attack on the World Trade Center and Washington, D.C.

And now that 9/11 was behind them, the whole world thought the Middle East was full of radicals. And that just wasn't the truth.

Sad, thought Ali, that the region will forever be tainted with the stench for which just a few of his countrymen were responsible.

Understanding all that, Ali shook his head in the Metro train car and thought about that young man at the Danforth Lab. Why did Islam have to kill him? The two could have gotten what they wanted, the files, without killing him.

The whole operation would have been a bloodless success. When they were interrupted, all we had to do was subdue the kid and tie him up, or even knock him out. There was no way that he could have seen their faces. Their clothes concealed them completely. It was a job that was done and dusted. It should have been just a matter of getting away.

But Islam wasn't content with just tying him up.

For some reason, Islam needed to kill.

No matter what.

"What sort of an animal had he gotten connected with?" thought Ali.

But then he thought of the way these Jihadists had treated his father, and the predicament they were all in. How did the Jihadist believe that this is what Allah would have wanted? He knew what sort of people these were. But he didn't understand them at all.

Sitting now in his subway car just more than a day after he watched a man die, and then kill the man responsible, Ali hanged his head and began to weep.

Back in Baghdad, Ali's family and people were a peaceful group.

They didn't experience the hate wars of those who wanted to destroy his country with jihads and phony jihads and tribal fights over money and oil rights. His was a family and a neighborhood that wanted to live and let live and grow old laughing with the grandchildren that he would someday have.

But that prospect seemed pretty dim at this point, as Ali thought back to the horrific memory of the previous night in St. Louis.

CHAPTER 16

In Baghdad, Qfar Mohammad clicked on the website www.stlouistoday.com. It is the city's local paper and Mohammad thought there might be a news story somewhere in the paper's City section tab about a curious little burglary on the grounds of the Danforth Institute that had local police baffled.

The police, thought Mohammad, would be so vexed by the seemingly pointless caper that they wouldn't really bother to investigate. Just some kids getting into some mischief, would be the reaction of the local constabulary.

What Mohammad didn't expect was to see the shocking headline "Two killed in Danforth slayings."

"What the fuck," Mohammad thought to himself. Something has gone terribly wrong.

He was right.

"How is this going to affect my plans? I've spent a year and a half putting this together. If my plans have been ruined, I'll kill Ali and his father and his family will starve looking for work," Mohammad thought.

Mohammad's eyes scanned down the story to see if Ali's or Islam's names were mentioned or anything else that may incriminate him or his efforts to become the richest Jihadist in Baghdad.

As he read through the details, it was clear the police didn't have much to go on. The killer or killers seemed to have left no clues at the scene.

"Excellent" thought Mohammad, "just as I taught that mindless, crazy Islam."

The news story noted that some computer files seemed to be missing, or at least duplicated and stolen from the lab's computers.

"Perfect," grinned Mohammad and he read on.

One of the victims was a twenty-five-year-old researcher who worked in the lab.

"Collateral damage," laughed Mohammad. He was so delighted that he said it aloud again, "Collateral Damage."

And the other victim was dressed in black and of Arab descent with no identification.

"Islam must have killed the weak Ali after the job was done in order to tie up any loose ends," thought Mohammad. "Very nicely done."

So, other than a little more publicity than the plan required, everything went perfectly, thought Mohammad.

But maybe, when the time came, the extra publicity might be good for recruiting more operatives. The unwilling can become willing more easily when you show the potential recruits that a possible side effect of refusing, is dying.

Matty and Benson finally got the joke.

Ha-Ha.

They could feel Lt. Jackson's mocking episode all around them.

Oh, very funny indeed.

What a kidder.

The two planned to give her a proper ass kicking when they return to St. Louis, but now they had to think.

They were interrupted by a buzz on Matty's phone alerted them that The Admiral was calling.

"Matty here," the agent said abruptly into his communicator.

"Contact with Ali?" asked the superior officer from St. Louis.

"Negative. Shit." Matty answered.

"Now, where was Ali going with that case?" asked The Admiral. "Come, come," he continued demanding input from his team. "Let's get down to it."

The Admiral didn't have time nor did he have the inclination to assign blame, or talk about how the two trained Intel officers were out run and out maneuvered by the son of a water district supervisor with no military training and no history of fitness.

That was all for another time.

Right now Guilbault-Johnson's two best men were trying to track down a killer. And those two men needed to be briefed on the current situation and they also had to tell him what they learned.

"Tired or fresh, we don't have time for panting and swearing. Losing one's head when the pressure is on betrays an untidy mind," Guilbault-Johnson barked in a firm, but not shouting tone.

Matty was starting to get his head about him.

"As you thought, Ali was exiting the USDA building when we marked him. What do we know about that? Who is his contact there?" asked Matty.

"Damn, I was sort of hoping you didn't find him there," said Guilbault-Johnson.

"Great, so now you're telling us that you're against us, and cheering for them? I thought we were the good guys," said Matty.

"You know this reminds me of that time in London when we were trying to get that guy who ended up getting shot and having that scar," jumped in Steve, starting a story that neither Matty nor The Admiral had the time or patience for.

"Really? Long story? Now? Shut up," Matty said putting his hand over the phone so his boss wouldn't hear Benson's tale.

"Remember? This guy I can't remember his name, shoot, we must have tracked in half way round the world. He was always wearing these high-collar shirts. We started calling him 'Big Neck.'"

The Admiral barked into the phone at Matty, "Let me talk with Benson."

Matty sheepishly handed the phone to his partner and said, "He wants to talk to you."

Benson took the phone and put his hand over the mouthpiece so The Admiral couldn't hear and said to Matty, "Oh, the Admiral remembers that caper, I'll bet. The Admiral always likes to hear about the old days. Great guy The Admiral."

Benson lifted the communication unit to his ear, "You remember that, sir? That time—"

"SHUT UP!" shouted The Admiral at Benson.

Benson's face went ashen and sheepishly handed the phone back to Matty.

"Now, as I was saying," The Admiral started again. "I was hoping that you didn't find him at the USDA. We sent you there on the outside chance that a person of interest there, Percy Montgomery, who we've been monitoring pretty closely, would be involved in this. Since you found Ali there, I am certain that Percy is involved. Damn shame. It turns out that Percy has had several contacts—via e-mail and phone —with the shadow group that we think is behind this whole business."

"Percy Montgomery, Percy…sounds familiar, but I can't place it," said Matty.

"He was the agitator for the Green Party of Maryland a few years ago," refreshed The Admiral. "He had some really odd ideas about how bringing some of the aspects of Jihad to the U.S. would be good for everyone. That's all fine, if that is your thing, but when I remembered that he was arrested for bombing a Metro station there in DC, he was really thrown to the top of my suspect list for this caper. He was acquitted at trail, but there were lots of questions about that."

A busy Metro station is a chaotic place. Commuters from the suburbs heading to their nice-paying jobs in the government sector and lobbyists sending vital text messages share train cars with unemployed drunks who stumble through life from government paycheck to government paycheck without any direction or plan. For the affluent subsections, the Metro is green, sustainable option for commuting. For the other, it is simply the easiest, cheapest way to get to the convenience store for more booze.

One morning as the well-aimed and the aimless commuters settled into their seats, a deafening explosion rocked the train car. In the aftermath, they counted fourteen dead and an equal number injured and broken. After an investigation, they tabbed a young USDA employee as the likely bomber. After a two-month trail, he was cleared by a jury of his peers when defense lawyers blamed a shadowy group that operated in stealth around the city.

In a city in which Al Qaeda's frightening specter can still scare people, the idea that a Middle Eastern group may be responsible made them sympathetic to the blond-haired defendant.

"Not guilty," they said.

"Oh sure, I remember that now," said Matty. "And what about that shadow group?"

"Well, it doesn't really have a name, or an ideology as far as we can tell," said The Admiral. "They sort of claim to be a Jihad movement when it suits them. Otherwise, they seem to operate more like any old organized crime group. Whenever they are active, they seem to want money more than anything else. We had them on the radar and we've been calling them the Jewelry Jihadists, since they are more keen on money than on anything else.

"And you suspect that Percy has been working with them? But the way you describe him, Percy seems like the genuine article. A true believer, so to speak. Would he get mixed in with some people who were just out for money?" asked Matty.

"Well, I said there lots of questions about his acquittal in that train bombing? What didn't come up at trail is that a passenger on the train was actually an envoy from the Iraqi embassy acting as courier for a pretty large cash movement—"

"And it turned up missing after the bomb?" finished Matty.

"Since it was not an authorized transfer, one of the millions of dollars that move through this city from embassy to investor to trading insider to connection, and since the Iraqis still won't admit that there ever really was a transfer, that money has never been counted as missing or stolen. And that was three years ago," The Admiral said.

"Sounds like there are too many coincidences for this to be unrelated. Why didn't you want Montgomery to be our man?" asked Matty.

"Don't know," said The Admiral. "I guess I was holding out hope that this guy actually didn't do it. He is quite a figure if you've seen his file. Just hoping that for once we were wrong about him and he was actually one of the good guys."

"Wow, strong evidence, boss" said Matty sarcastically. "You hoped he was a good guy? I mean, what the fuck?"

"I know, it is a feeble reason from a feeble old man," said The Admiral. "Maybe I've been doing this job too long. Sometimes I just hope we're wrong about some of these guys. I get tired of chasing the bad guys. And I get tired of always being right about them being bad guys."

"Well, if they weren't bad guys, we wouldn't need to chase them," said Matty.

Matty was being a smartass, which was his nature, but he actually felt for his boss. Matty spent his life out in the field chasing the bad guys wherever and whenever the government needs him. He liked to think he was a part-time government joy rider and a full-time rugby referee. Matty understood that it must get depressing at the top of the Intel food chain. Always suspicious, always questioning motives of those around you. 'Is the new janitor a spy? Is my secretary a foreign agent? Why is the junior officer taking out the classified trash to the burn center?' It must be awful to be on guard at all times, Matty thought.

It was odd that The Admiral would let down his guard on the phone with Matty too.

The moment didn't last, The Admiral collected himself.

"We'll have to get Percy on the tag and give him a closer look," he said.

When the Admiral puts someone on 'the Tag' he means to press him hard with surveillance. The Tag means that the suspect will know that he is being watched. This type of surveillance takes lots of work and lots of expense, but it gets results. Usually the suspect flees or exposes himself pretty quickly. If the suspect flees, they follow. If the suspect turns themselves in, they get a confession with little trouble.

If the Office of Directed Discretionary Operations was ever questioned about this tactic in court, it may be shown as harassment. But so far, every instance that The Admiral has put the Tag on a suspect, the results have been good.

Percy Montgomery lived in the very quiet northern suburb that straddled the D.C. and Maryland line called Tacoma Park. It was atypical in the capital area. Here in the middle of the seat of power in the Western Hemisphere was a neighborhood that looked decidedly like a town in the Midwest that time had forgotten.

Two-story, wood-frame homes situated on winding, hilly streets where children played and neighbors greeted one another with warm hellos and waves from well-kept yards that were always freshly mowed. Many in the area are longtime government workers with nice incomes and the type of job security that is better than a college professor's tenure.

So, as a group they tend toward community improvement and common welfare. Many trace their roots to the 1960s and the counterculture revolution.

It is among these people that Percy Montgomery had found a comfortable life. He worked at the Department of Agriculture in downtown D.C. Took the Red Line Metro train to his job each day. And rode his bike to the neighborhood cooperative to get his groceries whenever he could.

He didn't like the idea that the United States was involved in a war. He didn't like the idea that the U.S. military was killing people. He was sympathetic to the point of view that the people killed in the Twin Towers on 9/11 were "little Eichmans" and may have had it coming for all the evil they were doing, by going to work that day.

It was his comfort that led to his judgmental ways. People who had to work and work hard know that buying organic celery at three times the normal price at the local coop was not an option for everyone. Organic food is trendy and currently a wealthy indulgence for most shoppers. Montgomery didn't know that. Or, more likely, had long forgotten it.

To put it bluntly, Montgomery had grown up to become someone that the radical right would consider a "blame America first" type of guy.

His association with radical movements included a meeting about a year and a half ago.

Montgomery was at a USDA social/official function welcoming a delegation from Iraq in the main ballroom of the Washington Hilton. It was there that Montgomery met a member of the delegation named Qfar Mohammad.

Qfar was a likeable, gregarious fellow and Percy Montgomery liked him immediately. The Iraqi delegation was in the United States to visit with the Department of Agriculture to learn more about corn.

It seems that researchers in the Midwest had used some genetic engineering to develop drought-resistant crops. These crops could withstand high heat conditions and could produce a crop no matter how much sunshine the dessert could burn down on the plants. These corn varieties were not much use in the Midwest and the event was scheduled to discuss how to transfer this new technology to Middle Eastern countries so they could support their own population needs.

The USDA hoped to use the crops as an enticement to get better terms for the purchase of oil from the big producers who have plenty of sun and no real crops of their own.

At the soiree, Montgomery literally bumped into Mohammad while reaching for his drink at the open bar. The two started a social chat about the mission of the delegation, and how the USDA could help increase the food security of the dry nation. It was innocent enough chatter for a dinner party.

But as the conversation moved forward, Percy sensed that Mohammad didn't seem to know much about crop genetics or the availability of food in the dessert region. In fact, Percy began to wonder what this dignitary was doing on a junket like this. Despite his complete lack of background in the area of agriculture, Mohammad kept drawing the conversation to ethanol production and the idea that there would be lots of money for any U.S. company that solved the riddle of making green, renewable energy commercially profitable. The company or government agency that could develop profitable biofuels would have the answer to the question that the rest of the industrialized world wants solved.

"Sure there would be big profits in useable green energy," said Percy at the banquet table where the two were enjoying light finger snacks surrounded by more than 100 other delegation invitees from Iraq and the U.S.

"And that would allow the developing world to industrialize more quickly and without penalty for producing greenhouse gasses."

"Yes, certainly," replied Qfar Mohammad, happy to have a true believer to talk with. Mohammad had no interest in the drought-resistant corn that was supposed to be the star of the show. He would leave all that to the rest of the delegation from Iraq. Qfar Mohammad wanted only to convince Percy Montgomery that with a little help from a source inside the USDA, Iraq could help develop a green biofuel that will revolutionize how the world thinks about energy.

"I dream of a world where cars are filled with gas made of algae, and planes fly using the energy we get from the very sunshine that these large metal birds block out as they fly over us polluting our skies," said Mohammad in his most poetic voice. He had been planning this meeting for more than six months and he hoped that he was putting the close to a deal that would make him the richest man in the Middle East.

And that was a dream that was worth dreaming from for Qfar Mohammad.

Mohammad had not accidentally bumped into Percy Montgomery at the "Evening of Iraqi and U.S. Drought-Resistant Crop Engagement" as the evening was named by someone in the community relations department of the USDA.

Qfar Mohammad had researched a weak link, had killed to get on the delegation and was now setting the trap.

Mohammad had many contacts in the Washington area, many working at government jobs and some were part of a foreign cell of Middle Easterners. Although the cell was not an Al Qaeda group, it was originated not to kill Americans, but to rob them.

CHAPTER 17

Iraq and other oil-producing countries provide Western nations, like the United States, with the one product they have—oil. For that product, the United States pours trillions of dollars every year into these countries which, because of the huge fortunes at stake, are ruled by a small sector of the population—either a family or oligarchy that keeps the money—mostly for themselves. The leaders of the countries sometimes allow money to pass through them on to the rest of the population, but only enough to keep them from revolting and overthrowing the government.

On the other hand, the citizens of many of these countries are nomadic and have little use for material possessions or for that matter the very government that rules them.

If you can even call it rule, since these nomadic peoples often operate outside the law and have little interaction with law enforcement other than their own.

Because they are isolated by their nomadic lifestyle, the populations of these countries have always tended to cling desperately to religion as bonding and guiding principle in their lives.

It was among this tradition of self-sufficiency and religious zealotry that Qfar Mohammad was born.

He grew up in the nomadic fashion of a Bedouin without many creature comforts. He and his family didn't have much, but they didn't want for much either. Then there was the exception, Qfar Mohammad.

He wanted it all from an early age. When he was ten, he went to town for the first time with his father and with the adult men to collect supplies and trade some of the goods—skins mostly—that the family had been able to collect over the previous weeks. Since this first trip made such an impression on him, he remembered everything.

When his father's group sold their goods, they often took their money to the bar to get drunk. To finally be a part of the men's group in the city was a thrill for young Qfar Mohammad. And the trip to the bar was the special treat. Not because he wanted to drink, but because of the television set in the bar.

He was transfixed by the images on the screen.

Light-skinned people, drinking and laughing more than young Hussain had ever laughed. And the women…Oh, the women. He had never seen anything like them.

While the other men from his group were drinking and talking, Qfar was watching the rerun of "Dallas" from 1983. A grown-up member of Qfar's group saw the young man watching the Western show. He told Qfar that the entire theme of the show was evil. The man mocked the decadent Americans as weak and thinking only about pleasure.

Qfar didn't care, he was engrossed.

Qfar had to have that money, he needed to possess those women. He wanted it all and he would have it, all praise to Allah.

After that first trip, the images stuck with Qfar. And each time he went to town, he made sure he saw some more of this television.

So while he was growing up, Qfar Mohammad was always looking for a way to make money. Petty crime leading to larger crime which led to a small criminal enterprise in his adopted home city of Baghdad.

That small criminal enterprise, "The Gang" he called it, soon grew more and more powerful. Eventually the group got the attention of Iraqi President Saddam Hussein.

The president's security force made of habit of knowing what was going on in the Baghdad underworld, and in the underworld, young Qfar could not be ignored.

When President Hussain heard about Qfar, he was intrigued and wanted to learn more about his activities. Mostly Hussain was curious to observe how Qfar controlled his men and funneled money to the top with as little lost to bribes and corruption as possible.

Ironically, Qfar Mohammad had actually learned much of his craft from studying the rise to power of the dictator of Iraq himself.

In his ascent to power, Saddam had shown a ruthlessness and ability to kill without a conscience. That appealed to the young Mohammad.

As Qfar emulated Hussein, his business grew. From a neighborhood bully that brutalized old men and women in parts of Baghdad, to more sophisticated schemes targeting shop owners and protection money like the mob in the United States.

By the time Qfar was in his thirties, he was living the life that he had dreamed. He liked to charm young women, mostly from the West, whom he would he would fly to his Baghdad mansion.

He would travel to Europe to gamble in Monte Carlo and taste all the beauty that the city offered. Many of the women, were blond and built like Charlene Tilton from his favorite TV show. Short and buxom. He would often dress them in the cowboy-style clothes he had seen on Dallas years before.

And all during Qfar's ascension, Saddam Hussain was watching from his palace. At first Saddam was amused and interested by Qfar's efforts. Saddam felt toward the young man as a mentor would feel toward a student.

As Qfar's fortunes grew, Saddam started to get jealous and then a little nervous of Qfar's empire, as by the early nineties it was big enough to be called an empire. By then Saddam was distracted by his blunder into Kuwait and how badly he misjudged the reaction from the West.

He calculated that NATO and the United States would be upset. But he thought a few more sanctions, maybe or a meaningless embargo would be the worst the West would have had the stomach for.

GREEN WAVE

When the United States was able to organize and finance a full-scale invasion of Kuwait, including a coalition that included some Muslim nations, Saddam was astonished. Astonished not about the religious fratricide that he witnessed as Muslim Moroccan fighter pilots, flying NATO jets, paid for by American dollars, shot at his underpaid soldiers.

No, that didn't bother him. On the issues of religion and piety, Saddam and Qfar were very much pragmatists. If claiming yourself to be a devout Muslim allowed the leaders of Iraq to more easily bilk innocents out of their money, or made a policeman more vulnerable to decapitation, then that was the easy dodge to employ. If the results meant death to your enemy, more money or more women, then they would claim to be Muslims all the way.

Saddam's outlook changed with the liberation of Kuwait and the partial invasion of Iraqi in 1991. He was shocked when coalition forces stopped short of deposing him. Saddam was certain that the West was going all the way to Baghdad and he would certainly be killed along with everyone who was part of his regime.

As it turned out, most of Iraq and Saddam Hussain were spared. In the wake of the 1991 Gulf War, Saddam Hussain did two things.

First, he understood that his reign on his country was only as good as his ability to fool the West and test their will.

Two, he realized that he could use more internal allies.

Because he was already familiar with Qfar's work, Saddam brought him into his inner circle more and more. At state dinners and national affairs, Qfar was a frequent guest. Qfar was introduced to the globe's most powerful people in the energy sector.

Qfar's dream of becoming rich and banging blond women on a bed covered in American Dollars was already fulfilled a thousand times over. Now he was venturing into an area of power and money he had not previously considered…politics.

Some of these energy and oil contacts proved very valuable to Qfar. On one trip to Europe he was in Belgium on a junket to discuss the tariffs charged in the ports in Amsterdam and Rotterdam for the import of oil from Iraq. At least that was the story. It was really a chance to buy diamonds from the distributor in bulk to give to the latest blonde Charlene Tilton lookalike he was planning to conquer.

One particularly interesting aspect of the trip to Belgium was meeting a young blonde girl whom he immediately took a liking to. More than the other American bimbos, this one was smart, and savvy and she had a poise that the others didn't have.

Her name, Qfar would always remember, was Patty. Patty Johnson.

She was unlike the other women whom he had 'dated'. She was smarter, more composed. And so very hot. The long blonde hair, just like Charleene Tilton. The buxom body. The cute smile.

Everything was perfect.

Everything but one.

She didn't seem interested in going to the most expensive parties and meeting the most expensive people as Qfar's other women did.

She was interested in her school work. When she told fellow partiers that she was a student working her way through college, it was actually true.

When they did go to parties together, Qfar actually didn't feel as though he needed to dominate her as he had the others. He sort of liked her. It was a feeling he was not accustomed to with the blondes who found their way into his inner circle of partiers.

It was inevitable that the relationship would end. Qfar eventually resorted to his old ways and one night raped her repeatedly at his Baghdad mansion.

She barely survived the ordeal. The last thing she remembers for that night is three or four of Qfar's henchmen taking turns at her after the boss had finished off.

This how Qfar treated people for whom he had a fondness.

And because of that fondness, he bought her a ticket back to school and let her return to her normal life.

During this trip to Belgium, Qfar was to meet with scientists working on alternative forms of energy made from renewable resources. After years of research, the scientists from universities around the world were close to making a new kind of biofuel affordable and accessible. The consequences to such a discovery would have worldwide repercussions. Any group producing fuels in this way would be a threat to the stability, such as it is, to the governments in the Middle East. Qfar listened to the presentations and hatched a plan.

What if he, Qfar, could get his hands on the biofuels formula? Who would want it? What could he do with it?

After five years, the technology of the biofuels team in Belgium never produced the promised results, but the idea never left Qfar.

Now, when he met Percy at the party in Washington five years later, Qfar learned that a group at the Danforth Institute was closer than ever to solving the biofuels riddle once and for all.

And the interim years had only made the possibilities better. Not only was Saddam finally killed, leaving even more criminal opportunities for Qfar to explore domestically, but now there were more interested customers for the formula internationally.

China and India have booming fuel needs. Even the bumbling Russia had started finding its economic feet and needed to be fed energy wise.

If Qfar could get his hands on that formula now, he could realize a profit ten-fold more than he would have dreamt.

The problem now was, since Saddam was killed, Qfar's political influence had dried up considerably.

As the new government moved in and started selecting who was going to be part of the rebuilding of Iraq, Qfar was of two minds.

He could certainly approach the new overlords and ask for a job. After all, he was fluent in English—a language he needed as he traversed Southern Europe meeting "ladies" and gambling in the best casinos. But if he applied for a position in the new government, they would certainly do a background check and discover his previous activities that were unsavory, to say the least.

In the end, Qfar did was he always does. He acted boldly—if maybe a little stupidly—and asked the new government for a job.

And he got one.

But the job he had asked for, that of a mid-level administrator, from which he would be able to monitor the actions of the new government and look for opportunities to steal and bribe and obtain access to the higher ups, wasn't available. Instead, he was assigned to a more upper level position, Assistant Minster of Energy for Green Exploration.

It may have sounded odd for the new administration to name an administrator of green energy in a country where the oil nearly seeps from the ground and most of the population doesn't use cars.

There is an excess of oil here like almost nowhere on earth. The nation exports oil to the United States, Canada, and Western Europe by the billions of barrels. To spend time, money and manpower worrying about how a nation like this could be more green seems absurd.

It seemed absurd to Qfar also. But he took the assignment with his usual approach, by turning the situation to his personal advantage.

In one of his first acts as AME-GE, Qfar had some of his personal employees kidnap the wife of the Minister of Energy and demanded that he resign or his wife would be killed. The Minister, a man who had lived in Iraq his entire life and new that these threats were not idle, but was none-the-less an honorable man, resigned. His wife was freed.

Much to Qfar's surprise he wasn't named to succeed the minister. Instead, another man, a friend of Qfar's was named to the post and that was almost as good in Qfar's eyes. He would now have complete access to all the files, names, contacts that the new minster had, but without any of the responsibilities that come with the post.

For one of the few times in his life, Qfar had miscalculated, but for one of the many times in his life, Qfar's criminal actions had turned out better than he had anticipated. It didn't take Qfar Mohammad long to devise a plot that would make him millions, if successful, and might bankrupt the country of Iraq. That didn't matter to him as the only goal is to amass the greatest fortune he could and accumulate as many women as possible, before he went on to meet his friend Saddam in the afterlife.

After gaining access to the confidential files of the Ministry, Qfar looked for, and easily found, the "THREATS TO OIL PRODUCTION" on the Ministry's confidential files.

Most of the threats seemed benign to him, and for the most part they were. After all, President George W. Bush had said himself that the United States has an oil addiction.

One threat caught his eye, though. This threat seemed to be real and, more important, ripe for exploitation. It involved new sources of energy that were being developed at various research centers around the world. Qfar read in the files that if these biofuels were developed, they could pose a significant problem for oil-producing countries such as his. These files are highlighting next-generation biofuels that could be made from various sources.

The most promising of the new fuels was made from one of the fastest-growing types of vegetation known to exist, algae. But the file stopped there. In it, there was no mention of who was developing this fuel, or how far they were from developing the fuel, and would it even be financially feasible.

Qfar needed to find a way to do what the Saddam Hussain regime could not, or would not, or did not for whatever reason. He needed to retrieve that technology for making biofuels from algae and sell it to the highest bidder. Surely China, or Russia or even India would see the value in producing their own fuels for their growing economies.

The downside would be the Iraq would lose much of the value of its only product, oil, and the economy would crater. But these distractions were unimportant to Qfar as he dreamed only of banging some blonde homecoming queen in the presidential suite on a mountain of cash at a casino in Monte Carlo.

Over the next few weeks, Qfar tried to figure out where this research was being done. Where could he find out where this research is being done?

Finally, while sitting at his desk in his new job at the Ministry of Energy-Non Petroleum, he thought he would have to ask someone. But who?

During his Internet research on green energy, Qfar had found a weekly blog written by an American at the Department of Agriculture. The blog preached about the evils of American imperialism and the nation's dominance in the world that was undeserved and regrettable. "…our overconsumption of the world's resources is both immoral and unconscionable" was a passage that made Qfar think that he certainly had the right man.

Qfar immediately arranged a visit by members of his department to Washington to meet members of the Department of Agriculture. He made the purpose of the visit "to develop a cooperative framework for the two countries to move toward a greener future" so sappy that he didn't think the Americans would take it seriously.

But they did.

As preordained, Qfar met the blogger, Percy Montgomery, at the reception his first night in America.

Now Mohammad had to convince this American sap to get for him the secret to cheap oil from algae, so it could be sold to the highest bidder.

Qfar, as is his way, had another thought. "What if I offered to sell the technology to the OPEC nations in order to keep China or India from developing the biofuels," he thought.

"Now we are looking at a bidding war" he thought to himself, and that was good for business.

For his part, Montgomery, from the first meeting liked the Iraqi diplomat. And he liked even more the idea that he could help put an end to America's gluttony. The subject was like a drug to Montgomery. His expertise at the USDA wasn't biofuels. But through his connections, Montgomery was able to locate information on almost every aspect of the program that the USDA was currently funding and had funded in the past. Many of them showed much promise and many others didn't.

About a year before the murders in St. Louis, Montgomery found out that there was research about to be published about certain algal populations that may yield three of four hundred times the amount of biomass that current algae yield.

That amount of biomass converted into biofuels, including ethanol and others, could mean a green revolution that would put the planet back on the right road, in Montgomery's mind.

GREEN WAVE

When he was reading about the possibilities in the USDA files, Percy couldn't believe it. This could finally be the antidote to the carbon fuel dependence that was destroying the planet. Montgomery contacted his old friend, Qfar Mohammad at the Ministry of Energy, Non Petroleum, in Baghdad about the research.

CHAPTER
18

Farooq Ali looked up at the train map above the door and tried to make sense of it. He didn't know the words or the letters very well, but he knew that he had to meet his contacts, and they lived near the Brookland-CUA station.

He had gotten the contact's information for the Al Qaeda cell in Washington, D.C. from the packet of information in his pouch that he had acquired from the late Hussain Islam who met his untimely death recently in St. Louis.

The contact list doesn't have anyone's name listed. The Al Qaeda cell understandably doesn't quickly give away their names as they have learned that many people looking for them don't always have the best interest of terrorists in mind.

They know that it doesn't matter if a Republican or a Democrat was in the White House or what the latest political posturing was on Capitol Hill. Any time that anyone can claim to have killed an Al Qaeda member, or expose a cell of the group, that person will be considered a hero.

And Al Qaeda was trying its best to avoid heroes.

On the other end of the political spectrum, here in America, so many members of the local population openly profess to be on the side of Al Qaeda. More than a few times in the years since 9/11, complete strangers have approached members of the extreme Middle

Eastern group and, without reason, apologize to them for the treatment that they must be getting and the oppression they must be feeling.

Late at night, when the members of the group gather and discuss their next nefarious caper in a basement or warehouse, they often tell stories of how the Americans treat them so well. This always made the groups howl with laughter that they Yanks are so soft that they would welcome a cancer into their country and then apologize for not being welcoming enough. Oh, these Yanks are soft.

On the train, Ali took the paper out of his backpack and looked at it again trying to discern where he should be. He finally figured out that the Brookland stop wasn't on the train he was on. He realized his only chance to get to his train stop was by asking one of these soft locals to see if anyone could direct him how to get to the right train.

He managed to communicate with a tourist who was no help at all. It seems he was also lost. Finally Ali, who was quiet gentile man who only longed to return to his family, who he hoped were still in one piece, however broke, back in Baghdad, tried to communicate with another person.

This man looked more like a local as he didn't have a backpack and wasn't wearing the tourist uniform of khaki shorts from Land's End and a camera.

"Excuse, to help," he stammered.

"Whattup?" was the reply from a local.

Now this expression was not in the phrase book that Ali had purchased back in St. Louis, but when in Rome.

"Yes, ah whattup," he Ali returned in kind. "Do you know where the stop is for Brookland?"

"Brookland! Dude you are on the wrong, oh you mean Brookland-CUA station," the local responded suddenly enjoying the back and forth.

"Get off here and get on the Red Line to Brookland," he continued. "Here let me show you. I'm Jenkins."

From there Jenkins walked Ali down the car to the large map showing all the entire the Metro system and through pointing and talking, he showed Ali how to get where he was going. Ali understood about 10 percent of the words of the generous local, but the pointing and gesturing was very helpful.

"Right here, you got to get off," Jenkins said suddenly, and pointed Ali toward the door. "These train drivers ain't goin' to hold them doors long, brother. You better get movin'," he said while helping Ali maneuver through the train car towards the door.

"Here you go," he said as they parted.

Ali stepped onto the subway station platform while his new acquaintance waved from inside the car.

"Enjoy your stay here—" The doors closed.

It was a brief and hurried meeting with a local D.C. resident and a stranger from Baghdad. But after waving goodbye, Ali was a little sad at the parting.

"Now, back to work," Ali told himself as he concentrated on remembering what his friend Jenkins had told him about getting through the complex system of trains that was the D.C. Metro.

CHAPTER 19

As Ali sat on the Red Line seat, the train pulled away from the station he realized how tired he was. The thought occurred to him to just approach the police and tell them that he was the guy who had killed the prowler in St. Louis and that he was forced to do it by an evil mastermind who was intent on stealing and selling the formula for algae-based biofuels on the open market.

Then, Ali Jr. thought about that a little longer and decided that may not be the best idea. In his home country, confessing your sins and hoping the government would understand the stresses you are under and then giving you a break, is not really the way things worked.

Ali took the palm-sized spiral notebook containing the information he had copied from the phone he threw away in St. Louis. The information was meant for Hussain Islam. This was the information that had led him to Percy and now, hopefully, it would lead to him out of danger.

He noticed that he had written the word 'Friendlies' in the notebook next to some Arabic names. Considering his situation, he thought the word seemed out of place.

For what seemed like the first time, luck was on Ali's side. Ali looked at the address again. 1534 Florida Ave. NW.

This was his next step.

He was still hoping to get the formula to Montgomery and maybe the "friendlies" were friendly to Percy. Maybe they weren't.

Well, as his father once told him, "You got nothing now, so you might was well do it."

So, with a little help from another passenger on the train, Ali was able to figure out how to find the address in northwest quadrant of Washington.

He exited the train promptly at the Brookland-CUA station and found his way to the street. The streets were easy to navigate as the numbering system was well marked.

Before long, he arrived at the outside of the row of Federal-style townhomes and knocked as confidently on the front door as he was able.

Ali had no way of knowing who was on the other side of the door, of course, but he had nothing to lose, so he waited.

The door cracked open a few inches. A dark figure with dark features and a black beard was barely visible in the shadows behind the door.

"Yes?" asked dark figure in Arabic.

It was a little frightening, yet Ali was somehow comforted to be speaking with a familiar form in his familiar language.

"I got your address from Hussain Islam and Qfar Mohammad." He said, still trying to be confident. "I need help."

"Come in," the figure replied.

Ali didn't embarrass himself by asking who this man was and how he knew Islam and Mohammad. He did, however, strategically omit the portion of his introduction about how he killed Hussain Islam because he was repulsed by the violent act of that evil prick.

After Ali entered, his eyes took a few moments to adjust to the dark space. Ali could see there were several Arab-looking men in the room, but couldn't see much else.

The questions from his hosts began…

"How did you come to find us here?" asked the one who spoke first, so was likely the leader and because, although all their faces were covered, the others seemed to defer to this inquisitor.

"I, ah, well," Ali stammered out. He had been so cool with the woman at the St. Louis airport and at the USDA and at the train station.

He wondered why he couldn't put together a clear thought here in the presence of his own people in his own language.

"I got your address from Islam Hussain who got it from Qfar Mohammad," Ali said finally. He now knew why he was so nervous. In the other settings, a wrong answer may have ended up with Ali going to jail. A harsh treatment since he still didn't think he had any choices in the whole episode. Here, however, if his questioners didn't believe him, or he answers incorrectly, he would be dead before he hit the floor, his head separated from his shoulders.

Ali decided that his best plan was to tell the entire truth and only lie about the killing of Hussain, whose death he would blame on a security guard. That would be just one, manageable lie that he would need to remember. Of course, if his hosts knew the real story and caught him in a lie, then Ali would be dead. But he figured if they knew that he had killed Hussain Islam, he was dead anyway, so his one hope seemed to be to convince them he hadn't killed anyone.

"So, what do you want from us?" one of the scarfed men asked.

"I am on the run from the U.S. government," Ali responded.

"Aren't we all?" responded the man. And the entire room started to laugh quietly at the joke. The brief moment of levity took some of the tension out of the confrontation.

"What can we do for you,...what is your name?"

"I am Farooq Ali Jr. of Baghdad. I was recruited for a mission by Qfar Mohammad. I have not completed it although my leader, Hussain Islam, has been murdered by an infidel. I don't know where to turn. Can you help me get into the USDA to meet a man who will help me complete my mission?"

"Qfar Mohammad was a good friend of mine from our days fighting the Soviets in Afghanistan," said the leader.

Ali froze thinking that this was the precursor to the end.

"He must know," thought Ali.

He thought about bolting out the front door and making a run for it. But where would he go? In a city he didn't know. And everyone spoke a language he could barely speak.

He knew he couldn't stay here. He would certainly be…

"Of course I will help you," said the host after a dramatic pause. "I know how these Americans have a cold-blooded streak in them when it comes to killing Arabs."

By now Ali's eyes had adjusted and he could see more clearly. There were plainly three men in the room in addition to him. The leader of the group and the two other men stood on the living room rug in the home in Northeast D.C.

The group of four men exchanged more and more information. Ali seemed to be gaining the trust of the group and before long they were all sitting on the floor together cobbling a plan to get Ali in touch with Percy, the contact at the USDA he had already tried to meet today.

"Why did you go there on a Sunday to meet this American?" one of the men asked Ali.

"Well, I only had his work address and assumed that would be the best place to find him during working hours," replied Ali.

With that answer, the room roared with laughter. They hadn't seen an Arab this green for some time.

Sunday is not a work day in this country, my Iraqi friend," said the leader.

The ice was truly broken now, but not so much that the mysterious men would take off their scarves that hid their faces.

"Now," Ali was asked, "how soon do you need to meet with this contact? Is he a member?" asked the leader referring to a member of the Al Qaeda group.

"He is American and sympathetic to our cause," said Ali. He had almost blundered and said "your cause." Had he made that mistake, he was certain he would have betrayed himself.

"And I must meet him yet today," implored Ali.

"Why today?" asked the leader.

Another problem for Ali. He could hardly tell them that his father was in danger and Qfar would certainly kill his father if he learned the truth, which could be any minute.

Then, another lie came to him.

"Because my contact is leaving the country soon, later this week, and if I don't make contact now, there maybe not be another chance to get to him," Ali blurted out.

"Is this someone you've been sent to kill?" asked the leader matter-of-factly.

"No" Ali said startled by the question.

Ali continued, more composed, "I need to get some information to him and he should have information for me."

"And money?" asked the leader of the Al Qaeda cell.

Times were not good for Al Qaeda communities in the United States. While capturing the men from these shadowy groups hasn't gone as well as the federal agents would like, the government has succeeded in making it hard to move money to the groups in the country.

"Not now," said Ali. "But after the mission, my leader Qfar Mohammad has pledged to make me wealthy. If you help me, I pledge to share the bounty of Allah with you."

Ali was now in pretty stinkin' deep.

But, he felt that there was no harm at this point in embellishing the story. What could go wrong from here? Anything could mean instant death at the hands of these men, and they were really his only chance of getting the mission accomplished, so why not go all the way.

Ali was pretty proud of that Allah comment. He was starting to get the hang of the whole thing.

These guys who claimed to be all about Allah, are really, like Qfar Mohammad back in Iraq, just using the ruse of religion as a method to extract what they really wanted…money.

Ali wondered silently if other religions in other parts of the world would stoop to this?

"Hmmm…food for thought," pondered Ali to himself.

After a few minutes, the leader said quietly, "We will help you."

"First, we will act tomorrow. Here is what we can do," he said.

Within an hour, the plan, such as was, was laid out to Ali. It seemed like a long shot, but he didn't have much choice. He had put himself, his safety and his family's safety in the hands of these shadowy figures when he knocked on the door.

He was about to find out if that was a good choice.

CHAPTER
20

At exactly 10:20 a.m. Monday morning, a sudden, terrifying explosion sent a fireball into the air near Independence Avenue, outside the east end of the building that housed the United States Department of Agriculture.

The noise and chaos sent tourists on the mall scrambling for cover in every direction.

Many tried to run into the USDA building itself looking for something or some place or someone to protect them.

Flames shot into the sky while black clouds of smoke momentarily blocked out the sun. The security people who work on the Mall, some in plain clothes and some with uniforms on, sprinted towards the site of the explosion. The four contracted guards assigned to monitor the entryway to the USDA building left their posts and hurried toward the door. They looked outside to see what had happened and soon realized what was going on.

"We need to go," said one of them.

"We can't leave here, what about when people come through here?" said another.

"Let's shut down this entrance and go see what we can do," implored the third. Leaving one's post is a serious breach of security and is only to be considered under extreme circumstances. The four figured a bomb going off in the vicinity to be extreme.

With all the commotion, they had forgotten that in addition to security checking everyone who entered the USDA building, the team was also instructed to keep an eye out for one of the USDA personnel leaving the building. In particular, the team was supposed to keep an eye on Percy Montgomery.

All the security teams at every entry were given instructions and a photo of Montgomery first thing Monday morning and were told to keep an eye out for him. If anyone saw him, they were to radio their supervisor with that information.

These four had forgotten that order. They shut down the entrance and then left the building. They locked the door as they left in order to ensure no one would sneak into the USDA.

Percy was in his office when he heard the blast. He knew it was time to move.

Montgomery came out of his office to check out the situation. He walked down the hall to the east entrance.

There, the guards had heard the blast, but they had not left their area of responsibility. They had stayed put per their morning orders.

Montgomery then walked to the west entrance. The four members of the security group there couldn't help themselves.

They had left their post and were gone. Good luck for Percy Montgomery.

Immediately after they left to assist at the explosion site, Percy Montgomery walked through the abandoned exit doors, calmly let himself out the doors with the one-way locks, and went out onto the Mall.

Instead of turning right towards the commotion, Percy turned to his left and marched west toward the meeting site with the man who had attempted to see him yesterday.

Percy knew that the explosion was a diversion by the newfound 'friends' of Ali Jr. Earlier in the day, Percy had received a text to meet his contact at the intersection of Constitution and Seventeenth Avenue NW and to bring the information.

Percy texted back to the unknown number and indicated that he knew that we would be under surveillance and didn't think there would be any way that he could meet with his contact undetected.

The final text gave Percy the chills and made him a little uneasy about what he was doing.

"You will get us what we want. Or we will take it."

"Well, Goddamn it, where are they?" shouted The Admiral at anyone who was listening in the cavernous theater room at the headquarters of the Office of Directed Discretionary Operations in St. Louis.

And everyone was listening.

"We are efforting now, sir," reported his young admin, Petty Officer Molina.

Even though she had little to do with the tracking of the suspects, she always knew that stepping up and getting involved was the best way to get noticed and to get kudos if things go right. Nobody knew if this was going to go right.

Since Admiral Guilbault-Johnson had decided to let the suspect slip through their fingers on the streets of Washington in order to track his movements back to the bigger prey, things have not gone right.

In fact, things had gone very wrong.

First, there had been an uptick on traffic on websites that are known to be used by Al Qaeda operatives. When Guilbault-Johnson had heard about the increased Internet traffic, he had really thought that his plan had worked.

More traffic means more clues and that means more indicators pointing to the nest, what The Admiral calls the hideouts of the bad guys.

Second, there was an insider at the USDA who seemed to be helping the Middle Easterners. But that insider, Percy Montgomery, never had been involved with intentionally deadly activity prior to this one. And Guilbault-Johnson had always thought he was generally a benign figure among those who were considered "disrupters" and agitators on the grid.

Third, the picture of exactly what was happening was still not clear. In past cases, the Al Qaeda reps could usually be found, and detained without much problem. This case was certainly different.

The Admiral's best men, Benson and Mateus, should have had this wrapped up by now.

Last, there were reports coming in of an explosive detonating on the National Mall.

On the Mall! For Christ's sake. This is all wrong, thought the boss. This time was different, though, and The Admiral was starting to realize that.

The reports of a bomb explosion with casualties was deeply disturbing to Guilbault-Johnson.

Not only did he assume that this was tied to the Al Qaeda case that he was currently working, but he also assumed that his decision to allow the suspect to escape was also responsible for the injuries and heaven forbid, deaths that The Admiral was starting to get on his secure computer feed.

"Where can I get an answer around here?" he shouted, again to no one in particular in the theater room.

"What are these reports of an explosion? Where is it happening? Did our man blow himself to Kingdom Come? Jesus Christ, I would welcome that at this point," The Admiral continued.

That last statement caused a short pause and uneasy quiet in the room. The twenty-five, or so, Navy Intel officers and civilians all understood the profound power of that statement.

As much of a patriot as The Admiral always has been, he never liked the loss of life that so often accompanied real-life operations. Even as a younger officer on a riverine boat in the Mei Cong delta in Viet Nam, he accepted that realization that people died. And it was always better that the guys on the other side died, rather than his own boat crew. But he never killed anyone if there were any other choice. If there was a way to wound or disable without killing, even in the heat of action, he would take that option. But, of course, it wasn't always an option.

Admiral Ian Theodore Guilbault-Johnson didn't have time, of course, to mentally review the current situation vis-à-vis the historical aspects of the Intelligence business.

He was a man of clear thinking and action.

"Where exactly was the explosion?" The Admiral barked.

Almost instantly, and unseen hand pushed a button and the security cameras on the Washington Mall were put on the main screen in the theater room.

It was clear that the problem was on or near the east end of the Department of Agriculture building on Independence Avenue.

"Sir, we have the visuals for you on the main screen," said one of the assembled staff. It was not Molina who said this. She works closely the boss and knows he doesn't like the obvious said to him.

"Please request immediate visual confirm that Percy Montgomery is still in his office," demanded The Admiral in a strong, but controlled voice.

Without an instant passing, "Building security on voice connect, now, sir," came another voice from somewhere in the St. Louis theater.

"Hello, Admiral," said a voice from Washington. The video link with the head of security at the USDA was on a smaller screen on the wall to the right of The Admiral. Guilbault-Johnson didn't bother to turn to look at him.

"Travis, this is Admiral Guilbault-Johnson, we spoke yesterday on monitoring employee Montgomery today," said The Admiral.

"Of course, sir," responded Travis. "We are a little busy today, what can I do for you?"

Admiral Guilbault-Johnson was not accustomed to being treated so gruffly, but he understood that the civilian in charge of the USDA security was unaccustomed to military protocol. The Admiral also knew that Travis and was up to his eyeballs in problems right now.

"Travis, could you give me a visual confirm on the presence of Montgomery in your building?" said the Admiral getting right to it.

"Admiral, we have alerted our staff to monitor Montgomery. I have reminded them today. They haven't reported anything to me, I am certain Montgomery is in his office," said Travis.

"Understand, Travis," the Admiral was quickly growing tired of the smug Travis. "I say again, could you give me a visual confirm on Percy Montgomery?"

This time Travis understood the urgency in the voice of Guilbault-Johnson. Travis also understood that, even though the Admiral wasn't directly in his chain of command, one wrong step with this guy, and Travis could end up in a pile of crap.

"Will do soonest. Would you like to maintain communication or —"

"Maintain," interrupted The Admiral. "I'll wait."

The line went quiet. Travis had thought for an instant about getting on his intercom and directing one of his agents to Percy Montgomery's office. Then he thought better of it. He realized that he better do this himself and started walking up an empty corridor towards Percy's office.

While on the way, Travis had another idea. He would call assistance so when he got to the office and if Percy was in there, his staff would see his triumph.

"Officers available, meet me at space KM1231-99 for visual confirm on occupant," Travis said into his shoulder-mounted mouthpiece.

"Chief, I'm on break right now," a forlorn voice answered Travis's call.

"Brent, is that you? On break? There was an explosion on the Mall!" barked Travis.

"Union rules," explained Brent.

"You will have to break union rules to accompany me to Percy's office," ordered Travis.

"I am entitled to two breaks tomorrow," Brent explained.

"Get to Percy's office NOW!" Travis had run out of patience.

"That's an affirm," replied Brent.

When Brent tried to sound official at work as civilian cum military security, his expression were often a mish mash of official sounding jargon they had picked up over the years from movies and television shows. The phrase 'That's an affirm,' for instance, came from the movie Apollo 13 as far as anyone could tell, because it wasn't taught in any security course that anyone could remember.

"Now, Brent!" barked Travis in the closest thing he had ever come to issuing any phrase that carried the weight of an actual order.

The firmness of his boss's voice startled Brent. He decided that moment was best spent meeting his boss as ordered. Brent knew his break and his vending-machine-dispensed Hot Pocket would have to wait.

Brent took one more bite on his ham and cheese extreme, got up and headed out the door of the break room. He didn't rush to Percy's office. If Travis had gotten himself into trouble, he should get out of it himself.

"Don't drag me into your mess," Brent muttered to himself as he ambled down the passageway of the USDA building. "And don't make me report you to the union foreman either. I have rights. And this is a weekend Monday morning shift. Should be quiet here..."

Despite walking as slowly as possible, Brent actually arrived at Percy Montgomery's office a few moments ahead of Travis. But instead of entering the office himself, he waited for his boss. If something was wrong, he didn't want to discover it.

After a few moments, Travis arrived and knocked on the door. He talked through the door.

"Mr. Montgomery, sorry about the interruption, but could you please open up? I've got a request here from...Mr. Montgomery?"

Travis was still absolutely certain that he would be proven right and the subject would be in his office.

After another knock, he started to get a little nervous.

"Montgomery, open the door please."

Nothing.

Now he was nervous. The bravado he displayed to Guilbault-Johnson was evaporating quickly.

"Sir, I am going to force the door if you don't answer immediately," was Travis's last effort to verbally get the door opened.

"Let's enter with force," an excited Brent blurted out. He was almost going to bust at the possibility. In all his time with the force, he was finally about to see some action.

"Draw your instrument," said Travis, now genuinely nervous.

With that order, Brent's hand reached cautiously down until he felt the cool reassurance of his walkie-talkie.

"Ready, sir."

Brent turned the handle on the office door. The silver knob rotated without resistance. It was unlocked. Travis eased the door open to see a cluttered desk, a book case, and an empty chair. There was no Percy Montgomery.

Of course Percy had left fifteen minutes ago. Brent and Travis were immensely disappointed to see the office empty. Soon and especially, The Admiral was about to be even more so.

CHAPTER 21

Travis was at a loss.

While it was unacceptable that his staff had allowed this high-value target to slip through their fingers, the most disappointing aspect of this was going to have to eat his words to The Admiral.

Travis picked up the phone in Percy's office and punched in the number to pick up the line where The Admiral was waiting.

"Sir, I am standing in the office space assigned...," said Travis to The Admiral.

"Put him on," The Admiral interrupted.

"Sir?" replied Travis.

"I assume you found him, so please put him on the line, Travis," he said.

"Well, about that. I have something to tell you," Travis was starting to see the graveness of his two fuck ups. The first was the actions of his staff letting Percy go. The second was Travis's own bravado. And The Admiral wasn't going to let him off easy.

"Well, what is the matter? Did you beat him so badly that he can't talk right now? Did you have to kill him? Mmm, is that the problem? It must be one of those things, since there is no stinking way that you let him get away. Not with your crack staff," now The Admiral was verging on mockery. He had an idea that he was right, and he never liked these two-bit, quasi-military jerks getting too big for their camouflaged britches.

"No, sir, nothing like that…," stammered Travis.

"Yes? Yes, man, what is it? C'mon, let's get down to it," demanded The Admiral.

"Sir, Percy was not in his office," said Travis.

"Jesus Horatio Christ, you stinking nincompoop. What the hell kind of monkey zoo are you running down there? I am going to put on my office security specialist on the phone to get the details of this. Tell her every detail of this massive screw up, her calendar is clean for the remainder of the day…"

With that, Guilbault-Johnson nodded to Petty Officer Molina to take over the call. Molina, although a very good enlisted sailor, was neither a security specialist nor did she have the rest of her afternoon free.

Guilbault-Johnson got out of his chair in the center of the room and let Molina slide into it. Molina picked up the phone and said in her most gruff voice, "Molina here."

The Admiral nodded to her confirming that she should take over the bollocking that he didn't have to time to give.

Then he was back to the mission. He looked at the screen that was showing the explosion on the Mall in Washington, D.C.

To no one in particular he murmured, "Looks like we got a confirm on Montgomery as a contributor to the Al Qaeda cause. Now where is Percy and where is Ali Jr.?"

Then he said to Lt. Jackson in a louder voice, "Where is Percy and where is Ali Jr.?"

On the Washington Mall, Percy approached the man who was described in the message he received earlier on his private mobile phone. The message had described where to find his contact and what he would look like.

In the months before this encounter he was always convinced that this was a group he would proud to work with.

Now, seeing the aftermath of the explosion, and all the chaos it made, he was now quite certain that he was no longer proud.

He now faced the two men he was there to meet.

Percy's blonde mullet was in sharp contrast to the dark, thick hair on the heads, arms, and necks of his contacts, two swarthy someones who didn't offer names.

"Hello, are you Ali?" asked Percy to one of the men standing on the east side of the World War II monument.

"Islam could not make it," said the man quite gruffly, and with a thick accent that Percy couldn't distinguish.

Percy was immediately disappointed.

He had hoped that this foray into the world of international cloak and dagger would be more like James Bond, or even his Bond's poor man's equivalent, Matt Helm.

He could see immediately that this exchange with the poorly dressed pathetic figure in front of him would not be one filled with witty back and forth that Percy had seen so many times in the movies.

It would, in fact, be a blunt exchange very short on romance and memorable repartee.

"I am supposed to deal with Hussain Islam and only him," Percy may be a little disappointed in the nature of the meeting, but he was feeling like he would make up for that disappointment by taking the upper hand, after all, he had the information the man wanted and he was not about to deal with this fellow.

"Islam not here," came the guttural reply from the darker man.

"Well, who are you? I am not going to deal with anyone save Islam. He and I —"said Percy.

"Islam not here," said the voice again from the throat of the fellow.

"Perhaps I am having difficulty making myself clear," said Percy feeling as though he had gained that upper hand in the back and forth with this blunt instrument capable of only a few monosyllabic efforts.

"You see here. I will deal with no one else. Until you produce him, I will retain the information I have."

"OK," said the Al Qaeda cell member in the nation's capital, which is not a title one receives without being at least a little clever.

"You want to meet with Islam. I take you to see Islam. You come with me and meet with Islam."

Suddenly, Percy felt as though it was goodbye to the upper hand that he wanted so desperately.

He tried to regain it.

"Young man, what is your name?" Percy asked.

"Call me Sam, if that helps," was the reply.

Percy was unable to determine the Middle Easterners age, but by use of the word 'young', Percy thought he got an advantage by diminishing the other man. "I will not go with you. You will bring Islam here. At once."

"Islam cannot travel," said the man. "Islam is…immobile."

The last sentence was said with a permanence that conveyed the meaning that the Arab wanted it to convey.

"Oh, ahh, I see," stammered Percy who was now miles away from the witty back and forth and James Bond feel that he wanted. He was now focused on the chances of getting out of this with his life. Percy had seen the videos of what some of these people can do to those with whom they disagreed.

"Well, I have the information with me that you, or Islam, had wanted. And you know," he paused, "I really don't want anything for it. You can have it. I will be happy to be shed of you."

"OK, give it to me," said the dark-haired man. Truth was, he knew that he had no intention of paying Montgomery anyway, so now he was going to stiff the blond infidel with a clear conscience.

Percy Montgomery, the man who had pulled of the Train-Station bombings years ago without a conviction, who had spent the last two years coordinating what he thought would be the sweetest caper in his life, reached into his pocket and pulled out a piece of paper. On it was the name of a contact that Islam was to reach in order to complete his mission for Qfar Mohammad.

"Is that it?" asked the Middle Easterner.

"Maybe," said Percy trying, and failing, to be coy.

"Give it to me."

There was nothing left for Percy to do. He was powerless. He didn't insist on making the exchange with Islam. He didn't want any money. He didn't have anything left.

He handed over the paper.

With a happiness that bordered on glee, the swarthy one snatched the paper from Percy. Without even acknowledging the blonde man from whom he had grabbed it, he poured over the paper thinking that it would have some valuable information for him.

He was so engrossed in the paper, that he didn't see Percy Montgomery sliding away and blending into the crowd that continued to mill around the National Mall in the wake of that explosion.

So much had gone wrong during this caper—the St. Louis deaths that he had read about in the newspaper; the change in his contact; the explosion on the Mall.

Percy finally realized that he was in way over his head and thought walking away was the best, safest, and most healthful option.

CHAPTER
22

Ali was sitting in the dark, quiet living room inside the Al Qaeda safe house in northeast Washington. One other resident of the house had stayed behind to watch the new man from Baghdad and make sure that he wasn't an agent intent on turning in whatever information he gathered to the FBI or some other government agency.

The two men sat in the living room without talking. There was no radio on and no television playing.

The stillness in the house was suffocating for Ali. He knew from the conversations he overheard in the time he was there, that the phone would ring. That call would be from one of the men on The National Mall who was getting the drop from Percy Montgomery. If that man told the Al Qaeda man at the house that things had gone wrong, or that the information that Montgomery gave him was bad, or any other negative report, Ali would be killed immediately.

If the information was good, well, Ali assumed good news also meant he would be killed.

As predicted, the phone rang.

The man answered.

In a hushed voice, with his head turned away from Ali to ensure that he couldn't hear, the man talked quietly. He was clearly having a conversation on the mobile phone with the operative on the ground at the Mall.

With a quick glance at Ali, the man in the house took out a pad of paper, and started writing a few short notes. Ali tried his best to see what was being scribbled on the pad, but didn't want to look as though he was trying to see.

Finally after a few seconds, the man folded his phone in half and ended the call on the disposable mobile unit.

Ali tried his best to be casual…

"Who was it?'" he asked, trying to sound as though he didn't care.

"It was Jub…it was the Mall man," said the man. He had almost given away the identity of the Mall man.

"Oh? How is he?" Ali said. He was weak with fear and felt his knees almost buckle under the strain.

The man didn't answer and instead walked to the closet in the one-hundred-year-old house. With his back to Ali, he opened the closet door slowly and reached to the top shelf.

Ali was sweating as wildly as he ever had. He was certain the man was reaching for a gun and that he would soon be dead. That he would never see his family again and that his father would be killed. Well, he thought it might be just as well. These past few days had been too much. At least it would soon now be over.

Death may even be a relief.

But, he thought. The man wouldn't shoot him here, would here? Too many police in this area. Too many clues. Too many neighbors.

The dark man turned away from the closet and toward Ali. He walked right at him, directly toward Ali. Ali was staring at the man's hand looking to see if the gun was visible.

What is in his palm? What? Ali was about to scream.

Then he saw the large, manila envelope.

He came up to Ali and the two were face to face.

For a moment, the man hesitated.

Ali knew that this was the end. He closed his eyes and waited for death. A knife would come out of the envelope and he would he feel that knife in his throat? Would it be a gun? Would he hear a gun shot before he fell? A scimitar?

The man stopped. He was now nose to nose with Ali.

Then, instead of a gun, the man raised his hands and then embraced Ali with both arms. When he stopped, he shoved the manila envelope into the hand of Ali.

"Good luck to you, brother," said the dark figure to Ali.

Ali didn't know what he supposed to do. He saw the window of opportunity and turned and walked toward the door of the house.

He walked slowly…

Waiting.

Wondering if the man was going to call him back. Going to shoot him in the back. Going to do anything to stop him.

He never did.

Ali walked out the front door. Stopped and took a deep breath. And turned southeast toward downtown Washington. He was free.

Outside the house, in an apartment across the street, Stuart Mateus was looking out the window.

"…so the last time I was at Disneyland, it must have been a Wednesday, no wait, it was definitely a Thursday, I remember because my wife Jeanne was telling me that the Cubs had just finished off a three-game series against the Cards, and they had a rest day before starting another three game series with the Brewers. You know, I've never really gotten accustomed to the Brewers being the National League," Steve Benson was on a roll. "I understand the reasons why they wanted the National League to have an even number of teams, you know, so that when they have a full slate, all the teams have someone to play, that is, of course during the weeks when they don't have interleague play, which I have never liked, as you know…"

"I know," said Stuart.

"I mean, the two different leagues really had different personalities back in those days," said Benson. "Oh, my goodness, I'm sounding like an old person aren't I?"

"Yes," said Stuart still staring out the window without turning around.

"But it's true," Benson restarted. "The American League had the umpires with the big chest protectors, and the National League umpires had the ones that went inside their clothes. So, they always said the American League umps called the strike zone a bit higher because of the chest protectors. And the A.L. ball parks were a little smaller too. So there were a lot more home runs hit in the small band box ball parks in the American League. You know, Fenway was small, still is, of course. And the old stadium in Baltimore, before they built that new one down on the river. Minneapolis, Cleveland, Comiskey, they were all pretty small, so the hitters in the A.L. were really the power hitters. Teams would get and keep the hitters that had a little pop in the bat, you know. A little get-out-of-here in those sticks.

"Now the senior league. It was different. There were newer parks that were a little bigger. Vets, Three Rivers, the Astrodome. Those were parks that were built for the hit and run, for getting a run or two and then getting an insurance run. Then relaying on good pitching from Gibson or Seaver.

"Now there were good players in both leagues, of course, but by and large the bigger hitters were in the American League and the smarter ball players were in the National League…"

"Quiet," Stuart said in the voice that was more of order than a request.

Stuart's voice shut Benson up immediately. It was the voice that Stuart used when he needed complete compliance right now.

Across the street from the house Stuart and Benson were occupying, the door swung open. A man, the very man they were tracking, walked out of the door. He looked nervous.

That man, of course, was Ali Jr. leaving the house used by an Al Qaeda cell in Washington D.C.

Ali, still in the new outfit that he had bought Sunday as part of his attempt to fit in while on his trip to the capital city in search of the connection that will lead to the release of his father in Baghdad by Qfar Mohammad, started walking toward downtown D.C.

CHAPTER 23

Ali was exiting the house very cautiously.

He was so careful, that he never completely turned his back on the Al Qaeda member who was there still in the Federal row house with him. Even though he felt like he had escaped his closest call yet, he still was desperately uncomfortable.

Steve and Stuart remained across the street in the rented space watching the Al Qaeda house. The arrangements to use the house for surveillance had been made months ago by the CIA. They were already keeping tabs on the house and monitoring the group that lived there.

There had been at least three occasions in that time, the CIA agents told Stuart, that they were ready to bust into the place thinking there was a probable threat from the group. The CIA had gotten enough Intel about the group preparing to launch some attack, but the group always was able to conceal their activities just enough so the CIA agents felt they didn't have quite enough evidence to search the place. Among the agents who watched it regularly, the house had become known as the La Bomba.

Half the reason was that they knew there was some explosive activity going on in there. The other half of the reason was that they could never catch them. Every time they tried they just bombed out.

Now, however, the surveillance apartment was needed by the Office of Directed Discretionary Operations and they had asked the CIA to vacate for a time. The CIA, frustrated by the lack of progress, was eager to let someone else waste their time on surveillance outside the house and loaned the room, equipment and all, to the DDO.

So Steve and Stuart found themselves on this spring Monday afternoon in this run-down house in northeast D.C. It was a one bedroom place on the street level. There was one bed for the agents to rest in turn and a small kitchenette for the men to make themselves small meals as needed. The CIA men who had been practically living the apartment for the last month, had kept the place immaculately clean.

Every dish was washed, the bed was made and even the trash can was empty. So at least the two new occupants from the Office of Directed Discretionary Operations would have a tidy place to waste their day, they thought.

They had known their man Ali Jr. was in the house because the CIA men had watched him go in about an hour prior to the time Steve and Stuart arrived. But they didn't know much more. Was Ali a member of the group? A visitor? A guest?

While Steve and Stuart were recording everything that was said outside the house on Florida Avenue, they couldn't get any recordings of the conversations inside the house. They had the technology, but they were frustrated by not getting any recording gear inside the house due to the restrictions of the Patriot Act.

All the equipment was turned on and recording when they saw Farooq Ali Jr. back out into the street across from them.

Stuart was the first to spot him.

Stuart wasn't looking through the eye piece of the camera, on a surveillance job, he always preferred instead to watch with both eyes open and not tied to his equipment.

As Stuart watched, Ali turned and looked up and down the street.

"Yahtzee," Stuart said to get Steve's attention.

Steve was on the bed looking over the spare recording equipment and making sure that if they needed it, it was in good working order. It was.

"Roger that," Steve said and quickly came to the window to see what was going on. They both watched as Ali, with his backside to them, looked up the street, then down the street.

Then Ali turned and seemed to look directly across the street, right where Stuart and Steve were staking out the house.

Then, while looking towards Stuart. Ali winked.

Or at least it looked like he winked. Did he wink?

"Did he...? Naw," said Stuart Mateus. "He winked, right at us."

"What the...," said Steve also watching the Iraqi as he started down the street. "I think he just winked at us."

"Does he know that we are here? Does the whole operation, the cell, know that we are watching? That changes everything," said Stuart.

"Now hold on, we don't know what we saw. He may have been just, well, I don't know what, but there is no way that he...winked at us, at the CIA," said Benson.

"So, let's pretend he did," said Stuart moving on to what is next. "Why would he do that? To let us know that he knows we are here? How would that help him? If they know we are here, that gives them an advantage. Why would they relinquish that advantage if not for some reason?"

"He would not have done it, unless he wanted to tell us something" said Steve.

"Or will tell us something," said Stuart. "We've got to follow him to find out what he wants us to know.

"But if we walk out that front door to track him, we'll be forfeiting our position here, for us and for the CIA," said Steve.

"They already know, don't you think?" said Steve.

"Well, was that a wink or not?" asked Stuart.

Steve replied with the best answer he had.

It was the answer that had settled a thousand quarrels between the two over the years.

Each afraid to make the first comment, they would count in unison, and when they got to the count of three, they would both give their answer. This way, no one would have to give the first and often wrong answer, and force the other man to agree. This method of problem solving had been used in Naples when the two were in the service.

For instance, if the two servicemen were out on the town and they would meet two young Italianas waiting to be asked out on dates, each with dark, lovely hair and fully packed blouses and even fuller Capri pants filled with fanny, they could make choices. The two men needed, before they spoke to the ladies, to decide who would be paired with whom. The two men didn't yet know the names of the targeted girls. They only thing they usually knew about them was the color of the ladies' blouses.

To decide who got who, the two would count together "1…2…3…blue!" And this rudimentary method would determine which of the men would be assigned to which of the ladies. It was crude but effective and kept them from fighting beforehand or complaining afterward, depending on how things worked out.

Not that it always worked. Sometimes the girls wanted to change the pairing. If so, the boys always complied.

Sometimes the girls didn't like the men either way they were paired. Well, that happened a lot.

But the method of pairing soon worked its way into almost every decision the two shared. So it was used now in determining if they had seen a wink or not, Steve said, aloud, "Wink or no wink, in 1…2…3."

And then Steve and Stuart both said, "WINK."

"So, you thought it was a wink, too," said Stuart. "If it was a wink, then he was certainly trying to tell us something, right?"

"Well, if it WAS a wink—" Steve said.

"Look, you said 'wink' after a count of three," interrupted Stuart, as if the count of three had some sort of legal standing. "So, we are working from the idea that it was a wink. You know the rules."

"OK, OK. He would have been trying to tell us something, but we haven't really seen anything that he's done," said Steve getting into the spirit of the thing.

"Right, since we haven't really had any interaction with him in the past, he must be winking about something he is going to tell us in the future," said Stuart. "Is that what you are thinking?"

"Must be," said Steve. "That is, unless, the wink has a completely different meaning in Baghdad than it does in D.C."

"Yes, you're right," conceded Stuart.

"Maybe to them a wink means, 'be careful, or you're going to get killed,' or 'get the hell outta my business.'"

"He certainly wanted us to see him wink, right?" added Steve. "Even if it doesn't mean the same thing, it was clearly contact, an intent attempt to communicate. So, he knows we are here, one. Two, he wants us to know something. Three, by following him, we are not conceding anything and only stand to gain."

"Agreed," said Stuart. "We have to maintain surveillance on the target. Let's go."

Stuart and Steve each quickly grabbed their back packs they always have at the ready when on stake out duty. It was standard equipment with cash, IDs, money, change of clothes, weapon and all the things they might need for just this sort of moment.

They both put on ball caps and stepped out the door and onto Florida Avenue in northeast D.C.

They turned left, southwest, toward North Capitol Street. About a block ahead, was Farooq Ali Jr. He was easy to spot in the light pedestrian traffic and, besides, Ali was still wearing his odd-fitting tourist clothes.

Ali was walking pretty slowly, presumably to allow Benson and Mateus to catch up. The three proceeded down the street in some sort of peculiar, disjointed conga line with Ali in the lead and the two DDO agents a half block behind.

At the first stop light, Ali turned to see if he had attracted the attention of the two agents. He needed to know if they were following. He spotted them immediately. It was such a clear signal that Ali knew that Steve and Stuart were following him, that the two agents didn't even bother to conceal themselves.

The light turned green and Ali started to walk again. Now his pace a little quicker as he knew the agents were on his trail.

Ali, walked briskly through the afternoon heat on the streets of Washington. He strolled, if not confidently, at least with reason to think that finally something was going right.

As he walked, he reached into his inside breast pocket of his suit and retrieved the envelope that he was given by the Al Qaeda member. It was a large manila envelope that he had folded into half to fit inside his pocket.

Ali, with envelope in hand, paused on the corner of Florida and Capital streets. He made it a point not to turn around. He felt the wink that he gave his pursuers was enough. He wanted them to follow, but didn't know who else may be watching him.

Still walking, Ali slid his finger under the flap of the manila envelope and tore it open.

Inside he found a bundle of American money—not a neatly bound stack of money that a bank would hand out with a paper wrapper around a stack of twenties.

This was a bundle of bills of different denominations held together with a rubber band. Ali quickly stuffed the money into his front trouser pocket. Still walking, Ali also found inside the envelope a new passport with the name Kalil al Akbar, and a sheet of paper with a name and address on it. It was the same sheet of paper his host had written on during the call. The paper said:

> Joao de Costa
> 1435 Rua Agusto
> Pico
> Acores, Portugal

CHAPTER 24

Ali knew that this obviously was the name and address of the connection that Qfar Muhammad, the mastermind of this whole affair, had waiting in Portugal to help Ali and Hussain Islam escape after they had both arrived from St. Louis with the files on algae.

Ali was not experienced in international espionage, but he knew that keeping this paper in his possession for any period of time, would identify him as a member of the group and he would be targeted by the United States as an enemy combatant.

Ali, stopped walking for a minute and paused to think.

What should he do?

He realized that he had little time for contemplating his next move, so he began walking again and passed a dumpster, ironic to see the oversized garbage container in an area of the city that rarely cleans up after itself.

When Ali got to the dumpster, he slid open the side access panel, and threw the paper inside, making sure that he wasn't too wrinkled and didn't land in any liquid filth that would make it unreadable.

Then, he shut the dumpster panel and again started walking. This time directly south on Capitol Street toward, well, he wasn't sure. He did know what he was looking for: the quickest way out of town.

It had only been two days since Ali hade made an odd lonely, scary walk through an unfamiliar town. Ali had strolled through St. Louis only a few dozen hours before, and now this was his second solitary walk through a city in a country which he didn't know much of the language and few of the people.

And those few people he did know, the Al Qaeda cell that he had the misfortune of encountering, weren't exactly the most welcoming group in the world.

But Ali did what he had done for the last few months…he kept going through all the adversity. Capitol Street is a nice walk, at least it may have been a nice walk a century ago. The three-story townhomes that line the street are now mostly dilapidated and run down. Some still show the bones of their previous splendor. The English basements featured in many of the homes housed young, world-changers in the most powerful city in the world. These young people just a year or two out of college lived in these cramped apartments in bad neighborhoods and spent their days as interns for representatives and senators while they groomed themselves to someday become parts of the government machine. Maybe someday one of them might become president.

But for now those young interns live on Capitol Street in studio, 500-square-foot apartment for a cool $1,000 a month.

The townhomes along the street were interrupted every few blocks by what were hoping to be convenience stores, but were failing miserably.

There were liquor ads stuck to every broken window, each of them covered with chain-link fencing to keep the robbers out after hours. During store hours, they use the front door.

Ali had seen homes and businesses on streets somewhat like this in his Baghdad with houses that were just a few days' work away from being livable, and a few months' work from being very nice.

Ali would have felt a little comfortable in this neighborhood where few outsiders feel comfortable except for the feeling of depression and dread that seemed to hang in the air around him like a fog.

On Ali strolled southward on Capitol. He passed bums on the street, panhandlers who mostly left him alone since Ali himself seemed so out of place that the locals didn't think he would respond to their entreaties for change.

The sidewalks were narrower than Ali thought they should be. Over years and years of street widening, the walkways became less and less important.

The menagerie of streets that make up Washington, D.C. made it almost impassable in places.

The grid on which the city was laid out, included streets that run east and west. Of course there were also streets that run north and south. But there were also streets that ran diagonally, such as Florida Ave. Where two streets met, pedestrians found normal traffic patterns.

At the streets where a north-south meets east-west, meets northeast-southwest, little triangles were formed that were effectively little islands for pedestrians as they cross the street.

At the intersections where walkers encountered the north-south, east-west, northeast-southwest and northwest-southeast roads all converging, the little triangle islands, that were once, perhaps, green geometric shapes in a lovely pavement checkerboard, had been shrunk and nibbled at and asphalted over, until just these little triangles remained. Sometimes as small as a cocktail table.

The street layout was confusing to Ali, but after what he had been through in the last twenty-four hours, he barely noticed.

When, at last, Ali saw road side signage that included a picture of a train, he was relieved. Unknowingly, he had stumbled across Washington D.C.'s Union Station.

From here, Ali would be able to get the help he needed. There were information counters, ticket counters, and plenty of people who spoke his own language in the great melting pot of the magnificent building that was the hub of the city's rail traffic.

Built in 1907 for a rail system that served the few hundred thousand who commuted into the sleepy federal town of that era, the building has been cleverly and usefully updated when they built the new Metro rail system in the 1970s to serve the 3 million who had populated the city at that time and still seems to hold up well for the 7 million people who now call the city home, many of them, plus countless tourists who flock to the area, use the Metro daily for work and social transportation. The metro is now the second-busiest commuter rail in the United States, behind only the New York subway system.

Meanwhile a half block behind Ali, Steve and Matty approached the dumpster. They still couldn't believe that they had seen, or thought they had seen Ali Jr. drop something in there in plain sight of the two agents, who he may have already signaled to once with a wink just six blocks ago.

"I can't believe that he would have put something in there with the full understanding that we are following him and that we would easily find it," said Steve Benson stating the obvious.

"Yeah, it seems like he is making this trail pretty simple to follow," agreed Matty.

"I mean, what sort of crazy person would do that?" Steve continued. "Is this the same guy who we saw crease that cop's face after your game Saturday? Geez, and now you expect me to believe that he has become a friendly? No fucking way is that guy a friendly. Not after what he did to that cop. Hearing the guy's nose crack also almost made me hurl."

"I've been thinking about that," said Matty. "You know how we could have taken him out when we had him by the USDA building? Why didn't Jackson tell us to take the target when we had a chance?"

"Yeah."

"Well, what do they know that we don't know? What are they holding back? If Ali is a friendly, he is one of the most unfriendly friendlies I've ever tailed."

While Matty talked, Steve climbed the side of the dumpster to look down on the trash within. He had learned long ago not to open anything the same way that a target had opened it. That included a dumpster, apartment door or car door. Anything that the mark had opened, Steve knew must be opened another way.

Most of this was suspicion but some of it was based in good surveillance.

There had always been a story circulating around headquarters that during one operation, a mark had gone through the door of his duplex in Mexico, or Argentina (depending on who was telling the story) and an agent went in directly after the mark and walked in to an ambush that cost the agent his life. The door opening was the signal to the gang that the next person through would be a 'Federal' and was mercilessly slaughtered.

Now just because Ali had opened and closed the dumpster door without even a whimper, that didn't mean that the door was safe. It is easy work to rig a small explosive that would be detonated by a click of a ratchet or the closing of the door. So for all the love that Ali seemed to be showing Matty and Benson, he could have been setting them up for a little dumpster surprise.

So, Benson climbed up the outside of the dumpster so he could examine the container and looked around the nearly empty rusty garbage dumpster.

There it was. Sitting on top of a pile of old Playboy magazine's someone was throwing out, and as available and plain and easy to grab as if Ali had mailed the paper to them first class.

Without waiting or hesitating, Benson jumped down into the garbage dumpster and landed on his feet. He bent over and picked up the sheet of paper that Ali had purposely thrown there.

CHAPTER 25

"Hello, Admiral, this is Matty," Stuart said into the personal communication device or 'comm' that he always carried.
Stuart's tone was not disrespectful, but it wasn't as deferential as he usually was when talking with his superior whom had earned his respect over the years and, more to the point, he outranked him by a considerable margin.

"Admiral, I have, well, Steve and I have a few questions for you," Stuart said, his boldness was quickly leaving him now that he was actually talking with his director.

"Well, you know, Admiral, about that target you've had us tailing?" he had now lost almost all his nerve and was almost stammering as he went on.

Benson could only hear Stuart's side of the conversation, but he was getting the entire picture.

"Yes, him."

"Yes, and, and, well, we were thinking that there may be more to this case than what you've been telling, ahh, than the information that we've been given. Is there any chance that information has been overlooked that may help us crack this a little easier?"

"Mmmm hmmm," said Stuart, seemingly humbled.

"I see…is that right?…Mmm Hmmm. Well, sure, I see that," Stuart was clearly getting a verbal dressing down from The Admiral, who never liked his authority or decisions being questioned.

But this was beyond that. Stuart was questioning The Admiral's sincerity. This was inexcusable. And Stuart was getting an earful.

Meanwhile, Steve was still standing inside the dumpster with the paper in his hand. Once he realized that his friend was getting a reaming out from The Admiral, he did what any friend would do… He started to try to make Stuart laugh.

Benson, who was always the more expressive of the two, pounded on the inside of the dumpster to get Stuart's attention. Benson looked at Stuart directly through the access panel of the dumpster.

The two agents made eye contact.

When Stuart looked, Benson was still inside the dumpster and turned around pulled down his pants and was showing Stuart his ass in what the kids call the moon. Stuart glanced up and saw the pasty, round cheeks and smiled but turned away quickly, as he knew that if he laughed while The Admiral was chewing him out, that might portend the last assignment ever for Stuart.

For The Admiral's part, he was half angry and half bluffing. He really doesn't like his sincerity being questioned, but knows that any good operative would have lots of questions that way the last few days had unfolded.

The Admiral also knows that is always good to have your men fear you a little. It is always nice to share a glass of Scotch with the entire staff when assignments were successfully put to bed, but it is also good to let them know who was in charge from time to time. The Admiral chose this time to let Stuart Locke Mateus know who was in charge of this mission and this department.

The Admiral knew that doing this is good leadership and also good for the mission.

Sometimes he secretly wished he could be closer to his people and didn't have the mantle of leadership separating him from the group by rank and protocol and more practically age, but he had long since resigned himself to waiting until retirement before he allowed himself to grow closer to people.

At least he was hoping that friendship would still be possible for him then. He hoped that he would be able to talk with people instead of talking at them.

And he wanted to ask people questions and expect a sincere, truthful answer, not what the person thought you wanted to hear.

Heavy is the head that wears the crown, and part of the weight on The Admiral's head was his solitary life.

Back at the dumpster, Steve was now shoving his finger up his nose as far as possible—a move called the second knuckler—to get a laugh from his partner.

No luck. Stuart would not give out so much as a titter.

Steve, still looking directly at Stuart, was preparing to go for all the stops in order to get his friend to laugh…pull out his wiener.

He really wanted his friend to lose it while on the phone with The Admiral.

In a moment when the two had the eye contact, Stuart's eyes suddenly went shut and he fell to the filthy ground and onto the crumpled garbage, empty Gatorade bottles, and Snickers wrappers outside the dumpster.

From inside the garbage container, Steve didn't see what had happened.

He assumed Stuart was clowning around while getting drilled a new one by the Admiral. My butt must have done it, Steve thought to himself.

But as soon as he saw Stuart's limp body lying on the ground, he knew something was wrong.

Then, Steve, still looking through the access panel in the dumpster, could see the reason for Stuart's fall. A man in a taqiyah was holding metal pipe and he had just used it to crunch Stuart's ribs with one swing right in the lower side of Stuart's back.

And the Arab man was winding up and getting ready to clobber the agent again with a hit that may be fatal if he connected.

Without thinking, Steve jumped up and grabbed the top of the dumpster and pulled himself up. He planted his right foot on the rim of the dumpster.

When he got to the top of the container, he didn't hesitate. He kept going, almost flying over the side.

Pants still at his ankles, Steve jumped down to where his friend lay defenseless. As he jumped, Steve pushed himself downward to get to the ground faster.

While flying through the air on his way to the man below, Steve cocked his right fist down by his naked waist.

He twisted the upper half of his body to his right. And that caused the natural twist of his body to steer his lower body to the left.

As he neared the man, Steve uncoiled his body and shot out his fist from his waist with all the power he had.

Perfect.

Steve connected cleanly on the back of the man's head.

The man was stunned and staggered forward.

The feeling of connecting on a clean punch had always thrilled Steve, although he felt like he didn't get enough opportunities to use the training that he had gotten from the DDO. He landed perfectly on his feet.

And he just realized that his pants and underpants were down around his calves.

He bent over to try to quickly pull them up, but his fingertips only caught the waistband of his underwear. So he pulled those up as best he could.

Now, he looked at his target.

His fist hand landed squarely on target, the contact with his fist on the man's head didn't feel as sweet as he remembered.

In fact, it hurt.

The Arab had staggered forward from the hit and was now turning around to see what had hit him.

He looked Steve up and down quickly and realized that he just got punched by a half-naked man.

Steve threw another punch, a straight jab. This time with his left hand.

It was as hard as the first, maybe harder. Again, a perfect connection.

And now he cocked his right hand again. Wham. A third perfect connection. Right on the jaw.

The attacker was jarred by the impact and dropped the pipe he had used to hit Matty.

One more punch from Steve and the Arab man went face down, right on top of Stuart.

Steve moved quickly, now that his man was down.

He didn't want to give him a chance to turn around and get up.

The surprise was complete.

Matty was still in pain and shocked enough by the man landing on him that he went from a state of mild shock, to becoming a little more aware of his surroundings, but still groggy. He rolled a little to his left and that was enough to get the smelly man off of him.

While he clearly had the advantage and his prey was nearly unconscious, Benson was not through.

The Arab was face down flat on his chest in the trash.

Now, Steve did exactly as his training had taught him. He remained on his feet and stayed behind the man as he lay on the ground.

When he was entirely behind the man, Steve then knelt down and put his knee in the small of the back of the man.

The pain felt by the Arab, caused him to lift his head and groan. His presented a perfect target for Benson and his next blow was a crisp right hand right to the back of the man's head again.

The hit forced his head to whip forward into the pavement.

"Ahh," said Benson. "My hit on the back of your head and your face hitting the street.

"Nice bargain. Two hits for the price of one."

Whenever Steve felt uncomfortable—or really any other time—he made himself more comfortable by talking. It didn't matter what the topic was, Steve just liked to talk. And now, without thinking about it, he started to talk as the fight continued.

"You think this fucking fight is over, sleepy head?" he asked without expecting an answer. The word 'sleepy head' was punctuated by Steve's knee coming down hard into the man's back causing a muffled groan as the man face was still nose-first in the oily pavement.

Benson then came to his feet and thought it was safe to turn over the man. Benson knew that when you have the advantage, never allow the man to get back into the fight.

"When you have the advantage, keep the advantage," said Steve to himself, reciting a mantra from his training.

Steve leaned over and, with his right hand, grabbed the left shoulder of the Arab. He pulled on the fabric around the man's shoulder and began to roll him over. He now lay on his back.

In an instant, Steve thought, "What happened to his weapon? Did I ever secure that lead pipe he used to hit Stuart—?

His thought was interrupted by a flash of that pipe swinging toward the side of his head. The man wasn't as badly hurt as he pretended. He had fallen on the pipe by accident and quickly wanted to get back into this fight.

Steve jerked his head to his right and the lead pipe barely nicked him. Most of the energy of the blow was wasted. The man on his back rolled through on his swing and his momentum turned him over and onto his chest.

The fight started again and this time Steve would not lose his edge.

"What the fuck was that, douche bag?" shouted Steve as he came down again with the knee into the man's back again.

"I was trying to, wait, and where is that fucking pipe?" Steve said.

After one more particularly violent knee drop in to the spine, Steve dropped his full weight onto the man by sitting on the small of the man's back and then leaned forward putting his chest on the back of the man trying to keep him from moving. Then Steve's hands started feeling around the man. He gave the man a quick frisking and reached under him. He gave out a groan from the beating he was taking. Steve's hands quickly reached under the man's shirt, around the sleeves, into the shirt again.

"Ahh, there it is" thought Steve as he wrestled the tool away from the man. Steve came to his feet and raised it above his head like one of the monkeys from the opening scene of 2001: A Space Odyssey.

Steve was so focused on the fight, he still had his pants down.

"Now, let me show you how much this can hurt," and Steve brought the weapon down on the man.

THUD!

Directly onto the back of the man's right shoulder.

Steve knew that the man was unarmed. He knew he had at least broken the man's shoulder blade. Steve knew he had to keep cool. "This man may now be a good source of information if her were kept coherent," thought Steve.

In times of intense stress, sometimes all that a man knows is no match for all that a man feels. Steve wanted only to destroy this guy. He was so wound up that nothing could have stopped him.

In short, Steve Benson was in 'kill' mode.

"Hey, mother fucker, think swinging a lead pipe makes you tough?"

Steve rolled him over so the man would see him face to face. He punched him in the eye.

"You like that, huh? You like a little punch, huh?"

Steve stood over the man who was now lying motionless on his back. He kicked him in the balls.

"How is your little girl friend going to like that? Huh? Now that you wouldn't be able to bone her? Huh?"

The man, with the little energy he had remaining, balled up in pain from the kick. He muttered something but his breathe was just a whisper. Steve could be barely hear him, and if he had heard him, it would have just made Steve more enraged.

"Huh? What was that? You want me to kick your ass? OK? That's a big fucking 10-4, good buddy."

Meanwhile, Stuart groaned as he tried to get to his feet. He had recovered enough to see what was happening. He let out a grunt trying to get Steve's attention.

Steve didn't pay attention to his friend, however. He had work to do. Steve leaned over one more time and grabbed the man by the collar. He pulled on the man to lean him forward and get him up and away from the pavement to get some separation from the ground.

Steve's hand still clinched the lead pipe. He raised his hand, and smashed it down on the man's head.

He raised his hand to do it again. This would be the last one needed.

In a weak voice from 10 feet away, Matty grunted out a single-syllable…"Don't."

Steve heard his friend and looked over at Matty. He paused. His hand was still raised over his enemy.

Matty looked at Steve.

Matty, silently, shook his head no.

But Steve was blind and deaf with rage.

"Oh just one more, can't hurt can it?" and with that, Steve Benson brought down the pipe onto the side of the man's head making a sickening splat.

The man went suddenly limp.

Steve, as a trained veterinarian, knew the feeling of a lifeless patient. Many times, little girls and their moms would cry to Dr. Benson to get him "do something" when their little pet had lost the battle.

Because of his experience, Steve knew when all was lost.

In his rage, Steve had killed him.

The shock of the feeling the dead man in his hand, brought Steve back to his senses.

He pulled up his pants.

CHAPTER
26

Stuart Mateus came to his feet and picked up his phone. He pressed 'end'.

He approached Steve who was standing over the lifeless body.

Both stood there for a minute. Silent. Motionless.

Steve finally asked the obvious.

"Is he dead, Doc?"

"Yes." For the first time in his life, Steve used an economy of words.

"What should we do? It is your call on this one," said Matty.

"We have to get to this address in Portugal," Steve said matter-of-factly. "Here's our move. We will delay the reporting of this incident and remain in pursuit of the target. If we stop for this now, the DDO will call us in for reports and we will lose the scent of Ali, and his contact."

"They can get other people to track Ali," said Stuart.

"But Ali knows us. He winked to us, he is comfortable with us. Would you feel OK with letting someone else track him? Would you?" asked Steve Benson.

Stuart paused.

"I thought not," said Steve.

"OK, you win. Let's clean this up as we are able, and then get back to Ali," Stuart agreed.

Stuart was technically in charge of the operation and Steve was second in command.

If Stuart had wanted, he could countermand the plan, but he really felt that Steve, since he was the one who would fry if they found misconduct in the death, was risking more than he was, so he deferred to Steve's judgement.

Without any further consulting, the two moved to action.

Stuart still had a huge pain in his side from the pipe that found his rib cage in the attack, but didn't have any time to nurse it. Instead, he and Steve cleaned up the site as quickly as a team from Service Master ever did.

Steve leapt up onto the rim of the dumpster and surveyed the contents. He saw an old blanket down in the dumpster and jumped down into the garbage-y mess to retrieve it.

He quickly climbed out and came over to the body where Stuart was giving it a complete frisk down, looking for any identification on the man. He looked for two reasons. First if the man was an Al Qaeda operative, he may already be in the DDO database, and they could see what cells or groups are operating in the Washington D.C. area.

Second, since this was going to be an unreported death, Steve and Stuart wanted the body not to be identified for as long as possible. Someone, probably a sanitation worker, would eventually find the body and start an inquiry.

And since he may be part of a terrorist cell, friends of the deceased may not be eager to claim him. With the quickness and efficiency of trained military men, Stuart and Steve laid out the filthy dumpster blanket on the ground. They then rolled the body onto the blanket. Then they folded in both ends of the blanket and then rolled the body over until it was completely encased.

It looked like a filthy, 5 ½ -foot-long burrito.

With Steve at the head and Stuart at the feet, they lifted the body and walked over to the dumpster. They opened the side panel and shoved the body through the opening into the dumpster.

They climbed in after it and started grabbing what little garbage they found in there. They took the refuse and covered the body with old boxes and soda cans and whatever they could find. They even scattered some of the old Playboys on top of the body.

Then they climbed out of the dumpster, and took a look around the neighborhood to see if any more attackers were around or any witnesses.

Everything looked clear.

"Let's get moving to Union Station," said Stuart.

The two started to walk south on Capitol Street.

"How is your side? You hurt?" asked Steve.

"Not too bad, pretty painful, but I will be able to the work," said Stuart.

Stuart and Steve knew that when you are out on a job, that there is no time to be the hero and pretend you are not hurt when you are. Misleading a co-worker with faux bravery was a huge breach of etiquette. More important, it could get you both killed.

Not only are you endangering the mission because you could fail and be overtaken by pain when the team needs you to act.

Also, partners need to know the condition of partners. If an agent is dealing with a defective partner he or she needs to know the limitation of the partner.

Stuart told the truth as best he was able. He did have some pain, but he could go on.

Despite the pain, the short walk to Union Station was covered in just a few minutes.

They got to the counter.

"Two tickets for the Red Line to Reagan National," said Steve to the teller at the window.

Steve and Stuart flashed their badges at the security guard outside the access door to the secured area at Reagan National Airport in Alexandria, VA just across the Potomac River from Washington.

This airport was the biggest security risk in the nation. Each plane that comes in and goes out of the busy airport is a danger. When they start a descent or ascent out of Reagan airport, they are within 3 miles of the U.S. Capitol dome.

If a plane was being piloted by terrorists and was steered toward any of the monuments or buildings in Washington, D.C., the air traffic controllers on duty and the defense team working around the capitol area both on the land and in the air would have less than thirty seconds to recognize that an inbound plane was off course, identify that plane as a security threat, relay that information to the air defense team at Langley Air Force base south of D.C. which would then relay a kill assignment to Air Force jets in the air around the protected air space. The jets would then strike and eliminate the planes before they could contact their targets.

All in 30 thirty seconds.

Needless to say, the security detail in the Reagan National Airport was always a little jumpy.

And it takes more than a smile to get past the security detail at the door. Stuart and Steve didn't exactly look like a couple of spit and polished agents from the Department of Defense. They still were wearing their clothes that they wore while beating and killing a suspect near a dumpster in Northeast less than an hour before. They smelled of sweat, garbage and fatigue.

"We need to get in to look at security camera reels for the past two hours," Stuart said. He wasn't trying to sound official, but the tone of his voice was stern and firm.

"I'll have to see some DoD ID and a secondary form," said the security guard not about to bullied.

"Now is not the time to play like you're Chuck Norris in Uncommon Valor, OK?" Stuart said uncharacteristically short.

"Easy now, big boy," said the guard, who wasn't accustomed to being talked to like this, and besides, he had hours remaining on his shift, so it didn't bother him to get into an argument that lasted until his shift was over.

Either way, these boys weren't getting in without the proper authorization.

"We have procedures around here. I don't know what agency you're from, but you have to get clearance. You should know that—"

Stuart raised his voice, "No, I really need you to allow access—"

"And I really need you to show that you have a 'need to know' and an ID, or you aren't going anywhere," the defiant guard said.

"Hey, hey," Steve stepped in and talked to the guard. "Sir, we have authorization to use the facility and you only need to check this message on my phone and companion it with my security code Zulu, Golf, Hotel, 6, 4, 2. I say again, Zulu, Golf, Hotel, 6, 4, 2. Roger that?"

"Roger that," said the guard after checking Steve's secure phone and looking at his own phone for the authorization numbers.

The Admiral picked up the situation line in his office in St. Louis. After he heard just the first few words from the other end of the line, he motioned for Lt. Jackson and his Aide-de-Campe Marty Bishop toward him.

While still listening to the caller, the Admiral silently mouthed one word to Jackson and Bishop "Azores."

They both nodded and turned without comment toward the door. They walked smartly into the passageway, turned to the left and continued down the corridor until they got to the desk of Petty Officer Caty Molina, the admiral's flag writer and girl Friday.

Bishop, the higher ranking officer of the two, spoke first and efficiently. "What is transport status, destination priority 2, Azores, Portugal on request of N-00," he said, using all the slang required for letting Molina know that this was official business that needed attention, and not another bit of idle conversation that the two had so often enjoyed as they grew to be office friends over the previous year and half.

"Roger that," Molina replied in her monotone military voice. "Priority 2 D.C. for operative Bishop."

Bishop added, "And Jackson."

Molina said "Priority 2 D.C. for operative Bishop and operative Jackson."

"Correct, two operatives for D.C., priority 2," echoed Bishop.

"Will check and confirm with you soonest," Molina replied indicating that she will check to see if any of the DDO's planes are ready to make a flight of that distance right now.

Molina, picked up her phone and dialed a three digit number that connected her immediately with the night officer at St. Louis airport Lambert Field. The night officer responsible for keeping the three small planes owned by the DDO in one-hour operating status, meaning they should be ready to go anywhere in the world within one hour of notification.

Molina was relieved when she heard wing commander Richie Bower pick up the line. Molina got these requests only 3 or 4 times each year and always wanted them to go well.

With Bower on the line, she knew that it would.

Bower was an officer with the Royal Air Force who was working for the Office of Directed Discretionary Operations on an exchange program.

Bower was a little bit of a wild card compared to his American counterparts. He liked to go out after work, and often enjoyed the company of the enlisted members of his shop.

American officers would rarely if ever go for a night out and drink with the lowly enlisted. Bower was different enough that he often would.

After all, he figured, you're only in America for two years on an exchange program, why not have a pint with anyone who is willing. He was never wanting for anyone who is willing.

At work, however, Bower was the very definition of a spit-shined officer. He was always a full hour early for his shift assignment, even though sometimes he had a small headache as a reminder of the previous night's revelry.

"Bower here!" the wing commander snapped as he picked up the phone.

"Richie, this is Molina," said the cute young petty officer who had met Bower a few times over the previous year at different night spots around St. Louis. He always acted as though the encounters and ensuing chit chat were completely accidental. Molina wasn't so sure. And she would have been well pleased if they had been planned by him.

"Yes, how are you doing? Say, it was nice to bump into you at the Bootlegger Lounge—"

Molina interrupted, "Wing commander, got a priority 2 request from the top. What is your status?"

"Sorry, yes, status, is green. I say again, status is green. We can have go sortie within 5 minutes to destinations CONUS and go sortie within ten minutes for destinations EUR," said.

"Roger that. Initiate to Europe," replied Molina.

As she replaced the receiver and looked at Jackson and Bishop who were now sitting in two gun metal chairs across the hall from her office she addressed Bishop.

"We are GO. Repeat, we are go for CINCEUR, including Azores, Portugal. Can depart now."

The two came to their feet.

CHAPTER 27

Steve and Stuart got the green light from the security after arguing with him for what seemed like an hour. They were shown to the video surveillance room. The two sat down at a counter facing the front of a bank of television monitors. The screens weren't as nice or as numerous as the menagerie of high-definition screens at their headquarters back in St. Louis, but they room was still pretty impressive.

"On front screen, show TAP terminal counters, flight to Lisbon departing 6:23 or 18:23 hours," said Stuart to anyone of the agents in the room who could help him.

"Did you hear that, Tarpin," said the room duty supervisor with a patch on his chest that had the name Wilbur stitched on. Tarpin was at the main set of controls for the screens around the room.

"Easy day, sir," Tarpin responded to Wilbur.

Tarpin often had to track down nameless, faceless ghosts traveling through the airport using vague references to their destination. Now to have the flight time information and a specific airline TAP, Portugal's national carrier, made this job a piece of cake.

"Yes, sir. A flight on TAP would make that flight number 27. Is that right? Say I don't suppose you have the name of the target," said Tarpin jokingly.

He didn't want to look a gift horse in the mouth, but Tarpin figured it was worth a shot.

"That is what we are looking for," answered Stuart.

As much of a talker as Steve was, he always deferred to Stuart when they were in these types of situations. Stuart was the senior man. Trying to answer questions that Stuart knows the answer to would only increase crosstalk and possible confusion.

So, the mouth was shut for one of the few times today.

Tarpin said, "Well, I thought I would give it a try, sir. You seem to know everything about the guy anyway. And is it a male or female?"

"Male, Arab descent, late twenties or thirties, dark hair, dark eyes, about one hundred fifty pounds and five feet eight inches tall or so," replied Stuart.

After Tarpin punched a few quick numbers into the keyboard, the screen in front of the two agents showed the images from a camera placed behind the ticket counter of the TAP terminal looking directly into the faces of anyone stepping up to the counter.

For the flight 27 on TAP airlines Tarpin began to quickly fast forward through the images starting with the first person in line.

"Here are all the people who boarded that flight as they checked in at the TAP ticket counter for the flight you requested, sir."

The identification would be quick, but the security group didn't want to rush and forget about the procedure they were all taught at school. They began going through the faces of the people at the counter one by one.

Tarpin ID-ed the first in line. "Person 1, female, not target."

Stuart immediately responded, "Not target, Aye" signifying that he was in agreement with the assessment of Tarpin.

"Person 2, male, Caucasian, not target," said Tarpin.

"Not target, Aye," again was the curt response from Mateus.

And so went the process of ID-ing of the people in the line flying to Portugal on a plane that left fifteen minutes ago.

It only took a few minutes then, there he was. The target was on the screen.

"Wait," Steve interrupted the proceedings. "Go back two people."

Tarpin followed orders.

"Now that is someone you wouldn't mind meeting in a club in Lisbon, would you?" said Steve, when a particularly lovely Portuguese woman's image came on screen. "Oh, that reminds me of the girls we met in that club in Naples. Remember her…?"

Stuart muttered something under his breath. He didn't really know what to say, because he knew that Steve has suddenly turned into talk mode and there was nothing anyone could do to stop him.

"Right," continued Steve, to no one in particular. "We were out with some fellas from the base, and we were using the Kitty system, right Stu?"

"What is the Kitty system?" asked Tarpin.

"That's him. What is the name he is traveling under?" asked Stuart.

Tarpin replied, "I am checking the time code on the camera and will match against check-in manifest."

Without further explanation, Tarpin began typing at his keyboard accessing the database and the time codes on the check-in rosters. Through the TAP database he could also double-check with the airport database, which also had the same information.

While Tarpin went about his work, Stuart noticed something about the way that Farooq Ali Jr. was standing and holding his passport.

"Hey, doesn't that look a little curious to you, Steve?" asked Matty. "I mean look at how Ali is holding his passport. It's at an odd angle, almost like he isn't showing it to the counter guy, but he is showing it, well—"

"To us, to the camera," Steve finished Stuart's thought.

"Run that video forward a little bit would you? And can you get a freeze and isolation on the passport that guy is holding, maybe we could get his name right off that."

"That is weird," Tarpin added to the consensus. "I could pull that guy's name off the travel docs easily.

"And run it forward, too" Matty requested.

Tarpin reached for the cue dial and started to move the high definition video forward slowly, frame by frame.

There it was, the second oddest thing the two members from the DDO had seen that day. And these are two guys who had already killed a guy and threw him in a dumpster. So saying that this was weird, was really saying something.

"The guy fuckin' winked at us again," said Steve with amazement. That is the second time that guy has winked at us today."

"Either he thinks you're pretty cute," said Stuart, "or something fishy is going on here."

"Very fishy," added Steve.

"Yousef Blow, is the name your target is travelling under," said Tarpin. "I've never heard of a name like that."

"I don't know much Arabic, but isn't Yousef, like Joe?" asked Stuart.

"So you're saying he is travelling under the name Joe Blow? This guy at least has a sense of humor," Tarpin chimed in.

"And you can confirm that he boarded the plane, and that plane is bound for Lisbon, right?" Matty asked before he left.

"Seat 24D. Facial recognition software won't let anyone board who doesn't match the check-in photo," reassured Tarpin.

"The guy you are looking for is on that plane and he is traveling under the name Joe Blow."

"Thanks," Steve and Stuart said almost in unison as they started toward the door out of security office.

CHAPTER
28

Just that minute, the door to the security office popped open and in walked Lt. Jackson and Cmdr. Bishop.

"Where have you guys been?" asked Jackson. "Last time I saw you, you were chasing down a target on Independence Avenue. Say, did you ever catch him?"

Lt. She'Qlia Jackson couldn't help herself from laughing at his colleagues' expense.

"I think you're getting closer," mocked Jackson repeating her words from Saturday on The Mall.

"Say, I'd love to rehash the events of earlier, but I'm sure there is a reason you're here other than to give me a rash of shit," said Stuart in a rare loss of patience.

It had been a long weekend—one fire on the National Mall in Washington, one fight, one hidden dead body and an upcoming trip across the Atlantic. It can tire a person out.

"Where is target destination," asked Marty Bishop who had, as he normally does, slipped into the room almost unnoticed. "We have a plane waiting to transport."

At his desk in St. Louis, The Admiral leaned back in his brown, leather overstuffed chair and took a long pull on his Hupman cigar.

Exhaling the smoke, he sat quietly and lost himself in thought.

He thought for a long time while the people in his charge were flying across the Atlantic headed from Washington, D.C. to Portugal.

Something about this whole affair didn't seem right. Something was fishy.

He took another long pull on his cigar. He sat. Still. Motionless as a watercolor painting.

This was Intel the way he used to do it.

Thinking the situation through.

He knew the computers were valuable for working up psychographic profiles and running those profiles against a database of previous offenders and taking that information and checking against likely geographic offenders and then factoring in the most likely affiliates of those offenders to get to a list of the most wanted.

All that was valuable, The Admiral knew that. But nothing could ever replace the simple, tech-free process of walking through all the information available and sitting down with a perfectly aged cigar and a glass of single malt Scotch and noodling on it.

"What is Ali, or now Blow as he is calling himself, doing?" thought The Admiral. "Why is he trying to keep us on his trail? The winking...what is with that damn winking?"

The old Intel man leaned forward and buzzed his assistant on the intercom.

"Yes, Sir," the voice of Molina came on the line.

"Molina?"

"Roger that, sir."

"Good lord, woman, what are you doing here at twenty-one hundred hours? Did you get Jackson and Bishop out to D.C.? Don't you have some heart to break, or some boys to disappoint?"

"Yes, sir. Jackson and Bishop left from here on the DDO plane piloted by Richie Bower, I mean Wing Commander Bower. Steve Benson and Stuart Mateus will get on the plane and go from D.C. to destination. And no, sir," came the reply from the outer office. "I was doing some homework for class tomorrow, and I thought I'd use the work computer, my computer at home had a virus or something, and I figured it would be OK to use this one. Is that all right?"

"What? Sure, don't care. Say, would you have time to check on something for me? I am trying to…Well, could you just come in here for a minute?"

Without a response the line went dead.

In ten seconds The Admiral's office door opened and in walked Petty Officer Caty Molina.

"You're wearing jeans. I guess it is after hours and we should allow you to have some life outside of work," The Admiral enjoyed his time with the sailors in the new Navy.

"Thank you, sir," replied Molina coyly.

"Anyway, could you check on something for me? Our friend who was involved in the St. Louis killings, Farooq Ali Jr. Remember him? He came over here from Baghdad a month ago. Likely his ticket was purchased by his handler and boss on this job, Qfar Mohammad. You following me?"

"Yes, sir," said Molina who waited until The Admiral was looking at her and then slyly crossed her legs. Even though she was dressed in a casual pair of skinny jeans, she knew anything she could do to get the attention of the old man would be to her advantage.

"I'll need to go over his file again and look at all the tickets purchased by Mohammad for travel to CONUS," The Admiral said. "You know what CONUS is? Continental United States. What?"

Whenever The Admiral said things like "I'll need," he meant "This is your assignment."

It was the result of his sensitivity training teaching him not to be so forceful and try a little empathy when working around the office. Over time, talking like this became a habit. And it was a habit he sort of liked. He thought it took the edge off his otherwise gruff persona.

"Yes, sir. How far back should I go? Qfar Mohammad was pretty well known as an extensive traveler for many years, if I remember right," said Molina.

"Yes, you're right," The Admiral paused, thinking of an appropriate date for a parameter for Molina.

"Let's go back two months, no wait. Three months prior to the St. Louis attack. One name you will certainly find is Farooq Ali Jr.

right? We've seen his name on the list already, right? Well, as soon as we get an identification on the other body, we'll run a check for him. But for right now, l want you to look for the flights purchased and not for specific pre-identified personnel.

"I've found that when you start a search thinking that you know the answer already, you will find the answer you want to find. If you go into an investigation looking for any answer, you'll find more possibilities. Usually the right answer is among them."

"Yes, sir, three months prior to St. Louis incident, tickets purchased by Qfar Mohammad or any of his agents or agencies, for flights to the United States or CONUS," in Navy fashion, Molina repeated the order back to The Admiral in order to avoid any confusion and to confirm that she had it right. "Why three months and no longer?"

"Good Lord, Molina, I wish some of our field agents were as inquisitive as you," snorted Guilbault-Johnson. "Every day those terrorists are here for a mission, they are at risk of being found out. They are constantly at risk of a nosey neighbor turning them in. At risk of giving themselves away in any casual conversation. They get their mission specs, the mission target and the mission objective and then, of course plan the mission. Call it a gut feeling, but three months feels about right. And I will forward you the name of the other corpse when I get it. He may be on the manifests too. Got it?" he added.

"Richie Bower, here," the pilot said with his English accent from Sheffield. "Yes. Roger that. Roger. Lisbon. Roger."

The government plane had no markings on it as it started its decent into the Lisbon, Portugal airport. Usually Stuart didn't like airplane rides, but this one wasn't bad. Few bumps and little turbulence. Smooth as any he ever had.

He had never been to the Azores and looked forward to it. And for now his visit to the islands would have to wait. He had been redirected to Lisbon midflight.

The plane pulled up to the terminal and stopped. There was no jet bridge for the passengers to walk to the terminal. Just a set of stairs pushed out to the plane by the grounds crew and long walk to the buildings.

As he got to the front of the plane, Stuart paused to thank the pilot.

"Richie, right?" he said to the man he had known for just the 6 hours. "I like to sleep on planes and you drove this thing so well, I think I slept all the way here to the Azores."

"Well, cheers, mate," said Bower. "But while you were sleeping, we got diverted here to Lisbon, Portugal, we are not in the Azores. Something about the target coming here. Probably to get a connecting flight to the Azores. Anyway, I was ordered to transport you to Lisbon. Enjoy."

"Thanks anyway, I guess," replied Stuart. "Maybe next time we'll get to the Azores. Maybe later today."

"Wherever I'm ordered, mate," replied Richie.

Stuart thought this was a lucky turn. He always liked going to Lisbon, or Lisboa as his grandfather called it. His grandfather had immigrated as a boy from Portugal to Cranston, Rhode Island in the late 1800s and was fiercely proud of his Luso heritage. In the old country, his family was originally from the Alentejo, an area of Portugal that lies south of Lisbon. The Alentejo is not as far south as the beautiful beaches in the south. That area is called the Algarve, the southernmost region that had the kinds of beaches that make great photos for tourist brochures. For many years the Algarve has been the playground for British ex-patriots and holiday makers who come for the beaches, the weather and the relatively inexpensive real estate.

Stuart's grandfather would often talk about the beautiful Alentejo. It was quieter, and more genteel than the Algarve. And it also had a more relaxed feel than the busy life in the business, social and international center of Lisbon. The perfect spot in between the two.

GREEN WAVE

Lisbon itself was built on seven low-lying hills on the banks of the Tejo River that made its way lazily to the sea from the nation's inland.

Centuries ago, that river had been the launching point for some of the most ambitious and adventurous men in the world's history.

Bartolomeu Dias left for this harbor when he was the first European to sail around the southern tip of Africa, called going around the horn.

And even Christopher Columbus, as he left to discover America, sailed from Genoa, Italy, out the Mediterranean Sea, around Spain and pulled into Lisbon harbor as his last port of call prior to sailing east into the unknown.

Stuart's grandfather, Rui, would tell stories to young Stuart about the greatness of Portugal and the contributions to the world that the country had given to civilization. Portugal was, and is, the greatest nation filled with greatest, most adventurous, and bravest people on earth, he would tell his grandson.

Despite the heartfelt devotion of his grandfather, Stuart was always confused.

He thought Portugal was great. And yet, he never saw Portugal win the medal count at the Olympics, nor head the United Nations Security council, and no Portuguese ever seemed to win the Nobel Prize for, well, anything.

On the rare occasion when Stuart would ask his grandfather about the seeming contradiction, his grandpa Rui would fold down the newspaper he was reading, look over his glasses, and say to Stuart, "You know of the great things the Portuguese have given to the world, yes?"

"Yes," Stuart would reply that he did.

"You know that the Portuguese are the most industrious, hard-working people in the history of the world? Yes?"

Again Stuart would nod in agreement.

"Well," said Grampa Rui, "After all that…for now, they are resting."

"Stuart, we got a communication from the boss," Stuart was jarred back to the present and his memories were interrupted by Steve Benson nudging him on the arm and talking, always talking.

The hum of the airplane continued in the background as the group of four made their way across the tarmac heading for the terminal.

"Looks like The Admiral has set up a referee gig at a rugby match tonight. Bell-ass-ness against agronomy, or something like that," Steve continued.

"Belenenses against Agronomia," Stuart enunciated the team names, taking time to let Steve know that he had pronounced both incorrectly. "Bell-a-NEN-ses versus Ag-ron-a-ME-a, can you say that? Say it with me, OK?" Stuart was talking in Mr. Rogers-speak, a tactic he used when he wanted to let Steve know he was annoyed that Steve never made any effort to learn any other languages or even any phrases or words that would be helpful.

"Whatever dude," Steve replied not caring at all about the names and only wanting to get to the mission."

"There wouldn't be a real league match on a Monday, I don't think. Must be a scrimmage. You know Spain and Romania national rugby teams are both touring Portugal next month and the locals are probably trying to tune up by playing a couple extra matches."

CHAPTER
29

"Admiral," said Molina. "I have the Intel you requested on the flights and accommodations of all personnel that were purchased by Qfar Mohammad or through one of his known agents. Do you want a paper file or should I send electronically?"

"Do you have a print out? If so, I'll just have a look," said the old man in charge.

The Admiral likes sometimes to pretend that he is a technophobe and eschews electronic forms of communications, but it wasn't true. In fact, he actually sees himself as an early adaptor.

He often said to his IT team as he is getting outfitted with some new gadget or communications device, "Anything that helps get the job done."

And sometimes getting the job done was easier for him if he had paper copies and a large table top on which to spread them out.

Right now, a printout is fine.

He took the papers from Molina's hand and started setting them out on his desk. He was hoping to see something that would give him a clue as to what was happening to his team in Lisbon and what had happened right here in St. Louis a few days ago.

Something about having the crime committed in his hometown bothered him. He knows that the crime could have happened anywhere in the country. It was no shame that they occurred under his nose. But still, to have a major crime with international implications as this go undetected in the Gateway City was an embarrassment for the proud old man.

The Admiral took the papers with the flight information and spread them out on the desk in alphabetical order, hoping that some pattern would emerge.

The names on the tickets started with:

Afar, Mujadar 25 May Emirates $1365

Akeem, Muhammad 14 April Emirates $1400

And on the list went. Each flight on a separate piece of paper. The Admiral scoured the papers for a clue, a pattern that he wouldn't find by staring at a computer screen.

Nothing.

Then, he placed them all in chronological order looking for something that might tip him off.

Again, he couldn't find anything.

He looked at different arrangements of the papers and names. Nothing yet.

Not time yet to get frustrated.

It was time, however, to light another Hupman and tidy up his mind for a few minutes.

After a few slow puffs, Ian Theodore Guilbault-Johnson, known to all as The Admiral, put down the cigar in the ashtray he had picked up in Maldives thirty years ago.

He took a deep breath, and started again.

Then he put tickets for flights leaving Iraq next to the same passenger's return flights. Nothing. Or was there…

"Molina, come here for a minute, won't you?" asked the Admiral. "Do you see anything funny about this? And tell me this: Do you have all the flights? ALL the flights?"

"Yes, sir," she responded proudly. "I even included future flights that aren't scheduled to depart for up to two more weeks from now. The list should be complete. If there is something more out there, I don't know how to get it. After all, I'm not a trained Intel officer, so I'm doing the best that I can."

With that little dig at the old man, she glanced at him out of the side of her vision. He was glancing back.

"Point taken. Do you see anything?" asked the Admiral. "Or should I say, do you not see anything?

Molina was not a trained Intel officer, as she said. In fact, she was only an enlisted sailor and with no Intel training except what she picked up by being around the Intel community every day. But she was always willing to help and took any opportunity to show off her sharp wits to her boss.

"Sir, it's getting pretty late," she hemmed a little while trying to cover her own insecurities about not being able to pick up the hints that Admiral Guilbault-Johnson was giving her. "I really need to get going—"

"Hot date tonight?" the Admiral chided.

Molina bided her time while examining the papers.

"I was just thinking that I should get moving if I am to get away at all…Wait, I think I see what you are talking about. The man, Farooq Ali, or what are you calling him now, Jusaf Blow? Well, it doesn't look like he has—"

"Exactly what I was thinking," said the old man. "We'll make an Intel officer out of you yet. Nice work, Molina. And thanks."

The Admiral looked at the pretty young petty officer. He thought to himself that Molina always acted so tough at work with a hard shell and a guard around her feelings that she never let down. But right now, when this dark beauty discovered that she can think and deduce and apply logic as well as the trained officers, she showed vulnerability that The Admiral hadn't seen before.

She giggled a light giggle when the old man praised her and she felt proud of her work, and she was right to feel proud.

"Is that all, sir?" she posited as she was ready to leave, before her pride and accomplishment made her bust out of her already-snug sweatshirt.

"No, you can go," he responded.

She turned to leave and as she strode towards the secure hatch that leads to the hallway, she had to remind herself not to run and jump and skip. Despite warning herself, she thought she might do it.

Then, before she got to the door, she turned and said to Guilbault-Johnson, "Thank you, sir, for allowing me to work with you. Oh, and I almost forgot, I arranged for Stuart Mateus to referee a rugby match tonight in Lisbon. Two local teams. I can't pronounce, you know, they speak Portuguese and I speak Spanish. But it was supposed to be some high level scrimmage. I can look up the names of the teams and the specifics—"

"No, thanks. You've done more than enough for one night," he said. "Thanks for all your help."

"Now, what was I saying?" Steve said as he and Stuart sat in the secure area of the Lisbon airport. The room at the airport was very new and contained all the latest security features.

In fact, much about the Lisbon airport was newly installed and in better shape than similar-looking airports in the United States. This seemed strange to Steve and Stuart, but they didn't think too much about it. In a country that still has many farmers walking down country roads beside their milking cow which is pulling a wagon delivering dairy goods to the villagers, a high-tech airport with all the bells and whistles right out of the twenty-second century seemed just a bit incongruous.

And yet, because the Portuguese were part of the European Union, they got money from richer, more industrialized countries such as Germany. The idea is to get everyone up to the same standard of living, or at least try.

On the private military flight, the team had gotten in ahead of the commercial flight carrying Joe Blow, or Ali Jr. or whatever he was calling himself today and beat them to Lisbon.

The secure area in the airport was staffed with Portuguese security personnel who knew the Yanks were coming. The security staff were intent on showing that they had capabilities every bit as advanced as those that the Americans were accustomed to.

And they did have all the tools. One of the newest was a camera system that included facial-recognition software that recognizes people and compares the images to an international database to see if the person is wanted for anything from a traffic ticket in Hamburg to a sexual offense in Tbilisi. There were also communications systems that had not even been installed yet. The mobile units were all issued to security agents because the Portuguese like the way they looked when they clipped them to their lapels on their uniforms, but they didn't know one tenth of the capabilities of the devices which had GPS capabilities, laser guidance for night vision and impaired vision and even a 'shoot here' targeting system that can sense bodies by temperature and instruct the wearer if someone is out there and where to aim if you want to kill them.

"So this is where your dad was from, huh?" Steve continued as if he had been interrupted. "My folks are from Sweden, or maybe it was Switzerland. It was somewhere that gets mighty cold, I know that for sure. My dad used to say that he really didn't care too much about where he was from. You know, if you asked him where is ancestors came from, he would say 'Toledo' and he thought that was pretty funny stuff. Fact is, he had never in been to Toledo in his entire life, so he always got a laugh with that one. Well, he really didn't get a laugh out of anyone but himself, come to think of it, but he laughed like he was watching the Stooges. Boy he loved that one. So my mom was from somewhere that was warm, like Italy or something. You know, you can't keep those kinds of people apart. He was fair and blond and white as Casper's typing paper. She was dark and swarthy, is that the word they use for that? Swarthy? What is smarmy then? Huh? What does it mean to be smarmy? It's not the same as swarthy is it?" Steve waited for an answer, but not so long that anyone could respond. "Swarthy means dark, right?" he continued. "Like dark complexioned? Like pirates, or gypsies or Schmumfords. That's swarthy. And smarmy is what? Is that like real kiss-ups, you know, people who really lay it on thick when they want something from you. Like Eddie Haskell. Always pretending to be very nice and polite when it serves them, but are really sort of wankers and just trying to manipulate people. I've met a lot of them. They seem to be your buddy after only meeting them for a few minutes and giving you the real treatment, you know." Steve's voice got squeaky while he mocked smarmys. "You're right about that, buddy, boy you sure know a lot about football, never thought of that before,' and then almost in the same breathe, they need you to take them to pick up a friend who is getting off work and then that friend has a quick errand to run and the next thing you know, you realize that you've been smarmied right out an entire night and this jerk is just warming up—"

"Wait a second!" Stuart yelled.

"What do you see, Farooq Ali Jr.? What?" a stunned Steve asked. "Holy cripes, man, you scared the—"

"Who in the name of fuck are the Shmumfords?" Stuart laughed. "Dude, what in God's own name are you talking about? One second you are talking about your parents being from Sweden and the same breath you are yapping about some family called the Schmumfords—"

Steve stopped him. "The Shmumfords were a people from the area of what is now Bar Harbor, Maine, if I'm remembering right. They were much darker than the other groups around there at the time, of course most of them were British, because they figure these Shmumfords were from the Basque area between Spain and France on the Atlantic side. You've never heard of the Shmumfords? Boy I don't know what they are teaching you so long—"

"Oh, shut it," Stuart had seen the face he was looking for on the monitor. "There he is. Just as we thought. And standing in the line to get onto the flight to Pico."

Stuart turned to one of the Portuguese security team, "Hey, what is Pico?"

"Que," said the officer who seemed to have the best English.

"Onde e o Pico," Stuart surprised Steve and himself with the quality of his broken Portuguese.

"O senhor fala Portuguese?" the local asked of Stuart.

Stuart didn't think he spoke Portuguese, but he was eager to engage the man and it seemed like English was out of the question.

"Sim, eu falo," Stuart said with ease. "Onde fica Pico?"

"Pico fica no Acores. On mil kilometers do aqui. Acores e islands," said the security man.

"Nous precisamos ir la," said Stuart.

"Hey, what are talking about? And I didn't know you spoke Portuguese?" interrupted Steve.

"I didn't know either," replied Stuart. "I guess some it stuck from when I was young. My father used to tell me that he spoke to me in Portuguese when he I was a baby, but I really don't remember any of it. Weird. Anyway, I'm just asking Portuguese security where our Joe Blow is going. Seems he is waiting to get on a plane to the island of Pico on the middle of the Atlantic. We knew he was going to the Azores, but I just wanted to check with security team to make sure we are talking the same language. You ready to go?"

"We know he was going there, right?" said Steve.

The next flight from Lisbon to Pico wasn't until the following morning which meant that Stuart was going to have to referee the training match that night at a rugby pitch on the campus of the Universidade Agronomia in Lisbon. He was sort of hoping he could get out of it. All the running and flying and fighting over the last few days have gotten him feeling uncustomarily weary.

Steve and Stuart wanted to sit down and enjoy a few hours of rest knowing the target, Joe Blow, wasn't going anywhere until the following morning.

Stuart sat and asked Steve to contact headquarters to see if there were any more updates that they needed to know.

CHAPTER 30

"Admiral Guilbault-Johnson, this is Steve Benson in Lisbon, Portugal. Do you have a read on us?" asked Benson.

"Yes, young man. Where have you been?" replied The Admiral.

"You know exactly where I've been," responded Steve. "You've got the GPS coordinates on us everywhere we go with this tracking software. You even know what our altitude is at any time. You have our respiration, our heart rate. Good Lord, you probably know that I am hungry as can be right now. I wonder what makes a person hungry? I know the science of it, I guess with the stomach fluids causing the growling and so forth. But I've gone without eating for a day or two in the past and never felt hungry. I was on assignment at those times, but still, if hunger is purely a physiological response, then I would have been famished, right? And animals that I've examined, sometimes they are not hungry and their owners bring them in for a checkup because they are not eating. They shouldn't have emotional responses to anything, but they seem to be able to react to situations that are affecting the household in which they are living. "So what is this feeling of hunger? Something to think about for another day, I suppose."

"Finished?" inquired The Admiral.

"Famished? Well yes, but can we stop talking about food for a minute? I have some info for you," said Steve, not joking. "We just found out man Yousef Blow getting off the plane in Lisbon and tomorrow will get back onto a plane headed for guess where? Hmm? Can't guess can you?"

"Pico, Azores," replied The Admiral matter-of-factly. Same as the note you got from him in Washington D.C."

"Pico, Azores…yes, of course you know," stammered Steve Benson.

"Molina tracked down all the records for me of flights bought by Hussain Mohammad or known associates of Hussain Mohammad bought by themselves or on their behalf. It seems that a ticket was bought by Mohammad to go to Pico about three months ago," said The Admiral.

"Three months ago?" well that fits with what we were talking about earlier for the timeline of this whole thing, doesn't it?" replied Steve.

By now, Stuart was also taking part in the call on the comm device.

He jumped in, "So that means I don't have to ref the match tonight."

"No, you still have to ref," replied the Admiral. "In fact, since we have such good Intel concerning the meet and where it will take place, you have to ref the match and there seems to be little chance of losing contact with the target."

"Line out, Red put in." was the call from referee Stuart Mateus.

The field at the Agronomia rugby pitch was spectacularly groomed. As the two teams lined up for the throw in to restart the match, Stuart went to the back of the lineout. During a rugby lineout, the packs of both teams line up perpendicular to the point where the ball went out of bounds.

That is the point where the ball is to be thrown in.

The two packs of eight players each, form a long tunnel. It was at the back of this tunnel, that Mateus liked to stand during a lineout.

The team that should get the ball after the lineout, is the team that throws the ball in.

When the ball is thrown in, one of his teammates in the line tries to catch it.

While this is happening, the other team is also trying to intercept the ball.

The lineout looks a little like a jump ball in basketball, except instead of one jumper going after the ball, there are eight.

The only advantage that the throwing team has is they know which player they are trying to target. In order to make it easier for the thrower, he calls out signals, like a football quarterback at the line of scrimmage, telling his teammates where the ball is going to be thrown.

"Sete, Diez, Verde, Azulejo, Agora," was the shout from the Agronomia player prior to throwing the ball down the tunnel.

The thrower rocked back and shifted his weight onto his back foot. Then he leaned forward and gave the rugby ball a Joe Montana-style toss high above the tunnel that was easily caught by his own player who was jumping to make the catch.

The lineout had worked.

But, Stuart gave his whistle a short, decisive toot signaling an infraction. The ball was not thrown straight down the middle of the tunnel.

"Not straight, Belenenses choice, scrum here or line out," he said.

This call gave Belenenses team the option of taking a scrum at the point of infraction or they could have a line out again, this time they would be the team to throw the ball into the tunnel.

The Belenenses captain responded quickly, "Melee, er, scrum aqui, sir," indicating that he wanted his team to have a scrum to restart play as they are more dependable than a line out.

"Scrum here to blue," Stuart said smartly.

The teams took their pack positions to re-start play.

"Crouch, Bind, Set," said Stuart in his customary rhythmical cadence.

The two teams came together with the normal violence of a scrum forming.

After Stuart blew the final whistle, he jogged to the sidelines to get his bottled water. He reffed a very good match he thought. If this had been an international match, he certainly would have gotten a very high score from the rater who would have been there to judge his work.

But this was a match between two club sides on a week night and he doubted there would be a rater even assigned watch the match.

Anyway, it was time to start getting his mind thinking about terrorists and water department employees and not about rugby.

Stuart spotted Steve on the sidelines and started to make his way towards where Steve was standing.

Stuart was abruptly accosted by a swarthy man he had never seen before.

"Come with me please, quickly," was all that the stranger said to Stuart. The stranger took Stuart by the elbow and led him towards a more remote corner of the playing field where two other men waited impatiently.

"What are you doing?" Stuart asked, and got no reply.

They were walking so fast the Stuart almost had to jog to keep from stumbling. The man was very insistent and had a very tight grip on the back of Stuart's triceps. They were walking side by side with the man a half step behind the agent and pushing him forward.

As they moved, Stuart wondered if this was his contact here in Lisbon.

Had there been a change of plans? Had their target, Ali, gotten away or made contact with the local Intelligence community?

Or was this one of Islam's men who had gotten word of the chase for Ali and thought that the referee agent was a threat?

If this is one of Islam's men, then that was very good news indeed as that meant they were getting very close to the big target, and he and Steve were really rattling the cage of this animal.

It also meant very bad news as this possible killer had hold of him right now and he didn't have anywhere to run, and was unarmed. It is possible this would be the last rugby pitch he would ever see.

Stuart thought about this possibly for about two more steps, then he acted.

As the two marched quickly across the Agronomia rugby pitch, Stuart looked sharply over to his partner Steve who was engaged in an animated conversation with both Jackson and Bishop. They obviously weren't going to be any help.

As people do when they are walking together, Stuart and the man had started walking in sync. Left, right, left, right. It wasn't anything they planned on or were trying to do, but bodies naturally start doing it when walking closely so to avoid any clanging or bumping elbows and hips. The man was on Stuart's right side slightly behind him.

As his next left foot hit the turf, Stuart instantly changed his momentum and pushed backwards and to his right with all his considerable weight and strength. He also lowered his shoulder into the man's chest.

The quickness of the move took the swarthy man by complete surprise and the two stumbled back on the turf together. While they fell, Stuart knew that the only chance was to wrestle the man's weapon away from him before he could get to it. The swarthy stranger landed with a thud flat on his back.

Stuart started to frisk the man for the gun.

But where was he carrying it?

Stuart had purposely landed right on top of the man who was almost paralyzed by shock. This was going to be easier than he thought.

With years of experience guiding his hands, Stuart felt the man's pockets and around the man's waist to locate the weapon that Stuart was certain he carried. A few grunts came for the man who seemed completely docile and didn't resist at all. Odd.

"Senhor, referee," the man asked incredulously. "What are you doing?"

"Nice try, fella," Stuart responded "Now where is it?"

"I have it right here and will show to you if you can spare a moment," replied the man. The casualness of the man caught Stuart off guard. Stuart got off the man and sat beside him, still facing the swarthy man.

"What do you have then? I can't find anything." Stuart said.

"Well, your match report esta certo," he replied. Stuart recognized the thick accent as Portuguese.

"What?" asked Stuart.

"You're match report—"

"So you're here to give a report on—"

"On your refereeing well of the game. I thought you did a very nice job over all and had only a few small criticisms of your work... on the scrum downs you were calling, I think that...Say, may we stand up for this, I am muito uncomfortable here on the soil, or ground, grass how do you want to say, ground?"

"So if you are the referee grader, why are you hustling me way over here to this remote corner of the field?" Stuart asked.

"I only thought that you would not want everyone to hear my critiques. Since I don't know you, I didn't know if you wanted your friends and the players to hear my thoughts on your performance. Many people I critique don't like others to hear them and want only to hear themselves, which is of course not possible really as the comment are always available to all on our website and through the referee's council here in Lisbon and around Portugal, I think they are even linked to your country's site so all the members of your brotherhood, how do you want to say, group? Can see them to see on the improvement of each referee, you see?"

"Oh, yes, let's please stand up. Are you all right, by the way?" Stuart realized that this man was not, of course, an agent of Islam, but in fact a referee judge send there to critique his work during the game.

"So, why, senhor," asked the Portuguese gentleman, "do you attack me when I ask you to come over here for a quiet word about your refereeing work today?"

"Oh, ahh, that," Stuart stammered. "I slipped and accidently fell onto you. It was completely my fault. I am terribly sorry, I hope you aren't hurt."

"No, no I'm fine," said the man. "It was just so very odd that you were also grabbing at me and feeling into my pockets and tout, or all places that seem private."

"I was just, ah, trying to help you up. As I said, it was very much an accident and I am as sorry as I can be," Stuart said hoping the entire episode would go away. As quickly as he could, Stuart tried to turn the conversation away from the topic of the fall.

"Let me help you to your feet, Senhor…say, what is your name? I fell so hard that I seemed to have forgotten my manners. I really gave my leg quite a twist and I hope that it is nothing permanent. Let me try some rusty Portuguese on you, if I may. 'Como se chama?'"

"Oh, you speak Portuguese? How nice," said the man getting to his feet with the help of Stuart.

"No, not really, my family was from your country and I know only a few words and phrases, but I find it a beautiful tongue."

Stuart was now hoping that his praise didn't come across as flattery.

"Well, I was sent here to analyze your refereeing today against these two teams, by the way, my name is Senhor de Costa," said the Portuguese man. "I think over all your refereeing is very good, but I tell you the obvious as if you were not a talented referee, I would not be here to judge this game, right?"

"Well, that is quite nice of you to say, Senhor de Costa. I hope that I was good enough to deserve your confidence. I didn't know that I would have an analyzer for a simple mid-week matchup such as this," Mateus was more formal when dealing with the Portuguese as he knew they are a very formal and proper people.

"Very much so, senhor. I thought you were a very good referee. Shall I give you a quick verbal analysis in addition to the formal report I file with your organizing body at USA Rugby? On the plus or positive side, I thought your calls on the break down were very clear and players certainly clearly understood what you expected of them. As you know, the break down area around the tackle can be the most difficult in the game, and some say in all of sport. Players were coming into the rucks at speed, but always from an onside position and always getting guidance from you. For that, you will receive the highest score grade that I am allowed to give—"

CHAPTER
31

Stuart remained silent as a sign of respect to his grader.

"I found that you move around the pitch very well for an ample man..."

The voice of Senhor De Costa faded in Stuart's mind as he started thinking immediately about that phrase 'ample man' and thought that he was still moving pretty good, and the grader said so too. Ample? Maybe. But I am still nifty on my feet am I not? Why would de Costa bring that up? He could have left that out. Geeez, I am a mess, if this guy thinks am 'ample' then I really have some problems.

Stuart's attention came back to the present

"...and for this reason, I will also grader you as highly as the scale allows. Are you thinking these are fair comments, Senhor Mateus referee?"

"Oh yes, yes indeed, thank you for the feedback," said Stuart.

"On the negative side, and this is really muito pequeno, ah, ah, very small. I thought that there were times that you seemed to wonder in your head...oh how does it want to be called...not buying attention—"

"Paying attention," helped Stuart Mateus.

"Yes, thank you, paying attention. There sometime seemed to be in your thoughts something other than the game, the match right in front of you. Now this is something that is difficile, difficult to put into a report to the rugby authorities. It is more of a personal note to you. I think you missed no calls and I think you had control of the match at all times. I just could see, I think, a look in your eyes sometimes that I believe that you were not fully in the moment as you say."

"I see. I think I will give this some very serious thought, Senhor de Costa, I think you may be more accurate than you know," said Stuart. "I won't bore you with the details of my life off the field, but it is true that I have some very important matters that have been weighing on my mind lately. As you know, refereeing is a part-time occupation in rugby and we all have lives off the pitch and mine has been busy and complicated lately. I think you are very insightful and I do appreciate your giving me your thoughts. I also thank you for omitting these observations, however accurate they are, from your formal report to World Rugby."

"I don't omit these observations from the report as a favor to you, or because I am afraid to rate you badly," said the referee observer. "I would make note of it your distracted behavior in my report, but I simply don't know where or how to make the notation in the report. As I said, your efforts in the jogo, match were muito good, and I have no complaints. I just noticed the—"

"Everything OK, Matty?" Marty Bishop huffed and puffed out of his lungs as he and Lt. Jackson finally arrived after sprinting from the far side of the pitch to where the two were talking.

"We noticed you were having…we thought you may have hurt yourself in your fall," said Jackson. She was remembering from her training that an accidental fall is always the reason agents offer for any mistakes, miscues or misidentifications. That is according to the manual. And Jackson liked the manual when it served her.

"Yes, I stepped awkwardly and took a terrible spill. Senhor… ahh…ahh, outra vais"

"de Costa," the referee rater helped.

"Senhor de Costa has been very gracious in forgiving me for my terrible stumble. Senhor de Costa is the referee rater for this match and has been giving me a short verbal report highlighting the thrust of what he plans to put in his written report to the ref board. Pretty nice, huh?"

"Very nice of you, Senhor de Costa," said Lt. Jackson who was eager to get the awkwardness behind her.

Jackson reached out her hand.

"She'Qlia Jackson, nice to meet you, Senhor de Costa," said Lt. Jackson.

"Todo prazer para me," said de Costa.

"Marty Bishop, nice to meet you," he said as he extended his hand.

After a few minutes of small talk, de Costa excused himself so he could go to his office and write his official report while the events of the match were still fresh in his head.

"Where the hell are you all?" The Admiral was on the comm unit and he was pissed.

"Sir, we are all right here at the match," replied Benson who kept his responses short and military, the way the boss liked them. Benson was not about to heighten the stress on The Admiral while he was in one of his moods.

"Well why the hell didn't anyone contact me? For Fuck's sake, it's about twenty minutes past three Greenwich Mean Time, and I thought that someone would have the courtesy of calling me when my away team makes plans? Is that too fucking much to ask? Jesus Horatio Christ, what the fuck is wrong with you—"

"Sir, there was a little incident after the match, and we are not just getting ourselves together to talk with you about our next move," Benson tried his best to calm the old man.

"Well a message on the secure comm would have been adequate don't you think?" the boss was not easily mollified.

"Well in answer to your first question, we are all right here at the Agronomia rugby pitch as you directed, sir," said Benson who was becoming increasingly uncomfortable dealing with the boss. This was usually the job of Mateus.

Benson put his comm unit on mute and shout-whispered at Stuart "Matty, get your ass over here and talk to The Admiral."

Stuart was about thirty meters away in the parking lot near the rugby pitch. He deftly opened up the front and rear doors of his car to form a small, crude changing room that covered just enough of his mid-section and performed the function of not allowing gawkers to see as he was getting out of his sweaty rugby shorts and black compression shorts. Quickly and without notice, Matty slipped out of his game gear and just as quickly stepped into a clean pair of cotton shorts.

Stuart yelled back, "No way, I know what he's like when he gets his blood up. You can handle him."

With that, Stuart closed the car doors and walked over to the now-empty bleachers to change out of his cleats.

The Admiral hadn't let up on Benson, "I have had about enough of your crap, you know. I can make this whole thing go away if I like. Do you know that? Your little vacation to Europe can be over real quick."

Benson, with the comm unit still on mute whisper shouted to Mateus again, "he wants to talk with you, Matty, so come get this fucking phone."

"Bullshit," said Stuart not believing anything Benson said, knowing that he would say anything to get out of the conversation he was having with the boss. Stuart knew that The Admiral would have to let some steam off at least once each mission. Sometimes he would yell at his staff in St. Louis, sometimes it would be the group in Washington, and sometimes it would be directed at them, the boys in the field. The best thing to do was always to buckle up, take the shouting and get past it as quickly as you can. The Admiral always settled down and later, never apologized.

Stuart knew the whole thing would blow over, but it was always a little tense suffering through one of the Admiral's rants. But Stuart had heard it so many times that this time he even cracked a smile knowing what Benson was going through.

"…and another thing, you two. Have Jackson and Bishop gotten with you two about your plans yet? Those two can be as bad as you about keeping HQ informed about what the fuck you are up to." The Admiral's voice was losing its steam. He was getting tired of shouting and also starting to realize that he was making an ass of himself.

"So, when you decide on a plan, could you let me know? We have information about the destination of the target. Are you still on the line, Benson? And where in God's name is that Geeper Mateus?"

"Now he is really looking for you," said Benson to Stuart trying desperately to get out of the call.

"OK, give it to me," Stuart finally conceded to taking the call.

Stuart took the phone off mute.

"Yes, sir, Mateus here," Stuart said into the unit as official-sounding as he can could manage.

"Mateus, about time," said Guilbault-Johnson. "Now as I was saying to—"

"Benson, Bishop and Jackson and I are on station and we are all in conference on arranging next moves," said Mateus interrupting his boss. "Must discontinue comm as interception breach possible, do you roger? Out."

The Admiral replied, "Roger that."

The line went dead.

The four agents stood silently for a moment. Three of them: Bishop, Benson, and Jackson stared at Mateus with their mouths wide open. Had he just hung up on The Admiral? The most powerful man in the Directorate of Discretionary Operations? Did that really just happen?

After what seemed like several minutes, Mateus looked around at his colleagues and said in a deadpan voice staring at Lt. Jackson… "She'Qlia? Is that really your fucking name? Holy shit, what the fuck is that all about? I've never heard of crazier name. She'Qlia? Seriously?"

Between the pressure of having The Admiral yelling at them and the way Mateus handled the boss, the four immediately started to laugh uproariously.

Outside the Restaurante Miguel in Lisbon, the three men and one woman approached the door. Stuart led, not because the others deferred to him as the leader, in fact, if anyone would be considered the leader, it would be Marty Bishop who was the highest ranking.

Cmdr. Bishop wasn't the leader that Stuart was. Bishop was a desk jockey. A ranking member of the 101st Chairborne Division. A pencil sharpener.

Stuart led the group simply because he was the first to get out of the cab that brought them to this part of town. His hand reached out and grabbed for the door handle and pulled it open for the group.

Suddenly he stopped and turned to address his friends.

"Kitty tonight? He asked.

"Oh yes, the kitty must be in effect," said Benson.

"Absolutely the kitty is on," added Bishop.

"I wonder if the kitty is a worldwide phenomenon or is a local phenomenon?" wondered Steve. "I think the kitty is the best, absolutely the best way to go out, even if it means hanging out with you guys. I mean. What if you were in Russia and you were trying to put a few rupees together—"

"Rupees are from India, you tool," interrupted Marty, showing a rare ability to insult in a fun way.

"Whatever the fuck you want to call them, the dollars from India—"

"Russia, you nincompoop," said Bishop. "I mean rubles. Now you've got me all turned around."

"Right, Russia, that is what I was…anyway, I wonder while they are out buying their babushkas or whatever they buy on a Friday night in Moscow, do they all get the money together and buy as a team, or do they each buy individual babushkas? Huh, do you know?"

"Jesus you are a freaking idiot sometimes, you know," said Stuart.

The Kitty system was brought to the group by Stuart and Steve. They both learned it while they were in Italy and would party with the Brits who were also stationed in Naples.

The Kitty is when all the members of drinking party would put money into a common fund and then the group would all drink from this common pool of money. Say, you gave $100 bucks to the Kitty holder at the start of a night out with the gang, then the group doesn't have to worry about whose turn it is to buy, or whose round it is, or how much each should tip, or anything about the bills. The secret was getting a Kitty holder that you trust and to get also who would not spend all the kitty on food or drink that he alone liked.

So the group stood around deciding who…

"I'll be the Kitty master," volunteered Marty.

Everyone agreed because he certainly always seemed trustworthy and wouldn't spend anything on himself as the evening progressed.

"How much?" Marty asked to the group to determine the contribution.

"What do you think, about 100 euros?" asked Jackson.

Each person reached into their wallet to draw out the bills to hand them to Marty.

Jackson gave her 100 to Marty.

Stuart gave his 100.

When Steve opened his pocket and pulled out his 100 Euros. He reached out to Marty to give him two 50 euro bills.

"Hey check that out," Stuart's eyes were fixed on a young Portuguese woman crossing the road coming toward the Restaurante Miguel. She was about twenty-five, far too young for anyone in the group to have a shot at. She was hot. Her long brown hair fell straight from the top or her lovely caramel-skinned face, past her neck, and ending just at bosom level. Her legs were long. Long enough to reach the top, but not artificially accentuated by high heels or too-tight pants. Her face was tanned and brown with a perfect mix of European and Latin and possibly African features that were absolutely stunning. No, this girl's beauty wasn't glamorous. It was earthy. And it was powerful. And the boys could see it.

While everyone looked at the girl, Steve took his eyes off Marty as he handed him the bills and thought Marty had his money. Steve let go of the bills. Marty didn't have his hand on the money and was staring at the girl like everyone else.

When Steve let go, one of the bills slipped from their hands and dropped onto the sidewalk in front of Restaurante Miguel. A sudden gust of wind blew the 50 Euro bill quickly into a street grate and disappeared into the bowels of the city.

For a moment, nobody noticed. They were all still staring at the girl.

"Hello, I love you," said Marty. Marty loved classic rock music and had once seen on a Behind the Music-type show Ray Manzarik of the Doors recounting the origin of the song with that name and how it was he and Jim Morrison sitting beachside in California when a young beauty caused them both to pause. Ray said, "Hello, I love you" and Jim wrote a song about it.

Looking at this girl, Marty now knew what the Doors were talking about.

With a quick glance back at the boys, the girl turned up the street, never to be seen again.

Coming out of their trance, Marty said to Steve, "Where is your hundy?"

"I gave it to you," Steve protested.

"No way." I was standing right here. I would have known if you gave me a 100 Euro bill—"

"Well, I did, two fifties," Steve said.

"You gave me one 50," Marty Bishop was not backing down. "Here it is."

Jackson quickly interrupted this argument that was about to go juvenile.

"Look you two. Yes, he did give it to you, but you two idiots dropped one of the bills while you were looking at that lady."

Steve said, "Well that counts, I gave it to you. Jackson said so."

"That doesn't count," said Marty. "It never was introduced into the Kitty proper."

"The Kitty proper," Steve protested. "Are you fucking Garfield or something? The Kitty proper is that I gave you the cash and you blew it. That counts."

"Look, I hate to break up a discussion that is about to reach the 'I am rubber and you're glue' stage, but let's get inside and start eating and drinking and you jerks can start talking about that girl," Jackson urged.

CHAPTER 32

"Yes. Please. We'd like a bottle of Vino Verde," said Mateus to the waitress.

The four agents from the DDO were seated at a table in a restaurant in the oldest district of Lisbon known as the Alfama. The Alfama was just east of downtown Lisbon, or upriver on the Tagus, and has been there longer than the city has. When the city was dominated by Arabs or Moors as they were called, they built the Alfama.

Today, the Alfama remains a beautiful area of the city with narrow, winding streets that twist and turn as though they've never really decided where they want to take you. The three- and four-story buildings were built long before motorcars were invented. The buildings have faced each other across the skinny ribbons of streets for more than a millennia. So long that the tops of the buildings seem to lean towards each other—like two lovers leaning in for a kiss.

These buildings rise above the narrow streets and seem to grow closer as they grow taller. The upper stories seem to reach out across the streets to almost touch one another, blocking out the sun by day. At night, the ancient edifices form a roof over the streets that make the unlighted streets below a deep black and serene darkness.

Although it is black as coal in these streets at nights, there is little crime. The Portuguese people are too passive to be good criminals.

Although in recent years crime has grown slightly, it is still rare. The Alfama is still a neighborhood full of pride and old world ways where women walk safely from house to house in the blackest night with little fear.

Inside Miguel's, the restaurant the group chose for the night, the second of several vinho verde bottles is turned upside down and the last drop is poured out. Vinho verde is a green wine that is not found widely outside of Portugal.

It is called green wine, not for the color of the grape like red and white wines, but because the grapes are harvested prematurely, making for a tangy, sweet, wine that is almost like a wine cooler.

When the four American's heard the waiter recommend the green stuff in the Alfama restaurant, they knew immediately that the night was in trouble.

Bishop, Jackson, Benson and Mateus all liked the work they were hired to do. They all liked working for The Admiral. They all liked working for the good guys, and they all liked catching the bad guys. And when they had a night out with nothing to do, they all liked to party with a glass of wine and a good meal and a glance at the ladies, or men in Jackson's case.

"—so then I knocked him right on his ass," said Mateus in between bites of his grilled squid, a house specialty.

The group exploded in laughter.

"Where did this happen?" asked Bishop. "I didn't see any of this."

"I was fucking certain that this guy was going to kill me. I was trying to get your attention but you dicks were over by the parking lot doing some shit. I could have sent up a fucking flair and you wouldn't have seen it. What were you doing over there anyway?"

"That poor de Costa. He never knew what hit him," said Jackson. "With your fat ass coming down on him, I bet you broke some ribs—"

"My fat ass? Look She'Qlia…and what is a name like She'Qlia? You've never told me," shot back Mateus.

The agents work with a lot of stress. So when they are off duty, they let off steam, sometimes at the expense of each other.

And despite the fact that these four were well into their third bottle of vinho verde with no signs of slowing down, they were under pressure.

"Damn you all, I will have you fuckers killed," shouted Qfar Mohammad.

Mohammad's posse of six criminal henchmen roared with laughter at their boss's loud, drunken boast.

"That's what I told those pricks, and I'll tell you this, they all listened, even though I was the youngest Arab in his employment. My, God those were glorious times, weren't they my friends?

"Housef, you were there, don't you remember the time we told our former boss to fuck himself and we thought we were going to get our dicks handed to us? Huh? Don't tell me that he actually did get yours."

"That's right, Qfar," he got my dick," but he had to first fish it out of your mouth!" Housef's comment drew an intensely quiet reaction from the group gathered around the hookah pipe on the floor of one of the lounges in Qfar Mohammad's Baghdad home. All the underlings waited to see what the Qfar's reaction would be to this. Would he get angry and go into one of his occasional rages that sometimes ended in death to one of the party goers? Or would the boss laugh it off and enjoy the give and take with one of his longtime friend and allies, Housef.

There was a long pause. All eyes turned to Qfar.

Housef, of all the lackeys who took advantage of Qfar's generosity, was Qfar's most trusted. Likely because he has been with the boss the longest. But lately Housef seems to enjoy pushing the boundaries of that friendship, and the bonds of good taste, further and further and perhaps now, he has overrun even his own long leash and insulted the boss too much for him to forgive.

Five seconds pass...

Ten seconds pass...nothing.

All eyes remain on Qfar.

At last, the boss smiles and gives a laughing snort. Then falls into a full roaring laugh that cues the others in the room to begin laughing. To a man, they answered the call.

Housef smiled at the boss and the boss smiles back. All is OK for now between the two.

Housef asked, "Qfar, my friend, can I talk to you in private for a minute?"

"Of course, my friend," and Qfar looks around at the other five men, who all quietly get up and leave the two to talk in private.

"Qfar, sorry I was so rude in front of the others, but I have just gotten some news that you won't like."

"Will I like it more if you tell me later?" the boss asked as though he is the Godfather. "Then tell me now before the news gets worse."

"Qfar," says Housef, "The man killed in the algae job in St. Louis was not Farooq Ali as was planned."

"Who then? And who are we communicating with who claims to have the formula?" asked the boss.

"It seems that Ali survived the attack in St. Louis and the man killed was Hussian Islam. I can't understand how this could have happened."

"How do you know? Who has told you this? How do you know? And who then has the formula?" the boss was getting agitated.

"I don't know for certain, Qfar," said Housef, "but from the description I was given from the men in Washington, it seems that the man may be Farooq who is alive and the dead man is Hussain."

"Impossible. If there was violence in St. Louis, it was Islam who would have survived, unless, the Americans had known we were coming and ambushed the team. But that is impossible. What could have gone wrong?"

"I have been giving this thought, too, my master, and this is what I think," said Housef. "If we believe the reports of our men in Washington, then Ali lives and that means Islam is dead. So, if no one knew of our plan, it seems that Ali must have killed Islam while in St. Louis as a way to punish us for having his father fired from the water plant—"

"Wait," Qfar jumped in. "Are you saying that the mild mannered son of a water clerk could have turned into a killer at the first sign of trouble? I don't think this is possible."

"But look at the facts, sir," Housef replied. "How else could this have happened? The Americans could have killed Islam, but would they not also have killed Ali if there was a shootout or a gunfight or any other trouble? Ali lives and Hussain Islam does not. I think this is reason enough to say that Ali has killed Islam."

"Or worse, perhaps Ali was able to contact the American authorities while he was there in St. Louis and tell them of the plan," posited Qfar. "Perhaps the Americans set up an ambush where they killed Islam and allowed Ali to go free. Ali must be working with the Americans. He must be a plant that the Americans allowed to go free so they can follow him back to us."

"Yes, you're right, boss," agreed Housef. "You must be right. That is why the Americans have not detained him. He must be working for the Americans now. Or perhaps has been all along. Either way, he must die after he gives us the algae formula. And by the way, have we let his father live?"

"Yes, sire. He is allowed to live at home. We have never harmed him. And he doesn't even know that we are involved in this, let us say, misfortune."

"By the way, Housef, why did you choose Pico as a rendez vous point?"

"Your forgiveness, my master, if the location does not suit you," said Housef. "The location was chosen by our Hussain Islam prior to his death. He said that Portugal would have a relatively easy security to penetrate. I think he told me he had done jobs in Lisbon in the past without much difficulty and he thought that the island of Pico would be even more unprotected."

Housef was fast on his feet. Housef himself was the one who had suggested that he meet Islam at the island of Pico in the Azores. But when his unstable, paranoid, and violent boss asked a question like "who chose Pico?" Housef thought it was better to blame a dead man who could not defend himself than take the possible praise or more likely blame likely to come with the choice.

Fact is, Housef had always wanted to go to the island and though this would be a good way to mix a little business with pleasure. A quick exchange with Islam to get the formula, a few days on the beach, eh, why not?

CHAPTER 33

While discussing the situation in the United States and Lisbon, Qfar and Housef didn't rejoin the rest of the group in the party room.

The guests would be well entertained for many hours by the Lucy Ewing/Charlene Tilton look-alikes that Qfar had hired as 'escorts' from modeling agencies in Europe and the United States.

Qfar's home was extravagant and lavishly decorated.

Qfar Mohammad asked his most trusted advisor to join him on a short walk around the palace.

"Let's talk, my friend," he said.

"Yes, my lord," responded Housef, who still considered himself on thin ice after insulting and challenging the leader in public. He was nervous.

"I have been thinking," Qfar asked almost in a whisper. "What do you think we should do with this situation? We have a man, a rogue who cannot seem to take instructions, Farooq Ali. Jr. and who will not allow our plan to continue. Perhaps there would be ways to convince him that it is the best interest of the entire Ali family that the plan of Qfar Mohammad be completed as planned."

"How could we do that, my master?" an eager Housef begged.

"That is what I want us to decide," said the leader. "What means do we have to convince Ali Jr. to help us as much as his skills will allow? There must be some leverage that can be applied to this man, do you think?"

"I don't know, is there anything you have in mind?" asked Housef eagerly.

"Well, let us think it through. Certainly an answer will present itself if we look at the situation clearly and in the light of all the information." Qfar paused to take a drink of his scotch and stole a quick glance at Housef to see if he was at all worried at the tone of the conversation. Satisfied that his most trusted advisor was eager to please, he continued.

"What is it that members of this family respond to?" he posed to Housef. "It doesn't seem to be women, or necessarily money. However, the utter lack of money due to the series of unfortunate accidents that befell Ali Sr., caused the junior member of the family to act as an agent on our behalf."

"If it worked on one, it should work on the other," said Housef.

"How do you mean, my friend?" asked Qfar, pleased that Housef was taking the bait.

"I mean if we can get the troubles of the senior to control the junior, why can't we provide troubles enough for the junior to influence the senior?" Housef asked.

"Yes, I see what you are driving at," smiled Qfar. "So here is what I propose. We tell the senior that the younger Ali is in trouble and the only way to provide him with the security he desires is if the older Ali comes with me to Pico. While we are at Pico, he will prove to be a valuable resource for us as we accept the algae files from his son."

"Once we get the files, I have no doubt that we will ensure that the two of them will never get the chance to retell the tale."

"Exactly, my friend," Qfar said. "They will never leave Pico."

"I will invite Ali Sr. here to my home tonight and tell him that his son needs him to come to Portugal right away, that I have information that indicates that there is great danger for him. You will be in the next room. After I have talked with him for a few minutes, you must enter the room and tell us that you have news. Tell us that the younger Ali has found even more difficulties than we knew earlier and the situation has become even more dire. If he is convinced that his son is in real trouble, he will doubtless come with us to Pico."

"What news shall I bring, my master? What is it that he would fear most?" asked Housef.

"I think that you will know what to say, and you should devise it yourself and I should not hear it prior to the meeting," said Qfar. "The more surprised that I am, the more convincing will be the tale you tell."

"Your trust in me is truly comforting, my master," said Housef. "I had thought that after my ill-regarded remarks today that you would no longer find favor with me. I am relieved to know that your trust is unshaken."

"In fact, my friend, my trust in you is more strong than ever," replied Qfar. "I know that only one such as you who is strong enough to consider himself on the same level as I, well that man deserves the trust and confidence of Qfar. I will eagerly go further, Housef. Here is a gun which you should carry with you as you enter the chambers tonight. I don't know what Ali Sr. might do. As you know, he is a man desperate for money and may see tonight as a chance to behave as a highwayman and kill me and take my possessions. It would bring me comfort if you were armed and also knowing that you will be close by. Would you do this for me?"

"My master," said Housef. "I am humbled by your faith in me."

"Let this be our last discussion before our next meeting."

The final fourth and final bottle of vinho verde in the Miguel's Restaurant was turned upside down in She'Qlia's hand. She mimicked squeezing the last few drops down the neck of the bottle as if it were a toothpaste tube and laughing hysterically along with her friends and fellow agents working for the Directorate Discretionary Operations.

Benson was an oddity among the group. He worked hard, had a successful business outside the DDO and was doing pretty well with his family. He was the only married member of the group. Not normal for members of the organization. Of all the agents, he and The Admiral were the only family men.

He managed to find time for a family and a fairly normal existence outside of the crazy work life he had. That is, if one considers chasing robbers of stolen algae formula half way around the word to be a normal existence.

The other members of the group, Stuart 'Matty' Mateus, She'Qlia Jackson, and Marty Bishop had little time to pursue anything other than their jobs.

She'Qlia because he genuinely liked it, and felt as though destroying the enemies of America was a noble pursuit. Like the others, she was somewhat hyper-patriotic. You couldn't spend so much of your life doing this job if you weren't.

Marty Bishop, however, had another reason. He was always thinking in the rear of his mind how this assignment or that mission accomplished or objective achieved would affect his career. Sure he loved doing it, sure he loved the thrill. But he, more than the others, also loved the rewards.

"That's the way. Get the last drop out of that fucker!" said Benson, almost at a yell.

The group was getting a little drunk and they were getting loud. Not in a threatening way, but just a little more boisterous than other diners in Miguel's, who were about half tourists and half locals.

"Ya, squeeze it down to the last bit," said Bishop, the normally reserved member of the group who surprised even himself at his volume.

"Hey, settle down, everyone," said Mateus. "I've got a couple questions?"

The group started to quiet their voices and reel in their buzzes that were the verge of turning into run-away drunkenness.

"Why haven't we picked up Ali yet? Does anyone think about that?" said Mateus finally.

Benson joined in.

"Stuart and I were talking about this in Washington, and it doesn't make any sense that we haven't cloaked this guy and taken him to a secure location," he said using the euphemism for snatching a target and taking him to an international interrogation and holding site.

"When you were chasing the target on The Mall, The Admiral told us to order you not to detain," said Jackson. "Well it seems pretty clear to me that we are not cloaking him because The Admiral is going after someone higher up in the organization, right?" said Jackson. "You guys know that we do that all the time."

"Right," said Mateus, "but we can cloak him, get the information from him and get the next guy up the chain anyway. We've also done that many times. In fact, I thought I got a signal message this year sometime saying the DDO policy would be to cloak, detain, and extract as a priority now to avoid the possible target non-acquisition."

"You know why we are not picking up this guy?" said Bishop matter-of-factly. "Because The Admiral told us to trail and observe. So that is what we are going to do. T and O."

"Yes, of course, Mr. Company Man," smiled She'Qlia looking at Bishop, the career climber of the group.

She changed the subject quickly, "Hey, Bishop, if you ever had a bad report written about you and not following orders to the letter, you may not get your next promotion and put the bars on your shoulder boards as quickly as you'd like, huh?"

"I'm just saying, The Admiral has been doing this a long time and sometimes, we have to take his word that he knows what he's doing and let things play out the way he wants," said Bishop, not the least bit offended by Jackson's insult. "He wouldn't be the boss if he didn't know a little bit about this business."

"Yeah, I know, but this one seems to be a little dangerous," pressed Mateus. "I know that we aren't going to pick up Ali without the OK from the old man, but there are a lot of fucked up things happening on this case, don't you think? I mean, how many times have you had a target wink at you from his hideout? How many times? How many times have you had a target wink into a security camera that he should know is going to be seen by us? Huh? How many? I've never had it before and it is freaking me out a little. Is he luring us into some trap? Is he just fucking with us? Is he laughing while he leads us on a crazy chase to nowhere?"

"And after he winked at us at his hideout, we got blindsided by an enemy operative near a dumpster in D.C.," said Benson.

"It didn't end well for him," said Benson. "But it did end for him."

"And another thing," asked Bishop. "As long as we are airing our questions about this Portugal caper, why wouldn't target just send the algae formula to his bosses? I mean, we don't have to hand deliver stuff to people anymore. These aren't the days of the Pony Express. He could have sent it to his boss in any of one hundred different ways."

"Ali couldn't give Qfar the formula, or serum or fucking microfilm or whatever the fuck we are trying to recover. As soon as he gives the shit away, he won't have any leverage," said Bishop in a loud whisper.

"He—what's his name? Ali? Yeah Ali could get the formula shit to Qfar any time he wanted, but then what would he have to leverage with? Hmm? Nothing, not a freaking thing, so he has to keep it to himself," continued Bishop. "And if it's true that his father is being sort of soft tortured by Qfar, then junior could just kiss his dad's ass goodbye couldn't he?"

The other three sat stunned for a moment. They hadn't ever heard this kind of language out of Bishop.

Then, the entire table, including Bishop, broke into laughter. The stress, the booze and situation, had to find some release somehow.

CHAPTER 34

"Just a second, I'm getting a comm from The Admiral," Bishop interrupted himself to take a call from his boss.

Bishop opened his comm device and raised the unit to his ear.

The group paused and looked at Bishop while the aide to The Admiral nodded his head to whatever Guilbault-Johnson was saying. The group leaned toward Bishop looking for clues on his face of what the call was about. When they received a comm from the boss this time of night, it could mean anything and often did. They could be told to scramble to a new position, to carry on the search, to even quit the mission since maybe something else in the world will soon take precedence over the current mission.

The problem is that with all the options, most of them require that the group try to sober up quickly and get on the next phase of this mission, or the first phase of the next mission.

"Yes, sir," said Bishop emphatically from time to time. About the time the fourth "yes, sir" fired out of Bishop's mouth, the group started to think that The Boss had hung up already and Bishop was doing this to give some drama to the situation.

Finally, after what seemed like the longest phone call in Portuguese history, Bishop took the handset from his ear and pushed the 'End' button.

"What were we talking about?" Bishop asked the group.

"You were saying that Ali Jr. better mind his manners and keep his head down and deliver the algae shit or his old man will be toast," Jackson replied.

"Fuck that, what did The Boss say?" busted out a boozy Dr. Steve Benson.

"The Admiral said that he was worried that this whole thing is taking longer than he thought," answered Bishop. "He said that the plan in place should have already led to a detain."

"Well he told us NOT to detain, didn't he?" asked Benson.

"When you guys were chasing Ali Jr. in D.C. he told me to wave you guys off the pursuit. Yes." answered Jackson matter-of-factly.

"Right," said Bishop. "This is weird. The Admiral also said that Intel reports from the Baghdad contact said that Qfar is pissed at all this…"

"I bet he is," interrupted Stuart.

Steve added, "Right, his man has been killed and the formula he wanted so badly is floating out there on the edge of Europe."

"Well, he may not know that. I mean The Admiral may not know where the formula is," Bishop corrected himself. "OK, here is what we know. Qfar is angry. That should mean that Ali Sr. is in trouble. Possibly targeted for death. Certainly he is the only leverage that Qfar has on Ali Jr. to keep the formula coming. That's what makes The Admiral's news so odd. The big cheese said that Ali Sr. is now getting help from Qfar. You know, giving him money. Talking with the water authority to see if Ali Sr. can get his job back. Basically, he is undoing all that he did to get Junior to do his work."

Farooq Ali Sr. pushed back the curtain into the private living quarters of the one of the most notorious racketeers, thugs and murderers in the entire Middle East. He stepped cautiously and, as he was instructed, turned to his left. He walked slowly into the large room where Qfar Mohammad sat on fine pillows in his loose-fitting clothing.

"Come in, my friend," Qfar Mohammad came to his feet and beckoned to the humble civil servant in worn clothes who hasn't been able to afford many new things since losing his job due to the paperwork problem in post-war Iraq several months ago.

"Hello," greeted Qfar with a hearty welcome hug to his guest. "I am glad you could come, my colleague. Did you find your way here with ease? I suspect that you know well the city as you have been a loyal public servant for many years."

"It has been for many years, my good fortune to serve those who call Baghdad home," replied Ali Sr. Ali was quite excited to be in the spacious and lovely home of the notorious Qfar Mohammad, but also wary of what was in store. He had thought that perhaps Qfar was behind his string of very unfortunate occurrences as the new government took over for the Hussain regime. But Ali Sr. has always wondered why a simple civil servant like himself would be the target of the great crime boss.

Ali Sr. was a smallish man, about five feet eight inches with a thick head of black hair. There were a few gray hairs in the mix, but very few for a man of sixty-two. Except for the graying hair and aging skin, he looked very much like his son. He had a round mouth and a big-ish nose with too many hairs visible out of the nostrils.

"Have you seen my home before? Would you like to take a tour?" said the host.

"Very generous of you, sir. I would love to see how the successful and hard-working among us have the privilege of living."

"Good, good," replied Qfar. "If you will walk this way, you will see the main living quarters where I have had the honor of hosting parties for the late Saddam Hussain and, to show you that I have no political leanings either way, I hope to soon share my dinner table with the current head of state of our new country."

The humble Ali Sr. was surprised at the comment of the powerful man, "You say 'current' as though you may think there may be another head of state in the immediate future of the country, sir."

Qfar laughed out loud. Both at his guest's frankness and his guest's accuracy.

"Only Allah knows what awaits any nation in the future, my friend," laughed Qfar.

Qfar negotiated himself and his guest to an enormous davenport.

Qfar motioned his guest to sit.

As he took his seat, Ali Sr. knew that the time for small talk was finishing and soon he would find out why he was asked here. He was genuinely curious about the intentions of the powerful Qfar and his political ambitions.

Qfar remained standing, still in his bare feet.

"There are many worthy leaders in this country," posed Ali. "But few have the will, the friends and political infrastructure that you do, sir. Perhaps the future leader of our country would be a road well-traveled by a man who knows what success means and how to achieve it."

"You are very kind to me, my friend. May I call you my friend?" said Qfar. "But many of my actions in the past have often been misinterpreted by the press and the public. I am afraid the perceptions of me are very negative and these Western-style elections that have been imposed on the country seem to be a popularity contest rather than a measure of one man's ability to perform a public service."

"Or a public good," interjected Ali, glad to get a slight insult on his host, hopefully without notice.

No such luck.

"You may have noticed, my friend, that I have taken an interest in your plight at the water works here in Baghdad," said the host. "I am aggrieved when one of my fellow countrymen is wronged as you seemed to have been. Has there been any news from your son?"

When Ali Jr. left for America on what was to become his murderous mission to steal the algae formula from the Danforth Institute, he had told his family that he had a job that involved working with some members of the revolutionary guard, but that he was not involved in anything illegal. He said he would be back in a few months' time and not to worry.

"Why would you ask that? Do you have news of him?" Ali tried to hide his desperation. He was eager to get any news about his boy after months of no news.

"I have many ears and eyes throughout the world," said Qfar. "News often comes to my attention that may not come to the attention of others. For instance, I could tell you what is happening right now in certain areas of the city that you will not read in the newspapers or even see on the Western news television.

"It is my understanding that your son is somehow connected to the revolution, but not directly and may be doing some work for them. Is that what you understand?"

"Farooq Ali Jr. is not a revolutionary," insisted Ali. "He is doing what he feels he must to support his family after our recent unpleasantness. He is a man of honor and reputation. However humble we may be, we maintain our honor. That is the way of Ali."

"Certainly, certainly," said Qfar. "I hope you don't take my comments as an insult or a verdict in judgment of your family. Even those in power, perhaps especially those in power, know that doing what one must do to protect one's own interest is at the heart of the human condition. For you or your son to act in any other way would be inhuman, do you see my proposition?"

"Go on," said Ali.

"And acting humanely in this instance brings well intentioned men together. That is why I have asked you here today. Through my sources, I have learned that a young man, who matches closely your son's description, is now on his way to Pico Island in the Atlantic to meet with officials who are not to be trusted. They represent themselves as members of the United States government, but they are far more nefarious than that."

"Where did you hear this? Why is he there? How did he get to this place? Who is he working for? Where did you hear this?" Ali Sr. was delighted to know that his son was physically all right for now, but had no idea what Qfar was talking about. His head was reeling from the news. Perhaps his son was really a revolutionary and had been seduced by the money and power of those who are enemies of the new national order.

Qfar paused before he answered. He was hoping his guest was confused. By confusing Ali Sr. a little, Qfar hoped to get him off balance logically. Qfar wanted Ali to join him on a trip to Pico. Qfar thought that Ali Sr. may be a useful tool in getting the biofuel algae formula from Ali Jr. and avoid the formula landing in the hands of the Americans or Russians.

"My friend, you have so many questions, but I have so few answers," comforted the mastermind. "Let me tell you what I know and you can tell me how I can help you."

"Yes, any news of my son is welcome, of course, sir," said Ali Sr. with tears in his voice, but not in his eyes. He knows that a show of weakness would put him at a disadvantage with his host.

"How is it that you come to hear news of my son? The first born of a civil servant would be of little interest to man of your influence and power," said Ali. "And where is this Pico Island. I've never heard of it. I am not nearly as well traveled or worldly as you, sir."

Ali Sr. remained seated on the luxurious sofa. Qfar was still standing at the far end.

"The news of your son came to me by way of a friend who lives in America in that nation's capital city of Washington D.C.," said Qfar. "He has been a trusted ally for many years and enjoys the many benefits of my friendship, and I of his."

Qfar took a step closer to Ali and then sat on the sofa. He leaned in close to Ali Sr. and addressed him almost in a whisper.

"As you may know, in my business, it is important to keep all your business partners well informed and well paid to keep them happy. And if not happy, it least they know that if I stay healthy, they will be better paid than if something happens to me," said Qfar.

"Why do you say that 'if something happens to you'?" asked Ali Sr. "Well, I have heard this very day, that there are some in my employ who are not happy with the pay that they are getting, or the way this business operates. So I understand that some people, and I mean people right here in my own home are planning to confront me within a very short time," said Qfar.

"And what business, exactly, are you in, if I may ask?" queried Ali.

"Come over here" said Qfar completely ignoring his guest's question. "This photo on the wall is me, yes, that's me on the far right. Forty years have changed me little, no?"

Qfar didn't expect and didn't get a reply, but he couldn't help stroking his own vanity a little. He was still a good-looking man with jet-black hair and full beard. His jaw still sharp with a hint of a cleft in the middle. The scar on his right cheek was in the shape of moon. It was the only mark on his dark skin. Pretty lucky for a life spent in a violent business.

The violent face and his imposing six-foot-two-inch frame made for a dangerous-looking man.

Qfar laughed at his own vanity.

"You also see in this picture the man beside me there? Here?" Qfar touched the photo and continued without waiting for a response. "This is Housef, we won't worry with last names. It isn't important to you. Anyway, Housef and I have been friends, no, we have been more than friends. We have been family for more than forty years. We have fought wars together. We have sought our fortune together. We have found success together. We have been quite like the family Ewing on the American television show "Dallas." Do you remember it?"

"Of course," said Ali. "I was always a big fan of this show. The big American life and pursuit of dreams. You know, I always liked that girl who was the wife of Bobby. She was a good woman who would be a proud wife to a happy man. Now that slutty little blond, I would not like her to be any part of a family of mine. I thought she was the worst of America. Seeking immediate and physical pleasure and maneuvering herself between husbands and wives. Not a very honorable woman, I think. Lucy Ewing was her name right?"

"Quite right," said Qfar.

Qfar bristled at Ali's comments.

"Ha, I am glad you know the show. It was obviously a favorite of mine for many years as well," said Qfar. "What I was saying was that Housef, from the photograph, and I were like J. R. and Bobby. Family working together to achieve what we could not achieve alone."

"I see," said Ali Sr. "Qfar," Ali stopped his host. "Why are you telling me all this about your friends and your years of work to achieve such great things. It means nothing to me. I came here only because I thought you had news of my son."

"I am telling you all this because of two reasons, my friend," said Qfar, "I have heard of news that you may find of interest. As I said, I think I have heard news about your son."

"Yes, you said. You must tell me where I can find him? Has he been hurt? Is he healthy? Where is he? Take me to him," pleaded Ali.

"Now, now, now, my friend, I will tell you. I will tell you. First, I don't know exactly where he is. I have only heard some vague information about where he might be going. I understand that he is quite safe and unharmed. If you like, I will take you to the place where he is going and perhaps we can meet with him. If he wants, he can return with us here to your home within just a few days, at the longest," said Qfar. "Does this interest you?"

"Of course, my friend," gushed Ali. "I would be grateful for anything you could do for me. These past months have been agony for our family. We have begged Allah to return our son to us. Many nights my wife has cried at the thought that her oldest son has been… well…who knows what could have happened to him in that time. And now, to hear the word from you that you think he is well and unharmed? It is a gift from the heavens that you have given to me and to our family. Yes, my dear friend. I will go with you wherever you think is right. I will be happy to have you as my friend and a friend to my entire family."

Ali didn't embrace Qfar, but stepped toward him and offered his hand in friendship. Ali gave Qfar's hand a vigorous shake and with his left hand, he patted Qfar on his shoulder. Ali was as grateful to Qfar for this gift.

"Yes, I will give you all the details I have in a moment," offered Qfar. "But I want to tell you the second reason that I am telling you all this about my longtime acquaintance and friend, Housef. You see, when I heard the news about your son, I told Housef that I was hoping that we could bring you to him, that you might be reunited with your son. If I ever have a son, I should like someone with the means to make it possible would do the same for me.

"Well my dear friend of forty years, Housef, believes that we have no time to worry about the son of water administrator and that we should not work to reunite you two. Housef and I had planned to go to America to close a big deal this week. A deal that would make us both very rich men, again, he and I. Well, that was when my dear friend, Housef, refused to be my partner in helping you. It was then that I saw him in a different way after many years of brotherhood."

Ali still wasn't sure why Qfar, with his reputation for being a ring leader of a crime syndicate, would be telling him so much about the inner workings of his operations.

Qfar continued, "It is now that I know that my partner of so many years has a heart as black as the desert at midnight. He and I have made much money through the years, and now I hope that this benevolent act will provide my soul with some balance. I hope Allah will see that I am also a man of good will and not a man who sought only fortunes. My new friend, I have heard through my sources that my oldest and dearest friend Housef is coming here to my chambers tonight to discuss the matter further. I have asked you to be here, so you can show him that reuniting you with your son is a goal worth pursuing. That there is some goodness in the world. The world is not simply for the seeking of treasurers. Will you stay with me, Ali, and help me convince my partner that we are doing something good, and fair and right? Will you?"

"Of course," said Ali. "I hope that your mission of good will toward me will not destroy a friendship that has lasted so long. If there is something I can say to your partner, Housef, I will try to make him understand that you are doing a good and decent thing here."

Just then, the door opened and Housef came in just as Qfar had asked him to do earlier in the day.

Housef approached the two. He was moved by Qfar's comments earlier in the day. Housef reached out to embrace his friend.

"Hello, old friend…," started Housef.

BANG!

A shot rang out in the room and Housef fell to the floor.

Qfar had shot his lifelong friend through the chest at point blank range.

"What have you done?" yelled Ali almost before the gunshot's echo stopped ringing through the room.

"I've killed my friend," said Qfar inwardly marveling at how easy it had been, and how little emotion he was feeling at the moment.

Qfar and Ali bent down over the body that was now oozing blood onto the elaborate rug and onto the tile floor.

Farooq took a small step back from the body to avoid getting blood on his bare feet.

"I had to do it or he would have killed us both, such is his hate for this mission of mercy and his love of money," said Qfar.

"Why do you say that? He was coming to talk to us. I was going to talk with him about the great thing you are doing for me. Why did you kill him? He just wanted to talk."

Ali had never seen a man die before. In the era of Saddam Hussein, there were many murders in Baghdad, and Ali had experienced some loss among his coworkers. The bang of the gun and violence of the death struck him deeply. Seeing death this close, this violent, so intimate was very troubling.

"Why did you do this" Ali begged again.

"He came here not to talk with us, but to kill us," Qfar said. "Look here."

Qfar reached into the pocket of the dead man and pulled out a gun.

"You see, he was coming here with death on his mind, not to talk," Qfar said. "He was going to kill us both. Now, his hatred has killed him. Now, you go home. I will phone you tomorrow and we will find a time to go to the airport and fly to see your son. We should have additional information by noon tomorrow and we will leave as soon after as we can. Are you still with me?"

"I am, my friend."

CHAPTER
35

Farooq Ali Jr. of Baghdad pulled back the curtains covering the windows of his hotel room in downtown Lisbon and looked down the street southward from the fourth floor. He opened the window and stuck his head out the top of the double hung window. His eyes scanned the area around Praca Dom Pedro IV square that is the showplace in the center of the ancient city. He turned his head and looked north past the statue of Dom Pedro.

Nothing. No one suspicious. No one lurking. Nothing.

He turned his gaze back south. Nothing.

No matter which way he turned, he saw nothing. He pulled his head back inside the window, and breathed a quiet sigh. Then he sat down in the easy chair in the center of his room and relaxed for the first time in three days. Then, he looked around his hotel room.

Also, for the first time in three days he was able to think of something other than his father.

"This Marriot is awfully nice," he thought to himself. He pondered that the life of an international criminal wouldn't be so bad.

In fact, he could get used to this.

Too bad that he had come to be exposed to the world of international crime so late in life, he thought. The ripe old age of thirty-two seemed like it was past the prime of a true criminal.

If he had started at an earlier age, he would be wealthy by now and be able to stay in hotels such as this one whenever he liked. Either that or he would be dead.

But, he knows he is the honest child of an honest civil servant. In a city where corruption is everywhere, being honest is a poor man's game.

And things were not getting better. The city was becoming more and more corrupt as the influx of Western money—meant to rebuild the country—was used more and more to grease the palms of insiders to ensure fat government contracts with the American companies.

These companies were in Iraq to help re-build the nation. Over time, they became another corrupting force in the corrupt country. And what if he had been born into a family that had been more willing to 'compromise' its principles when it came to integrity and honor?

He certainly would have more of the comforts enjoyed by countrymen who were more willing to accept the new realities of the situation.

But his father had chosen not to respond to Qfar Mohammad when he was asked if he would be able to rig a construction deal contract worth millions to the city. And if he or his family had chosen a life on the other side of the red rope, the entire family would not now be facing this crisis at the hands of the one of the most ruthless criminals in the Middle East.

The only reason Ali Jr. was involved in this job was to help his father. His father, what a sucker. He had gone from a man who denied the powerful Qfar, to a man who could now lose his son and his own life.

However Ali Jr. chose to live, it would be with the lessons learned that his father taught him, even if that involved living the life of humble means that an honest civil servant lives.

Right. Enough idle nonsense, thought Ali.

"I've got to size up my situation," he thought to himself.

He looked through his bag.

"Money," he said to himself. "Check."

Ali figured that he had plenty for now and for after he got to Pico. About $50,000 USD left. And that's even after he paid the hotel bill…in cash.

"Plane ticket" he muttered. "Check."

"Contact name, place, and time…Check."

He had everything he could think of. Now it was time to relax a little bit.

Ali decided to take a walk to clear his thoughts. Just as he had done in St. Louis three days ago, Ali was a new man in a foreign city that is strange to him among people that were not his own and they all spoke a language that he little understood.

But, as Ali Jr. was discovering about himself, he was no shrinking violet. He was actually pretty bold. Now, unlike in St. Louis a few days ago, Ali walked the streets of Lisbon with a certain confidence that he previously didn't know he had.

He liked it.

A few days running from American operatives and living to tell about it were all doing great things for his self-esteem.

Ali wandered into a welcome-looking bar. He sat at one of the unoccupied small tables. Each table in the restaurant had four chairs that were also small. Four people sitting at one of these tables would be very crowded. The waiter approached and asked, "O que o senhor quer de pagar alguma coisa?"

Of course, Ali had no idea what was asked but he assumed it was something to do with an order and he responded that he would like glass of wine. Ali tried his broken English.

The waiter listened and seemed to understand a little.

The awkward exchange went on for a few volleys and then the waiter, happy that he had the order, retreated to the bar to get the drink.

A few minutes later, a glass of port wine was delivered to Ali. He had no idea what it was, but liked it and decided that this would be his Lisbon drink.

He was eager, excited, comfortable and feeling good for a man hurtling toward an uncertain tomorrow.

Mateus, Benson, Jackson and Bishop got out of the van at the private terminal of the Lisbon International airport. Each retrieved their rolling suitcase from the rear of the vehicle and thanked the government-supplied driver for the ride.

The four of them each had the slightest hangover from last night's revelry. But each made certain that they didn't get too out of hand last night.

For one reason, as comfortable as they were with each other, they are still on assignment. And they knew that they were being watched by superiors at all times.

Second, they were always aware when they are in a foreign country and everything is so unfamiliar, there were dangers that they don't see. When they are in St. Louis or Washington, they can often spot things that were out of place.

A new doorman at their apartment building or a strange barista where they buy coffee could raise their defenses.

In Portugal, or any place where they go for assignment, everything was new and they were unable to spot unfamiliar scenes.

"We meet him in Pico today, that's for certain," said Jackson, who was mentally the sharpest of the four since she had only a glass of wine or two, maybe three.

"Meet who?" asked Mateus. "I'm not even sure who we are supposed to be trailing, or arresting, or killing, or allowing to escape."

"Right," added Benson, while the four agents walked across the tarmac towards a waiting government-supplied aircraft so they could avoid any contact with local flight safety officials. "The Admiral didn't want us to get Ali at first when we could have had him in D.C. then we almost get killed by a guy that may have been tipped off by Ali. What the fuck is going on anyway?"

"You all know that The Admiral has his reasons for everything," replied Bishop. "He will reveal what the scheme is soon enough—"

"Well, he better hurry up, because this thing is going to be over soon. We should know what we are supposed to do before we get into a shootout with someone who isn't supposed to die," said Mateus.

"Like me," said Benson.

The four all smiled, but were too tense to laugh. They climbed up the three steps onto the waiting small jet that would be piloted by a Portuguese air force pilot to Pico.

"Bom dia, os senhors," greeted the pilot whose name badge said Daniel Luis de Silva. "I am your pilot to Pico today. We understand that you're hoping to meet with, but not be identified by man named Farooq Ali Jr. who is flying by commercial airliner operated by TAP today to Pico. Esta certo?"

"Yes, that's right," said Mateus.

"That commercial flight departs Lisbon at 9:15 and arrives just before midday," the pilot went on. "We now have 8:00 a.m. and will arrive at 10: 00 a.m. Are these times acceptable for you all?"

"Perfect," Mateus answered as he found his seat and buckled in. "We are ready when you are, capitaino."

"Perfeito," said de Costa. "Nous vamos."

With that, the pilot got on his radio and asked for a priority government official departure status. He was sent immediately to the front of the line for takeoff and was in the air within sixty seconds of the conversation.

CHAPTER 36

"May I call you Farooq?" asked Qfar Mohammad of his guest as they boarded his private plane to Pico Island. "I would like us to be better friends and I always find that dispensing of the formal titles is a good first step, don't you?"

"Yes, absolutely. And yes please call me Farooq." Farooq Ali Sr. was nervous about getting on board an aircraft with Mohammad, one of the best-known criminals in Baghdad. But, he thought, he did see Mohammad kill his number one criminal partner, Housef, and if Mohammad was willing to do that in front of him, then Mohammad must certainly be trustworthy because Farooq felt that he could put the gangster in jail. On the other hand, a man who would kill his friend of so many years so indiscriminately could certainly kill anyone. So, Ali was comforted and also afraid of his new 'friend.'

"As long as we are here, we might as well get some coffee," said Benson to the group as Marty Bishop steered the blue four door sedan out of the Pico airport parking lot.

The four of them were happy to be on terra firma after the two-hour ride.

After their late night out, none of them got sick from the plane ride. But none of the four were able to recuperate very well either.

"Sometimes I like to drink coffee and sometimes I don't, but I guess they have a really good choice of coffee here in Portugal, don't they?" Benson continued. "I go without coffee for months at a time sometimes. Don't miss it, don't get cravings for it. Nothing. I don't even want it. You know how some people can't go without coffee or they just claim they can't face the day. Well, I'm not like that at all when I am off coffee. I am fine without it and don't even miss it. When I am drinking coffee, I really love it. All kinds. Espressos, regular American coffees, lattes, mochas, you name it and I will drink it. I think it started when I was in the Army and we had to stand watch at the clinic, or even worse, when some asshole commander would make the veterinary staff stand watches with the regular Army guys. You know, we sometimes didn't have to stand watches with the regular Army. That was sweet. When we did have watches, we had nothing to do and had to stay up all night and I just had some coffee to get me through the night, well, from there it really gained momentum and before I knew it, I was practically an addict."

"Oh, too bad you had to stand watches. Boo hoo," said Mateus as Bishop he steered the car onto the road that led up the hill and to the small town of Vilanova. "The Navy stands watches all the time."

Bishop interrupted, "Just got a message from The Admiral. He has the contact name and location of the person who Ali is likely to look for when he gets to Pico Island. The Admiral also sent us GPS coordinates that will get us there."

"How did they get that info?" asked Jackson from the backseat.

"Sets up like this...I guess the Old Man was able to trace the body that Benson provided them back to an Al Qaeda cell in D.C. When they took that cell, they found Intel on the relationship between Qfar Mohammad, Farooq Ali Jr. and the guy named Hussain Islam. They found the address in that apartment. We've been instructed to get to the location, scout it, and wait for Ali to arrive," explained Bishop. "And, it is also the same address we got from Farooq."

"When Ali Jr. he gets to the location, we are instructed to take them both, alive if possible and package for shipment to a dark location for further Intel gathering," Bishop continued.

"So, that reminds me. What about that guy you snuffed in D.C.?" asked Jackson. "We never heard about that. What happened, Stuart? How was it? Give us some details."

"Don't ask me. I was getting my ass kicked. Benson did it all while I was passed out. After Benson destroyed this guy, he had the decency to throw the body into a dumpster. Fucking hilarious," said Mateus.

"Must have been jittery from all that coffee you were drinking, eh Benny?" joked Bishop.

The four laughed in spite of their nerves as the car sped down the winding road to the scene of what could be a deadly event.

The laughter was doubly loud because they were all beginning to get on edge about what they knew was directly in their future.

Rui Gomez sat in the front room of his small cottage on the hill overlooking a two-thousand-feet bluff over the Atlantic Ocean on Pico Island. It was a beautiful location with green hillsides all around and sunsets that he still doesn't believe even after living here his entire life.

Rui was one of the few people on earth who was living a wonderful life and he knew it. Not much money, not many problems, and not much to worry about.

The ocean waves rolled in all day making a hypnotic crashing against the rocks. Sleeping hours and waking hours seem to blend as the constant, undulating sounds of the ocean slowed down the pace of life and productivity on the island.

Paradise.

If someone gets too ambitious here on Pico, and upsets the natural order by going about their day too fast, they are brought to heal by the ocean's waves. Slowing them down, retarding their pace. Getting them back in the rhythm of the islands.

Today, though, Rui didn't have much time to enjoy his bucolic location. Rui was staring out the front window looking down his lane to the lonely winding street that provided the only access to his side of the island.

"Sweetie," he said, "what time is your amigo from Baghdad supposed to get here?"

Like many Portuguese natives from Pico, Rui Gomez had a dark complexion with thick, bushy eyebrows and a muscular torso. His legs were also powerful from years of walking up and down the hills of his home island. Growing up in a poor place provided most of the islanders a free workout each time they went to the store for some local home-baked bread or a bottle of wine or cigarettes, the three staples that locals seemed to live on.

"They will be here at 3:00 p.m. or fifteen as you call it, honey," said Susan who poked her head out from her bedroom and saw Rui in the front room enjoying the view. Susan was clearly not from this part of the world. First, she was tall and had striking long, blonde hair. No woman in Portugal had hair like this. And certainly no woman on the island of Pico. One other odd thing about her…she doesn't speak a word of the local language.

She called herself Susan Smith. Although Rui seemed to know that the name was fake, and he didn't care. She had arrived on the island a few weeks earlier while she waited for the file on algae that she was sent to collect, by whatever means necessary, from a courier who would likely be an Arab. That is all she knew.

On the island, she befriended Rui one afternoon soon after she arrived while they were both at the beach.

Susan had stood out because of her looks and her eastern European accent, likely Russian, Rui deduced, even though he had never been to Eastern European. In fact, other than traveling to the mainland to watch a soccer match with a couple friends when he was eighteen, Rui had never left the island.

He knew there was something about her that wasn't right. Her story of just being a tourist in the area was pretty remarkable. She didn't like to talk about her job back in wherever it was she was from, she never really said. As the two started a relationship, Susan always deflected questions about herself and never really offered any information to Rui.

He was suspicious that something more was different with her because she carried a large handbag that she was never without. He never looked in it. He joked about it once while they were walking on the beach and she looked at him and said "None of your business" in such a straight deadpanned voice that he almost burst out laughing. Then he realized that she was serious.

He never asked about it again.

Since her arrival, Susan had lived in a hotel downtown. But she spent more and more of her time with Rui at his house on the hillside.

Today, Susan had asked Rui if she could come to his house and meet a friend that is arriving from out of town. Rui, of course agreed, although he was a little afraid that the friend was a man, perhaps her boyfriend from her home.

He didn't know if she had another boyfriend back home.

Rui didn't know much about her.

In fact, Rui only knew one thing about her…she liked to have sex. And that was enough for Rui.

While gazing up the road that leads to the cottage, Rui spotted a car approaching. The road was gently carved into the hillside. Cars coming to his house looked suspended above the water on one side and covered by a green, lush mountainside on the other.

The contour of the hillside waved in and out, so Rui could see the car for only a moment or two before it followed the road back behind another bump in the hillside. Rui always thought that the contour of the hill was a little like a green curtain draped on the side of the island. Waving in and out like a huge, long window covering. Sometimes he thought that if he ever found the pull cord, he would open up those drapes and reveal whatever was behind them, whatever they were hiding.

The car kept coming up the road.

"Susan, your friend is coming," said Rui.

"No, no, it is too early for them to come. I am not ready," Susan responded.

"Well, they are ready. And I don't think they know that you are not," Rui said.

"Well, come here—" Susan beckoned.

"No…no, they went past," said Rui.

GREEN WAVE

The car didn't turn and come down the gravel lane to Rui's house. It didn't even slow down. It continued past the lonely house on the side of the hill.

CHAPTER 37

"Don't even slow down. They have to think that we just another motorist on the road looking for a nice place to eat or going home after a long day of work," said Jackson from the backseat to Bishop who was behind the wheel.

"Another motorist? If we are supposed to be another motorist, where the fuck is the first motorist?" asked Benson. "This place is deserted. I wonder if there are a lot of cops out here. I mean, what sort of laws could you really break out here. I suppose you could be speeding or drunk driving, but you could hardly hurt anything…"

The car was just about to pass the wide gravel drive way that opened into a large parking area. A large green open space surrounds the house on three sides where Susan and Rui were expecting their guest.

The driveway leads from the main road to the house and was about 50 meters long.

It would difficult for anyone in the house to see who was in the passing car, but just in case, precautions were still taken. Stuart needed to have glance.

"Don't everyone look at the house," reminded Jackson. "Since I am in the front back seat here, I'll just take a quick glance."

And she did.

The car passed the house while Bishop continued on the winding mountain road about one and half lanes wide by American standards.

After he was sure that the car was out of sight of the house, Stuart Mateus said, "Bingo, that's the one. Too easy. The Admiral's directions were just right. Did I tell you that when the Admiral called me today, he didn't sound like he was at his office in the perfect stillness of the underground bunker at the St. Louis Arsenal? Hey, Bishop, did he mention that he was going out of town for anything? Washington? Anywhere?"

"Not that I know of," replied Bishop. "He usually tells me if he is going to be out of the office for anything."

While they were talking about The Admiral, the passengers in the car— Mateus, Benson and Jackson—were studying the terrain on both sides of the road and up and down the hillsides.

"Any good spots to get out?" asked Mateus.

"I've seen a couple," said Jackson.

"What's the move?" asked Benson.

"OK, here's the approach," said Mateus while the others in the car quieted to hear him. The group is normally pretty loose when they are out on assignment. When the work starts, and lives are at stake, they know that they have to be deadly serious.

"We surround the cabin, two uphill and one downhill. And one stays with the car. Bishop, how is the car? Trustworthy? It's just a civilian rental. They don't have any unmarked military or police cars on this rock, so I had to take what I could."

"Seems OK, not very powerful, so any long-term pursuits or escape efforts will likely end badly. But it's solid and turns OK. This will work," replied Bishop.

"It has to work," said Mateus. "Bishop, I guess you are the first choice for wheelman, unless you object."

"Wheelman, right," said Bishop secretly relieved that he will be away from any action. All four agents were dressed in fairly drab civilian clothing. The colors were mostly dark greens, blues and blacks. They couldn't wear fatigues as they sometimes do. This job would have been perfect for camouflage clothes. But the group didn't wear them because they needed to give the brief illusion of being tourists if they were stopped.

"I'll go downhill," continued Mateus, "Jackson, you and Benson go uphill. Bishop, you drive into the nearest town and keep your ears open. We can't have that car around here. And you may be able to see or spot someone or something from the town. OK? Last, we don't know when this is going to happen. But like we talked about on the plane, if we can keep everyone in the group alive, we have to do it. If we can retrieve the algae files, do it. But priority one is to keep ourselves safe, and priority two is keep civilians safe. Now, whenever you're ready, Bishop, pull over and take the car into town. We'll get to our places. The Admiral said the best guess is a 2:00 p.m. event, that's 1400 hours, Bishop. But that is best guess. Gentlemen, we ready?"

"Gentlemen?" joked Jackson.

"Let's get this done," said Benson.

A few moments later, the car pulled into a scenic lay-by, and the four got out and stretched their legs and arms as tourists might do after a long trip, even though they were on an island the size of tiny Pico, and there isn't anything that is a long drive.

The phony stretching session was to give a little cover for the group as they began their exercise. With one last check of his revolver, Stuart Mateus waded into the dense brush below the road that clung to the hillside. After a few steps, he turned back to his team.

"Good luck, my friends," and he and his dark clothes disappeared down the hill into the greenery. Benson and Jackson looked at each other. Without comment, they started up the hill and into the forest. Bishop climbed back into the blue Vauxhall four door and drove into town to wait at a café and maybe have some coffee.

"This is all you have?" Ali Jr. tried his best to communicate with the man at the car rental counter at the Pico airport.

Farooq Ali Jr. was not an experienced traveler and was certainly not a member of any frequent flyer group. He got to the car rental counter and found that he had little to choose from. It seemed there were more travelers than the island usually expects and there was only one unclaimed vehicle remaining to be rented. And it didn't look too reliable.

GREEN WAVE

"OK, I'll take it," he finally said in his best English, which wasn't very good.

"He reached into his bag and retrieved a stack of American dollars and Euro notes to pay. He had changed money at the Lisbon airport not knowing what currency he would need next.

"Sim, o senhor," at the sight of the cash, the car rental agent was immediately more helpful and eager to assist Ali.

"Also," asked Ali, "Can you help me find this address?" Ali grabbed a piece of paper and wrote down the address given to him by the man from the Al Qaeda house in Washington, D.C. the man he thought might kill him, the man he didn't know. He had the address in his head since he dropped the paper into the dumpster in Washington. He had been too scared to write it down since then for fear of leaving evidence. Now, he wrote it down to ensure he could communicate the exact address since he didn't speak Portuguese.

Ali Jr. had risked his life for that address. It felt good to finally put it to use.

"Sim," said the counter man.

After a few more minutes of negotiation, the man behind the counter offered the keys to a nice mid-sized Ford that would easily get him Ali up and down the mountain where he was told to meet his connection. Ali thanked him and gave him an extra 100 Euros for his help. "Being rich ain't so bad," he thought.

With car key in hand, Ali went to the small parking lot and located his car. He got in and began the ten-minute drive toward house as the car rental man had directed.

The large private jet came to a stop at the end of the runway and Qfar Mohammad and his guest Farooq Ali Sr. stepped down onto the tarmac.

The car immediately sped off down the tarmac and out of the airport gate onto the access road that led to the road that would take them to Rui's place.

"We will be there soon," Mohammad said to his guest. "I hope we are not too late to find the boy."

"Are you sure he is here?" asked his father.

"What can anyone be certain of these days? But I think if he is anywhere, he is here," relied Mohammad cryptically.

CHAPTER 38

"Susan, I think your guest has arrived," said Rui.

He had been the sentinel at the window for more than three hours. Susan was in the kitchen pouring herself a small vodka.

"Now is about right," she murmured to herself.

To Rui she said, "I'll be right there."

The Mercedes pulled in the lane and began the 50 meter trip down the gravel road toward the house.

Bishop decided that a cup of coffee is exactly what he needed. So he found his way into the town of Vilanova and pulled over near one of the omnipresent cafes that dot the Azorean island of Pico.

He put his car in park and walked the few steps over a cobblestone street into the shop. The Pico Cafe was small and obviously locally owned. As the driver, Bishop was known in the caper as the wheelman. He knew that he shouldn't make himself conspicuous, but he shouldn't try to hide either.

If people kept their distance from this stranger, he would be more likely to avoid any encounters or entanglements that would keep him from focusing on his job.

He ordered the coffee—and was surprised that his newly learned Portuguese actually passed muster with the barista in the shop. And he also asked for a small custard-looking pastry.

He did not know the name, so he simply pointed at it through the display case.

"Sim," replied the shop keeper. "O senhor quer um pastas de Belem?"

"Yes, or si," stumbled out of Bishop's mouth trying not to cause a scene but trying to be friendly. Bishop reached over the top of the counter to accept the drink and the pastry before settling into the corner table. He picked up his communicator to look for any messages from The Admiral, Stuart or Benson.

Stuart Mateus had done this sort of thing a couple times before. But this time getting where he was going took a lot more physical work than he remembered. He was working up a pretty good sweat.

The climbing along this hillside through the greeny thickness was about all he could take. Or maybe he was just getting a little older and the jobs seem to be getting harder. And maybe he was carrying more weight than he had before so it seemed harder.

"Carrying weight" he said to himself and then laughed at this thought.

"Jesus," he said in a mumble to himself. "Just say it, boy. You're getting fat. The politically correct police have really mandated martial law. I now think in PC terms."

He was smiling to himself as he inched closer to the house. He was about one hundred meters downhill from the target house and could now make out the layout of the house and driveway.

It was informative to get the satellite maps from The Admiral and headquarters, but was always best to see it with your own eyes.

He trudged a little further up the hill to get closer to the action.

The house was a modest Azorean Portuguese home probably about seven hundred square feet with two bedrooms. And despite its spectacular perch on the hillside overlooking the Atlantic Ocean, it sat oriented toward the road with almost no windows facing the breathtaking vista.

The house was built when people sought protection for the sea and the wind and the rain. Of course, if the house were built today, it would have huge windows facing the sea.

This was an advantage to Stuart. No windows facing his side of the house meant it would be difficult to see him from inside. He still had to move carefully, but he didn't have to be quite so cautious as if the windows were facing him.

Mateus could see a beautiful blonde girl come out of the front door and wave her hand in a greeting to someone down the lane. He had to stretch his neck and get up on his tiptoes to see the approaching Mercedes Benz luxury car that was cautiously making its way toward the house.

"Come on out, fofino. It's my friends. The ones I was telling you would be coming today. I want them to meet you," said Susan, looking back toward the house and Rui who was still inside.

Rui walked out of the house about the same time the impressive, black Mercedes Benz pulled to a stop about ten meters from the place where Susan stood. The car was pointed directly at the house.

Inside the Benz, Qfar Mohammad looked at his guest, Farooq Ali Sr. and then excused himself. He asked Ali Sr. to wait in the car as he would be right outside. His son should be here shortly, he comforted.

Mohammad got out of his car and shut the door so Ali Sr. couldn't hear his conversation with Susan. Mohammad waved to the attractive blonde, but he didn't approach her. He knew how these encounters worked. He didn't yet know if he was the only guest at the house, or if she had brought friends. Friends who may not like seeing her approached by someone they didn't know.

"Hello, my dear Susan," he said just loudly enough for his voice to carry to her and no more.

"Hello, Qfar," replied Susan. "I hope that all is ready and we will have nothing unexpected."

"No, nothing unexpected. At least not from my side," said Qfar. "This must be your friend you were telling me about, yes?"

"Yes, his name is Rui and he is a native of the island. We are very close. We talk about everything," said Susan.

"Everything? Hmm. How interesting," Qfar said to Rui, "I am looking forward to getting to know you much better."

"Sim, eu tembien, I mean, yes, me too," said Rui who was a little startled to be invited into the conversation. "So how do you two know each other?"

Qfar ignored Rui and said to Susan, "How much is everything?"

Susan without word or warning reached into her handbag, wheeled around to face Rui and pulled a gun out.

"Que?" stammered out a stunned Rui just before a loud crack filled the air and a bullet pierced his chest.

Rui fell face first on the driveway. He wasn't alive to feel the impact of his head on the black gravel.

"He is nothing and knows nothing," said the killer.

"What the fuck?" said Mateus. He was now standing in the woods below the house on the side of the hill. He was inching closer to the house and was now about 5 meters away from the back of the building.

He was surprised that he said it so loudly and was afraid that he might have been heard by the group. The scene unfolded so quickly that he didn't have any time to react. Even if he thought it was the right move, he wouldn't have been able to save an innocent local.

And, in truth, with The Admiral's insistence on getting Qfar, Mateus probably would not have interfered anyway.

Mateus started to move closer to the house. Slow careful step, after careful slow step.

He couldn't see his feet through the thick underbrush, so he had to walk very slowly to make sure he didn't step on any twigs or branches that would snap and alert the group to his presence.

Slowly he crept through the shoulder-high bushes on the hillside, through the thick greenery. A slight vibration alerted him that he had a message on his comm.

The message was a simple "?" from Jackson.

With a few touches of his thumb on the screen, Mateaus replied to the text with his own "?"

Then Mateus added, "Is" meaning "eyes."

He was getting closer for a better look and he assumed Jackson and Benson would be doing the same.

In the Pico Café, Bishop was too far out of earshot to hear the one bullet fired. Even if he were closer, the sound was drowned out by the crash of waves against the rocky shoreline stretching all the way around the island.

He had been at the café twenty-three minutes, he made note of the time for his report he would later prepare for The Admiral.

During that time, only four or five other customers had come in the café and none had tried to start any conversation, for which Bishop was relieved.

Bishop was drinking his coffee and remaining vigilant on his comm device. He could barely see the screen due to the bright sunshine coming in through the café window.

He saw the two "?" messages from Mateus and Jackson, but didn't understand their meaning.

Suddenly, a huge shadow covered his device.

"Odd," Bishop thought to himself.

He glanced up to see who or what was standing over him blocking his sun.

"Jesus. What are you doing here?" blurted out Bishop.

"I don't think I ever heard you swear," said a familiar voice. "Let's go see if things are unfolding in a tidy way up at the cabin, shall we?"

The two walked out of the café and slid quickly into the rented Vauxhall.

"So, you are the wheelman today?" asked Bishop's companion.

The two sped off down the cobblestone road and up the hill toward the Rui's house.

CHAPTER 39

In the driveway at the hillside house, Farooq Ali Sr. had just witnessed a murder. He was staring out the windscreen of a Mercedes Benz and saw a woman shoot a man in cold blood without provocation.

Out of instinct, he opened the door and started to get out of the car.

"What is going on? Where is my son? You promised we would find him here."

Qfar tried to wave the frantic gentleman back into the car.

"The dead man was a conspirator with the man in Baghdad," said Qfar. "He was an enemy of mine and he was out to kill us both, along with Susan. We are lucky to be alive. Get back into the car. Right now," insisted Qfar.

The tone of voice made Ali Sr. genuinely frightened. He had seen Qfar kill once already in the past twenty-four hours and now he had witnessed another killing. He retreated to the safety of the car.

This trip was becoming a lot more than he had asked for. But still he hoped to find his son.

Stuart thought to himself that if he enters the scene up on the driveway by the house right now, he may ruin the entire operation. The woman, Susan, would be easy enough to convict, or at least detain, but the rest of the people involved, including the main target, Qfar Mohammad, may not be so easy to arrest and successfully prosecute.

If he didn't enter the crime scene, if he stayed in the brush and waited for something more too happen, that may mean more people would die before he could could stop them.

"What should I do?" he thought.

After just a moment of reflection…

"I'm going in," said Stuart to himself.

"Hold it!" Stuart Mateus yelled to the blonde murderer as he stepped from the dense greenery and revealed himself to the people in the driveway.

Stuart was holding his service revolver level and steady and aiming directly at Susan, the blonde woman who just gunned down her lover, Rui.

"Ma'am, please drop the weapon!" he said in a firm voice meant to convey his confidence and his determination. "NOW!"

Susan turned to the unexpected crasher to her formula-buying party.

"But, sir, I've done nothing wrong," said Susan with her gun still in her hand and still pointed at the dead Rui. She moved slightly to face Stuart.

"Don't move. Drop the weapon," reinforced Stuart. He straightened his arm with his service weapon aimed at Susan, bringing the gun closer and his aim sharper. "NOW!"

Susan was a young agent but she had been in dangerous situations before. She wasn't the least put off by the orders this American was shouting.

"You don't want to shoot me," she said demurely hoping to distract him while she thought of what to do next. She was hoping that Qfar would shoot the American, but knew that this wasn't likely. Qfar knew better than to get involved in this. If Qfar did get involved, Susan wasn't sure on which side Qfar would be.

Susan, still holding the bag she brought from inside the house, quickly moved her arm. She was gesturing while she spoke. "I don't—"

Blam!

She didn't get to finish. Stuart shot her as she moved. She fell backward hard and fast.

The purse she had been holding fell to the gravel beside her. It was chock full of American dollars and a few $100 bills spilled out of the bag as it hit the ground.

Just then a Ford turned into the driveway and started making its way down the lane. Ali Jr. was finally arriving after having lost his way on the curvy mountain roads.

Ali Jr.'s car approached with caution. He could see both the dead man and woman in the driveway.

Qfar beckoned for the young Ali to drive closer.

Ali parked his car ten meters behind the Mercedes and twenty meters from the house. He didn't know what had happened before he arrived, but he could see that it was a deadly situation.

Ali Jr. got out of his car and walked slowly toward the motioning Qfar.

"Farooq, great to see you," said Qfar Mohammad in Arabic. "You've come at just the right time. Quick, give me the algae files. I need them right now."

"How do you know me?" asked Ali Jr. answered in his native language.

Meanwhile, back in the Mercedes, Ali Sr. spotted his son. But he didn't get out of the car. He was desperate to follow Qfar's instructions this time. He could now see that the situation could be a deadly one.

"Boy, come quickly, I need the files," Qfar said again as he tried to get the boy to bring him the files.

Qfar figured that if he did this right, he might be able to get the money and keep the algae files. He could then sell the files again to the next highest bidder now that the first bidder was dead.

"Don't believe him, Farooq," Stuart said to the boy. Stuart also spoke in Arabic. "He is the man who is responsible for getting your father fired and getting you mixed up in this mess. We know that you didn't do anything."

"Give me the files, Junior," said Qfar, "and I'll tell you where to find your father."

"Don't believe him! He is the man who sent you to the USA and connected you with Hussain Islam," said Stuart.

"What does this man think you are a fool?" said Qfar. "He is trying to turn countrymen against each other. He will not succeed."

"How do you know about Islam?" asked Farooq Jr. breaking his silence.

"I was the American agent who was watching you in D.C," responded Stuart. "I was the man following you through the airport. I was the man you looked at and tipped off when you left the Al Qaeda house."

"Don't listen to him," said Qfar Mohammad. "You were supposed to come back with the algae formula and you did. Now get your reward."

"You know what your reward was?" Stuart asked Ali Jr. "It was getting killed. Your friend there didn't intend for you to come back from St. Louis."

"Why do say that?" asked Ali Jr.

"Because we checked the airlines," said Stuart. "There was only one plane ticket back from St. Louis. And the name on it was Hussain Islam."

"What?" Farooq didn't understand.

Stuart explained, "After you got the files at the Danforth Institute, Islam was going to kill you. Don't you see? There was only one ticket back to Iraq. Islam was supposed to kill you."

Farooq looked at Qfar. "You were going to kill me?"

"My son," said Qfar slyly as he walked closer to the boy.

"Careful, Junior, don't let him get too close," yelled Stuart as he saw what was happening.

When Ali Jr. turned his head to look at Stuart, Qfar took the final two remaining steps and grabbed junior and wrestled with him. It took just a moment for the older, larger Qfar Mohammad to subdue the boy and get behind him with his gun at Junior's head.

Until now, Ali Sr. had stayed inside the Mercedes as instructed by Qfar. Now, he could stay there no longer. He opened the car door and stepped out.

"Sonny, it's me, Dad!" he shouted in Arabic and then started running toward the boy and Qfar.

"Don't take another step," shouted Qfar at the older man.

"Stop, he'll kill you," yelled Stuart in Arabic trying to help.

BLAM! A single shot rang out, and Farooq Ali Sr. fell faced first onto the gravel drive.

"DADDY!" shouted Ali Jr.

Junior struggled to escape Qfar's grasp, but a lifetime of fighting and hard living had given the criminal strong arms and stronger determination. He had no problem keeping the boy detained.

"Well, 007, seems like we have a situation here," said Qfar, mocking the agent. "I have the boy and he has the files, and you ain't got shit, as I believe you Yanks like to say."

"Well, you got no way off this rock," replied Stuart coolly. "In fact, you don't really have a way out of this driveway. I have two rifles up the hill behind you and if I say the word, you'll be shot, killed and dead before you hit the ground. No money. No algae files. And no more options."

"Well, I don't see any more rifles behind me. I think you're bluffing," said Qfar. "And another thing, I know you Yanks get queasy when it comes to —"

Qfar was cut off in mid-sentence as Stuart casually waved his hand as a signal to Jackson and Benson. The muzzle burst from Jackson's rifle was barely visible. The sound of the gun was unmistakable, though.

The shot from Jackson's rifle shattered the window of the Mercedes-Benz setting off the car alarm.

"Oh, I've got rifles," Stuart had to shout above the sound of the car alarm. "Now, should we talk about ending this mess? I think enough people have died today on this hillside."

"I agree with you, my friend," responded Qfar sensing that he could get out of this yet. "Why do we need to have bloodshed? I want only to collect what is mine and leave you in peace."

Stuart wasn't about to let Qfar dictate the terms of this.

"You listen to me," said Stuart still pointing his pistol at Qfar. "You leave the boy, go, and leave the algae files, and you can walk away. Drive down the hillside and fly back to your castle. I will tell my team to give you free passage for twenty-four hours. These are the terms. Yes or no, right now. As you saw from your friend Susan, I am not very patient."

Qfar thought about it quickly. He really had no good options.

"I will leave the boy, and the files, but will take the Russian money. Sweet Susan would have wanted me to have it," said Qfar.

Stuart shrugged, looked at the bag of bills beside Susan's dead body.

"It's not my money. Let the boy go now," said Stuart.

Qfar released the boy who ran immediately to his father's body.

"Do you have the algae files?" Stuart asked Junior still speaking Arabic.

"Yes, I have the stupid files. They are in the glove box of my stupid rental car," replied Junior. "He's dead. My father is dead."

Qfar still kept his gun trained on Stuart as he walked cautiously toward Susan's body and bent down to get the satchel of money. He picked it up.

Still with his gun still on Stuart, walked over to Ali Jr.'s rental car and opened the passenger door. He reached in and opened the glove box door. He saw the jump drive that contained the files.

"Leave the files, Qfar," shouted Stuart.

Qfar did as he was told. He got out and walked toward the Mercedes. He reached into his pocket and retrieved his key fob and turned off the alarm.

He then opened the car door, got inside, turned on the car and drove away without another word. The car didn't have a rear windshield. It was pretty clear that when he returned the car, he wasn't getting back his deposit.

Qfar had gone, Stuart ran over to Farooq Jr. where he crouched over the body of his father.

"Why did you let him go?" asked Junior. "He killed my father."

"There has been enough killing for today," said Stuart. "We'll get him."

Just then Benson and Jackson revealed themselves and came out of the green hillside.

"We heard you offer him free passage," said Benson, "So we let him go. "You better tell Bishop not to engage Qfar."

"You're right," said Stuart. Then into his communicator Stuart said, "Bishop, you there?"

"Bishop here," came the reply.

"Bishop, I've given Qfar, a pass today. Do not engage. I had to offer a deal to save some life up here, and part of the deal was Qfar getting out alive. Doesn't taste right, but sometimes you've got to swallow the shit pie."

"I understand and roger that, Bishop out," replied Bishop.

Suddenly, from down the hill, out of sight, the sound of a gunshot rang out.

"What the fuck was that?" barked Benson.

Stuart shouted, "I gave Qfar a freebie! Did Bishop engage him?"

"Or did Qfar, take one more scalp on his way out and kill Bishop?" asked Jackson.

Mateus, Jackson, and Benson all ran to the Ford that Ali Jr. had driven to the house. They all quickly piled in.

A step behind them was Ali who got caught up in a moment and jumped in too.

Jackson was in the driver's seat. She started the car and turned it sharply out the drive. The car's tires sprayed black gravel in all directions as it pulled onto the road.

The trip down the hill was a quick but wild ride reaching speeds of more than 100 kilometers per hour on the dangerous hillside roads.

When they reached the bottom of the hill, the four of them saw Qfar's Mercedes.

The criminal mastermind was inside slumped over the wheel with a bullet hole exit wound in his back. Dead.

Standing alongside the car were Bishop and The Admiral.

"Admiral Johnson? What are you doing? What happened?" blurted out Stuart as he got out of the Ford.

The three agents and Ali Jr. crowed around the car to see the dead Qfar.

"Gentlemen, it looked like this fugitive was getting away," said The Admiral calmly.

"He wasn't getting away," replied Stuart. "I offered him an escape in exchange for the boy's life. And I told Bishop."

"But you didn't tell me that you gave him free passage," said The Admiral coldly. "I've been after Qfar Mohammad for 20 years. He was not getting away again. That would have been untidy."

"So, that's why you kept allowing Ali Jr. to escape. Why you didn't let us bring him in?" asked Jackson.

"That's right," said The Admiral. "I knew Junior would lead us to Qfar. And he did."

"But why?" asked Bishop. "Why was Qfar so important to you? Twenty years? We've had worse targets and had to let them go for various reasons. Political or tactical. Why this one?"

The Admiral took a deep breath.

"My little girl was on vacation once with me in Monaco about twenty years ago. Well, she met a rich man in the casino who took her out to dinner a couple times. I didn't mind. Well, turns out what he did to her physically and emotionally took five years of counseling to get over. I've never forgotten that name when she mentioned it in one of her sessions. Qfar Mohammad. When I heard that he was wrapped up in this, I knew this was my chance to get some payback. Now, he's dead."

"So, it was simple revenge?" asked Stuart. "You killed a man for revenge?"

"No, sir," barked The Admiral. "I killed a fleeing suspect. I didn't know about your deal. To kill for revenge would be savage. An act such as that would truly betray an untidy mind."

The group stood silently for a moment while they digested The Admiral's admission.

Ali Jr. didn't understand everything that The Admiral had said, but knew something serious was going on. Just then he spotted the bag full of Russian money sitting in the passenger seat in the Mercedes.

He reached into the car and got the bag. He held it up in front in Stuart Mateus knowing that he could speak his language.

Stuart paused for a minute, then said in Arabic.

"Like I said, it isn't mine."

Ali Jr. took the bag of cash and made his way back to the car.

He slowly slid in, started it and drove to the airport to return home. He had the money he had dreamt of, but lost something more.

As Ali Jr. vanished, Jackson broke the silence.

"All the way to this little island," she joked, "and I didn't get a chance to shoot anybody. I just got to kill a car. Pitiful."

"Me either," echoed Benson. "And when you were up in the woods, did you get any bugs crawling up your pant leg? Must have a hundred little critters climbing up my leg toward my privates. But we were so close that I couldn't make a noise. Wow, that really was driving me crazy. Now, I can get a good scratch for these itches—"

While Benson started into his story, Stuart Mateus was staring hard at The Admiral.

The man who built a career on an emotional detachment from his work, made one of the most emotional actions Stuart had ever seen.

"You OK, old man?" Stuart asked.

"Not yet, but this was a big step to getting myself, and my family tidy again," replied Guilbault-Johnson.

"Think it is too early to have a beer?" asked Stuart.

"My treat," said Guilbault-Johnson. "My treat. Now, let's get down to it."

ABOUT THE AUTHOR

From journalist and broadcaster for the U.S. Navy, to advertising copywriter, to science writer at a major research university, Dan Kuester has been a professional communicator for many years. He forever seeks new creative challenges and finds new adventures.

Dan also spent much of his time as a young man playing rugby around the Midwest, Canada and Europe. At his peak, many regarded him as one of the most average players in recent memory. After playing days were over, Dan decided he had not inflicted enough damage on the sport he loves, and spent a few years as a referee. Combining his love of creative writing with his passion for sports, Dan developed his characters for this book from many of the colorful people he encountered in the service and in organized sports from the U.S. and elsewhere.

During his time in the Navy, Dan lived in the Azores, Portugal; Newfoundland, Canada; and Lisbon, Portugal. In the United States, Dan and his family have lived in Des Moines, Iowa; Washington, D.C.; and Newport, R.I.

Dan wrote this book in between taking his kids to soccer practice, while waiting for them outside band rehearsals and in the spare hours when quiet was available. He is married to his smoking hot wife, Monique. They have two children.

CPSIA information can be obtained at www.ICGtesting.com
Printed in the USA
BVOW08s0935010616

450317BV00001B/81/P

The Hermetic Kabbalah

Colin A. Low

Digital Brilliance

© Colin A. Low 2015
The moral right of the author has been asserted.

All rights reserved. No part of this publication may be reproduced, stored in a retreival system, or transmitted in any form or by any means without the prior written permission of the author, or as expressly permitted by law.

Published by Digital Brilliance, www.digital-brilliance.com
Enquiries can be made to enquiries@digital-brilliance.com

First Edition 2015

ISBN 978-0-9933034-0-1

Cover Illustration: *Partzufim* by Colin Low, 2009

Table of Contents

Preface iii

Major Themes

    Introduction 3
    Foundational Ideas 11
    The Tree of Life 21
    Partzufim 43
    The Primordial Adam 61
    The Four Worlds 75
    Evil 83
    The Soul 105
    Ascent 115
    Theurgy 129
    Emanation & Emergence 155

The Tree of Life

    Genesis 183
    The Sefirot 195
    Malkhut 199
    Yesod 215
    Hod & Netzach 227
    Tiferet 239
    Gevurah & Chesed 251
    Binah & Chokhmah 265
    Keter & En Sof 281
    Da'at 291
    The Paths 309

The Rectification of the Soul

    Rectification 337
    The Soul and its Parts 351
    Intelligence 365
    The Society of Mind 381

Awakening 399
Death and Rebirth 421
Epilogue
Epilogue 433
Index 439

1

Preface

There are a great many books about Kabbalah, and they fall into three principal categories.

Firstly, there are books written by Jewish authors for an audience familiar with Jewish culture and tradition. The last few decades have seen a resurgence in interest in Kabbalah from within the Jewish community, and a proliferation of books elaborating on Kabbalah from a Jewish perspective.

Secondly, there are scholarly texts, the majority written during the last thirty years. These are intended for an audience familiar with complex issues of interpretation and obscure technical concepts. They often require deep familiarity with the subject matter.

Thirdly, there are popular introductory texts intended for a non-Jewish, New Age or occultist audience. For the most part these present a standard core of ideas in idiosyncratic ways and are often ungrounded in an historical context or tradition.

My goal was to write a book about Kabbalah that would be accessible and interesting to each of the three groups of readers. I wanted a Jewish audience to feel their traditions had been acknowledged and respected and presented with accuracy. In addition I wanted them to experience a sense of surprise at the substance and depth of the Hellenistic influence - the Hermetic part of the story - that provides a context not only to Kabbalah but to the overall pattern of European intellectual thought for more than a thousand years.

For the scholar I wanted to leave a record of substance and coherence of my own inherited tradition, because records of substance and coherence are what scholars like. I also wanted the scholar to feel they were in moderately safe hands.

For the non-Jewish, New Age or occultist audience I wanted to provide an intermediate text on Kabbalah at a level I have not found in my own reading. Indeed, part of my motivation was the memory of my younger self searching for a book such as this.

I began to articulate my thoughts on Kabbalah about twenty-five years ago and initially created some *Notes on Kabbalah* that were circulated on the early Internet. I edited and expanded the *Notes,* and in 2001 I published a completely new revision as an online book, *A Depth of Beginning*. This book is now my third attempt to plough the same field, and I hope that at each attempt my writing and presentation have improved.

The task of representing Hebrew words in English has caused me many headaches. I have attempted to be consistent with most modern scholarly books, although even in the world of scholars one finds variants. So for example: *Malkhut* and *Keter* and *Tiferet* because the 't' sound is hard, and not 'th'. I have used 'f' instead of 'ph', because it is intuitive. I have used 'k' rather than 'q' for the same reason, hence *klippot* instead of *qlippoth*. I have used 'ch' for *chet* because it is similar to the 'ch' sound in the Scottish 'loch'. I have mostly used 'i' instead of 'y', hence *chaiim* rather than *chayyim* or *hayyim*. The Hebrew *bet* is sometimes hard like 'b' and sometimes soft like 'v', which explains why some older books use *Geburah*, while I prefer *Gevurah*. I am reasonably certain I have muddled my spelling in places, a reflection of the fact that I changed my mind several times during editing, and I must ask the reader to forgive any lapses or inconsistencies.

Some people have been important to me during the eight years I have spent writing. I have never met Don Karr, but we have corresponded for many years. I feel certain this book would have been different and inferior but for the invisible presence of Don watching over my shoulder as I wrote. I am grateful for his unfailing support.

I would like to thank Fabienne for respecting my need to spend so much of my time writing during the past decade. My sons Gwion, Owen and Dougie have often wondered what Kabbalah was, and I hope this book will reduce rather than increase their incomprehension.

Preface

I would like to thank Duncan Fleming and Suzanne Cohen of the Rockwax Foundation for their continued friendship.

Lastly, Kabbalah is often communicated from mouth to ear. This is the tradition, and some people give much of their lives to keep a tradition alive. I would like to thank those who have done so, especially my teacher Margaret, who died twenty years ago. We must make these deserts live.

Colin Low, Gloucestershire, 2015

The Hermetic Kabbalah

Part 1

Major Themes

The Hermetic Kabbalah

2

Introduction

Kabbalah is an exploration of the relationship between human beings and God. It is an attempt to understand the divine context of existence. It originated in Jewish communities in medieval Europe towards the end of the twelfth century CE[1], at about the time of the Third Crusade. It draws on many ancient mystical traditions from the Middle East dating from the time of the late-Roman and Byzantine Empire.

A significant part of the content of Kabbalah is a vastly expanded conception of God. Most people of Jewish or Christian origin will have some familiarity with the Biblical God, the God of Jewish history. The *Bible* describes the relationship between God, the patriarchs, and the people of Israel. This relationship is described in the form of narratives, such as the stories of Abraham, Isaac, Noah, Jacob and Moses. God is an actor in the world, participating in the history of the Jewish people.

Kabbalah takes the view that Biblical narrative is the manifestation of a larger reality. The actions of God as they appear in the sacred literature of Judaism are the phenomena, the outward appearance of an inner realm of the divine. The inner realm of the divine is described and accessed via a complex interplay of symbols, and new

---

1. Common Era. Although the 'AD' and 'BC' designations are still used for dating, many authors now prefer CE and BCE.

kinds of narrative emerge, narratives of symbols. Kabbalah contains many overlapping and entangled symbolic narratives. The best known is the Tree of Life, but there are others equally important.

Just as we view the actions of a human being as the coherent manifestations of a personality, so Kabbalists have viewed the actions of God as the integrated and coherent manifestations of divine being. There is a sense in which the Tree of Life represents the internal psycho-dynamics of the divine.

Kabbalah does not stop with its symbols and often startling metaphors and allegories. It attempts, using language and symbol, to go beyond language and symbol. It repeatedly transcends itself. It provides us with a new vocabulary of symbols, and just as we believe we have understood what they signify, we discover they are slippery, fluid and limited.

Gershom Scholem, the distinguished scholar of Jewish mysticism and Kabbalah, titled a collection of his essays *The Mystical Shape of the Godhead*. It is a phrase that is poetic in its strangeness and opacity. 'Shape' conveys so much more than vision - it suggests a tactile and multi-dimensional quality, like a blind person learning to recognise a face by touch. 'Shape' is an emergent, a *gestalt* of many interactions as one feels one's way around, like the parable of the blind men and the elephant. This apprehension is possible because in Kabbalah the 'mystical shape' of the human soul is congruent with the 'mystical shape' of the Godhead.

The shape that Scholem had in mind is not a tangible three-dimensional shape. It is the shape of something beyond sensory perception, a shape apprehended by a faculty of the human soul. Neither is it a static shape; it is a dynamic, a living society of parts that move in and out of alignment like a sun and its planets.

The 'shape' that Scholem refers to is not conveyed by any one diagram, metaphor or analogy. A book about the core subject matter of the Kabbalah - not its textual tradition or its history - has to confront this difficulty in communication. The mystical shape of the Godhead is an integral experience that gives rise to a cartographer's workbench of partial outlines. There is a tendency to become lost in the maps. To return to the story of the blind men and the elephant, it would seem that a good strategy is not to stand in one spot, but to keep moving around, feeling the legs and the trunk and the tusks and the tail. This is the approach adopted here.

The first part of the book is an attempt to outline the 'mystical shape' by outlining several of the most important ideas in Kabbalah:

Introduction

the Tree of Life in its many forms and interpretations, the Cosmic or Primordial Adam, the family of divine archetypes known as *Partzufim*, the four (or five, or six) levels of reality, the nature of evil (which was the motivating factor in the development of many radical kabbalistic ideas), the human soul, and one of the most important ideas in Hermetic Kabbalah, the nature and practice of mystical ascent.

The second part of the book is a more detailed study of the Tree of Life according to the traditions of Hermetic Kabbalah, in which I hope an outline of Scholem's 'mystical shape' will become tangible to the reader.

The third part of the book is its core and motivation. It provides a 'narrative of the soul' according to both ancient and modern traditions. The tradition from ancient times is that the soul has 'fallen'; that is, it has fallen from truth into deception, from clarity into obscurity. Like a broken glass, what was once whole is now broken in pieces. The challenge facing each human being is to recognise the fractured and fallen nature of the soul and to engage with the process of rectification - that is restoring the soul to its proper integrity, dignity, and apprehension.

So how is it sensible to talk about 'Hermetic Kabbalah'? Is it not the case that Kabbalah is an intrinsic part of Jewish religion, culture and history? In what way does the Hermetic tradition have anything useful to say about Kabbalah? Is it really Kabbalah?

These are awkward questions. If one possessed a hostile spirit one could ask analogous questions about many Christian sects, or for that matter, variant forms of Judaism such as the Samaritans or the Kairites. Rather than confront the questions head-on, it is useful to understand how Kabbalah is not the product of a single time and place.

Kabbalah had its origins during a period of time in Europe that is sometimes called the '12th. century Renaissance'. The Jews of medieval France, Spain and Germany who created and contributed to the classical literature of the Kabbalah were immersed in a vital culture. The three principal communities in the Rhineland, Southern France and Northern Spain were on old trade routes. The Provençal Kabbalists were distributed across some of the most important commercial centres of Southern France - Narbonne, Montpelier, Toulouse, Arles, Aix - ancient cities laced together with Roman roads and large rivers.

At this time all three major monotheistic religions from around the Mediterranean basin - Judaism, Christianity and Islam - were struggling to merge the 'timeless truths' of philosophy with the historical revelations of their founders. Important works by Islamic thinkers such as Avicenna, Alkindi, Averroës, Al-Ghazali, and the Brethren of Purity - in each case strongly influenced by Greek philosophy - were available in Moslem Spain. Many of the translators were Jewish, living in northern Spain and southern France[2].

It was a time for re-examining ancient revelations and scripture. There was a struggle for pre-eminence: should ancient scriptures have the final say in all matters relating to the human condition, or should philosophy, which is based on rational enquiry and argument and is essentially a product of the human mind, be given a place at the table? There was an issue in deciding just how much freedom was permissible in interpreting a text. Scripture was dynamite, and the freedom to interpret was a lit match; this became all too apparent during the Protestant reformation.

At approximately the same time as early traditions of Kabbalah emerged in southern Europe, an Egyptian Jew, Moses ben Maimon (normally known as 'Maimonides') (1125-1204 CE), published the classic *A Guide for the Perplexed*, which provided an Aristotelian interpretation of the *Bible*. It is still in print today, and it is still an important perspective on Jewish religion. A century later one of the most important Christian scholars, St. Thomas Aquinas, attempted to reconcile Aristotelian philosophy with Christian faith and divine revelation. Aquinas was a typical pan-European intellectual of the period, born in Sicily, and working in France, Germany and Italy. He was contemporary to a Spanish Jew, R. Moses of Leon (1250-1305 CE), who compiled the *Zohar*, the most influential of all the classics of Kabbalah.

The communities of southern France and northern Spain where Kabbalah emerged were exposed to the intellectual trends of the day. As Jews they had considerably more scope to interpret their sacred texts than their Christian neighbours, and so long as they displayed a sufficient mastery of *Torah* and *Talmud,* then they were more likely to be admired than condemned. Nevertheless, they were aware that they were playing with fire. R. Isaac the Blind (1160-1235 CE), often dubbed 'the father of Kabbalah' wrote an angry letter to the Kabbalists of Gerona in Northern Spain:

> demanding that Kabbalistic theories be kept secret and protected from the public forum. He forbade the dissemination of exoteric composi-

---

2. Hebrew, Aramaic and Arabic belong to the Semitic family of languages, and have the similarity one finds in French, Spanish and Italian.

Introduction

tions of Kabbalah because, as he wrote, 'a book which is written cannot be hidden in a cupboard.'[3]

At least, not hidden forever. They had good reason for caution. Although Kabbalistic exegesis tended to follow the traditional pattern, in which a respected text is quoted (for example, a verse from the *Bible*), and an interpretation is given, the overall structure that emerged was new and very different from anything that had previously existed within Judaism. Although it was framed as revelation, one can detect many generic influences from the intellectual culture of the period.

Core structural ideas in Kabbalah, such as emanation, the One and the Many, multiple worlds of reality, the structure of the soul, a hierarchy of divine beings, a divine pleroma with dynamic processes involving hypostasised entities with names such as 'intelligence', 'wisdom' or 'beauty', the power of divine names, procession and reversion, exile, theurgic ritual, and so on - these ideas can be found, in various guises, a thousand years earlier in the world of late antiquity. There is an substantial connection between many aspects of Kabbalah and the intellectual culture, fringe religions and proto-sciences of late antiquity: Platonist, Hermetic and Stoic philosophy, Neopythagoreanism[4], gnosticism, medicine, chemistry, astrology, divination, magic and theurgy. In their later developments these are often referred to as 'the Hermetic Tradition'.

The connection between Kabbalah and the Hermetic traditions of late antiquity was further cemented during the Italian Renaissance of the late fifteenth and early sixteenth centuries, when most of the surviving Hermetic literature was brought from Eastern Europe to Florence and translated. These documents had a massive impact on the intellectual culture of the period. At the same time, Jewish scholars and converts in Italy were commissioned to translate Kabbalistic works into Latin for the benefit of Christian scholars. It all came together at the same time.

Leading scholars of that period believed that there was an original ancient wisdom, a *prisca theologia*, that had originated in the figure of the ancient Egyptian god of wisdom, Thoth/Hermes. This ancient wisdom had found its way into Judaism (through Moses), into Christianity, and into Hellenistic philosophy (possibly via Pythagoras). It was believed that Kabbalah preserved traditions going back through

---

3. *The Early Kabbalah*, Joseph Dan & Ronald C. Kiener, Paulist Press 1986
4. One of the most influential source texts for Kabbalah, the *Sefer Yetzirah*, is believed by scholars to have been written by a Jewish Neopythagorean in Late Antiquity.

Moses to the Egyptian priesthood. This belief was incorrect, but it motivated the study of Kabbalah outside the Jewish community. From the late 15th. century onward, Kabbalah was adopted by scholars, mystics and esotericists outside the Jewish community for its symbolic vocabulary and integrated into an Hermetic mystical tradition that continues to the present day.

I hope this indirect answer will suffice to answer questions relating to questions regarding the conjunction of 'Hermetic' with 'Kabbalah'; the Jewishness of Kabbalah is not in question, but when it is situated in the broad sweep of European culture (of which it is an important and influential part) then it becomes part of a larger picture.

To talk of Kabbalah without God is largely meaningless. In the case of Judaism there is no issue, as Kabbalah provides a super-commentary and an expanded context for Jewish religion. In the case of Christian Kabbalah there is also no issue. Christianity diverged from Judaism, but it shares the Old Testament, and there is sufficient overlap that Christian Kabbalah is clearly well defined.

But what is the nature of God in the Hermetic Kabbalah?

This is usually not clear. Many popular books on Kabbalah mention God without reference to any religion, or mention Judaism in passing, but without an expectation that the reader understands anything about Judaism ... or needs to understand anything. It is as if God is an abstract ecumenical notion devoid of community, traditions, festivals, rites of transition, ethics, sacred literature or clergy. Many Jewish people feel this is a misleading and sometimes offensive way to present Kabbalah, and rightly so.

The detached and nebulous view of God found in the literature of the Hermetic Kabbalah may owe something to the systematic destruction of the Hermetic tradition since the Renaissance. It has not been treated kindly by Christian culture, which irrationally labels many of its beliefs and practices as 'black' or even 'satanic'. Heinrich Cornelius Agrippa (1486-1535 CE), the great systematiser of the Hermetic worldview, found it expedient to publicly recant his beliefs in an atmosphere of deepening religious mania and persecution - this is discussed in *Theurgy*, see page 129. Giordano Bruno (1548-1600 CE), who was perhaps the last of the great Hermetic scholars of the time, was burned at the stake in Rome's central market.

The Hermetic tradition has also been marginalised by the rational and scientific culture of the last two centuries. Hermeticism is the

Introduction

now-discredited science of antiquity. The practical tradition that survives has been fragmented into small groups working mostly in isolation, and with a strong element of individualism. This makes it nearly impossible to say anything about the nature of God in this tradition.

For myself, I have been much inspired by the Neoplatonic understanding of the divine as expressed in the surviving works of Plotinus and Iamblichus. Although I am not Jewish there is a great deal in Judaism I respect and admire, and I hope this respect and admiration is apparent in what I have to say about Kabbalah.

The Hermetic Kabbalah

3

Foundational Ideas

3.1 Introduction

There are a number of foundational ideas that underpin Kabbalah. I have not found these core ideas assembled together and elaborated in any other source. The descriptions here are terse; the intention is to reveal the ideas in a skeletal form and so prime the reader for their appearance later.

3.2 Being & Nothingness

We are limited beings, existing in space and time. Because we are limited, we must comprehend and experience the divine according to our limitations. The *Bible* depicts God as acting in time - a God who participates in human affairs. Leaving aside questions of historicity, we can understand these acts in the same way that we understand the actions of any person, and so we can view the actions of God as a *revelation of character*. We can attribute human feelings, and even a human appearance (such as the stereotype of an old man with a white beard sitting on a cloud). However, the inner nature of God is unknown and cannot be characterised in any way.

The part that cannot be characterised in any way is called by Kabbalists *En Sof*, 'limitless'. Any label or attribute we might use would limit and define *En Sof*, and so *En Sof* is beyond language and dualistic cognition. According to the *Zohar*[5]:

> Before He gave any shape to the world, before He produced any form, He was alone, without form and without resemblance to anything else. Who then can comprehend how He was before the Creation? Hence it is forbidden to lend Him any form or similitude, or even to call Him by His sacred name, or to indicate Him by a single letter or a single point. ... But after He created the form of the Heavenly Man, He used him as a chariot wherein to descend, and He wishes to be called after His form, which is the sacred name 'YHWH'.

The contrast between what can be cognised and comprehended, and what cannot be cognised and comprehended, is fundamental in Kabbalah. This contrast is sometimes described as being and nothingness, *yesh* and *ayin*. *Yesh* is being, all that has positive existence, everything we can potentially cognize and experience. *Ayin* is nothingness, the ultimate reality that gives rise to being.

In meditation *ayin* and *yesh* can swap places. *Yesh* is seen to be empty of autonomous existence, *ayin* is the only reality.

3.3 The One and the Many

The reality in which we live appears to be filled with a multiplicity of things – minerals, manufactured objects, plants, animals, people. These seem to have their own autonomous being and existence. According to Kabbalah this is an appearance[6]. All being is rooted in a single unique source, and that source is rooted in nothingness.

Early Kabbalistic literature uses the metaphor of a candle flame. When the candle is lit, one is able to see many things. The further we go from the flame, the less distinctly things are seen. If the light from the candle fails, then nothing exists - the light of the flame brings everything into being, and no thing has autonomous existence.

3.4 Duality & Antipathy

Reality as we experience it, with its boundaries, distinctions, oppositions, and antipathies, does not have the appearance of being rooted in one unique source. For example the goodness of God is compromised by the experience of evil, disease and death. Some have proposed that there are two primal and irreconcilable principles opposed

---

5. *Zohar* part ii., section "Bo," 42b
6. There is no doctrine in Kabbalah, and so statements such as "Kabbalists say" or "According to Kabbalah" can be taken as lazy shorthand for ideas that are relatively common and uncontroversial. As this is an introduction I feel this can be excused, and will attempt to be more specific in later chapters.

to each other, usually in the form of a Good and an Evil principle.

Kabbalah rejects this view, and insists on the underlying unity of all phenomena, proposing that the primal source of being manifests in a dual aspect. One becomes Two. The traditional titles for these two aspects are 'Mercy' and 'Severity'.

Mercy stands for an unattenuated flow of divine goodness, sustenance, providence. The universe is sustained by Mercy.

Severity is a 'holding back' of goodness, a restriction, attenuation or diversion of Mercy. The universe is defined by Severity.

The qualities of Mercy and Severity must manifest in balance for a universe (or any subsidiary situation) to be sustained, in the same way that steam must be contained under pressure to do work. An engine will not work if it lacks steam, and it will not work if the steam is not contained or restrained.

Sometimes Mercy is called 'Force' and Severity is called 'Form'. Force suggests activity and change, Form suggests definition and constraint. There are intriguing similarities between the duality of Mercy and Severity in Kabbalah and the well-known Yin-Yang symbol of Taoism.

The many examples of duality and antipathy we experience in daily life owe their apparent autonomous existence to this primal duality, visualised in the diagram of the Tree of Life by three pillars. The left and right pillars show the source of duality, and the central pillar exists because everything is connected, and nothing has an autonomous existence.

3.5 Reconciliation

According to Kabbalah, all duality is appearance. Because all duality and opposition are rooted in unity (see above), all oppositions are capable of being reconciled. There is always a 'third thing' which represents the reconciliation of two antagonists or extremes, a middle position in which opposites combine in a constructive way. This is an ancient idea found in Greek philosophy.

The progression (or emanation) in which One becomes Two, which are then reconciled in One, which becomes Two, which are reconciled in One (and so on), is a simple way to understand the structure of the Tree of Life (see Figure 1).

3.6 Divine Names

According to Kabbalah, all being or manifestation is a result of the

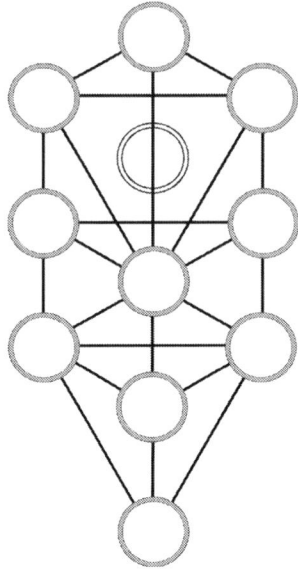

Figure 1: The lattice structure of the Kabbalistic Tree of Life. This illustrates a repeated application of the principle that one becomes two and two are reconciled in a third.

executive power of ten holy names of God. The 'character' of God acting in the world comes about through the agency of ten names. Each of these names manifests in its own way, and can be regarded as an aspect of divine being.

The Tree of Life is composed of ten powers or potencies organised in a lattice of relationships according to Unity, Duality, and Reconciliation (see Figure 1 above), and the 'simplest explanation' of these powers or potencies is that each one represents the executive power of a divine name.

3.7   Emanation

Emanation is a theory of mind, and begins with the assumption that the origin of all existence is rooted in the mind of One God or primal being. This theory proposes that the thoughts or ideas of a mind can assume an autonomous existence, and that these subsidiary thoughts can in turn spawn more subsidiary thoughts or ideas, which can also assume an autonomous existence. The fragmentation of a primal thought or idea is progressive and hierarchical, proceeding according to the principles of duality and reconciliation (see above).

Thoughts or ideas possess being and agency and executive power: they are living entities.

Emanation tends to be described in spatial terms, such as 'higher' and 'lower'. Entities higher in the hierarchy emanate entities lower in the hierarchy. The One - the primordial initiating mind - is the highest, and human beings are low in the hierarchy. A measure of distance is spiritual similarity; for example, beings that exhibit goodness are closer to The Good than beings that are not good. Sometimes distance is measured in terms of lightness and darkness, light being a measure of spiritual awakening (literally, 'enlightenment'). Darkness is associated with ignorance and evil.

Everything that can exist does exist (the principle of Plenitude), and everything has a designated place in the hierarchy, giving rise to a Great Chain of Being. There is a proliferation of entities as the 'distance' from the source increases, and an increase in ignorance, culminating in the material world, which contains a vast number of entities characterised by ignorance and delusion.

Emanation is layered. According to Plotinus (204/5-270 CE) the primary layers are: The One; the Divine Intellect; Soul, which comprises the World Soul and the souls of all animate beings; and Matter.

Emanation is part of a complex Theory of Everything developed by the followers of the Greek philosopher Plato for approximately one thousand years. It was influential in both Islamic and Christian philosophy. Its ideas are implicit in Kabbalah, especially in many descriptions of the Tree of Life and the Four Worlds.

3.8   Irrigation

In Kabbalah emanation is often likened to a flow of water as in a system of irrigation. There is source and a spring, and the water flows into a cistern (the Upper Sea) from where it flows into channels that water all aspects of existence before reaching a Lower Sea[7].

If the flow of water through a channel is blocked then that aspect of existence loses its flow of divine providence (*berakhot* - blessings) and may wither. If a channel overflows or is diverted then unhealthy aspects of existence may receive sustenance. The role of a Kabbalist can be likened to someone who tends a garden.

---

7. See the extract from the *Zohar, Essence and Vessels,* for a beautiful exposition of this, quoted in *The Wisdom of the Zohar*, Lachower, F., and Tishby, I., Vol 1, p.265, Oxford University Press 1991.

3.9 Worlds

According to the theory of emanation (see 3.7 above) reality is stratified into levels. The worlds are stratified according to their spiritual distance from God. Each world is populated by a characteristic kind of spiritual being (e.g. archangels, angels, *daemones*).

According to early Kabbalistic tradition there are four distinct worlds (or realms of being) named *Atzilut*, *Briah*, *Yetzirah* and *Assiah*. If the Heavenly Man or Primordial Adam is included (see 3.11) there are five worlds, and if the realm of the evil shells and the Great Abyss is included there are six worlds; however, the base position in classic Kabbalah is that there are four worlds.

3.10 Family

One of the most important symbols used in Kabbalah is that of family. There are four members: the Father, the Mother, the Son, and the Daughter. This family is equated to individual letters in the divine name of four letters, YHVH[8].

The symbolism is often sexual, and sometimes explicitly so. The Father and Mother are in continuous and eternal *coitus*; were they to cease, the cosmos would cease to exist. The Son and Daughter are also King and Queen, and Groom and Bride. The dynamics of their relationship provides an occult backdrop to human history.

This primal family is subsumed within a larger scheme of divine archetypes called *Partzufim*, or 'faces'. This is discussed in more detail in *Partzufim* on page 43.

3.11 Body

The first cognisable manifestation of God is often taken to have the form of a giant human body, the Heavenly or Primordial Man (see the quotation from the *Zohar* in 3.2). This Primordial Man is androgenous, neither male or female, and subsumes both the first man Adam and the first woman Eve. The parts of the body of the Primordial Man were of great interest to the medieval Kabbalist and the lobes of the brain, the hair, the beard, the eyes, nose and mouth, the arms and fingers, the torso, the heart, the sexual organs, the legs and the semen were subject to detailed discussion.

---

8. The divine name of four letters is often transliterated as *Jehovah* or *Yahweh*. Jews do not pronounce this name and substitute *Adonai*, 'Lord'.

3.12 Procession and Reversion

Procession and reversion is a key concept in the Neoplatonic model of emanation (see 3.7). According to this, all of existence *proceeds* from the One, which gives life and being to all things, like the light of a candle. Emanation is progressive. Each level of being gives rise to a dependent level of being, but, like the light of a candle seen through many panes of glass, it becomes more dim with each transmission. This is a key idea, as expressed by R. Moses Luzzatto[9] (1707-1746 CE):

> In order to reduce the too powerful downpour of His Light upon the nether beings, God established "Coverings" to shield them. These coverings consist of an arrangement of planes which restrain the Light and cause its successive minimisation and densification. Thus the Light is steadily decreased and densified, in a succession of condensations; and it is from the densest possible stage of Light that the body of man is created.

This chain, stretching from one to many, from light to dark, is called the Great Chain of Being.

The emanation of the ten *sefirot* in the Tree of Life is often described sequentially in this way, ten steps in which the pure quality of being is progressively diminished. This movement from singularity to multiplicity, or from light to dark, is *procession*.

Reversion occurs because every level of being has its origin in something greater and more inclusive. Each level of dependent being finds its perfection and completion in the level above it, and so there is a desire in all emanated beings to revert back, level by level, to the One. This is the explanation for spiritual ascent, as described in *Ascent* on page 115.

Kabbalah has its own conception of procession and reversion, expressed as the formula of 'run and return'. This derives from the influential *Sefer Yetzirah*, and is taken originally from the vision of Ezekiel as described in the *Bible*:

> Ten Sefirot of Nothingness
> Their vision is like the 'appearance of lightning'
> Their limit has no end
> And his word in them is 'running and returning'
> They rush to His saying like a whirlwind

---

9. *General Principles of the Kabbalah*, R. Moses C. Luzzatto, trans. Dr. Philip S. Berg, Research Centre of Kabbalah 1969

And before His throne they prostrate themselves.[10]

The creative energy of the godhead runs and returns, goes out and comes back to its source, like an echo.

3.13 Holographic Principle & Self-Similarity

A hologram has the property that any fragment can be used to reconstruct the original image, albeit at a reduced resolution. The fragment of the hologram need not be shaped like the original, and yet it 'contains' the whole.

A related idea is self-similarity; a part of something *does* look like the whole. We find this in many plants and trees, where a small piece can look remarkably similar to the entire plant, and this may remain true of even smaller pieces. A self-similar object may also be described as *fractal*. Pure mathematical fractals can retain the property of self-similarity down to extraordinary levels of magnification.

A property of fractals is *scale-independence*: it may be impossible to tell what scale one is looking at, just as, deprived of context, one cannot tell whether one is looking at a giant boulder or a grain of sand.

These are important ideas in Kabbalah. The Tree of Life, for example, describes reality at every level. Each *sefira* in the Tree of Life is itself an entire Tree, and so on recursively (just like a real tree). Each world (see 3.9) also contains its own Tree. The microcosm of each human being is a Tree. The soul of Adam contains all souls. Describing the Kabbalah of R. Isaac Luria, Lawrence Fine observes[11]:

> Significantly, the complete pattern of the divine is recapitulated in each one of its discrete manifestations, like mirrors set up in such as way that they endlessly reflect one another. The cosmos consists of a great chain of being, in which one can discern the whole structure of reality in any particular part of it.

There is no preferred scale, a property of scale independence. One might imagine that the Tree of Life has a top and a bottom, but Kabbalists have followed the *Sefer Yetzirah*, teaching that its "end is in its beginning, and its beginning is its end"[12] - there is no top or bottom, no beginning or end.

---

10. *Sefer Yetzirah*, Aryeh Kaplan, Samuel Weiser 1991
11. *Physician of the Soul, Healer of the Cosmos*, Lawrence Fine, Stanford University Press, 2003
12. *Sefer Yetzirah*, Ibid.

Foundational Ideas

3.14 Catastrophe and Exile

Existence is not as it might be. Everything *has* a place, but not everything is *in its place*. Some things have fallen off the shelf and broken.

The classical Hellenistic model of emanation is a smooth graduation from a source (see 3.7). All things are Good and all things are *in their place*. Kabbalah injects drama into this cosmic harmony with discrete moments of catastrophe. Whole worlds shift out of their proper place.

The sense of 'being out of place' gives rise to the feeling of being a 'stranger in a strange land'[13], of being in exile. This mirrored the historical displacement of Jewish communities throughout Europe, North Africa, and the Middle East.

When one believes one is in exile, there is a natural inclination towards return (see 3.12). One might attempt to 'put right' what is broken, to rectify what is crooked. This impulse may take material and spiritual forms - e.g. the Zionist return to the Holy Land; *devekut*, a mystical cleaving to the source of all being; *teshuvah*, a desire to turn away from evil and return to righteousness; and *tikkun olam*, the rectification of the cosmos. The entire third part of this book is devoted to understanding these feelings of crookedness and estrangement.

3.15 Life

The Tree of Life is also a tree of *Life*. It is easy to neglect this subtle switch in emphasis. Life: a multitude of interdependent living things that grow and interact and die.

In what follows much stress will be placed on the idea of organism: something that is self-organised and lives. There are interpretations of the Tree of Life where it is viewed as a 'map of organism', a blueprint for any living thing. If we are made, as many Kabbalists believed, in the "image of God", then it follows that the principles of divine governance depicted by the Tree of Life operate within us, and by extension, within all living things.

---

13. *Exodus* 2:22

The Hermetic Kabbalah

4

The Tree of Life

4.1 Introduction

The Tree of Life is a diagram of ten circles, called *sefirot*, and twenty-two lines, called paths, arranged in the form of a lattice. Most popular explanations of Kabbalah begin and end with the Tree of Life. The *sefirot* are enumerated, their names given, a convenient illustration is provided, and some explanation is attempted. Much of the context for the diagram is missing, and many people will go away mystified - they can grasp that they have seen a map, but the territory is unfamiliar and probably meaningless.

Figure 2: Title page from the 1516 Latin translation of Gikatilla's *Gates of Light*. This is an early representation of the Tree of Life.

The Tree of Life is most emphatically not a ladder of lights shining like a stained glass window in the sun. Anyone trying to find this picture in any of the early classics of Kabbalah will come away puzzled. There is no picture. Tishby, attempting to elucidate this confusion in his commentary to the *Zohar*[14] puts it very well:

> It is clear from the passage just quoted that the *sefirot*, which are finite and measurable, are not, however, static objects, like fixed, solid rungs on the ladder of the progressive revelation of the divine attributes.

---

14. *The Wisdom of the Zohar*, Isaiah Tishby, Oxford University Press 1991

The Hermetic Kabbalah

They are on the contrary, dynamic forces, ascending and descending, and extending themselves within the area of the Godhead. This dynamism is found both in their hidden existence, which is oriented upwards towards *En-Sof,* and also in their association with the lower world, as forces of creation and direction of the universe. They are in continuous motion, involved in innumerable processes of interweaving, interlinking, and union. Even their order changes as a result of their internal movement, and "their end is fastened into their beginning". The lower sefirot elevate themselves in their yearning to return and cleave to their source, and the upper sefirot move downwards in order to give sustenance to the lower, and to transmit divine influences to the worlds below.

Tishby also observes that the *Zohar* hardly ever uses the term *sefirot*[15]:

Instead we have a whole string of names: "levels", "powers", "sides" or "areas", "worlds", "firmaments", "pillars", "lights", "colours", "days", "streams", "garments", "crowns" and others. Each term designates a particular facet of the nature or work of the *sefirot*.

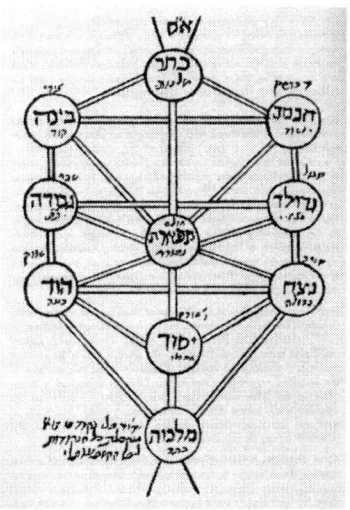

Figure 3: The Tree of Life from a *Zohar* manuscript.

Visual depictions of the Tree are sparse in the literature. One of the earliest images comes from the *Portae Lucis* of Paolo Riccio (see Figure 2), a 1516 Latin translation of Gikatilla's 13th. century *Gates of Light*. It has ten *sefirot* but it does not have the usual twenty-two paths.

The classic diagram of the Tree known to so many appears in the *Oedipus Aegyptiacus* of Athanasius Kircher (see Figure 4), a Jesuit priest, published in the middle of the 17th. century. This was some *five hundred years* after the first Kabbalists began writing.

The diagram of the Tree used by modern Jewish Kabbalists is usually based on the diagram published in the print edition of Cordovero's *Pardes Rimonim*, published in Cracow in 1591, and sometimes called the 'Safed Tree'. It can be seen in Figure 6.

---

15. *Ibid.*

The Tree of Life

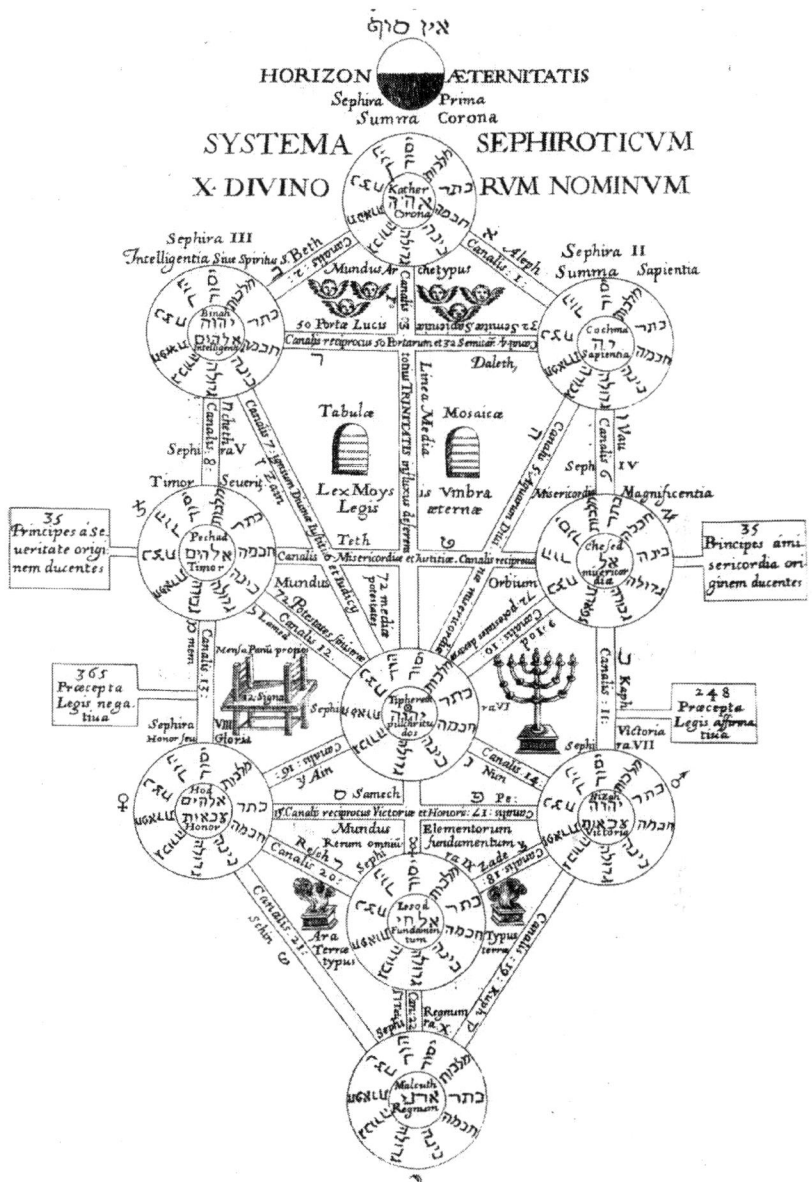

Figure 4: A Tree of Life published in the 1653 edition of *Oedipus Aegyptiacus* by the polymath Jesuit priest Athanasius Kircher.

This historic lack of imagery is all the more startling given the modern tendency to begin and end with the diagram of the Tree of Life. The lack of imagery may have something to do with the Biblical prohibition on images, but it may also be a consequence of the perplexing fluidity of traditional kabbalistic writing. Many modern readers will be looking for clarity and consistency, and will adopt a disjunctive and hostile view of conflicting metaphors and explanations, thinking "is it *this?* ... or is it *that?*".

The literature of Kabbalah tends to view each new perspective as additive, even when views appear to conflict. This is the traditional mode of Kabbalistic exegesis and will appear odd to the modern mind. It is useful to think of the Tree as a higher-dimensional construct that cannot be described from one single static viewpoint, and it makes sense at the outset to say that there are multiple views that do not need to be pruned or reconciled. With this caveat it is possible to begin to describe some of the many ideas that the kabbalistic Tree of Life is used to represent.

The Tree of Life is a *collection of views* of the dynamics of the relationship between God and the Creation. There are several views because no single view captures the complexity of the relationship. A view is dynamic because the relationship between God and the Creation is constantly changing. And the Tree provides a *view of relationship*, not a view of God, which kabbalists regard as unknowable, beyond any kind of imaginative or conceptual description.

Most importantly, each view is of a whole, not a collection of parts. Recall always the *Shema*: "Hear, O Israel: the Lord is our God, the Lord is One". The activity of God with respect to the Creation is always that of a whole, and the parts of the Tree, however described, however complex they may seem, do not act autonomously.

The activity of God is the prototype for all activity. The Tree of Life depicts relationship at every level. This is a key idea: parts mirror the whole, are an image of the whole. The activity of human beings, for example is also characterised by the Tree of Life. The 'activity of a human being' is the outward manifestation of an internal organisation, something we could call 'a soul' (see *Soul* on page 21), and so the Tree of Life describes the soul.

The Tree of Life is a fractal structure that appears at every level of reality. Every element of the Tree of Life, considered as a living thing, is another Tree of Life. R. Moses Luzzatto (1707-1746 CE) puts it concisely[16]:

Each of these *sefirot* [in the Tree] is constructed of ten Lights, each of which in turn is composed of an equal number of lights and so on ad-infinitum.

The recursive similarity at all levels of created existence leads to an additional complication: Kabbalists have a tendency to use the same terms when talking about different levels. Kabbalah has grown more complex over time, with more entities and distinctions reusing the same vocabulary, and this can pose a formidable challenge to the reader.

The basic skeleton for the Tree of Life comes from an ancient document that is often beautiful and poetic in its enigmatic brevity: the *Sefer Yetzirah*. The *Sefer Yetzirah* describes how God created the universe using number, language and speech:

> With thirty-two mystical paths of Wisdom engraved *Yah*, YHVH of Hosts, God of Israel, the Living God, God Almighty, high and exalted, dwelling in eternity on high, and his name is Holy, and he created His universe with three books, with text, with number, and with communication. They are Ten *sefirot* of Nothingness and twenty-two foundation letters.

The *Sefer Yetzirah* would seem to be a work of Hebrew Neopythagoreanism composed in the Hellenistic Middle East in late antiquity. It became the seed for highly original readings in the Jewish communities of southern Europe during the Middle Ages (that is, several hundred years later).

The ten *sefirot* of the *Sefer Yetzirah* became ten emanations of the divine, and the 22 Hebrew letters, grouped by the *Sefer Yetzirah* into 3 mothers, 7 doubles, and 12 elementals (based on Hellenistic cosmology), provides the framework of the Tree of 3 horizontal paths, 7 vertical paths, and 12 diagonal paths.

The *Sefer Yetzirah* states that there are ten *sefirot* but does not name them, or provide sufficient information to construct the familiar Tree of Life diagram. Even at the time of the *Zohar* (late 13th century CE) there was considerable fluidity in the relationships between the *sefirot*, and they were often masked behind a large number of titles and allusions. Nevertheless, it is possible to deduce the familiar Tree and the titles of the *sefirot*, which are:

- *Keter*, Crown
- *Chokhmah*, Wisdom

---

16. *The General Principles of Kabbalah*, Luzzatto, Moses, trans. Berg, Philip S., Research Centre for Kabbalah, 1969

The Hermetic Kabbalah

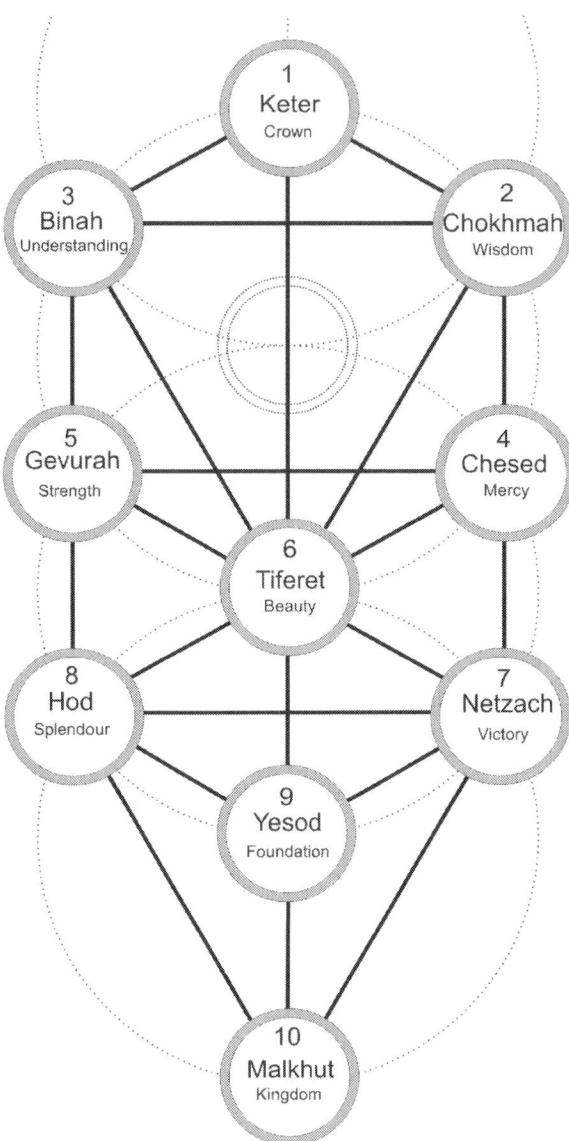

Figure 5: A Tree of Life with 10 sefirot and 22 paths - 3 horizontal, 7 vertical. 12 diagonals. This is an early version that is still favoured by Hermetic Kabbalists. It is sometimes called 'The Tree of Emanation'.

The Tree of Life

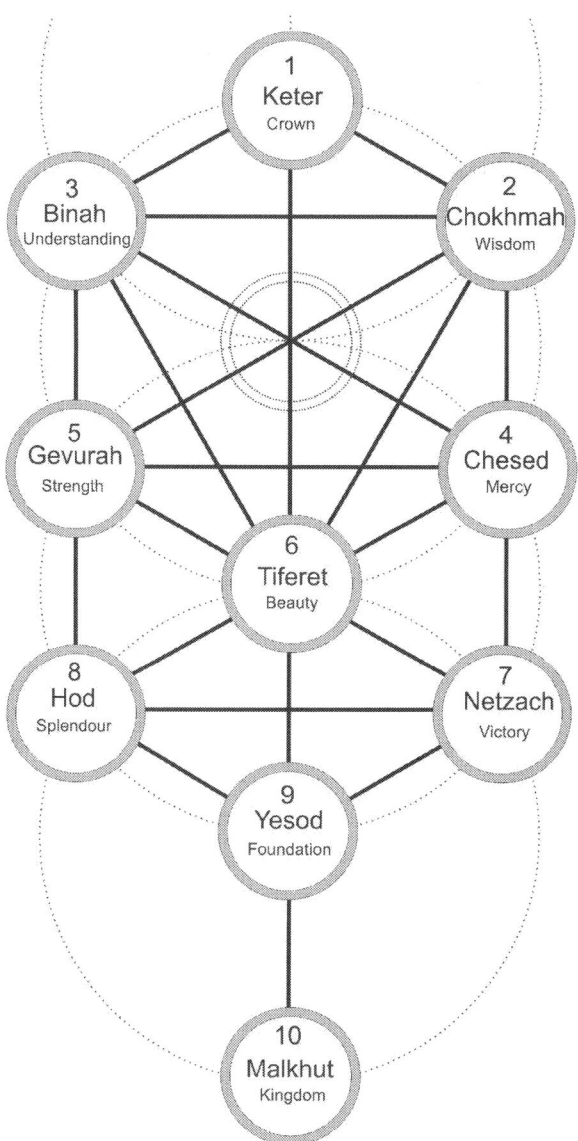

Figure 6: A Tree of Life with 10 sefirot and 22 paths - 3 horizontal, 7 vertical. 12 diagonals. This version appears as a diagram in R. Moses Cordovero's *Pardes Rimonim*, and is the preferred form in modern Jewish Kabbalah. It is sometimes called the 'Safed' Tree after R. Isaac Luria who described it, or 'The Tree of Return'.

The Hermetic Kabbalah

- *Binah*, Understanding
- *Chesed*, Loving Kindness, Mercy, also *Gedulah*, Greatness
- *Gevurah*, Strength, also *Din*, Judgement, and *Pachad*, Fear
- *Tiferet*, Beauty, also *Rachamim*, Compassion
- *Netzach*, Victory or Triumph, also Eternity
- *Hod*, Splendour or Glory
- *Yesod*, Foundation
- *Malkhut*, Kingdom, or Sovereignty

In some discussions *Keter* is considered to be concealed, a crystallisation within the *En Sof*, the unknowable inner aspect of God. In this case *Da'at*, Knowledge (shown as an unlabelled eleventh circle below *Chokhmah* and *Binah*) is substituted as the effective tenth *sefira*. Two frequently-encountered versions of the Tree of Life can be seen in Figure 5 and in Figure 6.

In what follows the Tree of Life is considered from a variety of different perspectives or views. Most are traditional, but some (e.g. holons) are a modern reframing of older ideas. These views are not always consistent with each other, and no attempt has been made to impose harmony upon them.

4.2 View - A Chain of Emanation

This view has the *sefirot* forming a sequential, causal chain of ten steps, so that *Keter* is the cause of *Chokhmah*, which is the cause of *Binah*, which is the cause of *Chesed*, and so on down to *Malkhut*. Each *sefira* 'contains' all subsequent *sefira* in a latent, undifferentiated form, in much the same way as an acorn contains an oak tree, so that *Binah* contains the dual qualities of mercy and strict judgement as possibilities that do not differentiate and manifest until the sefirot of *Chesed* and *Gevurah*.

The causal-chain ordering of the *sefirot* is sometimes called the 'lightning flash' order because their appearance is as a flash of lightning (this simile comes from the *Sefer Yetzirah*).

Figure 7: A calligraphic depiction of the 10 *sefirot* nested within each other, *Keter* on the outside, *Malkhut* on the inside. This design was published in the massive *Pardes Rimonim* by R. Moses Cordovero (1522-1570 CE)

The Tree of Life

This order is characterised by increasing differentiation, reification and structure, and what in Neoplatonism is called alienation, but in Kabbalah would be better termed attenuation. The sense is that the pure light of divinity is progressively attenuated. One of the common metaphors is a succession of veils, where each *sefira* in the causal chain veils the light of the previous *sefira*, so that the light is progressively diminished until one reaches *Malkhut*, at which point it is almost completely obscured, hence its title, "the mirror that does not shine".

R. Moses Cordovero (1522-1570 CE) gives the example of a craftsman who places a crucible in a furnace. The heat is too fierce, so he places a second crucible within the first, and then a third within the second, and so on. Each crucible attenuates the heat of the furnace, until finally, conditions are reached that support the creation of a viable cosmos. This metaphor suggests that the *sefirot* can be represented like the layers of an onion, and Cordovero provides a calligraphic depiction of this (see Figure 7), using the first letter of each *sefira* as a 'layer'.

This sequential production of *sefirot* is usually referred to as emanation. A *sefira* can emanate an inferior *sefira* because it contains within it every idea and structure necessary to suggest (emanate) a more detailed instantiation. For example 'a place to live' suggests 'a house', and 'a house' suggests a structure with four walls, a roof, a door and some windows. This kind of 'reification' (making real) within the mental realm is characteristic of that Hellenistic philosophy known as late-Platonism or Neoplatonism.

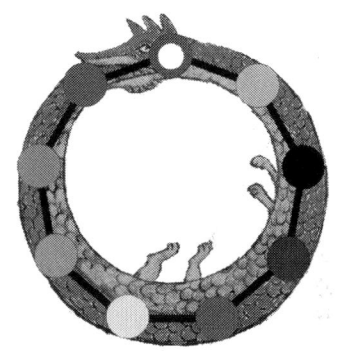

Figure 8: "The end is fixed in the beginning". The avoidance of duality by connecting *Keter* to *Malkhut*. This important idea is sourced from the *Sefer Yetzirah*.

Viewing the *sefirot* as an emanatory chain suggests that there is a top (*Keter*) and a bottom (*Malkhut*). Neoplatonic emanatory schemes (see *Emanation and Emergence* on page 155) have a top and a bottom, with the One, or the Good at the top, and Matter at the bottom. Matter is seen as an absolute alienation from the Good, and it is necessarily formless (because form comes from the divine mind) and so one is left with a strange, indescribable, shapeless goo that is nevertheless forced to carry the burden of all the defect in the cosmos.

Kabbalah avoids this unsatisfactory dualism by connecting *Keter* and *Malkhut*. Cordovero was well aware of the problem, and references a well-known verse from the *Sefer Yetzirah*:

> "Ten sefirot without substance, the beginning is fixed in the end, and the end is in the beginning etc". The Master is one and there is no other, and what do you count before one? Although the *sefirot* are ten in relation to the changing aspects, the end is fixed in the beginning. The head is the end, and the end is the head, for they are part of God's single substance. God is one with them and - God forbid - there is no duality.

In Kabbalah there is no terminal, unexplained 'stuff' at the bottom of the chain of emanation. Alienation occurs in ten progressive steps, and the quality of alienation is called *Din* (judgement) an abstract quality that defines and determines, and sets boundaries and limits on things. At each step of emanation the quantity of *Din* increases.

A way to visualise the Kabbalistic concept of emanation is shown in Figure 9. There is only light and darkness, but the interweaving of light and dark create the appearance of ten steps separated by levels of darkness. There is no final step because the light retraces its path back to the source - its end is in its beginning.

4.3   View - The Names of God

An important view of the *sefirot* is that they represent the executive powers of the Names of God. That is, the power of God manifests through His Names, and the nature of a *sefira* is essentially identical with the power of a Name. One of the most popular works of Kabbalah, translated into Latin in 1516 by a German Jewish convert Paolo Riccio, is the *Gates of Light* by Joseph ben Abraham Gikatilla (1248-1305 CE). This work is a series of essays on the Divine Names associated with each of ten Spheres or Gates. Gikatilla justifies these attributions by extensive quotation and interpretation of verses drawn from canonical literature, mainly the *Bible*, and it is obvious Gikatilla is collating views from an established tradition. His attributions have remained largely unchanged to the current period. The Names given

The Tree of Life

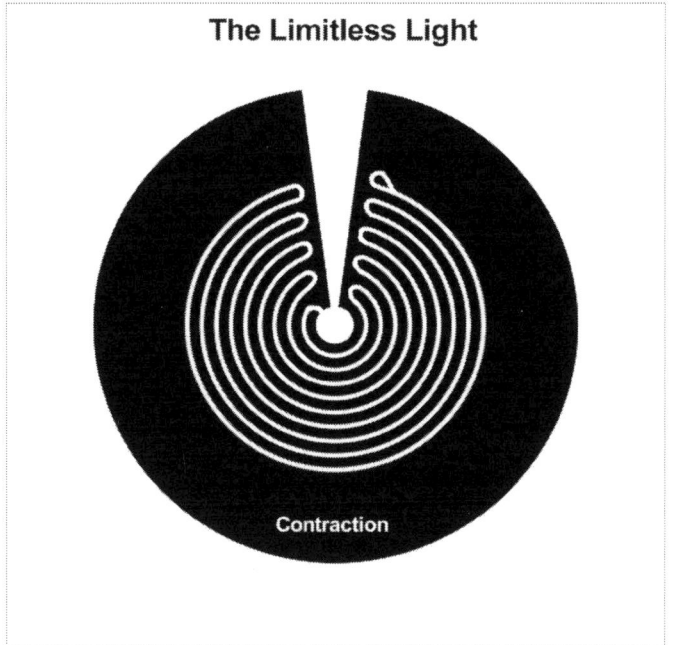

Figure 9: In *Isaiah* 45:7 the Lord declares: "I form the light, and create darkness: I make peace, and create evil". Kabbalists have interpreted this to mean that light and peace were already part of the divine, but that darkness and evil were not, and that the fundamental creative act was a withdrawal of God to create the possibility of distinction, of separation, and definition. This idea is paralleled in *Genesis 1*, where God manifests Light, and then separates Light from Darkness.

This primary duality has a technical definition in Kabbalah. Light is the power of life, benevolence, mercy, loving-kindness, and water, and is called *Chesed*. Dark is the power of death, holding-back, separation, distinction, constraint, boundaries and fire, and is called *Din*.

The diagram above attempts to condense several key ideas in Kabbalah. Light is separated from darkness, creating a space where the power of *Din* predominates. Light (divine creative energy) enters this space, and forms ten progressively attenuated 'layers' (i.e. *sefirot*), which shield the primordial intensity of the light. No part of the Light has autonomous existence - it is all connected, and even the end turns back on itself.

The structure of layers is created through the interaction of light with the power of *Din* (judgement), so that reality emerges from the interweaving. The Tree of Life embodies these ideas in the form of the interaction of the Pillars of Mercy and Severity.

by Gikatilla (see Table 1) are:

Sefira	Divine Name
Kether	Eheieh
Chokhmah	Jah
Binah	YHVH, vocalised *Elohim*
Chesed	El
Gevurah	Elohim
Tiferet	YHVH
Netzach	YHVH *Tzabaot*
Hod	Elohim *Tzabaot*
Yesod	Shaddai, El Chai
Malkhut	Adonai

Table 1 : The Divine Names according to Gikatilla

4.4 View - The Divine King

> Earthly kingdoms are like the kingdom of Heaven
> *Mishnah*

Many European cathedrals contain statues of kings sitting in state; that is, wearing a crown, and holding formal regalia - sword, sceptre, orb etc. Christ is often depicted as King in a similar way, sitting in his glory, surrounded by ranks of saints and angels.

This imagery is of great antiquity. God is depicted in the *Bible* as King, as Arthur Green comments[17]:

> The kingship of God is a central theme of the Hebrew Bible, and kingship is probably the most widespread single metaphor used to describe the relationship of God, His Creation, and His people.

There is an important view that the Tree of Life represents a King.

---

17. *Keter: The Crown of God in early Jewish Mysticism*, Arthur Green, Princeton University Press, 1997

The Tree of Life

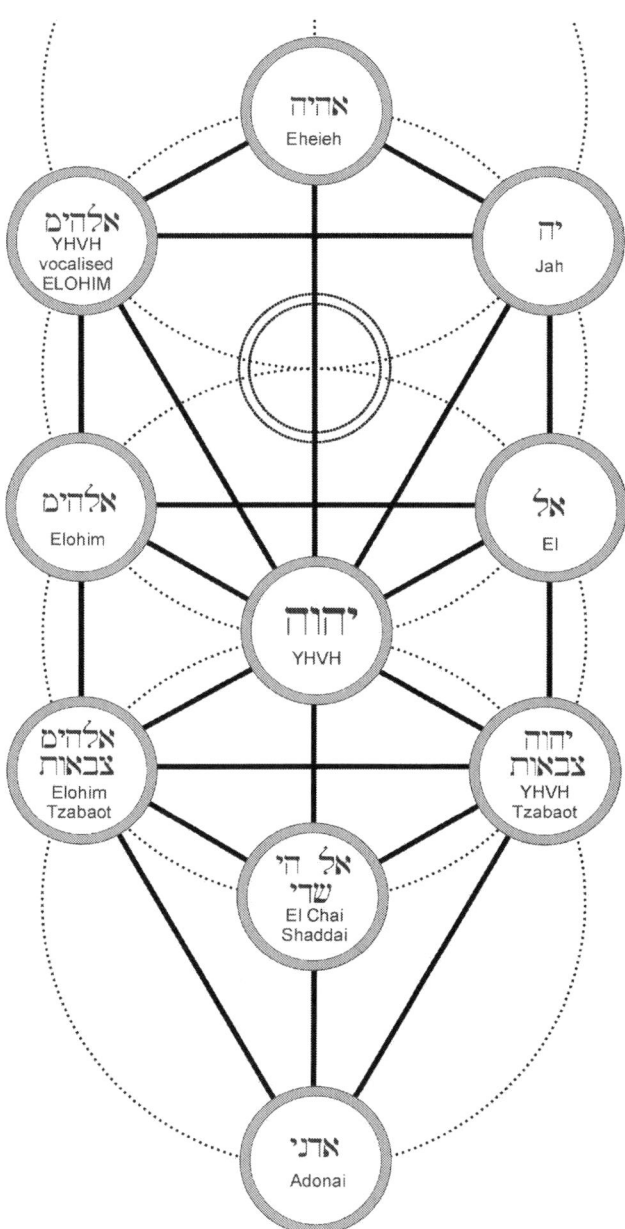

Figure 10: The Divine Names on the Tree of Life as given by R. Joseph Gikatilla (1248-c.1305 CE) in his *Gates of Light*.

Keter is the Crown. *Chokhmah*, and *Binah* are cognitive functions in the brain, but also Father and Mother to the King. *Chesed* is the right arm of authority and benevolence (sceptre) and *Gevurah* is the left arm of justice and retribution (sword). *Tiferet* is the King. *Netzach* and *Hod* are the legs, and also the hosts/armies (*tzabaot*) of the King. *Yesod* is the phallus. *Malkhut* is simultaneously the Kingdom, and the Queen, beloved of the King (see *Partzufim* on page 43). *Malkhut* might also be considered as the throne.

To a considerable extent this image of God as King is conflated with the image of the gigantic Primordial Adam (Adam Kadmon), and the *Partzuf* of *Ze'ir Anpin*.

4.5 View - Partzufim

Some *sefira* or groups of *sefirot* are viewed as possessing a quasi-autonomous identity. These are referred to as *Partzuf* - 'faces'. The *Partzufim* are divine archetypes overlaid and integrated into the Tree of Life. The best-known *Partzufim* are modelled after a family with four members. This is a major topic - see *Partzufim* on page 43.

4.6 View - The Human Body

A fundamental principle of Kabbalah is that human beings are made 'in the image of God'. This is taken from the creation story of *Genesis* 1:27 in the *Bible*. This led to speculation about the role of the *sefirot* in the body of a vast human figure known as the Heavenly Man, or the Primordial Adam (*Adam Kadmon*). This is a major topic - see *The Primordial Adam* on page 61.

4.7 View - Organism

An organism is a living thing. A more detailed definition that accords with this section is[18]:

> any complex thing or system having properties and functions determined not only by the properties and relations of its individual parts, but by the character of the whole that they compose and by the relations of the parts to the whole.

An organism is an emergent; it is composed of parts, but the coordinated interactions of the parts create a 'whole' that is much more than the sum of the parts. This obviously applies to human beings. We are composed of cells, and the cells differentiate into organs, but a

---

18. Dictionary.com

person is much more than a collection of cells or organs. One way to view the *sefirot* is to think of them as analogous to organs in a body, and the Tree as a living organism that emerges from their interactions.

A view that is expressed in the *Zohar*, and frequently repeated, is the need for the divine 'lights' and 'receptacles' that constitute the *sefirot* to find a 'balanced configuration'. This is a configuration in which each *sefira* receives light in proportion to its capacity to receive it, and exchanges light with other *sefirot* in proportion to their ability to receive and transmit. This balance is not a given; there is an old *midrash* (teaching) that God created many worlds and destroyed them. The *Zohar* interprets this teaching as a reference to prior creations in which the *sefirot* failed to achieve a balanced configuration. R. Isaac Luria developed this idea into *shevirah*, the Shattering of the Vessels (see *Evil* on page 83).

At issue is the dynamic equilibrium between the powers of *Chesed* and *Din*, light and dark. Too much *Chesed* and the receptacles cannot bear it; too much *Din* and we have what T.S. Eliot describes as "paralysed force, gesture without motion", the Tree of Death. The Middle Pillar of the Tree represents the dynamic equilibrium between these tendencies.

Since the time of R. Isaac Luria there has been a tendency to apply the Tree of Life at every level of reality. Every functioning microcosm can be described by a balanced configuration of *sefirot*. There is a kabbalistic holographic principle (see 3.13) that finds a Tree in every *sefirot*, so that reality can be decomposed at every level into the same, fractal, self-similar structure - not unlike many conifers, where each part has the same branching structure as the whole. This is an economy of means that is widely observed throughout the natural world.

According to this view, the Tree of Life is an abstract template of organism, any kind of organism: a carbon atom, an amoeba, the human psyche, society, the organism of God. Anywhere one finds a whole composed of a defined, dynamic equilibrium of parts, one finds a Tree of Life.

Similar ideas have been discussed outside the context of Kabbalah. Arthur Koestler[19], studying the emergence of complex systems, defined a *holon* as an autonomous whole that is itself composed of holons, and is capable of becoming a part of a larger holon. That is, a holon is a *whole* composed of *parts* which are themselves *holons*. For

---

19. *The Ghost in the Machine*, Arthur Koestler, 1967

The Hermetic Kabbalah

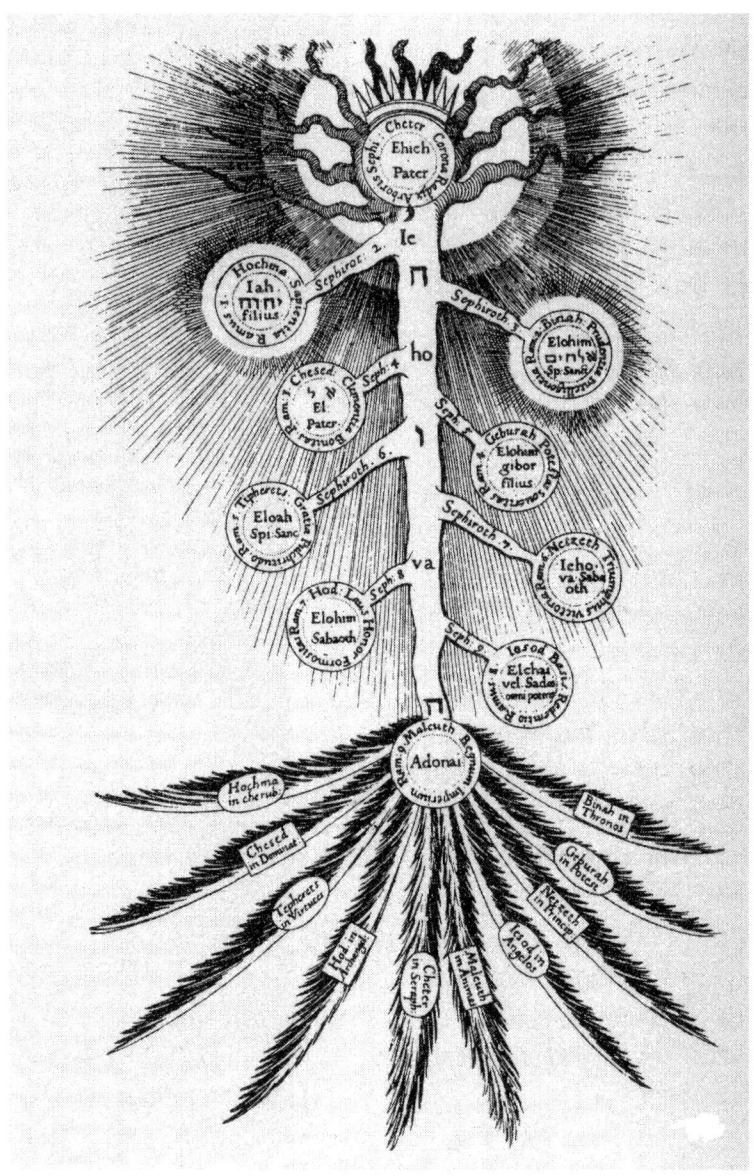

Figure 11: A Tree of Life showing the Divine Names published by Robert Fludd (1574 - 1637 CE) in his *Utriusque Cosmi Maioris* (1617). The Tree is rooted in *En Sof*, the branches show the angel orders.

example, atoms are holons that can become parts of molecules, which are holons that can become parts of proteins, which can become parts of cells, which can become parts of organs, and so on. Not only does this idea bear a strong similarity to the way in which the Tree of Life is used to depict organism, but the similarities go further.

Every holon must have two essential attributes. Because a holon is made up of holons, its component holons must be bound together. This binding is usually an active process, a homeostatic mechanism. The human body has many such processes, that maintain temperature, the ionic balance of the blood, blood sugar level and so on. Cells die and are replaced, injuries are repaired, and the immune system protects us from invasive organisms such as bacterial or viral infections. These active processes are the *agency* of the holon. When the agency fails, the holon disassociates or decomposes into its component holons.

A holon may also unite with other holons to form a larger holon, just as cells in the body unite to become an eye or a heart or a hand. This ability to connect is the *communion* of a holon. Because holons can come together into larger wholes, they can transcend themselves - this is the opposite of dissolution. These four necessary attributes - agency, communion, self-transcendence and dissolution - are shown in Figure 12.

The element carbon is a holon. It is composed of protons, neutrons and electrons. It also has the richest communion of any element, and can become part of a vast number of organic molecules. The elements with the lowest communion and the highest agency are the noble gases - helium, argon, krypton etc. These elements are almost unreactive and form very few compounds.

These ideas map onto the Tree of Life with surprising accuracy. The left-hand pillar, embodying the principle of *Din*, corresponds to agency. The right-hand pillar, embodying the principle of *Chesed*, corresponds to communion. The middle pillar corresponds to homeostasis at the centre: upwards it corresponds to transcendence, downwards to dissolution (or alternatively, embodiment via lower-level holons).

Communion is synonymous with the Platonic/Renaissance notion of *eros*, the teleological 'tie that binds'. Agency corresponds to will and self-determination. An extensive discussion of holons and their relation to an integral worldview can be found in Ken Wilber's *Sex, Ecology, Spirituality*[20].

The Hermetic Kabbalah

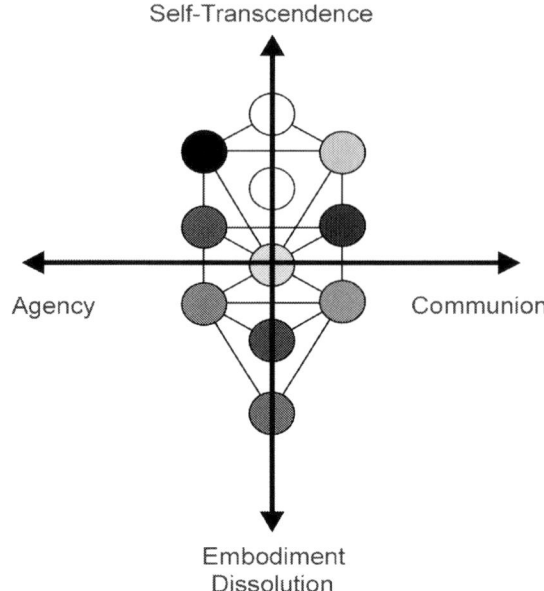

Figure 12: The Tree of Life as a Whole/Part (holon). On the left, Agency (self-definition, separateness, autonomy, individual), on the right, Communion (connectedness, relationship, group). At the bottom Embodiment and Dissolution (the Whole is composed of Parts which do or do not cohere). At the top, Transcendence (the Whole becomes part of a larger Whole).

4.8 View - Metaphysical Dovecot

In his massive survey of Renaissance occult philosophy[21], Heinrich Cornelius Agrippa (1486-1535 CE) provides tables of correspondences - 'scales' - for all the numbers up to twelve. His scale of the number ten is essentially a table of correspondences for the *sefirot* of the Tree of Life - divine names, angel orders, archangels, planets, animals, parts of the body and shells. This approach goes back to the various tables that can be constructed out of the *Sefer Yetzirah*.

This preoccupation with tables and lists derives from the ancient Hermetic notion of sympathies, the idea that certain things have an underlying sympathetic or harmonic connection that is rooted in a

---

20. *Sex, Ecology, Spirituality*, Ken Wilber, Shambhalla 1995
21. *Three Books of Occult Philosophy*, Heinrich Cornelius Agrippa, ed. Donald Tyson, Llewellyn 1993

higher world of planetary or divine essences (see *Theurgy* on page 129).

Since the time of Agrippa these tables have grown. The modern Hermetic Kabbalist is likely to encounter them in works such as Mathers' introduction to the *Kabbalah Unveiled*, Gareth Knight's *A Practical Guide to Qabalistic Symbolism*, Dion Fortune's *The Mystical Qabalah*, and Aleister Crowley's recasting of Golden Dawn teaching material, *Liber 777*. Because many modern students of Hermetic Kabbalah tend to learn about the *sefirot* ground-up from these lists, there is a tendency to view the Tree of Life as an organisational structure, a kind of metaphysical dovecot in which related ideas roost and synergise together.

Tables run contrary to the historical spirit of Kabbalah. A table instantly creates the question "what is the correct entry", and in many cases there is no single correct entry. Texts can have many meanings, and part of the richness of Kabbalah is the demonstration that a well-known text with a long history of interpretation can have a radically new meaning. This precisely what one finds throughout the *Zohar*. Tables also create a fixation with parts, and there is a tendency to lose sight of the *gestalt*, the essential dynamic wholeness.

Nevertheless, the allusive richness of the entire scheme of correspondences has many positive qualities, especially from a theurgic perspective, and the author has perpetuated this aberration in later chapters.

4.9   View - Days of Creation

In the account of the creation given in *Genesis*, God makes the world in six days, and rests on the seventh. The six *sefirot* from *Chesed* to *Yesod* - *Chesed, Gevurah, Tiferet, Netzach, Hod, Yesod* are often grouped together. They are sometimes called the six directions, after the section in the *Sefer Yetzirah* where God seals the six directions of space with permutations of the divine name YHV. These are the six *sefirot* that constitute the body of *Ze'ir Anpin*. They are also called the 'six days', and represent the six days of creation, as depicted in Figure 13. *Malkhut* is the seventh day and Sabbath, the day of rest.

This view relates the *sefirot* to the book of *Genesis* and the Biblical account of creation. It deflects a possible criticism that the story of creation told by means of the Tree of Life is a different story.

The Hermetic Kabbalah

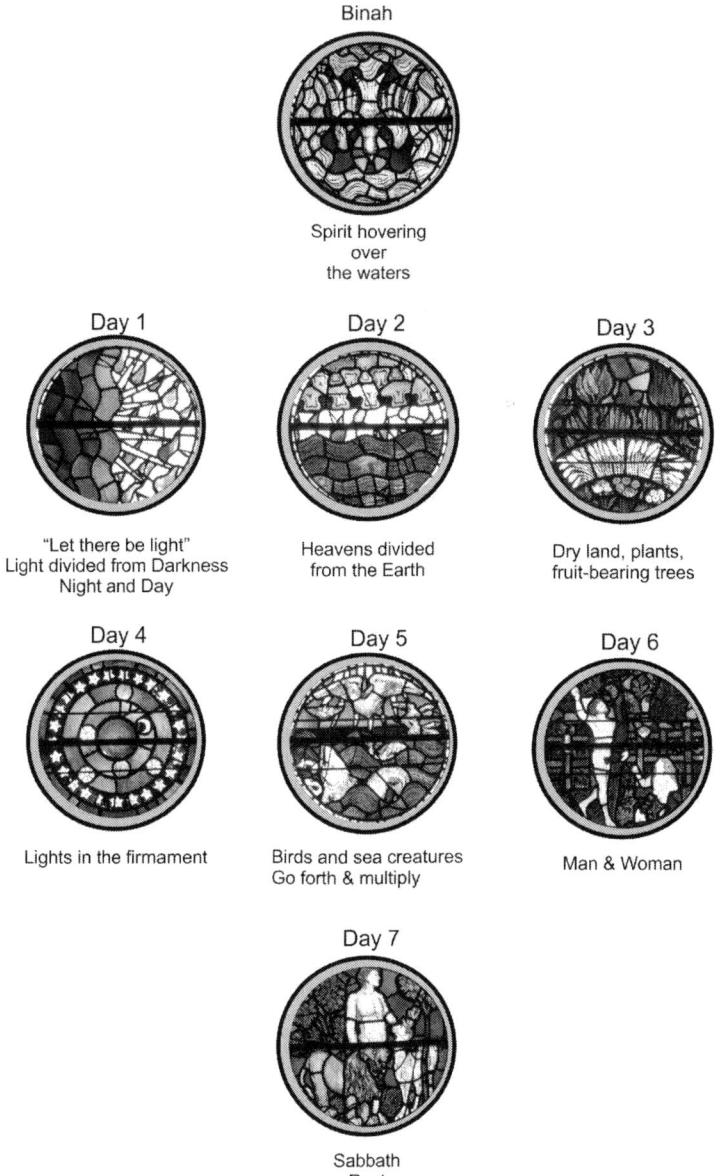

Figure 13: The *sefirot Chesed* to *Malkhut* as the Seven Days of Creation. Illustrations from stained glass in All Saints Church, Selsley: the *Seven Days of Creation* by William Morris and Philip Webb.

The Tree of Life

4.10 Summary

Many books on Kabbalah introduce the Tree of Life as a collection of parts, the *sefirot* flying in a loose formation like so many ducks. The emphasis of presentation is on the parts, not the whole.

The purpose behind this chapter is to introduce the Tree of Life as a *whole*, according to several differing traditional viewpoints, while saying almost nothing about the individual *sefirot*. This is consistent with tradition, which tends to focus on dynamics and interactions. However, a detailed description of individual *sefirot* can be found in Part Two.

The Hermetic Kabbalah

5

Partzufim

5.1 Introduction

Partzuf means a face or visage; it is sometimes translated as countenance, persona, personality or configuration. Probably the most accurate modern translation would be adopt the terminology of the Swiss psychologist C.G. Jung and translate it as 'divine archetype'. In the broadest approximation there are five *partzufim*: *Arikh Anpin, Abba, Imma, Ze'ir Anpin* and *Nukva*. Their relationship to the Tree of Life is shown in Figure 14. This relationship to the Tree of Life is more complex than one can easily depict; each *partzuf* corresponds to one or more *sefirot*, but each *partzuf* is also a complete Tree, because each *partzuf* is a complete configuration of living energy.

The *Partzufim* are central to some of the most complex and mysterious visionary descriptions in Kabbalah, and although their dynamics can be outlined briefly, the details as found in the *Zohar* and in the teachings of R. Isaac Luria are intense and bewildering, and require much study and meditation.

One can perhaps view them as the outcome of a collision of two alternative descriptions of the divine. The first was a Neopythagorean scheme of ten emanations grounded in the *Sefer Yetzirah*. The second, primarily anthropomorphic, was an attempt to unite various theophanies or visions of the divine found both in the *Bible* (the visions of the

The Hermetic Kabbalah

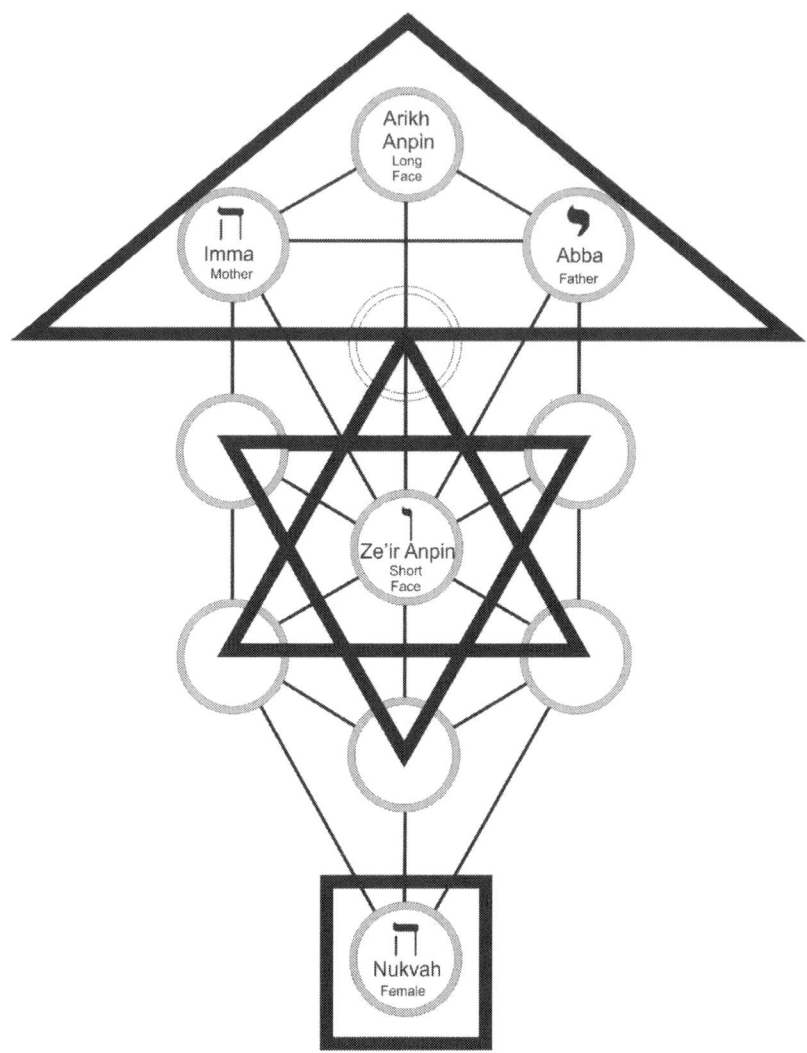

Figure 14: The *Partzufim* on the Tree of Life, showing the attribution of the divine name YHVH to the *sefirot*. The Father (Y) is in *Chokhmah*, the Mother (H) is in *Binah*, the Son (V, which also stands for the number 6) in *Tiferet*, and the Daughter (H) in *Malkhut*.

prophets described in the books of *Isaiah, Ezekiel* and *Daniel* were all important) and in various non-canonical apocalyptic texts such as the the three surviving *Enoch* texts, the *Apocalypse of Abraham*, the *Shi'ur Komah*, and other *Hekhalot* texts. The *Revelation* of St. John in the New Testament, although not a part of the Jewish tradition, contains many familiar elements in common with the theophanies of the period. A common feature of these theophanies is a description of the divine throne and the entities surrounding it.

An view of the divine as it presented itself to the medieval Jewish mystic contained three levels. There was a *transcendental* level characterised by remoteness and unknowability - this is represented by the upper triangle in Figure 14. There was an *immanent* level that came to be identified with the *Shekhinah*, God's presence in this world - this is represented by the lower square in Figure 14. Initially the *Shekhinah* was associated with the Ark of the Covenant and the Holy of Holies in the Temple, but from medieval times onward the *Shekhinah* is described as descending on any worthy person or group - the descent of the *Shekhinah* became a tangible experience.

Thirdly, there was the intermediate *visionary* level of the Throne of Glory as described in the theophanies. This is represented by the six-pointed star in Figure 14. The visionary level caused some discomfort. Were these visions of God, or of some intermediate being? Was this intermediate being a created angel such as *Metatron*? Could it be the giant Primordial Adam? According to R. Judah ben Samuel the Pious (1140-1217 CE), who was writing in Germany at approximately the same time as the beginnings of the Kabbalah in Provence, there was an intermediate aspect of God, an aspect of the Divine Glory (*kavod*), to whom prayers could be addressed:

> ... the Kavod has two "faces", one turned up toward the supreme Godhead and beyond human perception, and the lower one which is turned towards creation and serves as a focus for revelation. Yet the totality of the Kavod still retains its anthropomorphic characteristics, and the dimensions of God described in the ancient Hekhalot and *Shi'ur Komah* texts are attributed to it[22].

This threefold scheme of transcendent, intermediate or visionary, and immanent, is a wide-angle view of the *Partzufim*. The detail is considerably more complex. An early systematic treatment of the *Partzufim* is found in the *Zohar* in the sections known collectively as the *Idrot* (see 6.5); that is, the *Sefer de-Tzeniuta*, the *Idra Rabba*, and

---

22. *The "Unique Cherub" circle: A school of mystics and esoterics in medieval Germany*, Joseph Dan, Mohr Siebeck (1999)

the *Idra Zuta*.

The outline is presented in the *Sefer de-Tzeniuta*, a dense and cryptic midrash on the creation story of *Genesis*. Its title, usually translated as *The Book of Concealed Mystery* could not be more accurate. Perhaps the greatest mystery is why something so terse, enigmatic, elitist, and forbidding was written in the first place. The enigmatic hints in the *Sefer de-Tzeniuta* are expanded, firstly in the *Idra Rabba* (a description primarily of *Arikh Anpin*) and then in the *Idra Zuta* (the formation and dynamics of *Ze'ir Anpin*). The revelation of the content of the *Idra Zuta* coincides with an account of the death of R. Simeon bar Yochai, and is regarded as the most esoteric and sublime part of the *Zohar*.

5.2 Arikh Anpin

Arikh Anpin derives from *Exodus* 34:6 "And the Lord passed by before him, and proclaimed, YHVH, YHVH!, merciful and gracious, long suffering, and abundant in goodness and truth". The key phrase is *arikh appayim*, translated as 'long suffering' or 'slow to anger', but literally 'long of nose'[23]. It is usually translated as Long Face, or in Latin, Macroprosopus; the association is with patience, and the epithets merciful, gracious, goodness and truth. This is in contrast with *Ze'ir Anpin*, Short Face, Microprosopus, 'the Impatient' or quick to anger. While *Arikh Anpin* has only the quality of loving-kindness (*chesed*), *Ze'ir Anpin* is defined by judgement (*Din*).

Alternative titles for *Arikh Anpin* are *Atika Kadisha* (the Ancient Holy One) and *Atik Yomin* (the Ancient of Days). Originally the alternative titles appear to have been used as synonyms, but in time they were used to make subtle distinctions in the level of emergence and crystallisation from *En Sof*. *Arikh Anpin* is described as a vast head. The *Idrot* describe the cranium, the brain, hair, the beard, the nose, forehead, cheeks and lips of *Arikh Anpin* in considerable detail.

The hair and beard are white and luxurious, and precisely specified. The imagery would appear to derive from *Daniel* 7:9

> I watched till thrones were put in place,
> And the Ancient of Days was seated;
> His garment was white as snow,
> And the hair of His head was like pure wool.

Vast numbers of worlds depend on the influences emanating from

---

23. This is intended to convey the image of someone whose face is calm, as opposed to the grimace of an angry person.

every part of the Great White Head. In particular, thirteen streams of pure dew (thirteen aspects of Mercy) descend from *Arikh Anpin*; four of these are retained and nine descend and provide the influx that (how can one express this?) 'animates' *Ze'ir Anpin*. Although there are two eyes, they have the appearance of one, and only the right side (that is, the quality of Mercy) is seen. For this reason *Arikh Anpin* is sometimes depicted as a head seen in profile, the left side being hidden in *En Sof*. If the eye of *Arikh Anpin* were to close for an instant, the universe would cease to exist.

Arikh Anpin is the first crystallisation of the *En Sof*, and one of the most common epithets is 'concealed', or even 'concealed of the concealed'. This manifestation is identified with *Keter* on the Tree of Life. Much play is made with the idea of 'brains' concealed within the Great White Head, based around medieval ideas of physiology.

An internal aspect of *Arikh Anpin* is revealed as the *sefirot Chokhmah* and *Binah*, which manifest as the *Partzufim Abba* and *Imma*. *Abba* and *Imma* (Father and Mother) are an intermediate step in the manifestation of the child and son, or (alternatively) son and daughter.

5.3 Abba and Imma

A compact way to describe the *Partzufim* as they relate to *Ze'ir Anpin* is to imagine that each letter in the Tetragrammaton, the divine name of four letters, is a living being in its own right. Each Hebrew letter in YHVH is an irreducible part of the whole, but also has its own life in respect of its relationship to the other letters.

Yod is spelled *yod, vav, dalet*, that is, יו״ד. Put the *vav* and the *dalet* together and you get a *heh* ה. This shows how *yod* contains all the letters of the name of four letters. This also shows how *heh* has a *vav* 'inside' it. *Yod* represents the Father, and the seed that impregnates the mother *Heh*. The seed is born as *VavHe*, Son and Daughter, and *VavHe*, although two halves of one being, become separate *Partzufim* (a midrash contains the vivid image of them being sawed in half). *Binah*, the sefira of the Mother, is spelled BYNH, which can be rearranged as YH (Father and Mother) and *Ben* (the Son). An alternative title for *Binah*, *Tebunah* (also translated as 'understanding') can be rearranged to disclose Father - *Yod*, Mother - *Heh*, *Ben* - Son, and *Bat* - Daughter.

This kind of exposition (but more succinct, so terse it barely qualifies as exposition) is characteristic of the *Sefer de-Tzeniuta*. The overall picture is multi-dimensionally allusive and almost impossible to communicate, and perhaps with good reason - it is subversive, strange, and unexpected. At its heart is the creation of God against a background of destruction and the beginnings of cosmic evil. The Kings of Edom had no mates (they were unbalanced configurations) The first stable configuration of energy balanced male against female, and it is from this that the Son, *Ze'ir Anpin* emerges. *Ze'ir Anpin is God*. When I first understood this I thought that perhaps I had misunderstood. But I had not misunderstood: *Ze'ir Anpin*, is the Holy One, Blessed Be He, the God of Abraham, Isaac and Moses, the God of the *Bible*.

The Father and Mother sustain reality. Their *coitus* is eternal; were it to cease for a second, the illusion of reality would end.

5.4 Ze'ir Anpin

The Great White Head of *Arikh Anpin* is only a head. With *Ze'ir Anpin* we have a full male body. Where the hair and beard of *Arikh Anpin* are pure white, those of *Ze'ir Anpin* are black (*Song of Songs* 5:11):

> His head is pure gold -- fine gold,
> His locks flowing, dark as a raven ...

The *Sefer de-Tzeniuta* retains the long-standing ambiguity concerning the nature of this humanoid figure, playing with Exodus 15:3 "YHVH is a man (*ish*) of war". That is, YHVH, the name that expresses the nature of *Ze'ir Anpin*, 'is a man', and a source of judgement. There is a similar subtlety and evasiveness around the name *adam* (human). The great Jewish scholar Maimonides thought the *Shi'ur Komah* should be destroyed, and yet here in the *Zohar* we have the giant humanoid shape of God reappearing in an even more radical form.

The first word of *Genesis*, the first word in the entire *Bible*, is *bereshit* - 'In the beginning'. The *Sefer de-Tzeniuta* reinterprets this as *bara shit*, 'created six'. That is, *Elohim*, the name of God connected with *Binah* and the quality of judgement, 'created six'. The 'six' is the letter *vav* in the Tetragrammaton, which in Hebrew is used to represent the number 6. The 'six' is also the *sefirot Chesed, Gevurah, Tiferet, Netzach, Hod* and *Yesod*. These *sefirot* constitute the body and limbs of *Ze'ir Anpin*, as depicted in Figure 14.

Arikh Anpin is entirely *white*, the colour of *Chesed* and lovingkindness. The dominating character of *Ze'ir Anpin* is *Din*, judgement. Every phenomenon in the world that has a distinct, fixed and determinate aspect derives its nature through the quality of judgement.

Partzufim

The reality we experience is the outcome of a 'pulling-apart' that we characterise in various ways: a big bang, space, time, expansion, cooling, symmetry-breaking, causality, discreteness and isolation. We understand this 'beginning' in a different way than the writers of *Genesis*, but the essential story - that things were pulled apart and separated - remains the same.

Tradition views *Ze'ir Anpin* not only as demiurgic, but administrative, with an active role in reward and punishment. R. Moses Luzzatto explains[24]:

> As we have learned, Ze'ir Anpin is the measure of the Creator's judgement. It represents the root of the measure of judgement. Judgement is the result of the concealment of the Creator's goodness. But in the measure of judgement itself we may discern two types: first, severe judgement, which is wrath, contempt and abandonment; second, emended judgement, which is tempered judgement. Hence, Ze'ir Anpin embraces all the various aspects of judgement. When we analyse the progression of this judgement, we shall recognise it to be first of all, utter, severe judgement. Following that, we distinguish modification and a trace of emendation in it. Thereafter more modification and more emendation is presented until it becomes completely perfect.

The idea of a progression and emendation in judgement from severe to less severe may reflect the story of the extermination of life on Earth and God's covenant with Noah not to do it again. The traditional view is that sinfulness arouses the quality of judgement in *Ze'ir Anpin*, and righteous behaviour arouses the quality of loving-kindness. This dynamic is related to the relationship between the King (*Ze'ir Anpin*) and Queen (*Nukva*).

An important part of *Ze'ir Anpin* is his penis, represented by the sefira *Yesod*. The penis is sometimes described as a pillar; righteous behaviour causes the pillar to strengthen, an idea based on a sentence in the *Talmud (Hagiga 12b)* and expanded in the *Bahir*:

> We learned: There is a single pillar extending from heaven to earth, and its name is Righteous (Tzadik). [This pillar] is named after the righteous. When there are righteous people in the world, then it becomes strong, and when there are not, it becomes weak. It supports the entire world, as it is written, "And Righteousness is the foundation of the world." If it becomes weak, then the world cannot endure. Therefore, even if there is only one righteous person in the world, it is he who supports the world. It is therefore written, "And a righteous one is the foundation of the world."[25]

---

24. *General Principles of Kabbalah*, R. Moses Luzzatto, trans. Dr. Philip S. Berg, Research Centre for Kabbalah 1969

The causal connection between righteousness and the maintenance of the world is one of the more important ideas in Kabbalah.

5.5 Mother, Sister, Daughter, Bride, Queen

The final *Partzuf* of the five has many titles: mother, sister, daughter, bride, and queen are often used. Each title contributes a small part to a larger picture. The larger picture is that God's immanence is personified as a woman. This is a Kabbalistic innovation, and one of Kabbalah's most striking influences on Judaism.

The tangible presence of God in the world is called *Shekhinah*, a feminine noun which means presence or resting or indwelling. Prior to the medieval period *Shekhinah* meant simply God's immanent presence in the world. According to aggadic tradition the *Shekhinah* was originally fully manifest in the world, but the disobedience of Adam and Eve ruptured the flow of divine energy and the *Shekhinah* withdrew. The Biblical patriarchs caused a partial descent of the *Shekhinah* (it was pictured as riding on their backs) but it was not until the time of Moses and the Covenant between God and the Jewish people that the *Shekhinah* had a home in this world, resting between the two Cherubim on the Ark of the Covenant. The *Shekhinah* accompanied the Jewish people on their journeys, and found a permanent home with the building of the First (Solomonic) Temple.

When the second Temple was destroyed by the Romans in 70AD, the Holy of Holies was destroyed, and the Shekhinah no longer had a home. From the Kabbalistic (medieval) period onward the *Shekhinah* was depicted as being in exile with the Jewish people. Sometimes she was identified with Rachel weeping for her children (*Jeremiah* 31:15), and with the black-clad figure of Mother Zion.

During the early medieval period the *Shekhinah* was treated as identical with the divine Glory (*kavod*), an imminent, outward-facing aspect of God (in the sense of "The whole world is filled with his Glory"). However, there was still no sense of an internal relationship between aspects of God and the *Shekhinah*. It is in the early kabbalistic work, the *Bahir*, that God and the *Shekhinah* appear in relationship, usually in the form of allegories concerning a king and his daughter.

The evolution of the concept of God's immanent presence in the world towards a quasi-autonomous hypostasis within the divine

---

25. *The Bahir Illumination*, Aryeh Kaplan, Samuel Weiser 1979

Partzufim

Divine Syzygies in Kabbalah

A syzygy is male-female pair that may be regarded as a dual manifestation of a single being (or cause of being). Syzygies are commonplace in ancient cosmogonies, especially those that attempt to explain how structure and duality emerge from a single source. They can be found in Egyptian cosmogonies such as the Heliopolitan Ennead, and in many gnostic cosmogonies. The *Zohar* orients much of its discussion of divine dynamics around three pairs of syzygies.

The first pair is *Abba-Imma*, literally "Father and Mother". *Abba* and *Imma*, although exhibiting some degree of separation, exist in an eternal state of sexual union. If their coitus was interrupted for a moment, the universe would cease to exist. On the Tree of Life, *Abba* corresponds to *Chokhmah*, and *Imma* to *Binah*.

The second pair is *Ze'ir Anpin* and *Nukva Ze'ir*. *Ze'ir Anpin* is the son of *Abba* and *Imma*, and *Nukva* is simultaneously his emanation and their daughter. *Ze'ir* and *Nukva* sometimes embrace, and sometimes turn away from each other. The flow of divine energy from the higher to the lower worlds depends on the condition of their relationship. It is this pair that is most commonly associated with the *Song of Songs*, hence their epithets of King and Queen, or Groom and Bride. *Ze'ir Anpin* is associated with six *sefirot* on the Tree of Life (*Chesed, Gevurah, Tiferet, Netzach, Hod, Yesod*) and *Nukva* with *Malkhut*.

The third pair are Adam and Eve, the progenitors of the human race. Adam and Eve are initially one being (the Primordial Adam) that separates and then falls into a condition of complete separateness. It appears that the impetus for the metaphoric use of divine couples in Kabbalah derives from several ancient traditions about Adam and Eve merged with the symbolism of the *Song of Songs*.

Much of the discussion of syzygies in Kabbalah relates to the manifestation of separateness and evil. It is often unclear whether these ideas are being used allegorically, or relate to the literal existence of an intermediate level of reality (sometimes called a pleroma) that has a quasi-autonomous existence within the divine Glory (*kavod*).

pleroma is one of the most distinctive features of medieval Kabbalah.

The Kabbalistic traditions concerning the *Shekhinah* are complex and multi-faceted, and because they interconnect at so many points, they are difficult to dissect. However four key themes stand out:
- the *Shekhinah* as the *sefira Malkhut* in the Tree of Life.
- *Shekhinah* as a divine *Partzuf*, often called *Matronita* or *Nukva Ze'ir* (the female of *Ze'ir Anpin*)
- the *Shekhinah* as the divine archetype of Bride according to the imagery of the *Song of Songs*.
- the *Shekhinah* as Queen of Creation.

Shekhinah as Malkhut

The Tree of Life is a progressive emanation of divine being through ten emanations or *sefirot*. In traditional sources these emanations are represented as the active potencies of the names of God. The Tree of Life provides a template of energies and internal relationships that form the basis for the rest of the creation, usually represented in the form of Four Worlds. *Malkhut* is the final and tenth emanation in the Tree, and as such, is the interface between the dynamic energies of the Tree and the rest of creation.

It is necessary to understand the internal dynamics of the Tree to understand the role of *Malkhut*. A key insight is that the Tree is a dynamic between two kinds of manifestation, both of which are positive when properly balanced, and both of which are negative when unbalanced. These manifestations are judgement (*Din* - setting boundaries, defining limits, restriction, punishing wrongdoing) and mercy or loving-kindness (*Chesed* - blessings, love, grace, giving, abundance). Traditionally judgement is regarded as the more intrinsically negative of the two, because it represents a holding-back of divine love[26]. *Malkhut* is the full and final manifestation of these two tendencies, and so regulates the flow of divine energy to the rest of creation.

Our experience of the world is dominated by its harshness, its hardness, its unyielding abrasive quality. When I bump into the edge of a table it will hurt every time. When I touch the edge of the grill it will burn every time. Reality is not entirely abrasive. There is an elusive quality we call luck or providence, but our baseline for judging luck or providence is the near certainty of being hurt in so many situ-

---

26. However, it is also pointed out that an excess of mercy is a sanction for wrongdoing and evil.

ations. There is also kindness, a willingness to aid those who have fallen into misfortune - the quality Kabbalists call *Chesed*. We cannot ignore its importance in this world. Nevertheless, we recognise how close we stand to sickness, pain, poverty, death, and how close we are to the active and intelligent presence of evil. This is the traditional view of *Malkhut* - a little *Chesed*, a lot of *Din*. *Malkhut* provides life with a foothold into existence, but the price we have to pay is a harshness that we alleviate as best we can.

According to tradition a key influence is human behaviour. When human beings neglect their spiritual obligations, the positive aspect of *Malkhut*, the flow of *Chesed*, is choked-off, and so the harshness of judgement is the dominant experience. When human beings are kind and charitable and cognisant of the divine within, the opposite occurs and divine blessings and abundance flow into the creation. The character of *Malkhut* is, to an extent, determined by the moral and spiritual character of human beings.

In traditional literature this reciprocal relationship is used to explain historical events, such as the destruction of the Temple, and the Exile. On occasions when the conduct of human beings has been very bad, *Malkhut* has been drawn into the influence of the realm of the evil shells (unbalanced forces left over from the first failed attempts to manifest a stable configuration of *sefirot*) and the energy of *Malkhut* has then become demonically destructive. In this condition the *Shekhinah* is depicted as wearing the black clothes of *Lilith*, the evil demonic counterpart of the *Shekhinah*.

Many sources discuss two *Shekhinahs*[27]. This derives in part from the creation story of *Genesis* in which God divides the firmament into an upper firmament and a lower firmament. These are the waters above, and the waters below. In terms of the Tree of Life, the waters above refer to the *sefira Binah*, and the waters below to the *sefira Malkhut*. The waters flow from the great sea of *Binah* through the channels and emerge in *Malkhut*, often depicted as a spring of pure water (e.g. *Be'er Sheva*, the 'well of seven', referring to the seven *sefirot* flowing into *Malkhut*). Both *sefirot* share the epithet 'Mother': *Binah* is the superior Mother, and *Malkhut* the inferior (not in the derogatory sense) Mother. Sometimes *Binah* is called the 'mother of form'. *Binah* contains all the preconditions necessary for form. According to this viewpoint, *Malkhut* is the realisation, the completion of a process in which form becomes manifest.

---

27. properly, *Shekhinot*

This relationship and dynamic between *Binah* and *Malkhut* is also apparent in the divine name of four letters, YHVH. Both *Binah* and *Malkhut* are associated with the letter *heh*, so that there is a '*heh* above' and a '*heh* below'. *Binah* is at the head of the left-hand Pillar of Form/Severity, and manifests the quality of judgement in its archetypal form. *Malkhut* is the manifestation of that judgement. We experience the manifestation of judgement as the world we live in.

As the final *sefirot Malkhut* only receives - that is, *Malkhut* is the polar opposite of *Keter*, which only gives, and so is furthest from the divine ideal. For this reason *Malkhut* is "the mirror that does not shine", and so is black. And yet *Keter* and *Malkhut* are one, a paradox represented by the serpent that eats its tail.

Shekhinah as Nukva

In the system of divine archetypes known as *Partzufim*, the *Shekhinah* is equated to the *partzuf* known as *Nukva Ze'ir* (literally, 'the woman of *Ze'ir Anpin*'). The primary source for this imagery is the *Song of Songs*, as extensively interpreted by the *Zohar* and again by R. Isaac Luria. *Nukva* is Bride (*Kallah*, as in the *Song of Songs*) and Queen (*Malkah*) of the kingdom, which is *Malkhut*. Her colour is black - "I am black, but comely, O ye daughters of Jerusalem".

The central dynamic is that of the King and Queen (who are also Son and Daughter, and Groom and Bride). When they face each other in divine *conjunctio*, all the channels open and blessings (often depicted as a flow of pure spring water) flow into the world. When they turn away from each other the powers of evil are able to gain ingress. *Samael*, prince of evil, attempts intercourse with *Nukva* and she then becomes *Lilith*, his evil consort. At this time the *Shekhinah* is filled with darkness and terrible judgements flow into the world.

Some of the symbolism of *Ze'ir* and *Nukva* comes from the Sun and Moon, and shows an understanding of basic astronomy. The Moon has no light of her own, and is lit by the Sun. Each month the Sun 'withholds' his light and the Moon is darkened. This is equated to female menstruation, at which time, according to Jewish law, she is ritually impure and must stay apart (*niddah*). This complex of analogies is translated into the cosmic realms as an explanation of history: the cosmic Sun, which is *Ze'ir Anpin*, turns away from the cosmic Moon *Nukva*, and she is immersed in a realm of impurity in which evil has the upper hand. There are connections here with the Jewish lunar calendar and the monthly sanctification of the Moon (*Kiddush Levanah*).

Traditional Kabbalah contains many negative characterisations of women. The female is associated with the quality of *Din*, which in its pure form is evil. According to Jewish law women are impure for some part of each month - that is, they become a part of the realm of impurity. Purely biological metaphors - the emission of semen into a woman, pregnancy, birth, menstruation - are given a metaphysical dimension. Various social prejudices and perceptions from the medieval world are carried through into the modern world. The entire notion of the divine is tilted in favour of the male. The anthropomorphisms of the *Partzufim* provide a ready avenue for various kinds of deeply rooted and probably unintentional misogyny. I am aware of this, and for myself, I try not to confuse a map with the territory - that is, the *Partzufim* provide us with a map, and I do not lose sight of this.

Shekhinah as Bride and Queen of Creation

> Enter in peace O crown of her husband
> Even in gladness and good cheer
> Among the faithful of the treasured nation
> Enter O Bride, enter O Bride.
> Among the faithful of the treasured nation
> Enter O Bride, the Sabbath Queen.

Every Friday evening, the eve of the Sabbath, millions of Jews worldwide welcome the Sabbath Queen into synagogues and personal dwellings. The *Shekhinah*, the divine Glory and Holy Presence is welcomed in her dual aspect as Queen (*Malkah*) and Bride (*Kallah*). As Queen she is a stately presence, as Bride she is the centre of celebration and rejoicing. The verses above are from the final stanza of the *Lekha Dodi*, a song to welcome the Sabbath Queen composed in the sixteenth century by R. Solomon Alkabetz, teacher and brother-in-law of the great Kabbalist R. Moses Cordovero.

The *Zohar* is effusive in its praise of the Sabbath, saying "The Sabbath is equal in worth to the whole of the *Torah*, and whoever observes the Sabbath is like someone who observes the complete *Torah*". With regard to the preparations for the Sabbath Queen it observes:

> One must prepare a comfortable seat with several cushions and embroidered covers, from all that is found in the house, like one who prepares a canopy for a bride. For the Sabbath is a queen and a bride. This is why the masters of the Mishnah used to go out on the eve of Sabbath to receive her on the road, and used to say: 'Come, O bride, come, O bride!' And one must sing and rejoice at the table in her honour ... one must receive the Lady with many lighted candles, many

enjoyments, beautiful clothes, and a house embellished with many fine appointments ...'

The Sabbath is not only a day of rest, of celebration and worship - it is suspension of cosmic business. All the negative judgements flowing into the creation are suspended, the *Shekhinah* is freed from the power of the malign shells, and she is able to turn towards her husband and embrace him. Blessings flow into the world, and each person celebrating the Sabbath is gifted with an additional soul. It is considered a sacred duty for a husband and wife to join the supernal Sabbath Bride and Groom in consummating their relationship at midnight on the Sabbath Eve.

5.6 Later Developments

The anthropomorphism of the *Partzufim* provides an anchor for the narrative, mythological and visionary themes of the *Bible* in a way the *sefirot* do not, and they provide a natural story-telling device. The outline of the *Partzufim* as it appears in the *Zohar* was enormously elaborated by R. Isaac Luria in the sixteenth century, and the dramatic and catastrophic features were exaggerated. Some scholars have attributed this to the trauma of the Spanish expulsion (1492 CE) - Luria's theogonic drama provided an explanation for why God's chosen people were being subjected to the dominion of evil princes and terrestrial powers in a broken universe. The drama of the *Partzufim* became a metaphysical prehistory that defined the world we live in, and set the stage for the dramas of the present, in which human beings are not just inhabitants of a divine universe, but actors. This was a revolutionary shift in perspective.

Luria added many more levels and steps and processes which are not discussed here. He did not record his ideas himself, and his several pupils who did have left us with a vastly complex and baroque narrative of creation. His model has become the accepted interpretation of the core of ideas found in the *Idrot*, and modern treatments of the *Partzufim* tend to follow Luria, not the *Zohar*.

The gnostic aspects of the *Partzufim* have been observed by a number of scholars. These are apparent in the *Zohar*, and glaringly obvious in Luria's elaborations. There is a remote 'true' God (*Arikh Anpin*), a divine pleroma of syzygies (complementary male-female pairs), a cosmic catastrophe (death of the Kings/*Shevirah*), a demiurgic figure (*Ze'ir*), upper and lower female archetypes (*Malkhut/Binah*), a female figure (*Nukva/Shekhinah*) exiled in the domain of evil, and a redemptive relationship.

Partzufim

Figure 15: Jacob meets Laban and his daughters Leah and Rachel.

The redemptive relationship in early Christian gnosticism was that between Christ and Sophia; in Luria's system it is *Ze'ir* and *Nukva*. Luria makes extensive use of the story of Jacob (who corresponds to *Tiferet/Ze'ir*), his two wives Rachel and Leah, and father-in-law Laban, to explicate cosmic dynamics. Despite scholarly investigations, no link to the gnosticism of late antiquity has been uncovered, and we appear to be dealing with genuine archetypes.

The notion of the divine in the *Zohar* has the structure of a trinity. When parts of the literature of the Kabbalah began to be disseminated in translation during the Renaissance, Christian readers interpreted the figure of *Arikh Anpin* as God the Father; *Ze'ir Anpin* as the Son Jesus Christ; and the figure of *Nukva/Shekhinah* as the Holy Spirit. This was an exciting discovery, for it meant that Kabbalah proclaimed the truth of Christianity! This distortion became another weapon in the arsenal of those seeking to pressure Jews into converting to Christianity.

5.7 Further Reading

The *Partzufim* are such a deeply esoteric part of Kabbalah it is difficult to separate the medium from the message; that is, the *Idrot*, with their intricacy, ingenuity, allusion, drama and enigma are an inseparable part of the insights they attempt to convey. The English reader has been poorly treated in this respect, and throughout the twentieth century the only accessible translation was taken from the Latin of Knorr von Rosenroth's 1677 compilation *Kabbalah Denudata*:

The Kabbalah Unveiled, S.L. Macgregor Mathers, Routledge & Kegan Paul, 1970 (originally 1887).

Recently an excellent scholarly translation of the *Zohar* has become available, and both *Idra Rabba* (vol. 8) and *Sefer de-Tzeniuta* (vol. 5) are available with excellent commentaries:

The Zohar: Pritzker Edition, Daniel C. Matt, Stanford University Press 2003-2014 (edition incomplete at the time of writing).

For an insightful analysis of the messianic drama of the *Idrot* one can consult Liebes in:

Studies in the Zohar, Yehuda Liebes, State University of New York Press, 1993

For an organised digest of the *Zohar* with excellent section introductions and commentary:

The Wisdom of the Zohar, Fischel Lachower & Isaiah Tishby, Oxford University Press, 1990

For an extended discussion of published material on the *Zohar* available in translation refer to:

Notes on the Zohar in English, Don Karr, 1985-2014, http://www.digital-brilliance.com/contributed/Karr/Biblios/zie.pdf

To understand the complexity of the traditions behind Mother, Sister, Daughter, Bride, Queen, one can refer to

The Hebrew Goddess, Raphael Patai, Wayne State University Press, 1990

The narrative underpinning to the *Partzufim* was massively elaborated by R. Isaac Luria and recorded by his students in several not-entirely-consistent versions. Luria's Kabbalah speaks very directly to the experience of being Jewish, which may account both for its immediate popularity and a lack of accessible material in translation. A text which is in translation is:

Kabbalah of Creation: Isaac Luria's Earlier Mysticism, trans. Eliahi Klein, Aronson 2000

One can also consult the first volume of a translation of Hayyim Vital's famous *Etz Hayim*:

Tree of Life: Chayyim Vital's Introduction to the Kabbalah of Isaac Luria, V. 1, the Palace of Adam Kadmon, Hayyim Vital, trans. Donald Wilder Menzi & Zwe Padeh, Arizal Publications

Partzufim

2008

Some of R. Moshe Chaim Luzzatto's (1707-1746) explanations of Luria are in translation, and are valuable both for their insights and as historical documents in their own right:

General Principles of Kabbalah, R. Moses Luzzatto, trans Dr. Philip S. Berg, Research Centre of Kabbalah, 1969

The Kabbalah of the Ari Z'al, R. Moshe Hayim Luzzatto, trans. R. Raphael Afilalo, Kabbalah Editions 2005

The Hermetic Kabbalah

6

The Primordial Adam

> And above the expanse that was over their heads, like the appearance of a sapphire stone, was the likeness of a throne, and on the likeness of the throne, was a likeness *like the appearance of a man...*
> Ezekiel 1:26

6.1 Introduction

The Kabbalistic lore concerning the Heavenly Man, Adam Kadmon, the Primordial Adam, derives from the most ancient strata of Jewish mysticism. The full extent of this archaic lore is now lost to us, but remnants of related lore can be found in texts that derive from Egypt, from the Holy Land, from Syria and Eastern Turkey, from Iran, and from India. The most relevant and interesting survivals come from the intersection of Judaism, Hermeticism, Zoroastrianism, and Islam in a belt that stretched from the ancient city of Harran in Turkey, to the equally ancient city of Babylon in a region that was once called Chaldea, then Mesopotamia, and now Iraq.

A synthetic, composite outline of this lore might be composed as follows:

> In the beginning of all things, the first creation was a configuration of primordial light-energy with the 'shape' of a human being. This configuration was the archetypal pattern for all that followed. The pattern of

light-energy (or spiritual being) has many names, most of them secret. The most common name is Adam or Adamas, which in Semitic dialects means 'human being'. In Kabbalah a 'well-known' secret name for this energy is YHVH, or YHVH-ALHIM. In the gnostic *Pistis Sophia* the name is *Jeu* or IAO. Other names are the Heavenly Man, Primordial Adam, Light-Adam, Man of Light, Adamas, or Anthropos. The Primordial Adam is vast beyond comprehension and contains uncountable worlds of light. Adam is dual and androgenous - that is, considered in terms of human biology, Primordial Adam is neither male nor female, but both.

This being is the first emanation of an unknowable first cause. Just as we distinguish between the mind and body of a person, so we can think of the light-energy-Adam as the 'body' of a mind that is beyond our understanding. As a 'body' it can 'act', and its 'actions' are creative. This Adam has a dual nature, and as a consequence of this duality, it is demiurgic, and manifests worlds of duality.

There is an inherent structural instability within the light-energy-Adam. Although the archetype figure is eternal, it is infinitely mirrored and reflected and repeated within itself, like a fractal, so that it is both one and many. These fragments of light-energy-Adam are called 'souls', and the totality of their relationships is called the World (or Reality).

The Biblical story of the fall of Adam and Eve and their expulsion from Eden is sometimes interpreted as a secret teaching on the fall of souls into 'nature'. The Fall has a fractal or holographic quality - each soul manifests the pattern of the Primordial Adam. Souls 'fall' because they forget their origin.

Each soul retains its relationship with light-energy-Adam, and so it can, through secret knowledge or grace, retrieve the knowledge of its origin and reunite with its source.

Because the primordial Adam is the archetypal pattern for all that exists, knowledge of the 'parts' of Adam - eyes, ears, hair, beard, nose, lips, arms, fingers, torso, penis, legs - conveys great mystical and magical power. One might use this knowledge, for example, in a magical ritual to create a body of light for the soul, so that it might survive death.

The light-energy-Adam exists outside of time and fate and necessity. As a timeless being (s)he exists equally at the beginning and end of time, and has been linked to the end times in which evil powers will be subdued, and fallen souls redeemed to worlds of light. In this sense Adam becomes identified with the Messiah, or Christ, or the Gnostic Redeemer.

The sources for this lore are many. There are several Jewish *midrashim* (teachings) from late antiquity filled with curious lore about Adam that directly influenced later Kabbalah. Some can be found in

The Primordial Adam

the Hermetic lore of Hellenistic Egypt. More can be found in the ancient Iranian religion. It surfaces in many gnostic writings attributed to sects that are now nothing more than names. St. Paul writes as though he was familiar with the idea of a heavenly and earthly Adam. Some of this tradition survives to this day in an ancient baptismal sect, the Mandeans, whose history tells of a migration from the Jordan valley to the marsh region of Iraq in the vicinity of Basra. They maintain traditions of a giant heavenly Adam in a relatively pristine form[28].

6.2 Two Adams

In *Genesis* Adam is created twice. In *Genesis* 1:26-27 man is created, male and female, in the image of God. In *Genesis* 2:7 man is created from the dust of the earth. This provided fruitful material for speculation. The ancient *Bereshit Rabba*[29] records the suggestion that humankind possesses a dual nature, part celestial, part material:

> There were two formations, [one partaking of the nature] of the celestial beings, [the other] of earthly creatures. R. Joshua said in the name of R. Hananiah, and the Rabbis in the name of R. Eleazar: He created him with four attributes of the higher beings [i.e. the angels] and four of the lower creatures [i.e.beasts]. [His attributes of the lower creatures are]: he eats and drinks, like animals; procreates, like animals; excretes, like animals; and dies, like animals. [His celestial attributes are]: he stands upright, like the ministering angels; and speaks, understands, and sees, like the ministering angels. But does not a dumb animal see?

> This one [man] can see from the side. R. Tifdai said in R. Aha's name: The celestial beings were created in the image and likeness [of God] and do not procreate, while the terrestial creatures procreate but were not created in [His] image and likeness. Said the Holy One, blessed be He: "Behold, I will create him [man] in [My] image and likeness; [thus he will partake] of the [character of the] celestial beings, while he will procreate [as is the nature] of the terrestial beings" R. Tifdai [also] said in R. Aha's name: The Lord reasoned:

> "If I create him of the celestial elements he will live [for ever] and not die; while if I create him of the terrestial elements, he will die and not live [in a future life]. Therefore I will create him of the upper and the lower elements; if he sins he will die, and if he dies he will live [in the future life]"

The Alexandrian Jewish philosopher Philo (20 BCE - 50 CE) and

---
28. *The Secret Adam*, E.S. Drower, Oxford University Press 1960
29. *Midrash Rabba*, H. Freedman and Maurice Simon, Soncino 1961

The Hermetic Kabbalah

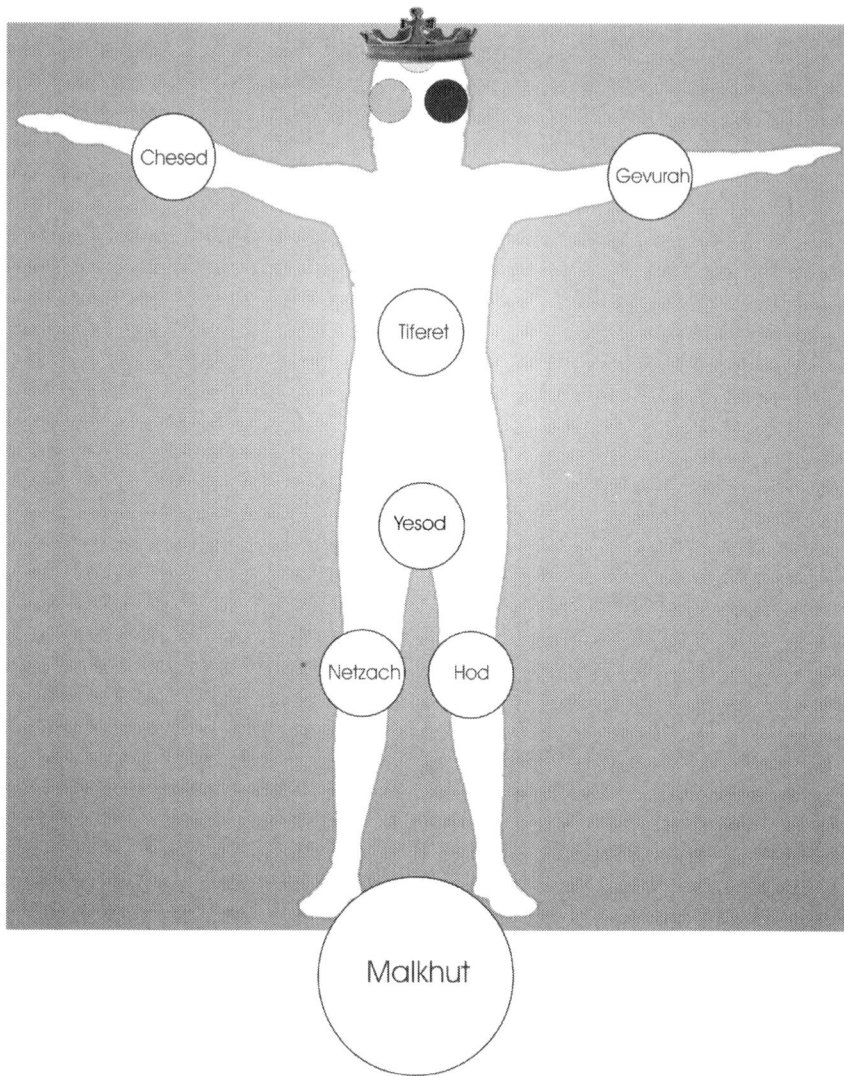

Figure 16: The Primordial Adam, Adam Kadmon. The *sefira* of *Keter* is the crown of the King. *Chokhmah* and *Binah* correspond to the cerebral hemispheres of the brain, and perhaps more properly to the mind. *Chesed* and *Gevurah* correspond to the right and left arm respectively, *Tiferet* to the trunk, *Yesod* to the genitals, and *Netzach* and *Hod* to the right and left legs. Note that the figure faces *into* the Tree, to place the left side of the Tree and the left side of the body into correspondence. The human figure is shown standing on *Malkhut*.

The Primordial Adam

St. Paul (5 CE - 67 CE) were both familiar with speculations of this type, and attest to the antiquity of these ideas. In *Corinthians* 15:45 Paul plays with these ideas of an earthly and a spiritual Adam:

> And so it is written, The first man Adam was made a living soul; the last Adam was made a quickening spirit.
>
> Howbeit that was not first which is spiritual, but that which is natural; and afterward that which is spiritual.
>
> The first man is of the earth, earthy; the second man is the Lord from heaven.
>
> As is the earthy, such are they also that are earthy: and as is the heavenly, such are they also that are heavenly.
>
> And as we have borne the image of the earthy, we shall also bear the image of the heavenly.
>
> Now this I say, brethren, that flesh and blood cannot inherit the kingdom of God; neither doth corruption inherit incorruption.

Another variant of the 'two Adams' theme is that initially Adam was a vast luminous being brighter than the sun who filled the whole of creation. The angels were alarmed to find such a powerful being, and went to God saying 'there are two powers, one in Heaven and one in Earth' and so God shrunk Adam[30].

Later Judaism would become uneasy about an early stratum of tales dominated by a vast, creative light-being in the shape of a human being. Was it God? Just what was that figure with the likeness of a man seated on the throne-chariot in the vision of Ezekiel?

The theophanic vision of a figure on the Throne of Glory was a staple of early Jewish prophetic vision and mysticism ... but what was seen? If it was not God, what kind of entity was it? This was an important point of speculation in select Jewish circles in early thirteenth century Europe[31]. The verses from *Isaiah* 6:3,

> And one cried unto another, and said, Holy, Holy, Holy, is the LORD of hosts: the whole earth is full of his glory

suggested that there was something outside of God, his Glory (*Kavod*), and medieval German pietists, the Ashkenazi Chassidim, saw the figure on the throne as the visible externalisation of God's Glory.

And who made the world? There exist untidy and fragmentary scraps of legend that suggest an intermediate being - *yotzer bereshit*,

---

30. *Tree of Souls - The Mythology of Judaism*, Howard Schwartz, Oxford University Press, 2004.
31. *The "Unique Cherub" Circle: A school of mystics and esoterics in medieval Germany*, Joseph Dan, Mohr Siebeck 1999

the creator of the beginning - did the heavy lifting. Sometimes this demiurgic being was an archangel such as *Metatron*, or *Akhatriel*, or *Yahoel*, or *Michael*, or *Anafiel*, but sometimes it was Adam, the divine regent. The suspicion of heresy was later removed by editing the tales to show the intermediate being diminished or crippled. For example, it was stated that angels cannot sit, and so it could not be an angel on the Throne of Glory. When the mystic Elisha ben Avuyah saw *Metatron* on a throne and mistook him for God, *Metatron* received sixty lashes with rods of fire to show he was only a servant.

The contemporaneous gnosticism of late antiquity was less restrained, and Adam or Adamas or *Jeu* or Anthropos was seen to be a vast secondary *aeon* intermediate between a remote god and the world. Something similar to this idea is still preserved in Kabbalah in the form of the *partzuf* of *Ze'ir Anpin* (see *Partzufim* on page 43).

According to ancient tradition the Primordial Adam was dual in another sense, a sense that is both appropriate and perhaps unexpected. It is that Adam was both male and female combined[32]:

> When the Holy One, blessed be He, created Adam, He created him an hermaphrodite [bisexual], for it is said, male and female created He them and called their name Adam (Gen. 5:2). R. Samuel b. Nahman said When the Lord created Adam He created him double-faced, then He split him and made him of two backs, one back on this side and one back on the other side.

6.3 The Shi'ur Komah

Medieval Kabbalists were intensely interested in the structure and dynamics of the 'world behind the world' - that is, the super-celestial realm of the divine throne and the various angelic functionaries surrounding it. They had at their disposal canonical texts, such as the *Bible* and the *Talmud*, and in these they found the canonical theophanies - those of Moses, Isaiah, Ezekiel, and Daniel for example.

The *Talmud* contains a terse mention of the four who entered paradise, a fragmentary allusion to a secret visionary tradition that existed in Palestine at about the same time as the first generation of Christian apostles - that is, the latter half of the first century CE. This period was so fascinating and important to medieval Kabbalists that both the *Zohar* and the *Bahir* were written as if they were authentic works of the period, and feature historical characters. They present themselves as mystical revelations from the sages of that time handed

---

32. *Midrash Rabba*, H. Freedman and Maurice Simon, Soncino 1961

The Primordial Adam

down in secret. Many orthodox Jews continue to believe this, and challenge scholarly opinions to the contrary.

Medieval Kabbalists did possess a number of genuine esoteric texts from that time period. They are often difficult to date, but are typically in the range of 100BCE to 500CE. The *Sefer Yetzirah* is an example of a cosmogonic work. In the *Hekhalot* texts the central feature is an ascent through the heavenly realms and a vision of the Throne of Glory. Several of these mystico-magical texts would appear to have been preserved into the medieval period by Jewish families living in the Rhineland. These texts, preserving the remains of an earlier stratum of Jewish mysticism, were of extraordinary interest.

One small collection of fragments is called the *Shi'ur Komah* - 'the measure of the body'. In one fragment the narrator, a famous Tannaitic sage called Rabbi Ishmael, receives part of the experience from the angel *Metatron*; the rest would appear to be visionary and it enumerates the parts, the dimensions and the secret names of a vast humanoid figure. The figure is associated with the Throne of Glory and is named as *El*. The figure would seem to be the God of the *Bible*, something that caused great unease, as the *Shi'ur Komah* comes close to a depiction of God, and idolatry. The great Egyptian rabbi Moses Maimonides believed it was a forgery and expressed his belief that it

> ... would be a highly meritorious deed to snuff out this book and destroy all memory of it[33].

Despite this opinion one finds detailed descriptions of vast human figures occurring in some of the most mysterious portions of the *Zohar*. The most extraordinary thing about *Shi'ur Komah* is the inclusion of substantial quotations from the *Song of Songs*. Of all the texts in the Bible, why the *Song of Songs*?

6.4 The Song of Songs

The early Christian theologian Origen (184-253 CE) quarrelled with his bishop in Alexandria and moved to Caesarea in Palestine. He was acquainted with local Jewish teachers, and when he wrote the first Christian commentary on the *Song of Songs* he followed Jewish tradition and interpreted it as an allegory of the love of the community (in his case Christian) towards God. In the prologue to his commentary he wrote[34]:

> It seems to me that this little book is an *epithalamium*, that is to say, a

---

33. *The Mystical Shape of the Godhead*, Gershom Scholem, Schocken 1991

The Hermetic Kabbalah

marriage song, which Solomon wrote in the form of a drama and sang under the figure of the Bride, about to wed and burning with heavenly love towards her Bridegroom, who is the word of God.

He was also familiar with another tradition of interpretation:

It is said that the custom of the Jews is that no one who has not reached full maturity is permitted to hold this book [i.e. the *Song*] in his hands. And not only this, but although their rabbis and teachers are wont to teach all the scriptures and their oral traditions to the young boys, they defer to the last the following four texts: The beginnings of *Genesis*, where the creation of the world is described; the beginning of the prophecy of *Ezekiel*, where the doctrine of the angels is expounded; the end [of the same book] which contains the description of the future temple; and this book of the *Song of Songs*[35].

One thousand years later and the list had not changed: *Genesis*, *Ezekiel* and the *Song of Songs* - any medieval Kabbalist would have understood the significance.

Taken at face value, the *Song of Songs* appears to be a compilation of erotic poetry of indeterminate age. Its traditional association with King Solomon might place it as far back as 900BC. It is a strange document, simultaneously beautiful, moving, erotic, and enigmatic. In places it is disjointed, in others repetitious, as if verse fragments have been deleted and other fragments copied and transposed. Some sections are connected and sustained. It is written in the first person, but the viewpoint is female one moment and male the next. Attempts to ascribe an overall meaning are unconvincing - we do not know whether it is a complete work, a complete work that has become jumbled, a single work with portions missing, or a collection of fragments from complete works now lost.

The world it evokes is one of fixation with the beloved, a youthful love filled with a passionate intensity. Everything in the sensual world leads back to the beloved, even a sight as unlikely as a flock of goats or sheep. There is a backdrop of luxury: precious stones, metals, fragrances, spices, wine, food, time. The *Song* expresses an overwhelming and unreasonable passion - there is nothing measured about it.

Set me as a seal upon thine heart, as a seal upon thine arm: for love is strong as death; jealousy is cruel as the grave: the coals thereof are coals of fire, which hath a most vehement flame. Many waters cannot quench love, neither can the floods drown it: if a man would give all

---

34. Origen, the Song of Songs Commentary and Homilies, trans. R. P. Lawson, Longmans, Green 1957
35. *Jewish Gnosticism, Merkabah Mysticism, and Talmudic Tradition*, Gershom Scholem, The Jewish Theological Seminary of America, 1960

Bride and Groom

Christian and Jewish mysticism draw from many of the same texts and traditions and so it is hardly surprising that sometimes they share similar ideas. For example, St. Paul envisaged Adam and Christ as duals, the one leading humankind into mortality through sin, the other leading humankind into eternal life through sacrifice. He even refers to Jesus (1 *Cor.* 15:47) as the "Last Adam".

As the Divine Son, Jesus Christ is a spiritual intermediary occupying a similar place to the *Ze'ir Anpin* in Kabbalah. Many Christian interpretations of Kabbalah place Christ in *Tiferet* (with the divine name YHShVH) in a manner that has many parallels with the Jewish tradition. There are also parallel traditions concerning the *Song of Songs*.

The symbolism of the Bride and Groom comes directly from passages in the New Testament. In a traditional Jewish marriage the groom first enters into a covenant with the bride and her family, and then, after a period of time that can last several months (during which the bride prepares for marriage) the groom returns and claims the bride. Christ is the Groom, and the Christian community is the Bride - hence the well-known phrase "Bride of Christ". This is interpreted in terms of the second coming of Jesus, who comes to claim his bride.

Christian mystics have interpreted this more directly and personally, viewing themselves as the Bride. For example, St. Bernard of Clairvaux (1090-1153 CE) writes in his extensive commentary on the *Song of Songs*:

"With good reason then I avoid trucking with visions and dreams; I want no part with parables and figures of speech; even the very beauty of the angels can only leave me wearied. For my Jesus utterly surpasses these in his majesty and splendour. Therefore I ask of him what I ask of neither man nor angel: that he kiss me with the kiss of his mouth."

the substance of his house for love, he would be utterly despised.

It is unclear why the *Song of Songs* became part of the sacred canon. Modern commentators agree that it is likely to be exactly what it appears to be: erotic poetry. Nevertheless, at the time of Origen it was being read allegorically by Jewish commentators, who interpreted it as an allegory of God's love for the people of Israel. Origen gave this allegorical interpretation a Christian gloss and published his own commentary, establishing the *Song* as a classic of Christian mysticism (see *Bride and Groom* above).

Origen's observation that its study was restricted suggests there was another tradition of interpretation, something more controversial, something for the select few. In the *Talmud* it says defensively:

R. Akiva declared, "Heaven forbid that any man in Israel ever disputed that the *Song of Songs* is holy. For the whole world is not worth the day on which the *Song of Songs* was given to Israel, for all the Writings are holy and the *Song of Songs* is the holy of holies."

R. Akiva, who was contemporaneous with the first generation of Christians following the death of Jesus, is one of the most famous figures in the Jewish mystical tradition. He is a leading figure in traditions concerning a generation of Jewish sages who were able to ascend through the worlds and the heavenly palaces to behold, seated upon the Throne of Glory, the appearance of a Man (literally, Adam). Akiva's disciple was R. Simeon bar Yochai, reputed author of the *Zohar*.

Scholem[36] connects this secret tradition with the *Shi'ur Komah*, a text where the *Song of Songs* is quoted directly, and it is clear that the lyrical description of the male lover, the bridegroom, is the likeness of God:

His cheeks are like a bed of roses
As banks of sweet herbs;
His lips are as lilies,
Dropping with flowing myrrh.
His hands are as rods of gold, set with beryl.
His body is as polished ivory, overlaid with sapphires.
His legs are as pillars of marble,
Set upon sockets of fine gold.
His aspect is like Lebanon,
Excellent as the cedars.
His mouth is most sweet.
Yea, He is altogether lovely.
This is my beloved, and this is my friend,
O daughters of Jerusalem

---

36. *The Mystical Shape of the Godhead*, Gershom Scholem, Schocken 1991

The Primordial Adam

We can perhaps begin to appreciate the unease that filled Moses Maimonides, why he wanted to snuff out the *Shi'ur Komah*. His unease was acknowledged and ignored: the tradition continued into the medieval period, so that the *Song of Songs* would become one of the foundational texts of Kabbalah.

6.5 The Idrot

The *Zohar* contains two unusual texts, the *Idra Rabbah* ('Greater Assembly') and the *Idra Zuta* ('Lesser Assembly'), and a third text often associated with them, the obscure and mysterious *Sepher de-Tzeniuta* ('Book of Concealed Mystery').

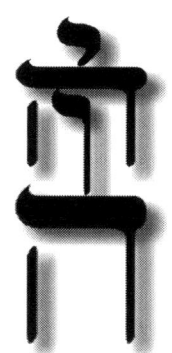

Figure 17: The letters of the Tetragrammaton form the shape of Adam. According to gematria the letters *yod, he, vav, he*, written in full and added together, sum to 45, the same as Adam (*Zohar*).

The word *Idra* (plural *idrot*) comes from the Aramaic for a threshing floor. The *Greater* and *Lesser Assemblies* are works of high drama in which the Rabbi Simeon bar Yochai and his closest disciples gather together to present the most secret mysteries at a level of consciousness so high that their descriptions trigger changes in the upper worlds. This connection is so direct that in the *Greater Assembly* three of the disciples die in a condition of mystical ecstasy. One could liken their actions to bringing together high-tension power lines. In the *Lesser Assembly* Shimon bar Yochai also dies.

Arthur Green describes the *Idrot* as the "most radically anthropomorphic section of the *Zohar*"[37]. Much of the discussion relates to vast human 'appearances', with a special emphasis on the faces, hair and beard. The *Idrot* and the *Sepher de-Tzeniuta* signal the appearance of the *Partzufim*, one of the most recondite aspects of Kabbalah, and one that would reverberate like a giant bell when it was given a radical reworking in Safed by the great Kabbalist R. Isaac Luria. Again, one finds many references to the *Song of Songs* throughout the *Idrot*.

As the 'appearances' or *Partzufim* are discussed in the previous

---

37. *A Guide to the Zohar*, Arthur Green, Stanford University Press, 2004

chapter, this section is merely a place holder for the more complete presentation in Chapter 5.

6.6 R. Isaac Luria

According to tradition, the cosmogonic teachings of R. Isaac Luria (1534-1572CE) are a consequence of deep and sustained meditation upon the *Zohar*, and in particular, the *Idrot*. His mystical insights and interpretations have been widely accepted within Judaism, to the extent that Kabbalah, as it is expounded in modern Jewish circles, tends to follow his insights.

According to Luria the first divine act was a withdrawal of light (*tzimtzum*) to create an empty space (*hallal*) which was then penetrated by a ray of light (*kav*). This produced the first crystallisation of light-energy in the form of the primordial man.

This was an exceedingly remote crystallisation within the *En Sof*, and from this light-crystallisation four light-impulses came forth, from the eyes, ears, nose and mouth of the primordial light being. These new configurations would eventually form the prototypes for four energy configurations corresponding to four articulations of the divine name of four letters, and correspond to the energy configurations of Father, Mother, Son and Daughter. However, as this stage precedes the shattering of the vessels, and precedes any stable energy configuration, we should see these light-impulses as transient energy dynamics - they are like embryonic prefigurations of the *Partzufim*.

Luria's cosmogony can best be described as visionary, and so its immense complexity and many stages of development are difficult to grasp outside of mystical vision. His Primordial Adam is more remote and abstract than the Primordial Adam of earlier speculations.

6.7 Run and Return

A consequence of the congruence between the greater and lesser Adams - that is, the giant primordial Adam and the individual human being - are practical exercises using the microcosmic Tree of Life. The *sefirot* are imagined superimposed on the body, and awakened by vibrating the appropriate divine names. These practices have some similarities to Kundalini Yoga, and were probably inspired by it.

A well-known method for doing this is called the Middle Pillar exercise. It is described online and in many books following the Golden Dawn tradition[38] and so it is only outlined here.

The Middle Pillar exercise is an example of the way in which the

The Primordial Adam

formula of 'run and return' can be used. An impulse of light is brought down from *Keter* (imagined as being at the crown of the head) and moved down the middle pillar of the Tree of Life, where it intersects and energises each *sefira/nexus* on the Pillar -that is, *Keter*, *Da'at*, *Tiferet*, *Yesod* and *Malkhut*. These are superimposed on the body and aligned approximately with the spine. A divine name is vibrated in each *sefira* as the light moves down. The light is then circulated up the Middle Pillar from *Malkhut* and returns to *Keter*. It is important to circulate the light, creating a complete circuit between *Keter* and *Malkhut* with the human body as the bridging element.

It is possible to create other exercises along these lines; for example, each of *Hod-Netzach*, *Gevurah-Chesed* and *Chokhmah-Binah* have a path crossing the Middle Pillar and these can be added making seven (or eight, depending on whether *Da'at* is used) focal points on the Middle Pillar. In this form it is similar to the better-known *chakras* in yoga.

6.8 Further Reading

There are books so filled with detail, insight, relevance and clarity that they inspire a kind of devotion. I feel this about most of Scholem's writing, but this collection of essays in particular goes straight to the heart of some of the most profound ideas in Kabbalah:

On the Mystical Shape of the Godhead, Gershom Scholem, Schocken 1991

The *Idrot* are difficult texts, and an insightful companion text is this extended essay that throws light on the events that take place during the disclosure of the most sacred mysteries of the Upper Worlds, events that culminate in the death of R. Simeon bar Yochai:

The Messiah of the Zohar: On R. Simeon bar Yohai as a Messianic Figure, in *Studies in the Zohar*, Yehuda Liebes, State University of New York 1993.

The next reference is not about Kabbalah but should be on the reading list of anyone interested in the most ancient and recondite traditions in Kabbalah. Drower's *The Secret Adam* is like a lost treasure from the ancient world, an authentic record of Mandean gnosticism pieced together from a disappearing culture.

The Secret Adam: A Study of Nasoraean Gnosis, E. S. Drower,

---

38. For example, *Circles of Power,: Ritual Magic in the Western Tradition*, John Michael Greer, Llewellyn 1997

The Hermetic Kabbalah

Oxford University Press 1960

7

The Four Worlds

Kabbalah contains the idea of a chain of four worlds. These are *Atzilut*, the world of emanation, *Briah*, the world of creation, *Yetzirah*, the world of formation, and *Assiah*, the world of action or making. They are sometimes referred to using the acronym A'B'Y'A'.

The Kabbalistic notion of four worlds employs space to represent important distinctions. Kant suggested that space and time are pure forms of intuition, which means that all knowledge and experience is necessarily represented within the context of space and time. Space is a natural intuition. The important question is: what is space being used to represent? There are three recurring themes, mixed in various combinations, themes that might be termed the literal, the spiritual and the cognitive.

The *literal* view is derived from ancient cosmogonies that viewed the realm of the divine as a real place that could be reached by travelling upwards (although paradoxically the *Merkavah* mystics travelled down). There was a sub-lunary realm, the spheres of the planets, the fixed stars, and then various divine realms. The divine realm was structured into heavens, or experienced as the palace of a king that had to be negotiated in a manner somewhat like the protagonist in Kafka's *The Castle*. In this view the four worlds are an organisation of real space.

The *spiritual* view is well-expressed by R. Ashlag[39] when he observes that distance in spiritual realms is expressed by similarity of form. Things are close when they are similar, and far apart when they are different. He gives an example contrasting two extremes: the first is 'giving', an energy that is directed entirely outwards, and the second is 'receiving for oneself alone', an energy that is directed entirely inwards.

God is entirely giving, and dead things or inanimate objects are entirely receiving. Distance from God can then be expressed in terms of a mixture of giving and receiving, which translates into a collection of related polarities: charity and selfishness, love and anger, selflessness and narcissism, holy and impure, life and death, good and evil. *Keter* represents the quality of pure giving and *Malkhut* represents the quality of receiving. Using this model of spatiality, the four worlds are strung out like four Trees of Life, with the *Keter* of one Tree overlapping the *Malkhut* of another.

The *cognitive* view derives from Neoplatonism, which also recognises four worlds or realms: The One, The Intelligible or Divine Intellect, the World Soul, and Matter (see Figure 19).

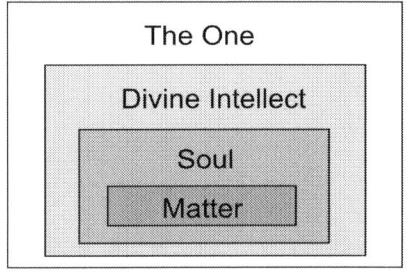

Figure 19: A layering of reality following Plotinus. Each level corresponds to a narrower view of the totality, as if one was seeing the world through a slot. This narrowing of view is also associated with forgetting.

The basis for this view is the observation that the reality we perceive depends on our capacity for organising and structuring perception. An animal can observe what human beings do, but is excluded from the entire cultural sphere because it lacks language. A person can be fluent in the human cultural sphere and still have no contact with the realm of the Intelligible (which was closely associated with pure mathematics and direct, timeless apprehension of truth).

According to this interpretation the four worlds are aspects of attention, where one can choose to attend to the external world of sense impressions, to the internal world of human culture, to the world of pure forms and ideals, or to the undifferentiated One. This view is close to that of the philosopher Plotinus, and has modern

---

39. *In the Shadow of the Ladder, Introductions to Kabbalah*, R. Yehudah Lev Ashlag, trans. Mark Cohen & Yedidah Cohen, Nehora Press 2002

The Four Worlds

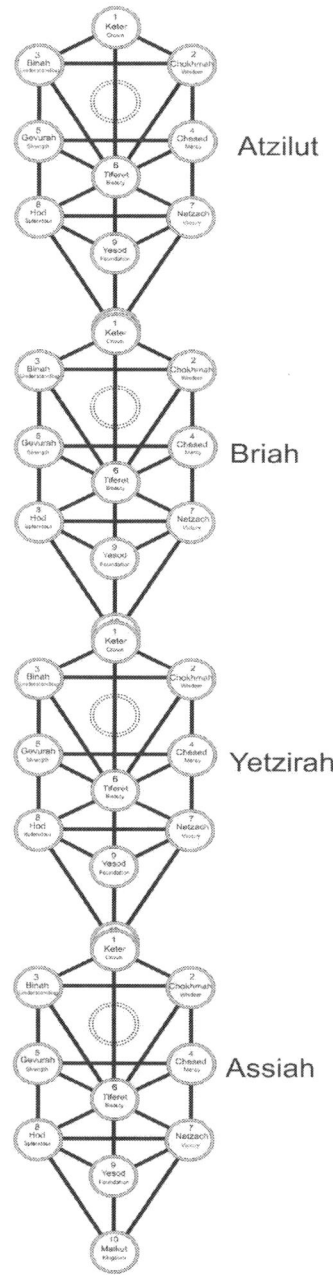

Figure 18: The Four Worlds depicted as four Trees laid end-to-end.

adherents such as the philosopher Ken Wilber, who posits seven levels of cognition[40]. This view overlaps with representations of the soul - see *Soul* on page 105.

The most consistent and enduring interpretation of distance/space in Kabbalah is the spiritual one, although one finds clear evidence of the cognitive view derived from Plotinus or Aristotle, or the literal view of the *Merkavah* mystics. The spiritual view distinguishes between that which is 'most like God', and that which is 'most unlike God' (and so had to be created). That which is most unlike God is a realm of impurity within the creation, and although it is part of the overall scheme of things, it should be avoided.

Various commandments (*mitzvot*) within Jewish law can be interpreted as prohibitions on contact with the realm of impurity. A person who follows the impulses of the animal soul and sins frequently through contact with the realm of impurity is a *rasha*, an evil person. A person who tries to follow the commandments but who sins occasionally and repents is a *beinoni*, an average person. A person who is able to avoid sin entirely, even in thought, is a *tzaddik*, a righteous one or saint. This view, from the *Tanya* of R. Shneur Zalman[41], is probably the dominant view of spirituality in modern Jewish Kabbalah, and gives us a sense of what the spatiality of the four worlds represents - it represents distance from the divine.

A traditional view of the occupants of the four worlds[42] is that *Atzilut* contains the realm of the *sefirot*, *Briah* contains the Throne of Glory, the seven Palaces and the powers of the Chariot (*Merkavah*), *Yetzirah* is the abode of *Metratron* and the angels, and *Assiah* is the physical world of the planets and the elements, this planet Earth, human beings, and the habitation of the husks and shells (*klippot*).

This stratification shares a great deal with contemporary Christian and Islamic culture, where similar schemes derived from the philosophy of late antiquity can be found - see *Ascent* on page 115. There is also a correspondence with the parts of the soul: the *Neshamah* corresponds to *Briah*, the *Ruach* to *Yetzirah* and the *Nephesh* to *Assiah* - see *The Soul* on page 105.

In addition to the linear representation of the Four Worlds (see Figure 18), there are alternative representations, shown below. Two

---

40. Sex, Ecology, Spirituality, Ken Wilber, Shambhala 2000
41. *Opening the Tanya*, R. Adin Steinsaltz, Jossy-Bass 2003
42. See Tishby's commentary in *The Wisdom of the Zohar*, Fischel Lachower & Isaiah Tishby, Oxford University Press, 1990

The Four Worlds

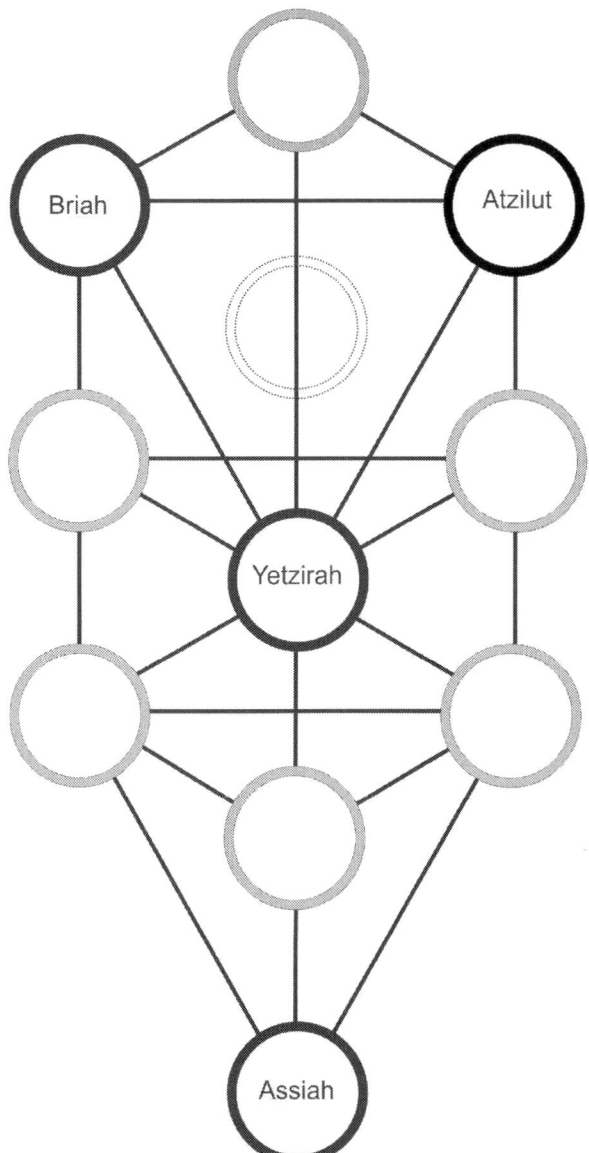

Figure 20: A traditional view of the Four Worlds mapped onto the *sefirot*. Following the Kabbalistic holographic principle, each of the Four World maps onto the Tree, but each world is a full Tree in its own right.

The Hermetic Kabbalah

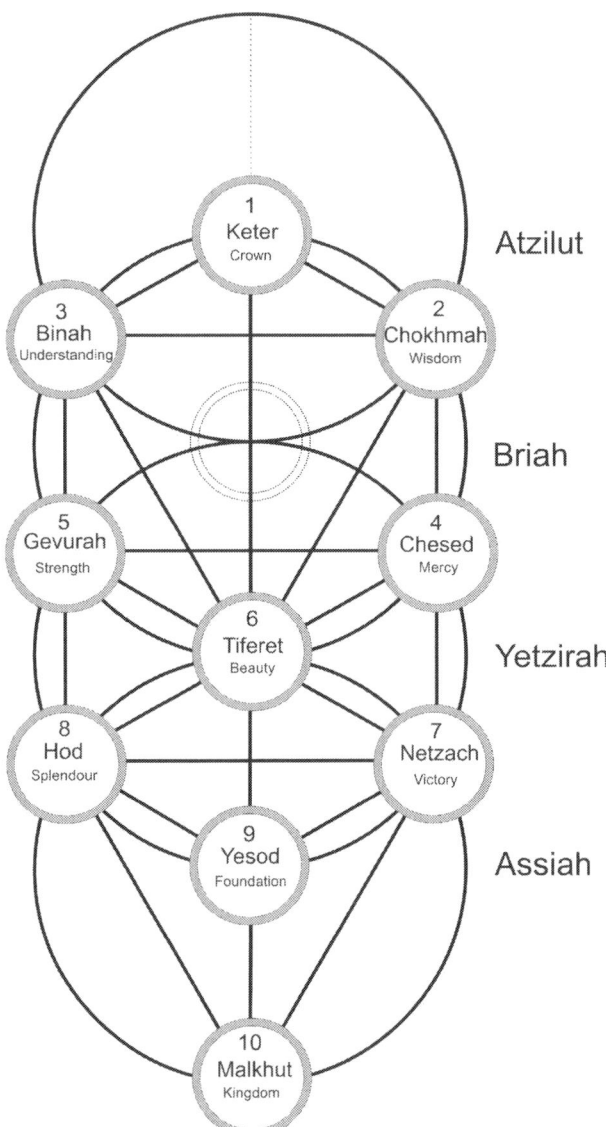

Figure 21: An alternative modern view of the Four Worlds mapped onto the Tree. This view follows the construction of the Tree as four adjoining circles, and shows the worlds overlapping and interpenetrating, a view shared with the Extended Tree.

The Four Worlds

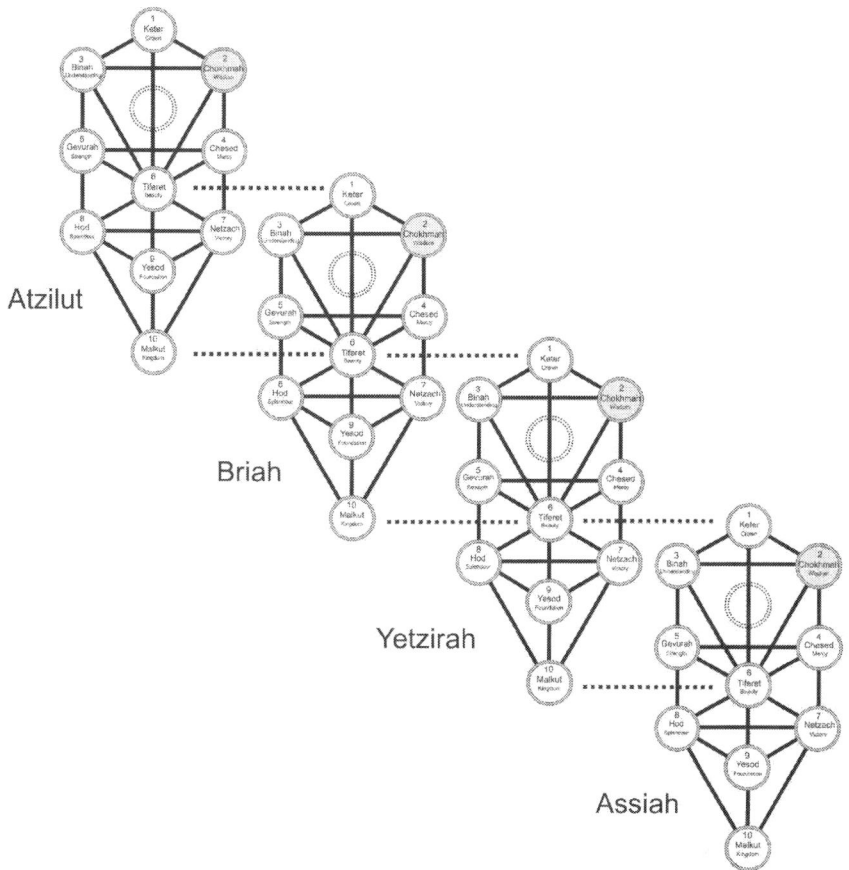

Figure 22: The Extended Tree, a view that extends the Tree of Life through four worlds in a way that highlights deep connections between *sefirot*. *Keter*, *Tiferet* and *Malkhut* overlap, as do *Da'at* and *Yesod*, *Chokhmah* and *Netzach*, and *Binah* and *Hod*. This view illustrates the flow of energy between worlds, and elucidates the cognitive transition from one world to another.

modern views are especially interesting because they view the worlds as overlapping; that is, a *sefira* can exist in two or more worlds simultaneously. Figure 21 exploits a common method of drawing the Tree using four overlapping circles. Each of the four circles then corresponds to a world, and most *sefirot* have an aspect in two or more worlds. For example, *Tiferet* exists at the intersection of *Briah*, *Yetzirah*, and *Assiah*, and this can be given as a justification for three aspects of *Tiferet*: that of King in *Assiah*, Sacrificed God in *Yetzirah*, and Child in *Briah*.

The Hermetic Kabbalah

Figure 22 shows four overlapping Trees, the Extended Tree. This is an extremely productive diagram, and reveals important relationships between *sefirot*. In particular, *Da'at* in one world appears as *Yesod* in another, *Malkhut*, *Tiferet* and *Keter* 'fasten' worlds together, and *Hod/Binah* and *Netzach/Chokhmah* are seen to be duals in which the macrocosm is reflected into the microcosm.

The value of a diagram like this is not superficial - its value is something that tends to emerge (for example) in meditation and contemplation, when symbols begin to reveal multiple coherent meanings of increasing subtlety.

8

Evil

8.1 Introduction

The word 'evil' has lost much of its currency. Sometimes the word is bandied about in criminal cases where experienced police officers are shocked and sickened. Politicians use the word to describe regimes that oppose their dearest values. It retains some meaning among Hollywood script writers.

A modern viewpoint is to focus on behaviour, not metaphysical labels. An influential element in the community views behaviour as a product of nature, nurture and environment. 'Evil' is a convenient label to slap on people when one is too lazy or indifferent to analyse the complexity of cause and effect, or listen to many and various moral viewpoints. 'Evil' sounds irrational and rooted in the demonic. In the calm world of the intellect it can be reasoned away (as it was by Plato and his many successors) so that evil becomes a lack of function, a lack of integration, a lack of socialisation, a lack of intervention, a lack of care and nurture - always an absence of something good.

In opposition to this is the observation that the sum total of human misery is greatly increased by corrupt politicians, warlords and drug barons (to name a few), who do not seem in any way lacking in ingenuity, perseverance, creativity or financial resources.

A recurring theme in Kabbalah is the attempt to comprehend evil, evil that was organised, intelligent and focused on the Jewish community. For much of the period from the destruction of the Second Temple in 70CE, Jews in Europe were denied legal rights of citizenship and excluded from most forms of economic activity. They were subject to the whims of princes, which meant arbitrary expulsions and seizures of property. Sacred books were burned in public, and synagogues sacked. There were vicious libels and slanders, such the accusations that Jews poisoned wells, sacrificed Christian children, and spread the Black Death. There were terrifying and unpredictable outbreaks of mob violence in which thousands (latterly millions) were murdered.

From the time of the Venice Ghetto in the early 16th. century Jews were often forced to live in restricted areas, and identify themselves with a mark on their clothing. There were programmes of enforced conversion to Christianity, and institutions such as the Spanish Inquisition to root out backsliders.

The list of expulsions, massacres, slanders and humiliations is difficult to comprehend. One incident is sufficient to typify the whole story[43]. In 1290 several families of Jews were forced to buy passage on a ship out of England following the seizure of their property by the Crown. They were marooned on a sandbank by the ship's captain and left to drown in the rising tide, while the crew mocked them and urged them to call on Moses to part the sea.

It is against this background that Kabbalists struggled to understand why God's chosen people were so targeted and persecuted. Was it punishment for sinfulness? Would an unbending devotion to *Torah* and commandments alleviate God's wrath? Was evil woven into the fabric of things? Did it possess an autonomous existence?

8.2 Traditional Views

Four positions on the nature of evil are important in the traditional literature:

- **Philosophical**. This view, which derives from Hellenistic philosophy, envisages God as entirely good. Evil is simply a lack of good. The material world contains the imprint of divine ideas in Matter, and it is Matter that adulterates and obfuscates the divine goodness. Matter is the antithesis of being, and has no reality - no quality, including evil, can be ascribed to it - but nevertheless it obscures the essential goodness of all being. Evil is privation, alienation from the good, and is founded in human ignorance.

---

43. *History of the Jews Volume 3*, Heinrich Graetz, Elibron Classics 2005

Evil

- **Instrumental**. Evil is an instrument of God's governance, characterised in the *Bahir* as God's Left Hand. The powers of the left side have no autonomy, but act according to God's decrees. One function of evil is to punish evil-doing. Another is to test humankind, in the belief that righteousness has no substance unless it is tested against temptation.
- **Structural**. Evil is a potential that is realised in human action. If human beings did not act on the possibility of evil, there would be no evil. This view goes further than the philosophical by acknowledging the potential for evil within God's creation, but justifies it by observing that unless God provided the structural possibility of evil in the creation there would be no choice and no free will - that is, the world would function mechanically and resemble a clockwork automaton. The archetypal example of free will and its consequences was the disobedience of Adam and Eve in the Garden of Eden.
- **Dualist**. Evil has an autonomous existence within the God's creation, and is activated by a primordial catastrophic event that brings it into a parasitic existence. Evil derives its sustenance from divine energy that is diverted from its proper place by human perversity: this can be defined as "separating that which should be joined, and joining that which should be separate." Evil may be eradicated at some time in the future.

The default traditional position was the Instrumentalist, and a dramatisation of this can be found in the *Book of Job*. Early Kabbalah, up to the *Zohar*, moved sharply in the direction of Dualism, but the next few hundred years were much influenced by philosophy and the Philosophical and Structuralist views became popular, giving rise to a view characterised by Joseph Dan[44] as "No Evil Descends from Heaven" - that is, the realm of the divine is entirely good. Following Isaac Luria in the sixteenth century and the subsequent Sabbatian heresy, Kabbalah moved strongly towards the Dualist position, to an extent that scholars have compared it with the gnosticism of Late Antiquity. It is not uncommon to find some or all of these positions muddled together. The position taken in this book is that evil is Structural: it arises from our freedom and the choices we make.

8.3 Chesed & Din

Much of the discussion of evil in Kabbalah centres around the dual

---

44. *Jewish Mysticism: The Modern Period*, Joseph Dan, Aronson 1999

The Hermetic Kabbalah

concepts of *Chesed* and *Din*. The creative impulse that the Holy One emanates into the Cosmos is entirely good, but contains in a latent form a duality that does not manifest until after the *sefira Binah*. This duality manifests as two complementary impulses, characterised as *Chesed* and *Din*. *Chesed* is the quality of loving-kindness, mercy, and blessing. *Chesed* is creative and expansive and connective. *Din* is the quality of strictness, judgment, and punishment. *Din* is restrictive and conservative and destructive.

The right-hand pillar of the Tree of Life conveys the attribute of *Chesed*; the left-hand pillar conveys the attribute of *Din*. The central pillar of the Tree mediates between *Chesed* and *Din*, but partakes primarily of the quality of *Chesed*, except for the *sefira Malkhut*, in which the attribute *Din* dominates. Each *sefira* in the Tree of Life retains and restricts some of the divine light, and even though the *sefirot* are holy emanations of God, their character is determined by holding-back, by *Din*. The *Bahir* characterises *Chesed* by silver and *Din* by the more valuable gold, because the light that God holds back is more valuable than the light that God reveals.

Figure 23: the Taoist concept that reality is the interplay of the duality of *Yin* and *Yang* has many overlaps with the Kabbalistic duality of *Din* and *Chesed*.

A creation dominated by *Chesed* would never gain definition. Structure might form momentarily, but would not last long enough to build on. A creation dominated by *Din* would not develop, would not create new forms. It would be dead and mechanical, and lack emergence and novelty. Because *Din* restricts or holds-back the light of God, it is often represented by a covering, a veil, a husk, or the bark of a tree. This dead covering is usually referred to as *klippah*, meaning just that - a husk.

Din is a structural element in the Kabbalistic view of creation. It cannot be removed from the picture. *Din* is often portrayed as the source of evil. However, it is not *Din* as such that is evil. In an ideal condition there is dynamic balance between *Chesed* and *Din*, with energy flowing into appropriate structures, with neither aspect dominating. Evil occurs when *Din* and *Chesed* are out of balance in some way, when a working harmony is perturbed, especially in those cases where it is perturbed

Evil

by wilful action.

One way to understand the interplay between *Chesed* and *Din* is to visualise how a steam engine works. Steam under pressure is made by heating water in a boiler. Without the heat there is no steam, and without the boiler there is no pressure. The engine itself - a piston in a sleeve, a crank, a flywheel, some valves - is a way of converting pressure into useful motion. *Chesed* corresponds to the heat that makes the steam, *Din* to the structure that contains the pressure. If we wanted to continue the example, we could say the engine was *Malkhut* in the world of action. Three simple concepts: energy, a way to contain energy, and a mechanism to turn it into something useful.

The divine attribute that Kabbalists call *Din* is a form or structure that 'does something' to energy, so that the energy is simultaneously degraded (made less generally useful) and directed (made more specifically useful). Although *Din* degrades the goodness of God, it does so like a sunshade that prevents us from burning. It removes light, and creates shadow, but out of necessity.

This is a natural and intuitive idea with resonances as far afield as the dynamic duality of Love and Strife in the philosophy of Empedocles, and the well-known duality of *Yin* and *Yang* in Taoist philosophy.

8.4 Destroyed Worlds

One of the most extraordinary ideas in Kabbalah comes from an ancient midrash attributed to R. Abbahu of Caesarea:

> The Holy One, blessed be He, created worlds and destroyed them, until he created this [present] one, and said: 'This one gives Me pleasure, they did not give Me pleasure'

Why did the Holy One make worlds and destroy them? There are various clues that centre on the concept of righteousness. God agreed not to destroy Sodom if Abraham could find fifty righteous men in the city. Abraham bargained God down to ten righteous men, but could not find even ten, and Sodom was destroyed.

The *Talmud* contains the opinion that the world is only sustained for the benefit of thirty-six righteous men and women in every generation - these are the mysterious *Lamed Vav*, the *Tzadikim Nistarim*, the Hidden Saints.

The *Bahir* continues this idea as follows[45]:

> There is a single pillar extending from heaven to earth, and its name is Righteous (*Tzadik*). This pillar is named after the righteous. When

---

45. *The Bahir Illumination*, Aryeh Kaplan, Samuel Weiser 1979

there are righteous people in the world, then it becomes strong, and when there are not, it becomes weak. It supports the entire world, as it is written, "And Righteous is the foundation of the world". If it becomes weak, then the world cannot endure. Therefore, even if there is only one righteous person in the world, it is he who supports the world. It is therefore written, "And a righteous one is the foundation of the world".

Complementing these ideas are speculations by a famous medieval mystic, R. Eleazar of Worms, who lived in the Rhineland. He wondered why God made worlds and destroyed them, and concluded that it was an experiment. The quality of righteousness can only be exhibited in an environment where it is tested against evil, and so God made worlds of pure evil to see if any righteousness would manifest. None did, and he destroyed them. The present world is a compromise, a mixture of good and evil where only modest levels of righteousness are possible.

According to Joseph Dan, these ideas may have been a stimulus for one of the most influential documents in Kabbalah, the *Treatise on the Emanations of the Left*, written by the Castilian Kabbalist R. Isaac ha-Kohen[46]. R. Isaac not only accepts that the destroyed worlds were pure evil, he gives details of their demonic nature. He also suggests that the Tree of Life splits into two below the sefira *Binah*, so there are seven lower sefira of good, and seven lower sefira of evil - these are the emanations of the left and of the right. The worlds of evil are accorded a similar ontological status to the worlds of good.

It is this dualist view that influenced the *Zohar*. The destroyed worlds of pure evil are identified with the seven Kings of Edom who ruled before the kings of Israel (see *Genesis:36*). They are kingdoms of unbalanced force, of strict judgement (*Din*), and they were destroyed.

It was the elaborate mythological dualism of the *Zohar* that provided the basic elements for R. Isaac Luria's concept of the *shevirat ha-kelim*, the breaking of the vessels, the primordial catastrophe that provided the physical basis for the powers of evil. Because of the breaking, the lights and vessels of the *sefirot* 'dropped down' out of their original places, and so we live immersed in the realms of the ancient shells.

The idea that we live our frail lives against the backdrop of ancient realms of evil aligns Kabbalah with perennial myths of great power. One can cite Egyptian cultic rituals to preserve the sun on its nightly

---

46. A translation can be found in *The Early Kabbalah*, Joseph Dan & Ronald C. Kiener, Paulist 1986

Evil

journey through the demonic realms, Norse mythology, H.P. Blavatsky's story of the evil magics that destroyed Atlantis, and H.P. Lovecraft's fictional Old Ones of chaotic evil banished to an adjacent dimension.

8.5 Catastrophe

Two catastrophes disrupt the pleasingly abstract see-saw dynamic between *Chesed* and *Din*. The first catastrophe is the cosmic catastrophe of the Destroyed Worlds (see above). The Destroyed Worlds were kingdoms of pure evil, and so their remains weigh the nature of existence heavily on the side of evil. The shells (*klippot*) of the Destroyed Worlds form a demonic mirror to the Tree of Life, with averse *sefirot*, palaces, and a hierarchy of evil led by the archdemon *Samael* and his consort *Lilith*, who are the evil mirror image of Adam and Eve. *Lilith* is the enemy of women and childbirth, delighting in strangling babies. *Samael* is identified with Esau, with the planet Mars, and with the violent, oppressive, warlike power of Rome (although any warlike, totalitarian, gangster regime would be appropriate). The realms of evil possess some remnant of primordial life force, derived from sparks of divine light that fell into the abyss during the shattering, but gain much of their parasitic sustenance from human evil, which feeds energy directly to them.

The second catastrophe was the disobedience of Adam and Eve. By eating the apple from the Tree of Knowledge Adam 'cut the shoots'; he separated the Tree of Life from the Tree of Knowledge. There are many ways one can interpret this. One Kabbalistic view of the Fall is that it was a fundamental alteration in cognition.

Knowledge presupposes subject and object. It also presupposes representation, in the form of concept, symbol, sign, narrative and fundamentally, language. Our ability to know is the consequence of a privileged viewpoint that is always detached from what we know. We live in a world of surfaces, of exteriors. Each human being we encounter is another surface, another exterior, and we contact the unknowable interior through shared representations. We experience the other-as-phenomenon only, we cannot know the other-in-itself. When Adam and Eve chose to taste the forbidden fruit, they chose to fall out of a direct apprehension of the divine into a state characterised by duality. They could have knowledge, but only of a restricted kind.

In his introduction to the *Zohar*, Daniel Matt comments[47]:

---

47. *The Zohar*, trans. Daniel Matt, Vol. 1, Stanford 2004.

Once, as Adam, Humanity was wedded to God. The original sin lies in losing intimacy with the divine, thereby constricting unbounded awareness. The loss follows inevitably from tasting the fruit of discursive knowledge; it is the price we pay for maturity and culture. The spiritual challenge is to search for that lost treasure - without renouncing the self or the world.

Adam's sin was a primordial separation within human consciousness, a rupture of comprehension creating the appearance of self and other, subject and object, and it is the asymmetry between self and other that opens up the possibility of moral evil. We do evil because of a one-sided perspective.

R. Yehuda Ashlag's insights into this are both simple and profound[48]. He describes the nature of God as entirely giving. God wishes to give benefits and blessings to all beings. In order to do so, all beings must possess a proportionate capacity to receive. As God has no need of anything, this capacity to receive is something new and must be created.

One can read this in the context of *Isaiah* 45:7: "I form the light and I create darkness; I make peace and create evil" - that is, both evil and darkness were created, and are related to the capacity to receive for oneself alone. The capacity to receive, to give a shape to what is received, has the nature of *Din*. The capacity to receive is necessary (otherwise there could be no relationship with God, or relationship of any kind) but is also the root of that exaggerated sense of self-entitlement that leads to moral evil. The mutual competition between people (each being the centre of a universe of personal need) leads to conflict, and often results in a spiritual gluttony that demands unlimited space, money, honour, status, freedom, whatever.

The ethic of reciprocity is one of the oldest and culturally most pervasive principles that attempts to regulate selfishness and narcissism. A Jewish version of this principle is attributed to R. Hillel in the *Babylonian Talmud (Shabbat 31a)*:

> Once there was a gentile who came before Shammai, and said to him: Convert me on the condition that you teach me the whole Torah while I stand on one foot. Shammai pushed him aside with the measuring stick he was holding. The same fellow came before Hillel, and Hillel converted him, saying: 'That which is despicable to you, do not do to your fellow. This is the whole Torah, and the rest is commentary, go and learn it.'

A Christian version of this principle is "Love your neighbour as

---

48. *In the Shadow of the Ladder*, trans. Mark Cohen & Yedidah Cohen, Nehora 2002

yourself". A well-known philosophical interpretation of the idea can be found in the various formulations of Kant's Categorical Imperative:

> Act in such a way that you treat humanity, whether in your own person or in the person of any other, always at the same time as an end and never merely as a means to an end.

In other words, people are not resources to be used in the attainment of personal goals.

Returning to R. Ashlag, he characterises moral evil as arising from the desire to receive-for-oneself-alone. In its distilled form this desire is pure selfishness and egotism, where the balance between self and other is entirely weighted towards the self. He characterises an ideal situation as receiving-to-give-benefit, where energy is both received and directed outwards, and the balance shifts from self to other. If we stand in the divine light and fail to pass it on, we create a shadow. This idea links to traditions concerning the *sefirot*. Each *sefira* receives light and passes on some of it. Only *Keter* is entirely giving, and only *Malkhut* is entirely receiving (the "speculum that does not shine"). The symmetry is restored by the active participation of created beings, who turn the light around[49] so that a current travels from *Malkhut* back to *Keter*. This cannot be achieved when beings are receiving only for themselves: it is in giving benefit to others that one creates the return link back to *Keter*.

8.6 Near-Dualism

A turning point in the Kabbalistic understanding of evil took place in the Galilean hill town of Safed during the sixteenth century, during a period contemporary with the English scientist and occultist Dr. John Dee, and the playwright William Shakespeare. Safed was under a relatively tolerant Turkish rule, and the thriving wool industry was able to absorb and support large numbers of European Jewish families fleeing from near-universal European persecution. Two outstanding figures were the hinge on which the Kabbalistic understanding of evil swung from philosophical to primordially dual.

R. Moses Cordovero ('Ramak') was influenced by rational philosophy, and sought to unify nearly four hundred years of Kabbalistic speculative thought within a unifying framework. He reflects the 'mild' philosophic understanding of evil:

> the truth is that above, in the world of the divine emanations, no evil

---

49. "Run and Return".

thing descends from Heaven, for up there everything is absolutely spiritual.

He interprets the 'destroyed worlds' of the *Zohar* as the first evanescent flickerings of divine will - an idea strikingly reminiscent of quantum virtual particles in quantum field theory.

A pupil of the Ramak, R. Isaac Luria ('Arizal') turned this on its head by developing and elaborating the *Zohar's* treatment of the 'destroyed worlds'. As the Vilna Gaon commented:

> ... where philosophy ends, kabbalah begins, and where the kabbalah of the Ramak ends, the kabbalah of the Ari begins.

Luria located the origin of evil in the first moment of creation when *En Sof* withdrew His light in an act of self-contraction (*tzimtzum*), creating a 'space' in which some part of God's being and holiness had been withdrawn, leaving behind an excess of the quality of *Din*. The first attempt to emanate a system of *sefirot* resulted in a catastrophe, the shattering of the vessels, or *shevirat ha-kelim*. Like a series of explosions from a firework, sparks (*nitzotzot*), fragments of divinity fell into the dark to provide the activating power for the *klippot*, the powers of absolute *Din*. This irreducible, primordial, cosmic evil is the backdrop to all created existence.

A significant part of Luria's system is the integration of his cosmogony with traditional Jewish religious practices. The Mosaic law, the *halakhah*, the divine commandments and prohibitions that had governed Jewish religious life for millenia, were interpreted in the light of a realm of holiness and a realm of impurity. In his commentary on the *Tanya*, R. Adin Steinsaltz observes[50]:

> *Sitra achra* is the Kabbalistic term for evil. But the words literally mean 'the other side', that is, not the side of holiness. In other words, on the most basic level, there are two aspects to reality: the side of holiness and the other side. The domain of *halakhah* ('Torah law') contains a broad realm known as *reshut* ('the optional'), which is neither virtuous or sinful, that lies here between the divinely commanded *mitzvot* and the divinely proscribed *averot* ('transgressions'). However, in the Kabbalistic division of reality, there is no middle ground. Nothing is neutral; anything that does not actively relate to God is automatically on the other side. For there cannot be anything that does not relate, positively or negatively, to God.

The world of holiness is a world of unity, a world that manifests the truth that 'There is none else besides Him'. The conception of God as 'the Infinite' (*Ein Sof*) does not merely imply that He is Infinite Being:

---

50. *Opening the Tanya*, R. Adin Steinsaltz, Jossey-Bass 2003

Evil

being without limit and definition, being that embraces everything so that there can be nothing else. In contrast, the other side is rooted in the world of disunity, in which the light of the Infinite is not manifest, the exclusive unity of God is not recognized. Thus the essence of *sitra achra* is that there is (so to speak) something else besides Him. In its initial, most basic form, the other side does not deny the existence of holiness, nor is it hostile to it. It merely deigns to define holiness, to confine it within a set of parameters. It is willing to accept the existence of a lofty and superior realm of holiness, based on the assumption that there are other things as well.

The argument Steinsaltz makes is subtle and clever. He avoids outright dualism. He views the *sitra achra* (Other Side) as neither innately hostile or ignorant. It is simply a realm of being set apart from the unity of God, apparently by choice, and by inference it is perhaps too self-involved and inward-looking to care about a realm of holiness.

Despite a desire not to dilute the absolute unity of God with contrary impulses, there is still the nagging question of how *Din* makes its appearance in the very first moment of creation. Nathan of Gaza, prophet and apologist for the messianic Sabbatai Tzevi, and strongly influenced by Lurianic Kabbalah, may not have been completely misguided in postulating two contrary impulses within the *En Sof* itself, pushing back the source of duality to its only plausible source. The interested reader might like refer to *Kabbalah and the Art of Being*[51] by Prof. Shimon Shokek for a sympathetic treatment of the difficulties and unrevealed consequences of the Lurianic view of creation.

Despite the Lurianic view that life in the world is dominated - almost overwhelmed - by the powers of evil, the outlook is not world-denying as in many dualist gnostic systems. Far from it; the Chassidic outlook is joyful, as Steinsaltz explains[52]:

> A cardinal principle in the service of God is that it must be done with joy. It is said in the name of many Hasidic masters that there is something that is not listed in the Torah as a sin yet is worse than any sin and something that is technically not a *mitzvah* [commandment] yet is greater than all *mitzvot*. Nowhere does the Torah expressly forbid sadness and depression, yet this is the most virulent of sins, for it stifles the heart and mind, closing them to the service of God. Joy is not an express *mitzvah* but it is the greatest of all *mitzvot*, for it opens a persons heart and mind, enabling him to perform all the *mitzvot* and make a *mitzvah* of everything.

---

51. *Kabbalah and the Art of Being*, Shimon Shokek, Routledge 2001
52. *Opening the Tanya*, R. Adin Steinsaltz, Jossey-Bass 2003

Far from denying the world, Luria's Kabbalah emphasises the role of human beings in *tikkun olam*, the repair or rectification of the world. The divine sparks that fell into the realm of the shells can be reconnected with the world of holiness; that which should not have been separated can be reintegrated and unified.

R. Hayyim Vital, Luria's student, offered the opinion that in the period of time between the Ramban (Rabbi Moses ben Nachman, 1194-1270 CE) and the Arizal, no Kabbalah of consequence had been produced; that is, he implies that classic Spanish Kabbalah, with the production of the *Zohar* at its peak, was divinely inspired, as were the insights of the Ari. What lay between was little more than intellectual speculation. Luria's views spread rapidly through the Jewish community and have prevailed to this day.

8.7 Hermetic Views

Ancient Greece had an ascetic tendency that derived from the Pythagoreans. The philosophic ideal was the philosopher, who lived a simple and virtuous life. Materialism was not so much evil as irrelevant. There was no reality, no truth in it. Reality was accessible via the capacity within the human soul to apprehend the divine in contemplation. There was nothing in the material world of sustaining interest (it was here that Aristotle, a keen biologist, diverged from a general opinion that lasted until the scientific reformation in the seventeenth century).

In the *Nicomachean Ethics* Aristotle advocated the Doctrine of the Mean, a middle ground between the extremes of human behaviour. Virtue emerged as moderation and regulation of one's behaviour to self and others. This was an intuitive and influential view that was encoded as the four cardinal virtues: temperance, wisdom or prudence, strength or fortitude, and justice.

The cardinal virtues are to be found in the trump cards of the Tarot pack, and despite some absurdly fanciful interpretations, the imagery and meaning is traditional and well-understood. Wisdom/ Prudence appears to be missing from the deck, but as Robert Place has argued, The World card is probably a mutation of the traditional image[53].

There are two virtues that refer to oneself, and two virtues that refer to others. Temperance is the moderation of appetite and expression, avoiding excessive, obsessive, addictive or harmful patterns of

---

53. *The Tarot, History, Symbolism and Divination*, Robert M. Place, Penguin 2005

behaviour. Strength or Fortitude is moderation of self-concern, an avoidance of exaggerated reactions to life's inevitable problems and difficulties (i.e. "don't be a drama queen").

Justice is fair-dealing with others, the ethic of reciprocity discussed previously. Wisdom or Prudence is perhaps the most elusive until one places it in a social context. In the original context, it meant dealing with situations rationally, not impulsively (or imprudently): taking counsel, soliciting advice, weighing options, bringing experience to bear, and part of what we might now consider 'leadership' and 'consensus building'. Wisdom is a social attribute: one can be arrogant by oneself, but one cannot be wise by oneself.

There is a correspondence between the doctrine of the mean and a related concept of balance in Kabbalah. The middle pillar of the Tree of Life expresses the dynamic balance between the extremes of Mercy and Severity, and the triadic structure of the Tree diagram illustrates this idea of mean or balance.

Sefira	Virtue	Vice	Shell (*Klippot*)
Malkhut	Discrimination	Avarice	Inertia, Stasis
Yesod	Independence	Idleness	Vegetative state
Hod	Honesty	Dishonesty	Rigid Order
Netzach	Unselfishness	Selfishness	Habit, routine, sentimentality
Tiferet	Devotion to the Work	Pride	Hollowness
Gevurah	Courage and Energy	Cruelty	Bureaucracy
Chesed	Humility	Tyranny	Bigotry, Hypocrisy, Gluttony Ideology
Binah	Silence	Avarice	Fatalism
Chokhmah	Good	Evil	Arbitrariness
Keter			Futility

Table 2 : Evil on the Tree: Virtues, Vices and *Klippot*

The Hermetic Kabbalah

Hermetic Kabbalah, perhaps more so than traditional Kabbalah, sees vice not just in the interplay between the energy of the right side and the left side, but as excess. The Biblical account of Moses on the mountain has it that Moses could not look upon the face of God and live. In the *Zohar* various sages die in divine rapture. Like the shattering of the vessels, one can have too much of a good thing. Too much form or structure imprisons divine energy, but too much energy shatters the structure that contains it. This is developed into the idea that every *sefira* has a good and bad side, corresponding to too little and too much.

Aleister Crowley's 777, a compilation of Kabbalistic correspondences, has a table labelled 'Transcendental Morality', and this table is further developed in Dion Fortune's *The Mystical Qabalah*[54] into a duality of virtue and vice for each sefira. One can also view the *Klippot* not only as an evil, the opposite of a good quality, but also its original sense of the dead husk or shell of a *sefira*, empty, lifeless structure, form without force. These correspondences are presented in Table 2.

Dion Fortune's understanding of Kabbalah was heavily influenced by her initiation into the Alpha and Omega lodge of the Golden Dawn, and she is a useful counterbalance to Crowley, providing in *The Mystical Qabalah* a comprehensive, systematic and accessible explanation of its principles. Fortune's presentation on the *Klippot* and the nature of evil is influenced by the *Zohar*, and the 'destroyed worlds' legend in the *Sefer De-Tzeniuta*, which she quotes from S.L.Mather's *The Kabbalah Unveiled*[55]:

> ... these emanations [*klippot*] took place during critical periods of evolution when the sefirot were not in equilibrium. For this reason they are referred to as the Kings of Unbalanced Force, the Kings of Edom 'who ruled before there was a king in Israel', as the *Bible* puts it, and in the words of the *Siphra Dzeniutha*, the Book of Concealed Mystery, 'For before there was equilibrium, countenance beheld not countenance. And the kings of ancient time were dead, and their crowns were found no more; and the earth was desolate.'

She explains evil primarily in terms of unbalanced force. There is a primordial component of evil, the 'Kings of Unbalanced Force', and there is an additional component caused by human activity, according to the idea that "each thing evokes its opposite": we cannot manifest any quality without necessarily coming to grips with its opposite. Too

---

54. The *Mystical Qabalah*, Dion Fortune, Ernest Benn, 1935
55. *The Kabbalah Unveiled*, S.L. Mathers, Routledge & Kegan Paul 1981

Evil

much kindness permits evil to flourish; too much severity punishes both guilty and innocent. Each person is endowed with the faults of their strengths. A driven, energetic person may push others too hard and become overbearing; an over-kind parent may spoil a child and fail to imbue self-discipline.

Dion Fortune echoes the ancient tradition that the worlds of evil are a mirror of the worlds of good, the flip side of the coin, and uses the image of two trees reflected across the surface of a sphere. Too much movement in the direction of Severity or Mercy takes one around the surface of the sphere into the averse, *klippotic* tree on the other side. It is fascinating to see ancient traditions preserved and elucidated in a way that is both relevant and creative.

The idea that each *sefira* has a potential for imbalance that can manifest as too much (an excess of force without balancing form) or too little (an excess of form without vivifying force) is not novel to Fortune, and can be found in traditional sources, but it is a distinctive part of her outlook. It links strongly to ideas of physical health, to psychology, to ecology, to biology, to society, to any model of organism in which the function of the whole is dependent on the balanced and harmonious function of parts. Examples of this failure of balance in the context of health would be cancer, where a group of cells escape from the body's regulatory system and grow out of control (corresponding to the *sefira Chesed*), and auto-immune diseases, where the body's regulatory framework misidentifies and attacks its own organs (corresponding to the *sefira Gevurah*).

Her view on moral evil is based on an idea that the divine expresses itself in an outward current of emanation that is embodied in matter, and that there is a point at which all beings begin a journey (which she calls evolution) in which they acquire progressive knowledge of their divine origin, and eventually, a reunion with their divine source. This current of transcendent evolution (this is, a cognitive and spiritual evolution) defines an absolute direction: one may work with the flow, or against it. In her *Esoteric Philosophy of Love and Marriage* she states[56]:

> White Magic is distinguished as that exploitation of knowledge which aims at harmonising and uplifting existence along the lines of advancing evolution, and which, though it may concentrate its efforts upon a particular point, excludes from its benefits nothing which by its nature is capable of receiving them. Black Magic may be defined as that use of superior knowledge which endeavours to cause any section

---

56. *Esoteric Philosophy of Love and Marriage*, Dion Fortune, Aquarian Press 1988

of existence to return to a phase of evolution below that to which it has attained, or which attempts to benefit any special section of manifestation at the expense of the rest.

In other words, evil is not subjective, contextual, relative or non-existent. Evil exists, and it exists absolutely. It is receiving for the self alone, just as R. Ashlag suggested.

Another aspect of Dion Fortune's teachings on evil can be found in a channelled work, *The Cosmic Doctrine*[57], communicated during 1923 and 1924. She makes a distinction between Negative and Positive Evil. Negative Evil is structural, and appears almost identical to Cordovero's definition of *Din*[58]:

> It must be remembered that to the Kabbalist, judgement [Din - judgement, a title of Gevurah] means the imposition of limits and the correct determination of things. According to Cordovero the quality of judgement is inherent in everything insofar as everything wishes to remain what it is, to stay within its boundaries.

Positive Evil is the outcome of human beings employing Negative Evil to achieve their own goals. An example may clarify this. A boiler is designed to confine steam. The boiler without steam is just an empty shell. With energy and water, the steam and pressure created by a boiler can power an engine. A balance is required - too much energy and the boiler shatters; too little and nothing happens. In abstract, energy is confined and directed, and is put to use. A car bomb exploits the same principles as a boiler. The principle of confinement for the generation of useful work is an example of Negative Evil. The car bomb would be an example of Positive Evil.

Better, but more complex examples of Positive Evil can be found in the realm of human society and behaviour. Every society has the means to regulate and administer the behaviour of its members. This was the traditional value of the succession of kings - better a bad king than no king, and the collapse of civic order. A key issue in every human society is the extent to which the mechanism of the state exists to serve all equally, or whether it has been perverted to serve the interests of a privileged few at the expense of the many. Again, the 'confinement' of society by law and regulation can serve the greater good, or it can be perverted.

Fortune's abstract concept of Positive Evil appears similar to the traditional Kabbalistic notion that human action can drip-feed energy

---

57. *The Cosmic Doctrine*, Dion Fortune, Aquarian Press 1979
58. Quoted from *Major Trends in Jewish Mysticism*, Gershom G. Scholem, Schocken 1961

Evil

to the powers of the Left Side, and it is this energy that sustains the *Klippot*. Evil arises from the combination of an inherent structural possibility within the divine, combined with immoral choice, and the intention to serve oneself.

A student in Fortune's tradition, William Gray, devoted an entire book titled *The Tree of Evil* to exploring these ideas[59]. He contrasts two different outlooks. One outlook is directed outwards to material existence as the totality of existence, and the deification of the Ego (what he calls the pseudo-self) within that context, with a focus on acquisition according to temperament: material resources and power, honour and status, knowledge and its utilisation. The other outlook is directed towards relationship - that is, reality is not 'things', it is constructed out of the connections and relationships that we choose to make, and the connections we make can be entirely self-serving, or can serve others. The ultimate relationship is with the totality of all being:

> Good may fairly be defined as the intention or will to achieve identity or true self in the living spirit of cosmic creation. Evil can be contra-defined as the intention or will of remaining retarded in a state of pseudo-self for the sake of its own automatic aggrandisement.

and evil is the

> Deliberate or willed isolation of egoic autonomy at the material end of the self-spectrum for the sake of establishing an apparently independent condition of entity apart from the life-spirit of cosmos itself whereto we properly belong. In old-fashioned language, Man trying to set up apart from God in a state of self-sufficiency.

8.8 Da'at and the Great Abyss

Da'at means 'knowledge', and in the *Zohar* it is treated as a product of the union of wisdom and understanding. It is placed on the Tree of Life on the central pillar above *Tiferet*. It is not normally considered a *sefira*, but in some interpretations of Kabbalah, *Keter* is considered beyond any kind of conceptual understanding, and *Da'at* replaces it as a 'proxy'. For the most part *Da'at* appears on the Tree as a kind of 'gap'. It plays an important role in the modern Hermetic understanding of evil, and this is described in more detail in *Da'at* on page 291, but for completeness a summary is given below.

In the late 19th and early 20th century members of the Hermetic Order of the Golden Dawn dramatised the nature of this 'gap' so that

---

59. *The Tree of Evil*, William G. Gray, Helios Books 1974

it became 'the Abyss'. The Tree of Emanation (see Figure 5) has no path connecting *Chesed* to *Binah* via *Da'at*, and so the spiritual ascent of the Tree (see *Ascent* on page 115) required the aspirant to travel off-piste when transitioning from *Chesed* to *Binah*. This notion of an uncharted 'black run' was combined with ideas, current during that period, of a 'Guardian/Dweller of the Threshold', an encounter with a quasi-demonic entity that would confront the aspirant at a critical point in the spiritual ascent.

A successful crossing of the Abyss was considered to be a rare accomplishment. The (unknown) Secret Chiefs of the Golden Dawn were those individuals who had survived the encounter with the Dweller, and the transition to the spiritual plane of *Binah* ('crossing the Abyss'), and were regarded as virtually superhuman. S. L. Mathers described a supposed encounter with one of these beings as if he had met a god.

A member of the Golden Dawn who claimed to have 'crossed the Abyss' was Aleister Crowley. He used the Enochian Keys of the sixteenth century occultists Dr. John Dee and Edward Kelley to skry into the spiritual nature of each *sefira*, and documented these experiences in *The Vision and the Voice*. Crowley provides fascinating insights into his conception of the meaning of the Abyss and the Dweller, whom he named *Choronzon*, after a 'mighty demon' that is referenced once in Dr. John Dee's angelic communications.

Choronzon can perhaps be characterised as the zero-point energy of consciousness, the random eruptions of cognitive coherence that self-assemble into an Ego that believes itself the divine and autonomous centre of a personal universe - the Most High. *Choronzon* and the Most High are duals, the Most High being Ego at its most unselfconscious, arrogant, and self-centred, while *Choronzon* is the Ego decomposing back into its constituent whirls of awareness. Crowley describes the situation of the Ego in starkly dualist terms, the battlements and angelic legions of the Most High standing guard against the terror of the chaotic Abyss.

For Crowley, crossing the Abyss was an encounter with the fundamental nature of Ego. The Ego is a composite of parts whose interrelationships are tuned (in a multitude of possible ways) for survival in human society. When the Ego loses coherence (which feels like a descent into madness) the constituent parts have the potential to turn into obsessive forces. Crowley described and documented this process in considerable detail.

A significant event in the development of these ideas was Kenneth

Evil

Grant's *Nightside of Eden*. Grant developed the ancient idea of an averse Tree of *klippot* using notes left behind by Crowley[60], who had done a little work along these lines. *Nightside of Eden* is nothing less than a counterpart to the Thirty-Two paths of Wisdom (*Chokhmah*), using *Da'at* as an entry point into the reflected averse Tree and the thirty-two paths ... of Ignorance. The paths of ignorance are the obsessive and addictive kinds of false reality sustained by the *klippot*.

In today's consumer society, with its obsessive cravings for handbags, shoes, pornography, food, drugs and celebrity, these paths can be explored without an arcane catalogue of demonic names.

8.9 Summary

Joseph Dan has observed that a Kabbalist's position on the nature of evil is a litmus test for the rest. It is one of the defining subjects, and this survey has done little more than cherry-pick some views that seem representative of important positions. The influence of the *Zohar* has been paramount. Over time Kabbalists have zigged and zagged between various philosophical, structural, instrumentalist and dualist positions, but they have returned to the *Zohar*. It is the mythical dualism of the *Zohar*, amplified by the teachings of R. Isaac Luria, that has prevailed: that is, due to catastrophe and choice the worlds have descended into the realm of a primordial evil that manifested during the earliest moments of the creation.

Scholem uses the metaphor of childbirth[61]: evil is the placenta, the afterbirth, the support system, the other occupant of the womb, the second birth hidden from the mother and taken away for disposal.

But there was nowhere for it to go. It dominates perception so that nothing of the divine is visible, so that the appearance of 'stuff' - matter, material, substance, in every kind of appearance - is all that presents to the human mind. From our privileged interior viewpoint we look out on a world of surfaces and coverings, and it is coverings and surfaces all the way down, until we reach the realm of quantum mechanics, at which point the perceptual legerdemain vanishes and we are exposed to an underlying unity of mechanism where there is no more naive materialist 'stuff' - only structure and relationship, embodied in abstractions like fermions and bosons.

It is the duality of structure and relationship, under the guise of *Din* and *Chesed*, that dominates Kabbalistic ideas of evil and good.

---

60. *Liber CCXXXI*, Aleister Crowley.
61. *Major Trends in Jewish Mysticism*, Gershom Scholem, Schocken 1974

The Hermetic Kabbalah

From a moral perspective, evil is a product of focusing our relationships on structure, building relationships with 'stuff'. If all our aspirations relate to 'stuff' and we treat other people as further manifestations of 'stuff' (that is, means, not ends - see Kant's Categorical Imperative above), then we are creating personal empires of 'stuff' in which we are *de facto* deities. This is materialism in the fullest sense. It is a culture that attributes the highest values to manufactured goods, to tokens of wealth, and tokens of status.

The *Zohar* suggests that the powers of the Left Side derive their energy from human action. Everywhere people are trying to actualise their ideal lifestyle, bringing stuff to life by diverting life force into it, trying to behave like gods while simultaneously denying their fragility, mortality and God. There is nothing wrong in trying to achieve some level of material comfort, security, safety, and control over one's circumstances. It is the exclusive devotion to the arbitrary obsessions of an Ego dominated by aggrandisement that feeds the Left Side, and creates the readily comprehensible forms of evil discussed in the introduction.

There is substantial agreement between traditional views (e.g. as understood by R. Yehuda Ashlag) and Hermetic traditions (e.g. deriving from the Golden Dawn through Dion Fortune and her students). Both Ashlag and Gray identify two fundamental positions: receiving for oneself alone, and receiving to give benefit - relationship with stuff versus relationship with others and, through others, with God. In the Hermetic tradition the rectification of the world, *tikkun olam*, is relabelled as the Great Work, but it is the same process expressed using the language of alchemy: the refining of persons and situations to reconnect with the spiritual gold amidst the dross.

This is the nub of it: being able to see past coverings and surfaces to recognise the spark of the divine, and building a relationship with it, thus freeing it to transcend its identification with 'stuff'. R. Moses Cordovero puts it exceedingly well:

> The essence of divinity is found in every single thing — nothing but it exists.... Do not attribute duality to God. Let God be solely God. If you suppose that [Ein Sof] emanates until a certain point, and that from that point on is outside of it, you have dualized. God forbid! Realize, rather, that Ein Sof exists in each existent. Do not say, 'This is a stone and not God.' God forbid! Rather, all existence is God, and the stone is a thing pervaded by divinity.

Evil

8.10 Further Reading

This chapter has been strongly influenced by collections of essays:

In *Jewish Mysticism: The Modern Period*, Joseph Dan, Aronson, 1999
- *Samael, Lilith and the Concept of Evil in the Early Kabbalah*
- *'No Evil Descends from Heaven': Sixteenth Century Jewish Concepts of Evil*
- *Manasseh ben Israel's Nishmat Hayyim and the Concept of Evil in Jewish Thought*
- *Samael and the Problem of Jewish Gnosticism*
- *Nachmanides and the Development of the Concept of Evil in Kabbalah*
- *Kabbalistic and Gnostic Dualism*

In *Kabbalah*, Gershom Scholem, Dorset 1974:
- *The Problem of Evil*
- *Demonology in Kabbalah*
- *Lilith*
- *Samael*

In *The Wisdom of the Zohar*, Fischel Lachower & Isaiah Tishby, Oxford University Press, 1990:
- *The Forces of Uncleanness*
- *The Activity of "the Other Side"*
- *Demons and Spirits*

In *On the Mystical Shape of the Godhead*, Gershom Scholem, Schocken 1991:
- *Good and Evil in the Kabbalah*

I have also drawn heavily on the views of R. Yehudah Ashlag in

In the Shadow of the Ladder, R. Yehudah Lev Ashlag, trans. Mark and Yedidah Cohen, Nehora Press 2002

The Hermetic Kabbalah

9

The Soul

> But Mind the Father of all, he who is Life and Light, gave birth to Man, a Being like to himself, and He took delight in Man, as being His own offspring; for Man was very goodly to look on, bearing the likeness of his Father. With good reason then did God take delight in Man; for it was God's own form that God took delight in.
>
> *Corpus Hermeticum, Libellus 1 (Poimandres)*

9.1 Introduction

The ancient view of the soul was uncomplicated: the soul was the animating principle of the body. A living body and a dead body may look the same, but the dead body has lost its animation. The abruptness of death, like turning off a switch, provides the simple intuition that something has departed. The soul made the difference between a walking, talking human being, and a corpse.

Over the millenia metaphysical and religious speculations have accreted to this simple concept. Many rational people will be uncomfortable using the word 'soul', being unsure what it means, or believing that it has something to do with religion. Outside of religion the word is mostly unused at the present time. We seem more comfortable referring to the soul in Greek, *psyche* being the root of psychology and psychiatry, professions which (if we take the Greek root seriously) minister to the soul.

The word retains much of its original meaning when used in popular expressions such as "the life and soul" or "it ain't got soul". Here we can interpret soul as the coherence of disparate parts - party people, musicians, bodily organs - into something larger, something that transcends the sum of the parts. This idea of emergence, of parts cohering into a whole that exhibits a novel and unexpected richness, is one of the key ideas behind the ancient concept of soul.

9.2 The Structure of the Soul

An early development in the idea of the soul was the observation that it is multilayered, like a wedding cake. Attempts to derive a structure for the soul can be found in the philosophy of Plato and Aristotle, and were very influential. A simple way to explain this is that human beings can be viewed in several different ways.

Firstly, we are atomic matter, the chemical cookery of dead stars - carbon, oxygen, hydrogen, nitrogen, iron, sulphur, calcium, phosphorus, magnesium and so on. We obey physical laws. A human cannonball flies through the air in the same kind of parabolic arc as an iron cannonball.

Secondly, we are a collection of cells composed of a wide range of organic chemicals shared with all other forms of life - proteins, lipids, carbohydrates, DNA and so on. Our cellular processes are typical, and at this basic vegetative level we can be compared with jellyfish and beetroot.

Thirdly, we are mobile animals that seek food, reproduce sexually, defecate, groom ourselves, and try to be comfortable in the face of heat and cold.

Fourthly, we are people. We talk about concepts, like fairness and law and justice. We argue constantly. We make things for our comfort, for our amusement, and to kill. We enact laws, and punish offenders. We worship.

Lastly (and this viewpoint only became controversial in the 20th. century) we are divine sparks. This viewpoint is well expressed in the American *Declaration of Independence*:

> We hold these truths to be self-evident, that all men are created equal, that they are endowed by their Creator with certain inalienable Rights, that among these are Life, Liberty, and the Pursuit of Happiness.

What is this notion of 'equality'? On reflection it is not about the body or the brain, or about anything we can measure and compare. It is the equality of a divine soul that transcends material circumstances. Without a belief in a divine soul, the wording of this declaration makes no sense.

Further layering in the soul can be postulated, graduations of the divine essence. Discussions of this kind can be found in Kabbalah, and will be touched on below.

The subdivision of the soul, embodied in matter, into a vegetative or nutritive soul, sensitive or animal soul, and rational soul dates back to Aristotle (384-322 BCE). His views were widely promulgated in the medieval world and influenced Judaism, Christianity and Islam equally, so it should come as no surprise that the Kabbalistic understanding of the soul is strongly influenced by Aristotelian and Platonic thought.

In Kabbalah, as in Greek philosophy, the parts of the soul can be thought of as enclosing each other like Russian dolls, with the inner being closer to the divine than the outer. The souls are normally given as *Nefesh*, *Ruach* and *Neshamah*, and have an approximate relationship with the intellectual culture of the period as follows:

Kabbalah	Epistemic Faculty	Tree of Life	Approximate Scope	Neoplatonic /Aristotelian Tradition
Neshamah	*Noesis*	*Binah*	Divine spark, higher self, intuitive apprehension of truth	Intellectual Soul
Ruach	*Dianoia*	*Tiferet*	Discursive reason, conceptual and symbolic thought, language, self-awareness, morality	Rational Soul
Nefesh	*Aesthesis*	*Yesod/ Malkhut*	Sense perception, instinctive drives (sleep, food, reproduction etc.)	Nutritive/ Animal Soul

Table 3 : The Parts of the Soul

R. Moses of Leon (c. 1250-1305 CE) comments:
"You ought to know and think upon the mystery of the *nefesh*, the *ruach*, and the *neshamah*. The *nefesh* is the power that is associated with the sensations of the body in all matters that are connected with the blood, and in all the factors that sustain the body throughout its life, through perception of this world with respect to everything that the body needs. This preserves the body ..... The *ruach* is the power that enables the *nefesh* to maintain itself in the body, for the *nefesh* survives only through the power of the *ruach*, which acts like the breeze that blows. It is because of the *ruach* that man is sustained by the power of the *nefesh*, for if the *ruach* were withheld from the *nefesh*, this would bring death in its train, for the *nefesh* would not be able to maintain itself in the body. The *neshamah* is a matter of true intellect. It is hewn from the source of life, and from the wellspring of intelligence and wisdom [i.e. *Binah* & *Chokhmah*]. Glory comes to dwell in the body in order to sustain everything for the service of the Creator, in order to provide him with substance."

Later Kabbalah became much concerned with the soul: its origin in the upper worlds, its lineage and affiliation to other souls, its theurgic capacity, and the redemptive character of certain pure and enlightened souls, the *Tzadikim*. There were many elaborations, and in order to understand qualitative distinctions in the nature of the purest and most refined souls, more classifications were made, for example, the '*neshamah* of the *neshamah*', the *Yechidah*, and the *Chiah*.

9.3 The Dignity and Fall of the Soul

One of the fundamental ideas in Kabbalah derives from *Genesis 1:27*:

So God created Man in his own image, in the image of God created he him.

Human beings have the likeness of God. This is an extraordinary revelation, and there are many ways to interpret it. One way is to represent God as having the form of a human being, such as the gigantic deity of the *Shi'ur Komah*. Another way to interpret this is to suppose that the human soul has a dynamic and structure that mirrors the divine; that is, the human soul is a *simulacrum* of God.

This is a radical idea, so radical that R. Moses of Leon wondered how God could judge and punish the soul since 'it is actually He Himself'. If the dynamics of divinity can be represented by the Tree of Life, so the human soul - its image - can be represented using the same template. This is the basis for using the Tree of Life to represent both macrocosm and microcosm, manifest God and the human soul. One is the reflection of the other.

Another consequence of divine mimesis is the extent to which the human soul is dignified and empowered, almost to the point of hubris. Human beings are seen as possessing a legitimate divine power *within the bounds of divine law*. Human beings have a vital role to play in the Creation as part of a mutually beneficial relationship between God and humankind. A consequence of this is the legitimate use of *theurgy*, as described in a following chapter (see *Theurgy* on page 129).

This is a uniquely Jewish and Kabbalistic perspective that will seem alien to anyone raised in Christian belief. This view on the dignity of the human soul fed into Renaissance humanism, and created attitudes that are still with us today. Giovanni Pico, Count of Mirandola (1463-1494), an enthusiast for Kabbalah who commissioned translations of several Kabbalistic works, created a dramatisation of the dialogue between God and Man in his famous *Oration on the Dignity of Man*:

> We have given you, O Adam, no visage proper to yourself, nor endowment properly your own, in order that whatever place, whatever form, whatever gifts you may, with premeditation, select, these same you may have and possess through your own judgement and decision. The nature of all other creatures is defined and restricted within laws which We have laid down; you, by contrast, impeded by no such restrictions, may, by your own free will, to whose custody We have assigned you, trace for yourself the lineaments of your own nature. I have placed you at the very centre of the world, so that from that vantage point you may with greater ease glance round about you on all that the world contains. We have made you a creature neither of heaven nor of earth, neither mortal nor immortal, in order that you may, as the free and proud shaper of your own being, fashion yourself in the form you may prefer. It will be in your power to descend to the lower, brutish forms of life; you will be able, through your own decision, to rise again to the superior orders whose life is divine.'

Note that Pico assumes the capability "to rise again to the superior orders whose life is divine". This is a key aspect of the Hermetic tradition.

9.4 Awakening and Ascent

An important issue in Hermetic, Neoplatonic and Gnostic mysticism (and Kabbalah shares many characteristics with these) is the extent to which the soul knows itself. The ancient injunction to

The Hermetic Kabbalah

'Know Thyself", supposedly inscribed on the Temple of Apollo at Delphi, hints at what one might call 'epistemological mysticism'. At first sight the Delphic injunction seems ridiculous. How can one *not* know oneself? Descartes founded his epistemology on the principle that the only certain knowledge we possess is about ourselves. The implication of the Delphic injunction is that we do *not* know ourselves.

The idea that the soul has forgotten its true nature is ancient, and formed an important part of Plato's theory of knowledge. It is also found in Gnostic sources, such as the famous Gnostic *Hymn of the Pearl*, supposedly sung by the Apostle Judas Thomas while in prison.

The *Hymn* is a story of a young prince who is sent to Egypt on a quest, but he is seduced by luxury and forgets his origin and mission. He eventually recalls who he is and what he is supposed to be doing. This was taken as an allegory of the soul, which falls into material existence and forgets its true nature. *Libellus 1* of the *Corpus Hermeticum*, the so-called *Poimandres*, depicts the fall of the soul as a kind of narcissism[62]:

> And Nature, seeing the beauty of the form of God, smiled with insatiate love of Man, showing the reflection of that most beautiful form in the water, and its shadow on the earth. And he, seeing this form, a form like to his own, in earth and water, loved it, and willed to dwell there. And the deed followed close on the design; and he took up his abode in matter devoid of all reason. And Nature, when she had got him with whom she was in love, wrapped him in her clasp, and they were mingled in one; for they were in love with one another.

There are two primary views about the soul's forgetfulness. The first view, which we could label Neoplatonic, is that the soul forgets because of its attachments to the physical, which it takes to be 'real'. We can liken this to watching a movie, where we briefly 'forget' our larger concerns, and like the protagonist of the *Hymn of the Pearl*, we may need to be reminded.

The second view, which we can label 'gnostic', is that the soul is deluded by powers that are themselves ignorant and detached from the Real. A modern version of this idea is presented in the film *The Matrix*, where the protagonist Neo takes the Red Pill and awakens from a false reality into what he thinks is 'the Real': a devastated world dominated by machines that synthesise reality for captive humans. The final film in the trilogy reveals 'the Real' to be only the outward appearance of an even deeper 'realer-Real'. Neo is able to

---

62. *Hermetica: the writings attributed to Hermes Trimegistus*, trans. Walter Scott, Solos Press

cognise and interact with three, simultaneously-existing levels of reality.

The process whereby the soul comes to 'know itself' is often modelled as an ascent through the levels of creation. The soul may be accompanied by a being who acts as a guide and whose true nature may be revealed as the 'higher part' of the soul whose nature and existence has been 'forgotten'. This reuniting of the parts of the soul may be given a dramatic and literary form as an idealised sexual encounter, such as the marriage of the King and Queen in alchemy, the bride and groom in the *Song of Songs*, and Dante and Beatrice in *The Divine Comedy*.

9.5 They Met Themselves

There is a well-known painting by Dante Gabriel Rossetti titled *How They Met Themselves*, and it is famous as a representation of *doppelgänger*, doubles. A couple in medieval courtly dress encounter another identical couple during a walk in a wood.

There are ancient traditions that the highest level of the soul (*Neshamah*) presents itself in a revelatory form as an image of oneself. For example, the prophet Mani (210-276 CE), influenced by early Jewish mysticism and who founded what was possibly the first world religion, received revelations from his celestial twin, double, guardian angel or true self, the terms being conflated in a way that remains true today.

This experience was documented in medieval Kabbalah: the pinnacle of ecstatic trance was the vision of a *doppelgänger* who was simultaneously the bearer of prophetic revelation, and also a trance image of the mystic. This phenomenon has been labelled 'autoscopic', and is sufficiently well documented to have been investigated[63]. Scholem has collected these Jewish mystical traditions in his essay *Tselem: The Concept of the Astral Body*[64].

These traditions have survived to modern times. Various members of the Golden Dawn, Aleister Crowley in particular, were much influenced by a fourteenth century magical text, of possible Jewish provenance, called *The Book of the Sacred Magic of Abramelin the Mage*[65].

---

63. *Speaking with Oneself: Autoscopic Phenomena in Writings from the Ecstatic Kabbalah*, Shahar Arzy, Moshe Idel, Theodor Landis and Olaf Blanke, *Journal of Consciousness Studies*, 12, **11**, 2005, pp. 4–30
64. *On the Mystical Shape of the Godhead*, Gershom Scholem, Schocken, 1991
65. *The Book of the Sacred Magic of Abramelin the Mage*, trans. S.L. Mathers, Dover 1975

The Hermetic Kabbalah

This manuscript contains a description of a lengthy procedure used to summon one's Holy Guardian Angel, for purposes both of revelation and of practical magic. Crowley followed ancient tradition by conflating the Holy Guardian Angel with the 'Higher Self' and the *Neshamah*.

There are interesting overlaps with psychoanalysis. Freud's threefold layering of the psyche into Id, Ego and Superego can be compared with *Nefesh*, *Ruach*, and *Neshamah*. One could make a case for similarities between Id and *Nefesh*, and Ego and *Ruach*. Perhaps one could also make a case for the Superego resembling the *Neshamah*, at the cost of turning the *Neshamah* into something resembling the Wizard of Oz - an inner voice that has the timbre of power and authority, but is seen to be a fraud. This is how an atheist might view the idea of a divine soul.

Another interesting view comes from Freud's contemporary, C. G. Jung (1875-1961 CE) who made a lifetime study of Alchemy, Kabbalah and Hermeticism. He concluded that the *psyche* was composed of several parts that were dissociated and unconscious. Because these parts were dissociated, they appeared to the conscious Ego in dreams, images, fantasies, myths and projections as autonomous characters of great fascination and power. He named these figures 'archetypes', and the more important archetypes are the Anima, Animus, Shadow, Persona, Wise Old Man, and Mother. He also believed the psyche possessed an organising principle, a teleological attractor, which he called the Self. The Self appears to the Ego as a symbol of wholeness. It may appear in dreams and visionary experiences as a person or symbol of extraordinary power. It is identical with the ancient gnostic symbol of the redeemer or Emissary of Light that rescues the soul from the chaos of a world ruled over by evil daemonic powers - which in Jung's system are the dissociated archetypes.

The value in Jung is not that he supplants ancient traditions of the *psyche*, but that he understands them in sufficient depth to act as a modern taxonomist. His immersion in mysticism has been widely criticised, and his work has been viewed as unscientific, but it is difficult to study the strange mythic worlds of the *Zohar* and R. Isaac Luria, without respecting Jung's intentions and insights. One could take the view that Luria's dynamics of the *Partzufim* in a fractured creation, and Jung's dynamics of the archetypes and individuation, are narratives of a similar type and content, with only five hundred years and a thin slip of paper between them.

An important aspect of Jung's work is his understanding that the wholeness of the soul is a potential, not something one can take for granted. The soul, like an iceberg, is largely concealed, with only the Ego visible to self-consciousness. When we imagine the missing parts, we imagine externalised projections embodied as autonomous archetypes woven into mythic narratives - Satan, Gaia, Jesus, Abraham, Mary Magdalene, *Lilith*, Arthur, Orpheus and so on. Or to the modern cinema-goer, Neo, Morpheus, Cypher and Trinity, or Luke Skywalker, Obi-wan Kenobi, Princess Leah and Darth Vader.

9.6 Summary

The fundamental narrative of the soul is its fall, its awakening, its ascent, and its unification with its forgotten higher aspect. There may be accompanying revelations about the nature of reality.

This section is a foretaste of a more complete presentation in Part Three of this book. If this book can be said to have a purpose, then it is to show how Kabbalah is an intrinsic part of this drama. Kabbalah, taken together with ascent mysticism and theurgy, provides a practical method for awakening and rectifying the soul.

The Hermetic Kabbalah

10

Ascent

I am parched with thirst and dying:
let me drink from the ever-flowing spring on the right,
by the luminous cypress tree.
'Who are you? And where are you from?'
I am a son of Earth and starry Heaven
but my descent is from Heaven.
                Orphic burial gold leaf, translated by Ted Jenner

10.1 The Spheres

At the beginning of the 14th century the Italian poet Dante Alighieri wrote an imaginary description of a journey through the Cosmos as it was then imagined to be. In the company of the classical Roman poet Virgil he journeyed through the realms of *Inferno* and *Purgatario*, and then in the company of his ideal love Beatrice he journeyed upwards into Heaven - *Paradisio*. They travelled through the spheres of the planets, then the fixed stars, and finally into the Empyrean, characterised by nine concentric rings of angels surrounding the divine presence. This was a conventional view of the cosmos at that time, and is depicted in Figure 25.

Towards the end of the 19th. century a group of mildly eccentric

The Hermetic Kabbalah

Figure 24: Dante and Beatrice pass beyond the fixed stars and gaze on the nine concentric rings of angels. Illustration by Gustav Doré.

and individualistic British freemasons and occultists met at the Mark Masons Hall in London and ritually initiated each other into what could be viewed as progression through the *sefirot* of the Tree of Life. This was not play-acting. In their minds they assumed the forms of ancient gods. They believed they were concentrating the occult powers of the spheres into the *temenos* of a masonic lodge, using symbols and incantations to refract the divine light like a prism, splitting it into its component parts, and focusing it onto the candidate. They believed that profound changes in cognition and agency would occur, and in a vital sense, they would transcend their humanity.

Although it may not be obvious, Dante and the members of the Hermetic Order of the Golden Dawn shared an ancient worldview that is now almost forgotten, although anyone with a serious interest

Ascent

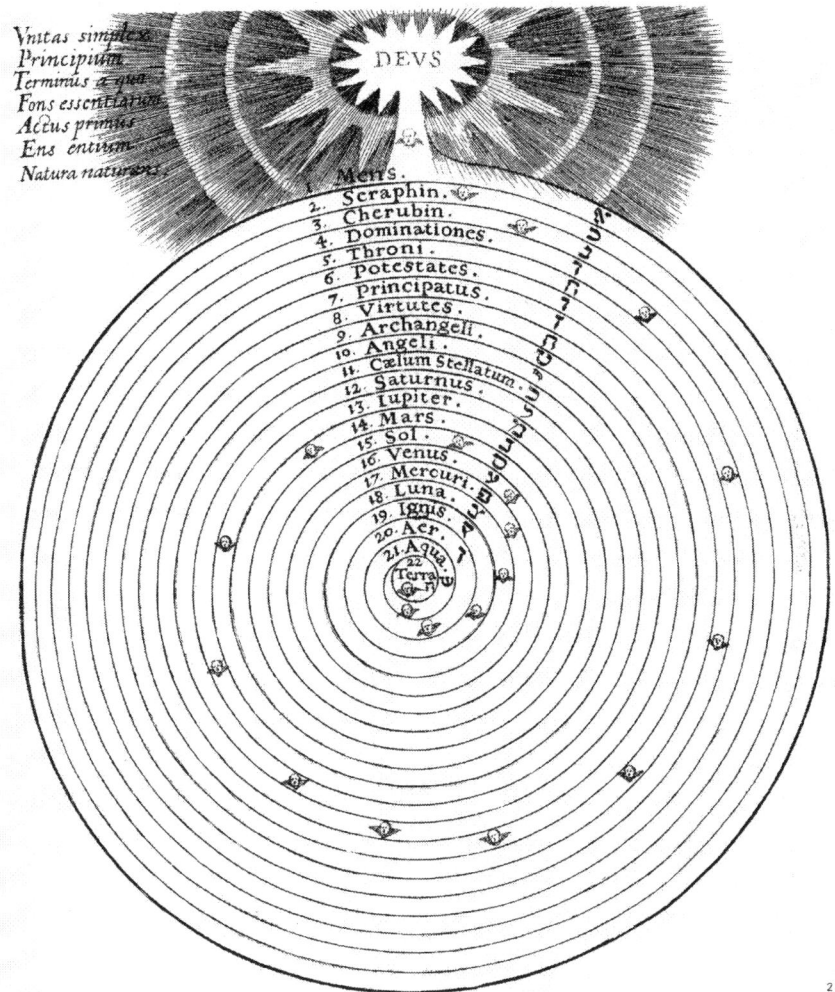

Figure 25: A pre-Copernican view of the Cosmos according as depicted Robert Fludd in *Utriusque Cosmi*, c. 1620 CE

in astrology is likely to be familiar with it. It is a composite worldview, part of it coming from classical Greek philosophy, part from the astronomy of late antiquity, part from a Neoplatonic forgery, and part from Christian theology (which was itself adapted from classical Greek philosophy).

This worldview is based on the simplest of observations: that human beings live under a sky that is filled with interesting things that happen regularly. The sun rises and sets. The moon waxes and wanes. The stars and constellations rotate around a fixed point in the sky. Wandering lights traverse the constellations.

By the time of Christ much of the detail had been worked out, and there was a consensus that the lights in the sky were the outward signs of the powers that ruled humanity. The sun, moon and planets were associated with gods, and there were cults and temples devoted to them. But there was more. According to Plato the mechanism of the cosmos had been set in motion by a craftsman, and behind the appearance of multiplicity there was a unique cause. The cosmos, glorious living thing that it was, was only the outward sign of a deeper reality. This deeper reality was the origin of human souls, which descended from on high, and accreted layers of substance from each plane of reality until they were immersed in gross matter. Because the human soul had acquired a portion of substance from every plane, it was like a little universe - literally, a micro-cosmos. At death, if the soul was not weighed down by matter, it would ascend once more. The layers would be stripped off. This is described in the ancient *Corpus Hermeticum* as follows:

> And thereupon, having been stripped of all that was wrought upon him by the structure of the Heavens, he ascends to the substance of the eighth sphere ...

There was a measure of world-hating puritanism in the idea that the soul had been sullied by its descent through the spheres into physical incarnation. The Platonists insisted that all was well, that the cosmos was perfect in every respect, but also believed that the soul was overwhelmed by the sensory impact of physical existence and had forgotten its divine nature. The most negative of the traditional Platonic views was that the body was the 'tomb of the soul'.

Some of the books that comprise the *Corpus Hermeticum* are explicitly negative and see the influence of the planets as the source of the passions that bind the soul to material existence. These are given as:

- Increase & Decrease (i.e. fickleness, inconstancy - the Moon)
- Machinations of Evil, Cunning (Mercury)
- Lust, whereby Men are Deceived (Venus)
- Domineering Arrogance (Sun)
- Unholy Daring & Rash Audacity (Mars)
- Evil Strivings after Wealth (Jupiter)
- The Falsehood which lies in wait to work Harm (Saturn)

Ascent

This list, which could be close to two thousand years old, would be recognisable to a modern astrologer as characterising negative aspects of the planets. The unknown author is blaming the planets for defects in our being.

The gnostics of late antiquity went further still and took the view that material existence is the domain of evil powers that hold the soul in subjugation. The planetary powers (*archons*) are administrators and captors that must be foiled and evaded if the soul is to rise to the realms of light beyond. To achieve this required divine grace, and often secret knowledge - seals, names, incantations - to control the daemonic spirits of the planetary aeons.

One of the most unusual and related sets of gnostic literature, the *Pistis Sophia* and the two *Books of Jeu* (IAO, or IVH), purport to be teachings given by the risen Jesus to his disciples. These are 'closed group teachings' to an elite. They are highly irregular from the perspective of normative Christianity, but consistent with the bare-bones historical picture of Jesus compiled by Prof. Morton Smith in *Jesus the Magician*[66]. The *Pistis Sophia* describes a Jesus who claims he has descended from the realms of light into the sphere of Fate to free the righteous from the demonic powers of the zodiacal regions, the planets, the 360 Egyptian demons of the calendar, and the world-serpent that circles the sphere of Fate. He performs magical rituals, utters strange incantations, and knows the dark arts used by the demonic powers to enslave the human soul by binding it to a 'counterfeiting spirit'[67]:

> And they put the counterfeiting spirit outside the soul, watching it and assigned to it; and the rulers bind it to the soul with their seals and their bonds and seal it to it, that it may compel it always, so that it continually doeth its mischiefs and all its iniquities, in order that it may be their slave always and remain under their sway always in the changes of the body; and they seal it to it that it may be in all the sin and all the desires of the world.

If Jesus did travel to Egypt to learn arcane magical arts, and return with his body tattooed with magical devices (as Prof. Smith reconstructs from various sources), then the *Pistis Sophia* and the *Books of Jeu* are the kind of secret tradition he might have taught his closest followers. But this is speculation and a digression ...

The mixture of Neoplatonic, Hermetic, Stoic, Gnostic and Ptolomaic conceptions of the universe that co-existed during late antiquity

---

66. *Jesus the Magician*, Morton Smith, Ulysses, 1998
67. *Pistis Sophia: A Gnostic Gospel*, trans. G.R.S. Mead, The Book Tree 2003

provided a rich palette of options for constructing metaphysical cosmologies, and were synthesised to form a 'standard model' that became the dominant European model of reality for over 1000 years. The cosmos described by Dante is a Christian fusion of parts: a hell where souls are imprisoned and subjected to torments, somewhat like the *Pistis Sophia*; the planetary shells of Ptolomy, complete with morally-ambiguous spiritual intelligences; a divine pleroma of angelic orders that follows the model of a late Neoplatonic forgery, *The Celestial Hierarchies* of pseudo-Dionysus.

This model is much closer to gnosticism than to Hellenistic rational speculation. The Church remained uneasy about the planetary powers, and saw them as primarily demonic. Under-the-counter grimoires such as the celebrated *Key of Solomon* provided instructions for communicating with the planetary spirits. There was a great deal of uncertainty about which parts of the cosmos were 'good' and which were 'bad', and there were learned debates by leading intellectuals (such as Marcelio Ficino - see 11.5) about the boundary between good (natural) magic, and bad (demonic) magic.

This is the ascent model of spirituality. The soul descends through the spheres, a cocoon of planetary stuff is wrapped about it like bandages, and it is embodied. At death it ascends once more, the mummy bandages are removed, and it returns to its home.

This is a huge shift from the most ancient beliefs in Greece and Mesopotamia, where the souls of the dead went to a dark place and ate dirt. In the ascent model the soul is a divine creature that descends into the world, and depending on many factors - divine grace, moral conduct, secret knowledge, ritual purity, or faith, it may rise to a blessed utopia, or it may fall into a place of torment.

10.2 The Mysteries

At some point in the ancient world there was a transformation in the status of the soul. The after-death experience went from eating dirt to quasi-divine. The origin of the shift in perspective lies in ancient mystery traditions associated with Orpheus, Dionysus and Demeter. The Neoplatonists subscribed to the myth of Orpheus, who was supposed to have brought mystery traditions to the Greeks, and who influenced Pythagoras and Plato, and was thus co-opted into their own lineage. Orpheus and the 'Orphic tradition' is still the subject of considerable academic debate, and may well be a late invention. What is known however is that the local mystery cults of Dionysus and Demeter offered an alternative to the dirt-eating, after-death experience. With suitable purifications and offerings the soul of the deceased might travel to a better place and become a companion to the gods. Over time the choice of afterlife destination became more extreme and dualistic, with a choice between a very, very bad place and a very, very good place. This is similar to the beliefs of many Christians at the present time (and it should also be noted that in rituals such as the *Viaticum*[68], Christianity has preserved ancient traditions for the in-flight care of the soul).

The famous Eleusinian Mysteries, celebrated at the small town of Eleusis near Athens, were not just a purification. They were an initiation into mysteries of life and death. Our understanding of what happened is imprecise because initiates were required to be silent about their experiences, and remarkably, they were. In well over one thousand years no-one revealed the central experience, although there are many informed conjectures. Central to the Mysteries was the myth of Demeter, goddess of growth and fertility, as told in the *Homeric Hymn to Demeter*.

Demeter's daughter Persephone is given by Zeus to Hades, king of the underworld. Hades seizes Persephone while she is picking flowers, and carries her off. Demeter searches for her daughter, and eventually goes into mourning. Nothing grows, there is no harvest, the human race is in danger of starvation, and Zeus is forced to intercede. A compromise is reached: Perspephone must spend six months of each year with Hades as queen of the dead, but is permitted to join her mother for the remaining six months. This myth is clearly related to the pattern of winter and summer in the northern hemisphere. We can infer (and there is some evidence to support this) that the pattern of death and regrowth in nature was applied to human existence: that in death there is also life. This is just the bare bones of the back-story - there was much more to the Mysteries than a simple idea. It was a vivid and life-altering experience.

The initiation must have been an exhausting event, as it was spread over several days, and began with purification rituals that included washing a pig in the sea. There were several days of fasting. There was a fourteen mile procession from Athens to Eleusis, and much lewd humour. There were all-night dances. The central part of the Mysteries was held in a large building known as the *Telesterion*, and the ritual roles were hereditary positions taken by members of one or two families. Much was done at night in the light of torches. It

---

68. *Viaticum* signifies 'provisions for a journey', and is the last sacred meal or eucharist given to a person when death is imminent.

is reasonably certain that tricks and illusions were used, and some have suggested that psychotropic substances were given in drinks.

Drugs were probably unnecessary, as people can be extraordinarily suggestible and malleable in groups - there are videos on the internet of charismatic Christians showing 'signs', such as speaking in tongues, of being 'slain in the spirit', and exhibiting many kinds of atypical manic, catatonic and convulsive behaviours.

10.3 The Golden Dawn

With this prologue it is now possible to understand the unusual things that members of the Golden Dawn were doing in the Mark Masons Hall at the end of the nineteenth century. The Hermetic Order of the Golden Dawn was instigated in 1888 by three members of a quasi-masonic Rosicrucian organisation called the *Societas Rosicruciana in Anglia* - SRIA. The SRIA requires[69] that its members be Master Masons, and provides an initiatory structure of grades. The founders of the Golden Dawn preserved the basic structure of SRIA grades and added a tenth so that the grade structure corresponded to the ten *sefirot* of the Tree of Life (see Table 4). The order of the initiations follows the reverse order of emanation of *sefirot* on the Tree of Life; in other words, initiations take the form of an ascent through the *sefirot* of the Tree of Life in reverse-lightning-flash order (see Figure 32).

Because each *sefira* is associated with a planet, the ascent of the Tree coincided with the traditional ascent through the spheres of the planets, and the order coincides exactly with that given by Fludd (see Figure 25, and many other sources, including Dante). In other words, the ancient view of the experience of the soul after death became a living experience, and in this respect Golden Dawn initiations resembled the Eleusinian Mysteries. The temple became a place where the soul could experience the operational forces of the cosmos while still alive.

Sefira	Planet	Grade
Malkhut	Four Elements	Zelator
Yesod	Moon	Theoricus

Table 4 : Sefirot, Planets and Temple Grades of the Golden Dawn

---

69. It still exists.

Ascent

Sefira	Planet	Grade
Hod	Mercury	Practicus
Netzach	Venus	Philosophus
Tiferet	Sun	Adeptus Minor
Gevurah	Mars	Adeptus Major
Chesed	Jupiter	Adeptus Exemptus
Binah	Saturn	Master of the Temple
Chokhmah	Fixed Stars	Magus
Keter	First Swirlings	Ipsissimus

Table 4 : Sefirot, Planets and Temple Grades of the Golden Dawn

The authors of the Golden Dawn initiation rituals were aware of these connections. The titles and roles of the temple officers - those entrusted with conducting rituals in the temple - were based on those of the Eleusinian Mysteries. The *Hierophant* ("who shows what is holy") represented the right-hand pillar of the Tree of Life, the quality of mercy, the east, and the forces of the 'right side'. The *Hiereus* ("priest") represented the left-hand pillar, the quality of judgement, the west, and the powers of the 'left side'. The *Hegemon* ("guide") represented balance, *Tiferet* and the Middle Pillar. The *Dadouchos* was the torchbearer. The *Stolistes* ("preparer") was the cup-bearer.

The rituals followed the ancient pattern of *legomena*, "things spoken", *dromena*, "things performed", and *deiknymena*, "things revealed". There were invocations, ritual actions, circumambulations, and solemn oaths. The temple officers conducted a ritualised initiation on the physical plane, and a more elaborate version of the same ritual in their imagination, in which they were embodying and channelling cosmic forces. In this sense the temple was a cosmic simulacrum designed to awaken and instruct the soul of the candidate. There are parallels with the theurgic ritual theory of Iamblichus, a Neoplatonist philosopher and theurgist who believed that the soul was so ensnared by material existence it required the 'shock' of theurgic ritual to awaken it to the powers of the cosmos. The soul required an intervention, it needed to be 'snatched out' of its short-sighted obsession with the life of the physical body and exposed to the larger reality from whence it had come. This is described in more detail in the following chapter.

The wording of the Golden Dawn rituals dramatically contrasts 'light' and 'darkness'. Darkness is normal physical existence, light is both the light of occult and spiritual philosophy, and the experience of being 'enlightened' through progressive initiation into the ascending levels of spiritual life. Neophytes were advised to 'quit the Night and seek the Day', with a spiritual dawn embodied in the rising sun symbol of the Golden Dawn itself.

The final goal of initiation can best be summarised by a quotation from the *Talmud* that has become a staple of greeting cards: "Every blade of grass has an angel that bends over it and whispers grow, grow". The is the tip of an ancient belief found in both the Hermetic and Jewish traditions: that everything in the world below has its reflection and origin in the world above. What is true of grass is true of human beings, and there is an angelic being in the upper worlds that is both the Holy Guardian Angel, the divine genius, and the true self. It also whispers "grow, grow!". The aim of the Golden Dawn rituals was to accomplish this unity.

There are legitimate questions about the extent to which these goals were met in practice. A spiritual hierarchy is an unstable social construct. *The Celestial Hierarchies* of the pseudo-Dionysus describes the ideal or prototype:

> For each of those who is allotted a place in the Divine Order finds his perfection in being uplifted, according to his capacity, towards the Divine Likeness; and what is still more divine, he becomes, as the Scriptures say, a fellow-worker with God, and shows forth the Divine Activity revealed as far as possible 'in himself'. For the holy constitution of the Hierarchy ordains that some are purified, others purify; some are enlightened, others enlighten; some are perfected, others make perfect; for in this way the divine imitation will fit each one.

The members of the Golden Dawn may have liked to imagine themselves as recreating the celestial hierarchy via an *imitatio dei*, with members higher in the hierarchy exemplifying the spiritual life to those further down the ladder. In reality the organisation suffered the problems of any newly-created hierarchy, and there were claims that members had not achieved their claimed levels of initiation - that is, a person had undergone an initiation but failed to achieve the corresponding level of spiritual awareness.

A collection of spiritual non-conformists is certain to experience difficulties with the concept of hierarchy. One of the most notably non-conformist of the members was Aleister Crowley, himself the child of fundamentalist Christian non-conformists (his parents were members of the Plymouth Brethren).

Crowley was an industrious student of the Golden Dawn system. Crowley's tendencies towards self-promotion, notoriety, ill-advised legal contests, drugs, sexual promiscuity, and spiritual grandstanding obscure the fact that despite being a member of the Golden Dawn for a short period of time, he remained faithful to their goals and methods throughout his life. He continued to work his way through the grades of the Order for decades after leaving, convinced that higher powers would provide the necessary initiations. His Holy Guardian Angel communication occurred in Cairo in 1904, his crossing of the Abyss to Master of the Temple grade occurred in North Africa in 1909, his assumption to Magus occurred in 1919, and in 1924 he accepted the grade of Ipsissimus while in Cefelau in Sicily. The Golden Dawn system of occult symbols and correspondences, including Kabbalah, became the platform around which he structured his life.

Crowley adopted the ascent model of spirituality from the Golden Dawn. As one of the Order's most prolific and engaging writers, he carried many of their ideas forward into the twentieth century. A later generation of writers - Israel Regardie, Dion Fortune, Gareth Knight, William Gray and many others - perpetuated the idea of a mystical ascent of the Tree of Life, often in conjunction with theurgical and magical practices, which are outlined in the following chapter.

10.4 Jewish Ascent Traditions

The Jewish tradition has descriptions of ascent (or puzzlingly, descent), the best known being those of the mystics who lived in-or-around Palestine in late antiquity. The focus of the *Hekhalot/ Merkavah* texts differs from the Hellenistic worldview of planetary spheres in that they resemble an attempt to gain audience with a great king in his palace, or alternatively, a vision of the divine throne. In modern terms we could compare this to admission to the VIP lounge of a celebrity night club. The purpose of these ascents was not to experience or pass beyond the powers of the spheres; it seems to have been the experience of nearness to the divine, with possible occult, theurgic and prophetic benefits[70].

The traditions of the *Merkavah* mystics were preserved into medieval times, but these literary remains do not seem to have reignited attempts to reenact ancient visionary techniques.

---

70. *The Ancient Jewish Mysticism*, Dan, Joseph, MOD Books 1993

The Hermetic Kabbalah

Figure 26: Jacob's dream (*Genesis 28:11*)

One of the most enduring symbols of ascent is that of a column or pillar connecting the higher and lower worlds down which souls pass at birth and ascend at death. There are descriptions of meditative ascents through the worlds/*sefirot*. Cordovero described this practise, the purpose of which was to ascend to *Keter* and draw down spiritual forces. One might also ascend in the imagination to perform unifications in the upper worlds. One finds nothing quite like the systematic ascents through the *sefirot* as practiced by the Hermetic schools. The interested reader is referred to Idel[71].

One of the most important and enduring symbols of the connection between earth and heaven is Jacob's Ladder, based on the dream of Jacob in which he saw angels ascending and descending from earth to heaven via a ladder. The shape of the Tree of Life, with its horizontal paths, does resemble a ladder, and even more so in the case of the

---

71. *Ascensions on High in Jewish Mysticism: Pillars, Lines, Ladders*, Moshe Idel, Central European University Press 2005

Ascent

Extended Tree (see Figure 22).

10.5 Summary

The ascent model of spirituality is a direct consequence of the cosmological models of late antiquity. The soul descends into this world at birth, and assuming it does not become bound within the spheres it will ascend out of it at death. This model remained valid until the seventeenth century, at which point the ascendancy of the new natural philosophy began to undermine the old metaphysics. It still remains an item of belief in major religions, including Christianity and Islam; for example, the feast of the Assumption of Mary is a public holiday in many countries.

A major innovation of the mystery religions was the belief that the soul could be initiated into the mysteries of life and death *before death*. The soul could ascend through the planes of existence while still connected with the body. This was an important part of the gnosticism of late antiquity, as we find in the *Pistis Sophia* and the *Books of Jeu*. It is intrinsic to the mysticism of Plotinus, Iamblichus and Proclus.

In the late 19th. century the Golden Dawn rescued ancient Hermetic and Mystery traditions and recreated a living theurgic and initiatory tradition. Much of 20th. century occultism has been a reaction to it in one way or another as more and more source material has become available to researchers.

The hierarchical approach to initiation had its social problems, as many of the influential offshoots of the Golden Dawn have experienced. Hierarchy may have appealed to the mentality of the late nineteenth century, but society has changed greatly since then, and this has led to a proliferation of individual approaches. Crowley attracted many people to the Western Esoteric Traditions, but obscured as much as he clarified - he was an effective proselytiser, but not a good historian. His sinister reputation has done nothing to restore the tradition to respectability.

10.6 Further Reading

Many books on Kabbalah (or Qabalah) were published by people connected to the Golden Dawn tradition, which did a great deal to keep public interest alive at a time when Kabbalah had been marginalised within many sections of the Jewish community[72]. While these are not great works of scholarship, they reflect a living, working,

The Hermetic Kabbalah

theurgic tradition of Kabbalah that is both well-developed and accessible. Among these works one could mention

The Kabbalah Unveiled (1887) by S. L. Mathers,

The Sepher Yetzirah (1887) by W. W. Westcott,

The Holy Kabbalah (1929) by A. E. Waite,

A Garden of Pomegranates (1932) and *The Tree of Life* (1932) by Israel Regardie,

The Golden Dawn (1934) by Israel Regardie,

The Mystical Qabalah (1935) by Dion Fortune,

The Equinox (1909-1913) by Aleister Crowley,

777 and Other Qabalistic Writings of Aleister Crowley (1909) by Aleister Crowley.

---

72. The unsympathetic opinions of the important Jewish historian Heinrich Graetz (1817-1891) reflect a (then) trend of hostility towards Kabbalah, which was seen as backward-looking and superstitious. Much has changed.

11

Theurgy

> There is a universal tendency among mankind to conceive all beings like themselves, and to transfer to every object those qualities with which they are familiarly acquainted, and of which they are intimately conscious.
>
> David Hume

11.1 Introduction

This chapter introduces what is sometimes called 'practical Kabbalah' - an aspect of Kabbalah that goes beyond speculative theosophy and cosmogony and puts theory and theosophy to good use. There are some who will say that this is not a part of Kabbalah, that it is an accretion or a distortion. Some popular books on Kabbalah state outright that 'real Kabbalah' is not connected to 'occultism'.

There is abundant evidence that the practical aspects were there from the beginning, and no less a Kabbalist than R. Joseph Gikatilla (1248-1305 CE) spells it out (see below) in unambiguous terms. There are theurgic aspects of Kabbalah in some of the most influential texts, for example the *tikkun* described in the *Idra Rabba* in which three participants die. There are many aspects that are less well-known and are 'occultism' in all but name.

It is possible to substantiate in detail the extent to which many of the most important figures in Kabbalah were linked to 'occultism'[73], but this would be a diversion from the purpose of this chapter. What one can say is that the Hermetic Tradition is more open and explicit about its practical aspect, and this makes some people uncomfortable.

---

73. Kaplan discusses documented practical techniques in *Meditation and Kabbalah*, Aryeh Kaplan, Samuel Weiser 1982

This discomfort translates into a desire to show clear water between an 'authentic' Kabbalah in which occultism (where present) is disguised or reclassified, and an 'inauthentic' Kabbalah in which disreputable foreign elements have been introduced.

A related area of discomfort is the attempt to distance the nobility of theurgy from the base and superstitious concerns of magic. This is a contentious distinction, much debated, and there is no more clarity in this debate than the many attempts to distinguish magic from religion.

The approach adopted here is less about classification and more about what one is attempting to achieve. The Hermetic Tradition presents human beings as having a dual aspect; one part, immersed in nature and clothed in skin, has forgotten its origin and place as a divine being. The soul can regain its original dignity. The embroilments and passions of this world, vivid though they may seem at the time, are secondary to the task of recovering the forgotten understanding of who and what we are. The practical aspects of this task are valued according to whether they aid us towards freedom, or embroil us further in murk and confusion.

11.2 History

Magic, the belief that one can influence one's environment using esoteric technical skills, is grounded in cultural assumptions about the nature and structure of reality. One of the simplest and geographically most pervasive of these assumptions is that everything that moves and acts is alive and so has a soul. These living souls exist within a larger ecology of being that subsumes what we might think of as our normal daily life. We can apprehend the 'living aspect' of the world directly in our minds, and it can interact with us directly, and become perceptible in dreams, during visionary experiences, and sometimes spontaneously. There is a vast terminology for identifying and classifying this extended 'ecology of being', but for the sake of brevity and simplicity I will follow common usage and refer to disembodied aspects of living power, experienced through our minds, as 'spirits'. The ancient Greek term, *daemones*, would do just as well. In practice, someone like Iamblichus (see below) recognised an extended hierarchy of beings, with *daemones* at the bottom.

The basic cultural model for relating to spirits differs in very few respects from the way that people deal with each other. We know that some people are kind and helpful. Some are neutral but prickly. Other people are mean and spiteful and vindictive. Most cultures view spir-

Theurgy

Figure 27: A talisman from the *Sefer Raziel*

its in the same way. A universal method for smoothing relationships with spirits is propriation via offerings, usually food and drink, or animal sacrifices. Problems with spirits happen because people are neglectful and fail to respect spirits, break taboos, or irritate those people who control spirits. The normal signs that one has angered spirits are misfortune and ill-health. Various classes in society specialise in understanding the relationship between spirits and people, and possess the subsidiary skills of identifying, communicating-with, propriating and manipulating classes of spirit.

The default term for working with spirits is 'magic', and the word is used here. It is a difficult term to define, in part because it overlaps with religion, and the interested reader is referred to Graf for a history of attempts to define what magic is[74]. Even the view that it is the

---

74. *Magic in the Ancient World*, Fritz Graf, Harvard University Press, 1999

techne of working with spirits is limited, but this is a useful definition within the context of this chapter.

Powerful technologies are normally regulated, partly to prevent harm, and partly to provide power and income to approved groups. We find this with medicine and pharmaceuticals, with weapons, and vehicles. The more potential harm in a *techne*, the more tightly it is controlled, and the more likely it is that its use will be restricted to a highly-specialised group of professionals. This is what occurred in the Roman Empire: magic was subject to legal restraints depending on the potential for social harm. Freelance practitioners of magic were routinely hounded off the streets. Certain kinds of divination were the preserve of the state. The principal concern would seem to have been social order; it was bad for business to have sorcerers throwing curses, or predicting the death of emperors. We can see similar legislation today in our 'hate crimes', actions that inflame relationships between social groups.

With the rise of Christianity a new concern emerged, that magic was bad for the soul. This was an inversion of the view of Iamblichus (see 11.4) where certain kinds of divine magic (theurgy) *were good for the soul*. The traditional *daemones* were transformed into entities opposed to the divine order, and commerce with them was seen as unambiguously evil. This view reached the level of social hysteria during the witch hunts of the late 16th. and 17th. centuries.

Little has changed. When the table-top role-playing game *Dungeons & Dragons* became popular there was a panic linking it to 'satanism'. The *Harry Potter* books by author J. K. Rowling were condemned by many different religious groups - Protestant, Catholic, Orthodox Christian, and Islamic - on the basis that the books were directing children towards dangerous occultism. Rarely have so many religious authorities been so united on a topic. The defence against this condemnation should have been that occultism is based on a legitimate and sophisticated worldview, with a history and tradition that precedes all of these religions. Instead, the defence was that what was depicted in *Harry Potter* was *not real occultism*.

The determination to suppress the worldview and practices of 'occultism' - that is, the Hermetic-Kabbalistic tradition[75] described in this book - is as real as it ever was.

---

75. Essentially, the fast-fading worldview that Agrippa attempted to capture and record in his *Three Books of Occult Philosophy.*

Theurgy

Magic depends implicitly on cosmology. The cosmology of Amazonian native peoples is not that of a Neoplatonist philosopher, and so assumptions about spirits - what they are, their nature, their likes and dislikes, where they reside, their internal relationships - are also different. As human society became organised and hierarchical, so did the spirits.

The world of late antiquity (i.e. the transitional period c. 200CE - 600CE) was dominated by large urban centres such as Alexandria at the eastern end of the Mediterranean. The Mediterranean and Middle East was dominated by empires - the Roman, Persian, Byzantine and latterly Islamic empires. This greatly increased the number of privileged, educated and urbanised administrative classes, classes characterised by a rigid hierarchical stratification, arcane and often incomprehensible ranks and titles. At at the pinnacle, ruling over all, was an emperor.

The shift from tribal cultures and animist beliefs to empires administered by privileged hierarchies and ruled by an emperor, caused a similarly dramatic shift in cultural assumptions about the nature of the cosmos and the spirit world. Taking ancient Greece as an example, as far back as 500BC animist beliefs were giving way to the belief that the Cosmos was the outcome of a creative process involving a single supreme source of all being. This change can be detected with Pythagoras, and becames pronounced and highly influential with Plato. The impact of this centralisation is that spirits became subordinate to a larger scheme. Instead of subsisting in an organic natural ecology, they became organised, stratified, categorised and increasingly dominated by larger concerns and hierarchies. The cosmos resembled a large wedding cake.

One can see this depicted in the entrance way to many larger churches and cathedrals in European cities. The arch above the main entrance (*tympanum*) is often arranged to show the spiritual structure of the Cosmos in the form of The Kingdom of Heaven. Christ is seated at the centre of the Heavenly Court, crowned as king, and surrounded by disincarnate entities: saints and angels, organised according to priority, and in many cases, various inferior classes of spirit such as demons and devils tormenting sinners.

The *techne* of magic evolved in parallel with this wedding cake view of reality, as did the categorisation of magic and its practitioners. One could distinguish between literate and educated practitioners, and illiterate and uneducated practitioners. There was the 'high magic' (*theourgia*) of urban Neoplatonist philosophers and the 'low magic' (*goetia*) of uneducated country folk. There were approved entities, and unapproved entities. There was state-sanctioned magic, and there were practices (even in pagan Roman times) that were illegal and treated as criminal acts. The state-sanctioned magic of priests was reclassified as 'not magic', while various itinerant mages, healers, fortune tellers and sorcerers were harassed by the authorities.

One of the greatest changes from earlier times was the increasingly clear-cut distinction between morally good entities (saints and angels), morally ambiguous or dubious entities (the spirits of the planets, zodiac and decans, days of the week, hours of the day, and so on), and morally evil entities (fallen angels and associated legions of devils, also organised in hierarchies).

When the Christian Church became the de-facto state religion of the Roman Empire in the early 4th century CE, there began a systemic suppression of other religions. Ancient sanctuaries and temples were destroyed. The Platonic Academy in Athens was closed by the Emperor Justinian in 529 CE, and he also closed the great temple complex of Isis and Osiris at Philae in Egypt. This marked the end of the ancient world - from this point on the great urban centres of the Eastern Mediterranean were controlled by Christian doctrine. The Church selected for itself a broad class of rites, ceremonies and ancient practices, reinterpreted and reframed them according to its own doctrines, and effectively reclassified anyone else as trafficking with evil spirits. Something similar happened within Islam, and one still finds people in Arabia being brought to trial on charges of sorcery and witchcraft[76].

The magical lore from late antiquity was preserved with its cultural and cosmological assumptions intact - that is, a single source of being; a layered cosmos; hierarchy and stratification; a realm of time and fate administered by subsidiary powers (the zodiac, the decans and the planets); and the magical importance of textual formulae, glyphs, and secret names of power.

The dominance of Christian culture made any further cultural development difficult and the lore was preserved in this form until the scientific reformation of the seventeenth century. The publication of Cornelius Agrippa's *Three Books of Occult Philosophy* in 1531-33 CE was essentially the last gasp of a thousand year tradition. With the increasing rise of humanism and atheism (in all respects a greater barrier to comprehension than Christianity) magic receded deep into

---

76. The penalty is death by beheading, and a man was executed on this charge in 2012.

the shadows (which is what 'occult' implies), and apart from romantically-inspired occult revivals among niche groups, it has remained there.

11.3 Gikatilla

R. Joseph Gikatilla (1248-c.1305 CE) is one of the central figures from the mainstream of classic Spanish Kabbalah. He unites two traditions. As a student of R. Abraham Abulafia he was deeply immersed in the practical techniques of the ecstatic Kabbalah, but his published works show him to be equally well acquainted with the theosophical Kabbalah. As a contemporary and probable acquaintance of R. Moses of Leon, he is of great interest to scholars examining the question of the authorship and sources of the *Zohar*. According to R. Isaac of Acre, Gikatilla had a deep interest in magic, and this may account for his sobriquet *Ba'al ha-Nissim*, Master of Miracles.

Although it would be wrong to generalise from such a unique Kabbalist, his opinion is interesting and important. In his *Gates of Light* he provides a detailed explanation of the 'applications' of divine names:

> Now you have been informed that the essence of faith and the basis for understanding the unity of God is to understand the applications for each name. For all His Names that are mentioned in the Torah are included in the Tetragrammaton YHVH, which is similar to a tree trunk. Each of the other names - those which I have compared to roots and branches and other hidden treasures - has a unique function.
>
> It is just like a storehouse which has several rooms. Each room within the storehouse has a specific identity: one room has precious gems, one has silver, another has gold, while another has different kinds of food and another has drinks. If a person needs food, he may starve to death if he doesn't know how to get into the room, even though the rooms are full. It is not because his request has been denied. He is simply not aware of which room he needs. So it is with the comprehension of the blessed Holy Names: there are names in charge of prayer, mercy and forgiveness, while others are in charge of tears and sadness, injury and tribulations, sustenance and income, or heroism, loving kindness and grace.
>
> If one does not know how to concentrate on the very Name which is the key to the answer of his request, then who is to blame if the request is not granted? It is his own foolishness and ignorance, as it is written:
>
> 'A man's folly subverts his ways and his heart rages against the YHVH.' *Proverbs 19:3*

For God is open to everyone. It is the foolishness of man that is to blame - the one who does not know to which room he should go and therefore returns empty-handed. Yet, man thinks this evil thought, that God thwarted him from getting what he needed. This, however, is not the truth, for his own foolishness has let him down. As it is written,

'It is your iniquities that have diverted these things, your sins have withheld the bounty from you.' *Jeremiah 5:25*

One must therefore familiarise oneself with the ways of the Torah and know the purpose of the Holy Names. He should be expert in them and when he needs to request something from God he should concentrate on the name designated to handle that question. If he does so, then not only will his request be granted, but he will be loved in the heavens and beloved in the world; he will inherit both this world and the next.[77]

Gikatilla is remarkably clear. Each of the names of God found in the *Bible* is related to the name YHVH just as the branches of a tree relate to the trunk, and each name has a 'unique function'. The key to effective use of the names is 'concentration', and that 'God is open to everyone'.

The remainder of the *Gates of Light* contains a selection of texts, readings and correspondences to point the reader in the right direction. He provides a context of understanding for each name organised under ten headings, the 'gates of light', that is, the ten *sefirot*. The result of this exercise is intended to be a divine mimesis, the construction of an internal microcosm that enables the practitioner to literally 'be like God'.

This is a style of magic that will be unfamiliar to many people. There is nothing in it concerning magic circles, black candles, sacrifices, arcane texts and conjurations, evil spirits, pacts, chanting or sinister robes - the kind of imagery that one can distil from the more lurid of the eighteenth century grimoires and summarised in Waite's *Book of Black Magic*[78]. There is no 'black' in Gikatilla's mind because he is Jewish and not Christian. His worldview does not contain the strange, quasi-dualism of Christianity in which the powers of evil have a near autonomous status and compete for the souls of humanity. The idea of "selling one's soul" in a Faustian pact would have seemed ludicrous. For Gikatilla "God is open to everyone".

The style of magic is so different from the stereotype it is called

---

77. *The Gates of Light*, R. Joseph Gikatilla, trans. Avi Weinstein, Harper Collins 1994
78. *The Book of Black Magic*, Arthur Edward Waite, Weiser, 1972

Theurgy

theurgy ('god-work'), a name coined by Chaldean Platonists in the second century CE to set it apart from the armchair speculations of *theology* ('god-talk'). Theurgy is based on the belief that human beings have a divine spark, that human beings share the same demiurgic capabilities as the creator, and there is a legitimate use of this power to participate in the dynamic unfolding of the Cosmos. When Gikatilla states:

> If he [the Kabbalist] does so, then not only will his request be granted, but he will be loved in the heavens and beloved in the world; he will inherit both this world and the next.

he obviously views this kind of activity not only as desirable, but as a fulfilment of human potential, an awakening to full stature. God wants us to walk tall and realise the full measure of the divine power granted for our use.

A key aspect of this Kabbalistic theurgy is the use of names. As Gikatilla states, names have a unique function. They are not merely signifiers; they are capabilities. One must know how to concentrate upon them, and for this one must become aware of the context within which they are embedded. For example, the name *Adonai* is associated with the *sefira Malkhut* and with the *Shekhinah*, and a vast association of symbolism, legend, scripture, history and ritual practice is evoked within the mind of the Kabbalist when this name is employed. There would almost certainly have been additional secret techniques used under the guise of 'concentration'; Gikatilla was for a time a student of R. Abraham Abulafia, a master of the discipline of *tzeruf*, a technique of sustained mental concentration in which the letters of words and divine names are permuted and combined.

The use of names as capabilities, somewhat in the manner of a platinum credit card, did provoke a sense of unease. In the *Sefer Chasidim*, attributed to R. Judah the Pious, it states:

> One may not say that the invocation of God's Name obliges Him to do the will of the invoker, that God Himself is coerced by the recital of His Name; but that the Name itself is invested with the power to fulfil the desire of the man who utters it.

So yes, as the good Rabbi Judah confirms, it *is* a platinum credit card!

11.4 Iamblichus

Theurgy is magic united with a belief in the dignity of the human soul and its place in the cosmos; that is, because we possess a divine spark, we can do God-work. Both the *Hermetica* and the Kabbalah provide related beliefs about human dignity: that the Primordial Adam was a glorious light-being almost equal to God in power and magnificence; that we are co-creators; that we have a demiurgic role to play in the unfolding of the world; that we have forgotten our place in the scheme of things; that we can recover our place in the scheme of things.

It is the belief that human beings have an essential role to play in the cosmos that make the events in the *Idra Rabba* and *Idra Zuta* comprehensible. The companions of Simeon bar Yochai, each taking the place of a divine aspect, describe the bodily parts of *Arikh Anpin* and *Ze'ir Anpin*, and in doing so, effect powerful changes in the divine realm. They are 'repairing God', restoring harmony and balance and connection within the upper realm of the divine.

The most influential spokesperson for theurgy was the Platonist Iamblichus of Apamea (c. 245-c. 325 CE). A descendent of the priest-kings of Emessa in Syria, Iamblichus had a peerless understanding both of late Platonism and the cultic practices of the time. Much of his writing is lost, but he made the case for theurgy in an important letter best known by the title given it by Marcelio Ficino: *On the Mysteries of the Egyptians, Chaldeans, and Assyrians*. It is often known by its abbreviated Latin title *De Mysteriis*.

De Mysteriis was written in response to a letter from Porphyry, the most important student of Plotinus (c.204/205-270 CE), who asked obvious rational questions about magic, cultic practices, divination and so on, and Iamblichus answered the questions point by point. It is a difficult document: often technical and tedious, prolix, didactic and patronising, and Iamblichus rarely says in ten words what could just as easily be said in twenty. This suggests that the loss of most of the works of Iamblichus may have been the vote of history, and not just Christian spite. Nevertheless, *De Mysteriis* evokes a sense of awe, not unlike finding an ancient tomb with all its treasures intact. It is the real deal.

Central to the discussion was the role of the world we live in, which we can conceptualise as 'Nature'[79]. Nature is not ideal. It is harsh and difficult and demanding. The tribulations of daily life suggest it falls far short of the ideal, and is (compared with an ideal) defective. The Neoplatonist view is that everything that exists is a consequence of divine emanation from the One, and the One is per-

---

79. Greek philosophy tended to follow Aristotle and use the term *hyle*, which just meant 'generic stuff'; the corresponding word today would be 'matter'.

fect, implying that Nature must be mixed in some way. Plotinus depicted Nature as divine forms made real by Matter, in the same way that a potter can make a beautiful vase out of clay. A potter can make many different pots out of the same clay, but the potter does not make the clay. The potter finds the clay and uses it. The model of divine forms being embodied in Matter was much inspired by a potter moulding clay. If we think of God as a potter, did God make the infinite diversity of the world out of a deposit of metaphysical clay, and if so, where did this mysterious stuff come from?

Plotinus (who was still alive when Iamblichus was a young man) struggled with this issue. Matter perplexed him; the more he withdrew divinity from it, the more he was left with an incomprehensible, defective, malignant nothingness. Matter was the furthest alienation from the Good, a mindless, formless, defect. His position was that Nature had nothing to offer the spiritual person, because the soul did not descend into Matter. It remained unsullied. His approach to the divine was the contemplation of the pure forms far removed from materiality.

This is an important argument that has resonated throughout history. If Nature is divine, then we live surrounded by and immersed in divinity. Everything we touch is sacred and holy, and part of God.

If Nature is not divine then we live surrounded by and immersed in filth. Everything we touch is disgusting and we should take stringent precautions to avoid polluting ourselves. We should be contemptuous of this world and place no value on it.

This position has much in common with extreme forms of Christian piety. We live with this legacy, and a dualist vocabulary that strongly opposes the 'spiritual' to the 'material'.

Iamblichus lived at the end of what we now call paganism; that is, a large number of diverse local and regional cults with their temples and holy statues, and priests that co-existed in relative harmony. The Emperor Constantine, who was to legalise Christianity, was born two years after the death of Iamblichus. Iamblichus could sense the coming end of the pagan world in southern Europe and the near-East.

Iamblichus disagreed with Plotinus in several important respects. It seemed to Iamblichus that philosophy was sucking the divinity out of this world with its world-denying emphasis on a remote, transcendental God of divine ideas and ideals, and was invalidating the local cults, which were firmly grounded in location and tradition and community. In his letter to Porphyry he sets out an alternative view. *De Mysteriis* was his attempt to show that cultic worship could be understood and dignified within the context of Platonic philosophy. He attempted to reverse a trend in Platonic philosophy that was simultaneously world-denying and so abstract that only a tiny elite could begin to understand the issues.

Central to his discussion was the status of the soul. Did the soul descend into Nature, or did it not? He believed (and his position mirrors that of the Hermetic discourses) that the soul has an aspect that does descend into Nature, and is fully engaged with Nature.

The soul, descended into Nature, sees only Nature, and loses sight of its divine origin and dignity. But if Nature is an aspect of the divine, then it will contain signs of its divine origin, signs recognised by the soul and capable of awakening the soul. This was the key argument made by Iamblichus: the soul can be awakened by physical ritual employing carefully chosen items to awaken it to the higher orders of reality.

The 'carefully chosen items' were *sunthemata*, items that had the property of revealing and communicating some aspect of the divine, and could be physical objects (stones, plants, animals), perfumes, divine names, music, actions, songs or poetry. *Sunthemata* were not just symbols or signifiers - they literally contained or channelled an aspect of divine energy. The One may have (at the level of Nature) become Many, but the Many were still One and retained their deep inner unity, so that every physical thing, even a stone, was capable of channelling an aspect of the One into this world (Cordovero makes this point in a quotation on page 102). Some things contained a more concentrated extract of divinity than others, and were used preferentially by the theurgist.

A ritual immersion in *sunthemata* had an effect, like that of a magnifying glass, of concentrating a divine aspect on the soul and awakening the corresponding aspect. Ritual was a natural adjunct to the worldview of Iamblichus: philosophy prepared the mind, and ritual awakened the interior eye of the soul to the natural orders of the Cosmos. In time the soul itself became *sunthemata*, a conscious channel for the divine influx capable of demiurgic action and co-creation:

> All of theurgy has a two-fold character. One is that it is a rite conducted by men which preserves our natural order in the universe; the other is that it is empowered by divine symbols (*sunthemata*), is raised up through them to be joined on high with the Gods, and is led harmoniously round to their order. This latter aspect can rightly be called 'taking the shape of the Gods'[80]

The experienced theurgist 'takes the shape of the Gods'[81] and acts like a god. This returns us to Gikatilla, where 'God is open to everyone'. This is unfamiliar territory to most people, stepped in centuries of belief that magic ritual could only be efficacious through the agency of evil demons. Iamblichus and Gikatilla, neither of whom were Christians, view the whole of reality, the human soul included, as pulsating with divinity, and tell us that we are entitled to use tokens of divinity to participate in the work of creation. Creation is not yet done, and we have an active role to play.

What of good and evil? The usual Kabbalistic view of theurgy is that evil occurs when human beings, through ego and wilfulness, attempt to disrupt the natural order by "separating what should be joined, and joining what should be separate". Iamblichus says something very similar:

> The influence from the Gods causes things that are furthest apart to move together according to the one harmony of the cosmos, but if someone who understands this tries to draw certain parts of the universe to other parts in a perverse way, the parts are in no way the cause of the perversion but the audacity of men and their transgression of the order of the cosmos, perverting things which are beautiful and lawful.[82]

He also adds that any damage caused by the theurgist "will fall on him personally"[83], so it is incumbent on the theurgist not to dabble.

The theurgist, by 'taking the shape of the Gods', can possess great power, potentially unlimited power, certainly the power of any sorcerer. To the outside observer there may be little obvious difference between the theurgist and the sorcerer, and we preserve that ambivalence today in literary characters such as Merlin, Prospero, Faust, Gandalf and Dumbledore. The difference between a Faust on one hand, and a Merlin, Gandalf or Dumbledore on the other, is the human difference between someone who is wrapped-up in personal lusts, passions and ambitions, and someone devoted to a larger scope of concern, usually beyond the limited grasp of other protagonists.

11.5 Marcelio Ficino

It is difficult to avoid some astonishment at the way so much of the important mystical and magical literature from late antiquity found its way to the desk of Marcelio Ficino (1433-1499 CE). There is

---

80. *De Mysteriis*, quoted in *Theurgy and the Soul*, Gregory Shaw, Pennsylvania State University Press 1995.
81. The assumption of god-forms was a ritual practice in the Golden Dawn.
82. Ibid.
83. Ibid.

a tradition in Tibetan Buddhism that teachings (*terma* - hidden treasures) may be concealed until, at some future auspicious time, they can be revealed to the world by a *terton*, who is usually an advanced adept. In some respects we can view Ficino as the *terton* of the Renaissance, the man who opened the box of forgotten magics lost for a thousand years.

The ground was prepared for Ficino by a seminal figure in the reintroduction of the Platonic/Pythagorean tradition to Europe. This was George Gemistus (1355-1452 CE), otherwise known as 'Pletho' or 'Plethon'. Deeply learned, a devotee of Plato, and a polytheistic pagan, he not only survived in the murky corners of the Byzantine world, he was well respected. In 1438, when the Byzantine Emperor travelled to Florence for an ecumenical council between the Roman and Orthodox Churches, Pletho and some of his students went along and provided lectures on Plato to the citizens of Florence. The works of Plato, unlike those of Aristotle, were little known or understood in Europe at this time, and for the most part were still untranslated out of Greek. The same was true for most of the later Platonists, especially Plotinus. According to the oft-recounted story, these lectures sowed a seed in the mind of the wealthy and powerful Florentine banker, Cosimo de' Medici, a seed that lay dormant for two decades.

Marcelio Ficino was the son of a physician and surgeon of middling means who had ministered to Cosimo de' Medici. Ficino was small, with a speech defect and a spinal deformity[84]. Early paintings show him with golden hair and curls in the style of the 15th. century; in later paintings he wears red clerical robes and appears careworn, fragile and pinched. He received an education in the humanities, and it would seem his father intended for him to practice as a doctor according to the tradition of Galen. He developed an enthusiasm for the Latin sources of Plato, and this may account for the fact that when his father introduced him to Cosimo de' Medici, the seed that had lain dormant in Cosimo's mind for so long came to fruit. Cosimo recognised quality in the young Ficino. They must have had a close relationship - Ficino described Cosimo de' Medici as his "second father".

There is some academic controversy about a supposed 'Platonic Academy' created by Cosimo with Ficino as its young 'director'. Rather than an 'academy', it would appear that Cosimo gifted Ficino with a villa outside Florence, and a modest income from an estate,

---

84. *The Life of Marcelio Ficino*, Giovanni Corsi, 1506

Theurgy

and in return for this generosity and patronage (especially gifts of rare and expensive books and manuscripts from Cosimo and his successors Piero and Lorenzo) Ficino spent his time translating and publicising the philosophy of Plato. In time Ficino acquired important students, the best-known being Giovanni Pico, who played an important role in promoting Kabbalah as an ancient source of divine wisdom.

Ficino's first major translation project was a manuscript of the *Corpus Hermeticum*. It would seem that Cosimo had whispered in ears about his interest in rare Greek manuscripts, and an Italian noble who travelled as "Father Leonardo de' Pistoia" uncovered an ancient manuscript in Macedonia. The manuscript was given to Marcelio Ficino, and when it was eventually published it caused a sensation.

Ficino believed it was a work of divine revelation pre-dating Plato, and possibly even Moses, that it was an ancient and authentic Egyptian teaching that *reappeared* in the later works of Pythagoras and Plato and (dare one say it) the *Bible*. He believed that what appeared to be the teaching of the Egyptian Hermes was ancient. He did not realise that its melange of Egyptian, Jewish and Neoplatonic ideas was a result of its relative lateness. What Ficino had on his desk was genuinely ancient and genuinely fascinating, but it was written at least 500 years after Plato.

Because the *Corpus Hermeticum* was believed to be an authentic divine revelation consistent with both the *Bible* and ancient philosophy, it provided a borderline respectability to Hermetic documents such as *The Perfect Sermon* (aka the *Asclepius*), and to the theurgic tendencies in later Platonists such as Iamblichus and Proclus. This is where Ficino began to go off-piste; he struggled to be a good Christian, and even became a priest at the age of forty-two, but he had an pronounced inclination towards theurgy and magic.

One reason for this was that he had medical training and continued to provide services as a physician to the Medici family. Medicine at that period, in the tradition of Hippocrates and Galen, was a much more esoteric subject than today, and preserved the worldview of late-antiquity in a practical form. Ficino's writing is saturated with the astrological wisdom of the period. He believed that stars and planets provided an intermediate veiling of the divine in the form of the *anima mundi*, the World Soul. Everything in this mundane world was imbued with stellar influences; an exceedingly fine medium (spirit or quintessence) communicated influences from soul into matter. The essence of medicine was to correct imbalances caused by malign influences by using benign aspects.

A second reason for his inclination towards theurgy was a melancholic disposition which he attributed to the influence of the planet Saturn. Today we would say that he had a tendency to depression, and at times this depression would appear to have been severe, affecting his overall health. He countered this by using the influences of the 'three graces': the Sun, Jupiter and Venus. Like the later Platonists such as Proclus he had a marked preference for the influence of the Sun to dispel the negative influence of Saturn.

Ficino has become famous for his 'Orphic singing'. Orpheus, whose skill with the lyre was legendary, was reputed to be the source of the teachings of Pythagoras, who was also known for his theurgic use of music to create effects. Ficino had resurrected the idea of *musica universalis*, the 'music of the spheres', which links reason, mathematics, harmony, proportion, and ratio. He could, by making music, draw down the influences of the stars.

We possess an idea of how the mage might perform an operation of this type in the description of a disciple of Ficino, Francesco Cattani da Diacceto[85]:

> If for example he wishes to acquire solarian gifts, first he sees that the sun is ascending in Leo or Aries, on the day and in the hour of the Sun. Then, robed in a solarian mantle of a solarian colour, such as gold, and crowned with a mitre of laurel, on the altar, itself made of a solarian material, he burns myrrh and frankincense, the Sun's own fumigations, having strewn the ground with heliotrope and suchlike flowers. Also he has an image of the Sun in gold or crysolite or carbuncle, that is, of the kind they think corresponds to each of the Sun's gifts. If, for example, he wishes to cure diseases, he has an image of the Sun enthroned, crowned, and wearing a saffron cloak, likewise a raven and the figure of the Sun, which are to be engraved on gold when the sun is ascending in the first face of Leo. Then, anointed with unguents made, under the same celestial aspect, from saffron, balsam, yellow honey and anything else of that kind, and not forgetting the cock and the goat, he sings the Sun's own hymn, such as Orpheus thought should be sung. For here is the force, and as it were the life, of the conciliation of the planet's favour. He sings, I say, first to the divine Henad of the Sun, then he sings to the Mind, and lastly sinks to the Soul; since One, Mind, Soul, are the three principles of all things. Also he uses a threefold harmony, of voice, of cithara, and of the whole body, of the kind he

---

85. Quoted in *Spiritual and Demonic Magic from Ficino to Campanella*, D. P. Walker, Sutton 2000

has discovered belongs to the Sun: not one which by too much complexity produces wantonness, or which constantly displays gravity, but one which is the mean between the two, which both is joyful by simplicity and at times does not avoid a mood of gravity. To all these he adds what he believes to be the most important: a strongly emotional disposition of the imagination, by which, as with pregnant women, the spirit is stamped with this kind of imprint and flying out through the channels of the body, especially through the eyes, ferments and solidifies, like rennet, the kindred power of the heavens.

What we find here is the theurgic magic of Iamblichus adopted and elaborated. The use of solar *sunthemata* is paramount to this method of channelling solar influences. This is a more systematic and coherent application of the principle of sympathy than one finds in 'low' magic. There are causal principles. There is also an explanatory big picture, a reference to the standard Neoplatonic wedding-cake cosmos of One, Mind, Soul and Matter. This is a theurgic recipe of considerable sophistication.

Without attempting to over-rationalise *sunthemata*, we can see this as an attempt to organise *qualia*, our direct, incommunicable experience of the world. It places the subjectivity of the theurgist at the centre. For the theurgist the associative web of connections - the smell of beeswax, the colour of honey, the roar of a lion, the buzz of bees in the sun, the yellow of buttercups, the timbre of a sound - these direct the soul, turn it about, force it to look within while simultaneously looking out. Pletho understood this well[86]:

> May we carry out these rites in your honour in the most fitting manner, knowing that you have no need of anything whatever from us. But we are moulding and stamping our imagination and that part of us which is most akin to the divine, allowing it to enjoy both the godly and the beautiful, and making our imagination tractable and obedient to that which is divine in us.

Ficino's commitment to the Platonic tradition, and his productivity as a translator and commentator, was impressive. After completing the translation of fourteen tractates of the *Corpus Hermeticum* he went on to translate the works of Plato, and later in his life, the *Enneads* of Plotinus. He produced substantial commentaries on Plato, and taught and lectured. His impact on students, friends, and later disciples, was enormous. He had at his disposal most of the dangerous literature of late antiquity. Walker lists[87]:

---

86. Ibid.
87. Ibid.

Peter of Abano and other medieval writers on magic, such as Roger Bacon, Alkindi, Avicenna, and 'Picatrix', are probably sources for Ficino's talismans, and I would suggest invocations to planets. But far more important are certain Neoplatonic texts: Proclus' *De Sacrificiis et Magia*, Iamblichus' *De Mysteriis* and *Vita Pythagorae*, Porphyry's *De Abstinentia*, the *Hermetica*, especially the *Asclepius*. Most of these Ficino translated or paraphrased.

Ficino struggled to reconcile his Christianity with the marvellous philosophy of the ancients, and became a Christian apologist for Plato in his later years. He was protected by powerful patrons, and lived in the adventurous and seemingly tolerant[88] atmosphere of the Italian Renaissance, but still had to exercise caution. Both Ficino and Giovanni Pico emphasised the 'naturalness' of their natural magic, that there was a 'good' natural magic that operated without recourse to entities that might be interpreted as demonic, and there was a bad magic (using incantations, sigils, and barbarous names) that was demonic and illegitimate. This separation was defensive and self-protective. Their presumptions about the nature of the cosmos, suffused with soul and life and intelligence at every level, made a nonsense of this kind of thinking.

In 1484, at the instigation of the German Dominican inquisitor Heinrich Kramer, the credulous Pope Innocent VIII issued the Papal Bull *Summis Desiderantes Affectibus* recognising the reality of witchcraft and providing the authority to prosecute it by "correcting, imprisoning, punishing and chastising". In 1487 Kramer and James Sprenger published the infamous *Malleus Maleficarum*, the '*Hammer of the Witches*', a handbook intended to alert and assist the prosecutor tasked with exterminating witches. In the same year Pope Innocent appointed Tomas de Torquemada Grand Inquisitor of the Spanish Inquisition[89]. He also interdicted the *Theses* of Giovanni Pico. These events occurred within Ficino's lifetime.

11.6 Heinrich Cornelius Agrippa

Seeing there is a threefold world, elementary, celestial and intellectual, and every inferior is governed by its superior, and receiveth the influence of the virtues thereof, so that the very original and chief Worker of all doth by angels, the heavens, stars, elements, plants, metals, and

---

88. The flip-side to the Renaissance in Florence was the messianic lunacy of the populist preacher Girolamo Savonarola, who organised book-burnings and homosexual pogroms towards the end of Ficino's life.
89. Nobody expected that.

Theurgy

stones convey from himself the virtues of his omnipotency upon us, for whose service he made and created all these things: wise men conceive it in no way irrational that it should be possible for us to ascend by the same degrees through each world to the same very original world itself, the Maker of all things, and First Cause, from whence all things are and proceed; and also to enjoy not only these virtues, which are already in the more excellent kind of things, but also besides these, to draw new virtues from above.

This brilliant and irresistible opening sentence comes from the first paragraph of the first chapter of the first book of Heinrich Cornelius Agrippa's *Three Books of Occult Philosophy*. The entire Hermetic enterprise is contained within it. If any work could be said to contain the prospectus of 'real occultism' then this is it. Seek no further.

It is a compendious and encyclopaedic work that, in Donald Tyson's copiously annotated edition runs to 700 pages of core text, and nearly 1000 pages when Tyson's additional material is included. It was written by Agrippa in his early twenties and his original manuscript version from 1510 still exists - that is, it was written about ten years after Ficino's death. On the advice of Agrippa's mentor, the immensely learned Abbot Trithemius, it was not published for a further two decades.

The three books mirror the organisation of the cosmos. The first deals with the elementary world, substances, and the body, and corresponds approximately to the Kabbalistic world of *Assiah*, the World of Action. The second book deals with the celestial realm of the stars, planets, numbers, and the rationally comprehensible aspect of divine administration. This corresponds approximately to the Kabbalistic world of *Yetzirah*, the World of Formation. The final book discuss the intellectual realm and matters of religion, and contains (among many other discussions) a digest of Kabbalah taken primarily from the writings of Johann Reuchlin (1455-1522), who in turn was influenced by Giovanni Pico, whom he met in 1490. This third book corresponds to the Kabbalistic world of *Briah*, the world of Creation.

It is an astonishing work in several respects. Its structure, organisation into subject headings, and frequent summations of relevant philosophy suggest a mature ability to stand back from the subject and view it in its entirety. It references an immense quantity of background material directly, with thousands of quotations from, and reference to, classical literature; indirectly it is suffused with the spirit of Ficino, the Hermetica, and the Neoplatonists. It suggests proximity to a large reference library of arcane manuscripts, as well as access to

The Hermetic Kabbalah

the contemporary writings of Ficino, Pico, Reuchlin and *their* sources.

This raises the question of the involvement of Trithemius, who did indeed have an exceptionally fine esoteric library at the abbey in Sponheim ... but Trithemius resigned from Sponheim in 1506, and was in Wurzburg when Agrippa presented him with his first draft in 1510.

Although Agrippa tipped his hat in the direction of Christianity from time to time, his *Three Books* are essentially a distillation of the pagan magic and esoteric philosophy of the pre-Christian world of late antiquity, the world of Iamblichus, Proclus, the technical *Hermetica*, and the *Asclepius*. And he included the Kabbalah, added to the mix because, according to the humanist syncretism of the period, it was seen to be a part of the same big picture, another branch of an original *prisca theologia*.

A unique aspect of the *Three Books* is that they unite an intellectual comprehension of the nature and structure of reality with the technical aspects required for interaction. Most 'black books' or grimoires possess the structure of a cookbook, with instructions and recipes. They appeal to the practically-minded who just want to get on with seducing their neighbour's wife, suborning judges, souring milk, or spiriting away their neighbours' crops (a genuine concern in Roman times). The intimate relationship between cosmos and magic is reduced to empty formulae. The *Three Books* are more in the nature of a scholarly presentation of everything the youthful Agrippa knew about the organisation and mechanics of the cosmos. The subtext is "everything you wanted to know about the cosmos but were really afraid to ask". Agrippa might seem archaic and boring to the modern reader because he devotes so much effort and detail to a view of the cosmos that is now obsolete, but to anyone with a genuine interest in the esoteric, the *Three Books* possess a charm that grows and grows.

It is unclear how much effort Agrippa devoted to magical pursuits. He accumulated a considerable reputation during his chaotic and hectic life, and stories associated with him became a part of the legend of Faust. He recanted his work of youthful folly in later life, raising the question of how sincere his *volte-face* was. He probably was sincere, but it is worth noting that the *Constitutio Criminalis Carolina*, the penal code for the Holy Roman Empire, ratified in 1532 (three years before Agrippa's death), sanctioned death by burning for those guilty of sorcery and witchcraft. Europe was being torn apart by the Reformation, in a climate of religious mania and hysteria. It was not a safe

Theurgy

place, and would be dominated by a religious furore for more than a century.

11.7 Modern Theurgy

The theurgic tradition of late antiquity, the tradition that has come down to us from Iamblichus and the Neoplatonists via Ficino and Agrippa and many others, continues today. Very few people are aware of the tradition, squeezed as it is between the mainstream religions and a combination of atheism and scientific rationalism.

The modern scientific understanding is that the world is mechanistic and dead. This would seem to signal the end of various kinds of magic, but this has not been the case. The occult revival of the 19th. century, which began with spiritualism and achieved enormous visibility through the activities of Madame Blavatsky, had the effect of bringing about a revival of interest in the Hermetic tradition. One can cite for example G. R. S. Mead (1863-1933 CE) who was for a time Blavatsky's private secretary, and who published an excellent collected edition of *Hermetica*[90].

The most important filter for these traditions in the English speaking world was the Hermetic Order of the Golden Dawn, who captured much of the syncretic spirit of Renaissance humanism in their rituals and teaching, and did much to popularise Kabbalah at a time when it was almost unknown outside of relatively closed Jewish circles.

The twentieth century has seen an expansion of interest in the subject, and the publication of a large number of books on Kabbalah, the Hermetic arts, and magic. One can (using the Pillars of the Tree as a guide) group this interest under the three headings of *agency*, *gnosis*, and *communion*.

Under agency one can include the renewed and very active interest in the grimoire tradition, what one might loosely term 'Solomonic Magic' or *goetia*. This is a conservative and results-oriented tradition, and has a strong flavour of the kitchen recipe book, with formulae for obtaining specific results. It can be traced back in an almost unchanged form to the ancient world, and shares many cosmological assumptions[91]. The classic grimoire describes how to summon and dismiss various spirits, may contain descriptions of spirits and how they may be employed, and may contain a miscellany of magical

---

90. *Thrice Greatest Hermes, Studies in Hellenistic Theosophy and Gnosis*, G.R.S. Mead, Weiser 2001

methods for achieving various results, the most popular of which tended to concern women, hidden treasure, and judges. The *goetia* tends to appeal to the solitary practitioner. Closely related to this, and subject to much analysis, are the spirit or angelic workings of Dr. John Dee and Edward Kelly.

Under communion one finds a large and active neopagan community, with an emphasis on seasonal ceremonies. These are modern re-enactments of traditional, pre-Christian religious communities, an attempt to reconnect the present with the past. It is now understood that many of the traditions and practices drew heavily from the late nineteenth century occult revival, but have evolved over time into distinctive communities.

Under gnosis one finds many offshoots of the Golden Dawn, using quasi-masonic group rituals and complex and innovative ritual formulae. These are syncretic and combine many traditions (including Kabbalah) for the purposes of ascent mysticism, and can be classed as gnostic, as the overall purpose is the rectification of the soul.

One must suspect that for any given person one would find a combination of agency, gnosis and communion according to temperament - these are not sharp boundaries. Wiccan witches are as likely to be as results-oriented as the most ardent solitary practitioner of the *goetia*. Some traditions tend to be dominated by men, others have more appeal to women. Some people are solitary practitioners, others prefer to be in a group.

Non-conformist religious belief and practice has always been characterised by a fierce individuality, and one finds this in the countless gnostic cults of late-antiquity, in the hydra-like fragmentation of the Protestant reformation, and in the many ways the Hermetic tradition has been used and adapted during the twentieth century. Perhaps the most extreme in its individuality, and rejection of hierarchy, authority, and cosmology, would be the Chaos Magic of the 1970s and 80s. Chaos magic, in its rejection of the tradition, forms the postmodern and nihilistic limit of the tradition.

Theurgy continues in a form remarkably similar to what one might obtain were one to combine Iamblichus with Gikatilla. This book is an outcome of one such tradition; that is, the author received a tradition of theurgic Hermetic Kabbalah, and this book reflects four

---

91. The 'howlings' or *goetia* can be studied in an original form in T*he Greek Magical Papyri in Translation*, ed. Hans Dieter Betz, University of Chicago Press, 1992. See also the collection of Coptic texts published as *Early Christian Magic*, ed. Marvin Meyer & Richard Smith, Harper 1994

Theurgy

decades of working within the tradition. Although the author is bound by the traditional requirement of silence regarding the details of the tradition (a traditional requirement that can be found in the *Corpus Hermeticum*) it is possible to provide a synopsis, and much can be inferred from the totality of the book.

The overall goal is gnostic, as described in Part Three, *The Rectification of the Soul*. It is more overtly Kabbalistic than many other traditions, but contains much that would be immediately familiar to Iamblichus nearly eighteen hundred years ago.

An important aspect is the use of *sunthemata* - colours, perfumes, sounds, ritual actions and so on - to awaken the soul and guide it into those aspects of its reality to which it would be otherwise unconscious. The rich symbolism associated with the Tree of Life suggests many *sunthemata*, and *colour* is one of the most important.

Malkhut is associated with earthy colours, in particular, brown. *Yesod* is a deep aethyric purple suggestive of a moonlit night, of things half-seen. *Hod* is the orange of mercuric compounds, especially mercuric oxide. *Netzach* is the green of copper, metal of *Venus*. *Tiferet* is the yellow-gold of the Sun. *Gevurah* is the red of blood. *Chesed* is the blue of the sky. *Binah* is the blackness of the tomb. *Chokhmah* is the sparkle of the *mazlot*, the zodiac, the starry sky. *Keter* is the pure white of bright light. These colour correspondences derive from Hermetic tradition and are associated with the planets. They have come down to us through the Golden Dawn and have become ubiquitous in representations of the Tree of Life.

Colour, the ritual use of perfumes and incense, the correct intonation and *focus* on divine names (as in Gikatilla), and the overall structure of ritual constitute the most important physical *sunthemata*. There are other *sunthemata* however, those of the soul. The organisational structure of the soul determines how we live our lives, and determines the kind of person we are. According to tradition we are little gods, and the smallness of our demiurgy is determined by the narrowness of our souls. We are like those workers who handle dangerous substances through a wall using heavy rubber gloves - reality feels dangerous, and our souls keep us at a remove.

Each *sefira* possesses a positive quality that 'widens' the soul and makes it more capable of receiving divine emanations. These are the virtues. Each *sefira* possesses a negative quality that 'narrows' the soul and makes us even less capable of receiving the divine emanations. These are the vices and the illusions. To the extent that divine emanations fail to reach the soul, so the soul feels dead, empty, soiled, and trapped in sterile routines. These experiences are the *klippot*.

The work of the theurgist is not limited to the ritual space and great stress is placed on opening gates in the soul to let light in, so that inculcating virtue and banishing vice becomes a permanent discipline. For example, the virtue of *Netzach* is unselfishness, and the vice is selfishness. The selfish person is closed to *Netzach*; the selfish soul is not *sunthemata* for the divine emanations of *Netzach*. The arrogant soul is not *sunthemata* for *Tiferet*. The avaricious soul cannot ascend to *Binah*. This task of rectification, shaping a soul that can manifest some small part of the divine in this world, is a distinctive aspect of theurgical work; one can liken it to creating a Tree of Life in the microcosm.

Further insight into these methods can be found in Part 2, which discusses the correspondences for the *sefirot*, including virtue, vice, illusion, klippot and several others, and in Part 3, which attempts to explain and justify what must seem to be a strange idea: the rectification of the soul.

11.8 Further Reading

For insight into Iamblichus, one of my favourite books:

> *Theurgy and the Soul: The Neoplatonism of Iamblichus*, Gregory Shaw, Pennsylvania State University, 1995

For insight into Ficino and his impact:

> *Spiritual and Demonic Magic from Ficino to Campanella*, D. P. Walker, Sutton 2000

> *Eros and Magic in the Renaissance*, Ioan Couliano, The University of Chicago, 1987

Agrippa is essential reading for anyone who wants to understand the continuation of the Hermetic tradition into modern times, and this is an outstanding edition:

> *Three Books of Occult Philosophy*, Henry Cornelius Agrippa, ed. Donald Tyson, Llewellyn 1993

For a scholarly treatment of the grimoire tradition of thaumaturgy:

> *Grimoires: A History of Magic Books*, Owen Davies, Oxford University Press, 2009

The practical aspects of theurgy and thaumaturgy overlap to a significant extent. For a throrough practical introduction to the classical techniques of thaumaturgy:

> *Secrets of the Magical Grimoires*, Aaron Leitch, Llewellyn 2005

Theurgy

For an introduction to ritual magic with a theurgic bias along the lines of the Golden Dawn:

Circles of Power, John Michael Greer, Llewellyn 1997

Authentic practical or occult aspects of Kabbalah are often deprecated, frowned-upon, or assumed to be non-Jewish. Nothing could be further from the truth. Kaplan's book (below) is more 'occult' than the title might suggest.

Jewish Magic and Superstition, Joshua Trachtenberg, University of Pennsylvania 2004

Meditation and Kabbalah, Aryeh Kaplan, Weiser 1982

The Hermetic Kabbalah

12

Emanation & Emergence

12.1 Introduction

Emanation runs through Kabbalah like wire in an automobile - you can't always see it, but it is part of the inner working. Emanation is not the only story; there are alternative perspectives, such as the dynamics of the *Partzufim*, or the body of Adam Kadmon, or the agency of Divine Names, or the seven days of creation, and so on. Each way of thinking about the Tree of Life imparts its own flavour, and part of the charm is that none of these perspectives is necessarily consistent or coherent with any other. Nevertheless, emanation is one of the outstanding intellectual relics of the world of late antiquity, and it is an important aspect of Kabbalah, and so we must, if we aspire to be serious about Kabbalah, grasp its main ideas and implications.

There is a problem however, and its seriousness may not be apparent to the reader at this point. The problem is that emanation has gone the way of the stagecoach. It was an essential component of intellectual understanding until the beginning of the seventeenth century CE, and then it was gradually replaced by a new understanding in which complexity *emerged* out of blind, mechanistic interactions. A key point in the acceptance of this new understanding was Darwin's model of the evolution of species by heritable variation and environmental selection. This pulled the rug out from under the Biblical story of creation because it showed that species were not fixed and new species could evolve in response to environmental pressure. When this understanding is combined with the geological record and the evidence from fossils it is possible to create a picture that shows life evolving and adapting over billions of years.

What is presented here is not an attempt to favour one position over the other. The theories of emanation, and subsequently emergence, represent the considerable efforts of intelligent people doing their best to understand why the world has the character that it does. Emergence is a tricky and unintuitive idea, and had it been intuitive, people would have arrived at it much sooner than they did. Emergence proposes that complex living organisms can emerge spontaneously from a primordial soup of simple chemicals. Without the scientific understanding gained over the twentieth century this idea is no more credible than believing in a Maker. It is only within the lifetime of the author that emergent complexity began to take shape as a coherent theory, and even today it is not widely understood by the public.

If I viewed Kabbalah as an obsolete view of reality then I would have focused on emanation and ignored emergence. This is not my view, and so I took the decision to contrast the two models. This may seem like a major digression into unfamiliar territory, but I believe it is worth pursuing.

12.2 Dead or Alive?

Throughout history the default understanding of the world was that it was *alive*, and was the visible manifestation of *unseen agency*. This outlook is still common in children, and some may recall what it feels like. One can still find this belief in many cultures around the world, and until the seventeenth century it was the dominant understanding in Europe.

When the world is alive the dominant *techne* is an understanding of the diverse modes of relationship required to deal with spirits and gods. There are social classes - shamans, priests, cunning-folk, diviners etc. - who specialise in these relationships, and provide a diagnostic service in cases of sickness and ill-fortune. They will tell you what spirit you have offended, and how to make things right.

When the world is alive nothing is truly determined (unless Fate has decreed that it should be so). Miracles can happen. Prayers, sacrifices and offerings show that outcomes are negotiable, and ill-fortune can be set aside for a price, because the world is held in place by *will*, and can be shifted out of place by will.

Emanation & Emergence

At the beginning of *The Godfather*, guests pay their respects to Don Corleone. It is his daughter's wedding, and according to tradition, they can make requests. For millenia people have treated the unseen agencies of this world in this way, honouring the day, showing respect, giving gifts, asking for favours.

Because outcomes are determined by will, we are not permitted to ask 'how things work'. Folk tales are filled with miraculous creations that violate any sense of deterministic causality - flying carpets, magic bean stalks, cloaks of invisibility, seven-league boots, magic rings. We are told what they do, but we are never told how they work. They are the creations of will and intelligence, not mechanism. For millenia Christians believed that the smooth running of Nature could be suspended at any time; the sky would open and the End of the World would begin.

The view that the cosmos is alive and the product of unseen agency is like a story; we cannot expect full or consistent explanations because we can never know with certainty what a living being will do.

A more recent understanding that has come to prominence over the last three centuries is that the world is *dead*. It is mechanical, like a machine. According to this understanding, the world behaves in the way it does because its constituent parts follow simple rules. After three hundred years of careful experiment and observation we now have a good understanding of these rules.

When the world is dead the dominant *techne* is understanding the rules and how to apply them to real-life situations. To do this we use language in a formal way - what we call reason and mathematics. The classes of people who understand this formal use of language we call physicists, chemists, biologists and engineers.

Because the rules are invariant in the circumstances experimentalists have devised and encountered so far, we are able to talk about *laws*, such as Newton's laws of motion and gravitation, Maxwell's laws of electrodynamics, and the various conservation laws such as those of energy, momentum and angular momentum.

When we aggregate all the rules that work consistently and dependably we find that a large part of the behaviour in the world is determined. Some would say *all* the behaviour in the world is determined, even human behaviour. It is determined by principles that are comprehensible, principles that do not vary. There is no agency (except Hollywood) that can suspend or modify these rules. In evidence of this extraordinary claim, one can exhibit the mobile smartphone, a small, mass-produced device of astonishing complexity that subsumes a large part of the technology we possess in one small object. It works, therefore our understanding is good. *Quod erat demonstrandum*.

From the seventeenth century onwards Europe was in a quandary. One one hand there was the age-old belief that the world was alive, and that the human soul was part of a disincarnate ecology of being. On the other hand there was a rapidly emerging technology based on the understanding that the world followed rules like a machine (i.e. was dead). This was an era of increasingly complex and lifelike clockwork automata - the simulation of life. Traditional religion saw the world as a product of divine agency. A small but persuasive band of natural philosophers saw the world as a product of mechanism and accident.

At the centre of the debate was the status of the human soul - did it belong to the world of life, or like the body, did it belong to the world of death. A half-baked compromise was to make the assumption that the soul, a ghostly apparition and the seat of personal identity and consciousness, was connected to the body with a piece of aethyric wet string anchored somewhere in the brain (Descarte famously proposed the pineal gland). Naive proposals of this kind form the basis of the famous mind-body problem.

A loose formulation of the mind-body problem is that the mind exists autonomously and aphysically, but somehow maintains a causally efficacious two-way connection with the brain. In the opinion of the author the idea is ludicrous, completely daft, for reasons that should become clear in Part Three, where I discuss the physical nature of intelligence and consciousness. I believe there is no coherent notion of mind, intelligence or consciousness that is not embodied. To talk about a disembodied soul is an error of the same kind as talking about dehydrated water.

If we reject quasi-dualist solutions (i.e. a realm of life bonded to a realm of death) then we must confront monist solutions. There are two major variants of monism. In the first variant, everything is derived from Mind. In the second variant, everything is derived from Matter. The first is usually called Idealism, and the second Materialism. Idealist models begin with One Thing that fragments, and can be characterised as 'top-down'. Materialist models begin with Many Things that combine, and can be characterised as 'bottom-up'.

Naively, one would have thought that there could be only one kind of monism (if everything is One, does it matter whether we call it mind or matter or jello?) but this is not the case. Top-down and bottom-up models look completely different, and people have extremely polarised feelings about them. The first model is 'emanation', and the second 'emergence'. It is important to understand how they differ. It will then be possible to see how Kabbalah fits into the picture.

12.3 Neoplatonic Emanation

European and Middle Eastern mythology contain many accounts of the creation of the world. In Norse mythology the giant Ymir is killed by Odin and his brothers, and Ymir's body is dismembered and used to create the world. In Babylonian mythology the God Marduk kills the monster Tiamat, and again her body is used to create the world.

There is no logical structure to these narratives. Various entities - Giants or Titans or Elder Gods - appear without explanation, and implausible events take place which culminate in the creation of the world and the birth of various cultic gods and goddesses.

The *Bible* states that God made the world over the course of seven days. Kabbalists have scoured the *Bible* and traditional literature for insight into the creative process. What they were looking for was more insight, more explanation, more detail. How *did* God make the world? Was creation an essentially miraculous sequence of acts, or was there a process that one could comprehend rationally?

The doctrine of emanation marks a shift from the earliest mythology towards monotheism and rationality. It is closely associated with the Platonic tradition, but it has its roots in the quasi-legendary figure of Pythagoras. There are old stories that suggest Pythagoras obtained some of his traditions from Jewish sources (or that he was Jewish!) during many years of travelling throughout the near-east and Egypt. It is probably not wise to give the detail of these stories too much credence, given that we have so little credible information about him. What we are told is that Pythagoras believed in one God who is the source of all things. If the record of his extensive travels is accurate then it is likely that he talked to Jews who believed the same thing.

Emanation appealed to the rational mind because in place of pure story-telling it substituted a quasi-rational development. It eliminated an *a priori* assemblage of unaccountable giants, monsters and elder gods doing dark deeds at the dawn of time, and substituted a single source for all things. In this it coincided with the rise of monotheistic religion and so was able to piggyback itself onto the three major faiths that dominated the history of Europe and the Middle

The Hermetic Kabbalah

East.

The introduction of a single source for all things seems like a major simplification, but the rational development of this proved to be anything but simple. This is the traditional problem of the One and the Many: how does a single source of all Being develop into multiplicity? How does a process that takes place outside of time become temporal? How does perfection become imperfect? How does the Good and the Beautiful manifest evil and ugliness? The theory of emanation attempted to provide a rational explanation for what appeared to be irreconcilable dualities, and it became more and more complex over time.

It was Plato who created the outline structure of emanationism, but his ideas cannot be dignified as a theory because there are too many loose ends, too many undeveloped hints, too many contradictions. Plato was more interested in presenting arguments than answers. The successors to Plato developed his hints and arguments over a period of one thousand years, during which Rome and Byzantium displaced Greece as a dominant power, and Christianity displaced a large number of regional cults that we now refer to as paganism.

A classic exposition of Neoplatonic emanationism is found in the *Enneads* of Plotinus (204-270 CE). Two hundred years later a valiant attempt to provide a rational and axiomatic development in the style of Euclid's geometry can be found in the *Elements of Theology* of Proclus (412 - 487 CE). Proclus was the last of the notable pagan Neoplatonists because the Platonic Academy in Athens was shut down by the Byzantine emperor Justinian in 529 CE, and the descendents of the Platonic tradition dispersed. Nevertheless, Neoplatonic ideas became an integral part of the intellectual and mystical superstructure of Christianity, Islam and Judaism, where they were merged and harmonised with the revelatory traditions of each religion, so that they became the pervasive 'standard model' of intellectual thought until the scientific reformation in Europe.

The key idea that informs emanationism is that everything that exists depends upon a single source for its being. There is an ontological dependency that proceeds via a number of discrete steps, and with each step, the level of *alienation* increases. One might imagine a flow of water from a spring or fountain, or the emanation of light from a candle (and these images are often used in kabbalistic literature), but there is no actual flow or movement. There is no diminution of the source. The *Zohar* likens this dependency to lighting one candle from another. There is a *great chain of being* that proceeds from a source in discrete steps until it terminates in the world as we experience it.

By definition, the source (characterised by Plato as The Good, and by Plotinus as The One) represents complete unity, infinite creative potency, and absolute self-knowledge. Each successive step in the hierarchy is marked by an increase in multiplicity, a decrease in creative potency, and a decrease in self-knowledge. This is because each level emanates a subsequent level according to its creative potency, and this creative potency diminishes in proportion to the degree of alienation and ignorance. In their normal state human beings are characterised by a perception of multiplicity and fragmentation, very limited creative potency, and almost complete ignorance of the interconnectedness of all things.

Why discrete steps? Why not a continuum? The Greeks of the classical period lacked the tools for conceptualising continuous change - these would not be developed until Newton and Leibniz formulated the infinitesimal calculus in the seventeenth century. During the Hellenistic period, mathematics was concerned with natural numbers and with ratios of natural numbers. The Pythagoreans had grasped the connection between mathematics and physical phenomena through the observation that strings clamped according to certain ratios of natural numbers would produce harmonious or discordant sounds. There was a *relationship* between the length of the string and the pitch. In retrospect this was a profound observation, and it could have led to a scientific revolution, but it did not.

Instead, natural numbers were held to possess *intrinsic qualities*, and the progression of numbers from one to ten was assumed to possess a cosmological significance. That is, individual numbers acted as the roots of fundamental qualities in an emanational scheme.

An example of this can be found in the Pythagorean *Tectatrys*, where the numbers from one to ten are arranged in four rows within an equilateral triangle (see Figure 28). Another example of this thinking can be found in that seminal and influential work of Jewish Neopythagoreanism, the *Sepher Yetzirah*, where the first ten counting numbers and the twenty-two letters of the Hebrew alphabet are taken to be the ontological foundations of manifest existence.

The emanational scheme according to Plotinus exhibits four levels. The first three are The One, The Intelligible or Divine Mind, and Soul (specifically, the World Soul). The fourth level or entity is Matter, a difficult concept, and Plotinus struggled with it.

The One is the source of all emanation. It cannot be characterised

The Hermetic Kabbalah

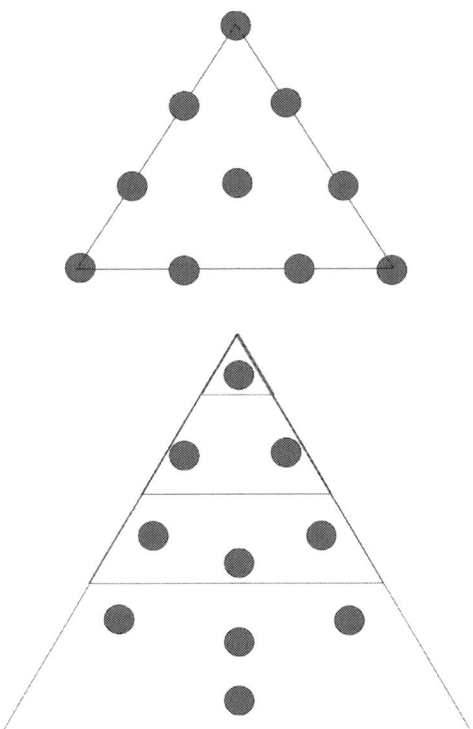

Figure 28: Above: the Pythagorean *Tectatrys*, the numbers one to ten arranged in an arithmetic series with four rows (1+2+3+4 = 10) to form an equilateral triangle. Below: a minor rearrangement of the four rows to form the Tree of Life, and showing one of the variant attributions of the *sefirot* to the Four Worlds.

by language. Any descriptive term would imply a limit or structure, and the One is beyond limit or structure. In Kabbalah the title *En Sof* ('no end' or 'no limit') is used, and this also denotes limitlessness.

The next level, the Intelligible, is the mind of God. It contains the forms of all existents. Plato wondered how we could know or recognise anything given that the world we experience is in a constant state of flux. Everything changes, nothing is stable. According to Plato's theory of knowledge, the abstract forms of everything we are capable of knowing exist within the mind of God. We are able to recognise beauty because our souls have encountered the Form of Beauty in the realm of the Intelligible. We know what is good, or what is just, in the same way. Even simple things such as a table or a chair have their correlates in the realm of Form.

Emanation & Emergence

Although the Forms may sound like dry, mathematical abstractions, they live in the mind of God, and are imbued with creative power. They are demiurgic within their own limits, and it is better to conceive of them as quasi-autonomous living beings integrated and harmonised within an overall divine purpose[92].

Soul provides the interface between Idea and Embodiment. On one hand it contemplates the form of which it is a realisation, and on the other hand it organises matter into a living being. It is the soul that provides vitality and coherence to matter that would otherwise be disorganised and formless. In the absence of soul (as in death) matter reverts once more to its natural state. Soul is torn between two realities. On one hand there is the eternal reality of the Intelligible realm, and on the other hand there is the shadow reality of the material world. The soul can be corrupted by its attachment to the material world, and 'forgets' its divine origin.

This 'forgetting' occurs because the soul attaches values to material things, and these values give rise to passions which blind the soul. The soul forgets its origin in the divine, and is unable to see that the material world is the shadow of a higher reality. In *The Republic*, Plato gives the allegory of the cave. A group of people are chained in a cave and can only see the wall in front of them. A troupe of players carry objects and act out scenes behind the chained people, and the shadows of these actions are projected on the wall by the light of a fire. The chained people have only the experience of shadows, and mistake them for reality.

The worlds of being that emanate from The One are good, in that all things possess correct measure and proportion; they are rationally ordered according to the divine reason-principle, and they exist in harmony. The emanations from the One are ideal, because they derive from the form of The Good as described by Plato in *The Republic*, and later Platonists would equate The Good with The One. There is no place in this worldview for anything that is deficient or superfluous. Everything that emanates from The One is both perfect and necessary.

This is inconsistent with the imperfect world that we experience. The fourth concept in the worldview of Plotinus is Matter, the matrix for the embodiment of form. It is Matter that must bear the entire burden of the deficiency we find in the natural world. An intuitive

---

92. The first part of Tolkien's *Silmarillion*, called *Ainulindalë*, is a creation story in which divine thoughts (the *Ainur*) elaborate musical themes of increasing autonomy and complexity while still harmonising around a divine purpose.

way to think about this is to imagine the designer of a mechanism, such as an automobile engine. The designer would design every part according to its function and its relationship with every other part. Gears would necessarily mesh, and fasteners would necessarily fasten. There would be no superfluous parts, each part would contribute to the overall function of the machine. But a real engine must use real materials, which break or bend or stick. They *wear out*. The entire Plotinian view is contained in this example: the designer (The One), the ideal components (the Forms), an integrated and functioning whole as ideally conceived (Soul), and the defective realisation (Matter).

Because of the way that Plotinus sets up Matter in opposition to The Good, he produces a perplexing concept that appears to be intellectually void[93]. According to Plotinus all form emanates from the One, and so Matter is formless - it possesses no structure. It is characterised by privation, need, and estrangement. It is the principle of *alienation* - the separation of things that belong together, and the antagonism of things that should be in harmony. Sometimes Plotinus characterises Matter as the theoretical limit-point of emanation, like parallel lines that meet at infinity. Matter is emanation that has become so estranged from its source and so weakened that it is no longer capable of further emanation, and is purely *receptacle*.

The order of emanation, from the One to the Many, establishes an order of priority and dependence. Emanation is a 'top-down' model. Because the soul is rooted in the divine it does not depend on matter and has its being *independently of a material basis*. It is the soul that organises matter into a living form, and when it departs, that matter decomposes. This view is still pervasive in many religions and in popular belief.

Emanation also provides the basis for a *hierarchy of being*, often depicted as a sequence of concentric circles (Figure 25). An understanding of the hierarchy of intermediate intelligences, along with secret names and sigils, is the basic for invocatory and petitionary magic, and the surviving textual tradition is often referred to as *magical grimoires*[94].

---

93. Matter: a substance devoid of substance or being.
94. Given the pervasive nature of dualism, it is unsuprising that the demonic realms were also organised according to hierarchy. It is probably redundant to point out belief in emanation and hierarchy coincided with sharply delineated social stratification and the institution of divine kingship. The rise of belief in emergence coincides with liberal democracy.

Emanation & Emergence

There are important differences between the classical emanationism of Plotinus and emanation in Kabbalah. The dualistic tendency in Platonism, in which Matter is opposed to The Good, is avoided in Kabbalah. In Neoplatonism the principle of alienation appears as an end point of emanation. In Kabbalah, especially Lurianic Kabbalah, alienation is the essence of the first creative act where God withdraws his being to create a void.

Kabbalah avoids the dualistic tendency of Plotinus by linking all potentially dualistic elements into dynamic unities through the structure of the Tree of Life. The three Pillars represent pairs of contraries and their reconciliation. Even *Malkhut* is dual to *Keter* and *Tiferet*. This reconciliation is dynamic - that is, there is continual flux and change which provides a cosmic backdrop to events in this world, but, like a swinging pendulum, things balance out.

Much of the discussion of Matter in Neoplatonism is duplicated in Kabbalistic discussions of the *sefira Malkhut*. Each *sefira* on the Tree of Life is characterised by receiving and giving, except for *Keter*, which only gives, and *Malkhut*, which only receives[95]. Like Plotinian Matter, *Malkhut* is also characterised as needy and lacking, and when the flow of divine beneficence is interrupted, estranged and alienated.

As a model of how the universe came into existence, emanation has been remarkably pervasive and persistent. Neoplatonic ideas became an integral part of Judaism, Christianity, and Islam, and provide a model for mystical praxis, the *ascent* model of mysticism, in which the practitioner ascends through the various wedding-cake layers of reality to reunite with God. Many of its key ideas still pervade New Age mysticism, often in a disconnected mish-mash. Emanation is psychologically satisfying: it states that the individual human soul is a component in a vast and integrated system of cosmic harmony, and if we can overcome the passions that create a state of confusion and ignorance, we can participate in the cosmos.

Neither is it a foolish model. Human beings are creative. Even in classical times artisans had the skill to produce works of the most astonishing intricacy and delicacy, and Grecian artists and architects are still a source of inspiration and instruction. If there are greater minds than human minds (and there probably are) then it is likely that they will also create.

---

95. Although *Malkhut* is characterised as only receiving, it nevertheless originates and sustains countless worlds in its guise as Mother and Queen.

It seemed to the Greeks that the complex but comprehensible movements of the celestial sphere - the motions of sun and moon, the movement of the planets, the patterns of the stars, the predictable occurrence of eclipses - required rational design. It could not possibly be accident. The world we live in and the celestial spheres could only have been *made*. This is why, in the *Timaeus*, Plato refers to the demiurge as the Craftsman or Artificer. He must have seen skilled craftsmen at work, and would have understood the processes of rational deliberation, measurement and integration that underpin any complex manufacture.

The ancients concluded that creation was the result of the expression and operation of a *cosmic reason principle*, and that human beings possessed, by virtue of their divine souls, a part of that divine reason. This was that basis for the important Hermetic principle that human beings are a microcosm, quite literally 'a little universe'. The abiding belief in the rational comprehensibility of the cosmos was an important influence at the start of the scientific reformation.

12.4 Emergence

If emanation is a top-down theory, then the 19th. century saw the introduction of 'bottom-up theories', the most famous component of which is Darwin's theory of selective evolution, which shows how new species can evolve through heritable variation and environmental selection. Evolution was a mechanistic theory of novelty that did not depend on a divine craftsman - accident and selection were sufficient. The popularity of such theories gathered pace through the 20th. century and can be loosely grouped under the headings of 'self-organisation' and 'emergence'.

A key understanding was that structure and complexity can emerge spontaneously. Let us suppose we have a large bag of parts from a child's construction set[96]. When the bag is shaken there is a possibility that some parts will stick together by chance. If the bag is shaken gently only a few parts will stick together, and if it is shaken too hard, parts that have stuck together will fall apart. There is an optimal shaking regime where parts stick together into complex assemblages, just as atoms form into molecules. As the bag is shaken there is a chance that larger assemblages of parts will separate out from smaller complexes of parts, like pebbles on a beach.

---

96. The author has in mind a well-known brand where parts can be pressed together and pulled apart.

This is what we find with the Earth's geology: atoms like silicon and oxygen and calcium and carbon have 'stuck together' to form molecules, and these molecules have differentiated into ores. Our planet was formed in this way. Differentiation through heat and pressure and physical movement can produce complex crystalline formations, such as quartz clusters, the extraordinary inorganic polymer forms of asbestos, and the glass-like sheets of mica. All this is a natural self-assembly. No craftsman is involved.

This much is understood and can be replicated in the laboratory. Living organisms present more of a challenge; from the self-assembly of complex inorganic molecules to the self-organisation of simple living cells there is a gap in our understanding. It is a significant gap. However, it is not a gap that requires the introduction of a mysterious, external 'organising principle', which is how the ancients imagined the soul. They could not envisage how simple components could come together into complex and interlinked assemblages and processes without an external organising power. They suspected agency. Wherever they found nests they found birds. When they found hives they found bees and wasps. When they found tracks and trails, they found animals. It appeared obvious that complexity and organisation required a power of agency to make it happen.

Modern biochemists have been able to observe processes within the living cell to an extraordinary level of detail and find that they are machine-like and comprehensible[97]. They have not encountered phenomena that require a mysterious external agency. The only significant missing piece in the picture is an understanding of the conditions under which the first forms of cellular life emerged. The difficulty is not conceptual - there are many good proposals, perhaps too many. The problem is that living organisms have had billions of years to evolve, and even the simplest are unimaginably complex and sophisticated. The problem is like studying a modern automobile without knowing the developmental history of wheeled vehicles and their manufacture. We would probably not be able to deduce that the immediate predecessor was the horse and cart. This is the difficulty in trying to understand the origin of the first living cells.

An essential feature of all living organisms is the ability to extract free energy from the environment. Plants extract energy from sunlight and bacteria living kilometres underground extract energy from metallic ores. Human beings extract energy from pizza. The chemis-

---

97. An excellent presentation can be found in *Biochemistry,* Lubert Stryer, 4th Edition, Freeman 1995

try of energy extraction is well understood, but it is a complex multi-part process, and it *takes* energy to just to build this complex energy extraction apparatus. There is a chicken-and-egg problem: how to build a complex, self-contained energy extraction apparatus without already having a complex self-contained energy extraction apparatus. This is essence of our current gap in understanding. This is the 'origin of life' problem[98].

Living organisms self-organise to solve several essential problems, such as:

- metabolism, that is, free energy extraction from the environment via complex metabolic pathways, leading to ...
- growth and reproduction, and a ...
- a membrane or boundary, leading to ...
- homeostasis, the ability to maintain a stable internal environments (such as acidity or temperature) in spite of external changes, which is necessary for ... metabolism, growth and reproduction.

From bacteria to complex multicellular organisms our story is much more complete. Despite fundamentalist religious opposition to the idea of evolution, it is readily observed in the laboratory, and the continuing evolution of pathogenic organisms is one of our greatest public health hazards. Anyone who doubts the power of environmental selection can easily study the influence of selective breeding on animals (such as dogs) and crops (such as the potato).

In more detail: the story of emergence begins with a soup of hydrogen and helium atoms that condense to form stars. The stars pressure-cook the hydrogen and helium, causing them to fuse into the entire periodic table of elements, and then spew them out in huge supernova explosions. Eventually there is enough 'atomic muck' to form not only new stars, but planetary systems. Planets are at sufficiently low temperatures for chemical differentiation to occur, leading to (taking our own planet as an example) continents, seas and atmosphere. It is in this environment that we believe that carbon-based life originated. This process is shown in Figure 29.

The next step is a separation into organisms that extract energy directly from the environment, and organisms that extract energy

---

98. One might wonder how one could build an electric power station without having electricity to run the factories that make the parts. But we know that industrialisation and manufacturing began with manual labour and then steam, so there is no 'power-station problem'.

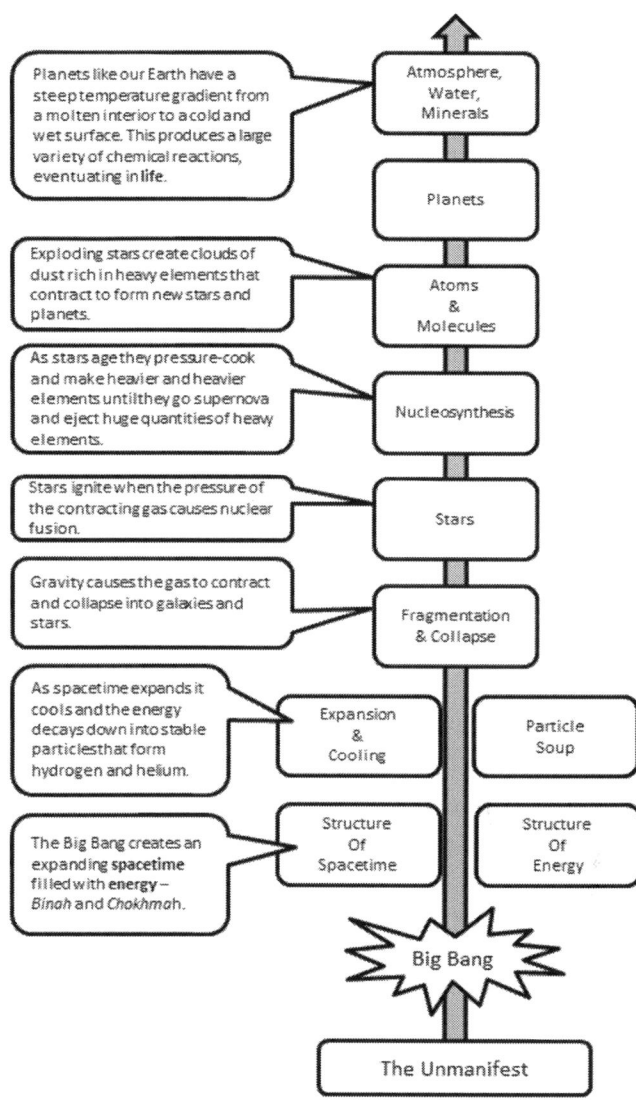

Figure 29: The Steps of Emergence Part 1 - from the Unmanifest to the Inorganic.

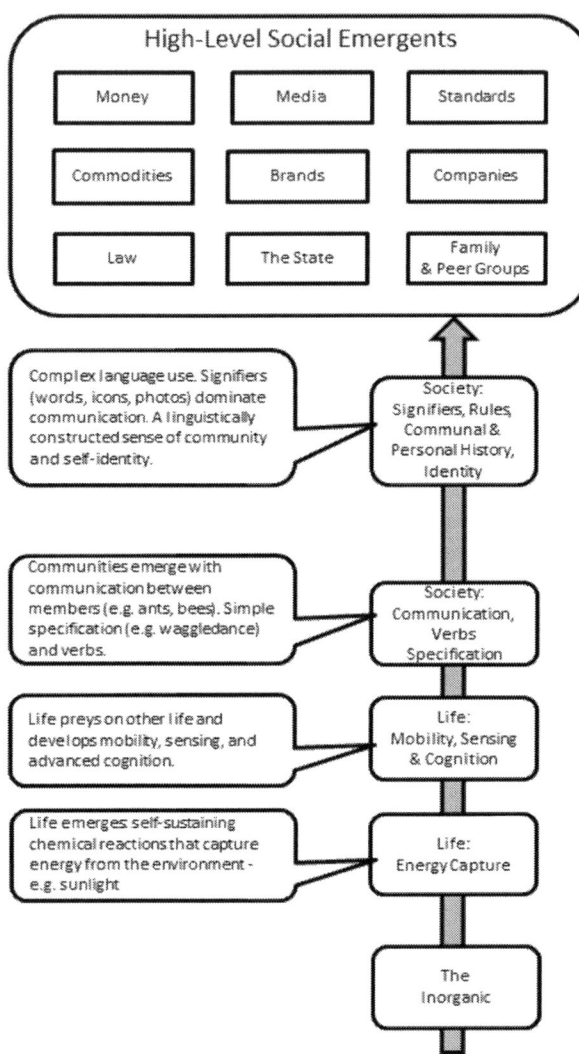

Figure 30: The Steps of Emergence Part 2 - from the Inorganic to the Economic.

from other organisms. Even simple bacteria know how to *hunt*. This requires motility and the ability to recognise prey. Another step is the emergence of societies. Societies require communication between members, and communication enables collective behaviours. In general, a society can shape the environment in favour of its members in a way that an individual member cannot do. Both of these innovations are found in bacteria, which indicates the powerful selection pressures involved, not to mention a radical rethink of the complexity of what we have regarded as 'simple' life forms.

A key indicator of emergence is the use of a specialised vocabulary. Emergents possess a distinctive morphology, so that it is possible to lose sight of the parts and talk about the structure of the whole. This is an unintuitive idea: parts form wholes, and these wholes have new behaviours distinct from the parts.

We know intellectually that every cell in the body (apart from the vast mass of symbiotic gut bacteria) is derived from a single egg cell, and under a microscope this is exactly how tissue looks - a collection of individual cells. This is not the first thing a doctor sees. The classic anatomical text *Gray's Anatomy* exposes the organs of the body (and their Latin names) in exhaustive detail. A physician who sees only cells would have trouble understanding a broken leg, astigmatism, or a heart murmur. None of these complaints have much meaning at the cellular level. A short-sighted eye is almost identical to a 20/20 eye - the difference is dimensional, not cellular.

Another aspect of emergence is the creation of artifacts that facilitate the newly emergent functionality. Examples might be: bacterial mats and films, ant-hills, bee-hives, roads and cities. Probably the most singular emergent in the human sphere is language, followed closely by money. Emergents arising from language are literature and certain kinds of performance: poetry, novels, plays, songs, religious ritual and liturgy. Emergents arising from money include markets, commodities, brands, advertising, banking, exchange rates, taxation, and so on. The steps of emergence from simple cellular life to the modern economy are shown in Figure 30.

12.5 Determinism and Freedom

It is surprising that two versions of monism turn out so differently. One version begins with The Many and works up to the most complex entity in our corner of the universe, the human brain and mind. The other version begins with an abstract, superlative mind and works down towards The Many. Both versions struggle to eliminate dualism

The Hermetic Kabbalah

(or pluralism). Neoplatonism begins with unity but contains no convincing account of Matter. It attempts to account for multiplicity and alienation, but produces a proliferating complexity of explanations[99] that seem as endless as the plurality it seeks to explain.

Modern science begins with the physics of sub-atomic particles and fields, and the atomic theory of matter, and provides convincing and useful explanations of the world at the human scale, and even up to the scale of stars and galaxies. At the current time it is not complete. There is an intractable and unexplained residue: four fundamental fields, energy, space-time, quantum field theories, several fundamental constants, and a standard model of sub-atomic particles that clearly share a common cause, but no linking theory. Einstein spent the latter part of his life on a fruitless quest for a unified theory, and many since have gone down that road to no avail. A science with autonomous, disconnected and unexplained first principles is not satisfying. At the other extreme of complexity, although science is working towards an explanation of how mind arises from the structure of the brain, the story is is still incomplete.

Monism is awkward because we are not adapted to think about monist models of reality. We are limited by our biology, perceiving each thing by virtue of its contrast with something else. Even where reality is shaded and graded, language dissects it into perceptual chunks, so that the infinite gradation of hues in a rainbow becomes seven discrete colours. Our perception is innately dualist - without contrast we cannot perceive, and language follows perception. *Monism presents itself to us as dualism*. Whether we progress in a top-down or bottom-up manner, there is a residue that we cannot explain and cannot sweep under the carpet.

Although Kabbalah is an emanationist monism, dualism becomes apparent at the outset in the form of the right and left hand Pillars of the Tree. Unity only exists at *Keter*, and even in *Keter* the seeds of duality must be present otherwise it could not emanate *Chokhmah* and *Binah*. If the seeds of duality exist in *Keter*, they must (according to some) also exist in *En Sof*[100], which leads to an apparent contradiction, but it is a contradiction that illustrates the boundary past which human thought cannot go.

Kabbalah makes a fundamental break with the emanationist

---

99. An example of this tendency can be found in *The Elements of Theology*, Proclus, trans. E. R. Dodds, Clarendon 1992
100. See the outlines of R. Nathan of Gaza's theosophy summarised in *Sabbatai Sevi, The Mystical Messiah*, Gershom Scholem, Princeton 1973

structure of Neoplatonism with the idea that *Keter* and *Malkhut* are two aspects of one thing. This is an elegant idea; taken together with the interplay of *Chesed* and *Din*, it avoids some of the intractable difficulties found in Neoplatonism. This overlap of *Keter* and *Malkhut* is not something one can justify intellectually (although monism demands it logically): it is part of the mystical component of Kabbalah accessible to direct apprehension.

Kabbalah highlights something that is implicit in the models of emanation and emergence described above: that there is in every aspect of reality a living, mind-like quality (symbolised by the right-hand pillar of the Tree and *Chesed*) and a dead, matter-like quality (symbolised by the left hand pillar and *Din*).

The dead, matter-like quality can be comprehended because it is fixed and determinate. Because it follows fixed rules, we can calculate the future from the present. One of the first practical applications of physics was the computation of trajectories for artillery. Another early application was the production of celestial tables and the computation of eclipses. Physics is exceptionally accurate at predicting orbits and trajectories. It is this precise determination of the future from the present that allows NASA to launch rockets, steer them across millions of miles of space, and land a probe on another world with a precision of a few hundred metres.

We can understand the mind-like quality by taking the opposite of determination. It is non-determination. It is freedom, choice, free will. This is a spooky notion that seems unphysical: freedom to choose. Is there anything in modern physics that has this property?

The answer would appear to be yes; this is what one finds in quantum mechanics. The behaviour of a particle like an electron is determined by its environment, but only up to a point. An electron appears to be free to choose from any future state that is not prohibited, and so for any *individual* electron[101] one cannot predict the future from the present.

This apparent freedom or non-determinism has resulted in a century of debate among physicists. Einstein found the idea abhorrent. It is spooky and unexpected. Many have thought the electron's behaviour must be a manifestation of a lack of knowledge; it is in fact deterministic, but it follows secret deterministic rules we do not yet understand, and it only *appears* to be non-deterministic. Many experiments have been carried out in an attempt to resolve the issue. At

---

101. One can predict the behaviours of sufficiently large numbers.

the time of writing the evidence favours non-determination; the electron (and other particles) *do* appear to have 'freedom to choose' from any possible future state not ruled out by current knowledge.

Whether this has any implication at the human scale is still unclear. The behaviour of electrons over very short distances and very short timescales may have no impact on the overall function of the human brain. It is too early to say. Nevertheless, most people would like to feel that they are genuinely free agents, and hence morally responsible, the position that Kabbalah has always adopted. This freedom that we believe we possess comes from *Keter*, the first point of emanation, which is traditionally associated with will (*r'tzon*).

12.6 Free Will

Will is an everyday word, but a difficult concept. A wilful person is someone who sets his or her mind on doing something and persists with that intention in spite of obstacles or disapproval. Likewise an 'iron will' cannot be deflected from a course of action. When a person has no 'will-power' we mean that they are easily tempted away from an intention or goal.

Implicit in the idea of will is freedom to choose. People feel they have freedom to choose. If I approach you in the street and I offer you a deal, you can say "no thanks", or "I'll get back to you", or "yes please". Even if I carry a big stick and look threatening, you can still make these free choices (although your choice would now factor in the big stick). Likewise with ideas; you can accept an idea, query and debate an idea, or reject an idea.

We are bombarded with offers, suggestions and ideas. We pick our way through them, deciding what we want and don't want. It is our wilfulness, our self-determination, that helps us to resist a 'hard sell'. We are a wilful species. We choose our own paths.

When the ancients tried to identify the difference between animate and inanimate objects it was the autonomous and self-determining quality of living things that stood out. A technical term for this is *causa sui*, being 'the cause of itself'. Every kind of life is 'the cause of itself'. We don't think of stones in the same way. Throughout human history we have been throwing stones at each other, and at no point has autonomous or self-determining behaviour[102] been an issue - they all fly through the air in a very predictable way. When I throw a stone I do not wonder whether it is going to pursue its own agenda (like the

---

102. As I write this I am aware of the development of intelligent ordnance.

Golden Snitch in *Harry Potter*).

It was clear to the ancients that living things contained a self-determination that stones did not, and as living things decayed back into dust, it also seemed obvious that the internal factor was not material. This intuitive reasoning led to the belief in a soul, and what one might call 'naive dualism' - a belief that the soul and matter belonged to different realms of being. Will became a faculty of the soul. It seemed to the ancients that Will was one of the most fundamental aspects of the soul, the point at which pure being changed from stillness into motion. This, in outline, provides the sense of why *Chokhmah* follows from *Keter*.

Over the course of centuries Will has became the centre of debate. Are human beings genuinely autonomous? If we are, how could God be omniscient? And if we are not self-determining, how can we be punished for breaking commandments? The entire presumption of resurrection, reward and punishment hinged on the idea of moral freedom. This debate went on for centuries.

The water was further muddied by the rise of the physical sciences and our current understanding of the deterministic nature of physical law. How can we be free if the future is entirely determined by the present? This led to a search for 'wiggle room' in nature, a core indeterminacy that would permit free will to operate.

We are still at this point. Some believe that free will is incompatible with determinism, and so it must be an illusion. Others believe it is compatible. There are many finely-honed philosophical positions and the literature is huge. Overshadowing the entire issue is the ancient belief that free-will is a divine faculty of the soul.

From a personal perspective I find the debate on the freeness of will unnecessarily metaphysical. When I am required to make a decision about a complex matter, I draw up a list of actions I might take. I associate with each action a collection of *pros* and *cons*, and with each *pro* and *con* I associate a weight - a valuation of how good or bad each of these factors might be. I talk to other people to try find out if I have missed something, and to find out how they might weight the *pros* and *cons*. I might do some reading. If I am wilful I might decide I have 'no choice' and ignore other people (who might be offering alternatives that I have chosen to dismiss). Out of this internal debate I reach a decision.

The freeness is not just in my final decision; it is distributed throughout the process I use to decide what choices I have, and how I weight my choices. The most creative people seem to be able to 'see' a wider range of possibilities than the rest of us. The word 'vision' is used extensively in business marketing, and leaders are often described as 'visionary'. It would seem that the true extent of our freedom has less to do with the laws of physics (without which we simply would not exist) and more to do with our internal limitations. If we cannot see out of the box then we cannot choose out of the box.

12.7 A Hybrid Model

In this section three models of monism have been outlined. Each handles determinism differently. Neoplatonism pushes it out towards the periphery and calls it 'matter'. Kabbalah introduces it progressively. In modern science it is the principal subject of interest (because the search for laws must necessarily begin with the study of determinate phenomena). Neoplatonism and Kabbalah use an emanationist top-down model, whereas modern science uses an emergent bottom-up model.

There are other models. In the early 90s the author described a model that was part emanation, part emergence. The motivation for this was not so much to combine the two models; it arose out of a dissatisfaction with the conventional step-by-step model of *sefirotic* emanation (the lightning flash model) found in many introductions to the subject. While the progressive step-by-step model is an useful explanatory device, it also has shortcomings.

In the realm of mind, a thing and its negation do not appear sequentially, they manifest simultaneously. So it is with *Keter* and *Malkhut*, and *Chokhmah* and *Binah*. The idea that *Keter, Chokhmah* and *Binah* could manifest without *Malkhut necessarily* manifesting seems as implausible as 'up' without 'down'. Once the quaternary has come into being simultaneously, emergence is a natural continuation. According to this picture, the quaternary of *Keter, Malkhut, Chokhmah* and *Binah* emanate in a single symmetry-breaking event, and the microcosm emerges out of *Malkhut*. This is shown in Figure 31.

The big difference between Figure 31 and the normal picture of the Tree is that there is no 'higher' or 'lower'. The quaternary of *Keter, Malkhut, Chokhmah* and *Binah* define a space in which dependent being is possible. They are connected into a unity and represent four aspects of one thing. *Keter* is the *being* of a universe, and *Malkhut* is its *realisation* through the interplay of the *determination* of *Binah* and the *expressive freedom*[103] of *Chokhmah*.

The universe is a living entity where every part, down the smallest

Emanation & Emergence

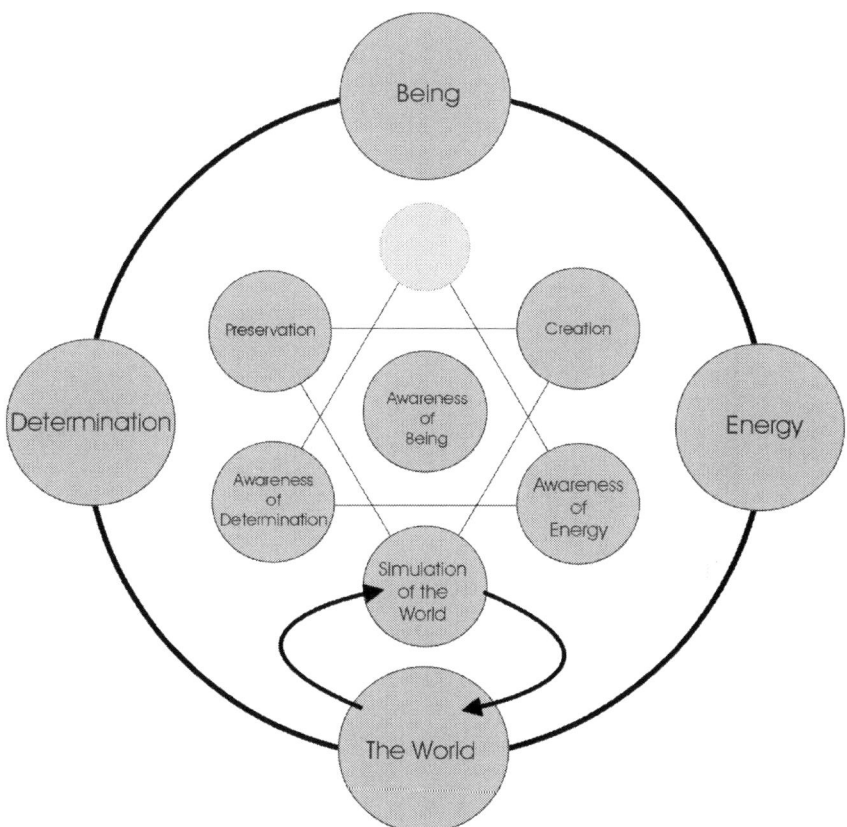

Figure 31: A minor restructuring of the Tree of Life, with the quaternary of *Keter, Malkhut, Chokhmah* and *Binah* forming the macrocosm, and the six sefirot centred on *Tiferet* as the microcosm. The macrocosm emanates, the microcosm emerges, forming a hybrid of two important approaches to monism.

particle, is both expressive and determined, and out of the interaction of the parts arises (or emerges) in turn reactive intelligence, sentient awareness, and self-reflective awareness that embodies and reflects the raw being that gave rise to it. This is the cluster of six *sefirot* centred on *Tiferet*.

---

103. There is no exact phrase or word for this idea. It is the potential of the present to discover new future states, like a spring flowing abundantly into all the channels it can discover. The idea combines the physical idea of energy with that of expressive freedom.

The microcosm reflects the bounding principles that give rise to it. On the right there is the potential for novelty, and all that goes with it: adaptation, growth, playfulness, creation, and the entire world of new possibility that comes from connection and relationship. On the left is the need for structure and stability, and processes that monitor and preserve and protect.

On the middle pillar, the primary requirement is to simulate. *Yesod* is the microcosmic simulacrum of *Malkhut*. In simple forms of life it is reactive, nothing more than *sense, evaluate and respond*; in higher forms of life more complex simulations come into play until all six *sefira* of the microcosm are active, and the microcosm becomes aware of its being in respect to the outer. This awareness takes four forms: consciousness of being (*Tiferet*), consciousness of many determinate things (*Yesod*), consciousness of many sentient beings as an interdependent whole (*Da'at*), and consciousness of unity (*Keter*).

12.8 Summary

Both emanation and emergence are theories of novelty: how do new things arise out of a state of simplicity. In emanation, novelty arises through a progressive fracturing of the One; in emergence novelty arises via a progressive organisation of the Many. They are beautifully complementary theories.

Emergence explains why there are living beings on this world. It makes sense of the history of our planet up to the point where human beings began to make pictures and fashion tools. It is less successful at explaining the novel *Finnegan's Wake* by James Joyce, or *Toccata and Fugue in D minor* by Bach. Countless new things are appearing every day, in the form of videos, advertisements, products, films, TV series, books, works of art, new sports and so on. To explain novelty in the human sphere one has to take into account the creativity of the human mind.

Modern humans live in a world that is almost entirely a by-product of the human mind. The world that surrounds us is, for the most part, novel. It did not exist ten years ago. Each new thing began as an idea in the mind of a person. Ideas are imagined, refined through social interaction, and brought into being. After 4,500 billion years of slow geological change, the agency of mind has altered the planet in fundamental ways in only 200 years. We have little conception of just how important or fundamental 'mind' could be.

The Hermetic tradition takes mind to be the most important cosmic principle, and views matter as a subsidiary concept; forms are conceived in mind and are instantiated in matter. This book has been written at a time when both views - emergence and emanation - seem equally important.

The Hermetic Kabbalah

Part 2

The Tree of Life

The Hermetic Kabbalah

13

Genesis

13.1 Introduction

The first line of the book of *Genesis* is *B'reshit bara Elohim et ha-shamayim v'et ha-aretz*: "In the beginning God created Heaven and Earth". This sentence has been subjected to interminable analysis in Kabbalistic texts. What is incontrovertible is that there was a beginning; there was a transition from a 'before' into an 'after'.

In Kabbalah the 'before' is called *En Sof*, which means "endless" or "limitless". The word is used to represent to our minds a condition that is beyond characterisation or dualistic cognition. It represents an aspect of God that is hidden and inaccessible to us, as it is beyond our means to grasp, and is often characterised by *ayin*, nothingness.

The 'after' is the creation of Heaven and Earth and the beginning of duality. It is at this point that descriptions of the progressive emanation of the *sefirot* of the Tree of Life begin.

Emanation means "to flow from". The creative force of an entity is sufficient to create a new entity. This is not an intentional act and the emanating entity loses no part of itself, just as we can light a candle from another candle without depleting the first. Emanation is a natural consequence of creative energy or force.

An emanated entity is inferior to its parent, in that it contains more self-definition or form, and so it is more constrained in its crea-

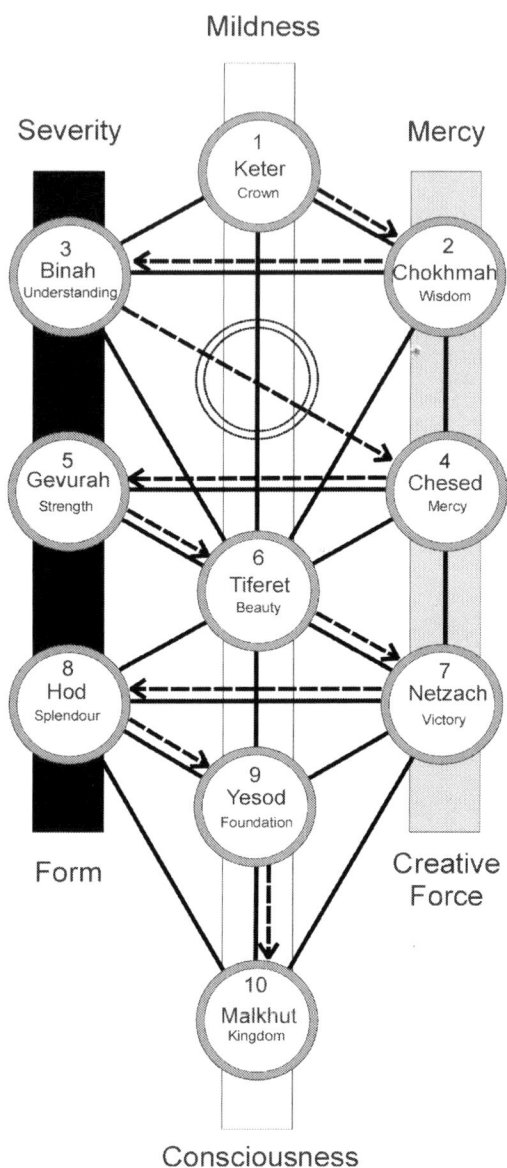

Figure 32: The Pillars and the Lightning Flash on the Tree of Life.

tive expression. This is so because the parent entity itself has limitations which constrain its creativity and so it must always emanate something less than or equal to itself. The creative process requires a diminution of the divine, else nothing would be distinct from God.

This view of emanation naturally gives rise to a chain of emanating entities, each one more limited than the one before. One can see the chain of emanation in Figure 32. The source of emanation is a condition of being barely differentiated from *En Sof*. Kabbalists call this *Keter*, Crown. Because *Keter* is the first, it signifies the divine will, the will to create.

The end point of emanation is a condition in which no further emanation is possible and the possibilities of 'creative becoming' are fully expressed. Kabbalists call this condition *Malkhut*, Kingdom.

Why is creative energy exhausted? In the Kabbalistic model of emanation, creative energy is limited by form, and one cannot exist without the other. Form limits or focuses creative energy so that it is more directed and intentional, but also more constrained. With each step of emanation, the creative energy becomes more limited. Eventually the energy is so limited it loses the capacity to relate - it becomes disconnected. Once it is disconnected it exists only for itself and it is effectively dead, what Kabbalists call a shell or a husk (*klippot*). A husk is fully determined and cannot become more determined. It is reactive and has the quality of mechanism - its behaviour can be specified by rules.

Nothing is ever *completely* disconnected (that would be outright dualism), and the *klippot* retain a residual connection with the divine, even if it is parasitic (taking without giving).

To summarise, emanation in Kabbalah is a discrete progression from a state of complete unity and pure creative power to a state of multiplicity in which creative power is exhausted. There are ten steps of emanation, and each step is given a name. These are the titles of the *sefirot*.

We can liken emanation to the conception of an idea. The mind is constantly flickering with evanescent ideas. A very few of these ideas awaken the will and take on a vague shape of possibility. The idea then needs to become personal; one has to engage with it, 'bring it down', make it more precise, produce a detailed plan, and finally make it happen. Whenever we plan something new (e.g. a holiday) we go through these steps, from vague concept to detailed itinerary and bookings, and finally, the execution of the plan in the form of taxis, planes, hotels and so on. There are three elements working together:

increasing detail (form), increasing commitment (force) and increasing attention and focus (consciousness).

13.2 The Pillars

The normal presentation of emanation on the Tree of Life uses a diagram of the Tree in which three vertical pillars are indicated, and a zig-zag line like a lightning flash moves between them (see Figure 32). The zig-zag line shows the order of emanation; that is, the order of priority among the *sefirot*. The side pillars show what one might call 'the primary duality' and the central pillar their reconciliation.

The traditional titles for the pillars are Mercy on the right, Severity on the left, and Mildness in the centre. Mercy is associated with giving, generosity, paternalistic love, and abundance. Severity is associated with judgement, punishment, constraint, limitation, and holding back.

Mildness is a balance in which the negative qualities of abundance and the negative qualities of restraint are balanced with the positive qualities of abundance and the positive qualities of restraint[104].

The traditional titles are anthropomorphic, and symbolise a wise king who is generous to the deserving, merciful to those who have transgressed, and severe with evil-doers. The overall tendency is mildness. Severity is not the natural state; it is a potential that is awakened through transgression.

The Hermetic tradition also uses the titles Force, Form and Consciousness (see Figure 32). Force is creative force, the ability to instantiate something new. Form is structure and definition. As Scholem[105] comments:

> It must be remembered that to the Kabbalist, judgement [Din - judgement, another title of Gevurah] means the imposition of limits and the correct determination of things. According to Cordovero the quality of judgement is inherent in everything insofar as everything wishes to remain what it is, to stay within its boundaries.

Consciousness is tricky to define, and I have tried to be consistent throughout in defining consciousness as awareness-of-something - awareness of an idea, a person, a feeling, a pain, a touch, a memory, or in the case of self-consciousness, awareness of self.

The Pillar of Mildness/Consciousness contains the *sefira Keter, Tif-*

---

104. The Biblical plagues of Egypt were balanced between abundance (e.g. locusts, frogs) and severity (death of livestock, first born).
105. *Major Trends in Jewish Mysticism*, Gershom Scholem, Schocken 1961.

eret, *Yesod* and *Malkhut*. The Pillar of Mercy/Force contains the *sefirot Chokhmah*, *Chesed* and *Netzach*. The Pillar of Severity/Form contains the *sefirot Binah*, *Gevurah* and *Hod*. In Masonic tradition the Pillar of Severity is called *Boaz* and the Pillar of Mercy is called *Jachin* after the pillars of the Temple of Solomon[106].

The classification of *sefirot* into three Pillars is a way of suggesting that each *sefira* in a Pillar partakes of a common quality that is 'inherited' in a progressively more developed and structured way from of the top of a Pillar to the bottom. *Tiferet*, *Yesod* and *Malkhut* share with *Keter* the quality of 'awareness-of', but in each case it is expressed differently according the kind of limitation placed on awareness. Likewise, *Chokhmah*, *Chesed* and *Netzach* share the quality of force, or creative energy, or expansiveness. *Binah*, *Gevurah* and *Hod* share the quality of form, definition and limitation. As one moves down the Tree from *Keter* to *Malkhut*, force and form are combined together.

13.3 The Lightning Flash

The *sefirot* first appear in the ancient *Sefer Yetzirah*, where they are one of the three elements with which God made the universe:

And he created His universe
with three books (*Sepharim*),
    with text (*Sepher*)
    with number (*Sephar*)
    and with communication (*Sippur*)[107]

The word *sefira* is associated with number and counting, and the tradition is that the *sefirot* emanate in sequence from one to ten in what is called the Lightning Flash order, as shown in Figure 32.

The process of emanation begins with the limitless and eternal ground of Being that Kabbalists call *En Sof*. In a way that need not concern us at this time, the *En Sof* gives rise to the undifferentiated point that is the *sefira* called *Keter* (Crown). *Keter* denotes the will-to-become. It is the seed that will become the Tree of Life in the same way as an acorn contains an oak tree. For many Kabbalists the *sefira Keter* is so far from conceptualisation it is not thought of as a *sefira*, more as a part of *En Sof*.

---

106. Conspicuous twin pillars were a feature of the Phoenician god Melqart, identified by the Greeks with Hercules. This may be the origin of the ancient name of the Strait of Gibraltar: the Pillars of Hercules.
107. *The Sepher Yetzirah*, trans. Aryeh Kaplan, Samuel Weiser 1990

The Hermetic Kabbalah

The second *sefira* is *Chokhmah* (Wisdom). *Chokhmah* is at the head of the pillar of force, and it denotes the creative energy that continuously sustains the creation. *Chokhmah* is the beginning: the beginning of creation, the beginning of duality, it gives rise to its partner and emanation the *sefira Binah* (Understanding or Intelligence).

Chokhmah and *Binah* are beyond space and time. It would be wrong to imagine that there was a 'time' when *Chokhmah* existed by itself. *Chokhmah* comes into being, and although *Binah* is a consequent of *Chokhmah* it comes into being simultaneously. *Chokhmah* is often symbolised by a spring, and *Binah* by a sea fed by the waters of *Chokhmah*. *Chokhmah* is the source, and *Binah* accepts the waters of *Chokhmah* and gives them shape.

The most common symbols used for *Chokhmah* and *Binah* is that of the *Partzufim* of Father and Mother (see *Partzufim* on page 43). The Father (*Abba*) ejaculates continuously into the Mother (*Imma*), who receives the creative seed and gestates it in her womb. *Chokhmah* is the Father of Life, *Binah* the Mother of Form. They are continuous in embrace and sustain the entire Creation.

Because *Chokhmah* is the Father, the Pillar of Force/Mercy is usually regarded as male, and because *Binah* is the Mother, the Pillar of Form/Severity is usually regarded as female.

The seven *sefirot* that follow *Binah* are sometimes called 'the seven days of creation'. Sometimes they are thought of as seven rivers flowing out of the great sea of *Binah*. The *Bahir* likens *Binah* to a mother bird sitting on a nest of seven eggs.

Form exists within *Binah* as a potentiality, not as an actuality, just as a womb contains the potential for a baby, or a seed the potential for a flower. Without the possibility of form, no thing would be distinct from any other thing and it would be impossible to distinguish between things, impossible to have individuality or identity or change. The Mother of Form contains the potential of form within her womb and gives birth to form when a creative impulse crosses the Abyss to the Pillar of Force and emanates through the *sefira Chesed*, which in turn emanates its dual *Gevurah*.

Chokhmah and *Binah* are eternal, but *Chesed* and *Gevurah* mark the beginning of change, which implies time and space[108]. *Chesed* (Loving-Kindness) and *Gevurah* (Strength) denote the qualities of

---

108. There is an element of ambiguity about the role of time in traditional sources. The Tree of Life exists in *Atzilut*, the highest of the four worlds, yet it is clear in the *Zohar* that the *sefirot* from *Chesed* down are involved in change, because changing relationships between the *sefirot* are used to explain historical events.

Genesis

Mercy and Severity that are fundamental to Kabbalistic thinking.

Mercy denotes the fundamental goodness of God. We associate goodness with giving without qualifications or conditions, and with a freedom from limitations, imperfections, failure and suffering. If the Creation was entirely Good it would not be distinct from God, and so, if it is distinct from God then it must in some way be deficient in goodness. According to the Kabbalistic way of thinking the Creation is initiated by a *withdrawal* of God. Some part of God's goodness is held back, and the Creation is marked by an absence of God's essential goodness. This absence has the character of Severity, and is often known by the alternative name of *Din* (Judgement).

Chesed is the first *sefira* of manifest form. The creative energy of *Chesed* brings inspiration into the world and is often associated with leadership, inspiration and genius. Gandhi, Einstein, Mandela, Pankhurst, and Picasso are examples of people who transformed the outlook of their time, so much so that it is difficult to imagine how we might be had they not lived.

Creative novelty must be given shape. This is an active and interactive process in which ideas that are overconstrained (i.e. do not work, worlds of pure *Din*) are discarded. We are familiar with the image of the writer tossing sheets of crumpled paper into an overflowing bin. Some ideas don't work, they don't stand up, they are defective, they have to be thrown away. These are destroyed worlds.

No change comes easy; as Cordovero points out "everything wishes to remain what it is". The creation of form is balanced by the preservation and destruction of form in the *sefira Gevurah*. Any impulse of change is channelled through *Gevurah*, and if it is not opposed then something must be destroyed. Paper requires trees, and omelettes require broken eggs. The sefira *Gevurah* is the quality of strict judgement which opposes change, sets boundaries on the new, destroys the unfamiliar, and corresponds in many ways to an immune system within the body of God.

There has to be a balance between creation and destruction. Too much change, too many ideas, too many things happening too quickly - this can have the quality of chaos (and can literally become that), whereas too little change, no new ideas, too much form, structure and protocol - this can suffocate and stifle. For growth and development to take place there should be a balance - a golden mean - and this harmony is expressed in the *sefira Tiferet* (Beauty).

Tiferet reconciles right with left, and above with below. It represents the agency of the divine name of four letters (YHVH) and is symbolised by the Son of *Chokhmah* and *Binah* who is also King. He wears the crown of *Keter* and *Chesed* and *Gevurah* are his right and left arms. *Tiferet* is the centre of the Tree of Life.

In the human sphere *Tiferet* denotes the integration of the quasi-autonomous functions of the *psyche* into a self-aware and balanced whole.

The *sefirot* of *Netzach* (Victory, Endurance) and *Hod* (Splendour, Glory) receive a minimal treatment in traditional sources. They are associated with the legs of the King, in the same way that *Chesed* and *Gevurah* symbolise the right and left arms, and *Tiferet* the upper torso and heart. They are associated with multiplicity.

In Hermetic sources they receive detailed treatment. *Netzach* denotes emotional responses to things and situations and people, and includes aesthetic judgements and valuations. *Netzach* manifests the quality of creative energy in a world of 'given elements'. The creativity of *Chesed* is inspirational, whereas that of *Netzach* is compositional, in the sense of composing or arranging known elements in the manner of an interior decorator. It is centred on personal judgments. It is as if everything in the world was coloured by the unconscious mind: things that are disliked are coloured red, things that are liked are coloured green, and everything else is grey or invisible.

Hod is the emanation of *Netzach* and denotes language and abstraction and the constructed reality that we spend much of our childhood assimilating. Examples of 'constructed reality' would be money and finance, law, good manners, and theology. *Hod* is on the pillar of form, and a key aspect is definition, usually linguistic, using a formal syntax, such as circuit diagrams, blueprints, musical scores, and any kind of writing.

We acquire the syntax and semantics of a specific human culture through education. Asking for '500 grams of cheddar cheese' requires an understanding of number, of weight and measure, and of varieties of a traded commodity, cheese.

We live in a culture where it is important (often essential) to give reasons for the things we do, and *Hod* is the *sefira* of form where it is possible to give shape to our desires in terms of reasons and explanations. *Hod* is the *sefira* of abstraction, reason, logic, language and communication, and a reflection of *Binah*, the Mother of Form in the human mind. We have a innate capacity to abstract, to go immediately from the particular to the general, and we have an innate capacity to communicate these abstractions using language, and it should be clear why the alternative translation of *Binah* is 'intelligence'; *Binah* is the 'intelligence of God', and *Hod* underpins what we generally recognise as intelligence in people - the ability to grasp complex abstractions, reason about them, and articulate this understanding using some means of communication.

The classical tradition of ancient Greece valued reason over feeling, but Kabbalah places *Netzach* before *Hod*, according to the maxim that "feelings tell us what to think". I can choose between an apple and an orange because I know what we feel like eating. A rational decision would require me to examine my extended eating history and overall health and metabolic needs in order to assess benefit. A feeling does this instantly. A purely rational being (like Spock in *Star Trek*) would find survival time-comsuming and difficult.

From *Hod* the lightning flash returns to the central pillar and the *sefira Yesod* (Foundation). *Yesod* is the *sefira* of interface. If *Tiferet* is the King and *Malkhut* is the Queen, then *Yesod* is the connection between them, the sexual organs. *Yesod* is sometimes called 'the Receptacle of the Emanations', because it interfaces the emanations of all three Pillars to the sefira *Malkhut*, and it is through *Yesod* that the final abstract form of something is realised in *Malkhut*.

Each *sefira* on the Middle Pillar has the quality of 'awareness-of'; that is, awareness-of-something. In *Yesod* the awareness is narrowed down to the specifics of personal survival. In the Hermetic tradition *Yesod* denotes the instincts and drives necessary for survival - the animal need for food and drink, sex, status, safety and comfort. It also corresponds to the imagination. The imagination can create a simulation of the world so real it may delude us; we can experience this in vivid dreams, hallucinations, and intense waking meditations.

Form in *Yesod* is no longer abstract. It is explicit, but not yet individual - that last quality is reserved for *Malkhut*. *Yesod* is like the cookie-cutter in the kitchen - the cookie-cutter is a prototype of the cookie, it has the shape of the cookie, but there is no cookie until it is pressed into the cookie dough.

The final step in the descending process is the *sefira Malkhut*, where God becomes flesh, and every abstract form is realised in actuality, in the 'real world'.

The "lightning flash" presentation shows how the order of *sefirotic* emanation zigs and zags across the Tree from the Pillar of Force to the Pillar of Form and back again. The overall progression is an increase of form (which equates to an increase in multiplicity and definition) as the lightning flash descends from *Keter* to *Malkhut*. Force becomes increasingly fragmented and defined (as it is in *Netzach*) while form becomes increasingly animated and alive to the point where Sherlock Holmes, Ellen Ripley, Elizabeth Bennett, and James T. Kirk possess a more tangible reality than most of the living and the dead.

Figure 33 is an attempt to show this progression. Going vertically down the Pillar of Force, the creativity of *Chokhmah* is unconditioned, the creativity of *Chesed* is conditioned, and the creativity of *Netzach* is second order, an aesthetic response to the creativity of *Chesed*. Descending the Pillar of Form, the fundamentals of space and time and the laws of nature are conceived in *Binah*, and are experienced in *Gevurah* as a response to duality - me and you, inside and outside, included and excluded, right and wrong, alive and dead. Moving down into *Hod*, form is entangled with the emotional binding of *Netzach*, leading in some to a geek-like fascination with complexity and structure, or in others to a sense of being overwhelmed by detail.

The experience on the pillar of consciousness is one of increasing alienation from the One. In *Tiferet* there is an experience of internal wholeness, but a sense of isolation and separation that seems impossible to bridge. In *Yesod* even the experience of wholeness is gone, and a key experience of the Ego is incompleteness and fragmentation. The Ego is restless and only temporarily happy, and tries to find anything - a career, a guru, a purchase, an experience, a drug - that will take away its feeling of incompleteness. At the same time it feels fragmented by its attachments and fears, being constantly buffeted by events, desires and contradictory, often self-destructive impulses.

These feelings of incompleteness, fragmentation and loss of self increase to the extent that one can be aware of *Malkhut*. Paradoxically, these feelings may be dissipated by the understanding that *Malkhut* is the revealed aspect of *Keter*.

Genesis

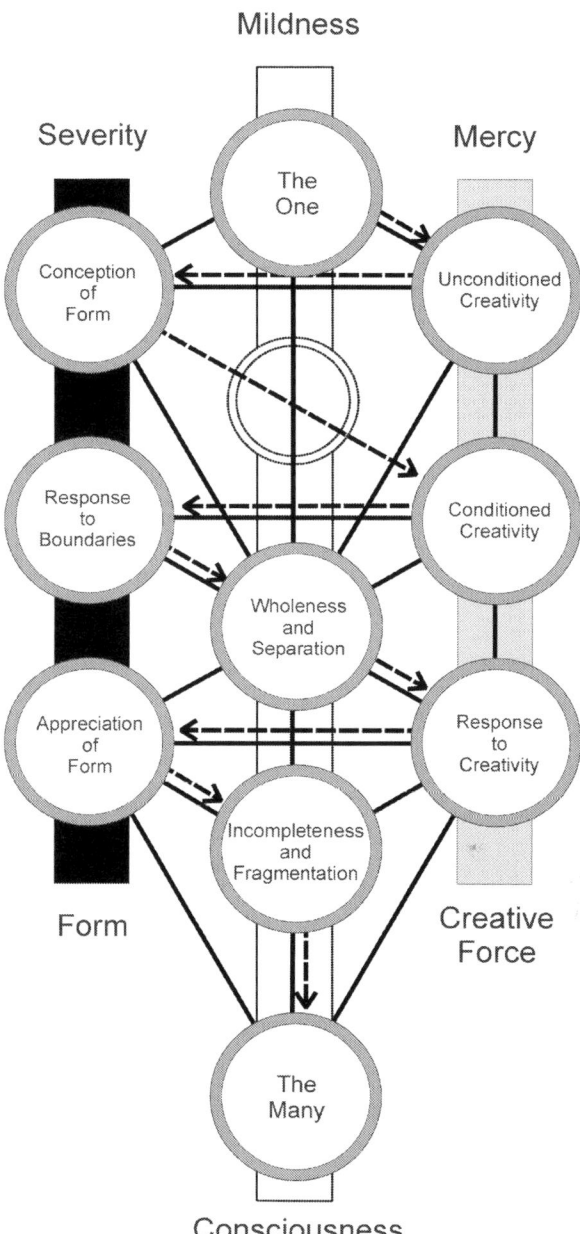

Figure 33: Emanation from One to Many.

The Hermetic Kabbalah

14

The Sefirot

14.1 Introduction

The approach taken in Part 1 was to describe the Tree of Life as a functioning whole. The *sefirot* appear as components in larger structures. This was the approach in Chapter 4, *The Tree of Life*, Chapter 6, *The Primordial Adam*, and Chapter 5, *The Partzufim*. These chapters discuss the relationships, images and associations most commonly found in the traditional literature. This approach views the Tree in terms of its dynamic wholeness.

There is a place however for describing the *sefirot* individually. This approach is widely used, especially in the Hermetic tradition. Sometimes they are described in emanation order, *Keter* to *Malkhut*, and sometimes they are described in ascent order, *Malkhut* to *Keter*. When the *sefirot* are described in emanation order it is often as part of a cosmogonic explanation - how things came to be in the beginning. These can become very complex, especially when following R. Isaac Luria's elaboration of texts in the *Zohar*[109]. When the *sefirot* are described in ascent order, it may be part of an initiatory ascent tradition as described in Chapter 10. This is the case here.

One of the oldest sources to provide a detailed exposition of this

---

109. See, for example, *General Principles of Kabbalah*, R. Moses Luzzatto, Research Centre of Kabbalah 1969

The Hermetic Kabbalah

kind is Joseph Gikatilla's (1248-1305 CE) *Gates of Light*. Published in Mantua in Lombardy in 1561, it is still in print today[110]. Gikatilla takes the traditional view that the *sefirot* represent the executive powers of the names of God, and he uses a large number of traditional sources to illustrate the point. The early translation and publication of this work in Latin (1516) by Paolo Riccio (with its well-known front piece - see Figure 2) has meant that it is an important source for the Hermetic tradition. Because of its length, detail and systematic treatment, the *Gates of Light* is a fascinating resource for classical Kabbalah.

The presentation given here is an amalgam of three influences. The first influence is traditional, especially the imagery, the divine names, archangels and angel orders, planets, and the dynamics of the *Partzufim*. The second influence comes via the late-nineteenth century Hermetic Order of the Golden Dawn, and in particular I use the colours and planetary attributions which have become canonical in 20th. century Hermetic Kabbalah (these are not a part of the Jewish tradition however). The Golden Dawn's elemental attributions are *not* used. The third influence is the author's own lineage of instruction, which (obscured by the mists and *lacunae* of time) would appear to derive in part from the Golden Dawn via the pre-WW2 traditions of Dion Fortune. It must be judged on its own merits.

The presentation is based loosely around tables of correspondences and is biased towards the microcosm - that is, many of the correspondences are related to human experience. A discussion oriented around tables of correspondences works well for practical learning, but produces a presentation that is often disjointed, for which I can only apologise. This mode of presentation can be found in Agrippa's *Three Books of Occult Philosophy* (see Figure 34), and the format has been widely adopted during the 20th. century, for example, in Crowley's *777*, in Dion Fortune's *The Mystical Qabalah*, in Gareth Knight's *A Practical Guide to Qabalistic Symbolism* and more recently, John Michael Greer's *Paths of Wisdom*.

The emphasis on the microcosm is deliberate. An important Kabbalistic principle is scale-invariance (see 3.13); that is, the same abstract principles and processes can be found in operation at every scale. We are most likely to observe them in ourselves, and by abstraction and experience we can progress to larger scales and concerns. This conveniently coincides with the initiatory ascent of the Tree and

---

110. *Gates of Light*, Joseph Gikatilla, Avi Weinstein (trans), Altamira Press 1994

The Sefirot

self-transcendence (see *Ascent* on page 115).

There is another reason behind the strong emphasis on the human microcosm and psyche. An innovation of the Hermetic tradition has been the attempt to 'beef up' the mostly symbolic initiations of Freemasonry and other similar initiatory societies of the eighteenth and nineteenth centuries to produce genuine initiatory experiences, modelled on the mystery cults of antiquity. To do this the grade structure had to follow the natural order of the universe. The soul, descended into matter, had to be conducted back through the spheres, so that it would experience and recall those factors that had blinded it to its true origins. The genius of the founders of the Golden Dawn was to combine the ancient traditions of initiatory ascent through the planetary spheres with the *sefirot* of the Tree of Life, and to create ritualistic initiations that borrowed much of their structure from the symbolic initiations of Freemasonry (see *Theurgy* on page 129).

There was a genuine expectation that results would follow, that the soul really could "quit the night and seek the day". This expectation was so real that one of the greatest causes of strife during the organisation's short life was the perception that individual members were not manifesting the level of attainment suggested by their grade. This is a problem that has dogged the use of symbolic initiation throughout the twentieth century.

At some point during the middle part of the twentieth century an understanding grew among descendents of the Golden Dawn tradition that the soul was resistant to initiation, and symbolic interventions were not sufficient in themselves. Initiations could be used to trigger a process, but the soul would resist, fight back, dissemble, and do everything it could to acquire the paraphernalia of initiation and social prestige without disengaging from its narrow view. We now find ourselves close to the viewpoint of the gnostics of late antiquity, who believed soul had been imprisoned in the world by dysfunctional powers that must be actively engaged and overcome.

If parts of the *psyche* are resistant to initiation then it is necessary to understand why, and one consequence has been the use of the Tree of Life to model the parts and dynamics of the *psyche*.

This can give the appearance that the Tree of Life and Kabbalah have been translated from the sphere of theosophy to that of pop psychology. This is not the intention. The purpose is to provide accessible concepts and models that people can relate to in their daily lives, so that the dynamics of the *sefirot* in the microcosm can be experienced at first hand.

The Hermetic Kabbalah

LIBER SECVNDVS.						CXXIX.
NAR II.						
יוד הא tenſum decem literarum		אלהים צבאות Nomen elohim Sabaoth				Nomina dei decem literarum
אלוה Eloha	יהוהצבאות Tetragrāmaton Sabaoth	אלהים צבאות Elohim Sabaoth	שדי Sadai	ארני Adonai melech		Decem nomina dei
תפארת Tiphereth	נצח Nezah	הור Hod	יסור Iefod	מלכות Malchuth		Decem Sephiroth
Virtutes	Principatus	Archangeli	Angeli	Animæ beatæ		Decē ordines beatorū ſecundum Dionyſium
Malachim	Elohim	Bne Elohim	Cherubim	Iſſim		Decē beatorū ordines iuxta traditiões Hebræorū
Raphaël	Haniel	Michaël	Gabriel	Anima Meſsihæ		Decem angeli præſidentes
Schemes	Noga	Cochab	Leuanah	Holomieſodoth		Decem ſphæræ mundi
Sphæra Solis	Sphæra Veneris	Sphæra Mercurij	Sphæra Lunæ	Sphæra elemē torum		
Leo	Homo	Serpens	Bos	Agnus		Decem animalia ſanctitatis ad ſuperos relata
Cor	Renes	Pulmo	Genitalia	Matrix		Decem artus intrinſeci hominis
Aēreæ poteſtates	Furiæ ſeminatrices malorum	Criminatores ſiue exploratores	Tētatores, ſiue inſidiatores	Animæ prauæ & damnatæ		Decem damnatorum or dines

Figure 34: A portion of the Scale of the Number 10 from the 1533 CE Cologne edition of Agrippa's *Three Books of Occult Philosophy*. Note the rows containing the divine names, ten *sefirot*, the angel orders, the archangels, and the heavenly spheres (both Latin and Hebrew titles). This is the prototype for many similar tables.

15

Malkhut

The Hermetic Kabbalah

Meaning	Kingdom
Number	10
Colour	Brown (citrine, russet red, olive green, black)
Briatic Correspondence	Stability
Magical Image	A young woman crowned and sitting on a throne
Titles	The Gate; Gate of Death; Gate of Tears; Gate of Justice; The Inferior Mother; *Malkah*, the Queen; *Kallah*, the Bride; the Virgin
Element	Earth
Virtue	Practical Wisdom, Discrimination
Vice	Avarice; Inertia
Illusion	Materialism
Klippot	Stasis
Obligation	Discipline
Command	Keep silent
God Name	*Adonai ha Aretz, Adonai Melekh*
Archangel	*Sandalphon*
Angel Order	*Ishim*
Planet	*Cholem Yesodeth* (The Breaker of the Foundations, the sphere of the elements)
Spiritual Experience	Vision of the Holy Guardian Angel
Keywords	The real world, physical matter, determinism, the Earth, Mother Earth, the physical elements, the natural world, sticks & stones, possessions, faeces, practicality, solidity, stability, inertia, heaviness, bodily death, incarnation

Table 5 : Malkhut

Malkhut

Malkhut means 'kingdom'. Related words are *melekh*, 'king' and *malkah*, 'queen'. As the endpoint of emanation, *Malkhut* is the full and final expression of a creative impulse that manifests in *Keter*. *Malkhut* is *Keter revealed*. If *Keter* is the seed, then *Malkhut* is both the earth and the flower. If *Chokhmah* is the well-spring, and *Binah* the upper sea, then *Malkhut* is the earthly garden of delights, well-watered and rich in abundance. But it is not the *Pardes*, the eternal heavenly garden. That is guarded. *Malkhut* has fallen out of its place in the upper worlds, leaving a hole behind where *Da'at* now is. In the world of *Malkhut* there are serpents and scorpions and many sorrows.

We look outwards at *Malkhut*. Here is a mystery, this looking out, our interiority, as if our eyes were windows in a house. We inhabit *Malkhut* as if we were not part of it, and even our bodies feel like strangers - friends at first, but as we grow old and struggle with simple things, strangers.

Just as we look out from the inside upon something we do not understand, so we see only the outsides, the surfaces of things we do not understand. The sun rises, the wind blows, the rain falls, crops grow, women have babies. With our eyes we see the outward surfaces of these phenomena; only with the inner eye of the mind do we see the structure of cause and effect and dependency, the underlying connections.

In the 21st. century it is difficult for an adult to experience *Malkhut* with untutored and innocent eyes. We know why the sun rises, why crops grow, why women have babies, but this richness of meaning is acquired. We learn it. Our inner eyes are always open, and we augment what we see with what we know. It was not always like this, this augmentation.

A inarticulate part of my hindbrain learns the immediate subtleties of cause and effect - I can catch a ball, run down stairs, play arpeggios, drive an automobile - but this is inarticulate knowledge. Without a guitar in my hand I struggle to recollect how to play a single chord. Even within my own body I often seem to be on the inside looking out. I feel like a ghost within a machine. This alienation, this seemingly intractable separation of subject and object, is a key experience of *Malkhut*.

If one had to characterise *Malkhut* with one word it would be determinism. There is a stable dependability of cause and effect. If this was not so, the sun would not shine. Bacteria would not have evolved a way to extract energy from sunlight. There would be no plants, or any other life. I would not know how to catch a ball, or run down stairs.

How much determinism is there? Is the immediate future completely determined by the present and the immediate past? Is there wiggle room for choice? Is the human soul free in some way that inorganic matter is not? If so, what is free will? How does it sneak into this world of determinism?

These are an ancient questions, and as hotly debated today as they were in ancient times. We feel uneasy about determinism. A fully determined world is a dead world. It may have the semblance of life, but it has no more life than a clockwork toy. Determinism takes away our sense of autonomy and freedom, and turns us into automata. The sublime frontiers of human culture and science and mathematics would then seem to be nothing more than the output of a long train of gears set in motion by a Big Bang. This is a difficult proposition to accept.

Many Kabbalists have thought that we must have free will otherwise there could be no righteousness. God wants us to have the freedom to choose between right and wrong, and so there is always choice and always the potential for good and evil.

Some theologians have felt threatened by the suggestion of human freedom, because it suggests we possess the power to make the future. For God to be omniscient, determinism must be absolute[111]. The Christian preacher and theologian John Calvin followed this to an extreme - he taught predestination, believing that God knew from the beginning of days who would be saved and who would be damned. Perhaps God is like the person who watches *Casablanca* knowing that Ingrid Bergman is always going to step onto the plane ... but I prefer to believe otherwise.

If determinism is the primary defining characteristic of *Malkhut*, then the next is evil. *Malkhut* is a mixture of emanations from the right and left sides of the Tree, but it is the emanations of the left side that predominate. In traditional Kabbalah the concept of *Din*, strict judgement, encompasses both determination and (when unbalanced) evil. Our experience of *Malkhut* is dominated by the experience of *Din*.

We live during a period where many people live in relative safety, are well fed, and have access to excellent medical care. Until the latter half of the twentieth century, war, pestilence, famine and early death

---

111. Like many theological absurdities, this is an artificial problem founded on its assumptions.

were commonplace. This has had a large influence on Kabbalah.

Jews in Europe lived an even more precarious existence than most. Banned from most occupations, they were subject to mass expulsions, seizure of assets, random violence and prejudice, book burning, segregation, and countless episodes of utter barbarity.

At first Jews believed these terrible privations and persecutions were their own fault. They blamed their communities, believing they had failed God in various ways. They believed that evil done by human beings ignited the power of strict judgement and brought it down into *Malkhut*. It was said that sin caused the *Shekhinah* to turn away from *Ze'ir Anpin* and don the black robes of *Lilith* - *Lilith* being the malign aspect of *Malkhut* and the *Shekhinah* when she is overwhelmed by the power of strict judgement.

As time went by this view darkened. Evil seemed to have a vitality of its own. A seed planted by an early work of Spanish Kabbalah, *A Treatise on the Emanations of the Left Side*[112], influenced the author of the *Zohar*, and the *Zohar* in turn influenced later Kabbalists, especially R. Isaac Luria. The Other Side, the Left Side, the powers of unmitigated *Din*, took on an increasingly autonomous and cosmological dimension. Luria proposed that the broken remnants of prior universes, universes of pure *Din*, still existed in the abyss. These fragments contained divine sparks, like the remains of an old fire that still glows when poked. In a deepening pessimism about the nature of existence, evil was no longer an instrumental reflex of divine justice that punished the wicked - it had an ancient and pre-existent life of its own. When Adam and Eve sinned by disobeying God's commandment and ate from the Tree of Knowledge, there was a cosmic catastrophe; worlds shifted out of place, and *Malkhut* descended into the region of the ancient shells, a realm of fundamental impurity.

The world can be an extraordinarily harsh place. It is resource-limited; that is, most environments are at the limits of their capacity to support life. We went forth and multiplied, and now *Malkhut* is all filled up. With few exceptions, non-photosynthetic species live off other species, and predation is the rule. Human beings have been able to expand the carrying capacity of the environment by ingenious schemes such as agriculture and irrigation, by ruthlessly using and eating other species, by modifying the environment on a planetary scale (felling forests for example), and, most importantly, by exploiting fossil water and fossil energy.

---

112. *The Early Kabbalah*, ed. Dan, Joseph, trans. Kiener, R.C., Paulist 1986

The Hermetic Kabbalah

This ruthlessness has created, for some at least, an illusion of abundance. Nevertheless most people are forced to spend a large part of their lives carrying out paid services for other people in return for the means to have a dwelling place and food. We live in a fragile situation, both individually and collectively. Human beings have an astonishing ability to pick fights with each other, and when this happens, much of the infrastructure that supports communities is disrupted and broken. We can witness civilized nations revert to a dysfunctional condition where commerce, law, education, medicine, and even the simple courtesy and kindness of neighbours, are forgotten in a bout of collective madness.

It would seem that suffering and death are the default states. Everything else requires unceasing effort, a social investment in knowledge, skills and infrastructure, and good luck. The 'good luck' component is paramount, and involves living at the right time, in the right place, having good genes and a good family, and possessing a temperament in tune with conditions in society. Even with the best of fortune we will all die of something, and in all likelihood it will not be quick or elegant or noble.

And if our condition is fragile and precarious, then that of most animals is worse. Is this *harshness* an irreducible aspect of *Malkhut*?

Throughout history human beings have sought to placate whatever beings they believed were giving them a hard time by creating temples, by complex ceremonials, and through sacrifice. In parallel they have imagined utopias, alternative *Malkhuts* in which the worst parts of this world are stripped out. The Norse idea of Valhalla, the Hall of the Slain, is typical: following their deaths, noble warriors would be plucked from the battlefield by warrior maidens and taken to a vast hall, where they would feast on limitless quantities of meat and mead, followed by fierce battle, at the conclusion of which their wounds would heal, and they could begin the cycle again.

There is a compulsive, obsessive aspect to this utopia that is reminiscent of computer gaming, where dull aspects of life are stripped out, and a small number of highly rewarded behaviours are repeated. This would seem to be true of all supernatural utopias: a small number of pleasurable activities are selected and repeated. Utopia is a free Las Vegas run by benign beings. Utopia is a good feeling, indefinitely sustained. For many people the short-cut to utopia is through drug use.

In some respects rational, materialist utopias such as those inspired by the writings of Marx and Lenin are more pernicious, in

Malkhut

that they appear plausible and achievable in a way that Valhalla is not. They assume that with suitable education and legislation it will be possible to produce a frictionless society in which negative experiences are progressively eliminated. This has never been demonstrated in practice; the level of social control required has been so repressive and restrictive it has created a power structure that has been exploited by a ruling class of officials, who have tended, over time, to become an elite class of hereditary feudal overlords.

It is remarkably difficult to imagine a better world, a world that is both complete and consistent, a world that is *not harsh*. Supernatural utopias are neither complete or consistent - they are fragments of this world with housework and toilet duties left out. Rational utopias are like this world, but with more training (that is, inner rules), more laws, and more supervision and control - that is, like this world but with *freedom* left out.

The Kabbalistic tradition of the Destroyed Worlds (see 8.2) is relevant here. These were worlds of pure *Din*, worlds of evil where moral choice and freedom were not possible, and so righteousness (self-consciously-adopted good behaviour) was also not possible. Attempts to create rational utopias tend in the direction of *Din* (that is, limitation or restriction); they require behavioural training and education during childhood, laws to mitigate every kind of harm, and overwhelming supervision and reporting (e.g. CCTV) to ensure that laws are obeyed. It would seem that human attempts to create better worlds are heading in the direction of more *Din* rather than more *Chesed*.

What would a world of greater *Chesed* be like? Sometimes science fiction attempts to portray an ideal world of 'good' people. It is rarely convincing. Either they seem weak and ineffectual in the face of strife, or they have a technology so advanced that no-one can mess with them - a steel fist in a velvet glove. Goodness is either balanced by strength, or it runs into the 'priests versus vikings' problem: that is, it is all very well living a life according to Christian ideals, but how does one deal with pillaging vikings? And if one does not deal with the vikings, who does? Whenever one finds a class of Eloi, removed from striving and strife, one has to look for Morlocks in the background.

It is natural to want to make a better world for ourselves. It is possible to imagine 'little worlds' that function perfectly - part of the attraction of the model railway (or similar) is that everything is in its place and functioning as it should - the sheep are in the field, the people are on the platform, and the trains are on time. Throughout history people have imagined that the cosmos could be or should be like this - a place for everything, and everything in its place. One of the medieval arguments for social stratification was that it was divinely ordained, that the poor (like the sheep) should be content in someone else's fields. From the beginning Kabbalists have debated the issue of rigid order versus freedom and rejected 'worlds of pure *Din*', accepting that a balance of *Chesed* and *Din* was a necessary aspect of the cosmos. A world of pure *Din* is not a *living* world, it is an automaton, a mechanism. God did not want a model railway. God wanted something else, something open and self-modifying.

It would seem then that harshness is an irreducible aspect of *Malkhut*. Good people do what they can to reduce it. It is always within our power to make things worse than they already are.

An aspect of *Malkhut* that would seem to be implicitly connected with determinism is that it is hard work to change anything. One can imagine the outlines of a fairy-tale castle in minutes, and sketch them out on paper within an hour. One could build a model in days. One would require the resources and determination of Mad King Ludwig to progress much further[113]. Ideas conceived in the imagination become progressively more difficult to achieve as we attempt to bring them into this world.

We would like to circumvent determinism but this is not so easy. One might like to make some mystical hand gestures and persuade a broomstick to carry pails of water, but outside of Disney animation, few people have the knack. There is more. Physical objects have mass: we have to push them to make them go, and push them to make them stop. There is friction, which we can alleviate with wheels and rollers and bearings and oil, but outside of a vacuum it is difficult to eliminate.

There is a general tendency for energy to spread itself around until it becomes so diffuse it is useless - this is the Second Law of Thermodynamics. There are conservation laws in physics that appear to be impossible to circumvent - those of energy, momentum, angular momentum for example. When we attempt to achieve anything in *Malkhut* we do so under the gaze of angels who have to account for every microjoule of energy in their ledgers.

From a psychological perspective something similar occurs. It is difficult to inculcate good habits, and difficult to remedy bad habits. We struggle with change. There always seems to be an endless list of

---

113. Neuschwanstein Castle took a little under 15 years to complete.

Malkhut

things to do, and we tire, and sometime we stop and don't want to start again. This is the background to the vice of *Malkhut*, which is Inertia. The word is used metaphorically. The meaning is that in both a physical and psychological sense it takes energy to cause change. It takes energy to transmit our intentions into reality. The situation is very different with imagination - in the imagination it usually takes effort and focus to *stop* things from changing.

The virtue of *Malkhut* is discrimination. Discrimination is an aspect of practical wisdom. The world is very particular about what it permits and what it does not permit. In myth, Icarus was able to strap on wings and fly. When the 10th. century monk Eilmer of Malmesbury read about Daedelus and Icarus and attempted the same thing, he plummeted to earth and broke both legs.

Discrimination is the ability to separate wheat from chaff, sheep from goats, and metaphors from similes. It is the ability to recognise a good idea, a workable business plan, a flaw in a proof, a watertight legal defence, a cock-and-bull story, or a scam. In the personal realm, it is the ability to detect when we are deceiving ourselves, or being selfish, or vain, or being arrogant or cruel. It is the needle that pricks the bubble of pretension. It is the first virtue required in the ascent of the Tree. Without discrimination we fall prey to an endless storm of subjectivity: what we feel, what we think, and what we imagine. Like Eilmer, we strap on wings and imagine we can fly.

Discrimination is a stance that is the psychological analogue of stability. We try to assess what will work and what will not work, what is truth and what is lie, what is sincerity and what is mendacious, what is real and what is not real. It is like a gate guarded by a suspicious watchman. There is a balance between being too accepting and open, and too pernickety and closed. When we are too open we are like a rudderless ship in a storm, changing direction with every new gust of wind. When we are closed, we are like a ship in a river, trapped by the channel.

According to tradition each *sefira* is the manifestation of a divine name. The divine name associated with *Malkhut* is *Adonai*, which means 'Lord'. During readings of the Torah, when the name YHVH is encountered, the reader vocalises *Adonai* instead. YHVH is not spoken. We can regard *Adonai* as the public persona of YHVH. This is not so different from the way kings and queens are addressed by their subjects. There are two variants of *Adonai*: *Adonai Melekh* ('Lord who is King') and *Adonai ha Aretz* ('Lord of the World').

The archangel associated with *Malkhut* is *Sandalphon*. According

The Hermetic Kabbalah

to ancient traditions that date back to the *Merkavah* period of Jewish mysticism[114] he was a vast presence who spanned the distance from earth to heaven. He stood behind the divine throne and worked the prayers of Israel into crown that would ascend by itself and crown the figure on the throne. Vast though he is, even *Sandalphon* is not permitted to see the figure on the throne. We can think of *Sandalphon* as part of the 'run and return' circuit that carries divine emanation from *Keter* down to *Malkhut* and then back to *Keter* again.

The divine beings associated with *Malkhut* are the *Ishim*. The *Ishim* are beings who can take a physical form and look like human beings. Sometimes in the Bible they are mistaken for human beings. According to some traditions they may be the souls of saintly individuals. *Ishim* is sometimes mistranslated as 'souls of fire'. This is an error found in several Golden Dawn offshoots and comes from a similarity between the words for 'fire' and 'human being'.

The primary Kabbalistic image for *Malkhut* is that of a woman. She appears in several guises that overlap with those of the *Shekhinah*, God's indwelling presence in this world, and overlap with the personification of the Sabbat (see *Partzufim* on page 43). The primary magical image is that of a young woman crowned and seated on a throne. This is *Malkah*, the Queen of the World. In so far as she is the spouse of *Ze'ir Anpin* she is also *Kallah*, the bride.

The imagery associated with *Malkhut* also overlaps with that of *Binah*, who is sometimes visualised as an elderly queen. *Binah* is *Imma*, mother. The overlap with *Binah* comes from the holy name of four letters, *YHVH*. *Binah* is the first letter *He*; *Malkhut* the final *He*. They are sometimes represented by the two daughters of Laban from *Genesis*: Leah is *Binah*, and Rachel is *Malkhut*. An ancient text associated with the *Sefer Yetzirah* states that *Malkhut* "sits on the throne of *Binah*". One of the titles of *Binah* is *Khorsia*, or throne. We can imagine *Binah* as 'upholding' *Malkhut*, that *Malkhut* is *Binah* 'reified'.

Malkhut is the sphere of the elements. This is often represented using an equal-arm cross inside a circle, the astrological symbol for earth. The four pie-segments representing the elements are coloured citrine, olive, russet red, and black.

The ancients had a straightforward view of the elements. They stood on the earth and the earth contained water in rivers and

---

114. *Keter: The Crown of God in Early Jewish Mysticism*, Arthur Green, Princeton University Press 1997

Malkhut

springs; they breathed the air, and the sun supplied heat and light. This led to a natural ordering of the elements: earth, water, air, fire. This also corresponds to four states of matter: solid, liquid, gas, plasma, a natural progression that results as the temperature increases. In its original form it was a simple kind of physics. Plato associated simple geometrical forms with the elements and tried to show how these forms accounted for their properties. For example, the tetrahedron was pointy and harsh and abrasive and the least complex of the regular solids, and so he reasoned that fire must be made up of tiny tetrahedrons.

In the course of time an extensive set of ideas grew up around the four elements, especially in medicine, alchemy and astrology. There were four humours, and four dispositions, and four directions, and four seasons, four Tarot suits and a great deal more[115]. As a result the four elements began to be seen as less physical and more subjective and metaphorical. For example, an earthy person would be stubborn and practical, an airy person would be vocal and opinionated, a watery person would be emotional and intuitive, and a fiery person would be energetic and daring.

Just as the planets were associated with the *sefirot*, so also were the elements. The Golden Dawn used a logical but unintuitive assignment based on the natural progression of the elements, so that *Malkhut* corresponded to earth, *Yesod* to water, *Hod* to air, and *Netzach* to fire. In other words, the elements ascended the Tree in order of density.

The Hermetic tradition recognises five elements, not four. The fifth is called spirit, aethyr or quintessence, and its primary attribute is *connection*. In the Golden Dawn tradition it is assigned to the fifth point of the pentagram and called 'spirit'.

Aethyr is the medium for the transmission of impulses, from the soul to the body, or from the stars to the world. It is an essential component of occult causality. In discussing the connection of the soul to the body, and how this is achieved Agrippa observes[116]:

> Now they conceive such a medium to be called the Spirit of the World, viz. that which we call quintessence: because it is not from the four elements, but a certain fifth thing, having its being above and beside them. ... By this Spirit therefore every occult property is conveyed into

---

115. Agrippa provides an overview in "The Scale of the Number Four", *Three Books of Occult Philosophy*, ed. Donald Tyson, Llewellyn 1992
116. *Three Books of Occult Philosophy,* Henry Cornelius Agrippa, Ed. Donald Tyson, Llewellyn 1993

The Hermetic Kabbalah

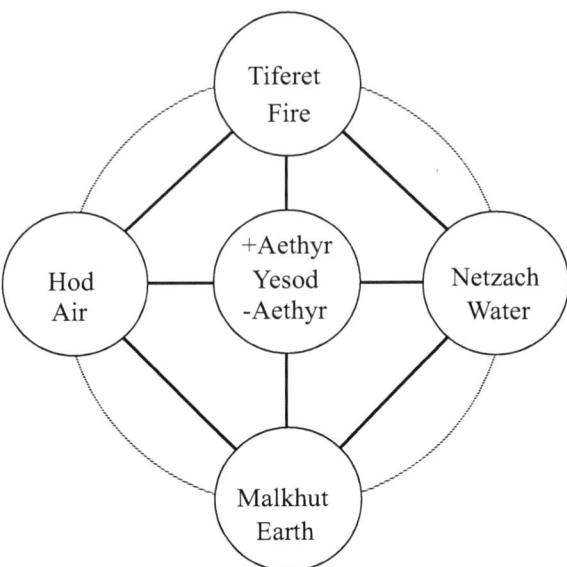

Figure 35: The Circle Cross of the Elements on the Tree

herbs, stones, metals and animals, through the Sun, Moon, planets, and through stars higher than the planets.

A surprising omission from Dion Fortune's *The Mystical Qabalah* (the published source for many of the correspondences given here) is that she does not give or discuss the attribution of the elements on the Tree. Concerning *Yesod* she states[117]:

Yesod is the sphere of that peculiar substance, partaking of the nature of mind and matter, which is called the Aethyr of the Wise, the Akasha, or the Astral Light, according to the terminology being used.

This differs from the Golden Dawn attribution of elements[118], where *Yesod* corresponds to Water, but is the same as that communicated verbally to the author. It is possible that Fortune possessed an alternative attribution that was unpublished and she chose not to refer to it directly[119]. It is illustrated in Figure 35. According to this attribution, *Malkhut* and *Hod* remain the same as in the Golden Dawn scheme, but now *Netzach* corresponds to Water, *Tiferet* Fire, and *Yesod* Aethyr.

---

117. *The Mystical Qabalah*, Dion Fortune, 1935
118. These had been published by Aleister Crowley and later by Israel Regardie.
119. Fortune was under a traditional oath of silence and only discusses esoteric material disclosed by others.

Malkhut

There are pleasing aspects to these attributions. Water would

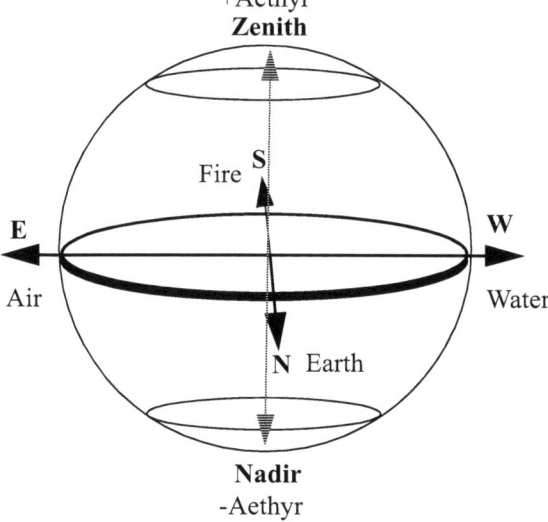

Figure 36: The Elements and the Cardinal Points

seem to be a better match to Venusian *Netzach* than fire. Aethyr is an excellent match to *Yesod*, the Foundation. The solar fire of *Tiferet* is now included. Using these correspondences the elements now form a *magic circle* or *mandala* on the lower face of the Tree (see Figure 35).

A near-universal magical practice is for a magician to create a ceremonial sacred space (*temenos*) in the form of a circle[120]. A convention widely adopted by Western magicians and neopagans is to attribute air to the East, fire to the South, water to the West and earth to the North. Aethyr or spirit corresponds to the operator who holds or binds the circle.

Aethyr is sometimes thought to have two aspects, a positive aspect that binds, corresponding to the zenith, and a negative aspect that unbinds, corresponding to the nadir (see Figure 36). This creates a space of six directions, and corresponds to the six permutations of

---

120. The fifth book of the gnostic *Pistis Sophia* describes Jesus and his followers performing a recognisable magical ceremony in which Jesus addresses the four quarters and his followers take ritual stations around an altar - see *Pistis Sophia*, trans. G.R.S.Mead. The *Pistis Sophia* may be as old as the canonical gospels of the New Testament.

The Hermetic Kabbalah

YHV as given in the *Sepher Yetzirah*:
> He chose three Elementals, and set them in his great name. And with them he sealed the six directions.

The attribution of elements to the lower face of the Tree in Figure 35 follows the pattern of Figure 36; that is, the order of elements as one turns around *Yesod* is the same as their attribution to the cardinal points. This is the *circle-cross of the elements*, one of the most important glyphs in the Western tradition.

A mysterious aspect of *Malkhut* is its relationship with *Keter*. An aspect of this mystery is artificial, created by the conventional depiction of the Tree, in which *Keter* is at one end, and *Malkhut* at the other. If we draw the same diagram on a cylinder, then we have exactly the same diagram, but *Keter* and *Malkhut* can overlap. If we can do this so simply with a piece of paper, then we can also do it in our minds.

A simple argument given by Proclus in the 5th. century is that whenever two things are connected or related - in space, in time, by causality, by inclusion, whatever - then they are united by whatever connects them. We can view the world of tangible objects in *Malkhut* as being separate and perhaps even discrete, but we can only do this by deliberately excluding everything related to these objects. Our attention focuses on a foreground, and neglects the presence of a background. Nothing real that we can point at is genuinely disconnected or isolated in this way. We can always find a context that objects share, even if it is all of space and all of time.

This is a basic exercise in unification - finding a larger context that connects apparently disjoint things. Jewish mystics developed exercises they called *yichudim* - unifications. The aim was to unify things that, due to the fallen nature of reality, had the appearance of being separate. We can carry out our own unifications in everyday life by looking for unity wherever we see opposition and duality. When we do this we may begin to look past the Many and perceive The One.

This impulse to discover unity in multiplicity is important in modern physics. The proton, a tiny particle of matter, interacts with all four of the known fields: the gravitational field, the electromagnetic field, and both the weak and strong interactions. It necessarily follows that all four fields are connected. It is difficult to imagine a complete explanation of any one field that does not involve the existence of the proton and the other three fields. They form, in some way we do not understand, a unity. This has resulted in decades of research into *unified field theories*. Einstein spent much of the latter part of his life

Malkhut

exploring theories of this kind. The belief in an underlying unity is not confined to Platonists and Kabbalists.

If we can 'look through' the multiplicity and particularity of *Malkhut* and see an underlying unity in the eye of the mind, then there is more we can do to perceive and (ultimately) experience this unity. For example, we can try to avoid thinking of objects or ideas or situations or events in isolation. There are times when isolation can be useful (in scientific thought experiments for example) but in general this disconnection creates an abnormal perception. We can avoid thinking disjunctively: for example "we can do this, *or* we can do that". Disjunctive thinking creates dualities, creates polarisation, creates antipathies. We are sometimes told to "think outside the box". Disjunctive thought *creates boxes* - usually where there are none. It is useful to practice conjunctive thought: for example, "we can do some of this, *and* some of that".

Exercises like this illustrate the extent to which there is a cognitive aspect to *Malkhut*, that things may appear more separate than they are. Even physicists acknowledge the possibility of an underlying unity that 'explains' multiplicity. If this is so then we must accept that the appearance of reality, what we experience as *Malkhut*, is an aspect of the unity of *Keter*; likewise the unity of *Keter* is never separate from its appearance as The Many. They are the same (but different), just as Kabbalists have maintained. It seems appropriate at this point to recall the *Shema:*

Hear, Israel, the Lord is our God, the Lord is One

To summarise, *Malkhut* is stubborn. It has its little ways. It has its routines. It doesn't like being pushed around. If by chance something does begin to move, best not stand in the way - it will take some stopping. *Malkhut* keeps us at arms' length to the point of alienation. We are inside looking out. We can watch, we can wonder, but we can never quite grasp what Kant called the *noumenal*, things-in-themselves.

This stubbornness, this fixity, has a side-effect. Determinism makes life possible. Freedom makes emergence and variety possible. One cannot play a game without rules, and *Malkhut*, sitting on the throne of *Binah*, provides the ground rules of freedom and determination that make the game of life possible.

Malkhut is harsh and abrasive and unyielding, so that it dominates our perception of reality. It hurts us. It overwhelms us, so that we cannot see an underlying unity that lies behind it.

The Hermetic Kabbalah

16

Yesod

The Hermetic Kabbalah

Meaning	Foundation
Number	9
Colour	Purple
Briatic Correspondence	Receptivity, perception
Magical Image	A beautiful man, very strong (e.g. Atlas)
Titles	The Treasure House of Images; the Receptacle of the Emanations; *Tzadik* - Righteous
Element	Aethyr
Virtue	Independence
Vice	Idleness
Illusion	Security
Klippot	Zombieism, robotism
Obligation	Trust
Command	Go!
God Name	*Shaddai, El Chai*
Archangel	*Gabriel*
Angel Order	*Cherubim*
Planet	*Levanah* (Moon)
Spiritual Experience	Vision of the Machinery of the Universe
Keywords	Perception, interface, imagination, image, glamour, the Moon and tides, the unconscious, instinct, illusion, hidden infrastructure, dreams, divination, anything as it seems to be and not as it is, mirrors and crystals, the Astral Plane, Aethyr, glue, secret doors, tunnels, sex & reproduction, the genitals, cosmetics, instinctive magic (psychism)

Table 6 : Yesod

Yesod

A succinct way to think about *Yesod* is that it is the "inside of the outside". Examining the Tree of Life, both *Yesod* and *Malkhut* have connecting paths to *Hod* and *Netzach*, and both are on the Middle Pillar. They are like duals, and that is one way to think about them. *Malkhut* is like the "outside of the inside", and *Yesod* is like the "inside of the outside"[121].

Yesod means "foundation", and the *sefira* represents the many ways in which the unseen supports the seen. It is the "receptacle of the emanations" the hidden (or occult) substructure whereby the emanations from the remainder of the Tree are transmitted to the *sefira Malkhut*.

Just as a large building has air-conditioning ducts, conduits, electrical wiring, hot and cold water pipes, attic spaces, lift shafts, service tunnels, winding rooms, storage tanks, and a telephone exchange, so we can visualise the unseen 'other side' of the phenomenal world. Meditations on the nature of *Yesod* tend to be filled with secret and concealed mechanisms, as if the cosmos was a gothic mansion with a door behind every mirror, a passage in every wall, a pair of hidden eyes behind every portrait, and a subterranean world of forgotten tunnels leading who knows where. For this reason the Spiritual Experience of *Yesod* is titled "The Vision of the Machinery of the Universe".

Many *Yesod* correspondences reinforce the notion of a foundation, of a substructure that lies behind, supports, and gives shape to phenomenal reality. The magical image of *Yesod* is of "a beautiful naked man, very strong"; an image often used is that of a man with the world resting on his shoulders, like one of the (mis)representations of the Titan Atlas (who held up the heavens, not the world). The archangel is *Gabriel*, the Strong or Mighty One of God, and the divine name is *Shaddai El Chai*, the Almighty Living God.

One of the oldest ideas about *Yesod* is that it represents the point where two different levels of reality intersect. Without that intersection they would be disjoint; there would be no communication between them. For example, the internal communication of the brain uses electrical potentials, but the external world requires movement in space, and so a large part of the human body is composed of muscle and mechanical levers. Muscles and bones are transducers; they transform the brain's language of electrical potentials into one of

---

121. See also *The Soul and its Parts* on page 351 for a more detailed explanation of the "inside of the outside".

pushing and shoving. Even speech is muscular and mechanical, as is hearing. So *Yesod* represents the interface, the 'imprint' of one level upon another. It is not the communication of abstract notions via language. It is more direct, like a punch in the face.

The image used frequently in the literature of Kabbalah (although it is often phrased in allusive language) is that of the male penis. For example, the *Bahir*, the oldest specifically Kabbalistic text, provides many of the key ideas[122]:

> A column goes from the earth up to heaven, and its name is righteous (*tzadik*), after the [earthly] righteous. When there are righteous upon the earth, it is strong, but when there are not it grows slack; and it bears the entire world, for it is said "the righteous is the foundation of the world." But if it is slack, the world cannot exist. That is why it is said in the *Talmud*, Yoma 38b: Even if there were only a single righteous man upon earth, he would maintain the world.

There is a complex of allusions here. The most overt is theurgic: the behaviour of the community of righteous individuals upholds the world. Their behaviour has a direct impact on the condition of a pillar (also called "righteous") that exists in the middle realm between earth and heaven. It can grow strong or slack.

This theurgic assumption predated Kabbalah[123], but it became fully developed and explicit in later Kabbalistic understanding: the mindful fulfilment of God's commandments plays an essential role in what Idel calls 'universe-maintenance'. What is not explicit in the *Bahir*, but is alluded to in other sources, is that the column that grows strong or slack is the penis of *Ze'ir Anpin*. When *Yesod* is depicted on the human body, it corresponds to the sexual organs: the penis in the case of *Ze'ir Anpin*, and the Holy of Holies in the case of *Nukva Ze'ir*. *Yesod* is the point of contact between *Ze'ir* and *Nukva*. *Yesod* is the gateway whereby life (*chaiim*) is communicated into this world.

An unusual medical idea that can be traced back to classical Greece is that semen is produced in the blood, concentrated in the brain, and runs down the spine into the testes. The verse "You are a garden fountain, a well of flowing water streaming down from Lebanon" (*Song of Songs 4:15*) can be interpreted as referring to *Chokhmah*, which according to Kabbalistic imagery, is often depicted as a spring or fountain. Lebanon can also be read as *laban* - white, a reference to the white matter in the brain, the whiteness of the spinal

---

122. *The Bahir*, quoted from *The Origins of the Kabbalah*, Gershom Scholem, Princeton 1990
123. See *Ancient Jewish Theurgy* in *Kabbalah: New Perspectives*, Moshe Idel, Yale 1988

Yesod

cord, and the whiteness of semen. A stream of souls flows down the Tree of Life, from *Chokhmah* to *Chesed*, from *Chesed* to *Tiferet*, from *Tiferet* to *Yesod*, and (all being propitious) from *Yesod* into *Malkhut*.

The column stretching from earth to heaven is also the means whereby souls may return to their divine source - the column (the symbolism is multivalent) is also the Middle Pillar, or the Tree of Life itself[124].

Yesod is the point at which life enters the world. Medieval Kabbalists followed the Neoplatonist view that matter was dead; it was animated by contact with *souls*. In Kabbalah, life, shape and causal autonomy are communicated through *Yesod*. *Yesod* communicates and upholds whatever it is that 'vivifies' matter. The name *El Chai*, "Living God" or "God of Life" can be interpreted in this sense. It is the aspect of God that vivifies.

Because we are surrounded by identical mass-produced commodities, it is difficult for us to imagine the world as it was a thousand years ago. Our historical dramas tend to focus on the lives of the rich, who had access to skilled crafts. Most people had very few possessions, and much of what they possessed would have been made locally, either within their families, or by local crafts-people. We would probably use the word 'rustic' to describe these goods - each would have been hand-made and one-of-a-kind. If one wanted to look for a consistent *shape* or *regularity* in the world, it would have been found in living things - plants and animals.

Living things were different from almost everything else in that they had a consistent and regular shape or form, and they were a source of autonomous action. Not only that, but when a living thing died, it lost its shape, and it stopped being a source of action. This encouraged the simple idea that life, shape and autonomous causality had their origin in a sphere of being independent of the physical. This is an idea that permeated European culture for millenia. Although modern science has discounted vitalist theories of living organisms, there is still a strong cultural attachment to the idea that a human being is an autonomous causal nexus, and hence responsible for good or bad behaviour.

An important influence on modern ideas about *Yesod* came from the 19th. century spiritualist movement. Spiritualist mediums demonstrated a wide range of inexplicable physical phenomena - floating

---

124. *Ascensions on High in Jewish Mysticism: Pillars, Lines, Ladders*, Moshe Idel, CEU Press, 2005

trumpets, mysterious music and bells, knocks and thumps, levitation, and materialised objects ('apports'). Early photographers produced photographs of what was supposed to be evidence, such as ghostly figures, and pictures of a strange substance that was named 'ectoplasm'. Mediums were weighed during the production of ectoplasm, and it was reported that they lost weight. There was a widespread belief that something connected with the physical body - a finer, less dense kind of matter - was coupled to the mind and capable of causing effects at a distance.

This was combined with older ideas, such as the idea that there is a medium that connects the stars to things in this world, an 'astral' medium[125] - one can trace ideas of this kind through Alkindi and Marcelio Ficino. The nineteenth century French occultist Eliphas Levi wrote about something he called 'the Astral Light', a connective and communicative medium that carried influences into the physical. According to Levi an occultist could influence the physical by building forms in the Astral Light. What Levi proposed (or modified - one can trace ideas like this back to classical times) was a very influential model of occult causality. It was influential because it provided an intuitive explanation for how traditional magic might work. It was proto-scientific, in that it hypothesised mechanisms and causality. A ritual, for example, was efficacious because it was a means to 'build a form' in the Astral Light. Instead of following a bizarre prescription in a grimoire, a magician could *design* a ritual using the Hermetic doctrine of signatures and correspondences to shape the Astral Light according to intention.

Concurrently with Levi, Countess Helena Petrovna Blavatsky, author of the sensational *Isis Unveiled* and founder of Theosophy, was combining Hindu and Buddhist metaphysics with traditional Hermetic and Platonic ideas of the soul to produce a multi-layered conception of 'subtle bodies'. The writings of Blavatsky and her successors mention the 'double' or *doppelgänger*, the etheric body, the *Akashic* body, the astral body, the mental body and the causal body, along with analogues from Eastern traditions. Descriptions of these subtle bodies are often conflated, especially in the later New Age literature, and the double, etheric body, Akashic body and astral body are often interchangeable.

Darwin's *On the Origin of the Species* was published when Blavatsky was 28 years old. Her Theosophy was an attempt to challenge the

---

125. See the discussion on spirit/aethyr/quintessence in the section on *Malkhut* above.

Yesod

threat of materialist science. She attempted to outflank science by creating an 'occult science' in which mundane science was only a tiny part of a much larger and older tradition. She hijacked Darwin's theory of evolution and harnessed it to the Neoplatonic idea of *procession* and *reversion* - the belief that we are an endpoint of a process of emanation, and it is our destiny to return to the source via a progression of more advanced spiritual states. The Theosophical movement attempted to use the language of science and re-enacted the downfall of Neoplatonism by creating an enormously complex ontology and causality. One finds quasi-materialist accounts of the various 'planes' and their interactions.

The net effect has been the introduction of Theosophical ideas into Kabbalah, and nowhere is this stronger than in descriptions of *Yesod*. Dion Fortune, who was greatly influenced by Theosophy, elaborates these ideas in her chapter on *Yesod* in *The Mystical Qabalah*; *viz*:

> But although we no more know the ultimate nature of the astral Aether than we understand the ultimate nature of electricity, nevertheless we know by observation that it possessed certain properties ... The first of these properties is the capacity of the astral Aether to be moulded into forms by the mind; the second is the capacity of the astral Aether to hold the molecules of dense matter in its mesh-like lines of tension as in a rack of pigeon holes.
>
> ...
>
> Sensation must always be an affair of both mind and matter, inexplicable in isolation. To explain neural sensation we must posit a substance that is intermediate between mind and matter; to understand purposive movement we equally require the existence of a substance - that is, which possesses the power to receive and hold the impress of thought and to influence the position in space of the atomic units of matter.

The substance "intermediate between mind and matter" is the quintessence of Agrippa. What impresses here is the essentially Neoplatonic procedure of introducing an intermediate entity (in this case, 'astral Aethyr') as a connective and causal medium[126]. Astral Aethyr connects mind to matter in a very traditional resolution of the mind-body problem.

Modern theories of the astral light, ectoplasm, and various causal bodies, have added weight to the theurgic importance of *Yesod*. The roots of the Tree of Life are embedded in the *Ungrund* of *En Sof*;

---

126. Modern physics does something almost identical by introducing 'fields' as the connective and causal medium between particles.

Yesod represents the seeds that will take root in the soil of *Malkhut* (a soil which may seem different from that of the roots of the Tree, but is not). The sexual symbolism leads directly to theurgic practices involving the sexual act between a man and a woman. Although it is not generally known, such practises exist in Judaism, in which the union of King and Queen is celebrated on the Sabbath. They also exist within the Hermetic tradition; the most public exponent would probably be Aleister Crowley[127].

An important symbol for *Yesod* is the mirror. A mirror reflects the world, and provides the illusion of a second world that seems to be identical to this one ... but may not be. A mirror is often used as a device in fantasy and horror as a portal between this world and another. We can think of *Yesod* as being the 'mirror' of *Malkhut*. The mirror also links *Yesod* to perception and the imagination, as perception is like a mirror of reality; 'simulacrum' would be a better choice of word, but mirror is intuitively reasonable. Imagination uses the syntax of *Malkhut* but is unconstrained by the shackles of determinism. We can imagine a talking tree or a hybrid beast, or a face in smoke - imagination is free to follow whatever path it takes without concern for logic or explanation or even meaning. Following a similar intuition, *Yesod* is connected with scrying and divination, and especially with magic mirrors and crystal balls.

In modern Hermetic symbolism *Yesod* is usually connected with the Moon, according to an ancient astrological scheme that orders the Sun and planets according to their apparent motion - Moon, Mercury, Venus, Sun etc. This differs from traditional Jewish Kabbalah, where *Malkhut* is associated with the Moon and *Tiferet* with the Sun (using the correspondence of *Tiferet* with *Ze'ir Anpin*, the King, and *Malkhut* with *Nukva Ze'ir*, the Queen).

The divine marriage or *conjunctio* between *Sol*, the king, and *Luna*, the queen is one of the oldest symbols of European alchemy, going back to the *Emerald Tablet of Hermes*: "Its father is the sun and its mother is the moon". The Moon has a twenty-eight day lunar cycle of waxing and waning, a cycle that was identified with the female menstrual cycle. The lunar cycle was taken to indicate the nature of *Malkhut*, at times bright, at times occluded, drawing from both the right and left sides of the Tree.

---

127. There is an underground stream of tradition that may connect the false Messiah Sabbatai Zevi, the bizarre antinomian cult of the Frankists, and European quasi-Masonic organisations - see *Why Mrs. Blake Cried*, Marsha Keith Schuchard, Century 2006.

Yesod

The Hermetic association of *Yesod* with the Moon inclines more to the idea that the daytime is the world of appearances or *phenomena*, and the night-time is the world of essences or *noumena*. The former is revealed, the latter is hidden (or occult). The former is experienced by the senses of the body, the other with the inner senses of imagination and intuition. It is the imagination that reveals what the eyes do not show, augmenting the world of appearance with the richness of the Hermetic worldview, a world of hidden life, of connection and relationship. The imagination is like the sea, often stormy, rarely still, and filled with strange life.

How do we avoid being swept away by vision and association? By employing discrimination, the virtue of *Malkhut*. Discrimination is like a harbour, with its lights, breakwaters and orderly quays, where a ship may tie-up without the buffeting of every random wind or tide.

On the Pillar of Consciousness, *Yesod* corresponds to the Ego. The Ego is primarily protective. It knows everything we need to survive in human society. It provides what we need to build trust, win friends, find a sexual partner, recognise offence, deal with threats, and provide a home and livelihood. Each human society has a unique way of going about its business, and so the Ego has to be able to adapt to the specifics. Human society is competitive, and the Ego has to be able to strike a balance between building relationships (which are usually the key to prosperity) and fending-off rivals. Because the Ego exists in a network of relationships, its coherence and stability is of great concern to many people, especially friends, family and employers.

Yesod does not correspond to the whole of the Ego, but it is centred there. The Ego extends down towards its defining environment in *Malkhut*; in *Hod* we find opinions, ideas, and all the stories the Ego tells itself; in *Netzach* we find values and attachments and projections (an instinctive tendency to use ourselves as a fundamental point of reference); in *Tiferet* the Ego senses the possibility of transcending its limitations and growing into something larger.

The Ego, depending on the person and the occasion, centres itself somewhere on the lower face of the Tree[128], and shifts according to circumstances. In the face of hunger, thirst, and exposure we are driven by bodily needs. As circumstances improve we ascend the hierarchy of needs and behaviour becomes more open, less self-protective and less self-interested.

The virtue of *Yesod* is *independence*. The illusion is *security* and

---

128. The five sefirot centred on *Yesod*.

The Hermetic Kabbalah

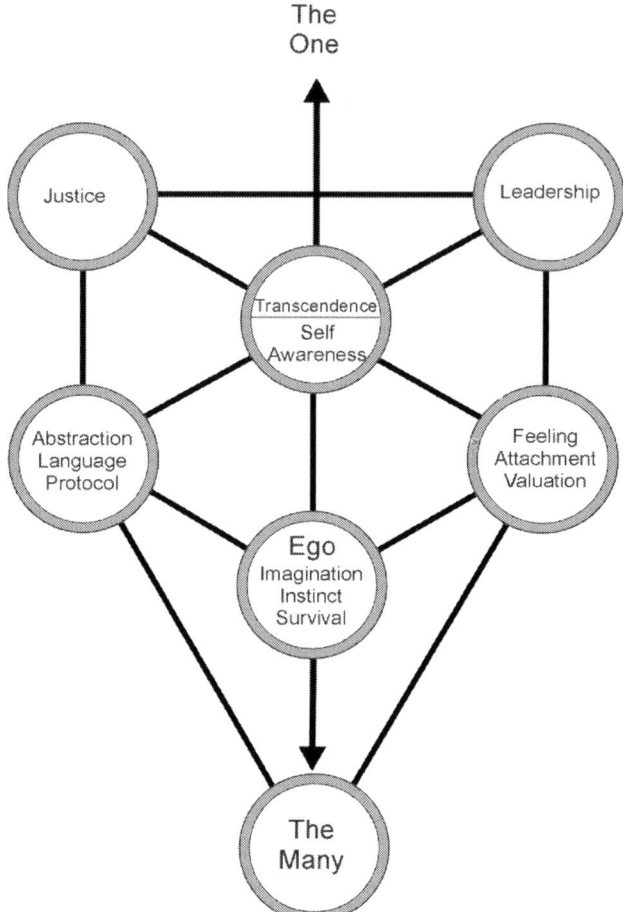

Figure 37: *Yesod* on the Pillar of Consciousness corresponds to the Ego. The Ego constructs an internal model of *Malkhut* (the Many) according to genetics and unconscious social cues. From *Netzach* comes the sense of what is important and valuable and how to feel about things and situations. From *Hod* comes conceptual knowledge and language, and an understanding of formal protocols (how to do stuff). From *Tiferet*, a growing sense of self-awareness and autonomy that may be transcended as one is willing to become a part of larger wholes - that is, there is a shift from taking the Many at face value, and viewing it as a manifestation of a larger unity. *Yesod* itself corresponds to the instinctive needs of the animal soul - food, shelter and reproduction. It is the mirror of *Malkhut*.

the vice is *idleness*. These follow from the dilemma of the Ego: on one hand it may wish for growth and change, to become independent of contingent factors, and on the other hand there are risks involved and it is easier to do nothing and remain in a condition which provides security and stability. This is like the man in the leaky boat. He is unhappy that the boat is leaking, but he is happy that he can bail fast enough to prevent himself from sinking. On the other hand, he realises he would travel faster and further if he could be bothered to do something about the leak ... but this would interrupt his routine and he can't be bothered.

To summarise, *Yesod* is spooky. It is spooky because of what it hides. *Yesod* is like walking down a moonlit street in the suburbs and wondering what is happening behind closed doors. Sex probably, and television, and lots of normal human rituals we tend to keep hidden from other people. The natural world has its own sense of privacy, private interactions we cannot discover without giant atom-smashing machines buried under Geneva.

Yesod is spooky because it is the black mirror of the world, what we call the imagination. There are many strange things in there, and some of it is terrifying. We require strange rituals to guard us as we confront the alien shapes that form in our interior vision. Some of this escapes into reality via comics, books, television, and film. This fountain of novelty and weirdness is *Yesod* as the receptacle of the emanations, impregnating the world of the material with new shapes. Today's *Yesod* is tomorrow's *Malkhut*.

The Hermetic Kabbalah

17

Hod & Netzach

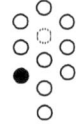

Meaning	Glory, Splendour
Number	8
Colour	Orange
Briatic Correspondence	Abstraction
Magical Image	An hermaphrodite
Titles	-
Element	Air
Virtue	Honesty, truthfulness
Vice	Dishonesty
Illusion	Order
Klippot	Rigidity, rigid order
Obligation	Learn
Command	To Will
God Name	*Elohim Tzabaot*
Archangel	*Raphael*
Angel Order	*Bene Elohim*
Planet	*Kokab* (Mercury)
Spiritual Experience	Vision of Splendour
Keywords	Reason, abstraction, communication, conceptualisation, logic, the sciences, language, speech, money (as a concept), mathematics, medicine & healing, trickery, writing, media (as communication), pedantry, philosophy, Kabbalah (as an abstract system), protocol, the Law, ownership, territory, theft, 'rights', ritual magic

Table 7 : Hod

Hod & Netzach

Meaning	Victory, Firmness
Number	7
Colour	Green
Briatic Correspondence	Nurture
Magical Image	A beautiful naked woman
Titles	-
Element	Water
Virtue	Unselfishness
Vice	Selfishness
Illusion	Projection
Klippot	Habit, routine
Obligation	Responsibility
Command	To Know
God Name	*Jehovah Tzabaot*
Archangel	*Haniel*
Angel Order	*Elohim*
Planet	*Nogah* (Venus)
Spiritual Experience	Vision of Beauty Triumphant
Keywords	Passion, pleasure, luxury, sensual beauty, emotions - love, hate, anger, joy, depression, misery, excitement, desire, lust; nurture, libido, empathy, sympathy, ecstatic magic, addiction

Table 8 : Netzach

> We speak not strictly and philosophically when we talk of the combat of passion and of reason. Reason is, and ought only to be the slave of the passions, and can never pretend to any other office than to serve and obey them.
>
> David Hume

"Feelings tell us what to think."

The twin *sefirot* of *Hod* and *Netzach* are often glossed-over in traditional presentations. Their titles give little away: *Hod* means Glory or Splendour, and *Netzach* means Victory or Endurance. They form the legs in the body of the Primordial Adam, *Adam Kadmon*. In traditional literature they are associated with mystical states connected with the phenomenon of prophecy.

In the Hermetic tradition they have clear and straightforward interpretations based on planetary and elemental correspondences. *Hod* corresponds to Mercury and Air, and *Netzach* to Venus and Water. This is not the whole story however; as *sefirot* they are a part of the overall dynamic of the Tree of Life, so that *Hod* at the base of the left-hand pillar communicates multiplicity of form, and *Netzach* at the base of the right-hand pillar communicates of multiplicity of force.

Why multiplicity? We can understand this in two different ways. Firstly, according to Neoplatonist understanding, an increasing degree of emanation (that is, alienation from the source of all being) is combined with an increase in *multiplicity*. Alienation becomes synonymous with *disunity*; it becomes increasingly difficult to discern unity, even though it is still there. This is very much apparent in *Netzach*, and more so in *Hod*.

Secondly, a King (*Tiferet*) has his hosts (or armies or servants) who carry out all the 'legwork'. The King decides strategy and direction, others worry about the detail and execution. The traditional divine names for these two *sefirot* reflect this: *YHVH Tzabaot* for *Netzach*, and *Elohim Tzabaot* for *Hod*. In both cases the name can be translated as 'God of Hosts'.

Netzach is at the base of the Pillar of Force or Mercy, and so combines *expressive* or *creative force* with multiplicity, like a decorative fountain where water is forced through a hundred jets. We can liken this to the Chinese saying "let many flowers bloom". There is force, but it is going in countless directions.

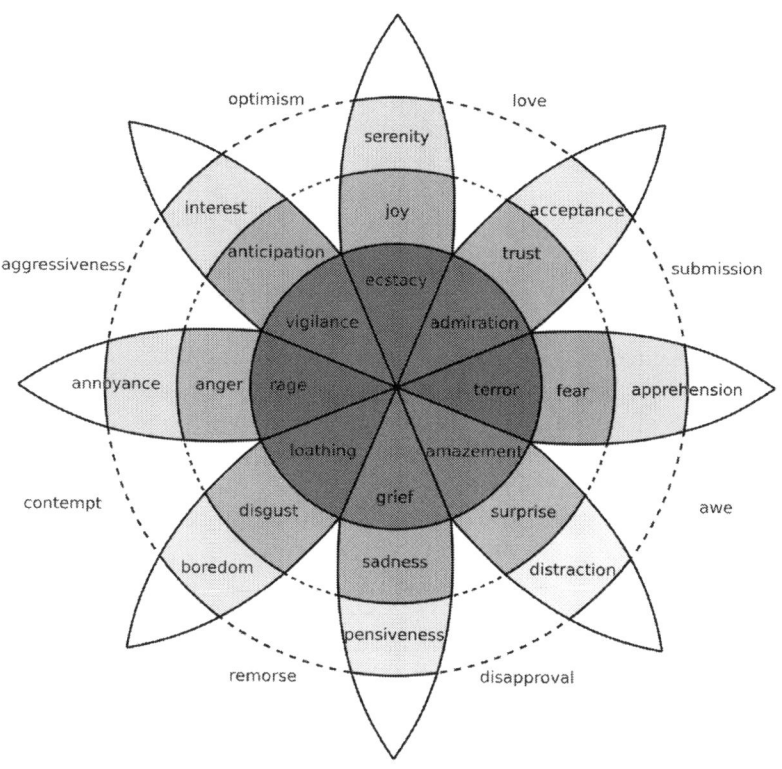

Figure 38: Robert Plutchik's 'Wheel of Emotions', one of the best-known attempts to categorise the internal states we experience as feelings. This provides a breakdown of how we might value situations as they arise. These valuations have an unconscious impact on how we think and behave.

Netzach refers to the mind's capacity to attach itself to things or situations. This attachment manifests in three abstract ways: to move (figuratively) *towards* something; to move (figuratively) *away from* something; or to be *indifferent* to something. There is an essential restlessness in every situation that becomes a need to create a new situation. *Netzach* expresses this restlessness, a need to respond to every situation with a new situation.

The 'expressive creativity' of *Netzach* may encompass what we consider artistic creativity but goes far beyond that. It is rooted in dissatisfaction. Dissatisfaction gives rise to restlessness, which gives rise to an impulse to change the *status quo*. Many causes of dissatisfaction arise from physical needs - we are hungry, cold, tired, or feel unsafe. Some are due to feelings of incompleteness - we would feel more complete with a music player, or a newer car, or shinier hair.

Some kinds of dissatisfaction and incompleteness go to the heart of one's being: a lack of meaning or purpose, a lack of achievement, an inchoate sense that something is missing or unexpressed, or a yearning for a place or time or person that is forever gone. The restlessness of *Netzach* is most apparent when we are bored. It will fasten on to any passing form or idea and try to bring it to life. This is the creative aspect of *Netzach*, symbolised by the many-breasted mother goddess of Ephesus.

Netzach can also refer to the connective tissue of reality. Every aspect of reality, from the smallest to the largest, must be in relationship. This is what reality is: the set of all relationships. The universal connective tissue is sometimes called *eros*, and derives from the notion that all things desire to be reunited, that every kind of relationship, even dysfunctional relationship, is rooted in a primordial unity. We can interpret sexual attraction (ruled by Venus) as a specific manifestation of a universal principle.

Hod is at the base of the Pillar of Form, and so combines *form* and *separation* with multiplicity. We can interpret this in terms of an irreducible requirement to perceive reality in terms of objects and patterns. This occurs because the brain has to abridge and condense reality. It does this by abstracting; that is, it quietly removes superfluous and unnecessary details, and in the process, turns continuous variations in contrast, colour, density and texture into objects. *Hod* reduces the world to chunks, chunks that can be named and defined. This abridgement of reality becomes most apparent when we are asked to recall a scene. Most people will remember key elements, elements which come together to create meaning (for example, a couple kissing, or a crying child) and fail to recall an enormous amount of peripheral detail.

It is abridgement and abstraction that enables one of the key correspondences for *Hod*: language and communication. Languages require small worlds. Natural languages are limited in size and complexity, even when one includes specialist vocabularies. When a world is not small there are tricks to reduce the complexity, for example, by labelling points in space using coordinates, or by approximating a surface using a mesh of triangles. This is routine in geology and the oil industry, in weather forecasting, in cinematic special effects and in computer gaming - the trick is to turn an unmanageably large world into a describable smaller world by cutting it into a manageable number of pieces.

Language is almost as natural to human beings as breathing. We are immersed in stories from infancy. We absorb much of our knowledge of the world second-hand via narrative accounts in the media. The opinions people form, and many fundamental motivating beliefs, are (more often than not) derived from written sources. Many of the anxieties that people possess are based on internal dialogue, stories they tell themselves. To the extent that reality is formed out of the abstractions and stories we tell ourselves and each other, language provides the medium for a 'simulator' that 'creates' the consensus reality we share. We are often unconscious of this, and we mistake *Hod* for *Malkhut* (the map for the territory).

Hod and *Netzach* create the illusion of a world. It is an illusion because the component parts, the elements we can talk about and think about (*Hod*), are elements of our cognition, and the values we place on these elements (*Netzach* - moving towards, moving away) are likewise internal to ourselves and not necessarily shared by other people. We can easily imagine (in the world simulator of *Yesod*) complex situations involving many elements, and conduct imaginary conversations and experience real feelings, but this is simulation, not reality. This kind of simulation is so intrinsic to the way we function as human beings, we may lose sight of the radical, unbridgeable gulf between what is happening in our heads and what is happening in reality.

The planetary and elemental associations of *Hod* and *Netzach* round out the picture that emerges from the idea of combining force, form and multiplicity. The planetary association with *Netzach* is Venus, and the elemental association is water. The planetary association with *Hod* is Mercury and the elemental association is air.

Venus suggests love and beauty and the emotional complexity of relationship. Water suggests feeling, intuition, and nurture. Many of the associations with *Netzach* can be subsumed within the idea of *aesthesis*; we like some things, and we don't like other things. It is as if everything in the world was painted in traffic light colours. The green we like, the red we dislike, and the rest we don't care about one way or the other and can ignore. We readily use spatial metaphors to communicate our feelings: "I feel close to you", or "you seem distant", or "we have grown apart". At heart these feelings are pre-verbal: some things we like and want more of (moving towards) and some things we dislike and want less of (moving away from).

Mercury suggests quickness and communication. Mercury was the *kerux* of the Gods. A *kerux* was a herald who travelled between kings and leaders, representing policy in the same way as a modern ambassador. His status as a *kerux* is symbolised by the wings on his feet, and by the *caduceus*, the rod or staff that he carries (the association of the *caduceus* with medicine, especially in North America, is partly through confusion with the rod of Asclepius). Mercury had a reputation for cunning, and so he was the god of thieves and merchants. As the syncretic Thoth-Hermes-Trimegistus he was the god of revealed knowledge such as astronomy, medicine, chemistry and the occult arts - the so-called Hermetic arts.

The element of air suggests language, communication and quickness of mind, and vocations where the use of language is paramount, such as journalism, law, media, politics, computing and mathematics.

The virtue of *Netzach* is unselfishness. The vice is selfishness. Few of us exist in isolation (and certainly no person reading this book). Our lives affect other beings in countless ways, and most of the things we need to live - food, clothing and so on - come via complex relationships and interdependencies with other people. There is a balance between living for myself (as if my life had an intrinsic value in isolation from all other beings) and living for others (attempting to be a part of a larger whole). Human society is a bewildering balance between pathological selfishness and spontaneous acts of kindness, generosity, and selflessness. Selfishness may be tolerated when power and status are involved (one can cite the near-universal tendency of leaders to live in opulence) but we may become deeply upset by a lack of fairness in simple domestic chores.

The essence of unselfishness is an awareness of others. The pragmatics of living with other people dictate a shifting balance of self-concern and selfless help. We admire selflessness - up to a point. Past that point we begin to wonder whether a lack of self-concern might be a mask for self-destructiveness.

The essence of selfishness is an exaggerated self-importance that can become predatory and ruthless, and is often masked with dishonesty and deception - narcissism must be rendered palatable to those who are being used and exploited. When the balance tips too far towards self the situation is isolating and unstable - it is difficult to be selfish without also being dishonest (especially to oneself) (*Hod*), deceptive and cunning (*Hod*), arrogant (*Tiferet*), intimidating (*Gevurah*), and hypocritical (*Chesed*). One vice rules them all.

Hod & Netzach

The virtue of *Hod* is truthfulness, and the vice is dishonesty. It is sometimes said that "animals cannot lie"[129]. Dishonesty is innate to the use of language: it can represent, and so it can misrepresent. Although no representation is every completely accurate, some are less accurate than others, often intentionally so. A lie enables us to separate ourselves from reality, or to synthesis a new reality. In Kabbalah separation has the quality of *Din*, which, unmitigated and unbalanced, is the ground in which evil flourishes. In the New Testament Jesus refers to the Devil as the "Father of Lies".

The illusion of *Netzach* is projection. This refers to the tendency to interpret the world in our own terms, to 'project' our interpretations, feelings, valuations, opinions and explanations onto situations and insist that these subjective judgements are *objectively present* in the situation. There is a large measure of unconsciousness in projection, and people often feel threatened or badly offended if their projections are undermined. This is easily observed in matters of personal taste, such as clothing, decor, choice of vehicle, music, television viewing and so on - one of the fastest ways to cause offence is to criticise a person's 'lifestyle choices'. Projection tends to set one person against another, and an extreme form of this can be found in the variety of 'hate crimes', where people are stereotyped and vilified according to broad criteria such as ethnicity, sexuality, gender, religion, wealth (or poverty) and many other factors.

The illusion of *Hod* is order. Order is often seen as virtuous - the neat desk, a smart tie and polished shoes, the tidy house, soldiers on parade, the completed collection, synchronised swimming. Some countries enjoy vast displays of identically-dressed people moving in orderly patterns. Order suggests efficiency and attention to detail. Order is often an adjunct to reason - reason is most efficient when dealing with the uniform, the consistent, the orderly mass, and reason is least effective when dealing with the arbitrary and the chaotic.

As in the case of *Netzach* the illusion is based on an inability to distinguish between what is subjectively imposed and what is objectively present. An example of how we impose order is the tendency to see patterns in uncorrelated events. We see evidence of luck or skill or obstruction when none are present. Investment managers are massively rewarded for good judgement when evidence shows that nothing more than happenstance is present.

---

129. This is a complicated assertion. Some birds will mimic injury. Some animals attempt to conceal food. Then there is Koko the Gorilla's sign-language untruth: "the cat did it".

The Hermetic Kabbalah

Why is order an illusion? It is an illusion when it is employed unconsciously in an attempt to simplify, when it is imposed in the interest of rational efficiency, when it is publicised as an achievable ideal. Most people have a utopian 'if I ruled the world' scenario depicting what things would be like if they were 'done properly' and not 'run by idiots'. Nature is typically not ordered according to human ideals. It is rational, but it is the reason of selfish genes, not of philosopher kings.

The vision or spiritual experience of *Netzach* is that of 'Beauty Triumphant'. This is an extremely biased view in which things are judged according to personal aesthetic criteria. This obsession with aesthetic valuation, whether trainers, tattoos, handbags, wine, restaurants, art, music and so many other things, is often associated with membership and the assumed superiority of specific social groups.

The spiritual experience of *Hod* is that of Splendour. A colloquial way to express this feeling is "a place for everything, and everything in its place".

The God names of *Netzach* and *Hod* both convey the idea of multiplicity. The name for *Netzach* is *YHVH Tzabaot* and that for *Hod* is *Elohim Tzabaot*. Both names mean 'God of Hosts'. The name *Elohim* is perplexing. When used with plural verbs and endings it is usually translated as 'gods' (as in a divine pantheon, such as 'the children of *El*') or angels. When used with singular verbs and endings it is usually translated as 'God'. It is associated with the left-hand pillar of the Tree, where it denotes the quality of judgement. In both cases *Tzabaot* signifies 'hosts': the divine hosts, countless as the stars in the sky.

The archangel for *Netzach* is *Anael* or *Haniel*, which can be translated as 'joy of God'. Haniel is the ruler of Venus, the evening star. The archangel for *Hod* is *Raphael*, 'healer of God'[130]. The angel order for *Netzach* is *Elohim*, which we can translate simply as 'gods'. We can think of these as the gods of the ego, the ruling passions. The angel order of *Hod* are the *Bene Elohim*, which we can translate as the 'children of the gods'. We can think of these as passions attached to specific ideas - the phrase 'bee in one's bonnet' springs to mind.

The angel orders confirm the sense of multiplicity. We are dealing

---

130. Some lists place *Raphael* in *Tiferet* and *Michael* in *Hod*. This divergence can be found in lists dating back many hundreds of years. Both *Raphael* and *Michael* have been associated with healing. *Michael*, the warrior who overcomes the serpent of chaotic evil, is perhaps better associated with the moral dimension of the central pillar.

with multitudes, and where we have multitudes we find distinction and difference and, like as not, contention. We can observe this easily in the microcosm of the human soul. Our passions are fluid like water, flowing from one turbulent extreme to another. Our attachment to ideas is rarely logical or consistent. This multiplicity is justified, examined and explained in more detail in Chapter *27, The Society of Mind*.

In summary, *Netzach* is that restless aspect of life that, like a shark, has to keep moving. Every situation demands that we make a new situation, according to how we feel. When we are happy we throw parties, grow flowers and build fountains. When we are fearful we watch for enemies, build a fortress, and buy guns and locks and alarms. Rarely are we truly still.

Hod is a world of representation, things that stand for other things, things that point at the complex using the simple. 'Cat!'. Three letters are all it takes to call forth an image - in the mind at least. This is the magic of representation: one can evoke the complex with the simple, play with the simple rather than the complex.

With representation we can use and create stories to translate us out of time and place. More profound still are the stories we construct about ourselves, the constant inner commentary making sense of experience like a voice-over on reality television.

Most profound of all is a Cosmos that contains storytelling. It is assumed by materialists to be dead, determinate matter, but we find there are seven billion voices all with something to say about themselves.

The Hermetic Kabbalah

Figure 39: Aphrodite (Venus) bathing, a favoured theme of artists from the Classical period onward. In her hand she holds a copper cup filled with wine. She may be offering the cup to the viewer, or showing what a good time she is having - she may not care that you are thirsty. The servant on the left mimics her behaviour but looks insecure. The servant on the right looks dour and unhappy.

18

Tiferet

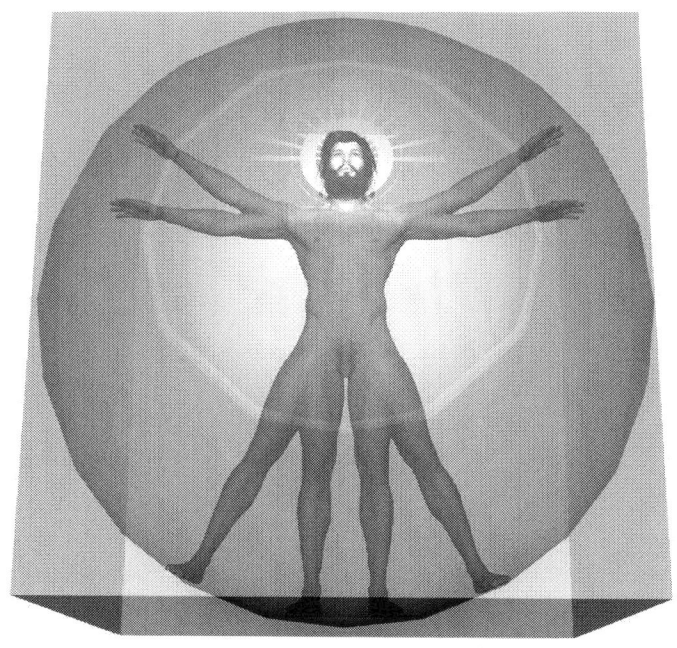

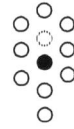

Meaning	Beauty
Number	6
Colour	Yellow
Briatic Correspondence	Centrality, wholeness
Magical Image	A Child, a King, a Sacrificed God
Titles	*Rachamim*, charity; *Melekh*, the King; *Ze'ir Anpin*, the lesser countenance; the Microprosopus; the Son
Element	Solar Fire
Virtue	Devotion to the Great Work
Vice	Pride, self-importance, arrogance
Illusion	Identification
Klippot	Hollowness
Obligation	Integrity
Command	To Dare
God Name	YHVH, *Aloah va Da'at*
Archangel	*Michael*
Angel Order	*Malakim*
Planet	*Shemesh* (Sun)
Spiritual Experience	Vision of Harmony, Knowledge & Conversation of the Holy Guardian Angel
Keywords	Harmony, integrity, balance, wholeness, centrality, the Self, self-importance, self-sacrifice, devotion, identity, the Son of God, a King, the Great Work, the Philosopher's Stone, the Sun, gold, the solar plexus

Table 9 : Tiferet

Tiferet

> Therefore, let each become godlike and each beautiful who cares to see God and Beauty
>
> Plotinus

Tiferet corresponds to the letter *Vav* in the Tetragrammaton (YHVH), the divine name of four letters. In Hebrew the letter *Vav* is also the symbol for the number six. In Kabbalah this is taken to denote the complex of six *sefirot*: *Chesed, Gevurah, Tiferet, Netzach, Hod and Yesod* (see Figure 40). This complex corresponds to the *Partzuf Ze'ir Anpin*, the Short Face, or impatient one.

The nature of *Tiferet* is difficult to communicate and the reason is simple. *Tiferet is* like health.

What happens if you go to the doctor for a full health check? Tests - a physical examination, blood analysis, electrocardiogram, electroencephalogram, X-rays, CAT and MRI scans, and so on. A full battery of tests would probably take weeks, and at the end of it the doctor would say "I can't find anything wrong with you. You seem healthy to me".

And that is health, defined by elimination. We are, for the most part, unconscious of health (that is, until we become old and infirm). We *are* conscious of unhealth, what we call illness or disease. It is when we depart from health that we become conscious of it, and having departed from it, we are by definition, not exhibiting it.

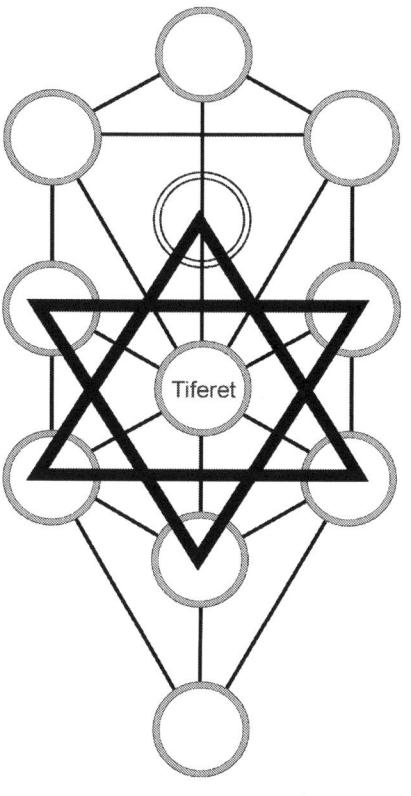

Figure 40: The Microprosopus, a complex of six *sefirot*. Although the upper point of the hexagram includes *Da'at*, *Da'at* is not a *sefira*.

Tiferet shares with good health some of the quality of unconsciousness. We don't notice it until it isn't there. Like health, *Tiferet* it is real enough, but it isn't a 'thing'. There is no 'thing' that makes a good party, a good film, a pleasant day, or a tasty meal.

Tiferet means 'beauty'. Although we are conscious of beauty when we encounter it, it is difficult to specify, and notoriously subjective. Ugliness is easier to achieve - ugliness does not seem to require much effort. In any case, the beauty of *Tiferet* does not signify an aesthetic or sensual beauty. It signifies the beauty of a soul that has achieved an harmonious balance of aspects. One could liken it to an instrument like a guitar; when six strings are fingered correctly and one plays a chord such as C major, then it sounds bright and pleasing. When six strings are fingered randomly, then many jarring and discordant sounds are produced. So it is with the soul. When the complex of six *sefirot* that constitute the Microprosopus exist in an harmonious dynamic, then beauty is communicated into the world.

In traditional Kabbalah *Tiferet* is seen as the centre of the interplay between the dynamic of *giving,* and of *holding-back*. Although the nature of God is giving, the creation could not exist in a state distinct from God without holding back, and so the manifestation of God (*Ze'ir Anpin*, the Microprosopus), the public face as it were, is a dynamic between these two tendencies.

This dynamic is present in every aspect of our lives. In every situation there is a sweet spot, a balance between too much and too little. Like Goldilocks we go through life noticing when things are too hot, or too cold, or too hard, or too soft, looking to find the compromise that is just right. The aspect of our lives where we are most likely to compromise is when we seek to find a balance between giving time, energy and resources, and not giving time, energy and resources. It is difficult to know how much time to give to employment, to parents and family, to children, to friends, to hobbies. Because we are finite beings with finite time, energy and resources we must measure out our lives (as T. S. Eliot put it) "in coffee spoons". The problem is not only in our lives: it is in the heart of existence.

One can see this dynamic in operation in art. Art is also creation. A painting that was entirely of the nature of *Chesed* would be a white canvas of unlimited extent. As the artist added black lines, so *Din* would enter the canvas. If the artist had skill then at some point we would see beauty emerge out of the interplay of white and black. If the artist added black lines to excess, then that beauty would be lost, and we would end (paradoxically) back at *Chesed*, for an excess of black is no different from an excess of white (and so it is that *Din* is subordinate to *Chesed*).

The Platonist philosopher Plotinus devoted a chapter of his *Enneads* to 'Beauty'. He was writing one thousand years before the

Tiferet

heyday of medieval Kabbalah, so it would be daring to suggest that his thoughts had a direct bearing on the understanding of *Tiferet*, but this is certainly not impossible: an Arabic version of the *Enneads*, published as *The Theology of Aristotle*, was influential in Islamic philosophy and mysticism, which in turn had considerable influence on medieval Europe.

For Plotinus, beauty was the beauty of a soul that had disengaged from material concerns through a life of moderation and virtue, and had turned its gaze to the source of all beauty, which he identified with the Good and the One. The qualities he admired were:

> ... righteousness of life; disciplined purity; courage of the majestic face; gravity, modesty that goes fearless and tranquil and passionless, and shining down upon all, the light of godlike intellection.

In contrast to the soul guided towards supernal beauty through a life of virtue and moderation, he characterised the ugly soul in the language of disgust:

> Let us then suppose an ugly soul, dissolute, unrighteous: teeming with all the lusts; torn by internal discord; beset by the fears of its cowardice and the end these of its pettiness; thinking, in the little thought it has, only of the perishable and the base; perverse in all its impulses; the friend of uncleaned pleasures; living the life of abandonment to bodily sensation and delighting in its deformity. What must we think but that all this shame is something that has gathered about the soul, some foreign bane outraging it, soiling it, so that, encumbered with all manner of turpitude, it has no longer a clean activity or a clean sensation, but commands only a life smouldering dully under the crust of evil; that sunk in manifold death, it no longer sees what a soul should see, may no longer rest in its own being, dragged ever as it is towards the outer, the lower, the dark?

Although I cannot endorse his suggestion that the soul is outraged by a "foreign bane", there is much in his depiction that is accurate, especially the phrase "torn by internal discord": the soul, fastened to the external, is driven by the external, and so has no overall coherence or unity. His remedy for this uses the example of the artist, depicting the interplay of *Chesed* and *Din*:

> But how are you to see into a virtuous soul and know its loveliness? Withdraw into yourself and look. And if you do not find you yourself beautiful yet, act as does the creator of a statue that is to be made beautiful: he cuts away here, he smoothes there, he makes this line lighter, this other purer, until a lovely face has grown upon his work. So do you also; cut away all that is excessive, straighten all that is crooked, bring light to all that is overcast, labour to make all one glow of beauty and never cease chiselling your statue, until there shall

The Hermetic Kabbalah

shine out on you from it the godlike splendour of virtue, until you shall see the perfect goodness surely established in the stainless shrine.

When you know that you have become this perfect work, when you are self-gathered in the purity of you being, nothing now remaining that can shatter that inner unity, nothing from without clinging to the authentic man, when you find yourself wholly true to your essential nature, wholly that only veritable Light which is not measured by space, not narrowed to any circumscribed form nor again diffused as a thing void of term, but ever unmeasurable as something greater than all measure and more than all quantity - when you perceive that you have grown to this you are now become very vision: now call up all your confidence, strike forward yet a step - you need a guide no longer - strain, and see. This is the only eye that sees the mighty Beauty.

In the space of two paragraphs Plotinus has provided a prescription for the Great Work: *viz.* one cannot behold Beauty until one has "straightened all that is crooked" - that is, rectified the soul - by moderating the passions with virtue, and by doing so, create "an inner unity". It is from the standpoint of the unity within that one can perceive the unity without.

I find the commentary on Beauty that Plotinus provides strikingly apposite to *Tiferet*, but it is only part of a complex picture. To summarise: *Tiferet* signifies the executive power or agency of YHVH, the divine name of four letters, and the letter *vav* specifically; it is the heart of the personality (*Partzuf*) of six *sefirot* known as *Ze'ir Anpin*; it signifies the idea of dynamic balance or homeostasis between a fundamental duality (*Din & Chesed*) at the heart of existence; it also signifies the rectification of the soul, a programme of personal self-transcendence that has come to be known as The Great Work. This latter aspect requires so much context and explanation it forms Part 3 of this book, and complicates the attempt to communicate what *Tiferet* represents - that is, a large part of my explanation lies in the future. As a symbol of self-transcendence, part of the explanation of *Tiferet always* lies in the future.

Anticipating the broader and deeper explanation of Part 3, one can say that the ascent of the middle pillar of the Tree of Life from *Yesod* to *Tiferet* signifies a shift from a narrow awareness defined by emotional responses to objects, people, situations, goals, ideas and physical needs (the "ugly soul" of Plotinus) into a broader awareness. One can also contrast a fragmented conscious centred in *Yesod* and looking down into *Malkhut*, with a unified consciousness entered in *Tiferet* and looking up to *Keter*. Looking down, one sees Many; looking up,

Tiferet

one sees The One. These views can co-exist, so that *Yesod* and *Tiferet* represent complementary modes of cognition transcending an apparent duality - the One and the Many being aspects of an ultimate source of reality and being.

It is because *Tiferet* is used to denote a programme of rectification that its virtue is Devotion to the Great Work - the "perfect work" outlined by Plotinus eighteen hundred years ago. Some of the most important symbolic aspects of *Tiferet* are connected with the self-transcendent ascent from a smaller view symbolised by *Yesod* to a larger view symbolised by *Tiferet*. For example, *Yesod* corresponds to the sphere of the Moon, the sphere of the unconscious mind and of primitive and quasi-autonomous sub-minds operating on the periphery of conscious awareness. *Tiferet* corresponds to the sphere of the Sun, the bright, midday sun where all is seen and ruled and harmonised into a unity (like the strings of a lyre). This is one of the reasons why the symbol of the nineteenth century Hermetic Order of the Golden Dawn was that of a sun rising out of the primordial waters of the unconscious mind.

The idea that "all is seen and ruled and harmonised into a unity" suggests the social institution of kingship, and this is connected to an ancient tradition of kingship: that the vitality of the kingdom is connected to the vitality of the king, and so it is the fate of divine kings to be sacrificed[131]. This explains the trio of magical images for *Tiferet*, that of Child, King and Sacrificed God. There is a threefold aspect to *Tiferet*, that of King (rule, stability), Sacrificed God (instability and self-transcendence), and Child (rebirth and growth). For the same reasons *Tiferet* is associated with Jesus, whose primary representations are those of divine king, crucified son of God, and infant child.

The redeemer aspect of Jesus overlaps with gnostic traditions of light-beings who descend from light-worlds to bring divine gnosis to select members of humanity, an influence that may derive from the Zoroastrian religion of Persian Empire. Far from being geographically remote, the Persian empire was adjacent to the nascent Christian communities in the Middle East. It is plausible to suspect an influence in early Christianity, and also in sectarian Jewish beliefs such as those expressed in some of the Dead Sea Scrolls.

It is this aspect of Jesus that is developed in several of the gnostic gospels of antiquity, such as the *Pistis Sophia* and the eerie and enig-

---

131. These ideas probably entered the Hermetic tradition following the publication of Sir James George Frazer's popular and highly influential *The Golden Bough* in 1890.

matic *Books of Jeu*. Jesus is depicted as an envoy or emissary from another realm of being, and is equipped with the arcane knowledge necessary to move between worlds, and to undo the shackles that bind us to this world. It is from this that one can begin to understand the spiritual experience of *Tiferet*, which is the knowledge and conversation of the Holy Guardian Angel (HGA). The HGA is a personal light-being that may be summoned (or appear spontaneously) to provide guidance. The HGA is often interpreted as a manifestation of a higher aspect of one's being.

Although related to *Tiferet*, the further expansion of these themes - rectification of the soul, sun and moon, kingship, death and resurrection, gnostic revelation and redemption - can be found in Part 3.

The vice of *Tiferet* is pride, or pride as it drifts into arrogance and eventually contempt. This attribution may seem counter-intuitive. The answer is that the cognitive level associated with *Tiferet* does not always imply an absence of Ego. The elements that constitute Ego have been dragged out into the light of day and subjected to balance and limitation and some measure of coordination and rulership. There is a reduced tendency to undermine oneself with impulsive behaviours, and a reduced tendency to engage in self-deception through the construction of evasions and rationales. The excesses of feeling have been moderated by a sense of responsibility to others. Pride emerges quite naturally under these conditions.

This pride, which is a kind of self-love, comes under two influences, that of *Gevurah* and *Chesed*. From *Gevurah* comes an increased sense of agency and direction, and a tendency to tilt at windmills. From *Chesed* comes a messianic need to protect and save and nurture through leadership. These are legitimate manifestations of divine kingship, but they also sow the seeds of hubris and nemesis. Leadership is a tricky business, and the teeming masses are not going to be on the same page; the flip side of pride is arrogance and contempt. The 'Sacrificed God' aspect of *Tiferet* is often the outcome of a collision between pride and reality, a collision that cracks the smug assumptions of the Ego.

This may lead towards the *klippotic* aspect of *Tiferet*, which is hollowness. When the bonds of self-love are broken it may seem that there was nothing at the core of one's being *but* a nucleus of self-love. Upon analysis one may conclude that every act of decency and kindness was a covert gesture of self-affirmation[132]. When this Egoic fulcrum disappears, there is a void, and there is no traction against

Tiferet

nihilism.

Nihilism is rarely far away at this level. Self-knowledge may sound like an obviously good thing, but it resembles the fabled acid that eats through every bottle used to contain it. The Ego attempts to be safe (for good pragmatic reasons) and fortifies itself with myths and stories and social verities and self-deceptions, and is able to do an excellent job of pulling itself up by its own boot laces, but self-knowledge eats through the mechanisms of deception and may expose the Ego to truths it finds difficult to assimilate. It may begin to suspect (in the manner of the Buddhist idea of *dependent origination*) that it has no substance beyond the causes and perceptual impulses that give rise to its activity. It may find itself staring into an abyss. Nihilism is a valid response, and it is not pathological - it takes courage and honesty to step away from every kind of support.

However, it is at this point that pride and self-opinion can progress into contempt - having seen too much and known too much, the shocked and scattered remnants of Ego may coalesce around an alienated identity that looks down on humanity. Nietzsche is an example of this - despite the perceptiveness and the unflinching honesty of his writing, one must suffer through a withering contempt for much of the human race.

The illusion of *Tiferet* is identification. Identification is an antidote to a feeling of hollowness. A person identifies with a goal or outcome or purpose and comes to believe that he or she is an instrument of destiny or 'chosen one'. The history of Kabbalah has many instances of individuals who believed they were the chosen one who would lead the Jewish people out of exile. Within the Hermetic tradition there is a tendency for people to announce that they have a message for humanity, that they have been selected as the mouthpiece of Greater Powers.

The obligation of *Tiferet* is integrity. Integrity requires an internal wholeness that manifests in an external consistency of behaviour. There can be no integrity when one is at odds with oneself, when there are inconsistent factions within the soul. When we see a person at odds with themselves - saying one thing and doing another for example - we call this hypocrisy.

The integrity of *Tiferet* is an internal consistency that requires an internal rule or self-measure that can usually be articulated as moral

---

132. After the manner of Little Jack Horner: "he put in his thumb, and pulled out a plum, and said 'what a good boy am I'"

principles, such as "be truthful" or "don't steal" or "acknowledge the contributions of others". It is more difficult to be consistent without simple rules. Hillel's summation of the Torah springs to mind: "What is hateful to you, do not do to others". There is also the injunction of the Hippocratic Oath: "do no harm".

It is not enough simply to have rules; one also requires self-awareness to know when one is, or is not, following them. Also, there is no guarantee that integrity will manifest in the form of a 'nice person' - the influence of *Gevurah* may be strongly felt.

The archangel for *Tiferet* is sometimes given as *Raphael* and sometimes as *Michael*. This schism goes back hundreds of years; for example, Agrippa gives *Raphael*, but Robert Fludd, that gifted illustrator of the Hermetic worldview, gives *Michael*. The Golden Dawn and its tributaries have preferred *Raphael*. An eloquent case can be made either way. Both archangels have long associations with healing and medicine. The author prefers *Michael* on the middle pillar (and in *Tiferet* specifically) because of his role as an executive proxy for God. His name is usually construed to mean 'who is like God' (*mi* means 'who' in Hebrew) and he is traditionally depicted in combat with, and overcoming, the powers of evil in the form of a serpent or dragon. This combat myth, in which a solar entity establishes order and dominion over powers of darkness and chaos, is timeless, and is one of the consistent themes of ancient myth. It can be interpreted psychologically; the wayward elements of our animal nature are brought to heel through the agency of the divine soul.

The angel order of *Tiferet* is the *Malakim*. This is sometimes translated as 'kings' (from *melekh*), but this would appear to be an error, and the translation should be 'messengers' (from *ma'lak*), as in *ma'lak elohim*, a 'messenger of God'. When the Bible was translated into Greek, *ma'lak* was translated as *aggelos*, a messenger, and later romanised to *angelos*, so a colloquial translation of *malakim* would be 'angels'.

In summary, *Tiferet* is like a balance. It balances up with down, right with left. When we balance on a bicycle we know that we are balanced. When we attempt to balance our lives in this world, there is little to guide us. We need to stand back. We need to be able to see ourselves. *Tiferet* is standing back, being able to see oneself.

When I began to write this chapter, I realised that *Tiferet* was a place holder for too many important ideas and they would not fit in one chapter.

Tiferet is at that level at which it is possible to stand back from everyday concerns and take a good look at what remains. This means talking about concepts such as intelligence and consciousness, setting out my view on what these words mean, and navigating around many pitfalls that are traditional to these topics. I wanted to talk about the unconscious, and why it is so important. I wanted to describe the strange glimpses of the unconscious we experience, and the numinous power of symbols and archetypes. I wanted to discuss an ancient tradition associated with *Tiferet*, that of Redeemer, or Emissary of Light, aka the Holy Guardian Angel and the Higher Self. I needed to talk about death, chaos and rebirth.

I summarise these topics in Part Three. They comprise what appears to be a massive digression from the core topic of the Hermetic Kabbalah. They are not a digression. They are an expansion of the inner core of what is concealed and revealed in *Tiferet*.

The Hermetic Kabbalah

19

Gevurah & Chesed

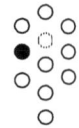

Meaning	Strength
Number	5
Colour	Red
Briatic Correspondence	Power
Magical Image	A mighty warrior; a judge.
Titles	Severity; *Din*, justice or judgement; *Pachad*, fear, dread
Element	Destructive Fire
Virtue	Courage and energy
Vice	Cruelty
Illusion	Invincibility
Klippot	Bureaucracy
Obligation	Courage and loyalty
Command	-
God Name	*Elohim Gevor*
Archangel	*Kamael* (sometimes *Samael*)
Angel Order	*Serafim*
Planet	*Madim* (Mars)
Spiritual Experience	Vision of Power
Keywords	Power, justice, retribution (eaten cold), the Law (in execution), cruelty, oppression, severity, necessary destruction, catabolism

Table 10 : *Gevurah*

Gevurah & Chesed

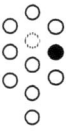

Meaning	Loving-Kindness, Mercy
Number	4
Colour	Blue
Briatic Correspondence	Authority
Magical Image	A mighty king
Titles	*Gedulah*, magnificence, love, majesty
Element	-
Virtue	Humility and obedience
Vice	Tyranny, hypocrisy, bigotry, gluttony
Illusion	Being right (self-righteousness)
Klippot	Ideology
Obligation	Humility
Command	-
God Name	*El*
Archangel	*Tzadkiel*
Angel Order	*Chasmalim*
Planet	*Tzedek* (Jupiter)
Spiritual Experience	Vision of Love
Keywords	Authority, leadership, creativity, inspiration, vision, excess, waste, secular and spiritual power, obliteration, birth, service, spiritual love

Table 11 : *Chesed*

Any living organism with a means of locomotion will tend to move towards what is good for it, and move away from what is not good for it. Even bacteria can propel themselves towards nutrients and away from toxins. It is also the case that any living organism will have a boundary[133] (membrane, skin) and this boundary will conduct what is beneficial and stop what is not, like a walled city that opens its gates to friends, and closes its gates to enemies.

These are two simple intuitions that appear to be fundamental to life: moving towards and moving away from; being open and being closed. If something is beneficial then an organism would tend to be open and move towards it. If something is harmful then an organism would tend to be closed and move away from it.

Beneficial and harmful depend on the organism but the responses appear to be universal. We do not need to talk to a cell to discover whether it prefers more or less acid, or more or less glucose. We have only to watch to see what it does. It is reasonable to assume that any form of life in this universe would behave in the same way: if something is good then it will tend to be open and move towards it. If something is not good then it will tend to be closed and move away from it.

This provides a measure of good and evil. It is not universal or metaphysical, it is particular and objective and measurable. For any given organism and any given circumstance we can observe what it does in response. In the case of human beings (whom we can consult) we will find some circumstances correspond to positive feelings - pleasure, enjoyment, happiness, fun - and other circumstances correspond to negative feelings - fear, disgust, pain, sorrow.

In a very loose sense we can relate *Chesed* to moving toward and being open, and *Gevurah* to moving away from and being closed.

A traditional image from the medieval period, found throughout the Europe, is that of a king on a throne[134]. In his right hand the king holds a sceptre, in his left hand a sword. Sometimes the hands are interchanged, sometimes there is an orb instead of a sceptre, but for simplicity let us assume that the right hand holds a sceptre and the left a sword. The sceptre corresponds to *Chesed* and the sword to *Gevurah*. The sceptre denotes legitimate authority and the sword denotes justice and the defence of the realm. *Chesed* (loving-kindness) is the king's obligation to care for his people and create a good world

---

133. There are basic thermodynamic reasons why this must be so.
134. Given the preponderance of male kings the figure is usually a man, but in what follows please assume that the sex of the figure on the throne is irrelevant.

Gevurah & Chesed

for them. *Gevurah* (strength) is the king's obligation to protect his people and uphold law and justice.

An aspect of both the sword and sceptre is that the sceptre denotes not just temporal authority but divine authority; the king has been chosen and appointed by birth and sacred ritual to act as divine proxy on earth. The laws upheld by the sword are not just any laws; they are the divine laws given to the people by God. This is the essential understanding: the kingdom is *Malkhut*, the sun-king is *Tiferet*, and his right and left arms are *Chesed* and *Gevurah*. The king in this world is an intermediary between heaven and earth, holding the balance of mercy and severity. One can trace ideas of this kind back through time to the dawn of human history. Specifically, the Egyptian pharaohs were considered to be descended from the sun god *Ra* and their authority and status was marked by regalia such as a crown, sceptre etc. (with the mace used as a symbol of power instead of a sword).

The mix or balance of *Gevurah* and *Chesed* are critical to the quality of existence. This is analogous to the mixing of petrol and air in the carburettor of an automobile. Too much petrol and too little air, or too much air and too little petrol, or too much air and petrol together, or too little air and petrol together - each of these is dysfunctional. The engine will cough and splutter, or fail to start, or run too hot and seize. There is an optimum mixture, and if we push the analogy, the carburettor is like *Tiferet* mixing the pillars of mercy and severity, and the engine itself is *Malkhut*.

The 'Goldilocks Principle' - not too much, not too little - is important in Kabbalah. The pathologies associated with the *sefirot* are those of too little and too much. This recalls the Golden Mean of Aristotle, where Aristotle gives the example of courage: too little courage is cowardice, too much becomes recklessness or foolhardiness.

Tiferet corresponds to YHVH, *Ze'ir Anpin*, the Short (or Impatient) Face, the executive face of God in relation to a creation that is defined, limited and actively administered. This is the God of Abraham, Isaac and Moses, the God of the Ten Commandments.

The Ten Commandments are well-known outside of Judaism, but less well-known among non-Jews is that the Mosaic Law contains 613 commandments (*mitzvot*), divided into 248 positive commandment (things one should do) and 365 negative commandments (things one should not do). These commandments form the basis for Jewish law (*halakhah*), one of the oldest, continuously-developed and sophisticated legal frameworks in the world.

The Hermetic Kabbalah

Law and religion are inextricably intertwined in Judaism. Christian communities have tended to divide over matters of belief; Jewish communities have tended to nucleate around the interpretation of law and the extent of observance of the *mitzvot*. A rabbinical court is a *Bet Din*, literally, a 'house of judgement'. Prepared foods are often supervised and approved by a *Bet Din*, to indicate that they have been prepared according to Jewish dietary law (*kosher*), and the name of the court will be shown on the label.

Halakhah is pervasive and central to Judaism, and it is the importance of law that has to be understood when trying to grasp the nature of *Gevurah*. Jewish law covers every aspect of life, from the personal through the societal to the religious. Law is the means through which the individual person, society and cosmos achieve an harmonious regulation according to divine mandate. *Gevurah* is the oversight and execution of the law.

In civil life the law is a vast system that includes judges, attorneys, officers of court, police, and a system for the punishment and rehabilitation of certain kinds of offenders. Only a small part of the law is criminal. Every area of life - employment, motoring, domestic, family, death and wills, health, business, finance and so on contains the possibility of disputes that need to be arbitrated to avoid people "taking the law into their own hands". There is a general consensus in every part of the world that almost any system of law is better than lawlessness. If law is about achieving impartiality and fairness, then lawlessness is the most partial and the least fair because it favours the powerful, the violent and the rich.

When there is too much law we feel oppressed. This has been depicted many times in drama. George Orwell's *1984* with its Big Brother are synonymous with an over-controlled society. In *The Castle* and *The Trial*, Kafka depicts worlds in which rules and law have become dysfunctional, often arbitrary and incomprehensible. In *Bleak House* Dickens depicts how law can become a grinding, inexhaustible, end-in-itself. The complex, procedural aspect to law and administration, what we call bureaucracy and red-tape, is the *klippotic* aspect of *Gevurah*. When the law becomes unbalanced, law becomes oppression and cruelty. The law can turn people into slaves (as it did in ancient Rome), into serfs (as it did in medieval Europe), and into automata (on a factory floor).

Another difficulty with social law is its inevitable association with power. One cannot administer the law without power. If the administration of law is not itself subject to oversight and law (*Quis custodiet ipsos custodes?*) then the possibility exists for the arbitrary exercise of power through laws that serve the few at the expense of the many. On one hand the police are respected for their courage and energy (virtue of *Gevurah*) in pursuing dangerous individuals; on the other hand they are often suspected of abuse of power (false testimony, trumped-up charges, complicity in crime, bribes, and evidence extracted under duress). The cruelty aspect is the vice of *Gevurah*.

The interplay of 'good cop' and 'bad cop' is one of the most popular tropes in television drama. The good cop upholds society. The bad cop is corrupt, has fallen into the dark side, and is fearsome because he/she employs the law for personal ends. The popular 2000 AD comic-book hero Judge Dredd is an extreme view of 'good cop'; a hyper-moral, implacable and deadly Judge attempting to enforce and deliver law in near chaos. His name combines two titles of *Gevurah*: *Din*, judgement, and *Pachad*, fear or dread. Another character from the same comic book series, Judge Death, is essentially *Samael*, the traditional demonic angel of Mars. *Samael* (variously Poison of God, or The Blind Power) is the Prince of the powers of the left side, entities of pure *Din*.

Law tends in the direction of pure mechanism. In an automobile engine each part is necessary, and has fixed and determinate relationships with every other part. If a part did not have a necessary and determinate relationship with other parts, it could be removed with no loss of function. In the case of dirt, dead leaves, spiders and mice, removal can be a good thing.

There is a pronounced tendency in human beings to wish to design ideal worlds, worlds of pure, rationally-comprehensible mechanism that meet ideal goals. Within restricted domains this is often achieved. We expect air transport to be safe, we expect the telephone to have a dial-tone when we pick it up, and we expect water to come out of the taps. This is both astonishing and admirable; hidden behind these services are empires of complexity managed down to the finest details. On the rare occasions when they fail we are concerned and angry. The outrage caused by the 2008 banking crisis has led to many calls for increased regulation in the banking system. There was too much freedom to do stupid things. The obvious solution is to try to design more checks-and-balances, and bankers have been telling us how terrible this would be - they need freedom to make money. For themselves.

The struggle between law and mechanism on one hand, and freedom on the other, is one of the core aspects of the human condition.

We believe we can design perfect mechanisms, but to do so in the human sphere requires power to regulate and control. Before handing over power we have to trust that the good cop really is good. We know we need to be governed, but we rarely trust the governing class, who are often depicted as self-serving, mendacious and greedy. We hand off some part of our freedom to politicians who may be a bunch of rogues.

We are now firmly in the realm of *Chesed*. The key aspect of *Chesed* is freedom, and the key question is "what are you going to do with it?". The phrase "spend your time" shows how we see freedom as a kind of capital that we can spend. Freedom is not an abstract thing that flaps around like a flag in the wind. It earths itself. If freedom cannot earth itself it is not worth much - it is like having money and nothing to spend it on. The paradox of freedom is the extent to which we spend it or give it away, and the ferocity with which we defend our right to spend it or give it away.

The average person does not want to live in the Land of the Lotus Eaters. We give our free time to family, relationships, clubs, associations, events, charities, and countless projects. In many countries we take for granted the freedom to associate together and do whatever it is we think needs to be done. Every illness has its charity; every hospital has its charity; every cause has its willing band of dedicated supporters. Within a few miles of where I live there is a cinema run by volunteers, a public house run by volunteers, a library run by volunteers, a community arts project run by volunteers, thrift shops staffed by volunteers, and a parish council led by volunteers. This is the tip of the iceberg.

A willingness to give is the essential and core aspect of *Chesed*, which translates as loving-kindness. Loving-kindness is a stand against the *Din* of *Malkhut*. *Malkhut* is not kind. It is implacable. Overcoming the harshness and inertia of *Malkhut* tends to erode self-importance and winnow out Ego, leaving behind an authentic energy that is prepared to make sacrifices and suffer to make things happen. This happens at every level, from parents' sleepless nights to leaders scrambling from one crisis to the next. We know it when we see it. Some people, the people we respect the most, have the ability to set their own concerns aside and work for the common good. This 'setting aside' requires humility, and humility is the virtue of *Chesed*.

Somewhat at odds with humility is the planetary correspondence of *Chesed*: Jupiter/Zeus, King of the Gods. Neither Jupiter nor Zeus were notable for their humility. Zeus overcame the Titans with his thunderbolts and imprisoned them in Tartarus.

Gevurah & Chesed

Throughout Europe and the Middle East we find the leader of the pantheon of Gods is the victor of a combat myth, a defining combat against powers inimical to life. At a time before the cosmos as we know it came into being, there existed a state the book of *Genesis* describes as *tohu va-bohu*, a difficult phrase that is translated variously as 'formless and empty', 'chaos and desolation', 'ruined and uninhabited'. A god steps forward and accepts the challenge to battle chaos personified as a great monster or mighty dragon. Whether it is Indra versus Vritra, Zeus against the Titans, Thor versus the Midgard Serpent, *Yahweh* versus Leviathon, Baal versus Yam or Marduk versus Tiamet the story is similar. After a mighty battle against the powers of this desolate and broken state, the cosmos comes into being.

One of the most complete versions of this myth is the Babylonian *Enuma Elish*, which tells how the god Marduk fought the monster Tiamat and divided her body in two to form the earth and the sky. Although *Genesis*, being a much later composition, presents a combat-free version of creation, relics of combat can be found in early Biblical sources such as the *Psalms*[135]. An important aspect of the combat myth is that although evil and chaos have been routed, they have not been annihilated. Evil has been overcome to a sufficient degree that a creation becomes possible, but victory is not final or complete.

My view on this is very personal. It seems to me that a large part of my life is a struggle to stop things reverting back to their primal nature, to *tohu va-bohu*. Almost every day there is an appliance that needs to be repaired, a relationship that needs to be mended, an eruption of weeds in the garden, an activity that needs a push. I feel like I am battling the lesser minions of the powers of chaos. My family, my house, my vehicles, my garden, all my projects, even my own body, appear to be teetering on the edge. I have to be vigilant, and diligent.

My universe-maintenance is all 'small beer', as the saying goes, hardly something to sing about over a horn of mead, but nevertheless I have my own personal combat myth, and I suspect most people of a certain age will recognise the feeling that life requires unrelenting hard work. Chaos is always working away at the periphery.

The struggle against disorder may possess the character of *Gevurah*, but the impulse behind it, the caring and willingness to spend

---

[135]. *Creation and the Persistence of Evil*, Jon D. Levenson, Princeton University Press 1988

whatever it takes in time and effort, has the nature of *Chesed*. This interdependence and intertwining of *Gevurah* and *Chesed* is very apparent in this description of the Norse god Thor[136]:

> If as a warrior Thor was terrifying, to his own people he was benign: he cared for cattle and crops and harvests. He would act as patron to a settlement, both defending it against external enemies and ensuring its inner stability. Guardian of law, he was called to witness every oath. He also cared for individuals: he was the god to whom a person would most readily turn in the hour of need. And he watched over all the most important events of a person's life: at wedding and at death bed he was there, friendly and protective. At all times and in every way Thor was the upholder of order.

The impulse of loving-kindness is almost never a moment of sentiment following a disaster appeal. At the level of *Chesed,* loving-kindness is hands-on, and being hands-on, is almost never detached from struggle. The factors one must struggle against are easily characterised by the vices of all the *sefirot*: inertia, avarice, theft, idleness, dishonesty, selfishness, pride, cruelty, and the vices of *Chesed* itself, bigotry, tyranny, hypocrisy and gluttony.

Caring brings us face-to-face with the harshness of reality and the active and intelligent powers ranged against us. Not only is *Malkhut* stubborn and inert and addicted to the second law of thermodynamics, but our fellow human beings add a large share of avoidable chaos to the situation. Addiction, cruelty, theft, and violence are realities of everyday life. War turns good people into beggars, children into orphans, and men into sadistic monsters. The greed of unfettered capitalism creates unimaginable wealth for a few, while employees struggle to pay bills from a minimum wage.

Some evil may be structural and unavoidable - fire, flood, pestilence and so on - but much is created whole-cloth, and sustained with energy and intelligence. As I write this, Syria is being turned into rubble. A large area of central Africa is terrorised by militias. Israel continues to fortify the Left Bank. Car bombs are a daily occurrence in Iraq, Afghanistan and Pakistan. Tyrants are hiding billions of dollars of looted state revenue in Swiss bank accounts. Forests are laid waste, ecosystems obliterated, fisheries swept clean. These activities are planned and intentional.

The dysfunctions and pathologies of *Chesed* and *Gevurah* are often difficult to comprehend because of their scale. A million refugees. What does that mean? A million people have lost their homes, basic

---

136. *Cosmos, Chaos, and the World to Come*, Norman Cohn, Yale University Press 1995.

amenities like clean water or fuel for cooking, education for their children, health care, and pharmaceuticals. They have lost their dignity and their place in the world. The magnitude of these pathologies, dominated by gluttony (unrestrained greed and appetite), bigotry, hypocrisy and tyranny, belong to *Chesed*. When *Chesed* turns to the dark side, it does so on a gigantic scale. The brutality and cruelty of the warlord and the tyrant corresponds to the most negative aspect of Mars, the planetary correspondence of *Gevurah*.

This may be difficult understand. How can loving-kindness be malign? It happens because caring, unrestrained and given the means, will stop at nothing. Just as appetite, unrestrained, can become addiction, so protectiveness can become a terrifying force. *Gevurah*, the iron fist within *Chesed's* velvet glove, is what loving-kindness can become when threatened. It recalls Ripley's concern for the human race in *Aliens*: "I say we take off and nuke the entire site from orbit. It's the only way to be sure." This is the logic of *Chesed*.

Traditional Kabbalah tells it a different way, but the effect is the same: without *Din* to set proper bounds on *Chesed*, the universe would not be distinct from God. It would cease to exist.

Chesed corresponds to water. In *Genesis* it states:

Let there be a vault between the waters to separate water from water. So God made the vault and separated the water under the vault from the water above it.

This act of separation has the quality of *Din*; it made the space for creation to exist. According to *Genesis* God decided He had had enough of humanity and He undid the separation of the waters and flooded the world. Only Noah and his family survived. The God of *Genesis* was not so different from Ripley: He nuked us from orbit.

A related pathology of loving-kindness is where it becomes attached to the Ego and the concerns of the Ego. Ego sustenance is measured in yacht-metres: just how large a floating pleasure palace can one moor off Cannes during the film festival[137]. The needy Ego lavishes kindness upon itself. It is insatiable. A well-publicised example of gluttony was the three thousand pairs of shoes bought by Imelda Marcos, wife of the president of the Philippines.

The god-name associated with *Chesed* is *El*. The history of this name can be traced back through written records to Akkadian, a Semitic dialect used in Mesopotamia about 4500 years ago. It occurs

---

137. At the time of writing the largest yacht is the *Azzam* at 180 metres, owned by Khalifa bin Zayed bin Sultan Al Nahyan, ruler of Abu Dhabi

in an easily-recognisable form in most of the subsequent dialects in an area that includes Mesopotamia, Syria, the Holy Land, Arabia, and the Horn of Africa. Today, the best-known variant would be *Allah*, a contraction of *al-ilah*, 'the God', where *ilah* comes from the same root as *Elohim*. The Akkadian is *ilu*, and it signifies a god or divine being.

The word *El* as the name for a specific god occurs in the region adjacent to the east coast of the Mediterranean formerly known as Phoenicia and Canaan. *El* would appear to have been a supreme god at the head of a pantheon of subsidiary gods and goddesses (such as *Asherah*, his female partner). There is evidence in many mythologies for an older god who heads the pantheon, wise but inactive, and a vigorous younger God who actively fights to uphold the divine order. Scholars find some evidence to suggest that at an early, pre-Biblical period, *El* and *Yahweh* may have had this relationship, but were later conflated and used interchangeably, along with *Elohim*.

The archangel for *Chesed* is *Tzadkiel*, almost certainly derived from *tzedek*, righteousness (and also the Hebrew title for the planet Jupiter associated with *Chesed*). The angel order is the *Chasmalim*, a name taken from the vision of *Ezekiel*.

The word *chasmal* occurs only once in the *Bible*, and is translated as 'amber', a substance well-known in the ancient world for producing sparks when rubbed on silk or fur[138]. The modern Hebrew word for electricity is *chasmal*, and so we can think of *chasmal* as an electrical discharge, sparks, or lightning. We have recovered the idea of a god with thunderbolts.

The god-name associated with *Gevurah* is *Elohim Gevor*, 'strong god', that aspect of God that dispenses judgement, according to the verse:

'Judgement is for Elohim' (*Deuteronomy* 1:17)

Elohim Gevor is a difficult aspect, as Gikatilla observes:

Know that at times the attribute Elohim is sometimes referred to as Gevurah (power, might), the reason being that it often overwhelms in order to bring justice to offenders and sinners. It is the one who takes revenge against the wicked who rebel against YHVH, may He be Blessed ... it has the ability to judge, exact punishment, and to overcome everyone. For there is nothing that can stand in its path.[139]

The divine justice aspect of *Gevurah* is often misunderstood by novices who fixate on the Mars aspect and interpret this aspect

---

138. The Latin word for amber is *electricus*.
139. *The Gates of Light*, Joseph Gikatilla, trans. Avi Weinstein, Harper Collins 1994

Figure 41: *Gevurah* as Justice

beyond its relevance. The left-hand pillar of the Tree is often interpreted as inheriting a female quality from *Binah* at its head. At first sight this does not seem to square with Mars, the most bone-headed and stereotypically masculine of the gods. Mars - warlike, violent, destructive, and somewhat stupid - is a very limited aspect of *Gevurah*. A more traditional view is that *Gevurah* is divine justice. Today, justice is most often depicted as a female figure (sometimes with a blindfold denoting impartiality) holding a sword and a balance.

The archangel of *Gevurah* is *Kamael*, a name associated with Mars. Sometimes *Samael* is used, emphasising how the energy of the left-side, unbalanced by righteousness and mercy, tends towards the demonic. The angel order is the *Serafim*, the 'burning ones', an attribution that would seem to be based on *Gevurah's* association with destructive fire[140] (as in Sodom and Gomorrah).

---

140. The angel orders associated with the *sefirot* and used here are the ten orders of angels given in the *Mishneh Torah* of Maimonides, c. 1180 CE.

In summary, with *Chesed* and *Gevurah* we enter our own personal combat myth where we attempt to make a world out of chaos. We must sustain the energy and vision necessary to care for our world, and the strength to hold it together in the face of a inbuilt tendency to come apart. For many people this world is a family. For others it may be a business, or a political party, or a charity.

If we are successful the world we have created will subsume us, and in time, replace us. We must be humble in the face of this possibility.

20

Binah & Chokhmah

The Hermetic Kabbalah

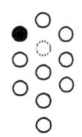

Meaning	Understanding, Intelligence
Number	3
Colour	Black
Briatic Correspondence	Comprehension
Magical Image	An old woman (possibly in mourning) on a throne.
Titles	*Imma*, the Mother; *Marah*, the bitter sea; *Khorsia*, the Throne; the Fifty Gates; Intelligence; the Mother of Form; the Superior Mother; *Tebunah*, Understanding
Element	-
Virtue	Silence
Vice	Inertia
Illusion	Death
Klippot	Fatalism
Obligation	-
Command	-
God Name	*Elohim*
Archangel	*Cassiel*
Angel Order	*Aralim*
Planet	*Shabtai*
Spiritual Experience	Vision of Sorrow
Keywords	Limitation, form, constraint, heaviness, slowness, inertia, old-age, incarnation, karma, fate, time, space, natural law, the womb and gestation, darkness, boundedness, enclosure, containment, mother, weaving and spinning, death (annihilation)

Table 12: *Binah*

Binah & Chokhmah

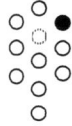

Meaning	Wisdom
Number	2
Colour	Grey, white flecked with silver
Briatic Correspondence	Revolution
Magical Image	A bearded man
Titles	*Abba*, the father
Element	-
Virtue	Good
Vice	Evil
Illusion	Independence
Klippot	Arbitrariness
Obligation	-
Command	-
God Name	*Jah*
Archangel	*Ratziel*
Angel Order	*Ophanim*
Planet	*Mazlot* (the Zodiac, the fixed stars)
Spiritual Experience	Vision of God Face-to-Face
Keywords	Creative force, life-force, the wellspring, the erect phallus and ejaculation, standing stone, fountain, water of life, a spring

Table 13: *Chokhmah*

The Hermetic Kabbalah

One of the most ancient and commonly-used metaphors used in connection with the Tree of Life is that of a flow of water. *Keter* represents the underground source, the aquifer. *Chokhmah* represents the spring where sweet water bubbles to the surface. *Binah* is the great sea, the upper waters. Water flows from the upper sea through the channels of the Tree of Life to water the whole creation - indeed, *Binah* is sometimes called *Be'er sheva*, the 'well of seven' (although the title is more often used for the Lesser Mother, *Malkhut*).

Water gives life, and life is symbolised by water. The Tree of Life is thus also the Tree of Water. This imagery is also associated with the *pardes* or garden where the Tree of Life stands:

A river flowed out of Eden to water the garden, and there it divided and became four rivers.

The flow of life has the nature of *Chesed*. The structure that encloses the flow has the nature of *Din*. Thus the nature of *Chokhmah* is primarily *Chesed*, and the nature of *Binah* is primarily *Din*, and this is why they appear at the head of the Pillars of Mercy and Severity (or Force and Form) respectively.

Another metaphor associates the bubbling spring of *Chokhmah* with the ejaculating penis of the Father, and the great sea of *Binah* with the uterus of the Mother. The primordial couple *Abba* and *Imma* are forever face-to-face, forever conjoined. Should their intercourse cease even for a second, the entire cosmos would cease to be. The womb of the Mother gestates the son or child, who manifests as *Ze'ir Anpin*, the cluster of six *sefirot* surrounding and including *Tiferet*.

The water of life that emerges in *Chokhmah* and descends the Tree is also the semen that ejaculates from the phallus of *Ze'ir Anpin* (*Yesod*) to impregnate the Holy of Holies of the Lesser Mother, *Malkhut*. The spermatozoa within the seminal fluid are *souls*. Sometimes the letter *Yod* from the Tetragrammaton, the letter associated with *Chokhmah*, is likened to a spermatozoön (the letter *yod* looks like an apostrophe ('), with a head and a tail).

Chokhmah means 'wisdom' and *Binah* means 'understanding' or 'intelligence'. The traditional interpretation of 'wisdom' and 'intelligence' tends to follow commonplace usage, but commonplace usage is complex and has varied over the millenia. Interpreting these words is less simple than it might seem. In addition, various communities of Kabbalistic understanding interpret the words in different contexts, and this can be confusing.

Many modern discussions of Kabbalah (especially those online) derive from the *Chabad* tradition, a Chassidic tradition whose name

Binah & Chokhmah

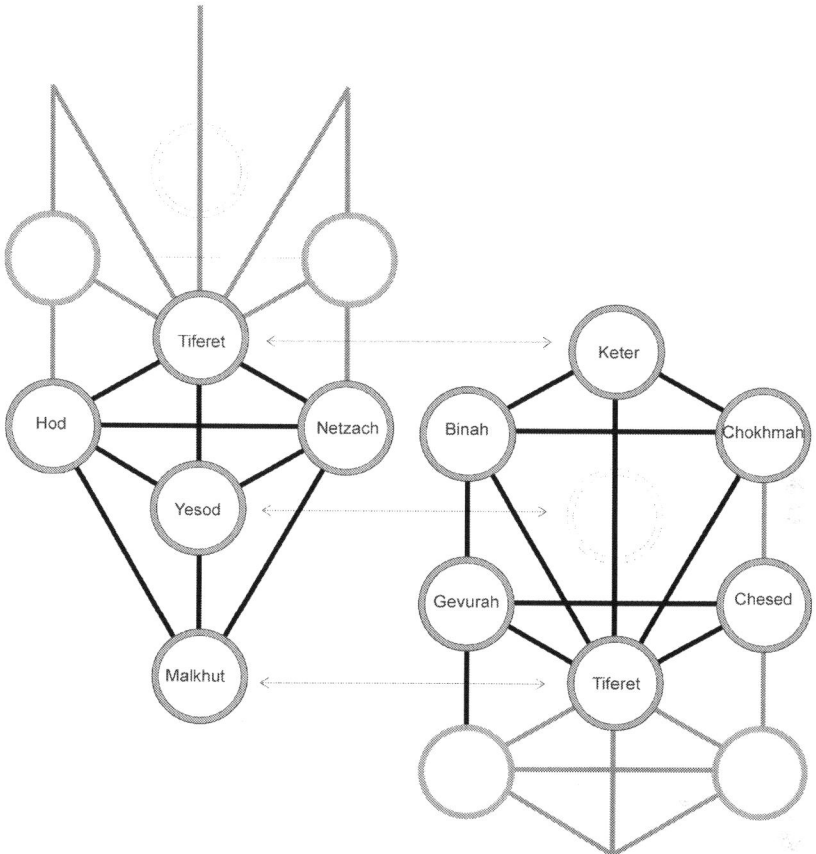

Figure 42: By symmetry, *Chokhmah*, *Binah* and *Da'at* in one world are *Netzach*, *Hod* and *Yesod* in the next, so that, for example, *Chokhmah*, *Binah* and *Da'at* in *Assiah* overlap *Netzach*, *Hod* and *Yesod* in *Yetzirah*. *Tiferet* overlaps with both *Malkhut* and *Keter*. These overlaps correspond to profound cognitive transitions, to 'moving between worlds'.

'ChaBaD' is an acrostic that derives from *Chokhmah, Binah, Da'at*, that is, wisdom, understanding and knowledge (*Keter*, as discussed previously, is considered too remote for comprehension and *Da'at* is substituted). This tradition tends to discuss wisdom, understanding and knowledge in the context of the microcosm, the human body, so that *Chokhmah, Binah* and *Da'at* constitute the human intellect (*sechel*) and constitute three 'brains'. In this view, *Chokhmah, Binah* and *Da'at* are primarily cognitive, and their meaning is expounded in the context of reading and comprehending sacred texts.

The Hermetic tradition, as given here, normally describes the trio of *Chokhmah, Binah, Da'at* in the *macrocosm* - that is, as aspects of the divine - and attributes much of the dynamic of the human intellect to *Netzach, Hod* and *Yesod* instead.

The difference between the two perspectives - Chabad and Hermetic - is much less than one might imagine, because the two trios of *sefirot* are dual on the Extended Tree (see Figure 42). That is, *Hod* can be viewed as a lower reflection of *Binah*, *Netzach* as a lower reflection of *Chokhmah*, and *Yesod* as a lower reflection of *Da'at*.

The words 'knowledge', 'understanding' and 'wisdom' enter Kabbalah from the book of *Proverbs*, one of the oldest texts of the Bible, and traditionally attributed to Solomon. The words are used together in a number of proverbs that are often referenced in the literature but offer little by way of insight to the reader. We are further distanced by translation into English. For example, "I know how to do it" and "I understand how to do it" could be used in the same context. I believe the best way to proceed is to discuss the core ideas, and hope not to labour the subject.

The simplest kind of knowledge is everyday factual knowledge, such as knowing where I have left my car keys, or whether it is currently raining. Then there is abstract factual knowledge such as one might find in a quiz, such as knowing the names of capital cities and the longest rivers. Licensed London taxicab drivers must acquire 'the knowledge', a thorough knowledge of streets, routes and destinations. It is common to see a person riding a scooter or moped with a clipboard on the handlebars - this is a prospective taxicab driver 'acquiring the knowledge'. This is knowledge as a mechanical accumulation of facts. We respect people with prodigious memories for facts, but do not confuse this with a broader intelligence. I will now attempt to separate this kind of factual knowledge from understanding.

I can observe many things without understanding, as if through the eyes of a child. A child knows that a parent 'goes to work' every day but does not understand 'work'. I can draw a picture of the phases of the moon without understanding what causes the twenty-eight day cycle of occultation, or the twice-daily cycle of the tides. Knowledge, in its most basic sense, is dead without an understanding of the deeper and larger context. Knowledge is something a machine can acquire. A computer could 'acquire the knowledge' of a taxi driver - this is more or less what a satnav does. Understanding on the other hand, is something human beings (and perhaps a few other species) are capable of

Binah & Chokhmah

possessing.

Understanding is the ability to look behind the surface of phenomena and see the pattern. Understanding (or intelligence) is the capacity to grasp (or make) new abstractions, the ability to comprehend the intricacies of cause and effect. Understanding relates one fact to another, shows how they depend, interact, influence and combine into larger facts. As time goes by understanding becomes more and more related, more and more connected, until it seems to be a world in its own right, a world-behind-the-world. It can seem, in moments of deep insight, that one is connected to the archetype of this world. This is what Plato felt, and many since. Kabbalists influenced by Plato have identified *Binah* with the divine intellect or intelligence, the mind of God that holds the core forms that determine the shape of this world.

Understanding tends towards vastness. The expert can see a web of relatedness and may be unable to value all the links and dependencies. There are so many *pros* and *cons*, no person seems capable of grasping the whole picture and making sense of it in a way others can understand. This situation is sometimes called 'analysis paralysis'.

One of the many stories told about Alexander the Great is that of the Gordian Knot, a knot of such intricacy that no person had been able to understand how to undo it. Alexander cut it with his sword. Wisdom is the social quality of being able to direct understanding like the conductor of an orchestra. One can have a room filled with experts but no direction or progress.

Wisdom is being able to traverse the web of understanding and not become lost or confused. Wisdom answers the questions "what do we do now?" or "how do we move forward?" or "where do we go from here?". Wisdom is the big picture, the whole kaboodle: a problem, the collective understanding of the problem, and a community of people looking for an answer. The answer could be as simple as "Head north in the morning". Wisdom brings understanding into focus. It turns understanding into something that can grow into action. It is as if understanding had been impregnated with a seed.

Chokhmah continuously impregnates the body of the Great Mother *Binah*, and out of that Great Deep of interconnectedness and relationship and potential - what we might call 'the realm of possibility' - something is born. Something is clothed in the flesh of *Yetzirah*. It is something *we* can relate to.

Chokhmah is associated with the first word of the book of *Genesis*, *bereshit*, which means, "in the beginning":

> In the beginning God created the heaven and the earth.
> And the earth was without form, and void; and darkness was upon the face of the deep. And the Spirit of God moved upon the face of the waters.
> And God said, Let there be light: and there was light.
> And God saw the light, that it was good: and God divided the light from the darkness.
> And God called the light Day, and the darkness he called Night. And the evening and the morning were the first day.
> And God said, Let there be a firmament in the midst of the waters, and let it divide the waters from the waters.
> And God made the firmament, and divided the waters which were under the firmament from the waters which were above the firmament: and it was so.
> And God called the firmament Heaven. And the evening and the morning were the second day.
> And God said, Let the waters under the heaven be gathered together unto one place, and let the dry land appear: and it was so.
> And God called the dry land Earth; and the gathering together of the waters called he Seas: and God saw that it was good.

In the beginning, primordial separations take place: heaven and earth, light and dark, night and day, evening and morning, the upper waters from the lower waters, dry land from the waters. There is a clear sense of 'things being pulled apart' where previously they had been undifferentiated. It is almost as if God's hands are tearing at the *En Sof* so that duality pours out. *Chokhmah* is the beginning where the primary dualities of existence are shaped.

Modern cosmology shares similar explanatory problems to Kabbalah: how to produce structure where initially there was no structure. According to modern physics the universe was in a completely uniform and symmetric state following the Big Bang. As it expanded and cooled, 'symmetries broke', and more and more structure emerged. The symmetry of the initial state broke because of forces or fields that caused clumpiness, making galaxies and stars and planets. We can see something like this in a snowglobe. When it is shaken the snow is evenly distributed, but when we stop shaking, it 'cools' and the snow begins to settle. Gravity breaks the symmetry.

Both cosmology and Kabbalah use a process of 'reducing symmetry' to explain how difference comes about. In *Genesis* God reduces the symmetry by *fiat*, as in "Let there be ...". In cosmology a small number of unexplained *a priori* 'fields' (five at the time of writing) break the symmetry of the universe as it expands and cools. There is

Binah & Chokhmah

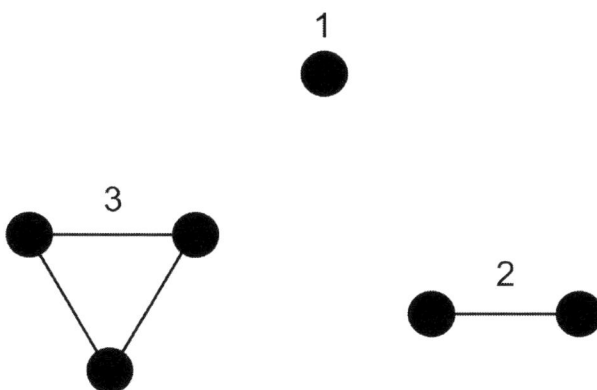

Figure 43: A geometric interpretation of the first three *sefirot*. *Keter* is a point, *Chokhmah* is a line, and *Binah* is a triangle. The line and the triangle are a common metaphor for the male and female sexual organs. The line breaks the symmetry of the point by imposing a direction. The direction is then given a 'shape' within the space of the triangle.

little more one can say to provide a rational or causal account of the beginning. There has to be some kind of symmetry-breaking mechanism, but where these symmetry-breaking forces come from we still do not know.

Chokhmah is associated with 'will' (*r'tzon*)[141] as it becomes oriented and directed. This direction can be depicted as a line (see Figure 43). Will is always directed towards a future state of affairs. We cannot will the past, and we cannot will the present. When I wake up in the morning I lie for a time imagining what I intend to do during the day. I make plans and decide how to organise my time. Many of my activities are connected with far-off goals that require sustained activity taking months or years (this book is one such). At some point in the past I would have imagined these goals and 'set my mind' towards achieving them. This is how Will works. In the abstract, Will is like the feeling 'what will I do today?', and in response a parade of possibilities is seen in the mind's eye. I decide which possibilities I want to move towards. This illustrates how *Chokhmah* is like a higher-level version of *Netzach*, less oriented towards the immediate

---

141. As *Chokhmah* emanates from *Keter*, and *Keter* is also characterised by Will, there is inevitably much in common. Much of the discussion of Will is reproduced at a more abstract level in the following chapter.

The Hermetic Kabbalah

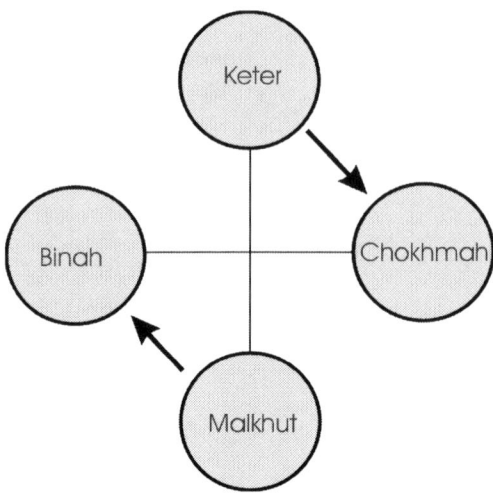

Figure 44: The will of *Keter* is directed towards a conception of *Malkhut* which instantly manifests as *Chokhmah* and *Binah*, so that *Chokhmah* is like a reflection of *Keter*, and *Binah* a reflection of *Malkhut*.

and the sensual, and more oriented towards the world of future possibility.

Binah emanates from *Chokhmah*. This is often described as if the emanation occurred sequentially, with *Keter, Chokhmah and Binah* popping out one after the other like Russian dolls. This is not the only way of thinking about it. Many Kabbalists have thought of *Chokhmah* and *Binah* as being outside of time, part of an eternal realm of existence that bounds human time and space. One of the titles of *Binah* is *olam ha-ba*, the World to Come.

An alternative way to think about this is that *Keter* and *Malkhut* are simultaneous, a single emanation we could call *Keter-Malkhut*, and like a mirror image or self-reflection, this instantaneously and simultaneously gives rise to the emanation *Chokhmah-Binah*, where *Chokhmah* is an 'expressive' image of *Keter* and *Binah* is a 'formative' image of *Malkhut,* as shown in Figure 44.

One can imagine *Keter* and *Malkhut* pivoting through 90° to form a dual pair of *Chokhmah* and *Binah*. The space in the middle corresponds to *Da'at*, and 'opens-up' to the next level of being, described by the six *sefirot* of *Ze'ir Anpin* (see Figure 31 for a more detailed representation of this). According to this picture *Malkhut* is set aside from the other six days of creation - the seventh day is special.

Binah & Chokhmah

Binah can be visualised through the image of the great or superior mother. There are two female images on the Tree of Life: the greater mother (*Imma*), and the lesser mother (*Nukva Ze'ir*, or the *Shekhinah*). Both mothers are represented by the letter *He* in the name of four letters, and both share many attributes. *Binah* is represented as an elderly queen on her throne wearing black. She is the queen of the universe, and stars are gems on her gown. Many of her attributes can be found in the Blessed Virgin Mary (for example, the letters of *Binah* contain *Ben*, the son). The BVM in turn subsumed many of the attributes of the great goddess Isis. Meditations on *Binah* turn to spinning and weaving; she is the Black Widow, spinning the fabric of space and time. Her sting is death.

Above the abyss she is neither robed in black or alone; she is forever clasped in the embrace of the Father.

Binah is closely associated with periods of time connected to the number seven. The word 'seven' comes from one of the oldest word roots in languages stretching across Europe to India. The S sound can be 'ess' or 'sh', and the V sound can be 'vuh' or 'buh' or 'puh" or even 'fuh'. The English 'seven' derives from proto-German *sebun*, and is related to the Latin *septem* and the Sanskrit *saptan*. The root in Hebrew is ShBA - *shin, bet, ayin*, and as *shin* can sound as 'sh' or 'ess', and *bet* can sound as 'buh' or vuh', there many words that incorporate this root but differ in sound. For example, 'seven' is *sh'va*, but the seventh day of the week is *shabbat*, which also means 'rest' or 'cessation'. The 'well of seven' is *Be'er Sheva*. The seventh planet in the traditional Ptolomaic order is Saturn (*shabtai*), the planet associated with *Binah*; interestingly, we also call the day of the Jewish sabbath Saturn's Day or Saturday.

The six sefirot of *Ze'ir Anpin*, *Chesed* to *Yesod*, are associated with the six days of creation as told in *Genesis*. The seventh day, *shabbat*, is associated with *Malkhut*. As *Binah* is like the supernal template for *Malkhut*, it is associated with 'super-cycles' of seven, specifically a period of time composed of 7 times 7 + 1; that is, 49 plus 1.

There are two super-cycles of particular importance. The first is a period of seven weeks and one day known as 'counting the *Omer*' and terminating with the feast of *Shavuot*. The second is seven cycles of seven years, with the final or fiftieth year being a *jubilee*, a Jewish term that is the indirect source for the same word in English.

The festival of *Shavuot* ('weeks') begins after Passover and marks the giving of the *Torah* by God and Moses to the Jewish people on Mount Sinai. The seven weeks comprising 49 days marks a period of spiritual preparation. This period of time can be used for daily reflection, and out of this has grown the idea that the Fifty Gates of *Binah* are fifty meditative gateways into the nature of created reality. The Fifty Gates are often contrasted with the Thirty-Two Paths of Wisdom associated with *Chokhmah* as described in the *Sefer Yetzirah*[142]. The difference is perhaps that the Thirty-Two Paths describe the structural building-blocks of creation viewed *from without*, whereas the Fifty Gates are aspects of the same creation as experienced *from within*.

One tradition interprets the Gates by using the association between the days of creation and the seven *sefirot Chesed* to *Malkhut*. According to this, the forty-nine days of the *Omer* signify seven Gates within each sefirot, so that *Malkhut* has seven Gates corresponding to *Malkhut* through to *Chesed*, *Yesod* has seven Gates corresponding to *Malkhut* through to *Chesed*, and so on up to *Chesed*. The fiftieth Gate is special, and, according to tradition, not given even to Moses.

According to Jewish law, every seventh year is a fallow year (*shmita* - release) in which the normal activities of agriculture are suspended. Crops are not planted. Such produce as does grow (e.g. fruit) cannot be sold and can be picked by anyone for their own use. Debts are remitted, and indentured servants released from their contracts. The seventh year resembles a year-long agricultural *shabbat*, and while there is less work to be done, there is also the concern that there is sufficient food in storage. A *jubilee* marks the end of a cycle of seven, seven-year periods - forty-nine years.

> This fiftieth year is sacred—it is a time of freedom and of celebration when everyone will receive back their original property, and slaves will return home to their families.
>
> *Leviticus* 25:10

There is debate as to whether the 49th year (which is a *shmita* year) is the jubilee year, or whether the *jubilee* is the following or 50th year. The traditional symbolism of *Binah* makes most sense if one follows the rule that the *jubilee* year is the fiftieth year, just as *Shavuot* falls on the fiftieth day.

The association of *Binah* with 50 comes from the *Talmud*:

> *Nun Sha'arei Binah* (Fifty Gates of Understanding) were created in the world, and all of them were given to Moshe except for one.
>
> *Rosh Hashanah* 21b

---

142. Ten *sefirot* and twenty-two letters, the letters divided into three, seven and twelve.

Binah & Chokhmah

Figure 45: A representation of the Fifty Gates of Binah, structured as 7 times 7. The fiftieth Gate is the totality.

The association of *Binah* with time is continued through its association with the planet Saturn (*Shabtai*). The Hebrew name of the planet comes from the same root as *shabbat*, the seventh day, the holy day of the week, which falls on Saturday, or *dies saturni* - Saturn's day. At an early period of human history Saturn was associated with agriculture, and one finds this in early texts on astrology, where Saturn has many earthy correspondences, and was portrayed with the scythe or sickle of a field worker[143]. However there was a shift in understanding, perhaps due to a confusion between Kronos, the Greek name for the planet Saturn, and Chronos, time. Chronos, with his scythe or sickle, became a symbol for old age and death. Some-

---

143. The sickle was also used to castrate his father.

times he is depicted explicitly as Old Father Time holding an hourglass. Both images can be found in the Tarot, as the trump Death, and as the trump The Hermit[144]. Modern astrology views Saturn as a Great Malefic, with associations that are primarily negative.

An important idea associated with Binah is *confinement*, such as a cooking pot with a lid on, or the pregnant womb. There are other words one could use - limitation, restriction, constraint, even imprisonment - but confinement conveys the human situation: that we find ourselves confined to an existence whose fundamental boundaries and limitations lie beyond our understanding.

Our conscious experience of this world begins at birth, and ends at death, and during the interim we are bound to an existence of a particular kind - a particular species of animal, healthy or not healthy, in pain or not in pain, hungry or not hungry, and so on, an endless list of particulars that define the unique peculiarities of our personal lives. Some people (and I would extend this to many species of animal) feel good about this kind of existence, but some do not and wish they were no longer experiencing[145]. Some are simply baffled by the contingent nature of it all. Why this? Why that? Why anything at all?

Jews, for the most part (and despite many appalling experiences), have been accepting of their situation and view their earthly lives as part of a larger relationship with a loving and merciful God. The book of *Job*, dated to between the 4th and 6th century BCE, explores the issues of loss and pain and faith with considerable skill and subtlety.

The gnostics of late antiquity viewed their confinement in a realm of suffering and death as the work of a deluded and ignorant creator entity, and sought to escape this confinement through divine *gnosis*; that is, direct intuitive knowledge of a redemptive character. The descended soul had two parts: an eternal and divine part, and a daemonic part formed during its descent into Nature through the spheres associated with the seven planets. The *gnosis*, a gift of divine grace, had the power to illuminate the understanding, and so the gnostic would *see* how the animal passions that bound his or her awareness to this world had been fastened to the soul by daemonic powers. The *gnosis*, which was often of an esoteric and magical nature, contained formulae that would break the bonds of nature and frustrate the daemonic guardians of the spheres.

---

144. In modern images the Hermit holds a lamp; in some older images, an hourglass.
145. Thomas Ligotti makes this case to great effect in *The Conspiracy Against the Human Race, A Contrivance of Horror*, Hippocampus Press, 2011

Binah & Chokhmah

It has been said that when a person dies, an entire universe is destroyed. It seems incomprehensible that so much richness could be lost, discarded, snuffed-out. It is entirely legitimate for us to ask what kind of Big Picture (*Binah*) is responsible for this kind of small picture (*Malkhut*). Do we live in a vast machine? Is God even more ignorant and arrogant than we are? Are we confined in a malign laboratory by malignant entities? Is our faith being tested? Will it all come right in the end? What is the big picture?

A result of this is that *Binah* takes on an ambivalent character. She is the Great Mother, the Mother of Form, but also the Gate of Death. In *The Cosmic Doctrine* Dion Fortune expands on this:

> For birth is death, and death is birth. All are born 'blind', which mercifully prevents them from knowing that they are dead ... Those who are in matter are in the grave, they are dead and buried. Death and Initiation produce the same results, therefore it is that all Initiations contain the symbolism of death and burial.

The language of the Golden Dawn Neophyte initiation contrasts night with day, darkness with light, and utilises the resonant symbolism of the gospel of *John*[146]:

> The voice of my higher soul said unto me, Let me enter the Path of Darkness, peradventure thus shall I obtain the Light. I am the only being in an abyss of darkness. From the darkness came I forth ere my birth, from the silence of a primal sleep, and the Voice of Ages answered unto my soul, I am he that formulates in darkness. Child of Earth; the Light shineth in the darkness, but the darkness comprehendeth it not.

The process is quite literally one of 'illumination': the neophyte is commanded: "Child of Earth, long hast thou dwelt in darkness. Quit the night and seek the day."

Some of the Neophyte ritual symbolism was taken from ancient Egypt, where it was believed that each day the sun descended in the West into the underworld realm of *Duat* or *Amenti*, a dangerous realm filled with hostile entities. Each morning the sun would rise again in the East. The Golden Dawn ritual symbolism imagined the soul as descending into darkness, and awakening once more to the world of light, this symbolism reinforced by ritual movements around the temple. The name of the order - Golden Dawn - says it all ... the dawning of the sun of *Tiferet*.

We are often challenged to see the big picture, to think outside the box. *Binah is* the big picture, *is* the outside of the box. *Binah* is so far

---

146. *The Complete Golden Dawn System of Magic*, Israel Regardie, Falcon Press 1985

The Hermetic Kabbalah

outside the box that the initiatory ascent tradition of the Golden Dawn placed the Great Abyss between *Chesed* and *Binah*. This is explored further in *Da'at* on page 291.

An important point to grasp is that *Binah* transcends every limitation placed upon our perception and experience as a result of being a particular species of animal living in a society at a particular time and place on one small planet. *Binah* is outside of that particular box.

In summary, *Chokhmah* and *Binah* are the brains of *Keter*, two complementary aspects of the inexplicable. *Chokhmah* is the beginning, the seed, our Father. *Binah* is our Mother; space is her womb and the stars are her children. The human race, a speck in the darkness, is made from the dust that collected in the corners.

Figure 46: The Father. His virility is denoted by the overflowing fountain. In the background are the *Chaiot*, the Holy Living Creatures, and the *Mazlot*, or sphere of the fixed stars and Zodiac.

21

Keter & En Sof

Meaning	Crown
Number	1
Colour	Brilliant white
Briatic Correspondence	Unity
Magical Image	A bearded man seen in profile.
Titles	*Atik Yomin*, the Ancient of Days; *Arikh Anpin*, Long-Suffering; the Greater Countenance (Macroprosopus); the White Head; Concealed of the Concealed; Existence of Existences; the Smooth Point; *Rum Maalah*, the Highest Point, and many more
Element	-
Virtue	Attainment
Vice	-
Illusion	Attainment
Klippot	Futility
Obligation	-
Command	-
God Name	*Eheieh*
Archangel	*Metatron*
Angel Order	*Chaiot ha Kodesh*
Planet	*Rashit ha Gilgalim* (the first swirlings, the Big Bang)
Spiritual Experience	Union with God
Keywords	Unity, union, all, Will, God, the Godhead, manifestation, emanation, point

Table 14: *Keter*

Keter & En Sof

God is the great urge that has not yet found a body
but urges towards incarnation with the great creative urge.
D. H. Lawrence

Keter is conceived as the first crystallization within the limitlessness of the *En Sof*. It is a crystallization so remote from our human cognitive capacity that it is often described as completely hidden and unknown. It is for this reason that "In the beginning" (*bereshit*) of *Genesis* is usually associated with *Chokhmah*. Sometimes *Keter* is depicted as a human head in profile so that the left side is hidden.

The *En Sof* (limitless) is an epistemological boundary. *En Sof* is not an object of knowledge. It is beyond thought, imagination, or feeling. We can depict it only in negative terms; any definition would limit it, and so we are forced to deny the validity of definition.

It is legitimate to question whether *En Sof* is an artifact of language and cognition, generated by taking any concept and sticking 'not' in front of it. One finds a similar approach in Vedanta, where *neti neti* - 'not this, not that' - is a negative characterisation of *Brahman*, which, like *En Sof*, is the ground of all appearance and becoming.

If *Keter* is the first intimation of finiteness, of appearance and becoming, set against the limitlessness of *En Sof*, it is also legitimate to ask whether appearance and becoming *require* a setting. Why cannot appearance and becoming be self-supporting and self-contained? Must we imagine them in the foreground, set against an incomprehensible background? The answer is no - we do not require this assumption, but the alternatives are no easier to digest.

There is a well-known story, based on oriental traditions, that the world is supported by four elephants standing on the back of a turtle. When an elderly lady was asked what the turtle stood on, she replied, "another turtle". And when asked again what *that* turtle stood on, her answer was "it's turtles all the way down sonny ...".

This answer is an example of infinite regress. A boundary condition is avoided by repeating the same elements an infinite number of times.

As an alternative to infinite regress, the lady could have answered "the turtle stands on the ground" and then ducked all further questions by saying "we cannot comprehend the unknowable nature of the ground".

A third way to answer would be to state that after a finite number of turtles, a turtle stood on the world. This circularity looks like cheating - if the world is supported by turtles, how can the turtles stand on the world? This is an example of self-reference[147].

These three positions - infinite regress, incomprehensible ground, and self-reference - occur time and again in philosophy and theology. The first avoids explanation by pushing the boundary off to infinity - this looks like evasion. The second denies explanation by introducing an inexplicable ground - this seems mysterious. The third explanation - self-reference - is intriguing because there is no *a priori* point of reference that explains the rest. An ideal science would aspire to this model of explanation, because it requires no external 'givens', no *a priori* assumptions. However, self-referential models are difficult to construct, being prone to paradoxes[148].

It is with this in mind that we return to Kabbalah. Kabbalah posits a beginning and it anchors the beginning on an incomprehensible ground. However, and most surprisingly, it also includes self-reference, based on an interpretation of a text in the *Sefer Yetzirah* that "their end is in their beginning, and their beginning in their end". This unity is centreless; the explanation of every part lies in the whole, and the explanation of the whole lies in every part. This can be difficult to understand, especially if one is accustomed to the linear, top-to-bottom representation of the Tree of Life - see Figure 8 for an explanation.

Keter means 'Crown'. A story that dates from the Merkavah period in late antiquity tells that the prayers of Israel ascend to Heaven where they are woven into a crown by the mighty archangel *Sandalphon*, and the crown ascends by itself onto the brow of the hidden figure on the throne[149]. This story illustrates a core idea in Kabbalah, that of "run and return", of circulation, in the same way that the lungs breath out and then breath in again[150], or blood flows from the heart to the extremities and back again. The universe is emanated, but the flow does not stop in *Malkhut*. It is the community of conscious beings in *Malkhut* who return the flow back to its source through their immediate awareness of the unity of all being. Hence the *Shema* - "Hear, O Israel: the Lord is our God, the Lord is One".

Keter is usually associated with Will (*r'tzon*), a strange and difficult

---

147. The Escher ascending staircases exhibit this circularity.
148. For example, Russell's Paradox in set theory.
149. *Keter, the Crown of God in Early Jewish Mysticism*, Arthur Green, Princeton University Press 1997
150. This derives from Ezekiel's vision of the Throne-Chariot via the *Sefer Yetzirah*, where "run and return" is stressed.

concept defined as "the faculty by which a person decides on and initiates action"[151]. It is closely allied to the concept of freedom; without freedom there can be no decision or choice, and hence will is reduced to deterministic mechanism. Part of the duality between *Keter* and *Malkhut* is the duality of freedom (*Keter*) and determination (*Malkhut*), a duality that is likewise mirrored by *Chokhmah* and *Binah*, and the right and left pillars of the Tree. In his commentary to the *Zohar*, Isaiah Tishby observes[152]:

> The first *sefira* is the primordial divine Will, the "Will of wills", the source of all volitional impulses, the power of the initial awakening within the Godhead. This inapprehensible will "that cannot ever be known or grasped, the most recondite head in the world above", is not directed towards any specific object. It is will in general without any separate, defined components - pure will, which acts on itself, and has no reference to the world outside itself.

Will and expressive freedom are spooky concepts. They do not belong in a world of mechanistic causality, where (by definition) one is able to explain how one thing causes another. They are *fundamentally spooky*; they cannot be reduced to an explanation. The spookiness of *Keter* is a difficult idea to communicate. At best one can attempt an analogy in the hope that it might provide an intuition. One such analogy can be found in the difference between a labyrinth and a maze.

Although a labyrinth and a maze may look superficially similar, a labyrinth offers no choice of path, whereas a maze offers both choice and multiple paths. In technical terms, a labyrinth is *unicursal*, whereas a maze is *multicursal*. A free agent can become lost in a maze, but not a labyrinth[153]. No matter how convoluted and infolded the path, a labyrinth can be untangled into a straight path. A maze cannot, and will contain branches, loops and dead ends.

A labyrinth, considered abstractly, is closed. It offers no choices. Similarly, a maze is open. It offers choices and multiple routes. A finite maze offers only a finite number of choices, and so one could also consider a finite maze to be closed - given sufficient time one can exhaust all the possibilities of a finite maze and become bored. An infinite maze, on the other hand, would offer infinite choices; one

---

151. OED.
152. *The Wisdom of the Zohar*, Isaiah Tishby, Vol. 1, Oxford University Press 1991
153. A non-free agent cannot become 'lost' in a maze - given identical starting conditions it must follow the same path each time. One could doubtless spend many unproductive hours debating what it means to set a clockwork rat 'free' in a maze, given that it is either constructed to find the centre (e.g. by wall-following) or it is not.

could imagine a fractal maze something like the Mandlebrot Set, both bounded and infinite in variety.

We could choose to model our universe as a labyrinth or a maze. It might be *closed*, offering no choices (this is *causal determinism* as articulated by Laplace) or it may be *open*, and contain a spooky element of freedom that cannot be reduced or explained[154]. A closed universe would be 'pure *Malkhut*', completely determined. An open universe would be 'pure *Keter*', free and undetermined.

One of the major issues of ancient theology and philosophy was the difficulty in reconciling something that was purely open (God) with something that was purely closed (Matter), an opposition that was never resolved with any clarity in Neoplatonism. Kabbalists also struggled with the issue. How can *Keter* 'contain' *Malkhut* and yet be completely open?

The material world as we understand it at the present time is like a labyrinth. We can determine with considerable precision how a physical system will behave over time. There is a path, and the world follows it without veering off or making choices. At the level of sub-atomic particles there are hints of spookiness, of a fundamental non-determinism, but we do not experience this in everyday life. It is difficult for us, immersed in a world that is closed and determined, to grasp the nature of *Keter*.

> **Symmetry Breaking**
>
> Modern physics also encounters difficulties in explaining how the simple can become complex. An example is a pencil balanced on its tip on a table top. It can fall in any direction (symmetric), but once the pencil falls it reduces the symmetry because it defines a direction.
>
> Symmetry breaking is now a core idea in modern physics, and it is useful to the kabbalist because it provides a conceptual framework for understanding how the simple 'conceals' the complex - for example, we could say that *Malkhut* is a 'reduced symmetry' of *Keter*.

Keter is the raw will to *be something*, where that *something* is concealed and indeterminate. With *Keter* we do not find a division into subject and object, a division that manifests with *Chokhmah* and *Binah*. *Malkhut* is concealed within *Keter* but *Keter* is still entirely *Keter* (see *Symmetry Breaking* above for an illustration of how Keter 'falls' into duality).

What we witness with our senses is *Malkhut*, and yet *Keter* lies

---

154. This is how things look according to quantum mechanics at the level of sub-atomic particles.

within it, *pushing it* into being. We cannot grasp this vast expressive urge because each one of us *wills-to-be* in a way that is bounded and self-centred, and parochial. It difficult to comprehend a will that not only *wills-to-be* each one of us, but also *wills-to-be* everything to which we are antithetical. *Keter wills-to-be* with a joyful lack of discrimination[155]. This is akin to the classical idea of *plenitude*, which means that anything that is logically possible will eventually come-to-be; there is a 'flowing-into' that, like a rising tide, fills every channel of possibility.

This is a radically different view of the divine when compared with popular or commonplace views of a god capable of personal relationships, and possessing attributes or qualities. It is Lawrence's "great urge that has not yet found a body".

Keter corresponds to *Arikh Anpin*, or "long face", a title that denotes patience, as opposed to *Ze'ir Anpin* or "short face", a title that denotes impatience and the fluctuating qualities of *Chesed* and *Din*. *Arikh Anpin* is remote and concealed, a conception of God for mystics and philosophers.

The name associated with *Keter* is *Eheyeh* or *Eheieh*. When Moses asked God for a name (*Exodus* 3:14) he was given *Eheieh Asher Eheieh*, usually translated "I am that I am". *Eheieh* is perhaps more accurately translated as "I will be". It is less a name than an assertion of existence without qualification, attributes or limitation, a transition from an eternal, unchanging state into a self-expression that is hinted at by the sense of becoming: "I will be".

In his discussion of *Eheieh*, Gikatilla emphasises that it manifests pure *Chesed*. In his view, *Din* enters our lives as a consequence of "sins and transgressions", which arouse a current of harsh judgement and anger. He believed that the prayers of a sufficiently righteous man could rise to the level of *Eheieh* and annul all harsh judgements, either against the individual or the community, by stimulating a flow of pure mercy. This is a strange and profoundly theurgic view. One could attribute his outlook to a quasi-mechanistic view of the middle worlds where *Din* and *Chesed* operate ... or perhaps think of it more in the nature of an appeal to a higher court (although the quasi-mechanistic view is perhaps the better interpretation)[156].

My view is both similar and different. The middle worlds are

---

155. Discrimination being the virtue of *Malkhut*.
156. *The Gates of Light*, Avi Weinstein, Harper Collins 1994

The Hermetic Kabbalah

indeed the realm of *Chesed* and *Din* because the duality of subjective consciousness will always interpret experience (seen as external and objective) in positive and negative terms. It may interpret positive experiences as a reward, and negative experiences as a punishment. Gikatilla is asserting the existence of an expanded level of awareness (*Keter*) in which *all* manifestations are viewed positively. This expanded level of awareness is not biased towards the experiences of one single person, and is not dual. In this sense it is pure *Chesed*.

The Archangel associated with *Keter* is *Metatron*[157], sometimes called "the Prince of the Countenance" or the "Prince of the World". There is a large literature and mythology surrounding *Metatron*, too much to recount here, as it comes from very old sources, and interpreting and reconciling the many views is a challenge in itself[158]. The lore is ancient, and there is no *coherent* account. Three traditions stand out however.

The first is that when the ancient sage Enoch[159] was taken up into Heaven, he became the archangel *Metatron*. The second is that *Metatron* is a demiurgic divine proxy sometimes referred to as "the lesser YHVH". This would appear to be a confused recollection of older traditions (now fragmentary) concerning an angel *Jahoel*, who did appear to exercise the executive power of God. This tradition caused unease; it was very close to heresy. The third tradition concerns a substantial identity between *Metatron* and *Sandalphon*. Both angels are described as vast, reaching from earth to heaven. Both are associated with the transmission of prayer. Both have odd names ending in '-on'. Sometimes they are depicted as twins or duals. This idea fits neatly with the dual relationship between *Keter* and *Malkhut*.

The angels associated with *Keter* are the *Chaiot ha Kodesh*, the Holy Living Creatures. They derive from possibly the most important source text in Kabbalah, the vision of *Ezekiel*, where *Ezekiel* has a vision of the divine throne-chariot (*Merkavah*):

> And I looked, and, behold, a whirlwind came out of the north, a great cloud, and a fire infolding itself, and a brightness was about it, and out of the midst thereof as the colour of amber, out of the midst of the fire. Also out of the midst thereof came the likeness of four living creatures. And this was their appearance; they had the likeness of a man. And

---

157. Early sources have two *tets*, hence *Metattron*. The origin of the name is unclear.
158. See for example the essay 'Metatron', in *Kabbalah*, Gershom Scholem, Dorset Press, 1987
159. If Enoch is identified with *Idris* from the *Koran* then he is substantially the same as the Graeco-Egyptian Hermes Trimegistus

every one had four faces, and every one had four wings. And their feet were straight feet; and the sole of their feet was like the sole of a calf's foot: and they sparkled like the colour of burnished brass. And they had the hands of a man under their wings on their four sides; and they four had their faces and their wings. Their wings were joined one to another; they turned not when they went; they went every one straight forward.

As for the likeness of their faces, they four had the face of a man, and the face of a lion, on the right side: and they four had the face of an ox on the left side; they four also had the face of an eagle. Thus were their faces: and their wings were stretched upward; two wings of every one were joined one to another, and two covered their bodies. And they went every one straight forward: whither the spirit was to go, they went; and they turned not when they went.

As for the likeness of the living creatures, their appearance was like burning coals of fire, and like the appearance of lamps: it went up and down among the living creatures; and the fire was bright, and out of the fire went forth lightning. And the living creatures ran and returned as the appearance of a flash of lightning.

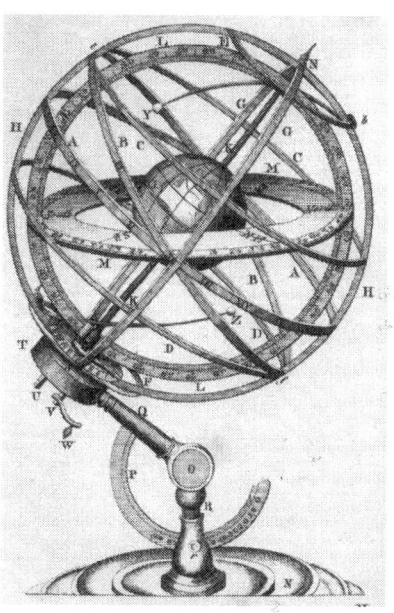

Figure 47: An armillary sphere, showing 'wheels-within-wheels'.

The vision continues with a description of mysterious "wheels within wheels", which some have interpreted as castor-like wheels for the *Merkavah* itself, somewhat in the manner of an office chair. Elements of this vision were incorporated into the foundational literature of the Kabbalah - the *Sefer Yetzirah* and the *Hekhalot* and *Merkavah* literature from Palestine and Babylonia, a literature that was transported into Europe and interpreted many hundreds of years later in the Middle Ages. It is not often noted, but the final book of the *New Testament*, the profoundly influential *Revelation* of John, contains many references to this literature:

And out of the throne proceeded lightnings and thunderings and voices: and there were seven lamps of fire burning before the throne, which are the seven Spirits of God. And before the throne there was a sea of glass like unto crystal: and in the midst of the throne, and round about the throne, were four beasts full of eyes before and behind. And the first beast was like a lion, and the second beast like a calf, and the third beast had a face as a man, and the fourth beast was like a flying eagle. And the four beasts had each of them six wings about him; and they were full of eyes within: and they rest not day and night, saying, Holy, holy, holy, Lord God Almighty, which was, and is, and is to come.

An interesting reference that connects this passage to the Jewish mystical tradition is not only the presence of the Holy Living Creatures, but also the "sea of glass like unto crystal" surrounding the divine throne. In the *Talmud* the famous mystic R. Akiva warns his fellows on the mystical ascent: "When you come to the place of pure marble stones, do not say, 'Water! Water!' for it is said, 'He who speaks untruths shall not stand before My eyes'". The mysterious substance surrounding the throne, so resembling water, is *chasmal*, a word that is now the Hebrew word for electricity. I like to imagine the sea of *chasmal* around the divine throne to be a rippling plasma similar to the aurora borealis.

The Holy Living Creatures and the interlinked wheels-within-wheels are strongly suggestive of Babylonian astronomy. The wheels are those of the celestial spheres viewed from the surface of the planet, in particular the projection of the Earth's equator, and the projection of the plane of the Earth's orbit, the ecliptic.

Taking this idea further, one can then interpret the Holy Creatures as the four fixed signs of the Zodiac: Aquarius, Taurus, Leo and Scorpio. The author of *Revelation* goes around the Zodiacal disc in a clockwise direction beginning with Leo, hence lion, ox, man and eagle. The origins of the identity of Scorpio with Eagle would appear to be lost in time.

With this interpretation the Holy Living Creatures represent the entire cosmos, supporting the figure of God on his throne at the centre.

In summary, *Keter* is spooky. It is free and inexplicable. It unfolds continuously into everything but is itself nothing - or at least nothing we can conceptualise or explain. It loves and sustains everything equally - even things we can't abide.

Keter contains the eventual possibility of *Malkhut*, which is unyielding and fixed. *Malkhut* is *Keter* when it has found a body.

22

Da'at

The Hermetic Kabbalah

Meaning	Knowledge
Archangel	The *Chaiot ha Kodesh*, the Four *Zoas*
Correspondences	*Da'at* does not manifest positively and it is not appropriate to think of it in the same sense as a *sefira*
Celestial	Sirius, *Sothis*, the Dog Star
Keywords	Hole, tunnel, gateway, doorway, Janus, black hole, vortex, prism. A condemned cell, the Empty Room.

Table 15 : *Da'at*

At the still point of the turning world. Neither flesh nor fleshless;
Neither from nor towards; at the still point, there the dance is,
But neither arrest nor movement. And do not call it fixity,
Where past and future are gathered. Neither movement from nor towards,
Neither ascent nor decline. Except for the point, the still point,
There would be no dance, and there is only the dance.

Four Quartets, T. S. Eliot

Da'at means 'knowledge'. Although *Da'at* is often shown on modern representations of the Tree of Life, it is not interpreted as a *sefira*. Some Chassidic traditions use *Da'at* as a proxy for *Keter*, as described previously, and in this case it *is* treated as one of the ten *sefira*, and replaces *Keter*, which is concealed in the *En Sof*.

Da'at forms a triad with *Chokhmah* and *Binah* - Wisdom, Understanding, and Knowledge - and is interpreted as the son (*ben*) of *Chokhmah* and *Binah*. The spelling of *Binah* - BYNH - shows that it is composed of *Yod*, *He* (the letters of the Father and Mother in the Tetragrammaton), and *BN* (*ben*), the son. *Da'at* is like the foetal stage of a child while still in the womb of *Binah*, before becoming manifest as *vav*, the Microprosopus, *Tiferet*.

There is a sexual connotation to *Da'at*. When the book of *Genesis* (4:1) states *ve ha Adam yada et-Chava ishtoo* - "And Adam knew his wife Eve" - the verb 'knew' (*yada*) is derived from the same root as *da'at*. Following this clue we can say that *Chokhmah* (the Father) 'knows' *Binah* (the Mother) - that is, 'knowledge' is synonymous with sexual union. Just as *Ze'ir Anpin* and *Nukva* are united in *Yesod*, so

Da'at

the Father (*Yod*) and Mother (*He*) are united in *Da'at*. An inspection of the symmetry of the Tree of Life (especially the Extended Tree - see Figure 22) reinforces the view that *Da'at* and *Yesod* are duals - *Da'at* in one world is *Yesod* in the next, and vice-versa. One can imagine them like wormholes connecting the worlds. This is shown in Figure 42.

Although *Da'at* is not a *sefira* it provides a place-holder for an intricate web of ideas. *Da'at* sits at the highest point of the microcosm, on the boundary between the interior and the exterior, just as *Yesod* does on the other side of *Tiferet* (see Figure 48). Like *Yesod* (*El Chai* - Living God) it marks the boundary between life and not-life, but in a more fundamental way.

In the *Timaeus* Plato lists the three irreducible characteristics of reality as space, becoming, and being. The *Sefer Yetzirah*, influenced by Hellenism, also frames reality in terms of space, time and being. It uses three dimensions of space (symbolised by the six sides of a cube), one dimension of time (symbolised by the movements of the sun, moon, stars and planets), and a dimension of being, which is the moral dimension of freedom (being able to choose between good and evil). These five dimensions - three of space, one of time, one of good and evil, correspond to ten 'depths' and to ten *sefirot* [160].

> Ten *Sefirot* of Nothingness: Their measure is ten which have no end. A depth of beginning, a depth of end; a depth of good, a depth of evil; a depth of above, a depth below; a depth east, a depth west; a depth north, a depth south.

In antiquity space, time and being were represented by a sphere. The interior of the sphere was space; the rotation of the sphere was time; and the axis of the sphere, T. S. Eliot's "still point of the turning world", represented being. The still point of the axis was the intersection of the infinite and spiritual with the transient and contingent.

This beautiful metaphor was inspired by the experience of looking up into the dome of the sky and feeling enclosed by the sphere of the stars. The daily rotation defined a day. The movement of the Moon defined a month. The motion of the Sun along the ecliptic through the zodiacal constellations defined the seasons and the year. The year was often represented by the *Tetramorph*, the images of a man, bull, lion and eagle - the constellations Aquarius, Taurus, Leo and Scorpio.

The axis, the Pole, the "still point", represented freedom from

---

160. The *sefirot* of the *Sefer Yetzirah* are conceptually much earlier than those of medieval Kabbalah.

The Hermetic Kabbalah

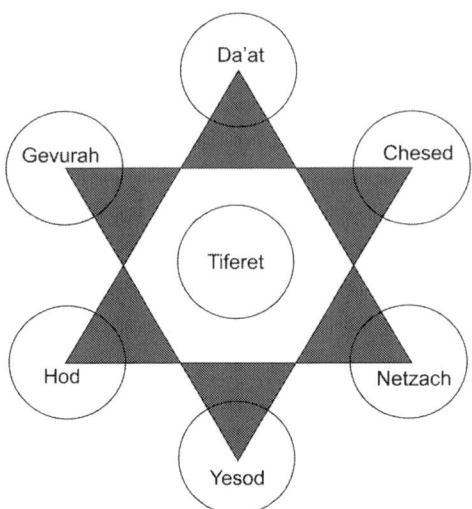

Figure 48: The Microprosopus, with *Da'at* at the 'top' and *Yesod* at the 'bottom', showing how our subjective universe is bounded by sense-perception and imagination (*Yesod*), and intellectual knowledge (*Da'at*).

Necessity, and that part of every ensouled being that comes from outside of the domain of Necessity. In the *Sefer Yetzirah* this axis is described as *Teli*. The axis, the *Teli*, the Pole, can be identified with *Da'at*. *Da'at* is the still point of the turning world.

Necessity is a term used in philosophy to describe the orderly progression of cause and effect. If a [*state-of-affairs A being true at time a*] necessarily implies the [*state-of-affairs B being true at time b*], then whenever we have A, we know that B must occur. This kind of necessity can be observed in physical processes. If I turn the winding handle then the bucket will rise out of the well. If I drop a stone it will hit the ground. An arrow, fired horizontally, will hit the ground at exactly the same time as the stone. The earth will continue to turn, the sun will continue to shine, and night will follow day.

There are other kinds of necessity, such as the biological necessities of water, food, defecation, urination, and sleep. We also experience the inner compulsions of our animal nature such as the sexual urge, jealousy, and the urge to compete and win. We can ignore these to a degree, but there are limits.

Because we are a social species and because we are capable of breeding prolifically, we have to find ways of living together. There are

Da'at

Figure 49: The *Yod* of the Father fertilises the womb of *Binah* to produce *ben*, the Son. The *Yod* grows into *Vav* (=6), *Ze'ir Anpin*, the six *sefirot* surrounding and including *Tiferet*. *Vav* exists within space and time, denoted by the circle and the four *Chaiot*, which mark the four quadrants of the Earth's orbit around the sun, and so represent the elements, the seasons and the year.

social and economic necessities, such as wearing particular styles of clothing, and having employment to pay for biological necessities. We have to stop at red lights, not lose our temper in public, pay taxes, and take turns to buy a round at a bar. There are rules for every occasion, and we can duck some of them, but there is usually a price to be paid. Even when we are outside of the public sphere, we are not free. There are personal morals that restrain us when no other factor holds us back.

Our freedom is limited at every level - physical, biological, animal, social, economic and moral. Philosophers in late antiquity used the term *heimarmene* to describe the necessities of the world-machine. This term encompassed not only cause and effect, but fate, destiny, and providence. They believed human beings lived in a turning world that was created, defined, limited and governed by external powers. They believed the animal soul was a creature of Necessity and the rational soul a creature of the divine, and the two were fastened together by some holy (or unholy) glue. The great ruling powers (*archons*) of Necessity lived in the sky and were visible as the stars, the planets, and the Sun and the Moon. A relic of these beliefs survives in the astrology pages of newspapers and magazines.

If the universe is created, defined, limited and governed by superior beings, then why is it a "vale of tears"? Plotinus, following Plato, argued that goodness permeates the Cosmos - it may become attenuated, but it does not vanish. Contemporaries of Plotinus (and even some of his students) were influenced by beliefs in which the powers of Necessity were *not good*. Plotinus picked up his stylus and wrote an essay *Against the Gnostics* that still survives.

The beliefs that irritated Plotinus were many and varied. Some arose from Jewish heresies that may have been influenced by dualist Zoroastrian beliefs of the adjacent Persian Empire. Some came from sectarian variants of a still-nascent Christianity. Others resembled a syncretic Hellenist philosophy, like Platonism turned on its head (e.g. some Hermetic texts), and it is for these that Plotinus reserved his special scorn. The modern term for these beliefs *gnostic*, after the Greek word *gnosis*, knowledge.

Although the word *gnosis* has a common technical usage in Platonic literature, the specific meaning of *gnosis* in gnostic literature is substantially similar to the word *da'at* in Kabbalah. *Gnosis* and *da'at* signify something special - not just any kind of knowledge, a special kind of knowledge. This knowledge is more in the nature of an illumination of the soul. Adam and Eve ate from the Tree of Knowledge and

Da'at

Figure 50: William Blake wrote:
"Four Mighty Ones are in every Man: a perfect Unity
Cannot exist but from the Universal Brotherhood of Eden,
The Universal Man, to Whom be glory evermore Amen.
What are the Natures of those Living Creatures the Heavenly Father only
Knoweth: no Individual knoweth, nor can know in all Eternity."

Blake called the 'four mighty ones' the Four *Zoas*, and they feature in several of his epic poems. They are identical with the four 'living creatures' that surround the divine throne as described in the vision of Ezekiel - indeed, *'Zoas'* and *'Chaiot'* derive from the respective Greek and Hebrew roots for 'life'. With characteristic intuition Blake places the *Zoas* on the boundary of human knowledge - they represent the *a priori* fragmentation of divine unity, and reflect the ancient tradition that the world of Necessity is bounded by space and time, represented by the signs of Aquarius (human), Taurus (bull), Leo (lion) and Scorpio (eagle). The axis or *Teli* represents unity and is cognate with *Da'at*.

saw that they were naked. They had been unconscious of their condition, and they became self-aware. They were cast out into the realm of Necessity and forgot themselves again.

We know very little about the people who were gnostics in late antiquity, and the manuscripts that have survived are often fragmentary, and filled with obscure terms whose meaning has been lost. The cosmogonies are rich and strange and some have similarities to Kabbalah, with progressive emanations of powers organised as pairs and triads. What we do know is that they wanted to be free of the domain of Necessity.

There is a duality between knowledge and ignorance. The gnostic believes the human soul incarnates into ignorance of its true nature and must be awakened with knowledge. In many gnostic systems it is Jesus who is the Emissary of Light, bringing secret knowledge to free the souls of those who wish to be freed. In some texts, like the *Pistis Sophia* and the *Books of Jeu*, the secret knowledge is magical - signs, seals, ritual formulae, secret names.

There is also another side to knowledge: knowledge has two faces. One face, that of the gnostic, looks out of this world and sees freedom; the other face looks into this world and sees Necessity. The implicit knowledge of necessity is what makes life possible. The human *ovum* is a bag of chemicals that *knows* how to make a child. Knowledge is dual with ignorance, but it is also the foundation to life.

This implicit knowledge is embedded in structure and processes. Life is a collection of physical processes that extract energy from the environment and drive chemical equilibria in the direction of complexity and structure. Part of that complexity and structure is the embedded knowledge coded into genes. There is a self-perpetuating circularity whereby the knowledge creates the processes and the processes recreate the knowledge. We can watch it happening through a microscope - we call it *mitosis*, or cell division.

Something similar happens at a higher level in multi-cellular organisms. Every organism, from a jellyfish to an elephant, needs to know how to survive in its environment. It has to survive long enough to reproduce. Any break in the transmission of knowledge, or a break in the processes that sustain it, and the organism or species or society will die. We possess abundant evidence that this can happen - many important species in the fossil record are now extinct. Many cultures are now little more than grave goods and bones. Life itself has survived planet-wide calamities, but it is fragile. We always stand on the brink of some event - war, disease, volcanos, comets - that will throw a

Da'at

spanner in the works.

This domain of the "spanner in the works" is the domain of *Samael*, the Poison of God. A poison is any substance that cripples a process, literally like a 'spanner in the works'. Poisons, because they can target key processes, can be astonishingly potent. This potency makes poisons peculiarly threatening and scary, a fear reflected in phobias concerning spiders, snakes, wasps, jellyfish and so on. If life is knowledge, then poisons are a different kind of knowledge, the knowledge of how to cripple or terminate life. Poisons are anti-life.

Samael is an important personification in Kabbalah. He is normally attributed to *Gevurah*, but he is also the personification of the 'other side' (*sitra achra*), the domain of parasitic unlife (the *klippot*) that exists because unbalanced energy 'spills' from the Tree of Life and provides nourishment. The *klippot* resemble fungus growing in the roots of the Tree.

According to tradition the 'other side' receives nourishment when we do evil. Kabbalah contains the core idea that life, the *entirety* of life as represented by the Tree of Life, is a collection of processes that could work harmoniously. This is represented metaphorically by channels flowing with water. There is a reciprocal relationship between *Keter* and *Malkhut* and an harmonious balance represented by *Tiferet*, and when the channels are clear all of creation is watered. The 'spanner in the works' is free-will, the ability to act for the self-alone, and it is this potential for self-isolation (individually or collectively) that leads to channels breaking, so that the water of life runs into the abyss to sustain the *klippot*.

Da'at represents an epistemological boundary, a transition from ignorance into knowledge, from freedom into necessity, from one state of being into another. It often appears in vision as a gate, door, portal or mysterious opening of some kind. Its magical symbol is that of *Janus*, the Roman god of portals. Because of its dual relationship with *Yesod* (that is, life *is* knowledge) its magical implement is also a mirror, but it is a black mirror[161]. In the film *2001 A Space Odyssey* a black monolith triggers evolutionary changes in the human race. The black monolith in orbit around Jupiter provides a portal to a new kind of being, represented by a star-child. This kind of imagery is characteristic of the archetypal content associated with *Da'at*.

The explanation or clarification of *Da'at* as a cognitive transition symbolised by a mysterious portal is one of the most interesting mod-

---

161. The 'speculum that does not shine' is also a symbol of *Malkhut*.

ern developments in Kabbalah. Within the last hundred years the view has arisen, almost entirely within the Hermetic tradition, that if the Tree of Life with its *sefirot* is the 'foreground' of being and existence, then *Da'at* must be a part of the 'background'. With this thought in mind *Da'at* becomes a kind of 'anti-*sefirot*', almost the opposite of an emanation (if such a idea makes sense).

According to ancient tradition the Tree of Life is set against the Great Abyss of the primordial creation, and in the modern view *Da'at* becomes a part of that background, a visible token on the Tree of an Abyss lurking in the background. It is like an orange safety barrier around a hole in the pavement. It suggests that one must pass cautiously or one might 'fall in'.

The Tree of Life diagram has no path following the lightning flash ascent from *Chesed* to *Binah*; logic would suggest that there must be a path, but there is no path, and so this off-piste transition was titled 'crossing the Abyss'. The phrase is usually attributed to Aleister Crowley, but it is likely he found the term in use when he was a member of the Golden Dawn.

The notion of 'crossing the Abyss' has antecedents that long pre-dated the Golden Dawn, the most obvious being the gnostic ascent of the soul through the spheres of the planets to the boundary of the cosmos, and the final transition to the realm of light. Some gnostic scriptures state that the daemonic *archons* bound a 'counterfeiting spirit' to the divine soul, a kind of evil twin, a creature of Necessity that was entirely attached to the material world. Today we would call it the Ego. It followed that as part of the ascent the gnostic must encounter and do battle with this counterfeiting spirit, in the manner of *Michael* versus the Dragon. In his 1842 novel *Zanoni*, Edward Bulwer-Lytton used a variant of this idea and the counterfeiting spirit appeared in the form of 'The Guardian of the Threshold'. A character in the novel states:

> "...Know, at least, that all of us – the highest and the wisest – who have, in sober truth, passed beyond the threshold, have had, as our first fearful task, to master and subdue its grisly and appalling guardian"

From *Zanoni*, the 'Guardian of the Threshold' found its way into late-Victorian Theosophical circles and would have been familiar to members of the Golden Dawn, and Crowley in particular. It is the case that Crowley framed the experience of 'crossing the Abyss' as an encounter with a daemonic entity he called *Choronzon*[162]. It is worth examining this encounter in detail because his picturesque description has been influential.

Da'at

The encounter took place in 1909 in the Algerian desert near Bou Saada in the company of his student and sexual partner Victor Neuburg. Crowley had been ascending the thirty 'Aethyrs' (a part of the angelic magic of Dr. John Dee and Edward Kelly) in a series of meditations that combined elements of Enochian magic with Golden Dawn Kabbalah. Crowley would perform an appropriate summoning and Neuburg acted as scribe, recording Crowley's visions. The record was published as *Liber 418: The Vision and the Voice*.

The Aethyrs form an ascending ladder from the thirtieth to the first, and although they can be placed in an approximate correspondence with *sefirot* and paths, this correspondence is not exact:

> But I reveal unto thee a mystery of the Aethyrs, that not only are they bound up with the sefirot, but also with the Paths. Now, the plane of the Aethyrs interpenetrateth and surroundeth the universe wherein the sefirot are established, and therefore is the order of the Aethyrs not the order of the Tree of Life. And only in a few places do they coincide[163].

Nevertheless, the intensely syncretic symbolism of Crowley's visions contain many overlaps with Kabbalah, and one obtains the clear sense that he is ascending the Tree of Life. If one takes three Aethyrs per *sefira* then the meditations consistent with *Chesed* would be those of the 12th, 11th and 10th Aethyrs, and this is what one finds.

The 11th. Aethyr provides the view out over the Abyss. There are vast legions of angels clad in brilliant armour, towers and battlements, and dire weapons to guard against the terrible desolation of the Abyss:

> Behold, a mighty guard against the terror of things, the fastness of the Most High, the legions of eternal vigilance; these are they that keep watch and ward day and night throughout the aeons. Set in them is all force of the Mighty One, yet there stirreth not one plume of the wings of their helmets. Behold, the foundation of the Holy City, the towers and the bastions thereof! Behold the armies of light that are set against the outermost Abyss, against the horror of emptiness, and the malice of *Choronzon*.

The encounter with Abyss and *Choronzon* took place in the 10th. Aethyr. Crowley decided the Scribe (Neuburg) required special protection and constructed the encounter in the manner of an evocation

---

162. *Choronzon* appears in the angelic transcripts of John Dee and Edward Kelly, and would appear from this context to be the same as *Samael* of Jewish tradition.
163. *The Vision and the Voice*, 12th. Aethyr.

of an evil spirit, using ritual elements from grimoires such as the *Key of Solomon*. The daemon was evoked into a triangle sealed with names of power, and soaked in the blood of three pigeons. Neuburg sat in a protective circle also sealed with names of power, and was armed with magical dagger. Unusually, Crowley was not in the circle.

Crowley is more than a little coy and evasive about the details of what actually took place. What he provides is not a frank account, and its ambiguities, evasions and blinds can be read in several ways, leading to arguments about 'what really happened'. There are also claims that Neuburg's original handwritten transcript was torn out of the record and the published version redacted by Crowley. Reading between the lines however there is ample evidence for the simple hypothesis that Crowley sat in the triangle and channelled *Choronzon*, and the various manifestations of *Choronzon* consisted of Crowley hamming it up in the sand dunes.

The bulk of the transcript describes a classic temptation, in which *Choronzon* mocks, threatens, flatters, seduces and variously attempts to trick Neuburg into opening the circle. Neuburg was able to thwart these attempts. When one considers that *Choronzon* is supposed to be the ultimate disorganised chaos he comes across as lucid, coherent, and literate. He quotes from Shakespeare, *Mad Tom O'Bedlam*, and gnostic scripture. He has a fine turn of phrase. He betrays none of the rambling, irrelevant, disconnected incoherence one can encounter so easily in drug users, alcoholics, the delirious, and the mentally ill. The average habitual drunk on a park bench does a better job of *Choronzon* than Crowley does.

Nonetheless, Crowley has some interesting observations to make about *Choronzon*:

> The name of the Dweller in the Abyss is *Choronzon*, but he is not really an individual. The Abyss is empty of being; it is filled with all possible forms, each equally inane, each therefore evil in the only true sense of the word – that is, meaningless but malignant, insofar as it craves to become real. These forms swirl senselessly into haphazard heaps like dust Devils, and each such chance aggregation asserts itself to be an individual and shrieks 'I am I' though aware all the time that its elements have no true bond; so that the slightest disturbance dissipates the delusion just as a horseman, meeting a dust devil, brings it in showers of sand to the Earth.[164]

These ideas are expressed again in a poem from Crowley's *The*

---

164. *The Confessions of Aleister Crowley*, ed. John Symonds & Kenneth Grant, Bantam 1971

Da'at

Book of Lies titled *Dust Devils*:
> In the Wind of the mind arises the turbulence called I.
> It breaks; down shower the barren thoughts.
> All life is choked.

The Ego has no centre or coherence. Each situation in life 'calls up' a complex of thoughts and feelings that briefly assume the mantle of 'I', before dissolving and passing-on the baton to another complex of thoughts and feelings. These are Crowley's dust devils. The 'turbulence called I' is *Choronzon*; in this sense we are all *Choronzon*, and here is an answer to the many critics who have assumed that Crowley must have been already insane to have invoked *Choronzon* in the way that he did. In his commentary to the vision Crowley adds:

> Various elements had been bound up into a "bundle" by the energy of the Call, and thus constituted a momentary unity capable of sensation and of expression. The obsessing idea of any such being, conscious that it is not a true organism, and threatened with immediate dissolution, which in its rudimentary psychology it is bound to dread, is of necessity, fear; and fear breeds pain, malice, and envy. Above all there is an insane hatred for the supposed creator because the supposed blessing of creation has been withheld from the "bundle".

The extreme dualism of Crowley's visions of the 11th. and 10th. Aethyrs - the motionless hosts of angels, with their battlements and thunderbolts on one hand; the swirling dust-devils of *Choronzon* stirring the sterile desert of the Abyss on the other - this is the 'terror of the situation' as it applies to the Ego. The Ego behaves like a god in its constructed universe - it is a gnostic demiurge - and creates almost insurmountable defences against the knowledge of its essential nature - that it is empty of being, that it is *Choronzon*. That Crowley understood this is clear:

> As soon as I had destroyed my personality, as soon as I had expelled my ego, the universe which to it was indeed a frightful and fatal force, fraught with every form of fear, was so only in relation to this idea 'I'; so long as 'I am I', all else must seem hostile. Now that there was no longer any 'I' to suffer, all these ideas which had inflicted suffering became innocent. I could praise the perfection of every part; I could wonder and worship the whole.

Although it is difficult to be enthusiastic about much of Crowley's life and behaviour, one cannot fault his insight here. He states that he crossed the Abyss before the *Choronzon* encounter (that is, reached an essential understanding about the nature of Ego), and advises in the strongest possible terms against attempting the encounter *unless one has achieved this understanding*. It is easy to see why. The Ego thrives on opposition and duality, and the more it feels threatened, the larger the bogeyman it will construct to explain its feelings and behaviour. This may explain why *Da'at* and the Abyss have developed into a kind of esoteric extreme sport, like free-climbing or base jumping or cave diving.

A major contributor to the twentieth century myth of *Da'at* was Kenneth Grant, who knew Crowley in his final days at Hastings, and who became a literary executor after his death. Crowley had done some work on the paths of the *klippot*, and published his thoughts in a terse document *Liber 231*[165]. Grant expanded on these ideas and published a book in 1977 called *Nightside of Eden*. It struck a chord.

Grant is a difficult and frustrating writer, and with each successive book he became more difficult and frustrating. His primary mode of presentation is a fire-hose of 'facts'. Each fact is presented with confidence and authority; self-doubt is absent. A small number of these facts are grounded in traditional esotericism, but the majority are validated by left-field gematria involving more statements of equally dubious validity, until a crazy house of invention is braced into a self-referential hypertext that floats magically in empty space, a linguistic exercise in painting by numbers. Even when Grant refers to objective history or third-party sources he cannot be trusted. In an excellent and amusing review the writer Alan Moore has this to say[166]:

> Each chapter an emetic gush of curdling chthonic biles and juices served up steaming, a hot shrapnel of ideas, intense and indiscriminate. A shotgun full of snails and amethysts discharged point blank into the reader's face.

The frustrating aspect of Grant is that he is can be intelligent, perceptive and discriminating. He will exit several pages of free association, hit the nail on the head with a paragraph of clarity and insight, and then resume his bog-snorkling through the left-over mud of creation. Trying to catch the authentic message of Kenneth Grant is like listening on shortwave radio to a faint voice heard through the roar of static, whistles and howls; he provides a more authentic *imitatio Chrorozonis* than Crowley ever could.

It is difficult to summarise (or comprehend) Grants ideas, but the

---

165. 231 is the number of pairs of Hebrew letters. The importance of this number derives from the *Sefer Yetzirah*.
166. *Beyond Our Ken*, Alan Moore, a review of *Against the Light: A Nightside Narrative* by Kenneth Grant (Starfire Publishing, 1997). First published in *Kaos* 14 2002.

principal purpose of *Nightside of Eden* is to provide commentary on the paths of the *klippot*, which he locates at the rear of the Tree of Life in a parallel or reflected Tree. This 'rear' is accessible by projecting one's consciousness through *Da'at* into the space beyond. Those structures analogous to the twenty-two front-side paths he names 'the Tunnels of Set'. It is as if there is an entire 'averse Tree' with 'averse *sefirot*' and 'averse paths' around the back.

Grant uses many dualistic contrasts to show that the back of the Tree is where all the action is, and in doing so reduces the 'front' of the Tree of Life to wallpaper, a *trompe l'oeil* painted over the Abyss. He fills up his Abyss with a rich selection of stuff - just about everything that is counter-cultural, spooky, threatening and horror-filmish is out there.

At this point it is worth reviewing what the Tree of Life represents. It is not just a diagram, a map, a treasure house of images, or a memory theatre. It represents a *dynamic*; a recursive 'dynamic of dynamics' that constitutes life. At every level this is what life is, an almost uncountable collection of interacting processes. Whether we focus at the level of proteins, cells, organs, organisations, societies or the entire ecology of the planet, we find processes within processes.

This is not a modern view of the Tree of Life. The focus on processes goes back its medieval beginnings, often expressed in terms of a flow and circulation of blessings into and through the worlds. The kabbalistic explanation of evil is heavily oriented around process disruption, often couched in the language of irrigation, of channels being blocked, or turned back, or overflowing into 'the Other Side' (the realm of the *klippot*). The traditional explanation is usually based around 'sin' - that is, violating the ordained divine harmony. The theurgic role of the kabbalist has always been to expedite this flow by attempting repair damage (*tikkun* - repair, healing). In keeping with this broad idea the 'virtue' correspondence of each *sefira* is an aspect that tends towards function in the personal and social sphere. The 'vice' and '*klippot*' correspondence is an aspect that tends towards dysfunction.

We could say that the Tree of Life is a representation of 'the working', and the Abyss is a representation of 'the broken'. Every divine impulse that makes it through to *Malkhut* is part of the 'working', and everything else is part of 'the broken'. Again, one can find this elaborated during the emergent phase of Kabbalah in the legends of the Destroyed Worlds and the Kings of Edom, the unstable worlds of pure *Din*. There is nothing avant-garde about the idea that the contrast between the Tree of Life and the Abyss is the contrast between 'working' and 'broken' (or dysfunctional).

The boundary between working and broken is not sharp. We are rarely completely healthy, and when we are we tend to be unconscious of it. We are conscious of being unhealthy, and there are thousands ways we can be unhealthy, some minor (like a rash), some major (like heart disease) - dysfunction is legion. In any discussion of function or dysfunction we must also consider the environment - fish survive very well in water, but not on land. Rats can live almost anywhere, gorillas almost nowhere.

There is no such thing as absolute function; a clock can run too fast, too slow, strike thirteen, or stop after twenty minutes, and it is up to me whether to keep it or throw it away. I can decide to keep it in the realm of the working, or send it to the world of the broken. In spite of defects each living thing is trying to retain its place in the world of the working, trying to find and create environments that are good for it and where it can function at its best. *Malkhut* is everything that has found a place. The Abyss is everything else.

Returning to *Nightside of Eden*, Grant has been inspired by the combat myths of ancient tradition in which the manifest universe was preceded by a pioneer phase in which reality was hacked out of primeval chaos, a chaos that still waits at the boundaries trying to find its way back in. One of the oldest original texts for this is the Babylonian creation myth, the *Enuma Elish*, which describes how Marduk waged war on the monstrous Tiamat and her kin and formed the universe out of her body. There are many similar traditions. In Greek myth the Olympian gods came to power after waging war on the Titans, who were banished to Tartarus. The Judeo-Christian tradition, as dramatised by John Milton, has Satan/Lucifer and a band of rebel angels waging war against the divine throne and being cast out of Heaven. A modern reframing that has exercised a profound influence on Grant is H. P. Lovecraft's fictional "Olde Ones" from beyond the stars, who once possessed the Earth but were banished to another dimension and seek to gain entry to this plane of existence. They will do so "when the stars are right".

For Grant the Abyss represents a part of reality that is prior to dayside existence, symbolised by the Tree of Life. He frequently uses 'phenomenal' and 'noumenal' to contrast surface and depth. He associates the front side of the Tree with surface and phenomena[167], and the reverse side with depth and noumena. He also associates the front side with Ego, and the reverse side with earlier phases of evolution -

animal or bestial phases that preceded the emergence of the linguistic neocortex. He uses *Da'at* as a portal between the front side and the reverse side, a gateway through which we sense the powers of the Outside, and a portal through which the adept can encounter the dark powers that lie behind reality.

These are ideas of extraordinary mythic power, suggesting that our cosmos is merely foam and waves on the surface of a dark sea filled with unknown shapes. He turns Kabbalah on its head, but is perhaps too B-movie or carnival-ghost-train in his attempts to rattle skeletons and brush our faces with cobwebs. It is chaotic and transgressive and (from my perspective) fun.

I began reading Grant in the early 1970s, and there is an aspect of his work which has always rung true to me. It is that the commonplace human perception of our world and our life is *too small*. When Kabbalah was conceived and elaborated the human being was the measure of all things. The core imagery in the Kabbalah is based on the human body, on marriage and sexual dynamics, and on family relationships. The ten *sefirot* are the ten fingers, five to the left, five to the right. It is *that* specific.

During the last century our understanding of our place in the universe has moved from the centre to a far distant periphery. Current theories of the Big Bang suggest that cosmic inflation would result in not one but countless bubble universes. In our universe alone there are an estimated 10^{24} stars, and the proportion with planets is likely to be around one-in-three. Not only is the probability of other life overwhelming, it may be that the process we call life is the dominant physical process everywhere, as it is on this planet.

If Kabbalah is to progress from its medieval perspective then it has to go beyond a parochial human perspective and confront a universe in which we are not the measure of all things. As one ascends towards *Da'at*, and the self-centredness of the Ego begins to assume a more modest proportion, then *Da'at* becomes the place where we can confront our smallness and insignificance in the face of reality, and knowledge really begins.

---

167. It is unlikely that most Kabbalists would used Kantian epistemological dualism in this way and characterise the Tree of Life as 'phenomenal'. The Tree of Life is normally considered to be the hidden source of reality, and Grant has turned its meaning on its head.

The Hermetic Kabbalah

23

The Paths

23.1 Introduction

According to the *Sefer Yetzirah* there are thirty two paths of wisdom: these are the ten *sefirot* and twenty-two paths. The twenty-two paths connect the *sefirot* on the Tree of Life into a symmetrical lattice or network. It is natural and intuitive to regard the *sefirot* as 'places' and the paths as 'connections' or 'transitions' between places, as if the Tree was a space-station-like structure of ten rooms and twenty-two corridors.

Whether this simple intuition is accurate is open to question. The paths could denote relationships and symmetries between *sefirot*, just as lines drawn between members of a group of people can be used to denote marriage or sexual partners, birth dates, astrological signs, food preferences, home towns or any one of a large number of potential relationships. In a possible confirmation of this view there are interpretations of the structure of the Tree which emphasise groupings of three *sefirot*, usually referred to as 'triads'. Larger-scale views of the Tree such as the Three Pillars and the two Faces also suggest that the 'paths as corridors' interpretation is not the whole story. It is an important intuition, but it is not the only way to think about the paths.

In a volume devoted to the paths[168], Gareth Knight takes the intuitive view that "while a sefira stands primarily for an objective state, a

The Hermetic Kabbalah

Path is the subjective experience one undergoes in transferring consciousness from one *sefira*, or state, to another". Dion Fortune interprets a path as the "equilibrium of the two *sefirot* it connects"[169]. Halevi[170] takes the view that as the Tree is a structure based on balance: an impulse of imbalance causes changes to propagate throughout the Tree, and the paths describe how imbalances are propagated and equilibrated, according to a process of thesis, antithesis, and synthesis. In his commentary on the *Sefer Yetzirah*[171], Kaplan comments that early Kabbalists viewed the thirty two paths as different states of consciousness. All of these views on the nature of the paths contain useful insights.

It is difficult to discuss the twenty two paths without referencing the *Sefer Yetzirah*, because it is from the few enigmatic chapters of the *Yetzirah* that much of the material associated with the paths is drawn:

Ten Sefirot of Nothingness
And 22 Foundation Letters:
Three Mothers,
Seven Doubles
And Twelve Elementals.

It was the *Yetzirah* which established the twenty two paths as the twenty two letters of the Hebrew alphabet; it was the *Yetzirah* which grouped the letters into three, seven and twelve (like the paths on the Tree); and it was the *Yetzirah* which established a large number of correspondences traditionally associated with the paths.

The primary association of each path on the Tree of Life is a letter from the Hebrew alphabet, and from the correspondences given in the *Yetzirah* a host of further correspondences follow. For this reason the study of the traditional correspondences for the paths begins with the Hebrew alphabet.

23.2 The Letters

The Hebrew alphabet is composed of twenty-two letters. Many Kabbalists believed (and still believe) that these letters are the instruments used by God to create the world. They are innately sacred and contain within them all the mysteries of creation.

---

168. *A Practical Guide to Qabalistic Symbolism*, Gareth Knight, Helios 1972
169. *The Mystical Qabalah*, Dion Fortune, Ernest Benn 1979
170. *Adam and the Kabbalistic Tree*, Z'ev ben Shimon Halevi, Rider 1974
171. *The Sepher Yetzirah*, Aryeh Kaplan, Weiser 1991

The Paths

According to *Aggadah*, the *Torah* pre-dated the creation of heaven and earth and formed a blueprint, written in letters of black fire on white fire. In the *Zohar* there is a story told of how the letters of the Hebrew alphabet individually petitioned God for the privilege of being the first letter in the *Torah* (the honour went to the letter *Beth*). The mysterious and holy names of God, which represent the manifestations of God in the Creation, can be expressed directly with this primordial script. To Kabbalists the letters glow with life and meaning, dancing in patterns, combining and recombining to spell out the secrets of the hidden realm of the divine.

Devout Jews believe in the sacredness of the *Torah* as the revelation of God's word. A measure of this is the reverence with which *Torah* scrolls are created, handled, and stored. A *Torah* scroll that has become worn or damaged is still considered to be holy and must be stored in a *genizah* (usually a dedicated storeroom in a synagogue) and eventually it will be buried, preferentially in the same place as a *Torah* scholar.

The letters of the Hebrew alphabet are all consonants. Even letters such as *alef* and *ayin* which at first sight appear to be vowels, are also classed as consonants.

The written language did not originally show the vowels; these were added between the seventh and tenth centuries CE by the Masorites, a group that standardised the texts of the *Bible*. Because the text was sacred and could not be altered, the vowels were indicated by adding various dots and dashes above and below the consonants.

The consonants represent different ways in which the pure sound of the larynx is modulated by movements made by the mouth, tongue and throat. The vowels are shaped by the consonants.

This interplay between vowels and shaping consonants resembles the interplay of force and form as a basic duality underpinning the Kabbalistic worldview. If the vowels are water in a river, then the consonants are the guiding river bank. The letters of the Hebrew alphabet can be viewed as twenty-two ways of shaping sound, as representations of form. This view is given substance in the *Yetzirah*[172]:

Twenty-two Foundation letters:
He engraved them, He carved them,
He permuted them, He weighed them,

---

172. *The Sepher Yetzirah*, Aryeh Kaplan, Weiser 1991

He transformed them,
And with them, He depicted all that was formed and all that would be formed.
Twenty-two Foundation letters
He engraved them with voice
He carved them with breath
He set them in the mouth
In five places
Alef Chet He Ayin in the throat
Gimel Yud Kaf Kuf in the palate
Dalet Tet Lamed Nun Tav in the tongue
Zayin Samekh Shin Resh Tzadi in the teeth
Bet Vav Mem Peh in the lips.

In the *Sefer Yetzirah* the consonants are not treated as arbitrary tokens, as individually uninteresting components of words. Each letter had a unique role in the formation of everything in the world, as if 'formation' was a twenty-two dimensional space with a letter allocated to each axis. They are classified according to the way in which they are shaped in the mouth. This suggests (unsurprisingly) that an important key to understanding the letters is in their sounds, individually and in combination. Each sound corresponds to an aspect of formation, and when this is understood and the correct internal connections are made, the letters can be used in various combinations in magical procedures. Each sound becomes a trigger for an aspect of consciousness which is active in determining the form of reality.

Magical traditions of this kind are attributed to the *Sefer Yetzirah*. The best known of these is the formation of an artificial being or *golem*[173]. The use of letter combinations and vowel sounds leads into complex, and by all accounts dangerous, meditative and magical practices called *Chokhmah ha-Tzeruf*, the science of letter combinations. The leading exponent of this method was R. Abraham Abulafia (1240-1295), who used these techniques to access the level of ecstatic consciousness where prophecy occurs.

Abulafia is one of the few Kabbalists to leave detailed accounts of practical meditative techniques. The publication of his techniques evoked considerable hostility from his contemporaries, to the extent that Abulafia was forced to move his residence on a number of occasions. Abulafia believed himself to be in possession of the same meditative techniques used by the Biblical prophets and produced several

---

173. See the essay *Golem* in *Kabbalah*, Gershom G. Scholem, Dorset Press 1974

manuscripts containing inspirational material received while in meditative states. He writes with authority and clarity. His descriptions of altered states and their characteristics (found in his works and also in records made by his disciples) have a convincing stamp of authenticity[174].

Abulafia states that there are two principle techniques in Kabbalah: meditations on the ten *sefirot*, and a more powerful technique based on the twenty-two letters. His technique was the latter, and he appears to have been the heir to an authentic tradition concerning the practical application of the *Sefer Yetzirah*. His techniques are complex and require an extensive immersion in Hebrew and gematria, as well as the ability to sustain concentration throughout lengthy meditations. They are not appropriate for a beginner.

Another key to the understanding of the letters is their formation from *root shapes*. Spoken words are formed from root sounds (phonemes), and written words/letters are composed of root shapes. This is obvious to the calligrapher, who makes the marks for each letter in a series of strokes. A simple technique is the decomposition of a character into its parts - an *alef*, for example, can be seen as two *yod*s and a *vav*. The numerical value (see below) of two *yod*s and a *vav* is 26, the same as YHVH. This connection between YHVH and *alef* is alluded to in the *Bahir*, one of the earliest texts connected with medieval Kabbalah.

Each letter of the Hebrew alphabet has a numeric value. Some letters have two numeric values depending on whether they occur in the middle or at the end of a word. Each letter also has a literal meaning (for example, the letter *shin* means "a tooth"). These letters are given in Table 16. The *Yetzirah* groups the letters into 3 mothers, 7 doubles, and 12 elementals as shown in Table 17. In the *Yetzirah* the three mothers have the correspondences shown in Table 18.

---

174. See *Abraham Abulafia and the Doctrine of Prophetic Kabbalah* in *Major Trends in Jewish Mysticism*, Gershom G. Scholem, Schocken 1974

Alef	Ox	1
Bet	House	2
Gimel	Camel	3
Dalet	Door	4
He	Window	5
Vav	Peg, nail	6
Zayin	Weapon	7
Chet	Fence	8
Tet	Serpent	9
Yod	Hand	10
Khaf	Palm (of hand)	20 (500)
Lamed	Ox-goad	30
Mem	Water	40 (600)
Nun	Fish	50 (700)
Samekh	Prop	60
Ayin	Eye	70
Peh	Mouth	80 (800)
Tzadeh	Fish-Hook	90 (900)
Qof	Back of Head	100
Resh	Head	200
Shin	Tooth	300
Tav	Cross	400

Table 16: The Hebrew Alphabet

The Paths

Mothers	Doubles	Elementals
Alef	Bet	He
Mem	Gimel	Vau
Shin	Dalet	Zayin
	Khaf	Chet
	Peh	Tet
	Resh	Yod
	Tav	Lamed
		Nun
		Samekh
		Ayin
		Tzadeh
		Qof

Table 17: The Letters according to the *Sefer Yetzirah*

Mother	Sound	Element	Season	Body
Alef	Breath	Air	Spring & Autumn	Chest
Mem	Hum	Water	Winter	Belly
Shin	Hiss	Fire	Summer	Head

Table 18: Mother Letters

Double	Planet	Day	Quality	Body	Direction
Bet	Moon	Sunday	Wisdom Folly	R. eye	South
Gimel	Mars	Monday	Wealth Poverty	R. ear	North
Dalet	Sun	Tuesday	Fertility Barrenness	R. nostril	East
Khaf	Venus	Wednesday	Life Death	L. eye	Up
Peh	Mercury	Thursday	Dominance Submission	L. ear	Down
Resh	Saturn	Friday	Peace War	L. nostril	West
Tav	Jupiter	Saturday	Grace Ugliness	Mouth	Centre

Table 19: Double Letters

The Paths

Elemental	Foundation	Zodiac	Month	Body	Direction
He	speech	Aries	Nissan	R.foot	Up.E
Vav	thought	Taurus	Iyar	R.kidney	NE
Zayin	motion	Gemini	Sivan	L.foot	Lo.E
Chet	sight	Cancer	Tammuz	R.hand	Up.S
Tet	hearing	Leo	Av	L.kidney	SE
Yod	action	Virgo	Elul	L.hand	Lo.S
Lamed	coition	Libra	Tishrei	gall bladder	Up.W
Nun	smell	Scorpio	Cheshvan	intestines	SW
Samekh	sleep	Sagittarius	Kilsev	pancreas?	Lo.W
Ayin	anger	Capricorn	Tevet	liver	Up.N
Tzadeh	taste	Aquarius	Shevat	stomach	NW
Qof	laughter	Pisces	Adar	spleen	Lo.N

Table 20: Elemental Letters

Double Letter	Planet
Bet	Mercury
Gimel	Moon
Dalet	Venus
Khaf	Jupiter
Peh	Mars
Resh	Sun
Tav	Saturn

Table 21: Golden Dawn Attributions

The correspondences for the seven doubles are in Table 19. The seven doubles are also associated with seven universes, seven firmaments, seven lands, seven seas, seven rivers, seven deserts, seven weeks, seven days of creation, seven years, seven sabbaticals, and seven jubilees.

The correspondences for the twelve elementals are in Table 20.

Different versions of the *Sefer Yetzirah* contain different correspondences for many letters; the correspondences above are from the Gra version[175].

It should be noted that the well-known Golden Dawn correspondences for the paths differ from all the sources listed by Kaplan when it comes to allocating the planets to the double letters. In the Golden Dawn scheme the double letters were written in increasing numerical order and allocated to the planets in order of increasing exaltation, as shown in Table 21.

This collection of correspondences is all very well, but what do they tell us about the Tree of Life? How do they fit on the paths as they are drawn, and can we ascribe a meaning to them that complements the rich and well-developed correspondences associated with the *sefirot*? Herein, as the saying goes, lies a mystery.

A commonly accepted scheme is the Golden Dawn attribution of letters to paths (Figure 51), but it suffers from a deficiency: the Hebrew letters are divided into 3 mothers, 7 doubles and 12 elementals, and the paths on the Tree are divided into 3 horizontals, 7 verticals and 12 diagonals. Tradition (for example, the attribution according to Isaac Luria) follows this by matching mothers to horizontals, doubles to verticals, and elementals to diagonals. The Golden Dawn scheme does not.

Given that the geometric structure of the Tree appears to be a direct interpretation of the text of the *Yetzirah*, this does seem perverse!

I had assumed for many years that the scheme used by the Golden Dawn had been devised by one of its founders, but this does not appear to be the case. The attribution would seem to have come via the mysterious Cipher Manuscripts, and is the same attribution of letters to paths as that found in the version of the Tree published by Kircher in 1653 (see Figure 4).

The Golden Dawn scheme has been much used, much written

---

175. *The Sepher Yetzirah*, Aryeh Kaplan, Weiser 1991

The Paths

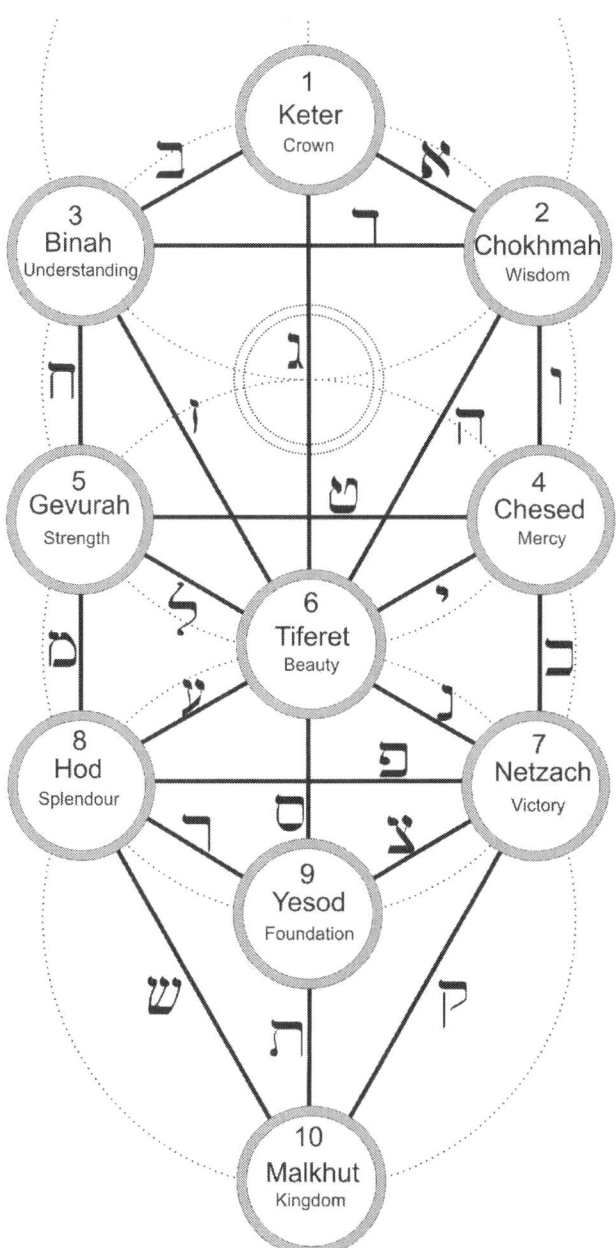

Figure 51: The Tree of Emanation with Golden Dawn Letter attributions

about, and one cannot deny that many people have found it useful, but it is open to the criticism that something vital has been lost along the way. I think it would be a mistake to approach Kabbalah with the view that the Golden Dawn attribution of letters to paths is beyond question.

Doubtless, many readers will have reached to point of asking (like the author) "well, what is the correct answer!".

There are many possible answers. One approach would be to pick an attribution associated with a well-known Kabbalist such as R. Isaac Luria (Figure 52). There are other attributions however, and then one is faced with the problem of balancing one authority relative to another. A possible solution might be to study the letters and wait for insight. While waiting, it would be wise to learn Hebrew, and study the *Torah*[176], on the basis that God helps those who help themselves.

23.3 The Paths

There are many presentations on the paths in the literature, most dating from the last century and strongly influenced by Golden Dawn correspondences. The following presentation on the paths is original, although the method is not. The method employed was to examine and describe the change in consciousness caused by traversing a path from one *sefira* to another[177].

The first step is to understand the nature of each *sefira* in as deep and fundamental a way as one can. This is essentially incommunicable (but I make the attempt nevertheless).

The next step is to meditate on the *sefirot* at either end of a path, and to make the transition in consciousness as many times as it takes to capture the essence of the transition. The nature of the transition depends on the direction in which one traverses the path, and in the examples below I have tended to give more weight to one direction.

There is no unique way to do this. Although the nature of the *sefirot* has been relatively well-established and stable for eight hundred years, the nature of the paths is much less established and should be considered a practical exercise for the individual kabbalist.

A characterisation of the *sefirot* and the paths according to this method is given in Figure 53.

---

176. One way to appreciate the complexity of the exercise would be to study *The Hebrew Letters*, Ginsburgh, R. Yitzchak, Linda Pinsky Publications 1990
177. John Michael Greer describes this in his discussion of the paths. See *Paths of Wisdom*, John Michael Greer, Llewellyn 1996.

The Paths

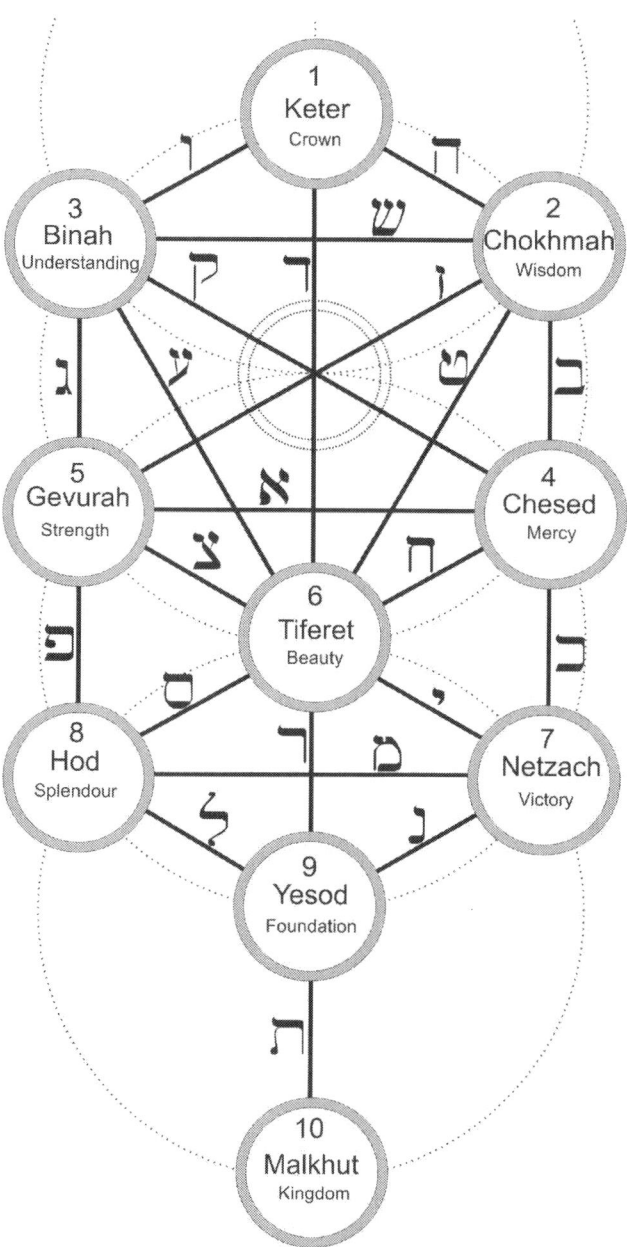

Figure 52: Letters on the Tree of Return according to R. Isaac Luria.

Keter is Unity. *Keter* is unity as it crystallises within the shroud of the Unmanifest. This eternal, unrevealed movement towards becoming contains a paradoxical and undisclosed duality.

Chokhmah is Unconditioned Creativity, the divine creative emanation in its purest form. Although *Chokhmah* is unconditioned, it contains within it the a desire for structure traditionally called *Binah*. *Chokhmah* is freedom falling into choice. This is its essential nature, the exercise of freedom in becoming *not free*. Freedom that fails to choose a form is evanescent; it returns back to the Unmanifest. *Keter* is like a bubbling in the Unmanifest, *Chokhmah* the point where a bubble chooses to fall into a universe of its own creation.

Binah is the Mother of Form and the possibility of boundaries. A boundary signifies difference, differentiation, form or structure. A boundary contains the idea of *separation* - The One becomes Many. *Binah* is the most abstract root of differentiation.

Chesed is Conditioned Creativity. It inherits the creative impulse of *Chokhmah* but cannot depart from the constraints imposed by *Binah*. *Binah* limits what is possible, and the creativity of *Chesed* must operate within these limits.

Gevurah is Response to Boundaries. The primary *Gevuric* concern is transgression. Cross the line and according to tradition, the Severity of God will discover you. The boundaries are everywhere: in the 613 *mitzvot* (commandments) of Judaism, in criminal law, in accounting rules and tax regulations, in social convention, and in the rules of soccer. Break the rules, and a *Gevuric* consciousness somewhere will call you to account.

Tiferet is Awareness of Self. This is a paradoxical and self-referential mode of awareness in which I am aware of myself. I am aware of my environment (*Malkhut*) and I am aware of myself as existing in relation to an environment. In *Tiferet* the unity of *Keter* is sundered into a plurality of awareness. Because consciousness is separate, it becomes concerned with its boundaries, self-definition, and unique identity. This narrative of identity coalesces and solidifies as the Ego in *Yesod*.

Netzach is Response to Creativity. The creative impulses of *Chesed* are evaluated at the level of basic emotional response and accepted or rejected. This is how we respond to the world, with a 'yay' or a 'nay'.

Hod is Appreciation of Boundaries. The boundaries between things *define* what a thing is, and as consciousness chooses one thing over another so it learns to value and appreciate boundaries. Novels,

The Paths

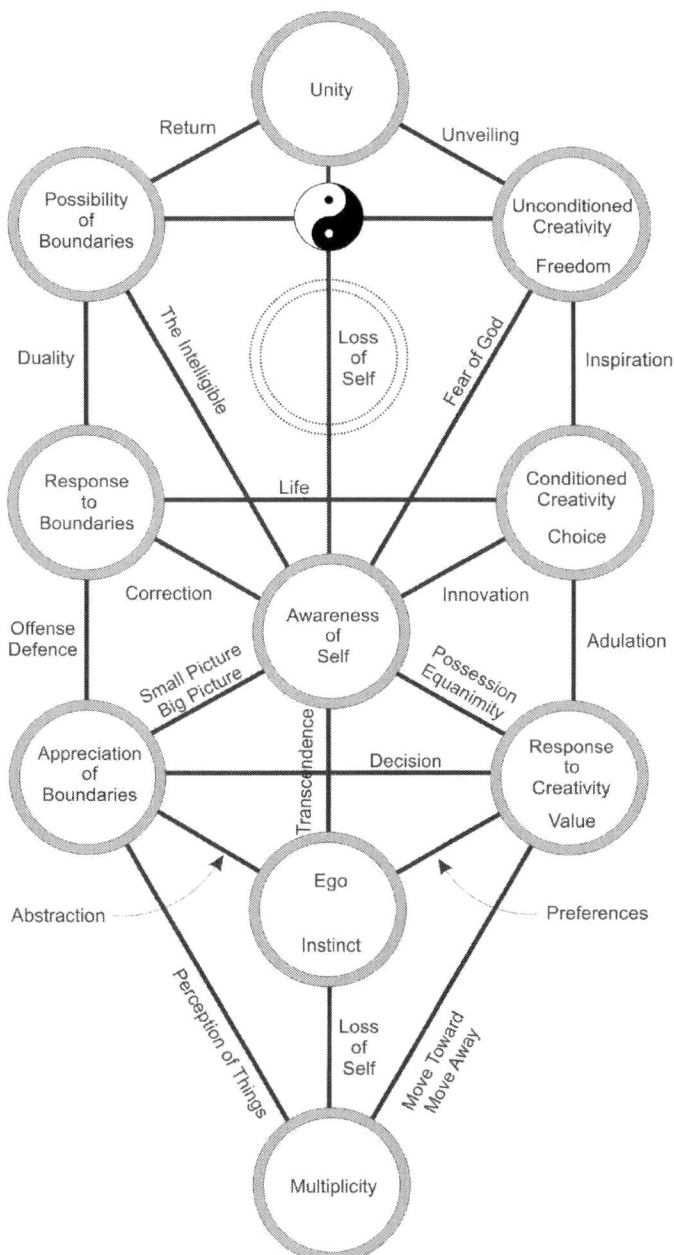

Figure 53: An interpretation of the Paths on the Tree

drama, dance, opera, music, fine art, law, culture, myth, and the entire corpus of human scientific knowledge, provide domains for consciousness to explore.

Yesod is Ego. The Ego is differentiated from Self by the inflexible affective responses of *Netzach*, the unquestioning intellectual fixations of *Hod*, and the treadmill of perception. Consciousness spins a web to run around on and becomes trapped in the web of its own manufacture.

Malkhut is Multiplicity, the culmination of a process of differentiation and increasing structure that begins with the Unity of *Keter*. If *Keter* is the One, then *Malkhut* is The Many.

The motivation behind this exegesis is a process of *separation*. The observant Jew will recite the *Shema Yisrael* twice daily. The *Shema* is usually translated as:

Hear, O Israel: the Lord our God, the Lord is One.

This declaration of unity is at odds with our perception of how the world is. The world appears diverse and fragmented. Figure 53 is an attempt to reconcile the One and the Many in a terse schematic, to capture how the unity of *Keter* is broken up and expressed through a process of reification, so that force is increasingly constrained descending the Pillar of Force, form becomes increasingly defined going down the Pillar of Form, and consciousness increasingly fragmented going down the Pillar of Consciousness.

With this characterisation of the *sefirot* it is now possible to explore the paths.

Yesod to Malkhut - Loss of Self

Malkhut is otherness, everything we experience outside of ourselves. We may be comfortable with otherness when surrounded by familiar things, such as our homes and possessions. Otherness can then become a part of the extended self.

Sometimes, through drugs, depression or fatigue, the sense of familiarity is dispelled and the otherness of the world is revealed. The mask slips, and we can see how we have invested the world with a personal meaning that no longer seems to be there. This may be experienced as a paralysing loss of self, an experience described by Sartre in *La Nausée*.

The Paths

Hod to Malkhut - Perception of Things

The normal perception of the world is of discrete things embedded in space and time. Language reinforces this perception because we have names for most things, and we can say how they are embedded - for example, "the cat is on the mat".

This is a synthetic perception; it is constructed by our senses. and by cognitive processing in the brain. Experimental physics, looking closer, does not see a cat on a mat. Experiments reveal little but empty space filled with a continuum of electromagnetic fields[178]. The 'things' we experience are given the shape by our nervous systems and by culture.

The initiation of this path is the conscious awareness of what Korzybski called "awareness of abstraction". This is a complex cognitive process that turns the emptiness of *Malkhut* into something the individual human consciousness finds tractable.

Netzach to Malkhut - Moving Towards/Moving Away

Bacteria can move towards a favourable environment and move away from a hostile environment. Movement is a primordial response to the world. We move towards food, friends, and safety. We move away from danger and discomfort. We do not view the world in a neutral light - we possess ancient instincts that steer us in a direction so that we thrive.

Hod to Yesod - Abstraction and Classification

This path is parallel to the path from *Hod* to *Malkhut*. Both paths are related to the imposition of structure and definition upon an unknown world. In the path from *Hod* to *Malkhut* we recognise a world of things. In the path from *Hod* to *Yesod* the world of things is larger, because each thing exists within a cultural context and web of associations.

For example, gold is not just a metal: it is a currency; it is a signifier of value; it is a basis for decorative jewellery; and it is a metaphor for what is finest and incorruptible. Gold is a close neighbour to the metal lead in the periodic table of the elements[179], but it arouses different passions. Gold stands for everything fine and superior; lead is

---

178. The emptiness of matter was demonstrated by Ernest Rutherford in 1911 when he observed alpha particles travelling through gold foil, and found that almost all of the foil was empty space.

considered 'base' and in Roman times lead sheet was used for making curse spells.

The idea of holiness demonstrates how material objects can be invested with qualities that make them more than material. A location can be holy, a book can be holy, a person can be holy. The high altar of a church is treated with a reverence that cannot be understood from its composition or the items placed on it. We see a similar reverence for flags and national symbols, for graves and consecrated ground, for historical sites and memorials.

The path from *Hod* to *Malkhut* is the first level in what we might call 'the construction of the material world'. The path from *Hod* to *Yesod* adds another level of complexity and substance on top of the first.

A word that is sometimes used to describe the extended world as it exists in the human mind and in human culture is *noosphere* - literally 'mind-sphere'. The path from *Hod* to *Yesod* is the path of the *noosphere*.

Netzach to Yesod - Preferences

The path from *Netzach* to *Malkhut* is about movement; away-from and toward. In this corresponding path from *Netzach* to *Yesod* there is still movement, but it is more complex and nuanced. Like the previous path (which it mirrors) it is grounded in the *noosphere*, and concerns the intricate system of values with which we relate to things in the world. The world is coloured-in according to how it relates to me - the *noosphere* is oriented around me, with me at its centre.

Perhaps the simplest expressions of these mostly-unconscious valuations can be found in our preferences for dress, decor, food and music.

Netzach to Hod - Decision

The path between *Netzach* and *Hod* is one of the three horizontal paths corresponding to the three mother letters (*aleph, mem, shin*) in the Hebrew alphabet. These paths express duality, the dynamics of force and form. The tension of manifestation is expressed through these paths: they are the 'mothers of form'. In this case we have the duality of two ways of responding to the world: by thinking, and by feeling.

---

179. The atomic number of gold is 79; that of lead is 82. Both metals are soft and heavy.

The Paths

There is a saying that "feelings tell us what to think". The justification for this is that a purely rational being (like Spock) would be incapable of making choices in real-life. To make a rational choice one requires a base of ground truth, assumptions one can depend on in any circumstance. Real-life is invariably situational and cannot be easily quantified. Feelings are Nature's way of speeding up decisions. By the time Spock has determined his ground truth, other people have moved on. But feelings are sometimes wrong. Like strong coffee, strong feelings can push us to make bad decisions more quickly. Spock may have the last laugh.

Whenever a person makes a decision, he or she determines the future of their world. In cases where we cannot make a decision then the Lightning Flash cannot travel from *Netzach* to *Hod*, and so it never reaches *Malkhut*.

Yesod to Tiferet - Transcendence

Yesod is the centre of the Ego, a product of the Necessity of the world. It is the outcome of an environment. It knows how to run our lives. It is limited however. Sometimes it realises how limited it is, and may voluntarily choose to transcend itself. This path is the intrusion of the greater into the lesser, and signifies the possibility of growth.

Tiferet to Hod - Small Picture/Big Picture

When a person seems to be lost in the details of a problem they may be asked to see 'the Big Picture'. The Big Picture transcends the Small Picture. The truths of the Small Picture are subsumed within the larger perspective of the Big Picture.

The level of awareness associated with *Hod* is fascinated by detail, by definition and classification, by fine shades of difference. There are antique specialists who can turn over a teacup and tell you the name of the designer, the year it was made, the name of the pattern, the name of the person who applied the pattern, how long the pattern was manufactured, its rarity value, and its current market value. This is an important skill in the antiques trade, but it is narrow in its focus. There are people in every walk of life who possess this narrow focus, and their skills are often extremely valuable, but there is a limited utility in a skill of this type.

There is always a larger picture. This path is about stepping out and looking around. Or conversely, it is about falling into the detail of a small world that seems infinite in its fascination and complexity.

The Hermetic Kabbalah

Tiferet to Netzach - Possession/Equanimity

Equanimity is the virtue of having presence of mind, composure, calmness, and stability, in situations that most people would find distressing or alarming. A key to equanimity is not being overwhelmed by feeling. When we are possessed by feeling, detachment vanishes, and we *become* our feelings. This often occurs with anger, love and fear.

This path is a mirror of the path from *Tiferet* to *Hod*. The descent from *Tiferet* to *Hod* is a descent into a small world of infinite fascination. The descent from *Tiferet* to *Netzach* is a descent into a small world created by strong feeling. Anger, love and fear are normally narrow feelings: they focus on specific people and situations[180]. Anger is an immensely disturbing feeling that can consume the mind to the exclusion of all else.

Mystical traditions tend to value equanimity, suggesting that we should be composed in the face of adversity. This undervalues the survival value of strong feelings. For most people their daily routines are underpinned by powerful feelings: fear of unemployment, fear of seeming incompetent, a desire to support friends and colleagues, love of friends and family, anger at transgression, taking care of oneself. People who have been socialised intelligently usually have feelings that serve a positive role in their lives. They have an instinct for good or appropriate behaviour that is most often seen when something unexpected happens.

This path is one of the most important paths on the Tree, because here we confront the organic necessity of the world head-on. Feelings are part of the organic necessity of existence. They seem to be a part of our core being, our essential identity. On this path we watch them, learn how they work, and try to mould them to serve us.

Tiferet to Gevurah - Correction

Any complex system, such as the cells in the human body, or the citizens of a nation state, are governed by complex processes. Some of these processes are corrective, and function like the captain and crew of a ship, holding the craft on a steady course in spite of sea or storm.

Corrective processes function via feedback; every part of the ship is monitored by the crew, and its condition reported to the officers, who may well interrupt the captain for new orders. When Norbert

---

180. When they are not narrow they may manifest as mental health issues.

The Paths

Weiner was looking for a word to describe the study of regulatory systems he chose 'cybernetics', from the Greek word *kybernetike*, which means governance, and comes originally from the word for the helmsman of a ship.

The paths from *Tiferet* to *Gevurah* and *Chesed* are paths of kingship (or in a more abstract sense, governance). The path to *Gevurah* is that aspect of governance concerned with correction - maintaining the *status quo*.

An important part of the regulation of the human body is the immune system. It can identify parts of the body that are misbehaving, either due to an error (e.g. a cancer) or infection. Something analogous operates in society with a justice system of police, courts and prisons.

Tiferet to Chesed - Innovation

An important aspect of governance is recognising when something has to change. Change does not come easy; the corrective aspects of *Gevurah* will tend to act against it. Any organism (at whatever scale) that cannot adapt to changes in its environment will eventually cease to exist.

This is a path of change, of innovation. One can associate it with leadership such as Ghandi, Martin Luther King, Mandela, or Emmeline Pankhurst. These are people who acted as a focus and catalyst for important social transformations.

Tiferet to Binah - The Intelligible

'The Intelligible' is a term that derives from the Platonic school of philosophy. It signifies that which can be apprehended through the inner eye of the rational intellect, an aspect of cognition that was sometimes called *nous*. It supposes that behind the appearance of the world (which we comprehend via our senses) there is another 'realm' of causes and principles that *gives rise* to appearances. With our *nous* we can perceive primary causes and rise to the level of the divine intellect or intelligence. Because there was an influence of Hellenistic philosophy on Kabbalah, we find an overlap between the *sefira Binah* (understanding or intelligence), and the Platonic Intelligible or Intellectual Principle.

The development of modern technology provides tangible evidence that there are indeed deep principles in the natural world. They are not apparent. They have been discovered through investigative disciplines - physics, chemistry, biology, geology and so on.

Tiferet to Chokhmah - Fear of God

In *Proverbs* it states that "The beginning of wisdom (*chokhmah*) is the fear of the Lord".

We are finite beings with small minds and limited concerns. As one moves from the root of personal identity in *Tiferet* towards the fount of cosmic manifestation, our personal frailty and insignificance become apparent.

Every person has felt the power of the sea, its immensity and unpredictability, its beauty and danger. How much more then can we experience the immensity of God's outpouring?

Tiferet to Keter - Loss of Self

Keter and *Malkhut* are duals by tradition, differing views of the One and the Many. The Many is concealed within the One, and the One is concealed within the Many. Perception is active, and it is an act of will whether one perceives One or Many.

For this reason the path from *Tiferet* to *Malkhut* (through *Yesod*) and the path from *Tiferet* to *Keter* (through *Da'at*) are also duals. The experiences are superficially different, but when experienced in depth they are the same.

Gevurah to Hod - Defence

This path is the transition from appreciating boundaries (*Hod*) to responding to them (*Gevurah*). For example, I may acknowledge that there is a parking restriction but decide to ignore it and risk a parking ticket. I may decide to ignore the parking ticket and risk a summons. I may decide to ignore a summons and risk being in contempt of court.

What began as an abstract notion of a parking restriction (*Hod*) has turned into a confrontation with power (*Gevurah*). It is a confrontation I am reasonably certain to lose.

Chesed to Netzach - Adulation

The experience of this path is the emotional response to creativity. It is creativity experienced at second hand. The subject of adulation could be music, art, film, dance, writing, or science. It is the feeling that brings eighty thousand people together to watch someone sing. It is what motivates people to visit art galleries.

The Paths

Gevurah to Chesed - Life

There is a tendency in Nature towards disorder. Wires become tangled, hair becomes knotted, and rooms become dirty and untidy. Empty a bag of chess pieces onto a chess board and the pieces do not spontaneously arrange themselves.

There is another unexpected tendency in Nature, what is sometimes called emergence, that causes organisation to appear in the midst of disorder.

The middle ground between order and disorder, a tireless chaos in which order and disorder are equally at home, is what we call life.

Binah to Gevurah - Duality

Binah is the Mother of Form, the root of distinction. Movement down this path is an awareness of separation, of the separation of one thing from another, the root awareness of being different and distinct.

The development of this awareness is noticeable in children as they become aware of siblings, possessions, and personal space. "It's mine!" is the dominant cry. This path is the authentic "root of all evil".

Chokhmah to Chesed - Inspiration

Inspiration means 'breathing into'. The ancients believed that the Gods 'breathed into them', and would pray to the Gods for inspiration. Creativity can seem miraculous, an external source that pours effortlessly through a person. Nietzsche wrote *Also Sprach Zarathustra* in just such a fever of inspiration, and afterwards he described the experience[181]:

> Has anyone at the end of the nineteenth century a clear idea of what poets of strong eras called inspiration? If not, I will describe it. If we had the slightest residue of superstition remaining in ourselves, we would scarcely be capable of rejecting outright the thought of being no more than a mere incarnation, a mere mouthpiece, a mere medium of overpowering forces. The concept of revelation in the sense that suddenly, with indescribable certainty and subtlety, something becomes visible and audible, something that shakes us to the core and knocks us over... All of this is involuntary unto the extreme but as in a storm of a feeling of freedom, absoluteness, power, divinity... This is my experience of inspiration ...

---

181. *Ecce Homo: How One Becomes What One Is*, Nietzsche, Friedrich, Penguin Classics, 1992

Chokhmah to Binah

The path from *Chokhmah* to *Binah* is the root of all duality and manifestation. One could imagine the path as a hose pumping water into a swimming pool - *Chokhmah* is the hose (traditionally the image was a spring or fountain) and *Binah* is the pool (traditionally the image was the sea, or supernal waters). Another related image is that of ejaculation into the womb of the Mother.

Figure 54: The Yin-Yang symbol of Taoism.

A symbol that captures something of the essence of this path is the well-known *Yin-Yang* symbol (see Figure 54) from Taoism. It suggests a mixing of two principles, with *Yin* being approximately cognate to the Mother, and *Yang* approximately cognate to the Father.

Binah to Keter - Return

A word often used in the mystical concept of return is *teshuvah*. It is a concept with many nuances. A common interpretation is that of turning away from sin and a return to God. A person who has sinned understands that he or she has sinned and wishes to return to righteous behaviour.

Teshuvah can also be interpreted as a return to the divine source. This could be personal, a mystical ascent of the Tree. It can also be general and universal, according to the formula of "run and return". Each impulse of manifestation that forms in *Keter* is reified in *Malkhut*; its impact is distilled through consciousness and returned back to its source.

It has been said that "God wishes to know God", and so all revealing into manifestation returns once more to the source. The act of living consciously and morally achieves this purpose. The closer we raise our consciousness to the source, the more we can return our experience of life. This, more than anything, dignifies life, dignifies even the worst suffering, and permits us to find joy even in pain, illness and death.

Keter to Chokhmah - Revealing

The path from *Keter* to *Chokhmah* is the beginning of the revealing that we call life, as it unfolds throughout the cosmos. We can know

The Paths

only the smallest part of its mysteries; the small part revealed to us is our personal existence. Meaning and purpose are emergent and transitory. They are stories we construct, narratives we weave around our projects. Our true revelation is in how we live, how we unfold our own being.

The Hermetic Kabbalah

Part 3

The Rectification of the Soul

The Hermetic Kabbalah

24

Rectification

24.1 Crookedness

> There was a crooked man, and he walked a crooked mile.
> He found a crooked sixpence upon a crooked stile.
> He bought a crooked cat, which caught a crooked mouse,
> And they all lived together in a little crooked house.
> Traditional
>
> Straighten all that is crooked
> Plotinus

Rectification means 'making straight' - putting right, repair, restoration. Its root can be found in 'rectitude' - moral uprightness - and it derives from the Latin *rectus* - straight. The word is still used in electronics, where it signifies the transformation of 'wiggly' alternating current into 'straight' direct current. Ultimately it derives from *regere* - to rule. In Hermetic Kabbalah the principal focii for rectification are the human soul (microcosm) and the cosmos (macrocosm).

Traditional Kabbalah contains related concepts. The technical term for an act of rectification is *tikkun*, and one often finds the phrase *tikkun olam*, the 'repair of the world'. Sometimes the term *teshuvah*[182] ('return') is also used. *Teshuvah* is connected with repentance, and may signify that someone has turned away from God, and now wishes to return to God and the Jewish community. In a

The Great Work

The Great Work is a term derived from alchemy. The aim of alchemy was a process of transmutation that would bring imperfect substances into a state of perfection. It was based on a belief that of all the material substances in the world, only gold was pure and complete and incorruptible. Gold was the spiritual essence of metals once they had been purged of dross.

For many alchemists and their wealthy patrons the motive behind the alchemy of transmutation was mercenary. Others saw it as indicative of a more profound transformation: just as the souls of metals could be rectified, *so could the human soul*. The Great Work became a metaphor for *rectification*. The principal focii for rectification were the human soul (microcosm) and the cosmos (macrocosm).

mystical context it can signify the desire to the soul to be whole, and to return to its source in the upper world (as one might wish to find the source of a river).

Why do the soul and the cosmos need to be rectified? Is everything - house, mouse, cat and stile - really crooked? In an essay *Against the Gnostics*, the pagan Neoplatonist philosopher Plotinus argued that the Cosmos was a divine creation and so inherently perfect and beautiful. This argument was still being articulated over one thousand years later when R. Moses Cordovero wrote:

> The truth is that above, in the world of the divine emanations, no evil thing descends from heaven, for up there everything is absolutely spiritual.

Since the time of the late Roman Empire people have tried to reconcile a belief in spiritual goodness and ultimate cosmic order with the reality of evil in this world, and at this point it is useful to recall the discussion in *Evil* on page 83. There are several alternatives to the Neoplatonist position.

The first is *catastrophe* (see opposite). In many myths, such as those originating in the gnostic cults of late antiquity, catastrophe was caused by a wilful act within the divine *pleroma*[183]. Often it was the divine wisdom Sophia who initiated calamity. Sometimes it was the primordial divine couple, Adam and Eve. In the view of R. Isaac Luria it was quasi-mechanistic - the universe began well but fell into an

---

182. Normally *teshuvah* is a traditional process of repentance for a sin (i.e. having turned away from godliness, one *returns*) but it can be used in a mystical sense of a return to the source of being.
183. Literally "fullness", but in this context "realm".

Rectification

Catastrophe

An influential view articulated by the famous kabbalist R. Isaac Luria is that there were two primordial catastrophes. The first, the Breaking of the Vessels, was caused by the inability of some of the first *sefirot* to contain the divine light. To use a metaphor, we might say that they lacked flexibility and elasticity, they were too solid, too massive, too brittle. Unlike palm trees that flex and bend, they were like oak trees uprooted in a wind. The *sefirot* were too rigid because the first attempt at creation was dominated by the quality of *Din*. When the *sefirot* shattered the shards fell into the abyss to become the *klippot* (shells, husks).

Despite this shattering, all would have been well had Adam obeyed the commandment not to eat from the Tree of the Knowledge of Good and Evil ... but he disobeyed, and this caused a second cosmic catastrophe. As a result the lowest world of *Assiah* slipped out of place and became immersed in the realm of the *klippot*. This displacement provides a metaphysical explanation for Jewish purity laws: we are immersed in a world that contains elements of fundamental and irreducible impurity.

There is a pronounced gnostic element in Luria's teachings. The details differ from the gnosticism of late antiquity, but there is the belief that the world we experience is not an outcome of an elegant exercise in central planning. It has been dropped on the floor. A key idea is that of *alienation*. The human soul is alienated because it has become displaced, and as a result of this displacement, distorted. As the familiar phrase puts it, we are "strangers in a strange land". We are alienated from our true estate. We have forgotten our origins.

The Kabbalistic view is that the situation can be repaired, and human beings must play their part. The first part is to rectify the soul. The second is to rectify the cosmos.

imperfect state, like the flow of water from a tap that begins smoothly but quickly breaks up.

A second alternative is *necessity*. It has been postulated that God created the universe to discover righteous individuals. A righteous individual would act well even when offered the opportunity for evil action. However, a person cannot choose to act well unless he or she possesses free will. Any universe in which free will is possible will, of necessity, permit evil. From this point of view, *God had no choice* but to include free will and hence evil[184]. Evil is structural, necessary, and it is centred in the individual freedom to act.

A third alternative is *dualism*. Many Christian sects have come to the view that evil is an autonomous metaphysical power with its own

---

[184]. A conclusion repellent to many theologians.

agenda, and while it will be overcome in time, we must live with it and avoid its snares and wiles. Judaism is fundamentally monist, but over the past millennium Kabbalah has gone from a philosophic outlook inspired by Platonism to a mythological outlook in which evil has autonomy, and (there is no way to wriggle out of this) evil does descend from heaven[185].

A fourth alternative is *divine justice*. There is an aspect of God beyond our understanding that sometimes causes bad things to happen, even to good people. This view was subjected to close scrutiny in the ancient book of *Job*.

A fifth alternative is the modern view: *mindlessness*. This is in direct opposition to the broad trend Hellenistic philosophy, where the quality of Mind was believed to manifest at every level of reality. According to the prevailing modern view the universe on a large scale is devoid of the quality of mind. There is no *mindful* process of creation. Complexity and order emerge in favourable environments via deterministic interactions between simple particles. This was outlined in *Emanation and Emergence* on page 155. The universe does not fall short of any plan or ideal, it does not evolve towards any goal. It does not encode meaning, nor is it is not the tip of a metaphysical iceberg. It just is. There are no privileged observers, and so all values are relative and contextual. Evil is contextual: a context that seems evil for one organism is probably a free lunch for another.

These are the most important viewpoints that one encounters in the Western tradition:

a). The universe is fine, we just don't see it.

b). The universe is not fine because it fell off the shelf and broke.

c). The universe could be fine, but evil is created by people exercising free-will and doing evil things.

d). The universe is divided between antagonistic powers.

e). The universe is administered by God, and the rationale behind punishment and reward is beyond human understanding.

f). The universe is neither fine nor not-fine, but it contains judgments made about it by people having either a good time or a bad time.

Kabbalah provides no clear view about which view is right, and from a personal perspective, I find them all interesting. According to

---

185. Hence the influential conjectures by the (heretical) R. Nathan of Gaza that the roots of evil may be found in the *En Sof*. See *Sabbatai Sevi, The Mystical Messiah*, Gershom Scholem, Princeton 1976

current scientific understanding, mindlessness is the most credible explanation. At the same time we find human beings altering the planet, and the best explanation for this is to understand what is going on in the minds of fellow human beings.

In what follows I have tried not to give too much weight to any one of the views given above. Where science is sound and well-grounded in fact and consensus I have used it, even though it best supports the view that the Cosmos is mindless. Nevertheless, I do not view the Cosmos as a whole as mindless (otherwise there would be no point in this book), and this leads to a tension and incoherence in my presentation. I am aware of this, and I apologise for it.

24.2 Rectification & Self-Transcendence

The impulse behind the rectification of the soul is often difficult to articulate. There is a sense of incompleteness. This feeling of incompleteness can take the form of a desire to *know* more, or a desire *to be a part of* something, or a desire to *be different* (attractive, charismatic, rich, powerful). If the feeling of incompleteness cannot be satisfied in any material or social context then one must go beyond the material. There is a tendency to characterise this as a search for the 'spiritual'.

'Spiritual' is an awkward word because of the diffuse metaphysical baggage that accompanies it, but we can ground it in the tangible social sphere of religion, mysticism, esotericism, and a world inhabited by the saints, shamans, prophets, and mystics. Time is extended into a timeless mythical past of revelation, and into a timeless mythical future of rectification and reward. Space is extended beyond the limits of the material. The spiritual becomes a way to transcend the here-and-now and the limited scope of who we are. In some to-be-defined sense we can become more than we are.

The details of this beatitude are often painted in glorious colours, and it is in the literature of the late 19th. and early 20th century that we find elaborate depictions of our full potential. We may acquire new abilities such as telepathy and clairvoyance, be seen in two places at once, have direct access to secret arcane knowledge, attain cosmic consciousness, and occupy a position in a cosmic administrative scheme not unlike the British Civil Service. We may emulate the sage Enoch and become as angels. There may be aliens involved. The sky is not even the limit.

It is tempting to point an accusatory finger at Countess Helena Petrovna Blavatsky (1831-1891), who pulled together many strands of esoteric tradition from West and East, and who gave shelter to the perennial wisdom of the ages under the umbrella of 'Theosophy'. She lived during the era of spiritualism, a craze that swept through nineteenth century society on both sides of the Atlantic. Spiritualism claimed to provide tangible proof of life after death, and undermined the ascendency of the materialist science that was providing so many new material benefits to the middle classes.

Blavatsky wanted to promote an occult science that was older and more inclusive than the materialist science of her day. Not only was she astonishingly successful and influential, she was the stimulus for a huge outpouring of spiritual revelation. Old words were harnessed to new meanings, and the spiritual landscape was reformed to mirror the hopes and prejudices of late 19th. and early 20th. century middle-class society.

Blavatsky created a confrontational opposition between occult and materialist science, and it was her vision of an occult science that lost ground. She was accused of making fraudulent claims, her reputation was destroyed, and she dropped out of public consciousness[186]. She had set herself up as the champion of ancient occult traditions that would transform the world, but it was the materialist scientific tradition she scorned that would transform the world during the next hundred years. Her vision of an occult science survived, but it was marginalised, fragmented and discredited, surfacing as 'New Age' spirituality in the sixties, and it has been much tarnished in the popular mind by a 'hippy-dippy' flight into drugs and unreason.

The active imagination (what Couliano has called 'phantasy'[187]) has been relegated to a role in entertainment, via science and fantasy fiction, film, the graphic novel, and games. A tradition of self-transcendence has been fractured into the slick marketing of personal growth and self-realisation workshops[188]. Although the Hermetic tradition lives on in many forms, the Hermetic tradition of self-transcendence is lost in a wilderness of forking paths.

---

186. Her primary works, *Isis Unveiled* and *The Secret Doctrine*, now seem dated, rambling, and often impenetrable. Set against this is a collection of the most extraordinary stories, often with extensive eye-witness testimony. Her personal correspondence and short articles reveal a person of considerable verve, sincerity, eccentric erudition, and charm.
187. *Eros and Magic in the Renaissance*, Ioan P. Couliano, University of Chicago Press 1987
188. The Tibetan Buddhist teacher Chögyam Trungpa is particularly insightful in showing how 'spirituality' is often the basis for what is simply another species of materialism - see *Cutting Through Spiritual Materialism*, Chögyam Trungpa, Shambhalla 1973

Rectification

For this reason I would like to step back from the 'spiritual' and the expectations the word creates. An accessible and meaningful way to think about self-transcendence is to consider how we grow into adults. Children spend up to a quarter of their lives learning how to enter the adult world. Throughout a period of twenty or so years, toddlers become children, and then become adolescents, and finally young adults. At this point society will consider them sufficiently mature to drink alcohol, drive a car, vote in elections, and choose sexual partners. They will still lack the full range of skills, social connections, and maturity of judgement necessary to participate at the top level in many professions.

Cognitive Limitation

When we compare human beings with other species, we find that each species possesses a cognitive limit. When we look at species that spend time in the company of people (e.g. dogs and cats) we find that while they can make excellent companions, there are parts of the human experience denied to them. They cannot enter into a discussion of a mathematical proof, a legal argument, debate ethics, or any subject that is primarily linguistic. Their understanding of *mechanism* - that is, complex causal interaction - is limited to the simplest devices.

We can infer that human beings also possess cognitive limitations. Some may be inherent, others may be a result of culture, education and experience.

We transcend ourselves routinely. We call it 'growing up'. 'Spirituality' is vague and ungrounded, but self-transcendence can be defined in a simple way. I define it to mean 'mastering larger and more complex environments'. We do this continuously through childhood, and typically peak at some point in middle-age. Self-transcendence (in the sense of 'mastering an environment') is an objective notion and it is routinely measured through testing and examination. A good example is learning to drive. It is a complex skill exercised in a dangerous environment, and we accept that lengthy training and testing is required.

The Hermetic/Kabbalistic tradition takes the view that although we may be adults in our human world, there are larger contexts. We do not see that this is so, and so we give too much weight to the priorities of this world.

Why do we not see that this is so? The answer would seem to be simple: survival. For five million years our ancestors hunted and fished, gathered berries and roots, had sex, talked, squabbled and fought. Merely staying alive required constant ingenuity. To accomplish these things we required an active administering intelligence within us - a soul. There is no obvious biological need for that soul to comprehend a big picture ... or even itself.

There may be excellent biological reasons why it *should not* comprehend a big picture or its own complexity. A feature of the 19th. century was the creation of vast insane asylums. Often built in a morbid gothic style, many of these were the size of small towns. Most now survive only in photographs.

According to a national survey published in the UK in 2009, one in four people will suffer a mental health issue *in a year*, the most common issues being anxiety and depression. Over a lifetime nearly one in five people will have suicidal thoughts. Around ten percent of people will require medical care for a personality disorder, schizophrenia or bipolar disorder.

It would seem that the soul is fragile; intricate, incomprehensibly complex, and easily knocked into a dysfunctional state. Perhaps, like a lifeboat, it has internal buoyancy to turn right-side-up. Perhaps it will resist attempts to tip it over?

Self-transcendence sounds like a good thing: growing into a 'bigger' or 'better' or more 'spiritual' kind of person, someone who is able to place his or her life within a larger context. However we must accept that for most people the self-righting and stabilising mechanisms built into the soul will oppose these efforts. We have evolved to focus on the here-and-now. Society plays its part in maintaining this focus, because society contains self-righting and stabilising mechanisms to hold its members within a consensus view. There are penalties for moving outside the circle of consensus: ostracism and isolation; removal from power; medical treatment; and incarceration.

It is easy to become indignant about this. The socially alienated invariably do. They want to drop out. They want to Stick It To The Man. They want to inhabit ideal pasts and ideal futures. But stability, consensus, and productive investment in the here-and-now has much more survival value than the many dysfunctional alternatives. Society, for all its ills, is a lifeboat. As Hobbes put it in his famous critique of 'the Natural Condition of Mankind':

> In such condition, there is no place for industry; because the fruit thereof is uncertain: and consequently no culture of the earth; no navigation, nor use of the commodities that may be imported by sea; no commodious building; no instruments of moving, and removing, such things as require much force; no knowledge of the face of the earth; no account of time; no arts; no letters; no society; and which is worst of all, continual fear, and danger of violent death; and the life of man, sol-

Rectification

itary, poor, nasty, brutish, and short.

We must consider the possibility (and experience would seem to confirm it) that although we may be capable of continued self-transcendence, there are also powerful mechanisms holding us back. The rose-tinted view of self-transcendence promoted by many books, workshops, courses and teachers may also be part of the general obfuscation - a societal misdirection, a cosy group-think, comfortable illusions, and an ego-affirming idealism. We want to feel better; we don't need the truth.

A hint of the genuine difficulty comes from the phenomenon of boredom. It is stressful to do nothing. People rant about waiting for hours, about hanging around, about the sheer awfulness of wasted time. We tend to shun the most simple of activities: sitting quietly and observing the mind. Experienced meditators will recognise the many ways in which the totality of mind and body 'push back' and become partitioned and divided by non-activity. There is an internal struggle, and one may even feel stressed and unwell. Doing nothing should be the easiest thing. It is not.

Courses, books, lectures - these are all *doing something*. We will pay to *do something*, especially if there is a diploma, badge, sash, handshake or interesting hat to celebrate attainment. Perish the thought that we should do nothing. If we are going to do nothing it has to be by choice and under our control (in a deck chair on the beach for example).

The idea that the soul is divided and contrary has a long tradition in Western culture. As we will see, St. Paul makes explicit reference to it, and Christian tradition has many accounts of the battle for the soul, often depicted as a dualist struggle between angels and demons, with Heaven and Hell as the final outcomes.

The very idea of self-transcendence implies movement, a 'before' and 'after', and so tension is inherent in the idea. There is a pull in two directions, with the Archangel *Michael* on one side and Satan (or The Great Dragon) on the other. This is how many people have depicted the struggle. While we do not have to accept this picture of a cosmic drama, it tells us that there is a struggle, and many people have experienced it.

What does the Western tradition maintain concerning transcendence and the rectification of the soul?

Two and a half thousand years ago Plato imagined the soul as descending into nature and losing sight of its autonomy and prior existence. He believed matter overwhelmed the soul, resulting in forgetting and ignorance.

If we take 'matter' to be a shorthand for 'worldly concerns' - that is, hunger, sexual desire, boredom, tiredness, pain, interruptions, deadlines, money and so on, then most of us will share the feeling of being overwhelmed and defined by the external.

Plato identified two factors as contributing towards the 'crookedness' of the soul. The first was *appetite*, and the second was *ignorance*.

Appetite signified a orientation towards the needs of the body and physical existence in general. We want things, sometimes obsessively.

Ignorance signified several things: unexamined opinion; the self-righteousness of opinionated people; a lack of awareness of our divine origin; an inability to grasp eternal truth.

Appetite and ignorance are complementary. Appetite creates a narrow focus that sees too much of too little. Ignorance signifies *the unexamined and uncritical acceptance of a world encompassed by the narrow focus of appetite*.

Plato believed physical existence was, for the soul, a befuddling condition like watching television. When we watch television we focus on the actions on the screen, and focus less on other parts of our lives. We forget the big picture while we focus on the little picture. To continue the analogy, our appetites are like television channels, and whenever we are satiated with one channel, we press the remote and switch to another.

Appetite and ignorance are two important aspects of the tradition that we should (and will) examine in more detail. Kabbalistic tradition identifies another element in the 'crookedness' of the soul. That element is *separation* - separating what should be joined, and joining what should be separate. Separation is an aspect of Kabbalah that diverges from the Platonic tradition, which viewed the Great Chain of Being as harmonious and continuous. In the Kabbalistic view, the correct relationships between all aspects of existence were broken when Adam and Eve tasted the apple in the Garden of Eden. This action separated the Tree of Life from the Tree of Knowledge of Good and Evil, and brought into being a dualistic consciousness in which all aspects of existence are perceived as *separate* and *dual*.

An important aspect of separation is the way in which the body seems separate from its environment, and the way in which mind seems to be separate from body. One can also cite the way in which the mind has turned away from any larger awareness in favour of a narrow focus in material needs - it is separate from that larger con-

Rectification

Figure 55: The Three Pillars of the Fallen State of Humankind

text, a context identified with the divine soul, the Holy Guardian Angel, or the Higher Self.

Ignorance, appetite and separation relate to the Pillars of the Tree of Life. Ignorance corresponds to the central Pillar of Consciousness. This ignorance is connected with a constructed sense of identity, the *Ego*. Appetite is concerned with what we don't have and want. It is about lack and need. It is always directed at something. Appetite is that dysfunctional aspect of relationship ("it's all about me") that is essentially predatory. Appetite corresponds to the Pillar of Force.

Separation is a fragmenting and isolating perception that is rooted in space and time. It shows a universe of *things* interacting via deterministic law. It corresponds to the Pillar of Form.

During the past one hundred years the word 'soul' has fallen into disuse. In its place, depending on context, we use several equally ill-defined and overlapping words, such as body, mind, brain, psyche, consciousness, self-consciousness, awareness, perception, cognition and so on. One reason for this shift is the modern focus on brain and mind, with the reasonable working assumption that mind is a manifestation of the physical working of the brain. There is considerable evidence from brain scanning, pharmacology, neurology, cognitive psychology, and brain trauma to support this hypothesis, and the idea of 'soul', with its metaphysical baggage, is seen as an unnecessary complication. This creates a profound dislocation with esoteric tradition, where the soul is seen as both autonomous and prior to the body.

The Platonic/Pythagorean tradition of the soul has been extraordinarily tenacious in Western culture, and holds that a root or seed of consciousness has become entangled with deterministic matter. The soul provides us with choice and free-will, powers of reasoning or intuitive knowledge, survival after death, and the ability to apprehend the archetypes of foundational knowledge - truth, beauty, goodness and so on. It is a tradition that has coiled around and through Kabbalah, hybridising with other Middle Eastern and European traditions of a similar nature. It is still a component of some current philosophical positions, and absolutely essential to almost every kind of New Age doctrine or philosophy. Even in respectable philosophical circles the argument continues, with philosophers such as David Chalmers[189] proposing that the physical brain does not 'explain' subjective experience at all, far less explain the richness, the complexity, and the creativity of inner experience demonstrated in music, poetry, art and mathematics.

The position adopted here is to take input from both sides of the debate. The dualist position, that mind exists independently of the brain, that it is non-physical - the classic mind/body problem - has been subjected to exacting analysis for centuries, and founders on the lack of a plausible causal model to connect mind and brain. There has been no breakthrough since the time of Descartes (1596-1650 CE). A great labour has been expended in trying to preserve the autonomy of mind (and by extension, the human soul) but in my opinion it fails to convince. The case becomes weaker year-on-year as brain mapping becomes more detailed and specific, showing how specific cognitive and affective functions are localised in the physical brain.

However, the idea that the mind is 'just the workings of the brain' also falls short. It is impossible to understand the Great Wall of China in any experiment involving a single human brain. As the human race continues to dig gigantic holes in the ground, erase forests, and blanket the globe in concrete, we have to admit the possibility that mind, not brain, is the most significant process operating on this planet.

In parallel, it is necessary to recalibrate our definition of materialism now that it is clear that the view of little particles banging into

---

189. *The Conscious Mind*, David J. Chalmers, Oxford University Press, 1996

Rectification

each other is too narrow. Matter can self-organise. Matter can assume stable patterns with behaviours of immense complexity, it can form patterns of intricate causal power. We used to call this life, but now we have to call it something else - intelligence - because there is a broader concept that subsumes many forms of organised matter. Intelligence, not matter *per se*, drives the world. Matter is at the dumber end of the spectrum of behaviour.

We can now experience embedded intelligence in our daily lives as we interact with smartphones, home media systems, smart fridges and washing machines. I even have a smart toothbrush. Automobiles are no longer just go-faster prosthetics, they are intelligent and autonomous; that is, they sense their environment, evaluate an appropriate response, and act. They are ready to drive themselves. Three hundred years ago people would not have hesitated to ask whether such objects contained an animating spirit. We no longer have a clear division between animate and inanimate; many objects that were once dumb are now smart, they have behaviour, they have an 'inside'.

It is this idea of soul as an embodied 'inside' that is developed in the following chapters. This is not a new idea; Aristotle, through his interest in biology, diverged from Plato over two thousand years ago. My treatment has been influenced by exposure to artificial intelligence, robotics, biology, and modern theories of cognition. I have attempted to tread a difficult path between the old and the new, avoiding the more obvious pitfalls of soul/body dualism and at the same time avoiding the tendency to reduce mind to neurons and chemicals.

It might seem that this is not a mystical treatment of soul, but it is, profoundly so. Soul is always referred back to the environment to which it is an adaptation. As we shift focus from the outer human world to the self-reflective inner world, and onward to the cosmos, we must at each step transcend our narrow focus, acknowledge a new and larger scope, and build a new kind of soul.

The Hermetic Kabbalah

25

The Soul and its Parts

25.1 The Composite Soul

A key idea used throughout this book is that a soul is an active administering intelligence that enables a living organism to remain *distinct from its environment*. So long as the administering intelligence is functional, the organism exhibits the kinds of behaviour we call life. When it stops being functional, the organism decays back into the environment and is no longer distinct - it dies. When we say "dust to dust", we recognise that we are distinct from the environment only for a time; we come from dust, and go back to it.

This definition does not convey what is meant by 'intelligence', a question that will be studied more fully in the next chapter. The brief answer: intelligence is the ability to sense a state of affairs in an environment, evaluate this occurrence with respect to an organism's current needs, and then act back on the environment. For example, I see an apple (sense), I ask myself "would I like to eat this apple" (evaluate), and then I pick it up and eat it (act).

Even bacteria and proteins can sense, evaluate and act. Within a single cell the active, administering intelligence consists of thousands of electrochemical feedback loops that individually sense, evaluate, and act, using the genetic code as an active computer. The embodied intelligence of a single cell - its soul - is extraordinary in its complex-

The Inside of the Outside

If a device or organism exhibits behaviour, then we assume there is an 'inside' that makes it work - levers or clockwork or motors or electronics or muscles - and some kind of control logic to tie things together.

The idea of a 'generalised control logic' became explicit with the invention of weaving looms, musical boxes and pianolas in the 18th. and 19th. centuries. A music box or fairground calliope could produce an almost infinite number of tunes using control patterns encoded on discs or rolls or cards. Although the control logic must always be embodied in a physical medium, and although it interacts with the rest of the mechanism (or 'body') using straightforward causality, it is separate. The drum of a music box can be removed and replaced with a different drum, just like a tape cassette or CD, or a program controlling a computer.

A more complex device can use the full power of computer technology (or DNA, or neurons) to produce tremendously complex behaviour, but the underlying principles are the same. We can make a conceptual separation between an 'outside' that acts in the world, and an 'inside' that controls it using a minimal or narrow interface. Whether the human brain is organised like this is unclear - it probably is not - but conceptually we can still think of the soul as a distinct, controlling entity without lapsing into metaphysical dualism.

ity.

The soul is in some sense a simulacrum of its environment. Sensing, evaluating and acting all take place with respect to something. Situations have to be *recognised* before they can be acted upon, and action requires an embedded knowledge of the environment in which action takes place. Before a fox can chase the rabbit, it must recognise the rabbit. It must model the rabbit, anticipate the rabbit, simulate the rabbit. And when it does chase the rabbit, the fox's brain and spinal cord and legs understand the physical dynamics of running at speed - bobbing, weaving, sprinting, all the things the rabbit does to throw the fox off. The better the fox is at simulating rabbits, the more likely it is to catch one.

Evolution has gifted the fox with locomotion, a way of running about on the surface of this planet. Foxes don't climb trees, or skitter about on crags, or swim in the oceans - there are better adaptations in the form of monkeys, goats and fish (whose bodies also reflect their environment). This also is a key idea: the soul does not stand alone, but always in a relationship with an environment, an environment it embodies through simulation.

There is an episode of *The Simpsons* where Bart sells his soul to Milhouse for $5. This is the popular view of the soul, a metaphysical

The Soul and its Parts

adjunct to the body that can be traded, wagered, sold or lost. It can travel, it can languish in purgatory, it can be prayed-for. This kind of soul may be useful for the purpose of generating large quantities of moralistic entertainment (and Dante's *Divine Comedy* provides much of the backdrop) but will not be useful here.

The ancients saw the soul first and foremost as the animating power in the body (see The *Inside of the Outside* above). They gave it a name because it seemed to have both identity and coherence, and it seemed to depart suddenly. It is at the point of death that the soul seems almost tangible. Something goes away. Whether we see the soul in materialistic terms as an harmonious organisation of parts, or whether we see it as a metaphysical cloud of animating power, one cannot doubt that at death, while the body remains apparently unchanged, something critically important has gone.

How does one explain this? There are two important intuitions. The first intuition is that something has fallen apart. Socrates gives the example of a lyre that been damaged through neglect and can no longer produce beautiful music. The second intuition is that something has departed. The first explanation is materialistic, the second dualistic. The first assumes the soul is a harmony of parts that can decay, the second that it is an entirely different kind of substance from the material body it inhabits.

Both views were important in antiquity. Facing death, Socrates rejected the 'harmony of parts' view in favour of the soul's immortality. In time, the dualistic view of the soul dominated Christian thinking, and so the word 'soul' fell out of use when modern science undermined the dualistic religious outlook. Perhaps if Socrates had chosen differently, the history of the West would have turned out differently.

In order to maintain continuity with tradition I will use the word 'soul' even when I am using it in the sense of a purely materialistic 'harmony of parts'. I do this because the phenomenon we call 'life' has to cover everything from a bacterium swimming through water to a mathematician proving a theorem. The ancients recognised that the human soul existed in multiple environments; sometimes we behave like animals with no thought for anything but food, shelter and sex; sometimes we are like frivolous social butterflies looking for status and recognition; and occasionally we exhibit an almost god-like apprehension of truth through geometry and mathematics.

It is as if the soul is stratified, like the layers of rock revealed by the cutting action of a river. Some of these layers are clearly mechanistic and organic and do not survive death; some are more mysterious. The idea that the soul has parts is an important aspect of Kabbalah, and derives from a union of Biblical exegesis and Hellenistic philosophy. This idea has a huge impact on how one might understand 'the rectification of the soul'.

For the purposes of this discussion I assume that the soul consists of four parts: the nutritive soul, the animal soul, the rational or social soul, and the divine soul.

25.2 The Nutritive Soul

The nutritive soul is concerned with issues common to all life. These are energy and metabolism, growth, self-identity and self-repair, and reproduction. We find these functions in single cells, and in any community of single cells. Human beings are, before anything else, a community of single cells that have been selected by evolution to live and die together.

The single most important thing a living cell must do is extract free energy from the environment. Free energy is available in sunlight, and in the chemical bonds of many kinds of molecule, especially sugars such as glucose. Free energy is converted into an internal energy store called a proton gradient, and this reservoir functions like a traditional mill pond, flowing through a protein water wheel to power all the processes inside the cell.

There are thousands of these processes running in parallel, processes of astonishing complexity and elegance. The mill workers are, for the most part, proteins, electrochemical machines that combine both the ability to *sense* and *act*. The decision-making ability to *evaluate* comes from computational abilities inherent in genetic code. Sensor proteins identify conditions inside the cell and interact with DNA. Genes can be switched off and on, and worker enzyme proteins can be made or destroyed. To find such directed intelligent activity occurring on a scale of a few nanometers is extraordinary.

All cells must repair themselves. Every chemical reaction is reversible, and so the cell uses energy to run forwards as its death runs backwards. A cell is always running up the down escalator. Things are made, and simultaneously, unavoidably, things are unmade. Nothing can be left alone, equilibrium is dynamic, not static. A cell can never sit and do nothing.

The most precious item in a cell is its DNA, its genetic code, and there are two copies, the simplest form of self-representation. There are scanning processes to keep it in good repair by fixing errors. The ultimate safeguard for identity is reproduction. With suitable nutrient a bacterium can reproduce itself in twenty minutes.

It is when cells form into communities that identity becomes a significant issue. There are advantages in being part of a community. Communities can create stable micro-environments, and exploit new methods to obtain energy. A huge survival advantage comes from novel forms of reproduction, such as wind-blown seeds. A disadvantage is that communities succeed or fail together. A single rogue element can bring down the whole community. It then becomes important to identify and eradicate cells that deviate from the norm. The human body contains a terrifyingly complex immune system that protects us from cancers, viruses, invasive bacteria and fungi, but when it goes wrong the immune system can attack and destroy any part of the body. It is a blessing for many, and a curse for some.

The issue of self-identity is common to all communities of living things and is related to self-representation and self-simulation. We find this in human society in the form of closed groups with membership requirements. Passports, visas, identity cards, immigration officials, military forces - these are part of the immune system of nation states.

Many key principles of Kabbalah can be found in operation at the very bottom of the Tree of Life where organisation emerges out of chemistry. One of the primary interpretations of the diagram of the Tree of Life is that it denotes the essential principles/components/dynamic processes of a *living organism*. It denotes a composite organism, a community of wholes that have cohered into a greater whole (a *holon*). In Kabbalah, *Chesed* is the energy that denotes things coming together through bonds of mutual relationship, while its opposite, *Din* (judgement) separates the wheat from the chaff - it is the immune system. *Tiferet* denotes homeostasis, the dynamic equilibrium or balance, and as such embodies the principle of self-regulation, self-representation and in humans, the self-simulation that we call consciousness.

25.3 The Animal Soul

A large group of organisms can extract energy directly from their environment. When energy is abundant, they prosper, and when it is not, they die. We recognise multi-cellular organisms of this type as plants. Plants have a very simple way of being alive, and while they will grow into the light or send out roots in search of water, they can do this with only the most basic forms of sensing, evaluating and acting.

Animals are a step-up in complexity. Animals ingest other organisms, such as plants, or each other. Because they eat other organisms, they are forced to move around, perhaps even to hunt or trap (like spiders). These survival strategies require much more sophisticated means to sense, evaluate and act, and so animals have evolved a brain and nervous system to facilitate this sensing, evaluating and acting[190].

With animals we lose the sense of 'community of parts'. Animals are so much more than a community of cells, because animals sense, evaluate and act at a level far above that of individual cells. An animal provides the appearance of behaving like a single integrated being. This is why we can talk about an *animal soul*.

The animal soul is probably the most important part of a human being. The animal soul runs the show. It knows how to talk, walk, type, drive an automobile, and catch a ball. It is excited by food, and disgusted by faeces. It becomes sexually exited by many stimuli, some exceedingly odd. It knows what it likes to eat, and it knows when it wants to sleep. The animal soul is able to pre-empt almost every consideration when its needs are paramount.

It can master physical skills with the extraordinary finesse found in elite athletes, musicians, artists and crafters. It learns by example and repetition and reward - we call this training. Sometimes it learns by punishment, but mostly it infers from punishment the power of intimidation and fear. For the most part, especially during childhood, it learns through observation of family members and authority figures.

Often it knows how to deal with a situation, and gets on with it. We call this 'habit'. Sometimes it does not know what to do and alerts the rational soul. We call this 'consciousness'.

The animal soul is, for the most part, pre-linguistic. It communicates via emotion, and through images. The animal soul creates the *base-valuation* for everything in the world. It provides a natural response to hot and cold, to crowds, to a street filled with restaurants and coffee bars, to the thrill of moving quickly, to repetition, to idleness, to pain, to dark places, and to many kinds of comfort. The animal soul *colours-in* the world with values, like a young child with a colouring book.

---

190. There are single-cell organisms that hunt and ingest other organisms. Clearly they do not possess a brain or nervous system.

The Soul and its Parts

The animal soul understands society at the level of many intelligent animals. It understands family. It understands dominance and hierarchy. It understand companionship, and it understands ostracism and loneliness. It understands survival and sexual competition. It will become violent in many situations.

The animal soul has had a negative press in Western culture. Its cruder forms of behaviour are sometimes referred to as 'bestial', because the animal soul has only a rudimentary sense of society. Much of the legal superstructure of society is alien to it, and it acts with indifference to the constraints on the social soul. This becomes apparent in many kinds of anti-social behaviour such as theft, violence, and sexual assault.

The automobile provokes some of the most atypical behaviours in normal people. It is as if the animal soul regards the car as a lair to be defended at all costs. Its response to minor traffic infractions can be a terrifying rage. Parking tickets, traffic wardens, overcrowded car parks - these are situations where people can explode.

One of the most powerful manifestations of the animal soul is sexuality. We know that the most adept and cunning of politicians will destroy their careers for sex. Infidelity in particular can destroy families, the bedrock of communities, and so traditionally there have been very strong sanctions against it.

Societies try to tame the animal soul during childhood by training and discipline. For adults there are laws and punishments. Lawgivers such as Solon, Moses, and Mohammed have been venerated because without laws there would be no orderly and peaceful communion between people.

The Mosaic laws that have shaped Western society are very simple: give one day per week to social worship; honour your father and mother; do not kill, do not commit adultery; do not steal; do not bear false witness; do not covet your neighbours' possessions[191]. To the social soul these commandments are obvious common sense. They restrain the animal soul. They keep the peace.

The animal soul poses a threat to social life, but it poses a much greater threat to the traditional religious vocation, because it drags the attention towards necessities of animal life. It is impossible to ignore. To paraphrase Oscar Wilde, we may be attempting to look at the stars but we are being dragged into the gutter. There is a dualism

---

191. The first few Mosaic commandments are meta-commandments that establish their authority in a unique God who is beyond human conceptualisation.

here that has had a sustained impact on Western culture, especially in its attitude to sexuality.

It is in the quasi-gnostic writings of St. Paul that we find the idea that the world and the body, and all its inelegant necessities, are the work of Satan, who has, through the disobedience of Adam and Eve, brought corruption and death into the world. The world as it is currently established, along with all its necessities (and we include here that part of the human soul that must deal with this world), is a source of corruption and death, and a product of an entity who fights against God.

Paul divided the soul against itself (*Romans 7:15*):

I do not understand what I do. For what I want to do I do not do, but what I hate, I do. And if I do what I do not want to do, I agree that the law is good. As it is, it is no longer I myself who do it, but it is sin living in me. For I know that good itself does not dwell in me, that is, in my sinful nature. For I have the desire to do what is good, but I cannot carry it out. For I do not do the good I want to do, but the evil I do not want to do—this I keep on doing. Now if I do what I do not want to do, it is no longer I who do it, but it is sin living in me that does it.

So I find this law at work: Although I want to do good, evil is right there with me. For in my inner being I delight in God's law; but I see another law at work in me, waging war against the law of my mind and making me a prisoner of the law of sin at work within me. What a wretched man I am!

The sentence "I see another law at work in me, waging war against the law of my mind" is as clear a statement as one is likely to find of what it is like to go against the will of the animal soul. Unlike Paul however, we do not have to regard this "other law" as inherently sinful. Nevertheless, we will discover, as Paul did, that there is a power within us, often unconscious and untamed, that was reared in a world of Necessity. It is allied to this world. If we love the world, we may come to love it. If we hate the world, we may come to hate it.

25.4 The Social or Rational Soul

The social or rational soul coexists with both the nutritive and animal souls. Its environment is human society, and it is as complex as human society. A precondition for its emergence was natural language, and it is for this reason that the ancients denied animals a rational soul. An animal may be cunning and subtle and intelligent, but it cannot explain its behaviour, even to itself. It cannot throw light on its motives, its goals, or its plans. It cannot recall the deeds of its ancestors or tell the stories of its tribe. Even if it feels moved by sunsets or flowers or scented breezes, it cannot tell us how it feels.

The social soul is the seat of identity. It knows its own name. It can provide an account of its life, and a recitation of its likes and dislikes. It has a predilection for talking and for interaction, wit, humour, gossip and scandal. It will natter all night about putting the world to order. It soaks-up information that might prove valuable in business, in sport, or in fashion. It is constantly engaged in making choices: should I buy this, or should I buy that? Should we eat out or stay in? Italian or Greek? Your car or my car? Audi or BMW? Petrol or diesel? An extra bedroom or a larger kitchen?

It believes it has a particular and unique discernment in music, furnishing, clothing, food and wine. It will justify extol these choices to the point of exhaustion, even when you (the captive listener) are biting your tongue with restraint. It is a font of explanation and rationale. It will talk about why it chose this school or that neighbourhood, to the limit of social etiquette.

The rational soul subsists on a diet of analysis. It compares, it contrasts, it weighs and evaluates, it asks questions. This is why boredom is such a fearful thing, and solitary confinement one of the worst punishments. We don't like to be bored. We would prefer to play a game, read a book, watch a film, or (and here is a clear sign of its nature) watch other people exercising judgement in an endless diet of reality television, panel shows, game shows and sport. This is what the rational soul evolved to do - exercise judgement in complex or novel situations.

Human beings use reason in every aspect of their lives. Much of it is common-sense and imparted in childhood. My mother would say "don't run with scissors", or "when you give a knife to someone, give them the handle", or "wash your hands before eating", or "always stop and look before crossing the road".

Reason is a linguistic method for encoding causality. We learn how to achieve certain effects, and how to avoid pitfalls and calamities. "Boil drinking water when possible or you may be very ill[192]" is a cardinal rule in many places. Along with these maxims we also acquire explanations, in this case: "because it kills deadly bacteria". They may be good explanations or they may be spurious explanations; what is important is that we try them out and test them for efficacy and learn how to understand the world in a flexible and extensible way.

---

192. When I was a child in Africa this was drummed into me. Today, bottled water serves the same purpose.

Even something so basic as the understanding of time, a year of three hundred and sixty-five days, with its seasons for planting and reaping, was a huge step forward for the human race. The yearly cycle is not something we understand intuitively; our ancestors had to learn how to simulate the patterns of the Earth's movement around the Sun, the movements of the Moon and stars, and encode this knowledge in social rituals. Much of the 'secret wisdom' of antiquity was astronomical.

Reason is not in any way a modern accomplishment. The 'Age of Reason' was the invention of European intellectuals with big wigs and scented handkerchiefs. The human race had been employing practical reason since it learned how to nap flint. Hunting, care of livestock, agriculture, trading, child-rearing, spinning, weaving and cooking, require a vast stock of practical reason. Observe any skilled craft worker and ask them to comment as they work; one will be overwhelmed with rationale. Examine their tools and you will see millenia of rational design. Why does a workshop have half-a-dozen different hammers? Why are there several different saws? Who decided the angle of the spiral of a twist drill? How many chisels does a woodworker really need?

One can find the same thoughtfulness in every practical skill: cooking, sewing and embroidery, garment design, blacksmithing, building, surgery, animal husbandry, forestry, automobile mechanics, computer programming, hairdressing and so on. There are countless skills that require years of learning and practice to acquire. All have received untold generations of careful thought and refinement.

The products of rational thought and design are so ubiquitous that we may not bother to examine them ... unless they are 'broken'. If an object (e.g. a cup) is broken we may attempt to 'fix' it. For something to be broken it has to conform to an ideal, and when we fix it we attempt to restore its ideal state. We have a clear sense of what that ideal state is. We like to buy new and unused things because they are more likely to conform to the ideal. Today, many of our everyday objects of utility - the laptop, the mobile phone, the music player, the washing machine, the dishwasher, the microwave, the automobile - are too complex for the average person to understand or repair. This was not always so - in times gone by most people would have been able to make or repair almost everything they used. There are many accounts of wooden sailing ships being severely damaged and almost entirely rebuilt by the crew[193].

It is probably the case that our ancestors had a clearer intuitive

The Soul and its Parts

grasp of practical reason than many living today, because they had to deal directly with the natural world. One cannot argue with a piece of wood, a cow, or snow, and one cannot argue with a fever. These people were not feather-bedded by modern life. They were not surrounded by mass-manufactured goods, or a vast array of technical specialists. They had to solve problems using whatever came to hand.

Today, our practical reason is more likely to be put to use in the social sphere. The difficulty here is that productive reasoning depends critically on good assumptions, and in the modern social sphere, one can assume whatever one wants. Reason dissolves into opinion. A craft worker can test an assumption very easily by making a prototype, but anyone can air an opinion, based on whatever arbitrary assumptions they choose, and that opinion is rarely put to the test. This breeds arrogance. There is little humility. Opinions are best heard when spoken loudly.

The rational soul then, is often afflicted. Its ability to compare, contrast, weigh and evaluate is often pointless when its conclusions are not put to the test. The ability to exercise judgement, so critical to our evolution, can descend into a mass of crazy opinions, and these can produce active hostility to self and to others. The rational soul may respond to situations with limited data and "jump to conclusions". It may be biased, weighing evidence unfairly, or it may be corrupt. It may overreach itself and try to reason in situations where it has no experience and then try to reason itself out of the resulting failure. Sometimes a person will blame themselves; just as often he or she will blame others. When things go very wrong the legal system has evolved to evaluate complex social situations with as much objectivity and fairness as possible.

Many of the negative aspects of religion have come about because *texts* have been used as *ground truth*; that is, statements are used to anchor complex chains of reasoning. These statements are not interpreted as allegory, metaphor, myth, legend, or tribal story-telling tradition. Reason has to begin with some base truth, and sacred texts such as the *Bible* and the *Koran* form the basis for complex systems of jurisprudence and social tradition that cannot be challenged without arousing intense hostility. This is called 'faith'.

If the rational soul is not trained and exercised it cannot distinguish good assumptions from bad assumptions, good reasoning from

---

193. One of the most dramatic of these incidents occurred in 1770 when Captain Cook and crew discovered the Great Barrier Reef by ripping a great hole in the bottom of the *Endeavour*. Far beyond any possibility of help, it took seven weeks to repair.

erroneous reasoning, or a testable conclusion from a barmy conclusion. It was this that Socrates and Plato set out to investigate so many centuries ago. The idea that reasoning should be tested is the basis of modern scientific thought and practice. Science is not so different in spirit from the suck-it-and-see, trial-and-error experimentation that has been the norm in crafting skills since human beings first picked up a piece of flint and began napping it.

The social soul is revealed in the way it chooses its entertainment. Puzzles, word games such as Scrabble, strategy games such as chess, and an entire industry of computer games where one must compete and survive in hostile situations. It is fixated on TV game shows, reality shows where people practice a skill, sport, crime dramas, and police and legal procedurals. The animal soul spends its time eating, drinking and having sex. The rational soul wants to be the best and win.

25.5 The Divine Soul

Throughout history, and as far back as we can infer from archeology, people have believed and acted as if some part of a human being survived death. Even today this is probably the dominant belief worldwide. Some believe the soul is reunited with those that have gone before, and others believe it is reborn into a new life.

I will say at the outset that the position adopted here is agnostic. Increased longevity and an aging population have exposed more and more of us to the neurological consequences of old age - strokes and degenerative illnesses such as Alzheimer's Disease. There are significant numbers of unfortunate people whose personalities do not survive life, let alone death.

In the *Phaedo*, Plato considered this idea. Socrates is in prison awaiting death. As Socrates and his friends debated the nature of the soul they considered the possibility that the soul is the *harmony of the body*, and used the analogy of a lyre. The lyre is an harmonious combination of materials, physical proportions, construction and tuning. The harmony of the lyre exists in the correct relationship of parts; 'harmony' is not an autonomous component that descends into and resides in the lyre. If the lyre, through decay or violence, loses its material integrity, then harmony also departs.

This is an insightful analogy. Our lives are filled with complex appliances. They work for a period of time[194], and then they stop

---

194. One month longer than the warranty.

The Soul and its Parts

working properly. When we say "it is broken", we mean the same thing as saying "the harmony of the parts has been disrupted".

Socrates rejected the "harmony of parts" hypothesis, arguing that anything that is a composite is subject to change. He was arguing in prison on his day of execution, and it is clear he was biased in favour of the soul's immortality. Despite Socrates rejection, the idea of the soul as "a harmony of parts" occurs many times in the Western tradition, and can be found in the symbolism of *Tiferet* in the Tree of Life.

The Hermetic tradition suggests that some parts of the soul do not survive death, but that some do. There is some consensus that the nutritive, animal, and social souls do not survive. The part that survives, the divine soul, the *neshamah*, the 'divine increment', is clearly not composed of anything related our normal experience - it is (by exclusion) something else. It lies outside of the entire sphere of being-in-the-world. One could speculate that it relates directly to basic reality, it may be as fundamental as energy or space or time. This is speculation. To the extent it can be grasped or apprehended, it cannot be described.

We know that each species on this planet has a cognitive limit. We must assume that human beings, separated from the great apes by only a few million years of genetic change, may be just as limited. This is a disappointing and disturbing thought. Some of the problems that perplex us may be as far from our understanding as a dog confronted by a textbook on tensor calculus. We must hope that whatever the human race becomes, it will be capable of understanding more than we can. The principal task in the rectification of the soul is to go as far as we can today, and lay down a path for others to follow.

The Hermetic Kabbalah

26

Intelligence

26.1 Intelligence

The word intelligence was used in the previous chapter at the point where the soul was defined as "an active administering intelligence ...". One of the ancient traditions of the soul that must be reconsidered concerns intelligence. There are strong reasons for doing so.

The Platonic tradition and its many offshoots saw mind and intelligence as a divine attribute that was diluted according to distance from its source. The cosmos was structured into layers of dependent beings according to their closeness to the divine ideal, giving rise to the celestial hierarchies of angels and spirits that were part of the European worldview until the age of reason. Even today occult literature discusses 'intelligences' in connection with the practice of evocation and invocation, as an alternative to using 'spirits' or '*daemones*'.

Christian theology, a descendent of Hellenistic philosophy, depicts God as omniscient, omnipotent and omnipresent, and so manifesting what is effectively an infinite intelligence. The Neoplatonic version of transcendence was an upward movement away from the distorting and obscuring effects of matter into an empyrean characterised by a clear view of root forms and causes, apprehended by a divine faculty of reason and intelligence.

There was an overwhelming consensus that intelligence diminished progressively when one compared human beings with animals, plants and rocks. This seemed obvious, and it was not until the latter half of the twentieth century that serious doubts emerged.

When computer scientists first began to experiment with the idea of artificial intelligence they began with the ability their Renaissance and Enlightenment forebears had identified as most clearly marking us out as intelligent: the ability to communicate using language. There were some early successes, such as Terry Winograd's SHRDLU (c. 1968-70). SHRDLU could understand sentences that referred to a world containing a small number of coloured geometrical objects, such as blocks and pyramids. It obeyed simple instructions to move and stack objects, and it could report what it 'saw'.

When computer scientists tried to extend this work beyond simple worlds, the results were disappointing. Researchers realised that words are grounded in a vast, interconnected mesh of knowledge, and tried to create 'ontologies' to ground this knowledge. The problem then was the astonishing difficulty in nailing-down the meaning of simple concepts like 'light' or 'heavy', and the prodigious quantity of computation required to chase down all the possible meanings of even simple sentences. One can build larger databases, but the larger the databases, the greater the computation. A certain amount of brute-force progress has been made, but one can debate the extent to which this work as qualifies as intelligence. 'Dumb on a spectacularly large scale' might be a better characterisation.

Some researchers abandoned the linguistic approach to intelligence and began to look at simple organisms, such as insects. Others looked at sub-systems of complex organisms, such as vision, or hearing, or locomotion. It became quickly apparent that even the simplest parts of the simplest organisms were immensely complex by the standards of our technology. Artificial intelligence researchers revised their expectations and learned humility. They began a phase of trying to reverse-engineer aspects of living organisms - the flight of insects, the locomotion of beetles, the cooperative behaviours of ants and bees, the flocking of birds and the shoaling of fish, the environmental navigation of houseflies.

It is difficult to emphasise how humbling it is to do this kind of research, to realise that many aspects of living organisms are optimised down the level of individual molecules. For example, the flagellar movement of a gut bacterium is determined by the number of methyl groups attached to a protein. The algorithm is: one methyl group, tumble this way; two methyl groups, tumble that way; three

Intelligence

methyls, don't tumble. Living organisms can build intelligence at scales we cannot resolve with the most powerful microscopes. This means that one single cell from the human body is more complex than any device or mechanism made by human beings.

It is an overwhelming thought that each neuron in the brain could be working to this level of complexity. There is a tendency to imagine that neurons are internally dumb and function as little electrical switches, like transistors in a computer. When one studies bacteria, which have a much simpler structure than the cells in our bodies, one discovers that bacteria are anything but simple or dumb, and they are capable of social behaviours. They can coordinate for mutual advantage. Individual brain neurons are more complex than bacteria, and it is possible that the brain is less like a computer and more like an integrated society of social organisms exploiting the considerable internal intelligence of neurons.

The evidence from modern research is that intelligence begins *right down at the bottom*. If we define intelligence as the ability to sense, evaluate, and act, then even individual molecules seem to qualify. It is cumbersome to talk about the way proteins act or behave inside cells without using an intentional vocabulary, as if they were intentional agents, and not just dumb chemicals. For example, there are *chaperone proteins* in cells that 'help' other proteins fold into the correct shapes, and they have actual behaviour, like lobster pots.

There are many other examples. The mechanisms that viruses such as the T4 bacteriophage (see Figure 56) use to find, dock onto, and penetrate cells can only be described in terms of intelligent protein mechanics. A bacteriophage is not very intelligent, but its small collection of proteins can still identify a host, grab hold of it, damage its membrane, and release the viral genetic code[195]. There are strong indications that some proteins are rudimentary agents, in that they can sense, evaluate and act. Their intelligence may not be much more than that of a central-heating controller, but it is surprising to find it at all.

If intelligence begins right down at the bottom then there is no point in trying to locate it anywhere. It doesn't *descend* from God and find a home in the ovum. It *ascends* from God.

---

195. This is what Giger's face-hugging alien did, and what is more, these proteins look like it.

Intelligence 'self-organises' out of the *Ungrund* at the level of atoms. There is no Cartesian 'seat of the soul' located in the human brain. Soul is seated everywhere. Each milligram of soil is packed with more intelligence than the entire computing infrastructure of the planet. This intelligence is mostly running in parallel: metabolising glucose, manufacturing proteins, pumping ions, and doing other cellular maintenance.

The same is true in our bodies; most of the intelligence is working down at the bottom. A small part of this activity is diverted into absorbing light, propagating electrical pulses, contracting muscle fibres and other activities of a more coordinated nature necessary for the global good - breathing in oxygen and regulating its level would be one such example.

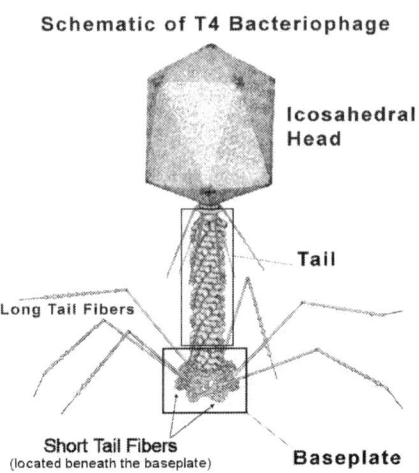

Figure 56: The T4 bacteriophage, which consists of nothing more than a few proteins and some inactive genetic material. *Credit: The figure has been adapted by Petr Leiman (Purdue University) from a drawing by Fred Eiserling (UCLA).*

A great deal of energy is used at the cellular level to process information. Although the human brain is 2% of the weight of the body, it uses 20% of the energy. It is tempting to suggest that only a trivial amount of intelligence is required to decide between items when choosing from the menu in a restaurant, but the energy consumption of the cerebral cortex suggests otherwise. A gigantic amount of intelligence is required.

There are about seven billion people on the planet at the time of writing, and in most cases we are not regimented and disciplined like the workers in *Metropolis*. We are actively coordinated by traffic lights and lane markings, and by time zones and business hours, and meal times, but mostly we are able to run our own lives.

In the same way the cells in the body are loosely coordinated. There are chemicals pumped around the bloodstream that provide various kinds of coordination, but cells and organs are mostly left to do as they please. Eyes do eye stuff, and ears do ear stuff, and the heart does heart stuff. One of the tasks of the brain is to coordinate all this independent activity and produce the kind of directed activity that keeps us alive. Computer scientists have thought about this problem and tried to model ways in which a large number of quasi-autonomous sub-systems can interact to control a single body. The answer may be very simple: the loudest shout wins.

A traditionalist might dislike the direction in which this argument is heading. Even if modern biological research does find 'intelligence' down at the level of proteins, it is an entirely deterministic and mechanistic intelligence. One might argue that there is no 'real' sensing and evaluating and acting, any more than a door key senses, evaluates and acts on a lock. This can't be *real* intelligence, can it? Perhaps it is not enough to consider complex behaviour; what about that mysterious adjunct to human intelligence, what we call consciousness and self-consciousness?

26.2 Consciousness

Consciousness is considered by many to be a great mystery, perhaps the last remaining unexplained mystery, a mystery that lies beyond the grasp of scientific explanation. Others think otherwise[196], and can point to many experiments that demonstrate that consciousness does not stand alone and free, a sovereign entity ruling the body. These experiments suggest that consciousness is more like a glove puppet, animated by an unseen hand.

The first necessary clarification is that when the word consciousness is used, in almost all cases it does not describe a thing. There is no 'thing' called consciousness. It signifies a relationship. The connection becomes much clearer when written as "Peter is conscious of Mary", or "Peter has consciousness of Mary". This has a similar form to "The cat is under the table", where "under" describes the relationship between cat and table. When consciousness is used to signify a relationship between a sentient observer and a sense impression then almost all the inexplicable mysteriousness of the concept vanishes.

There is a vast literature of sloppy usage where consciousness is treated as a light that shines in the absence of perception - a lamp of 'pure being', a consciousness that exists outside of a relationship with the external and material. The best argument against this sloppy usage is meditation. The second-best argument is also meditation - observe for yourself how the mind needs to synthesise worlds as part

---

196. *Incognito, The Secret Lives of the Brain*, David Eagleman, Canongate 2012. See also *Consciousness Explained*, Daniel C. Dennett, Penguin 1993.

of its dualist perspective of subject and object. Mystical traditions maintain that non-dualistic consciousness is possible, but this is emphatically *not* the popular usage of the word. The popular usage of 'conscious' equates to 'responds to sense impressions'. This is what is meant in a hospital when someone asks 'is she conscious yet?'.

The nature of our consciousness - what we perceive, the selectivity of perception, and the valuations we place on these perceptions - can be changed, often radically, by use of psychoactive chemicals. It can be changed by trauma and disease. It can be changed by tiredness, by food, by stress, and by exercise. It can be changed by something as simple as talking to a friend, or looking at an old photograph.

Much of our modern understanding has not come from elegant philosophical introspection in the manner of Descarte. It has come from psychology and neurology, and from a growing appreciation of *unconsciousness*. Unconsciousness here is used to signify all the things we 'can do without thinking'. It does not mean comatose.

Most of us can carry out tasks of considerable complexity without much thought, and there are activities in sport and music where having to think about what one is doing is an active impediment. Ask a golfer to relearn his swing - this is the fastest route to despair. When we have to focus on what we are doing, we become slow and clumsy. Trying to learn a new dance with a partner can be excruciating; there is no grace, no rhythm, no flow. Once the dance is learned it becomes as natural as walking. As for public speaking, few things are more awful and lifeless than a speaker who has lost the thread and has to fumble with notes.

The conclusion then, and this conclusion is easily tested by experiment and daily observation, is that the majority of our most important activities (typing this for example) are not only accomplished with a complete lack of awareness, they are actively impeded by self-observation. If a genie came out of a bottle and offered you unconscious mastery of a skill (for example, Olympic level gymnastic ability, concert-level piano playing, or fluency in Mandarin), would you turn it down because you had *no conscious understanding* of your new abilities?

I wouldn't. I do not even know how I am composing this paragraph. I can exercise judgement once I have written it, and usually rewrite it several times, but the fact is, I do not usually know what I am going to write. It is as much a surprise to me as it is to you. Unconsciousness is not a disadvantage; in many skills such as martial arts, unconsciousness (*mushin* = 'no mind' in Japanese) is a measure of attainment.

A current scientific hypothesis is that consciousness plays an important role in the overall dynamic of the psyche by popping into existence when we are confronted by anything that *cannot* be dealt with using unconscious routines. In the television series *Star Trek Voyager*, the ship does not have a doctor on board, and they are forced to rely on an artificial entity called the Emergency Medical Hologram. This construct pops into existence whenever there is a medical emergency. Then it goes away again. Consciousness is like this.

Consider sleep. During sleep we lack the directed activity of waking consciousness, but we are not unconscious. Sleep studies show that most people will alter their position many times during sleep. They may become sexually aroused, or babble nonsense, and some people walk around. There are episodes of the idiosyncratic quasi-consciousness we call dreaming.

Awareness of time is different during sleep. Hours can pass in a flash. Awareness of time is not entirely lost however; when I wake during the night I can often guess the time with reasonable accuracy.

A most interesting thing about sleep is the manner in which we stop sleeping. Anything that is intrusive - a strange noise, a need to urinate, daylight, being touched - will 'wake us up'. Like the Emergency Medical Hologram, consciousness springs back into existence. If we did not wake up then that would be a genuine concern.

An interesting phenomenon is 'nodding off'. This has happened to me countless times during lectures and seminars. Sometimes it happens when I am watching television. I nod off, sometimes only for a minute or a few seconds, but I realise there is a hiatus in my consciousness. My "wits have gone woolgathering" as the saying goes.

Another peculiarity of consciousness is attention. When I give my attention to something, I withdraw it from other things. I can read a book in a busy place and (to a greater or lesser degree) have minimal awareness of what is happening around me. When I am attending to something important or interesting I may experience this *surround inhibition* - I am less aware of my surroundings. I may resent an intrusion into my focused state of attending.

The conclusion one can draw from this brief introduction to consciousness is that it is variable in quantity and focus. Sometimes we have more of it (I am 'clear-headed') and sometimes we have less of it (I feel 'fuzzy-headed'). Sometimes we have very little (I am asleep, or drunk, or unconscious, or dead). It skips from focus to focus like a dragonfly hovering over a pond. Far from being the sovereign master of the flesh, it is the servant of the body, employed like a torch to throw light on situations where well-honed routines can no longer meet the need.

This is a modern view of consciousness as expounded by writers such as Dennett, Minsky, Damasio and Eagleman and I find it persuasive (see 26.5, *Further Reading* below).

Those who believe consciousness is a noble and divine faculty may find the modern perspective unsettling. It is a viewpoint that overturns many of the clichés one finds in spiritual literature. Plato thought our rational soul came from another level of reality and was dipped in the myre of material existence. It was overwhelmed by our appetites and our animal nature. Variants of this view can be found throughout spiritual literature.

According to the modern view, rational consciousness is *emergent out of our appetites and animal nature*, and serves their needs. It is primarily *practical*. It attends to problems that cannot be handled by unconscious abilities. The focus of attention that is presented to consciousness is manipulated by unconscious processes.

For most of human history reason was an instrument in sexual seduction, in manoeuvre, in wheeling-and-dealing (one of the early meanings of *ratio*, the root of rational, is concerned with financial accounting), in trickery, subterfuge, and cunning. Odysseus stands out in Homer's epics because he is shrewd, and we admire his practical intelligence just as much as we admire the physical prowess of Achilles. He was the man behind a classic stratagem, the Wooden Horse[197]. The Greek God Hermes manifests many trickster qualities, as do trickster figures in myth and folktale, such as Brer Rabbit. Reason is often just an adjunct to getting what we want, by fair means if possible, and by foul means if we have the stomach for the consequences[198]. Literature is filled with entirely rational villainy. Rationality is a practical and efficient means to practical ends.

Only later in history did reason become associated with just laws and fair-dealing, with science, and with abstract thought. It was seen as an antidote to superstition, to the oppression and unfairness of inherited privilege, to outdated beliefs of religion and social custom. Reason was like the stone of the philosophers - drop it into any old mess and it would turn into gold. Idealistic and utopian plans for the

---

197. We have not forgotten this tale. The generic term for a broad class of email malware is "trojan".
198. The simplest way to get what you want is to have the power to take it. Trickster figures do not have the power, so they outwit those who do.

Intelligence

rational restructuring of society abounded. Reason grew too big for its boots. It forgot where it came from. It thought it was god (or at the very least, a splinter of the divine). Hamlet, that exemplar of dithering Reason, could exclaim:

> What a piece of work is a man, How noble in Reason, how infinite in faculties, in form and moving how express and admirable, In action how like an Angel! in apprehension how like a god ....

It would seem that the consciousness we possess - a narrative consciousness, a consciousness that is always talking to itself, judging, assessing, weighing, poking fun, planning and fretting, is not the little god it might like to be. It evolved out of a need to compete against other members of the most intelligent and dangerous species on the planet. When it has nothing much to do it becomes bored, restless, fidgety, and often self-destructive. It loses sight of itself as a dependent part and imagines itself the centre and the whole. This is a central component of gnostic myth, that of an ignorant demiurge - *Ialdebaoth*, *Saklas* or *Samael* - who imagines himself to be the only god, and creates a blighted and dysfunctional universe in his own image.

In summary, consciousness is not the divinely-ordained master of the animal soul; rather, it is a late addition to the animal soul, an adjunct system (like the Emergency Medical Hologram) called into being when required. There are unconscious processes that *construct an environment for self-awareness*, in much the same way that a news team constructs the evening news. A news team scans news feeds for interesting news items, selects items that they decide are interesting, and constructs stories around those items, compiling this *narrow digest* into a 30 minute newscast. Almost everything going on in the world is ignored, and a few items of parochial interest are selected and deemed to be most interesting to a chosen audience. Most importantly, they don't ask you what you want to hear about. The news team make the choices, and you can either listen or switch off.

There is no name for the ever-changing collection of processes within my mind that constructs the environment for my self-awareness. It probably doesn't work like a news team. It probably works like the pit in a commodity exchange[199], where a bunch of traders with funny blazers and intense expressions yell prices at each other and make notes on scraps of paper. Commodity valuations and trading decisions of global significance emerge from the trading pit, and

---

199. Dennett proposes something along these lines with his 'multiple drafts' model of consciousness - see *Consciousness Explained*, Daniel Dennett, Penguin 1991.

are quoted in the press, but there is no central coordination. There is no little god making things happen.

26.3 The Ego

> "How to get rid of ego as dictator and turn it into messenger and servant and scout, to be in your service, is the trick."
> Joseph Campbell

Most social animals are competitive. Birds, such as seagulls, pigeons, hens and ducks, spend a significant part of their lives squabbling. There is a 'pecking order' for roosting spots, and when it comes to food, the fastest bird wins.

The author shares his house with a herd of guinea pigs, and they squabble and bicker constantly. There is a hierarchy among the females and it is constantly being tested and reinforced. Male guineas in the presence of sows will fight so savagely that it is usually not possible to keep them in the same enclosure. Guinea pigs will attempt to snatch desirable food out of each others' mouths, and a dominant sow will drive a lower-ranking pig out of a favourite sleeping spot. Often she will do it simply because she can. Guinea pigs have many different vocalisations, and they protest their feelings loudly - an indignant pig sounds and behaves exactly like an indignant pig. Watching guinea pigs is like watching an early prototype of human society.

This social structure - a small number of dominant males who compete for access to females, and a herd of females led by a dominant female who heads the pecking order - is widely replicated throughout the animal kingdom. Human beings may be different, and have many kinds of social organisation, but hierarchy, whether overt or covert, is common. Those at the top of the hierarchy usually have access to better food, finer clothing, and better housing. One can find corner-cases that do not follow the trend, but they are unusual.

The approach taken in the previous chapter was that a soul is an organisational structure necessary to survive in an environment. The environment for most people is one created by other people, and so it follows that there must be an organisational structure inside human beings that makes it possible to survive in a world of human beings. This structure is a combination of some parts of the animal soul and the social soul, and it is convenient to use the commonplace term 'Ego', because it is understood in expressions such as "he has an ego the size of a planet", "don't let your ego get in the way" and "egomaniac".

Intelligence

Ego enables us to survive in two ways. The first way is by copying other people. We blend in and conform. Consciously or unconsciously, we copy the worldview, opinions, fashions, aspirations, possessions, and language of particular groups we want to be part of. The second way is through competition. Most groups have a pecking order, and some way of acknowledging, denoting, or rewarding senior members. Sometimes the pecking order is subtle and unobtrusive, but in the commercial and professional world it is usually explicit and marked by pay grades, titles, and visible symbols of distinction (the luxury car, the chauffeur, the window office, the executive restaurant).

Each group has its own view of conformity and acceptable competition. The military insists on a homogeneous appearance of uniforms and haircuts, but values and recognises individual leadership when it is demonstrated in combat (in other circumstances it is designated mutiny). In sport, competitiveness is not only tolerated, it is essential. In the priesthood an overt competitiveness would be designated a lack of humility. In general we accept that we will have to compete for places at school and at elite universities, for admission to professions such as medicine or law, for jobs and promotion, for sexual partners, and for admission to circles of privilege, especially in certain aspects of politics.

There is a complex interplay between standing-out and blending-in. The fashion designer John Galliano belonged to a fashion elite where unconventional dress was permitted and admired, but anti-Semitic remarks were not. Throughout much of the Middle East the reverse is true. At a personal level the conventions of dress and behaviour make the difference between social acceptance and exclusion. There is an invisible line, and people cross it at their peril.

At a global level these social conventions seem arbitrary, and viewed over a timescale of thousands of years, even more so. We can laugh at the courtly dress of the 16th. century, with its huge ruffs and hanging lace and absurd pantaloons. At the same time we can be horrified by the virulence of religious disputation that racked Europe during this period. We live in a world just as idiosyncratic and just as serious. Four hundred years from now human beings will giggle at our fashions and obsessions, and be appalled by our misconceptions and prejudices. It is difficult to grasp the narrowness of perspective necessary to function in human society. We have little choice in the matter, and we are assimilated into society when we are too young to understand the essential arbitrariness of what seems so important and precious at the time when we are alive.

The Hermetic Kabbalah

The Ego, then, is constantly trying to make us look good in the eyes of our peers - it is trying to 'keep up appearances'. It is also alert to threat. Threat can take many forms: a disparaging remark, gossip, a leakage of damaging information from one social sphere to another (this is the bane of politicians), an encroachment on personal space, a lack of attention, a sexual competitor, an unwitting infringement of social convention, a broken commitment - the list is endless. The Ego is constantly alert and quick to respond. It will deny everything and attack anyone. Ego is arbitrary, self-protective, insecure, opinionated, attention-seeking, selfish, acquisitive, fearful, and it is often angry and delusional.

From an esoteric perspective, Ego is the Grand Daemon[200]. It is a constructed and derivative entity that is part of the *Necessity of the World*. It arises from circumstance. Its negative qualities, such as a propensity for anger and violence, dishonesty, selfishness, arrogance, obstinacy, and blame, are moulded by the environment in which it finds itself. It clings to a narrow view of reality with an iron grip, but internally it is inchoate and chaotic, a grab-bag of values, opinions and self-protective impulses that are rooted in the unconscious processes of the society of mind. It struggles to make sense of itself and fabricates deluded worlds of explanation. It wants to feel safe. It wants to exist in a realm where it no longer has to protect itself. It wants to be in charge. It wants to rule a world in which every day would be the first day of spring.

The gnostics projected the qualities of Ego onto their world-creating demiurge. In the *Secret Book of John*, the demiurge, who is known by the names *Saklas*, *Samael* and *Ialdebaoth*, is characterised by ignorance and arrogance. He does not know that he is an abortion, a mistake, an aberration, a dependent entity. He declares "I am a jealous God, there is no other God but me", and so reveals his fundamental insecurity. He creates further dependent entities to rule his cosmos, and these are the powers of evil Necessity - the negative feelings - that bind the human soul and imprison it.

This scenario has been played out many times in Hollywood movies. There is a psychopathic villain who creates a lair in an improbable place - a hollowed-out volcano, an underground complex, the Arctic wastes. He is served by unquestioning minions. He has a plan to rule the world - there will be no other gods. Often he has taken a woman prisoner. A hero is required to enter this alternate cosmos of evil, res-

---

200. In the literature of the gnostics it is sometimes called 'the Counterfeiting Spirit'.

cue the woman, and bring ruin upon the evil genius. This is one of the oldest legends we posses, and we can perceive it faintly in the ancient story of Orpheus and Euridice, a relic of the Orphic Mysteries. The human soul is trapped in a realm of dark necessity, and in thrall to evil powers. A light-being must descend into the darkness to redeem it.

Very few people are evil geniuses with access to hollowed-out volcanos, but the desire to create or inhabit a private cosmos is very strong. This is often seen in those who have been hurt, or those who find life stressful and difficult. A perfect example of this would be the model railway, the perfect microcosmic escape pod. One could also single out a devotion to the minutiae of the world of *Star Trek*, or an obsession with creating the perfect home. Indeed, the study of Kabbalah can be criticised in just the same way, and is perhaps an even more perfect example than the model railway.

The private cosmos is manageable in scale, unthreatening, open-ended, and absorbing. It is an antidote to care and toil. It provides the Ego with space to expand and to exert its natural powers of agency. The disadvantage is that it is private, and to an extent, incommunicable. These niche interests exist on the periphery of social life. There are groups, and societies and meetings, but they are often characterised by splintering and acrimony as private visions collide. Sometimes an artist or designer or writer will create a private cosmos that resonates with society at large, and their vision becomes a part of the status-quo. For every private vision that resonates, there are thousands that do not.

The Ego fears loss, and pain, and death. Old age and death are the ultimate insult that life can offer. Everything that one has accumulated is dispersed. One's home becomes the habitation of strangers. Achievements are forgotten, relationships are sundered, pleasures are removed, until only pain and extinction remain. It follows that the Ego will do everything it can to rewrite this script. It lives in denial. It fabricates ideal worlds in which the power of evil Necessity and its agents (and we might be speaking of the bourgeois lackeys of capitalism, or the evil spirits of Satan) are abolished forever, and the Ego can live in a world where swords have been beaten into ploughshares, and the lion lies down with the lamb.

Every genuine system of mysticism has to deal with the problem of Ego. The Ego views situations in terms of its core skills, which are blending-in and covert competition. It will camouflage itself with the patina of ancient wisdom. It will lust after every mark of attainment:

signs, symbols, handshakes, badges, sashes, degrees, scrolls and exalted honorifics. It will do so with innocence and conviction, satisfied as to the authenticity of its attainment. Social endorsement is enough for the Ego - that is what it seeks.

The Ego is often unconscious of its motives, unconscious of its deceptions, unconscious of its misrepresentations, its envy, and its overwhelming and irreducible narcissism. The self-conscious part of the Ego is the tip of the iceberg; there is a society of mind in operation and many of these autonomous and uncoordinated processes are under water and out of sight. The conscious mind is not the master of its house. It confabulates wonderful stories to present its behaviour in an acceptable, even commendable form. It did the right thing. It couldn't be helped. It wants to be praised and accepted, not rejected. When the Ego is under considerable duress and is presented with irrefutable evidence, it may cave-in and admit that it did something wrong, but criminal cases show that many remain obstinately self-righteous and belligerent even as they are led off to the cells.

There are many stories the world over where spiritual aspirants are treated in an appalling way by their teachers. The great Tibetan sage Milarepa spent years building and tearing down stone structures at the request of his teacher Marpa. After much suffering and "twelve fearful experiences" Naropa found the sage Tilopa and was asked to jump off a cliff to certain death. Gurdjieff required many student to perform menial household tasks. Crowley asked some students to slash their arms with a knife whenever they used the word 'I'. Students of Zen Buddhism may be struck with an 'encouragement stick' if they are seen to be flagging during meditation. Ego can be a problem, but fortunately there are alternative and gentler ways to confront it.

Returning to the issue of transcendence, why would the Ego seek its own extinction? I would suggest there is a restlessness, a dissatisfaction with what the world is offering. In my own case I can say that my unconscious mind made itself known in ways too powerful and immediate to ignore. From early childhood I was convinced that the phenomenal world was an appearance, and it subsisted on an occult foundation. Myths, legends and symbols evoked a powerful emotional response. There was no possibility of ignoring these feelings - they had to be drawn into the light and comprehended.

26.4 Summary

This chapter turns the traditional view of mind and intelligence on its head. The traditional view, as expressed via the Neoplatonists and variously embroidered, is that Mind is the primary organisational and creative principle in the Cosmos. Component parts of the One Mind, each possessing a degree of autonomy and organisational intelligence - what the tradition calls souls - fall into relationship with matter and animate it.

The view expressed here is that matter possesses an innate organisational capacity and intelligence that becomes apparent at an extremely small scale. It can be observed at the scale of the large molecules called proteins, and may exist at smaller scales. Intelligence is compositional; one can produce new, emergent levels of intelligence by composing many smaller units. We call these new levels 'nervous systems' and 'brains'.

The new story is even more mysterious than the old story. Intelligence not only makes itself, it makes its environment, organising nature to suit its convenience.

A part of the old story remains however. A part of us is a product of Necessity, a by-product of survival. This part would seem to be the same as the Counterfeiting Spirit of the gnostics. Another part of us sits outside of the world and looks at it in astonishment. What is this place? Why do we experience and feel? What else can we be?

26.5 Further Reading

Recent decades have seen extraordinary advances in our understanding of the brain - not just the human brain, but also the brains of other species right down to humble entities like nematode worms and lampreys. Advances in medical imaging have made it possible to study the active brain, and many kinds of experiments into cognition have been carried out while imaging live subjects. An aging population has focused research on diseases such as dementia.

A number of popular books have attempted to explain what has been learned about the relationship between mind and body. These are some that I have found useful. Dennett in particular has been prolific in writing about many aspects of the human experience, including determinism and free-will.

Self Comes to Mind: Constructing the Conscious Brain, Damasio, Antonio, Vintage 2012

Consciousness Explained, Dennet, Daniel, 1991

Incognito: The Secret Lives of the Brain, Eagleman, David, Can-

nongate 2012
The Emotion Machine, Minsky, Marvin, Simon & Schuster 2007
The Society of Mind, Minsky, Marvin, Pages Bent, 1988

27

The Society of Mind

27.1 Introduction

The previous chapter examined the notions of intelligence and consciousness and concluded that they are an intrinsic and emergent aspect of matter. Intelligence is compositional: it comes together in pieces to create larger intelligences, in the same way as cells and organs come together. Because it is compositional, there is a measure of autonomy between parts. What we call 'consciousness', the self-aware part that constructs a narrative sense of identity, is one of these pieces.

The idea that we might be composed of a crowd or society with consciousness as its elected *rapporteur* will seem odd to most people. In ancient times the Society of Mind was the explanation for the Cosmos, and many philosophers viewed Mind as emanating a vast hierarchy of being. In this chapter we discover a Society of Mind within us, and go some way towards understanding why it works as it does.

27.2 Sun and Moon

> Projections change the world into the replica of one's own unknown face.
>
>   C. G. Jung

One of my favourite images is that of the sun and moon in conjuction. By convention the sun has a male face, and the moon a female face. In alchemical literature they are sometimes represented by a king and queen, with the symbols for sun and moon used to indicate who they are. The couple may be seated on thrones, or found embracing in a bath of water. This is the *mysterium conjuctionis*, the divine union of King and Queen.

As with most symbolism, there are several ways to interpret it. I am going to follow a tradition still alive in astrology and take the Sun to denote our daytime social consciousness, and the Moon to denote its opposite, the night-time world of sleep and dreams, of flux and change, of what is hidden rather than revealed, in short, what we now refer to as the unconscious.

If our rational and social consciousness is, as I and others have suggested, emergent out of an animal nature that is largely unconscious, then it follows that consciousness will be forced to concoct elaborate stories to obfuscate its dependent status. Jewish tradition contains a fascinating story that tells of the *diminution of the Moon*.

According to this legend, the Sun and Moon were originally the same size and of equal brightness. They quarrelled, each maintaining that it was the brightest. Eventually the Moon complained to God, asking whether two kings could share the same crown. God told the Moon to make herself smaller, and commanded the Sun to grow brighter. The Moon refused, so God rebuked her, and spread part of her light over the sky in the form of stars. Tradition maintains that in time to come, the Moon will be restored to her former glory, and her light will be what it once was.

We could interpret this as a fable about the status of women. We could also interpret it as a fable relating the growing ascendency and autonomy of the Ego at the expense of the unconscious. As the Ego shines more brightly it loses sight of the night world, which becomes entirely shadow. The Ego loses sight of the basis for its being. The Ego is like a ventriloquist's dummy that from time to time becomes aware of a terrible occult mystery, the mystery of the Hand.

For much of human history the workings of the unconscious have been externalised and woven into the fabric of the cosmos. It is tempting to say 'objective reality', but there was no objective reality. Objective and subjective were one. One can see this with astrology, a fossil worldview that survives from late antiquity. In astrology, large parts of the human psyche, in the form of astrological constellations, planetary houses, and god-like planets are projected onto the sky. The sky is treated as a simulacrum of human nature and destiny, so that Venus does not just inhabit the human soul; she is up there in the sky ruling our passions directly.

When one looks into the magical and religious practices of the ancients, their beliefs were consistent with the world they believed they inhabited, and from this perspective, logical and rational. The cosmos was an extension of human existence on a larger scale - more good, more evil, more power, bigger CGI effects, but still explicable in terms of the dynamics of human society. The key word here is *projection*; the court of Olympus was like a human court blown-up in scale and projected onto an adjacent plane of existence. Likewise with Valhalla. The levels and tiers of reality that proliferated in Neoplatonic theology were like a projection of the tiers of fossilised status and bureaucracy in the late-Roman and early Byzantine empire.

Projection of inner onto outer was not limited to the gods. A dream encounter with a dead person was interpreted literally as an encounter with the dead. A gamut of mental health issues was interpreted as devils and evil spirits. Natural phenomena were seen as being animated by living intelligence. The phenomenon of inspiration was believed to come from external sources - as late as the 17th century John Milton began *Paradise Lost* with an invocation to the "Heav'nly Muse", and he was far from the only poet to do so, a recognition that the sources of creativity lie outside the conscious mind.

When one reads a seminal text such as the *Revelation* of St. John one is immersed in a narrative of striking power, and filled with images of extraordinary clarity - there will be an end to things, and (according to John) this is a revelation of what will happen. Even today the report of its author dominates the thoughts of millions. It is still interpreted *as a report* concerning events and processes taking place in a separate and superior realm of being. These events and processes (e.g. the breaking of the seals of the great book) will be causally efficacious in this world.

A grand debunking of this graphic-novel eschatology took place during the Age of Enlightenment. Suddenly Reason was king and the Moon was diminished almost to non-existence. It was not until the late 19th. century that Sigmund Freud brought her back into view as part of his quasi-mechanistic explanation of the workings of the psyche. Freud proposed the existence of the *unconscious*, a ill-formed Caliban lurking in the dark of the soul that causes us to deviate from the path of reason. And so we need to go into therapy ... and then we understand that a cigar is not just a cigar.

It was Freud's younger colleague, the Swiss psychologist Carl Gustav Jung who discovered numinous symbols in the visions, dreams and art of his patients[201]. He called these symbols *archetypes*, and used the word to denote autonomous living powers within the unconscious. In order to demonstrate the universality of these psychic patterns and so validate his ideas, Jung attempted to psychologise ancient myth. Jung trawled through the most recondite works of ancient literature as part of a lifelong quest to show that the unconscious spoke in a universal language of symbols. Jung was diligent in reporting his discoveries, and his collected works (though often verbose and tedious) provide an insightful exploration and commentary on ancient mystical and magical texts.

Jung's psychologisation of religion, myth and mysticism has been extraordinarily effective at the popular level. Jung performed a great synthesis. His work is appealing to anyone with an interest in the occult, for the simple reason that he took the literature seriously. It is not possible to write him off as a dilettante - his study of alchemical documents alone was obsessive. Too obsessive perhaps; the opinion of critics is that Jung lost his objectivity, that he fell into the "black tide of mud of occultism" (as Freud put it to him). I accept that, but given my outlook, I do not regard Jung's descent into the mud as an entirely negative thing - he returned to the Moon some part of her luminosity.

If there is a negative aspect to Jung's work (and the psychoanalytic trend in general) it is that pop psychology has become pervasive. Where once we attributed manifestations of the unconscious to divine powers, now, with equal facility, we explain the same phenomena as 'dissociated complexes'. There is a trivialisation of the profound within analytic structures that are, to an extent, dogmatic. A sign of discontent is the partial abandonment of these therapies in favour of medication and behavioural approaches such as Cognitive Behaviour Therapy. I interpret this as a tacit acknowledgment of the physical basis of consciousness; if consciousness is a manifestation of an underlying animal soul, then its pathologies cannot simply be 'talked away'. There is a downside however - the current trend of treating symptoms with drugs and behavioural therapy means that the deeper aspects of mind are ignored, and the Moon is diminished even further.

The positive aspect of Jung's work is that he viewed the unconscious mind as a living place filled with quasi-autonomous entities. It was not a dark place of dysfunction. The unconscious mind is like the sea; even though we can only contemplate its surface, from time to

---

201. And in his own inner life - see *Memories, Dreams, Reflections*, C.G. Jung,

time we find on its shores signs of a realm of great beauty and strangeness. Jung identified the creative life of the unconscious in works of imagination and creativity, in mystical speculations, in religion, in the Hermetic arts - anywhere the unconscious and the imagination is set free from the shackles of reason and convention.

Jung also saw that in many patients Sun and Moon had become estranged, often through trauma. The Moon was diminished, but only in visibility - its power was magnified in proportion, and the Sun, blinded by its own magnificence, was unable to see that it ruled nothing. In these circumstances emotions and moods and focus seemed to bear no reasonable relationship to circumstances. It was as if a succession of beings occupied the same flesh, all laying claim to the same identity, but working against each other, undermining each other, contradicting each other, so that goals, plans, relationships and even basic feelings of love and hate were unstable.

Jung believed that the human soul in this situation of internal chaos would manifest spontaneous symbols of a desired condition of harmony and wholeness. It was a condition in which Sun and Moon turned towards each other and embraced, a *conjunctio* that created a Child, a new kind of consciousness. He found evidence for this novel condition in visionary, mystical and religious works, especially in the symbol of the *lapis* in alchemy, and the *redeemer* in gnosticism.

What does it mean for the Sun and the Moon to embrace? To understand this it is necessary to enter into the society of mind.

27.3 The Society of Mind

In 1988 the cognitive scientist Marvin Minsky published a seminal work, *The Society of Mind*. It is a technical work and heavy-going[202], but the justification for his approach is simple to understand.

Minsky argued that attempts to find elegant explanations and models for the human mind were flawed because mind was neither simple or elegant. The brain and nervous system is an evolutionary accretion whose structure is coded by genes that have been modified over aeons by processes that had no regard for system or method. The underlying structure of the brain with its several lobes, cerebellum, corpus callosum, limbic system and so on, comes from our genes, not from Central Planning. Minsky proposed that mind is composed of a very large number of interacting agents, hence the inspired title of his

---

[202]. Minsky has published an accessible update of his ideas in *The Emotion Machine*, Simon & Schuster 2007.

book. He suggests that mind as we experience it in our daily lives is the interplay and interaction of many, many parts.

Neoplatonist philosophers proposed something similar. They believed that the entire cosmos was a society of mind, a hierarchy of dependent but quasi-autonomous mindful-beings that spanned the gap between the One, and the most lowly of forms embedded in Matter. They proposed what was quite literally a *cosmos* of mind.

Jung arrived at his society of mind by another route, but again, we find similar ideas expressed not so much mechanistically or theologically but *psychologically*, as experienced from the *inside*.

For a student of the Hermetic Arts the goal is not to explain mind. Whether one chooses to follow the explanations of Minsky, Proclus or Jung is, in the early stages at least, a matter of irrelevance. The initial goal is to experience mind from the inside, and to experience mind from the inside it is necessary to explore interior worlds that are a raw perceptual interpretation of the physical world - more pure, more basic, more intense, often disturbing, sometimes frightening.

In her introduction to an edition of Grimm's Fairy Tales, the novelist A. S. Byatt writes[203]:

> The best single description I know of the world of the fairly tale is that of Max Lüthi who describes it as an abstract world, full of discrete, interchangeable people, objects and incidents, all of which are isolated and are nevertheless interconnected, in a kind of web or network of two-dimensional meaning. Everything in the tales appears to happen entirely by chance - and this has the strange effect of making it appear that nothing happens by chance, that everything is fated.

In a fairy tale the nuances of character, incident, feeling, morality and causality that we have acquired with much pain as adults are diminished or entirely extinguished, and we enter a world of primal simplicity. The good are very good. The evil are exceedingly evil. Violence is extreme, but suffering is absent or symbolic. There is causality without mechanism, incident without sense. A queen consults a mirror with a panoptical view of beauty and the honesty of pure mechanism. In what workshop was this mirror made? By whom? From what? There is no backstory to consult, no culture to probe, and no assumption we can make. We probably do not think to ask (although we can garnish the simplicity of the tale with whatever imagination can supply). A princess has skin as white as snow, hair like ebony, and lips the colour of blood. This is a symbol, not a person. We are in a world of fragments, of half-formed people using symbolic

---

203. *The Annotated Brothers Grimm*, ed. Maria Tatar, Norton 2004

objects in half-formed landscapes. Material substance obeys no laws, but paradoxically, the consequences of riddle games, oaths, spells and promises are binding. A prince can be transformed into a frog, but to break a promise or a *geis*[204] is to trigger a doom that is inflexible as gravity.

Fairy tales provide a gateway into the society of mind. Things are flat and incomplete, but strikingly vivid and intense. In fairy tales we inhabit a juvenile cognition stripped of detail and nuance and perhaps this is the key to their universality. Perhaps they encode the deep structure of all story-telling; their transposition into animated cartoons seems entirely fitting.

From time to time a cherished Old Master painting goes into restoration, the discoloured varnish is removed, and the public recoils in disgust. What have they done! The subtle tones of age had been interpreted as mastery, but bright colours suggest immaturity. It may come as a surprise (or a shock) to learn that the glorious marbles of the Parthenon were probably painted in bright colours like a fairground carousel. As parents we can watch toddlers play in a world where every toy is a primary colour, where imagination trumps determinism, where narrative is as important as food, and feelings run out of control. As adults we have learned nuance and moderation and discernment. We try to create worlds for ourselves that are safe and controlled. It runs contrary to common sense that one should enter into a world of primal intensity where nuance and moderation cease to be important, a world where things are half-formed and incomplete.

The ancients intuited the incompleteness of angels, daemones, and the innumerable spirits that filled their world. There is the story, found both in the Jewish tradition and the *Koran*, that God asked the angels to bow down to Adam, who was made *in the image of God*. Satan (*Iblis* in the *Koran*) refused because he was created before Adam and felt he had precedence, and for this disobedience he was cast to earth with his angels. We learn from this that although Adam was created later then the angels, he possessed qualities that no angel possessed. The angels were incomplete.

There is also a tradition that each angel has one task only, and no angel can perform the task of another. There was considerable speculation about the nature of spirits in general, with suggestions that they were composed of only one or two elements, such as fire or air.

---

204. From the Gaelic: an idiosyncratic taboo, injunction, or spell that cannot be broken without dire consequences.

Demonic powers were also incomplete. A demon embodied a pure feeling - lust, rage, malice, jealousy, fear, destruction - with no possibility of balance or proportion. They were partial beings.

The Tree of Life is a decomposition into primitive parts. Each emanation is a part of a whole, and by itself, incomplete. The right and left hand pillars are emanations out of balance, and so should be invoked with the care that a chemist would use for concentrated acids and bases.

There are risks associated with entering into the society of mind. An important risk is obsession: one might encounter an entity so enticing, so seductive, so pure but incomplete, that it would dominate consciousness. Or to put it another way, one could go off the deep end and not know it. John Keats' poem *La Belle Dame Sans Merci* portrays the sense in which a mysterious entity that lives on the boundary between this world and the world of faerie can be both seductive and deadly: a combination of unearthly beauty and withering obsession. The ancients intuited the risks, and so constructed health and safety procedures, the equivalent of good laboratory practice, to protect themselves.

The most important method of protection was to cultivate protective entities. We find that many rituals have a quaternary of protective entities guarding the four quarters[205]. The magician would often call on the help and protection of a superior entity. It was common for the magician to wield a cutting weapon (sword, knife or *phurba*). The beginning and end of a ritual would be clearly bracketed in time. Physical space was used as a protective device, hence the familiar 'magic circle'. In the European grimoire tradition a spirit was often evoked into a triangle *outside* the magic circle, a procedure little different from the glove boxes used in biological laboratories for handling pathogens.

It is easy to both overstate and understate the risks. Just as some people fear spiders, some fear snakes, and some fear neither, it is impossible to know how any one person will respond when confronted with an influx of archetypal ideas, images, and feelings. Some people are over-cautious, some over-bold.

For many people this will be the level at which they first encounter the occult or esoteric. This level is very tangible, very anthropomorphic or theriomorphic. In every part of the world there are local cults that are much less abstract than the transcendent deities of priests

---

205. E.g. *Raphael, Michael, Gabriel, Uriel*, or Matthew, Mark, Luke and John.

and theologians. These cults 'idolise' entities that are tangible and accessible. People make offerings, light candles, and burn incense. They buy statues for their homes, and hang paintings on the wall. They create chapels in churches and temples for these intermediate beings, who in turn may appear in dreams and visions. There may be huge local cults, such as the pilgrimage sites of Lourdes in Southern France, Fatima in Portugal, and Santiago de Compostela in Spain.

Protestants fulminated at 'idolatry' in Catholic countries such as France, Spain in Italy, but it is a part of every human culture. One of the ironies of modernist architecture, especially that from the earlier part of the twentieth century, is the presence of friezes and monumental figures that depict, not the gods of antiquity, but the gods of modernism - Labour, Justice, Science, Agriculture, Reason, Industry, and so on. The US Library of Congress in Washington is a riot of nubile and sparsely-attired goddesses of the more progressive and modern kind.

This level of religion or esoterism is closely associated with the *sefira* of *Yesod*, the 'treasure house of images'. The society of mind erupts in a profusion of living images that are experienced as external and objective. Like the muse of the poet, they may speak in living tongues, and inspire the writer and the painter. They may communicate a terrifying revelation, like the *Apocalypse* of John of Patmos, a revelation that transfixed European culture for millenia. In this treasure house live the faery folk, saints and martyrs, bright angels, totem animals, the living Tarot, unclean spirits, and the products of romantic and gothic imagination. This is the realm of the dead and the undead, the eldricht, the skeleton rattle, the moonlit graveyard, and echoes of an unquiet past.

One can become lost in this world. It is rich and strange, and brings powerful inspirations. The Ego, gazing on the society of mind, becomes (variously) obsessed, seduced, or terrified. It may recoil out of the esoteric and swear to leave it alone from henceforth. It may choose to exist with one foot in the world of the Sun, and one foot in the world of the Moon, becoming a shaman or witch or seer, offering counsel and support, or (and this is surprisingly common) a counter-magic to the sorceries of others.

The Kabbalist should intend to pass into this realm, and through it. There may be a prolonged passage to the other side, and it may take years, or a lifetime.

27.4 Values & Virtues

Strong feelings makes the world a smaller place. When feelings run high there is a contraction, bright and fearsomely intense, like the image of the sun focused by a convex glass. Peripheral concerns are forgotten or ignored. Love, hate, fear, anxiety, disgust, grief, awe, attainment - the mind contracts and fastens on their object to the exclusion of other things.

Each one of us will have experienced overpowering feelings. I can recall lying awake at night, re-enacting encounters, unable to shift an endless replay of "I said, you said". Some people may recall feeling nauseous, sick, unable to eat, running to the toilet, even vomiting or collapsing. Others may remember doing things that in retrospect seem shameful and atypical.

It has been said that "feelings tell us what to think", and they do. Feelings are a summation of our circumstances, delivered by ancient parts of the brain whose development long preceded language. Feelings steer thoughts like a helmsman. An entirely rational individual like Mr. Spock would never know what to think about. He would require a gigantic database of explicit rules to cover every situation. Faced with a tiger, Mr. Spock would have to run through a thousand rules such as "is it leashed", "is it in a cage", "is there a ditch or moat", "am I looking at an image", "am I safe in a car", "am I looking at it through a telescope" and so on *ad nauseum*. Feelings short-cut this inefficiency by providing us an immediate thought context for every situation. Within a few hundred milliseconds we can say "like" or "dislike". In a few seconds we can be hiding, ordering a beer, or calling the police.

A strong feeling can guide thinking so completely that it is like a change in personality. Each feeling creates a different person. A person who is happy and excited may be bubbling over with fun ideas; a terrified person may have only one idea. We are so accustomed to experiencing feelings in ourselves and in others that we accept these startling shifts in personality as normal ... so long as they *seem appropriate*. Sometimes a person will be so much 'out of character' due to anger or lust or fear that we are forced to rethink our opinion of them.

Feelings that appear to be unrelated to circumstances, or wildly inappropriate to circumstances - anxiety, panic, paranoia, rage, sexual lust - can be alienating because we don't understand them. There may be no obvious or immediate cause. Sometimes these feelings seem to materialise out of thin air, and people may do unfathomable things. We may find it difficult to accept their subsequent rationalisations.

We understand feelings best when we see and understand how they relate to immediate circumstances.

Values are an adjunct to feelings. I value food in the cupboard because it may prevent me from feeling hungry. I value my house because I feel safe and comfortable in it. I value my friends because I am a member of a social species and I feel happy in their company. Commenting on the concept of value, Damasio[206] grounds it in biology:

> The values that humans attribute to objects and activities would bear some relation, no matter how indirect or remote, to two of the following conditions: first, the general maintenance of living tissue within the homeostatic range suitable to its current context; second, the particular regulation required for the process to operate within the sector of homeostatic range associated with well-being relative to the current context.

Put succinctly: things have value because they keep us alive. Their value is communicated through feeling. Situations that threaten our well-being produce negative feelings and situations that enhance our well-being produce positive feelings. The world is 'coloured-in' according to these valuations, colours that are constantly changing as our needs change. On Saturday I might look forward to friends, beer and a good time. On Sunday I might feel the opposite, that I have had "too much of a good thing".

Plato wondered what was good, and grounded it outside the human sphere. The modern view could not be more different. When I am hungry, food is good. When I am thirsty, water is good. When I have no food or water, money is good. When I have no money, employment is good. When all else fails, family and friends are good. 'Good' is very personal and situational. I pursue it according to the feelings I have moment by moment, and in pursuing my good, I bump up against others pursuing *their* good. There are occasions when most people will experience a powerful reaction to this bumping and jostling - feelings of covetousness and greed, envy and jealousy, indignation, misery and outrage. When shops have a sale, advertising and photos of queues drive up the perceived value until a mob develops.

We can now return to the assertion that strong feelings make the world a small place. We focus on objects, situations and people of high value. We may not be conscious of the ephemerality of value in the heat of the moment. Some will queue for days to buy a piece of tech-

---

206. *Self Comes to Mind: Constructing the Conscious Brain*, Antonio Damasio, Vintage 2012

nology that will be obsolete within a year. Others will sacrifice leisure time to meet deadlines on projects that become irrelevant as soon as they are complete. People declare they are best friends forever, and then stop talking over some trifle. There is an element of faddishness in society, often fed by blanket advertising, that promotes the perceived value of products and situations to the point that people become mildly deranged.

A holiday in a remote place often leads to a 're-evaluation of values'. People swear they are "getting out of the rat race", that they are "stepping off the merry-go-round". However, so long as one's survival depends on daily choices and activities, one is trading one restricted set of values for another. The world remains a small place.

What if one could reject the entire material world? What if one threw concern for survival to the winds? Europe and the Middle East have many traditions of asceticism. In *Matthew* 6:25 Jesus is recorded as saying:

> Therefore I tell you, do not worry about your life, what you will eat or drink; or about your body, what you will wear. Is not life more than food, and the body more than clothes? Look at the birds of the air; they do not sow or reap or store away in barns, and yet your heavenly Father feeds them. Are you not much more valuable than they? Can any one of you by worrying add a single hour to your life?
>
> And why do you worry about clothes? See how the flowers of the field grow. They do not labour or spin. Yet I tell you that not even Solomon in all his splendour was dressed like one of these. If that is how God clothes the grass of the field, which is here today and tomorrow is thrown into the fire, will he not much more clothe you—you of little faith? So do not worry, saying, 'What shall we eat?' or 'What shall we drink?' or 'What shall we wear?' For the pagans run after all these things, and your heavenly Father knows that you need them. But seek first his kingdom and his righteousness, and all these things will be given to you as well. Therefore do not worry about tomorrow, for tomorrow will worry about itself. Each day has enough trouble of its own.

This is heady stuff, and influential. One of the most powerful forces in early Christianity was fiercely ascetic monastic communities in Egypt. The Christian rejection of normal life could be carried to absurd extremes, such as the example of Simeon Stylites, who lived for thirty-seven years on pillar in Syria. In medieval times about a third of the arable land in England was administered by monastic institutions - an entire society thought it was reasonable to reject the world in favour of an ideal Kingdom of Heaven.

The Society of Mind

The view presented here is that the problem is not the world we live in. The problem is the way that growing up in the world creates an entity - the Ego - that is composed of values and feelings and opinions and behaviours that are for the most part *unconscious and specific to an environment*. Nature and nurture create an Ego that is (in the larger scheme of things) arbitrary and narrowly focused, but nevertheless actively self-protective. It is artificial (that is, manufactured by outside forces) and rather stupid (again, in the larger scheme of things). It is stupid because it is aware only of those things it values, and it fusses over this narrow set of concerns to an inconceivable degree. Because it is self-protective it goes to great lengths to resist attempts to broaden its field of view, or deepen its awareness of value, feeling and behaviour. Push it too hard and it finds ways to dig itself deeper, like a tick on a dog.

One answer is to rein-in feelings, to place reasonable bounds on behaviour, to set limits on the excess and melodrama of the Ego. The elements of this method can be found in classical philosophy. In the *Republic* Plato discusses the *cardinal virtues* Temperance, Fortitude, Prudence and Justice. The same four virtues (almost certainly derived from Hellenistic sources) appear in the Jewish *4 Maccabees*, which sets out the supremacy of reason over passion. Three of the four cardinal virtues (Temperance, Courage/Fortitude, and Justice) can be found in modern Tarot decks - Prudence/Wisdom has been lost.

Aristotle saw virtue as a mean between extremes. For example, there is a balance between indulging a child's every whim, and terrorising the child with rigid discipline. There is a balance between blaming oneself for every happenstance, and feeling belligerently self-righteous. People are angered by dishonesty, but recognise there are social occasions when it is better to be less than truthful - or at least, ingeniously evasive. We admire a confident assertiveness, but we are suspicious of pushiness or self-centred ambition. Cowards are scorned, but so is self-destructive or foolhardy behaviour.

There is some indication that Aristotle had watched craftspeople at work, and understood the importance of good judgement in dealing with the variability of raw materials. At his time nothing was standardised. An ancient baker had to be a judge of flours, yeasts, temperature and humidity, and the vagaries of a wood-fired oven. Likewise the smith, the painter, the potter, the leather worker, the tanner, the weaver and countless other craft workers. Each process depended on an ability to judge when things were 'just right'.

The Hermetic Kabbalah

The quality of good judgement is also called practical wisdom, or *prudence* (from the Latin *prudentia*). In classical times good judgement was considered the queen of the virtues because without it one was unlikely to exercise good judgement in matters of *appetite* (temperance), *fear* (fortitude or strength) or *fairness* (justice).

This idea of a mean or balance between extremes is important in Kabbalah. The Tree of Life can be seen as a dynamic between two extremes, one giving (*Chesed*) and the other holding-back (*Din*). It follows that there is an interplay between *Chesed* and *Din* within the microcosm, in our own feelings. When we view others as beings like ourselves, then this is of the nature of *Chesed*. When we view others as different from ourselves, this is of the nature of *Din*.

There is a well-known story in the *Talmud* where R. Hillel was asked to teach the whole of the Torah while standing on one leg. He replied: "That which is hateful unto you do not do to your neighbour. This is the whole of the *Torah*, The rest is commentary. Go forth and study". A version, which is widely attributed to Jesus but actually comes from *Leviticus 19:18*, is "love your neighbour as yourself".

This 'Golden Rule' or 'ethic of reciprocity' is recognised worldwide and in 1993 the Parliament of the World Religions agreed the form "We must treat others as we wish others to treat us". The second formulation of Kant's Categorical Imperative is especially useful: "Act in such a way that you treat humanity, whether in your own person or in the person of any other, never merely as a means to an end, but always at the same time as an end". I would reformulate it as "treat other people as equal partners in life, not as objects of utility".

A simple and intuitive morality emerges from this. The ideal for a majority of people is loving-kindness (*Chesed*), but most people will hold back a little (*Din*) for pragmatic reasons - we may have learned that some people do not reciprocate, and may use our kindness for their own ends. We may feel 'used'. Not everyone can be trusted with kindness. Ideals are often too extreme to be realisable in this world; we learn to set limits. This is *Din*.

Each *sefira* within the microcosm can exhibit too little or too much of its characteristic emanation. Virtue comes from the sweet spot between too little and too much. There are vices that derive from excess and vices that derive from holding back. At some point in the early part of the twentieth century characteristic virtues and vices for each *sefira*[207] were proposed. For example, the virtue of *Tiferet* is

Sefira	Virtue	Vice	Obligation
Malkhut	Discrimination	Avarice, Inertia	Discipline
Yesod	Independence	Idleness	Trust
Hod	Truthfulness	Dishonesty	Learn
Netzach	Unselfishness	Lust	Responsibility
Tiferet	Devotion to the Great Work	Pride, Arrogance	Integrity
Gevurah	Energy, Courage/Fortitude	Cruelty, Destruction	Courage, Loyalty
Chesed	Obedience, Humility	Bigotry, Gluttony, Hypocrisy, Tyranny	Humility
Binah	Silence	Avarice	-
Chokhmah	Devotion	-	-
Keter	-	-	-

Table 22 : Virtue and Vice on the Tree

'Devotion to the Great Work', that is, devotion to a cause beyond and greater than oneself. The vices are pride and arrogance, devotion to the deity that *is* oneself.

The purpose behind lists such as this (see Table 22) is not so much to create a moral checklist as to create self-observation and self-understanding. The untested Ego tends to idealise itself. When tested and found lacking it will often confabulate a version of events in which responsibility and blame for negative outcomes come from factors beyond its control, often other people. We cannot observe unconscious values and emotions, but we can observe the things we do (or don't do) as a consequence. .

---

207. The virtues are based on Crowley's *777*. The vices are based on those given in Dion Fortune's *The Mystical Qabalah*. The obligations were communicated verbally to the author and represent progressive goals for the Ego.

Ego	non-Ego
narcissism, control, blame revenge anger fear spite selfishness	freedom spontaneity relationship no-blame playfulness compassion sharing

Table 23 : Ego versus Non-Ego

When the Ego is confronted with events and denied the power to confabulate, it begins to understand that it is less of a single entity and more of an uncoordinated society rooted in animal self-protectedness Table 23 is an attempt to characterise two extremes of Ego. The first is the narcissistic Ego for which every other person is a means to an end. It's dominant model is that of control. What it cannot control it undermines, destroys or rejects. It hides its sociopathy behind a mask of charm, but is constantly insecure, constantly threatened by exposure, constantly threatened by loss of control[208]. The opposite of the narcissistic Ego is an (idealised) saint characterised by openness and a lack of self-protection, who sees no blame in any situation, who takes a joyful, playful, compassionate stance to situations as they arise.

People are a mixture of these two extremes. When we are in situations we dislike, when we are stressed or uncomfortable or ill, we tend to be more of the first, and when we are with good friends we tend to be more of the second.

27.5 Summary

The human brain is a haphazard evolutionary composite, and the human mind reflects this composite nature. There is a part of the mind (the Ego) that believes it runs the show, and it struggles to reconcile this idea with the experience of other powerful and autonomous components in the society of mind. These other parts are unconscious, and appear to the Ego as external and objectively real.

The Ego thinks it knows itself, but it does not. It creates an ideal-

---

208. In this we can recognise Frank Underwood in *House of Cards*.

ised model of itself - kind, decent, honest, generous - that is often contradicted by behaviour and the accounts of other people.

The Ego often will not accept its behaviour and will fight back - we call this 'denial' and 'blame'. Events are edited, important details are conveniently forgotten, the role of other people is stressed. Most of this is unconscious, and illustrates the aggressively self-protective nature of Ego.

It is easy to understand why the gnostics thought the soul was fastened to a Counterfeiting Spirit, a creation of evil beings. Sometimes it can seem as if we have an evil psychopath lurking within us, something like the shark in *Jaws*. We know it is out there, but we cannot see what it is doing and do not know when it will surface. If only we could look underwater ...

And this is what we can do. We can watch out for signs of the unseen fishy things glinting below the surface (for there are many) and try to understand what they are doing. A first step is to provide the Ego with a framework, a set of benchmarks such as Table 22, and let the stress of self-monitoring and increasing self-awareness work a slow alchemy. We can begin to *know ourselves*. We can also become more adventurous and proactive. One method is to solicit outside help using *theurgy*.

The Hermetic Kabbalah

28

Awakening

28.1 Theurgy

GLENDOWER
I can call spirits from the vasty deep.
HOTSPUR
Why, so can I, or so can any man;
But will they come when you do call for them?
                    Shakespeare, *Henry IV Part 1*

But will they come? Hotspur, irritated by Glendower's bragging, goes to the heart of the issue. The spiritualist movement of the nineteenth century maintained that they did come, and there were mediums throughout America and Europe who claimed to produce inexplicable physical phenomena such as knocks and raps, disincarnate voices speaking through floating trumpets, ringing bells, ectoplasm, apports and suchlike (although why spirits would expend their energy in this way was much a mystery as the claimed phenomena). The energetic and indefatigable Victorians created the Society for Psychical Research (SPR) in 1882 to investigate hauntings, poltergeist, premonitions, seances, ouija boards, table turning and many other claims that seemed to lie beyond conventional explanation.

I have a personal interest in this. In the early seventies I was an active member of the Cambridge University Society for Psychical Research, and I recall with great affection Tony Cornell, who was its president. Tony was also Vice President and Council member of the London SPR, and for decades one of the most energetic and experienced investigators in the British Isles[209]. I spent many hundreds of hours with him discussing cases and investigations. Credulity, misreporting, lazy journalism, pranks and hoaxes, financial gain, misinterpretation of natural phenomena, exaggeration, wilful dishonesty, attention-seeking, and mental health issues go a long way to explain the majority of cases. The results of a century of scholarly research in parapsychology under laboratory conditions have been ambiguous and controversial at best, but the general trend is that the most carefully designed experiments find nothing of interest[210]. Since 1964 the stage magician and psychic debunker James Randi has offered a prize for a demonstration of the paranormal under defined conditions. The prize now stands at one million dollars and remains unclaimed.

I chose to introduce theurgy in this way to balance and contextualise what follows. Many readers will not have summoned a spirit in earnest, and may wonder, like Hotspur, whether they do come. The occult community has a mixed reaction to the question.

The gold standard for evocation of spirits is "to visible appearance". There is a section of the occult community, typically working with *goetia* or grimoiric magic, who assert that visible appearance means 'objectively present', and that the evoked entities are "objective beings, with a life, will, consciousness, and an independent existence of their own"[211] The manifestation of a spirit may be accompanied by objective phenomena - sounds, odours, lights, and poltergeist-like effects, as if reality was tearing at the seams[212]:

> ... winds begin to stir in a sealed, windowless cellar room and blow objects around; green mists and blinking, multicolored lights of various sizes and shapes appear floating through the air; candles are extinguished and knocked over; moans and screams rip through the darkness; shafts of golden or different colored light appear out of nowhere and streak across the cement walls and through the air; these same walls are pounded on so violently by something that (at first) is

---

209. See *Poltergeists*, Alan Gauld & Tony Cornell, Routledge & Kegan Paul 1979, and *Investigating the Paranormal*, Tony Cornell, Parapsychology Foundation 2002
210. The current *Wikipedia* page on Parapsychology provides a scathing critique of both the subject and the history of research.
211. *Ceremonial Magic and the Power of Evocation*, Joseph C. Lisiewski, New Falcon 2004
212. Ibid.

invisible, and which causes the walls to begin to crack; in the rooms above there is the horrifying sound of something huge smashing against the floor over your head as if trying to get at you from above; and finally, an unmistakable form appears in the smoke of the Perfume of the Art (incense) and begins to cry and wail; it is then that you, the Practitioner, will become grimly aware of the objective nature of the being summoned forth.

An intermediate position is that the appearance of the spirit is subjective, and the spirit is seen "in the spirit vision" - that is, vividly and freely, but in the mind's eye. This was the method used by John Dee and Edward Kelly - Kelly saw the spirits in a glass, mirror or crystal, and Dee interrogated them through Kelly and kept a record of the proceedings. The *Talmud* mentions a practice called "the princes of the egg and the princes of the thumb" that refers to coating a surface (such as an egg or a thumbnail) with oil and calling on spirits to appear in the shiny surface. Water stained with ink could also be used. Some people have an aptitude for this kind of scrying, many (like Dee) have no talent for it. A number of grimoires specify a child as the seer, a tacit admission that many adults make indifferent seers.

The theurgists of late antiquity understood that the gods had no innate form, and took a form for our convenience, such as these solar images from the *Chaldean Oracles*:

> A similar Fire flashingly extending through the rushings of Air, or a Fire formless whence cometh the Image of a Voice, or even a flashing Light abounding, revolving, whirling forth, crying aloud. Also there is the vision of the fire-flashing Courser of Light, or also a Child, borne aloft on the shoulders of the Celestial Steed, fiery, or clothed with gold, or naked, or shooting with the bow shafts of Light, and standing on the shoulders of the horse; then if thy meditation prolongeth itself, thou shalt unite all these Symbols into the Form of a Lion.

Even at this early date it was understood that there was a measure of subjectivity in 'visible'. It is fascinating to observe that the child on the horse is still to be seen in modern versions of the Sun Tarot trump.

According to tradition spirits are immaterial (or less material than we are), and so it is difficult for them to assume a visible appearance. The received wisdom is that a materialising medium such as smoke from incense must be provided, and this is the rationale behind evoking incenses such as Dittany of Crete (a variety of oregano, with all the charm of burning newspaper).

According to Dion Fortune the spirit could manifest on the astral plane, a plane more akin to their nature[213]:

In the great majority of cases of evocative magick, the form is built up on the astral and can only actually be seen by the clairvoyant, though any sensitive person can feel its influence.

The initiated magician is usually engaged in some experiment or research, content to evoke to visible appearance on the astral, depending on his psychic powers for communicating with the entity evoked. He does not go to the trouble to evoke to visible appearance on the physical because, if he is an adequate psychic, astral appearance serves his purpose just as well; in fact, better, because it is more congenial to the nature of the beings ... and places less limitation on their activities.

A third interpretation of 'visible appearance' is that the spirits are entirely psychological, and their visible appearance can be attributed to an active imagination. One might say that the physically immersive nature of ceremonial magic calls out to dissociated components of the unconscious mind whose original evolutionary purpose was to engage with the world. Ritual becomes non-verbal communication with primitive entities in the society of mind. In his introduction to the *Goetia* Crowley writes "The spirits of the *Goetia* are portions of the human brain" and goes on to describe how the praxis of evocation is "a series of minute, though of course empirical, physiological experiments"[214]. This kind of explanation placates the modern mind. It retains the value of ritual and removes the embarrassing need to believe in spirits.

There is a great deal of tension between the objective and subjective positions, and it is a perennial subject of debate in forums. The objective position tends to be held by students of the classical grimoires who follow recipes to the letter. This leads to a 'grimoire fundamentalism' that asserts the textual purity and ritual efficacy of particular manuscripts, despite the fact that the manuscript traditions are patchy and variable (to say the least). The situation is reminiscent of those quoting the King James translation of the *Bible*; when challenged on the accuracy of the translation they respond that the translation was also divinely inspired. What is clear is that people obtain many different kinds of experience when evoking spirits. Some of these experiences are sufficiently vivid as to cross the boundary between subjective and objective.

My view is that we are more immersed in the cosmos than we are capable of understanding. In a non-dual perspective we cannot sepa-

---

213. Quoted from *The Truth about Evocation of Spirits*, Donald Michael Kraig, Llewellyn 1994.
214. *The Goetia: the Lesser Key of Solomon the King*, trans. S. L. Mathers, intro. by Aleister Crowley, Red Wheel/Weiser 1996

rate mind and matter; mind is self-organised matter. What we conceive of as 'the real world' is also organisation: geometrical patterns of atomic elements such as carbon and oxygen and hydrogen. In turn these atoms are patterns of waves organised in space[215]. There is no subtle line that marks the boundary between mind and matter, between soul and material. Likewise there is no obvious point at which intelligence or life begins. It is all one, and we are immersed and connected at every level.

Sitting at the peak of this immense pyramid of complexity and organisation and interconnectedness is an emergent homunculus. We call it the human Ego, the narrative sense of self. It believes it can nail-down a precise map of how things are. It makes distinctions between objective and subjective, imagined and real, mental and physical, mind and body, and so on. These are labels of convenience in the social sphere and they do not reflect the deeper reality.

I have spent decades summoning spirits from the vasty deep, for the most part using the ancient model of Iamblichus, Ficino and Agrippa, that of sympathy - *sunthemata*. As outlined in *Theurgy* on page 129, the ritualist uses perfumes, sounds, symbols, music, gestures, plants and objects that are connected through innate occult sympathy with a specific cosmic power, usually anthropomorphised as a spirit. As Tolkien puts it[216]:

> When we can take green from grass, blue from heaven, and red from blood, we have already an enchanter's power - upon one plane; and the desire to wield that power in the world external to our minds awakes.

The theurgist inhabits a reality augmented not only by his or her unconscious inner life, but also by symbols, myths and legends, traditions, religious imagery, and the spontaneous eruption of numinous symbols in dream and inner vision. There is the spontaneity of dream, and the terror of nightmare. There is life there, and not always as we know it. Sometimes - not always, but sometimes - things happen that are not simple to explain. The revelatory experiences of Crowley, Jung and Fortune described later in this chapter may convey a sense of what I mean.

On the balance, it is likely that some kind of subterranean rumbling will occur in the depths of the unconscious, a resonant response

---

215. The chemical properties of the elements are strongly influenced by the shapes of the electron orbitals, which are those of elegant mathematical functions called the Spherical Harmonics. These are the three-dimensional equivalent of waves on a guitar string.
216. *On Fairy Stories*, J. R. R. Tolkien, 1938

perhaps to some greater power in the cosmos, and in time it will make itself known in a way peculiar to its nature. Timing is often a sticking point; we expect the powers of the timeless realms to operate with punctuality, forgetting that natural processes (like pregnancy) have a timeliness of their own. A common experience is what Jung called *synchronicity* - an implausible sequence of events that lack a causal connection but are interpreted as related and meaningful. As always, we can provide a rational explanation such as selection bias and the black swan effect[217]. What matters is the sense of meaningful interaction - events can be strikingly apposite, and the personal impact can be profound.

In the previous chapter a structure of virtue and vice was described. The Ego is unconscious of the many forces that move it hither and thither, and so it confabulates, constructs rationales to explain behaviour. The focus on virtue and vice provides boundaries and improves self-observation. This approach is gentle, like a tourist guide book marking out the neighbourhoods of a foreign city. Theurgy is the next step, the transition from map to territory.

The theurgy outlined here resembles ritual or ceremonial magic only in its outward form. It differs in its cosmological assumptions, in its ontology, in its operational model, and in its purpose. I was instructed in its techniques in the late '70s, but my teacher would seem to have acquired the techniques at least twenty years earlier. Although there are some influences that would appear to come from various occult fraternities operating in the post Golden Dawn era of Britain between the two wars, its exact provenance is unknown. The theurgy is explicitly Kabbalistic; it contains none of the ritual syncretism of the Golden Dawn. There are elements that seem authentically Jewish in origin, but there are many correspondences that clearly originate from the same sources as Dion Fortune's *The Mystical Qabalah*.

The approach is essentially that described by R. Joseph Gikatilla in an extended quotation on page 135. Gikatilla likens the holy names of God (and by implication each associated *sefira*, which is its dynamic manifestation) to storehouses. Each storehouse has a specific identity and a specific purpose. He states that God is open to everyone; it is ignorance that thwarts intention. He urges a study of the Holy Names in the context of the *Torah* so that one can understand their operational efficacy.

---

217. *Fooled by Randomness*, Nassim Nicholas Taleb, Random House 2001.

Awakening

The essence of his technique is "knowing how to concentrate on the Name". This is what theurgic ritual provides. Gikatilla may have meant the mental concentration techniques (*tzeruf*) of his teacher Abulafia, but physical ritual using *sunthemata* in the manner of Iamblichus is also effective.

The technique is as follows. The theurgist creates a sacred space (*temenos*) according to tradition. Many modern practitioners have used a version of the Golden Dawn Lesser Banishing Ritual[218]. Within this *temenos* only a small number of ritualistic activities are permitted; all else is excluded. The *temenos* is dominated by *sunthemata* specific to the *sefirot* being invoked. Typically these would be colour, perfume and incense, certain ritualistic motions, but most importantly, the Holy Names and powers of the *sefirot*. The powers of the *sefirot* are called upon to assist and guide the practitioner in the name of the One God.

The attitude is one of humility and respect. The divine in the microcosm (the theurgist) calls out to the divine in the macrocosm for a unity in being and purpose. The ethos of the *goetia* is isolation and control, like somone catching rattlesnakes. This is not the ethos here.

An important application for this kind of theurgy is the experiential exploration of the *sefirot*. This is 'practical Kabbalah'. The *sefirot* are invoked, singly or in combination, for the purpose of becoming aware of the dynamics of the *sefirot* within the microcosm. One wishes to 'light up the lights' (which one could interpret as 'becoming aware of the dynamics of deeply unconscious processes').

This then, is a second, more powerful technique for knocking the Ego off its perch. A third and complementary technique is to use the techniques of theurgy to summon the Holy Guardian Angel, as described below.

28.2 The Holy Guardian Angel

> My god has forsaken me and disappeared,
> My goddess has failed me and keeps at a distance,
> The good angel who walked beside me has departed.
> *Ludlul Bel Nemequi*

---

218. This ritual appears to be derived from the Jewish practice of saying the *Shema* at bedtime, where angelic protectors are invoked. This is quite ancient, and its structure would appear to be based on a description of the *Merkavah* or divine throne in the 8th. century *Pirkei d'Rabbi Eliezer*. A ritual with a similar structure can be found in ancient Sumerian literature.

The Hermetic Kabbalah

A strange piece of lore that has survived from ancient times is that each human being is dual. There are three principal forms in which this lore is framed: that each person has a guardian spirit or angel that can disclose esoteric teaching; that each person has a spiritual twin; or that the soul is divided into two parts, and the lower is ignorant of the higher. In some cases a tutelary entity might be identified with a disincarnate spiritual teacher (*maggid*), such as Elijah.

On top of the bare ideas one finds an edifice of interpretation: philosophical (why is the soul divided); mythological (how did this separation come about); and psychological/physiological (is there a rational explanation for this phenomenon).

At the core of this strangely occult lore is the experience of an 'other' who seems at first to be separate, but, with increasing familiarity (knowledge and conversation) is revealed to be none other than a component of a larger aspect of the subject.

After many centuries of relative obscurity a version of this idea has re-entered popular culture through the novels of Philip Pullman[219]. In Pullman's novels each human being has a *daemon*, and in some universes (such a Lyra's) they take the form of animals. Pullman has chosen one of the earliest forms of this belief, that of a personal spirit/angel/daemon/animal guide/familiar spirit/*qarin*[220]/*yidam*[221].

The phenomenon at the heart of this lore is an experience, still common, of a personal guiding entity that intrudes on normal consciousness via dreams, visionary experiences, and auditory and visual hallucinations. This kind of phenomenon can be associated with mental health and physiological issues - schizophrenia, bipolarity, epilepsy and even certain kinds of migraine - but it is not always pathological and occurs in high-functioning individuals[222]. The Western tradition has a rich lore surrounding this phenomenon, and one of the central operations is the deliberate attempt to "acquire the knowledge and conversation of the Holy Guardian Angel". This is regarded as a significant step in the Work, and is associated with the *sefira Tiferet*. It is also associated with *Da'at*; the HGA is the Emissary of Light who guides the initiate towards another world.

---

219. *Northern Lights, The Subtle Knife, The Amber Spyglass*
220. *qarin* - an Islamic version of the guardian spirit.
221. In Tibetan Buddhism the *yidam* is one's own basic nature, externalised as a divine form.
222. See for example *Muses, Madmen, and Prophets: Hearing Voices and the Borders of Sanity*, Daniel B. Smith, Penguin 2008

Awakening

Before discussing the traditions as they have survived to the present day it is worthwhile to discuss interpretation, because interpretation is often at the heart of experience. These interpretations are often conflated in interesting ways depending on the precise experience, and may have revelatory component, a noetic component, and a redemptive component.

A number of gnostic systems from late antiquity believed that each human being had a heavenly twin. For example, *The Exegesis on the Soul*, a text associated with the tradition of Valentinus (an influential early Christian now labelled a gnostic) portrays the soul as a woman who has fallen into prostitution with the evil ruling powers of the world. The powers use and abuse her in what is clearly a metaphor for the way in which Ego is transfixed by worldly appetites and passions. Through an act of grace her womb is reversed (that is, turns away from appetites and passions) and so she is able to reunite with her heavenly brother and twin. Her brother in the upper worlds comes to her as the groom comes to the bride and they reunite in the bridal chamber.

This allegory has many resonances with medieval Kabbalah. As discussed in *Partzufim*, the metaphor of bride and groom and their union is important in texts such as the *Zohar*, where it is taken to describe the relationship between *Ze'ir Anpin* and *Nukva* (see *Partzufim* on page 43).

The belief that the soul has more than one part is an important idea within the Platonic tradition, and has many variants. An outline would be that a lower part of the soul is immersed in matter and bound by appetite, and hence ignorant of the higher part of the soul that regards the intelligible realm. When the lower part of the soul turns away from worldly appetites it is able to reunite with the upper part of the soul. But what would cause the lower part of the soul to turn away from appetite? Perhaps there is some aspect of the upper part that 'intrudes' upon the lower? Agrippa, much influenced by Iamblichus, described a "holy daemon" as follows[223]:

> The holy demon is one, according to the doctrine of the Egyptians, assigned to the rational soul, not from the stars or planets, but from a supernatural cause, from God himself, the president of daemons, being universal, above nature: this doth direct the life of the soul, and doth always put good thoughts into the mind, being always active in illuminating us, although we do not always take notice of it; but when

---

223. *Three Books of Occult Philosophy*, Cornelius Agrippa, ed. Donald Tyson, Llewellyn 1993

we are purified, and live peaceably, then it is perceived by us, then it doth as it were speak with us, and communicates its voice to us, being before silent, and studieth daily to bring us to a sacred perfection.

The *Ghayat al-Hakim* or *Picatrix*, one of the primary sources of the Western tradition, contains a ritual for contacting one's *perfect nature*. The ritual is taken from an undisclosed "book of Hermes". The perfect nature is described as a spirit that is connected with one's star, and is described as a perfect guide or teacher that opens "all the locks of wisdom"[224]. It is also related to the sphere of the Sun within the microcosm, a correspondence that has been preserved to this day in the Hermetic Kabbalah through the association of the Holy Guardian Angel with the *sefira Tiferet*.

The tradition of a connection between a person and their star is ancient, and was known to medieval Jews such as Eleazar of Worms, who wrote:

> Each person has his form above, who is his advocate ... an angel who guides that person's "star". And when he is sent below he has the image of the person who is beneath him ... And this is "and God created man in his own image, in the image of God created he him (*Gen.* 1:27). Why twice, "in his image/in the image of"? One is the image of man, and one is the image of the angelic being, who is in the form of that man.

The suggestion, justified through the use of a quotation from *Genesis*, that the Holy Guardian Angel is a *doppelgänger* or double of a man, is one of the most striking aspects of inner Kabbalistic tradition. It would be redundant to summarise these traditions, because Scholem has done so in illuminating detail in his essay *Tselem: the Concept of the Astral Body*. In this essay Scholem provides evidence that at the highest level of prophetic trance the kabbalist saw himself, and it was the double that spoke. The following is Scholem's translation from the *Shushan Sodot*[225]:

> The deeply learned Rabbi Nathan, of blessed memory, said to me: Know that the complete secret of prophecy to a prophet consists in that he suddenly sees the form of his self standing before him, and he forgets his own self and ignores it ... and that form speaks with him and tells him the future.

This phenomenon of splitting, where a person perceives a double, has been termed *autoscopy*, and occurs in many circumstances, not

---

224. *Ghayat al-Hakim*, trans. Hashem Atallah & Geylan Holmquest, Vol 2., Ouroboros Press 2008
225. *Tselem: The Concept of the Astral Body* in *The Mystical Shape of the Godhead*, Gershom Scholem, Schocken 1991

only prophetic trances. For a detailed discussion in the context of ecstatic Kabbalah the reader is referred to Arzy.[226].

There is a large modern literature that describes unusual states of cognition. Part of this literature is medical and describes disabling conditions such as schizophrenia, in which voices may be hallucinated. Part describes spontaneous and temporary experiences such as out-of-the-body (bilocation) experiences that can occur during light dream states and anaesthesia. There is a large anecdotal literature describing the use of recreational drugs - for example, ketamine is reported to produce, amongst other things, a sensation of bilocation. There is also an emerging literature on induced bilocation, usually by electrical or magnetic stimulation of part of the brain.

In the days of cathode-ray tube (CRT) televisions, there was a common problem. The television had to be adjusted to synchronise with the incoming broadcast signal. There were knobs on the back of the set to adjust the internal frequency of the television. If the television was out of adjustment, the picture would spin round like the wheel on a fruit machine. When the knob was adjusted, the spinning would slow down, and then suddenly 'lock-on' to the signal.

One can speculate that the brain has a thousand adjustment knobs that help it 'lock-on' to the senses, in particular, to the proprioceptive senses that monitor every aspect of the body. When some of these 'knobs' are out of alignment (and this can happen because of stress, tiredness, hunger, drugs, illness, genetic predisposition, and even intense exercises like *tzeruf*) a perception of bilocation takes place.

The modern view locates the cause of abnormal cognition and perception in physiological disturbances of the brain. Where the ancients would pin the cause on external agents such as spirits or daemons, there are now emerging mechanistic explanations that pin the cause on internal agents - for example, neurotransmitters such as serotonin, dopamine, glutamate and their receptors. As we will see, this does not reduce or explain the *creative content* of these abnormal states or the social repercussions.

When one begins to explore psychological mechanisms behind splitting it is difficult to avoid encountering Julian Jaynes' *The Origin of Consciousness in the Breakdown of the Bicameral Mind*.

---

226. *Speaking with One's Self: Autoscopic Phenomena in Writings from the Ecstatic Kabbalah*, Shahar Arzy, Moshe Idel, Theodor Landis & Olaf Blanke, Journal of Consciousness Studies, **12**, No. 11, November 2005

Beyond the controversy surrounding his ideas one finds a searching examination of the nature of consciousness. Jaynes argued that modern consciousness - the self-consciously rational, introspective, autobiographical consciousness - is a cultural artifact based on sophisticated patterns of language use that are learned. Prior to modern consciousness there existed a different kind of consciousness which he termed "the bicameral mind". The bicameral mind had two parts: a 'doer', and a 'reasoner', and the reasoner was not conscious as it is in the modern mind. The doer received instructions from the reasoner in the form of a godlike voice, and obeyed these instructions without question. As evidence Jaynes examined ancient literature such as the *Iliad* and the *Bible* and believed there was a transition from a non-self-reflective style where 'gods' were the principal decision makers, to a self-reflective modern consciousness.

What is interesting is the suggestion that modern consciousness is not a divine increment nor even a biological increment; it is a social increment. It is something that has developed out of an earlier form in which 'voices of the gods' were much more common than they are at the present time. Jaynes comments[227]:

> I also want to mention that the evidence from written texts, personal idols, cylinder seals, and the construction of personal names suggests that every person had a personal god. In Mesopotamia, it was his *ili*, which in Hebrew is perhaps from the same root as Eli and Elohim. In Egypt, the personal god which had the same function was called a *ka*, a word which has been an enigma in Egyptology until now.
>
> In connection with the personal god, it is possible to suggest that a part of our innate bicameral heritage is the modern phenomenon of the 'imaginary' playmate. According to my own research as well as other data, it occurs in at least one-third of modern children between the ages of 2 and 5 years, and is believed now to involve very real verbal hallucinations. In the rare cases where the imaginary playmate lasts beyond the juvenile period, it too grows up with the child and begins telling him or her what to do in times of stress. It is therefore possible that this is how the personal god started in bicameral times, the imaginary playmate growing up with the person in a society of expectancies that constantly encouraged the child to hear voices and to continue to do so.

If Jaynes is correct then one can speculate that some concentration exercises such as *tzeruf* paralyse or overload parts of the brain associated with language processing and induce a state of bicamerality. The *tzeruf* exercises of Abulafia were used to induce an autoscopic

---

227. *Consciousness and the Voices of the Mind*, Julian Jaynes

prophetic state, and it is possible we find here a connection between Jaynes' linguistic model of self-consciousness and the phenomenon of revelatory or prophetic voices.

The modern tradition of the Holy Guardian Angel derives from a text that purports to date from the fifteenth century, *The Book of Sacred Magic of Abramelin the Mage*. The text is found in Hebrew, French and German versions. Its true date and provenance have been subject to much discussion. Patai provides an overview of the issues and concludes that the text may be Jewish in origin[228]. Scholem began with this view and reversed his opinion. The surviving MS are late copies, which renders opinions speculative.

The text describes how a Jew called Abraham spent years searching for a teacher, and eventually found someone called Abramelin in Upper Egypt. He was given a body of teachings found in the text, which (as the text states) he now passes-on to his son Lamech. Part of the teachings describe a *pietist* operation to summon one's Holy Guardian Angel (HGA). The rest consists of a description of a demonic hierarchy, and large number of magic squares specific to solving many kinds of material problems, and in this it is conventional. So is this a genuine Jewish text for summoning one's HGA?

Piety is a response to a religious tradition, and it is socially defined. It cannot be abstract. The pious, by definition, go beyond the norm to the extent of over-fulfilling their religious obligations, so that (for example) they may spend more time reading sacred literature, spend more time praying, be fastidious about purity, sin, and the fulfilment of religious obligations, restrict their appetites to a degree (there is often an ascetic tendency), and may even invent novel forms of unpleasantness, such as the hair shirt, or Blaise Pascal's iron belt-of-spikes.

At the risk of over-generalising, there has been an historic tendency for the pious to be fastidious and self-critical, and by extension, critical of others. Pietist groups have tended to be isolationist, literal in interpreting texts, prone to splintering, and are perhaps the last of groups one might associate with an ecumenical tendency. There are pietist sub-groups in Christianity, Islam and Judaism to this day, and these tendencies are easily observed; it is very relevant to reference the current *Haredi* movement in Israel. Although piety in Judaism has varied over time, we have a record of pietist movements going

---

228. *The Jewish Alchemists*, Patai, Raphael, Princeton University Press, 1994

back to the Dead Sea Scrolls, and certain factors have been relatively invariant.

So what kind of piety is prescribed by the *Sacred Magic*? There is an element of seclusion, a withdrawal from social life, an emphasis on reading sacred texts, enthusiastic prayer, ablutions, a withdrawal from sexual intercourse and so on. It is clearly a progressive induction into *some kind* of piety. The most surprising thing about it is its non-specificity in most matters that are typically of utmost importance to the pious, such as specific texts, specific prayers, ritual intentionality, and maintaining and restoring purity. It is strangely vague. It feels like a one-size-fits-all ecumenical imitation of piety.

If, as some scholars have suggested, the ritual derives from a Jewish source, does it look like it might have been written by a pious Jew? Would a pious Jew believe the *Sacred Magic* exhibits a significant level of piety? I believe the answer to be an overwhelming 'no'.

> **The Sacred**
>
> Sacredness comes from the belief that certain objects, places and occasions 'belong to God'. In an emanational or graded cosmology there may be a graded sense of holiness associated with the sacred; objects, places, occasions and even people may become more holy as a result of activities such as prayer and sacrifice and service to God.
>
> A major issue with the sacred is defilement, and this can come about through contact with impure objects, or people, or through forbidden or sinful actions. In the *Hekhalot Rabbatai*, Rabbi Nehunya ben Hakkanah is in deep contemplation of the divine mysteries of the Throne and his followers wish to question him. A menstruating woman who has bathed twice to remove her impurity is asked to touch a cloth with the lightest touch of a finger, and the cloth is placed in the Rabbi's lap, He is immediately removed from the divine presence.

The mystical tendency among European Jews during the medieval period was inspired by a generation of pietists who lived in Palestine during the Tannaitic period (approx. 10 - 220 CE). These were the saintly heroes of the influential *Hekhalot* and *Merkavah* texts, and appear as protagonists in the *Bahir* and the *Zohar*. These were men of such remarkable holiness that they were able to regard the Throne of Glory. This was the context and standard of piety.

It would seem remarkable that a pious Rhineland Jew would publish a procedure for acquiring the purity to summon and communicate with God's Holy angels without a reference to this background. Not only does this seem unrealistic, but the Rhineland has an important place in the history of Jewish piety. Only a few generations prior to the supposed date of the *Sacred Magic* the region was home to Samuel ben Kalonymous the Pious, Judah ben Samuel the Pious (author of *Sefer Chasidim*, the *Book of the Pious*) and the famous Eleazar of Worms. These men were household names and the protagonists of fanciful bedtime stories for many generations to come[229].

The *Sacred Magic* may appear to be heavy-duty piety to the modern mind, accustomed to a thousand daily distractions and demands, but according to the historic trend of Jewish piety it is not. In the opinion of the author, the *Sacred Magic* was written by someone who lived in proximity to pious Jews, probably in the Rhineland, but was not Jewish, and was probably not a devout Christian either. This person observed the outward forms of Jewish piety, but was ignorant of the detail or inner substance. The content of the remarkably vague *Sacred Magic* reflects this[230]. It would seem to be an attempt to reverse-engineer the mystical technology of the wonder-working Rhineland pietists.

Leaving aside the question of its provenance, a French copy of the *Sacred Magic* was discovered by S. L. Mathers of Golden Dawn fame during his researches in the Bibliothèque de l'Arsenal. He translated it into English, published it in 1898, and the procedure described promptly excited the attention of fellow Golden Dawn member Aleister Crowley. Crowley observed:

> This book is written in the an exalted style. It is perfectly coherent; it does not demand fantastic minutiae of ritual or even the calculations customary. There is nothing to insult the intelligence. On the contrary, the operation proposed is of sublime simplicity. The method is in entire accordance with this. There are, it is true, certain prescriptions to be observed, but these really amount to little more than injunctions to observe decency in the performance of so august an operation. One must have a house where proper precautions against disturbance can be taken; this being arranged, there is really nothing to do but to aspire with increasing fervour and concentration, for six months, towards the obtaining of the Knowledge and Conversation of the Holy Guardian Angel. Once he has appeared it is then necessary, first, to call forth the Four Great Princes of the Evil of the World; next their eight sub-princes; and lastly, the 316 servitors of these. A number of talismans, previously prepared, are thus charged with the power of the

---

229. See *The Ma'aseh Book*, Moses Gaster, Jewish Publication Society 1961
230. It is interesting to contrast the piety of the *Sacred Magic* with that of the pietist community that formed around R. Isaac Luria - see *Physician of the Soul, Healer of the Cosmos*, Lawrence Fine, Stanford University Press 2003

spirits. By applying the proper talismans, you can get practically anything you want.

Crowley added that he would have preferred the *Sacred Magic* without the Princes of Evil (and the side-effect of worldly omnipotence), but when occasion required he did not demur from using the magic squares.

Crowley began the procedure in London in 1899, but decided he required a more remote location, and bought a property close to Loch Ness in Scotland. Some of the subsequent reputation of the *Sacred Magic* may derive from his lurid descriptions of the side effects of beginning the operation. Tradesmen, staff and friends were afflicted by emotional disturbances. There were also other phenomena:

> Besides these comparatively explicable effects on human minds, there were numberless physical phenomena for which it is hard to account. While I was preparing the talismans, squares of vellum inscribed in Indian ink, a task which I undertook in the sunniest room of the house, I had to use artificial light even on the brightest days. It was a darkness which might almost be felt. The lodge and terrace, moreover, soon became peopled with shadowy shapes, sufficiently substantial, as a rule, to be almost opaque. I say shapes; and yet the truth is that they were not shapes properly speaking. The phenomenon is hard to describe. It was as if the faculty of vision suffered some interference; as if the object of vision were not properly objects at all. It was as if they belong to an order of matter which affected the sight without informing it.

Crowley did not complete the procedure. A dispute within the Golden Dawn concerning S. L. Mathers' authority drew him away from Scotland to act on Mathers' behalf in London. The story did not end there however; about four years later, while Crowley and his wife Rose were staying in Cairo, Crowley received dictation during the course of three days from a disincarnate entity he called Aiwass. Crowley was later to identify Aiwass with his HGA. The dictation was published as *Liber AL vel Legis*, *The Book of the Law*. Crowley came to view Aiwass as an objectively existing entity possessed of knowledge he did not possess. Crowley spent years attempting to unlock hidden information coded within *Liber AL*, and made considerable use of *gematria* for this purpose.

An experience that resembles Crowley's in many respects, but also differs from it in respects, was that of the Swiss psychologist C. G. Jung. Jung possessed a powerful visionary sense that manifested partly through dreams and partly through waking visions. Jung does not appear to have employed any ritualistic techniques other than attentiveness; he was scrupulous in recording and analysing these experiences, and he was an accomplished artist. He also writes that he made things, such as a little town, to stimulate and engage his unconscious mind. The principal guide figure in his visions was an entity he called Philemon. Jung wrote[231]:

> Philemon and other figures of my fantasies brought home to me the crucial insight that there are things in the psyche which I do not produce, but which produce themselves and have their own life. Philemon represented a force which was not myself. In my fantasies I held conversations with him, and he said things which I had not consciously thought. For I observed clearly that it was he who spoke, not I. He said I treated thoughts as if I generated them myself, but in his view thoughts were like animals in the forest, or people in a room, or birds in the air, and added, "If you should see people in a room, you would not think that you had made those people, or you were responsible for them." It was he who taught me psychic objectivity, the reality of the psyche. Through him the distinction was clarified between myself and the object of my thought. He confronted me in an objective manner, and I understood that there is something in me which can say things that I do not know and do not intend, things which may even be directed against me.
>
> Psychologically, Philemon represented superior insight. He was quite mysterious figure to me. At times he seemed to me quite real as if he were a living personality. I went walking up and down the garden with him, and to me he was what the Indians call a guru.

Jung's interaction with what he characterised as components of his unconscious mind reached a crux during 1916 (only twelve years after Crowley's *Liber AL*)[232]:

> It began with a restlessness, but I did not know what it meant or what "they" wanted of me. There was an ominous atmosphere all around me. I had this strange feeling that the air was filled with ghostly entities. Then it was as if my house began to be haunted. My eldest daughter saw a white figure passing through the room. My second daughter, independently of her elder sister, related that twice in the night her blanket had been snatched away; and that same night my nine-year-old son had an anxiety dream. In the morning he asked his mother for crayons, and he, who ordinarily never drew, now made a picture of his dream ...
>
> ... Around five o'clock in the afternoon on Sunday the front door bell began ringing frantically. It was a bright summer day; the two maids were in the kitchen, from which the open square outside the front

---

231. *Memories, Dreams, Reflections*, C. G. Jung, Fontana 1972
232. Ibid.

door could be seen. Everyone immediately looked to see who was there, but there was no one in sight. I was sitting near the doorbell, and not only heard it but saw it moving. We all simply stared at one another. The atmosphere was thick, believe me! Then I knew something had to happen. The whole house was filled as if there were a crowd present, crammed full of spirits. They were packed deep right up to the door, and the air was so thick it was scarcely possible to breath. As for myself, I was all a-quiver with the question: "For God's sake, what in the world is this?" Then they cried out in chorus, "We have come back from Jerusalem where we find not what we sought". That is the beginning of the *Septem Sermones*. Then it began to flow out of me, and in the course of three evenings the thing was written.

This experience was the beginning of an outpouring of material that eventually became Jung's celebrated *Liber Novus*, or *Red Book*, an extraordinary self-illuminated manuscript containing examples of his powerful visionary art. The similarities to Crowley's experiences are striking: third-party emotional disturbances, psychokinetic phenomena, a deepening atmosphere, a sense of spiritual entities, and a sudden three-day outpouring of revelatory material.

A third example of occult revelation that makes an interesting contrast to both Crowley and Jung is Dion Fortune's *The Cosmic Doctrine*. *The Cosmic Doctrine* tackles the perennial cosmogonic question: how does something emerge out of nothing, how does complexity emerge out of simplicity. The content takes the form of a narrative cosmogony, and in this it is conventional, but in almost every other sense it is astonishingly original, using quasi-mechanistic metaphors, many taken from the physics of the day, to describe the evolution of an emergent multiverse.

The mechanistic metaphors owe more to inner vision than genuine physics, but this innovation removes the need for anthropomorphic projections of intelligence and agency within the emerging cosmos and its dependent universes. Unlike the many variations and combinations of Platonic and gnostic cosmogonies, mind is not a first principle. Mind and consciousness are emergents. With respect to its metaphors it declares:

> In these occult teachings you will be given certain images, under which you are instructed to think of certain things. These images are not descriptive but symbolic, *and are designed to train the mind, not to inform it* (sic).

This is certainly the case; in the author's experience it requires many readings and much time to begin to assemble the ideas that the text is attempting to express. It contains a prescient understanding of

Awakening

many ideas that have taken most of the twentieth century to become a part of modern physics, and are still not widely understood, such as the emergence of complexity out of the interactions of simple parts.

The Cosmic Doctrine is a channelled work communicated c. 1923-24. It was dictated to members of her esoteric group while Fortune was in a profound trance state. Fortune would lie horizontally on a couch, usually on an east-west axis in a protected space used as a temple. She would concentrate on a succession of symbols as part of a self-taught process of withdrawing from her body. Subjectively, she would journey to an inner-plane temple, where she would remain, subjectively conscious, during the communication. Objectively, her respiration would slow down, her pulse rate drop, and she would produce "a rather acid perspiration"[233]. Once the correct conditions were established, dictation would begin.

During some sessions there were reports of unusual phenomena[234]:

> The phenomena that occurred during trance were generally of two types: sound phenomena and changes in physical objects. One of the most common curiosities affected candles or altar lights where during the mediumistic sessions the flame would frequently well-up to enormous heights. These were physical phenomenon, they were not astral. On one particular occasion the altar lights' flame rose to about five or six feet in height where normally the light only came up about an inch. This occasion was during reception of certain parts of the *Cosmic Doctrine*. The scribe working the session almost fainted as there was also a great rush of wind within the room as the flame increased. Wind and air movement was not uncommon because the communication is basically an energy transference. In this one instance, the altar flame did not flicker but held absolutely steady as it increased up to a great height ...
>
> ... Other easily observable phenomena included very loud knocking sounds, bell-like sounds, and on several occasions pieces of paper used by the scribe were lifted and wafted around the room.

Channelling was in vogue at the time. Fortune had been influenced by the 19th. century craze for spiritualism, and the occult synthesis created by Madame Blavatsky and promulgated through the Theosophical Society. Fortune may be compared with her contemporary Alice Bailey, who, during the same time period as Fortune was receiving *The Cosmic Doctrine*, was publishing the first volumes of a huge corpus of channelled works. There are significant overlaps of

---

233. *The Story of Dion Fortune*, Charles Fielding & Carr Collins, Star and Cross 1985
234. Ibid.

The Hermetic Kabbalah

style and ideological background between Fortune and Bailey, and both develop ideas that had their origin in Theosophy. Bailey attributed her communications to "ascended Masters", Fortune to "inner-plane adepti". In Fortune's view these were highly-evolved humans who had passed beyond the need for physical incarnation, but rather than be absorbed in the divine had taken on a tutelary role, something like a *boddhisattva* in Buddhism.

Fortune does not appear to have made much use of the idea of the HGA, regarding it as a manifestation of the higher self, a mode of consciousness achieved once one acquired the ability to ascend up the middle pillar of the Tree as far as *Tiferet* and beyond:

> It is the prime characteristic of this higher mode of mentation that it consists neither in voices nor visions, but is pure consciousness. It is an intensification of awareness, and from this quickening of the mind comes a peculiar power of insight and penetration which is of the nature of hyper-developed intuition. The higher consciousness is never psychic, but always intuitive, containing no sensory imagery. It is this absence of sensory imagery which tells the experienced initiate that he is on the level of the higher consciousness[235].

Crowley, Jung and Fortune provide three differing views of the HGA. Crowley believed Aiwass was an objectively-existing entity. For Jung, his guide Philemon was a component of his subconscious mind. Fortune thought the HGA was a level of mentation above the normal egoic mode of internal narration and visualisation, but she believed the inner-plane adepts she channelled had an objective existence.

The experiences themselves have in common a revelatory component that seems to come from an external source, that knows things one does not know, and may adopt an unusual style - lyrical, didactic, prophetic, and often pompous. The Knowledge and Conversation of the Holy Guardian Angel would seem to take many forms. There may be a humanoid vision ... or there may not be. If human, it could be male or female. There may be explicit verbal communication ... or there may not be. If not human, it may be a symbol of extraordinary power. What one can say is that it is an experience of revelatory and redemptive power that conducts one into another realm of being. The exact framing will contain so many personal elements that one cannot be prescriptive about how it might occur, or over what kind of time frame.

The author's experience was of a sustained process that began in 1987 and completed in 2003. My guardian spirit was my syzygy, my

---

235. *The Mystical Qabalah*, Dion Fortune, Ernest Benn 1979.

Awakening

occult twin, and she was both guide and psychopomp, combining the roles of Dante's Virgil and Beatrice. I experienced an eruption of visionary narratives that I attempted to mould into quasi-mythological fiction, working at a computer late at night in a state that was almost dissociated. This fiction now seems banal, like fairy gold that turns to dust and leaves, but it was revelatory and instructive at the time.

Some of the content was consistent with Jung's notion of the collective unconscious - symbols and ideas and mythical narratives that seemed to come from beyond my personal knowledge and experience. I felt a need to integrate this material into my everyday life. This was not simple, but it was not until I did so that its archetypal power was discharged, and what had been autonomous psychic components became integrated.

The obligation *to know ourselves* comes with an obligation *to be ourselves*, and to integrate our new interior landscape with those around us. Jung seems to say something similar[236]:

> I took great care to understand every single image, every item of my psychic inventory, and to classify them scientifically - and above all, to realise them in actual life. That is usually what we neglect to do. We allow the images to rise up, and maybe we wonder about them, but that is all. We do not take the trouble to understand them, let alone draw ethical conclusions from them. This stopping short conjures up the negative effects of the unconscious.

There are dangers. The principle dangers are those associated with *Tiferet*: pride, arrogance, and identification. The Ego may become inflated with a sense of uniqueness, mission and self-importance. Like *Ialdebaoth* it looks upon its microcosmos and exclaims "I am God, and there is no other God but me", forgetting that even gods can be sacrificed.

28.3 Summary

To summarise, the threshold that separates the armchair Kabbalist from the practical Kabbalist is the moment one solicits the aid of non-physical beings. Prayer is one such method; theurgy using ritual and *sunthemata* as outlined here is a more physical and immersive method.

According to ancient tradition we have a guide in the upper worlds; this is our Holy Guardian Angel. The examples given here -

---

236. *Memories, Dreams, Reflections*, C. G. Jung, Fontana 1972

Crowley, Jung, Fortune - show that this communication can be a powerful and revelatory experience.

28.4 Further Reading

One of the more interesting theurgic rituals from Late Antiquity can be found in the *Great Magical Papyrus of Paris*, a text scholars refer to as the Mithras Liturgy. It is simultaneously a theurgic invocation, an ascent, and an encounter with a divine being identified with Helios. The god provides an oracle or prophecy.

The Greek Magical Papyri in Translation, PGM IV 475, ed. Hans Dieter Betz, University of Chicago Press, 1992

The source material on the theurgy of late antiquity is distressingly scant. For a thorough examination of surviving material consult:

Theurgy in Late Antiquity: the Invention of a Ritual Tradition, Ilinca Tanaseanu-Döbler, Vandenhoeck & Ruprecht 2013

Divination and Theurgy in Neoplatonism, Dr. Crystal Addey, Ashgate Publishing, 2014

Theurgy and the Soul, Gregory Shaw, Penn State Press 1995

29

Death and Rebirth

> Truly, truly, I say to you, unless one is born again, he cannot see the kingdom of God.
>
> *John* 3:3

29.1 Death and Rebirth

The word 'initiation' implies a beginning. In the context of Western mysticism[237] this is usually taken to mean the end of one kind of life, and the beginning of a new kind of life, and in some cases, of being 'born again'. The idea of being 'born again' may have been tarnished by revivalist evangelism to the point of parody and ridicule, but this should not detract from its significance. Dying and being reborn into a new life is one of the core experiences in the Western tradition.

Grave goods have been found in graves dating back tens of millenia. The belief that something follows death is old. It follows that a ceremony or ritual in which death and rebirth form a central component will tend to borrow from the rituals of actual internment. Initiates are symbolically killed and resurrected. For example, in the

---

237. And worldwide - see for example *The Sacred & the Profane*, Mircea Eliade, Mariner 1968

ceremony to make a master mason, the candidate is symbolically murdered, falls back into a symbolic grave, and is raised from the "horizontal to the perpendicular" by a lodge member representing King Solomon, using a special grip known as "the lion's paw"[238]. Rituals of this type, in which a candidate is ritually killed, or enters into the grave, or descends into the realm of the dead, followed by an awakening at the hand of an initiate, recall the raising of Lazarus by Jesus in the book of *John*.

This is the absolute core, stripped of exotic symbolism: one dies, one remains in a state of un-life for a period of time[239], and then one is raised and welcomed into a new life. The experience is an internal *eschaton*. If one regards the *Revelation* of John from the perspective of personal experience, the overall dynamic becomes clear: the day of judgement comes, there is a sorting and cleansing on a radical scale, and then a new world descends.

> And I saw a new heaven and a new earth: for the first heaven and the first earth were passed away; and there was no more sea.
>
> And I John saw the holy city, new Jerusalem, coming down from God out of heaven, prepared as a bride adorned for her husband.
>
> And I heard a great voice out of heaven saying, Behold, the tabernacle of God is with men, and he will dwell with them, and they shall be his people, and God himself shall be with them, and be their God.
>
> And God shall wipe away all tears from their eyes; and there shall be no more death, neither sorrow, nor crying, neither shall there be any more pain: for the former things are passed away.
>
> And he that sat upon the throne said, Behold, I make all things new. And he said unto me, Write: for these words are true and faithful.
>
> And he said unto me, It is done. I am Alpha and Omega, the beginning and the end. I will give unto him that is athirst of the fountain of the water of life freely.

There is great beauty in these verses. There will be a new heaven and a new earth. The former things, source of so much suffering, will pass away.

Towards the end of the nineteenth century there was a resurgence of interest in the esoteric. A spirit of syncretism, much inspired by H. P. Blavatsky, was in the air, and the industrious Victorians ransacked all the traditions of all the ages. There was a vogue for Egyptian culture and religion, and E. A. Budge, that indefatigable Keeper of the

---

238. Anyone recalling C.S. Lewis's Aslan at this point understands the symbolism.
239. Lazarus was raised after four days. According to tradition Jesus died on Friday and was raised on Sunday. Some sources cite forty days as the period required.

Death and Rebirth

British Museum, was publishing books on Egyptian culture and funerary traditions at a rate of about one book per year from 1885 to 1900. There were the mystery traditions of the ancient world, in particular the Eleusinian mysteries of Demeter and Persephone, and the Orphic mysteries that influenced Pythagoras. There was Freemasonry and the symbolism of the third-degree rite of the Master Mason. There were the Rosicrucian manifestos, and in particular, the symbolism of the vault of Christian Rosencreutz. An important influence was the publication of *The Golden Bough* by Sir James Frazer in 1890, which began as an investigation into the tale of the *rex Nemorensis*, the priest-king of the grove of Nemi who was fated to die violently at the hands of his successor. *The Golden Bough* popularised the idea of a quasi-divine figure who dies and is reborn in connection with the seasonal rituals of an agricultural society. As the song *John Barleycorn* puts it:

There was three men come out o' the west their fortunes for to try,

And these three men made a solemn vow, John Barleycorn must die,

They ploughed, they sowed, they harrowed him in, throwed clods upon his head,

And these three men made a solemn vow, John Barleycorn was dead.

People were like seeds: they had to go into the ground, but they would be reborn.

Another important element of tradition was that of alchemy, in which images of blackening or putrefaction were used to describe the early stages of a process in which dross or impure matter would be separated-out, and what remained would become the basis for the *lapis*, or stone of the wise. The first step in the quest for alchemical gold was a death process.

Above and beyond all these esoteric traditions there was the Christian tradition and its symbols. Death and rebirth is the central mystery of the crucifixion. Many churches have the stations of the cross, where one can meditate on the passion of Christ. In this way the passion of Christ is internalised; one can walk with Christ on the *Via Dolorosa* on the way to Calvary. It is a very small step from this to the idea that suffering, death and resurrection should be simulated or experienced in a ritualistic way.

An important influence was Dr. Anna Kingsford, for a time president of the London Theosophical Society, who tried to sway its members in favour of a Christian-Hermetic tradition rather than the oriental bias that had developed. Following differences, she left the Theosophical Society to form the independent Hermetic Society in

The Hermetic Kabbalah

1884. It's objectives were:
> 'Its chief aim is to promote the comparative study of the philosophical and religious systems of the East and of the West; especially of the Greek Mysteries and the Hermetic Gnosis, and its allied schools, the Kabalistic, Pythagorean, Platonic, and Alexandrian, – these being inclusive of Christianity, – with a view to the elucidation of their original esoteric and real doctrine, and the adaptation of its expression to modern requirements.

Kingsford was known and respected by the two most influential founders of the Hermetic Order of the Golden Dawn, W. W. Westcott, and S. L. Mathers. Had she not died at the age of 41 she might have played a much greater part (she died in 1888, the same year as the first Golden Dawn temple was founded in London). Another, later influence was Violet Firth (a.k.a Dion Fortune) who formed a Christian Mystic Lodge within the Theosophical Society and again left to form her own group, the Inner Light.

Christianity mutated as it moved through the fingers of these creative esotericists. It became less history and more allegory, in much the same way as it did in the hands of the gnostics of late antiquity. The Christ became a symbol of the divine Higher Self. The mystery of the crucifixion became personal. This esoteric Christianity was another element that went into the blender. The gamut of traditions - Masonic, Rosicrucian, Alchemical, Christian, Kabbalistic, Egyptian, Orphic and Eleusinian mystery traditions - were flat-packed into the rituals of the Golden Dawn in the belief that at some point they would self-assemble in the mind of the aspirant. Death and rebirth became the central mystery of *Tiferet*. It is all in there - you just have to look.

The denseness and interconnectedness of symbolism does tend to obscure a simple question. If death is enacted as a central experience, but it is not real death, if this late-Victorian theatre of symbolism signifies something, what is the signified? What does it mean to be reborn into the light, or the spirit, or born again? In the words of a Golden Dawn ritual, "quit the night, and seek the day". Are these just heady aspirations, or are they indications of a genuine inner transformation? What might those words mean today?

.When I discussed these matters with my teacher about thirty years ago she pointed out that the Magical Image of *Tiferet* is threefold: child, priest-king, sacrificed god[240]. The symbolism would appear to be taken from Christianity: Jesus the holy child, Jesus the King of

---

240. The earliest published source for this I have found is *The Mystical Qabalah*, Dion Fortune, originally published in 1935.

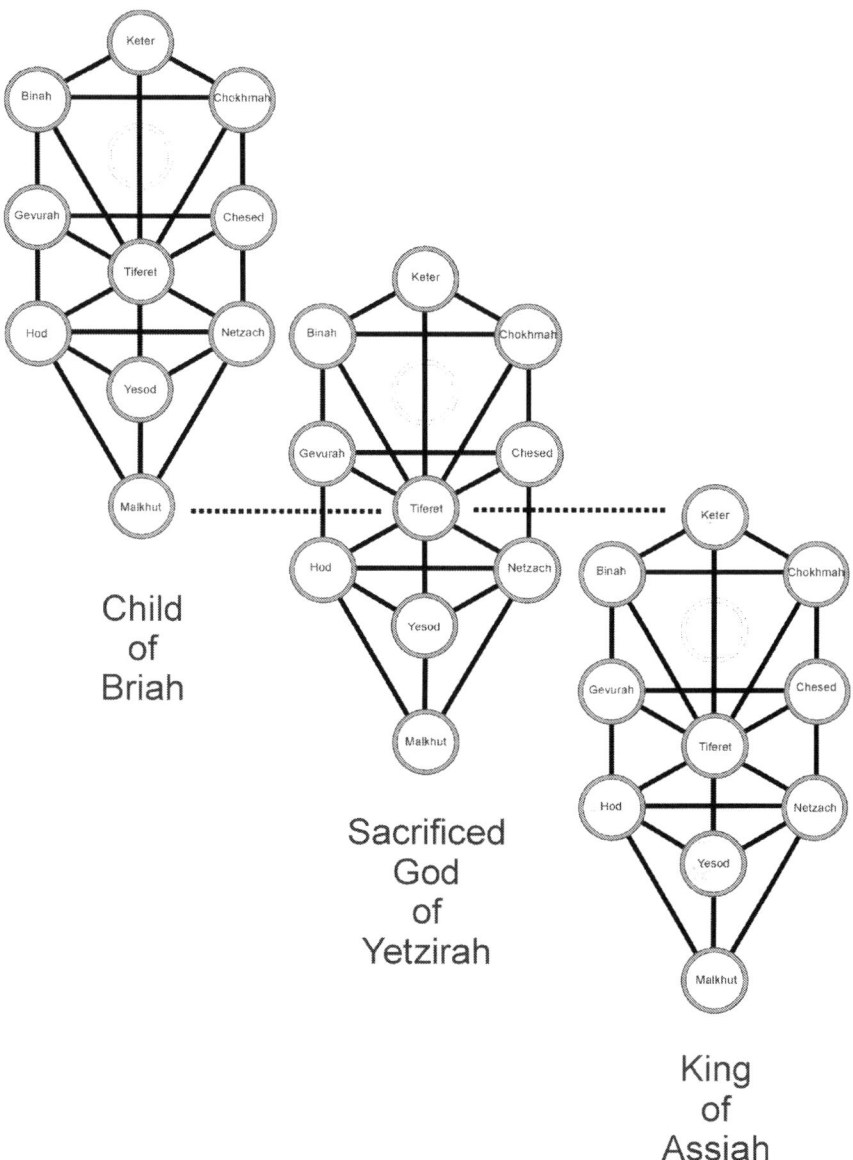

Figure 57: The Extended Tree, showing the worlds of *Briah*, *Yetzirah* and *Assiah*. When these Trees are overlapped, *Tiferet* takes on three overlapping but distinct aspects according to whether it is the *Malkhut* of *Briah*, *Tiferet* of *Yetzirah*, or *Keter* of *Assiah*.

The Hermetic Kabbalah

the Jews; Jesus the crucified Son of God. Her explanation was not Christian however, and referred to the Extended Tree, where four Trees representing the Four Worlds are overlapped to create a single, composite tree (see Figure 57). In this model, *Tiferet* of *Yetzirah* is both *Keter* of *Assiah* and *Malkhut* of *Briah*. It takes on three aspects. As *Keter* it is the crowned priest-king of *Assiah*, world of action. As *Malkhut* it is the child of *Briah*, world of creation. As *Tiferet*, it is the sacrificed god of *Yetzirah*. She told me that the god that is sacrificed is the Ego. The sacrificed god of *Yetzirah* is that part of us that has set itself up as a false god.

A parallel explanation is that the animal soul, the *nefesh*, is the master (king) of *Assiah*. The social soul, or *ruach*, believes it runs the show, but is largely in thrall to the animal soul. It has turned its face away from *Briah* towards *Assiah*, and so the higher part of the soul, the *neshamah,* becomes unknown and unconscious. To correct this the *ruach* must 'die', thus giving the *neshamah* the opportunity to be born into consciousness. In time this *Briatic* child, the *neshamah*, will grow into maturity - one literally 'grows a soul' as it grows into dialogue with the reborn *ruach*.

This is how I received the tradition. I do not claim this is the secret, 'correct' explanation of initiation through the ages, only that a tradition existed. This is the form I received it in, and, modern trappings aside, it would appear to be consistent with much older reports

29.2 Chaos

The central experience of *Tiferet* is self-sacrifice, and the corresponding virtue is "devotion to the Work". For a person to enter into the experience of *Tiferet* the Ego has to admit the existence of a scope larger than itself. The Ego may find a way to incorporate self-sacrifice and devotion into its sense of self-importance (hence the vice being pride or arrogance) but it is heading in the correct direction: it has admitted the importance of concerns outside of itself, and it has made a binding commitment to these concerns.

The Ego may have had a symbolic experience of death and resurrection. It may have understood the symbolism and what it implies. More importantly, it should have had an experience that fractured its integrity, a fatal blow to its autobiographical self-narrative. This is often caused by a life-event - the death of a friend, the ending of a relationship, the loss of a job.

There may have been non-fatal blows in the past, and the Ego will have picked itself up after a rejection, a failure, a loss of nerve, or a

Death and Rebirth

loss of control, and bottled the guilt, constructed evasions, and carried on. The primary purpose of the Ego is survival, and it is good at mending itself.

The fatal blow comes when the Ego no longer wants to mend itself. Like Scrooge in Dickens' *A Christmas Carol,* the Ego is forced to look at the past, the present and the future without the benefit of self-protection. The Ego stops trying to survive. One of the purposes of training and initiation is to prepare a person for this eventuality. It happens when one is ready to look at oneself with complete honesty, without using evasion techniques[241]. The magic mirror that reflects back what we want to see about ourselves, cracks:

Out flew the web and floated wide
The mirror crack'd from side to side
"The curse is come upon me," cried
The Lady of Shalott.

The curse that comes upon the Lady is the curse of looking beyond the magic mirror, and the death that comes with it.

What comes next is difficult to write about because it goes beyond commonplace experience, and the subjective nature of the experience depends so much on the framework in which it is interpreted. What follows is an attempt to synthesise the author's experience with clues and hints scattered about throughout the literature of mysticism. I believe it to be representative.

The short explanation is that the Ego begins to see that it has no substance, that it is a fabrication. Before this happens it may become aware of powerful forces that threaten it. It may project these forces onto the world. It may feel imperilled. It may have messianic feelings as it struggles to contain the powers of chaos that begin to engulf it. This is the combat myth of so many religions: a warrior god (Thor, *Yahweh*, Marduk etc.) who fights a never-ending battle against the monstrosities of the primordial deep. There is the ever-present influence of the Apocalypse of St. John, itself a combat myth. The Ego moves towards an immanentation of the eschaton, a personal endtime, the final confrontation with the forces of darkness.

An explanation for what is happening kabbalistically is that as one moves 'upwards' from *Tiferet* towards *Da'at* and *Keter* on the central pillar of consciousness, one is also moving 'downwards' from *Tiferet* to *Yesod* and *Malkhut* and re-experiencing these *sefirot* at a completely new level of awareness, as a child of *Briah*. Because *Da'at* and

---

241. i.e. blame, rationalisation, justification

Yesod are duals, the world of the broken below *Malkhut* can be imagined in *Yesod* as a terrifying encounter at *Da'at*.

As one attempts to work up towards *Da'at* from *Tiferet* the Ego begins to come apart. The actual causality is reversed; it is the Ego coming apart that enables the movement up the pillar of consciousness, but experienced from the inside, it feels like a gate has opened, and a strange mix of primitive and unpleasant entities threaten one's being. *Yesod* and *Da'at* begin to fuse as worlds begin to interpenetrate, and one may begin to become aware of worlds of chaos and evil. One may feel assailed; perhaps not so vividly as the many paintings of St. Anthony would suggest, but the feelings can be unpleasant.

One can become unwell. The author experienced about two years of increasing psychosomatic stress and nervous exhaustion. There are many descriptions in the esoteric literature of 'vampiristic entities' feeding on life energy, and of attempts to 'seal the aura' against these daemonic life feeders. This is one of the experiences that can occur when the armour of the Ego begins to deteriorate. I recall feeling abnormally sensitive to the energetics of situations, sensitive to the balance of gain and loss. Normal everyday occurrences would leave me feeling drained. I was so tired. Paradoxically, the more energy one puts into protecting oneself, the worse the situation can become. The psychosomatic nature of these feelings was revealed during an intense visionary experience, and from that moment I felt well again. I no longer felt threatened or drained by simple situations.

One could lose one's nerve and attempt to put the cork back into the bottle. This is difficult. One cannot unsee what one has seen, and the act of freely swearing an oath to undergo the process (which one will have done as a condition of initiation) may preclude this as an option. There may be a feeling of crisis or cataclysm, which again, one can project onto external causes.

Aleister Crowley gave this process a dramatic form when he encountered *Choronzon* in the company of Victor Neuburg in the sand dunes of north Africa (as recounted in *Da'at* on page 291). He provides wonderful descriptions of the two aspects of Ego: on one hand the Most High, with motionless legions guarding the Abyss, and on the other hand the dust devils and malice of *Choronzon*, who is *Samael* by another name. Intuiting the nature of this grand stand-off, he joined *Choronzon* in the triangle of evocation.

Crowley has been criticised for choosing to encounter *Choronzon* in the way that he did, by violating the basic principles of evocation[242]. This is subscribing to the drama of the combat myth, a fiction spun by the Ego in the belief that it has the power to control the shifting sands underpinning its bastions. The Ego has mighty incantations and seals. It has a circle of finest chalk, candles of beeswax, and a sword engraved with words of power. It has the power to compel the spirits.

This power exists only up to a point. The right hand can make a great noise about its ferocious struggle with the left hand ... until someone observes that they are both attached at the torso.

As for *Choronzon*, the mighty devil is only a threat when his swirling dust-devils are given energy to live for more than their natural span; that is, when they are cultivated and fed, rather than dissipated.

29.3 And After

There are many sayings from the Zen tradition of Buddhism that emphasise the complete ordinariness of what one had previously imagined to be a measure of spiritual attainment. A well-known paraphrase is "Before illumination I hewed wood and drew water. After illumination I hewed wood and drew water." A more elaborate version is:

Daily, nothing particular,
Only nodding to myself,
Nothing to choose, nothing to discard.
No coming, no going,
No person in purple,
Blue mountains without a speck of dust.
I exercise occult and subtle power,
Carrying water, shouldering firewood.[243]

The Ego tends to construct projects and grandiose plans based on a sense of manifest destiny or entitlement, and when the Ego goes down, so do the works of vanity.

There may be a listlessness, a lack of purpose, and it is easy to fall prey to the *klippotic* aspects of *Binah* (fatalism), *Chokhmah* (arbitrariness) and *Keter* (futility). In its worst form there is a collapse of meaning tending towards nihilism. This is a well-known pathology, and one can find elegant discussions countering this view in Bud-

---

242. This criticism is sound. An unprepared Ego should stick with protecting itself in the usual way.
243. *Two Zen Classics, "Mumonkan" & "Hekiganroku"*, trans. K. Sekida, Weatherhill 1977

The Hermetic Kabbalah

dhism.

There are compensations however, as Crowley observed in the aftermath of his encounter with the Abyss[244]:

> I understood that sorrow had no substance; but only my ignorance and lack of intelligence had made me imagine the existence of evil. As soon as I had destroyed my personality, as soon as I had expelled my ego, the universe which to it was indeed a frightful and fatal force, fraught with every form of fear, was only so in relation to this idea 'I'; so long as 'I am I', all else must seem hostile. Now that there was no longer any 'I' to suffer, all these ideas which had inflicted suffering became innocent. I could praise the perfection of every part; I could wonder and worship the whole. This attainment absolutely altered my outlook. Of course, I did not at once enter into full enjoyment. The habit of a misunderstanding everything had to be broken, bit by bit. I had to explore every possibility and transmute each base metal in turn into gold. It was years before I got into the habit of falling in love at first sight with everything that came my way.

The virtue of *Tiferet*, Devotion to the Work, can be a lifebelt when foundering in the vast expanse of the bitter sea (an aspect of *Binah*). The supernal waters may be much larger than we had imagined, but that does not mean that one should stop paddling. In the process of paddling one may discover that meaning and purpose are not a part of the external structure of reality; they are intrinsic to, and emergent from, the power to exercise choice and act in the world. The Ego tends to want more than this. In its vanity it cannot perceive the occult and subtle power in carrying water and shouldering firewood.

---

244. *The Confessions of Aleister Crowley*, ed. John Symonds & Kenneth Grant, Bantam 1971.

Part 4

Epilogue

The Hermetic Kabbalah

30

Epilogue

In his overview of the Western Esoteric Traditions[245], Professor Goodrick-Clarke characterises some of the important themes of the Hermetic tradition: non-dualism; the original dignity of the human soul; the Fall into Nature; Nature as the outward face of the divine; the Cosmos as a living creature; the interconnection and mirroring of different levels of reality; mentoring and initiation; ascent; the rectification of soul and Cosmos.

Many of these themes are also found (or have obvious parallels) in Kabbalah. The merging of traditions - Jewish Kabbalah, Hellenistic philosophy, and the magico-mystical traditions of late antiquity - has produced a modern esoteric tradition that is rich and distinctive. I hope this book has gone some way to justify this statement.

The tradition is overwhelmingly esoteric - that is, known only to a small number of people with specialised interests. My personal experience is that most people - and by most I mean the overwhelming majority of people - have no idea that such a tradition ever existed or that it continues to exist in a small and unobtrusive way. Images find their way into popular culture - disturbing, subversive and sometimes comical literary archetypes such as Faust, Prospero, Gandalf and Dumbledore[246] - but these figures are as remote from everyday life as

---

245. *The Western Esoteric Traditions*, Nicholas Goodrick-Clarke, Oxford University Press 2008

The Hermetic Kabbalah

the knights of Arthurian chivalry. They hint at something, but convey no idea of what the substance might be. The unreality and exaggeration of these figures has the effect of rendering an entire tradition unreal and implausible.

The heart of the tradition is *gnostic*, in broad sense of the word. A key idea is the belief (or perception) that a core aspect of our being ('the soul') is in a wrong situation. This is alluded to in the *Poimandres* with its description of the Fall into Nature (page 110). According to *Genesis* the parents of the human race ate the fruit of the Tree of Knowledge and fell out of one world ('Eden') into *another world*. They were exiled into flesh, and knew death. Their grasp of the infinite was shrunk to the immediate needs of the body. They forgot themselves.

There are three key aspects to this fallen condition. The first, *separation*, is the experience of embedding in space and time. There is an illusion of substance and solidity, of a multitude of substances and appearances.

The second aspect of our fallen condition is *appetite*; in its most general aspect we could call it *eros*, as the Greeks did. This is the desire to be in relationship with something that seems to be external to us. We are gluttons for experience of the world we inhabit, and this appetite, with all its subsidiary relationships and pleasures, binds us to a limited conception of ourselves.

The third aspect of our fallen condition is *ignorance*. We have forgotten that there might be a big picture. We can experience this 'forgetting' by going to the cinema and watching a movie. For a brief period we enter another world and forget ourselves. When we emerge into the daylight it can feel like waking from a deep sleep.

We seem to possess a natural capacity for absorption in small worlds. Each person inhabits their own unique small world, and like a movie, it is possible to exit from it and feel confused and unsettled.

The boundary between larger and smaller is represented on the Tree of Life by *Da'at*, Knowledge. *Da'at* is like going into the cinema and coming out of the cinema. It marks an epistemological boundary between a bounded world, and the world that contains it.

Da'at can also mark a gateway for an *emissary of light*. An entity from the larger world enters the smaller world. There is an encounter with a teacher, or an entity such as the Holy Guardian Angel, or (in Kabbalah) the prophet Elijah, and this encounter initiates a process

---

246. See *The Myth of the Magus*, E.M. Butler, Cambridge University Press 1948 for a scholarly discussion.

Epilogue

in which one recognises the smallness of the small world. The small world is transformed into a larger world, a larger world that includes the smaller world as a subsidiary element. This might be described as an *illumination*.

One of the most strikingly gnostic ideas in Kabbalah is that of the *Shekhinah*, the exiled presence of God. We are not exiled and alone in a Godless cosmos. In our collective moments of clarity and unity, we are the *Shekhinah*.

How has the tradition survived into the modern world? It survived the 20th. century in the way many craft traditions survive - by apprenticeship. If someone wants to learn the secrets of blacksmithing, clock-making, plumbing, cabinet-making and so on, then the time-honoured method is to learn the skills through an apprenticeship. An apprenticeship may last for several years, and will typically consist of a small group of apprentices of varying ability assisting a master of a craft.

This was the author's experience. In 1978 I came in contact with just such a small group, and this same teaching tradition continues today. It may seem odd that something as apparently abstract as Kabbalah should be taught like a craft skill, but there is precedent. This is the model for Hermes in the *Corpus Hermeticum*, Simeon bar Yochai in the *Zohar*, and R. Isaac Luria in Safed. It is the format in which Plato chose to present his Dialogues. For as long as there has been a tradition the model has been that of a master and a small group of associates or disciples. Perhaps disciple sounds better than apprentice; for myself, I found there were many practical aspects where active supervision by a person of greater experience was important, and it felt more like an apprenticeship.

Some parts of the tradition appear to possess what I can only describe as 'objective validity'. This is a quality one would hope to find in any transmission of knowledge, esoteric or otherwise. Much of the core material in this book reflects my personal experience of this 'objective validity' - that is, I discovered it for myself. One of the delights of my background reading was the realisation that others had been down the same road, and arrived at the same place. There was an internal coherence to the tradition that spanned millenia.

What of the future? A difficulty with a tradition having a *personae dramatis* extending back to Pythagoras, Orpheus, Moses and Zoroaster is a tendency to look backwards. Whilst looking backwards it is easy to ignore the fact that the world is being propelled forwards by those reading the Book of Nature, what we call science. The transfer of scientific knowledge into engineering and technology has produced a constant stream of innovations throughout the nineteenth and twentieth centuries, with confident predictions of a near-complete mastery of nature sometimes in the twenty-first. Madame Blavatsky chose to plant the banner of her 'occult science' in the path of this stampede into the future and was thoroughly trampled for her labours. We seem to want technology. It offers many benefits. It will bring new horrors as well as benefits.

One prediction can be made safely: the Three Pillars of the Fall - separation, appetite, and ignorance - show no sign of weakening. Despite the best efforts of liberals everywhere, the broad mass of people continue to define themselves by ethnicity and ideology, so that almost every day there are photos of beheadings, crucifixions, torture, bombings, and countless forms of mass murder; and these spread across large areas of our world.

The pathology of separation, based on nothing more than arbitrary labels, is illustrated by the 1971 Stanford Prison experiment, where some students were designated 'warders' and others 'prisoners'. What began as arbitrary labels became dysfunctional, and the experiment was terminated because it breached ethical boundaries. The sense of "us and them" extends into every part of society; people define themselves by attachments to novelties and ephemera of the most absurd kinds. These worlds of separation and attachment are often claustrophobic and sterile, and horrifying in their sparseness.

Appetite is an overwhelming force, especially our appetites for novelty and experience. The advertising industry cultivates appetite and we are deluged by messages to consume. We are bombarded by images of supposedly perfect experiences - perfect meals, perfect holidays, perfect partners, perfect homes.

The pathological endpoint of appetite - its *klippot* - is repetition, the repetition of addiction, where satisfaction is never achieved. Gambling, pornography, gluttony, alcohol - these addictions suck the life out of life. The perfect product is a pharmaceutical that makes people completely content for a few minutes at the cost of all their goods, forever. There is an inexorable logic behind the manipulation of appetite. It is to place us in the power of someone else.

Ignorance is the inability to comprehend that there might be an alternative to *smallness*. In a world dominated by separation and appetite, power flows to those who understand how to exploit our

Epilogue

attachments. This is what one finds in the burgeoning ecosystem of alternative spirituality. We have been educated to consume; this is what we understand. So we consume spirituality. The escape becomes the trap.

The experience of history would suggest that the tradition will remain what it has always been: a discipline for the few. This leaves it fragile and easily disrupted. I finish here in the hope that you have understood what the tradition is, and why some people are drawn to it. I leave you also in the hope that this book may inspire some readers to carry it forward into the incomprehensible future.

The Hermetic Kabbalah

Index

2001 A Space Odyssey 299

A Christmas Carol 427
A Guide for the Perplexed 6
A Practical Guide to Qabalistic Symbolism 196
A Treatise on the Emanations of the Left Side 203
Abba 43, 47, 47–48, 51, 188, 267, 268
Abraham 87, 113, 255
Abulafia, R. Abraham 135, 137, 312, 313, 405, 411
Achilles 372
Adam 16, 18, 50, 62, 63, 65, 66, 69, 71, 85, 89, 90, 203, 296, 338, 346
Adam Kadmon - see Primordial Adam
Adamas 62, 66
Adeptus Exemptus 123
Adeptus Major 123
Adeptus Minor 123
Adonai 32, 137, 207
Adonai ha Aretz 207
Adonai Melekh 207
aesthesis 234
Aethyr 209, 210, 211, 212, 216, 221
Against the Gnostics 296, 338
Aggadah 311
Agrippa, Heinrich Cornelius 8, 38, 135, 146–149, 196, 198, 209, 221, 403, 407
Air (element) 228, 230, 233, 234
Aiwass 414, 418
Akasha 210, 220
Akhatriel 66
Akkadian 262
Alexander the Great 271
Al-Ghazali 6
Alienation 160, 164, 165, 192, 230, 339
Aliens 261
Alkabetz, R. Solomon 55
Alkindi 6, 146, 220
Allah 262
Also Sprach Zarathustra 331
Amenti 279
Anafiel 66
Ancient of Days 46
Aniel 236
Anthropos 66
Antipathy 12
Appetite 94, 346, 347, 372, 394, 407, 411, 434, 436
Aquinas, St. Thomas 6
Aralim 266
Archetypes 43, 384
archons 296, 300
Ari - see Luria, R.Isaac
Arikh Anpin 43, 46–47, 48, 56, 57, 138, 282, 287
Aristotle 78, 94, 106, 107, 142, 349, 393
Arizal - see Luria, R. Isaac
Ark of the Covenant 45, 50
Ascended Masters 418
Ascent 150, 165, 195, 197, 244, 332, 420, 433
Asclepius
    Healer 234
Asclepius
    Hermetic Text 143, 146, 148
Asherah 262
Ashkenazi Chassidim 65
Ashlag, R. Yehudah 76, 90, 91, 98, 102
Assiah 16, 75, 77, 78, 81, 147, 269, 339, 425, 426
Astral Light 220
Astral Plane 216

Atik Yomin 46, 282
Atika Kadisha 46
Atlas 217
Atzilut 16, 75, 77, 78, 188
Autoscopy 111, 409
averot 92
Averroës 6
Avicenna 6, 146
ayin 12, 183

Baal 259
Bach, Johann Sebastian 178
Bacon, Roger 146
Bahir 49, 50, 66, 85, 86, 87, 188, 218, 412
Bailey, Alice 417, 418
bar Yohai, R. Simeon 46, 70, 71, 73, 138, 435
Be'er Sheva 53, 268, 275
Beatrice (Dante) 419
Beauty 240, 241, 242, 243, 244
beinoni 78
ben 292, 295
ben Avuyah, Elisha 66
ben Hakkanah, R. Nehunya 412
ben Joseph, R. Akiva 70
ben Judah, R. Eleazar (of Worms) 88, 408, 413
ben Kalonymous, R. Samuel (the Pious) 413
ben Nachman, R. Moses 94
ben Nahman, R. Samuel 66
ben Samuel, R. Judah (the Pious) 45, 137, 413
ben Shimon Halevi, Z'ev 310
Bene Elohim 228, 236
Bennet, Elizabeth 192
berakhot 15
bereshit 48, 271, 283
Bereshit Rabba 63
Bergman, Ingrid 202
Bet Din 256
Bible 11, 17, 30, 32, 45, 48, 56, 66, 136, 143, 159, 262, 311, 402, 410
Big Bang 307

Binah 28, 32, 34, 44, 47, 51, 53, 54, 56, 64, 73, 81, 82, 88, 95, 100, 107, 108, 123, 151, 152, 172, 176, 187, 188, 189, 190, 191, 192, 201, 208, 213, 263, 265–280, 286, 292, 293, 295, 300, 322, 329, 331, 332, 395, 430
Black Death 84
Black Widow 275
Blake, William 222, 297
Blavatsky, H.P. 89, 149, 220, 341, 342, 417, 422, 436
Blessed Virgin Mary 275
Boaz 187
boddhisattva 418
Book of Black Magic 136
Book of Concealed Mystery - see *Sefer de-Tzeniuta*
Books of Jeu 119, 127, 246, 298
Brahman 283
Brer Rabbit 372
Briah 16, 75, 77, 78, 81, 147, 269, 425, 426, 427
Bride 16, 50–56, 68, 69, 208, 407
Bruno, Giordano 8
Buddhism 430
Budge, E.A. 422
Bulwer-Lytton, Edward 300
Byatt, A.S. 386

Caliban 383
Calvary 423
Calvin, John 202
Campbell, Joseph 374
Canaan 262
Cardinal Points 211
Cardinal Virtues 94
    Justice 95, 393
    Strength/Fortitude 95, 393
    Temperance 95, 393
    Wisdom/Prudence 94, 95, 393
Cassiel 266
Catastrophe 19, 338, 339
Categorical Imperative 91, 102, 394
Cattani, Francesco 144

Causal Determinism 286
Celestial Hierarchies 365
Chabad 268
chaiim 218
Chaiot ha Kodesh 280, 288, 290, 292, 295, 297
Chaldean Oracles 401
Chalmers, David 348
Chaos Magic 150
chasmal 262, 290
Chasmalim 253, 262
Chesed 28, 31, 32, 34, 35, 37, 39, 40, 48, 51, 52, 53, 64, 73, 85–87, 89, 95, 97, 100, 102, 123, 151, 173, 187, 189, 190, 192, 205, 206, 219, 234, 241, 242, 243, 244, 246, 251–264, 268, 275, 276, 287, 288, 300, 301, 322, 329, 394, 395
Chiah 108
Child 81, 240, 245, 385, 424, 425, 426, 427
Chögyam Trungpa 342
Chokhmah 25, 28, 32, 34, 44, 47, 51, 64, 73, 81, 82, 95, 101, 108, 123, 151, 172, 175, 176, 187, 188, 189, 190, 192, 201, 218, 219, 265–280, 283, 286, 292, 293, 322, 330, 332, 333, 395, 430
Chokhmah ha Tzeruf 312
Cholem Yesodeth 200
Choronzon 100, 300, 301, 302, 303, 428, 429
Christ 57, 62, 69, 118, 133, 424
Christian Church 134
Chronos 277
Cipher Manuscripts 318
Circle Cross 210, 212
Cognitive Behaviour Therapy 384
conjunctio 222, 385
Consciousness 186, 369–374, 381, 416
Constantine, Emperor 139
Constitutio Criminalis Carolina 148
Cordovero, R. Moses 22, 27, 28, 29, 30, 55, 91, 98, 102, 126, 140, 186, 338

Corinthians 65, 69
Cornell, Tony 400
Corpus Hermeticum 105, 110, 118, 137, 143, 145, 146, 147, 149, 151, 296, 435
Couliano, Ioan 342
Counterfeiting Spirit 119, 300, 376, 379, 397
Counting the *Omer* 275
Craftsman (Platonic Demiurge) 166
Crossing the Abyss 300
Crowley, Aleister 39, 96, 100, 112, 125, 196, 222, 300, 301, 302, 303, 304, 378, 402, 403, 413, 414, 415, 416, 418, 420, 428, 429, 430
Crucifixion 423
Cybernetics 329

Da'at 28, 73, 81, 82, 99–101, 178, 201, 241, 269, 270, 274, 280, 291–307, 330, 406, 427, 428, 434
Dadouchos 123
Daedelus 207
daemon (personal) 406
daemones 130, 132, 365
Damasio, Antonio 372, 391
Dan, Joseph 85, 88, 101
Daniel
  Book of 45, 46
  Prophet 66
Dante Alighieri 111, 117, 120, 122, 353, 419
Darwin, Charles 155, 166, 221
Daughter 16, 44, 47, 50–56, 72
De Abstinentia 146
De Mysteriis 138, 139, 146
De Sacrificiis et Magia 146
Dead Sea Scrolls 245
Death (Tarot) 278
Dee, John 91, 100, 150, 301, 401
deiknymena 124
Demeter 121, 423
Dennet, Daniel 372
Dependent Origination 247
Descartes, René 110, 158, 348, 370
Destroyed Worlds 87–89, 92, 205

Determinism 171–174, 201, 202
devekut 19
Dickens, Charles 256, 427
dies saturni 277
Diminution of the Moon 382
Din 28, 30, 31, 35, 37, 46, 48, 52, 53, 55, 85–87, 89, 90, 92, 93, 102, 173, 186, 189, 202, 203, 205, 206, 235, 242, 243, 244, 252, 257, 258, 261, 287, 288, 305, 339, 394
Dionysus 121
Discrimination 200, 207, 223
Dittany of Crete 401
Divine Comedy 353
Divine Intellect 15, 76, 329
Divine Names 7, 13, 30, 32, 36, 38, 72, 73, 135, 137, 140, 151, 196, 198, 207, 230, 405
Doctrine of the Mean 94, 95, 393
doppelgänger 111, 220, 408
Doré, Gustav 116
Double Letters 316
Dragon 300
dromena 124
Duality 12
Duat 279
Dumbledore 141, 433
Dungeons and Dragons 132
Dust Devils 303

Eagleman, David 372
Eden 85, 434
Ego 223, 224, 246, 247, 258, 261, 303, 306, 307, 322, 324, 327, 374–378, 396, 426, 427
Eheieh 32, 287
Eilmer of Malmesbury 207
Einstein, Albert 172, 174, 189, 213
El 32, 67, 262
El Chai 32, 293
Eleazar of Worms - see ben Judah, R. Eleazar
Elemental Letters 317
Elements 122, 208, 209, 210, 211, 295

Elements of Theology 160
Eleusinian Mysteries 121, 122, 123, 423, 424
Elijah 434
Eliot, T.S. 35, 242, 292, 293
Elohim 32, 48, 229, 236, 262, 266, 410
Elohim Gevor 262
Elohim Tzabaot 32, 228, 230
Eloi 205
Emanation 14–15, 17, 19, 155, 159–166, 183, 185, 195, 230
Emerald Tablet of Hermes 222
Emergence 166–171, 331
Emergency Medical Hologram 371, 373
Emissary of Light 112, 249, 298, 406, 434
Empedocles 87
En Sof 12, 22, 28, 36, 46, 47, 72, 92, 93, 162, 172, 183, 185, 187, 221, 272, 281–290, 292
Enneads 145, 160, 242, 243
Enoch 288, 341
Enoch Texts 45
Enochian Keys 100
Enuma Elish 259, 306
Ephesus 232
Equanimity 328
eros 232
Esau 89
Euclid 160
Euridice 377
Eve 16, 50, 62, 85, 89, 203, 296, 338, 346
Evil 83–103, 305, 339
Exile 19
Extended Tree 80, 81, 82, 127, 270, 293, 425, 426
Ezekiel
  Book of 45, 61, 68
  Prophet 17, 65, 66, 262, 288

Fall 62, 89, 433, 436
Family 16

Father 16, 44, 47, 48, 57, 72, 188, 275, 280, 293, 295, 332
Faust 141, 148, 433
Ficino, Marcelio 120, 138, 141–146, 147, 149, 220, 403
Fifty Gates 266, 276, 277
Fine, Lawrence 18
First Swirlings 123
First Temple 50
Firth, Violet - see Fortune, Dion
Fixed Signs (Zodiac) 290
Fixed Stars 123
Florence 142, 146
Fludd, Robert 36, 122
Force 13, 186, 311
Form 13, 186, 311
Fortune, Dion 39, 96, 97, 98, 102, 125, 196, 210, 221, 279, 310, 401, 403, 404, 416, 417, 418, 420
Four Quartets 292
Four Worlds 15, 16, 52, 75–82, 162
Fractal 18
Frazer, James George 245, 423
Free Will 174–176, 202, 339
Freemasonry 423
Freud, Sigmund 112, 383, 384

Gabriel 216, 217, 388
Gaia 113
Galen 142, 143
Gandalf 141, 433
Gate of Death 279
Gates of Light 22, 30, 135, 136, 196
Gedulah 28, 253
gematria 414
Gemistus, George 142, 145
Genesis 31, 39, 46, 49, 53, 63, 68, 88, 108, 259, 261, 271, 272, 283, 293, 434
genizah 311
Gerona 6
Gevurah 28, 32, 34, 39, 48, 51, 64, 73, 95, 97, 123, 151, 187, 189, 190, 192, 234, 241, 246, 248, 251–264, 268, 299, 322, 329, 330, 395
Ghandi 329

Ghayat al-Hakim - see Picatrix
Giger, H.R. 367
Gikatilla, R. Joseph 22, 30, 32, 129, 135–137, 140, 151, 196, 262, 287, 288, 404, 405
gnosis 296
goetia 134, 150, 400, 402, 405
Gold 240, 326, 338, 372
Golden Dawn, Hermetic Order 72, 96, 100, 102, 112, 117, 122, 123, 124, 125, 127, 149, 150, 151, 196, 197, 208, 209, 245, 248, 279, 300, 301, 317, 318, 319, 320, 404, 405, 413, 424
Golden Mean - see Doctrine of the Mean
Goldilocks 242, 255
Golem 312
Gomorrah 263
Goodrick-Clarke, Nicolas 433
Grant, Kenneth 101, 304, 305, 306, 307
Gray, William 99, 102, 125
Gray's Anatomy 171
Great Abyss 16, 99–101, 280, 300, 301, 303, 304, 305, 306, 428, 430
Great Chain of Being 15, 17, 161, 346
Great White Head 47, 48
Great Work 102, 240, 244, 245, 338, 395, 406
Greater Assembly 71
Green, Arthur 32, 71
Greer, John Michael 196
Grimm's Fairy Tales 386
Groom 16, 51, 56, 68, 69, 70, 407
Guardian of the Threshold 100, 300
Gurdjieff, George 378

Hades 121
ha-Kohen, R. Isaac 88
halakhah 92, 255, 256
hallal 72
Haniel - see Aniel
Harmony of Parts 353, 363
Harry Potter (novels) 132, 175
Heavenly Man - see Primordial

Adam
Hebrew Alphabet 314
Hegemon 123
heimarmene 296
Hekhalot
    Texts 45, 67, 125, 289, 412
Hekhalot Rabbatai 412
Heliopolitan Ennead 51
Helios 420
Henry IV 399
Hermes 372, 435
Hermes Trimegistus 234
Hermetic Society 423
Hermit (Tarot) 278
Hiereus 123
Hierophant 123
Higher Self 249, 424
Hillel 90, 248
Hippocrates 143
Hippocratic Oath 248
Hobbes, Thomas 344
Hod 28, 32, 39, 48, 51, 64, 73, 81, 82, 95, 123, 151, 187, 190, 191, 192, 209, 210, 223, 224, 227–237, 241, 269, 270, 324, 325, 326, 327, 328, 330, 395
Holmes, Sherlock 192
Hologram 18
Holon 35–37, 38
Holy Guardian Angel 112, 124, 125, 200, 240, 246, 249, 347, 405, 405–420, 434
Holy Living Creatures - see *Chiaot ha Kodesh*
Holy of Holies 45, 50, 268
Homeostasis 37, 168, 244, 355
Homer 372
Homeric Hymn to Demeter 121
House of Cards 396
Hume, David 129, 230
Hymn of the Pearl 110

Ialdebaoth 373, 376, 419
Iamblichus 9, 124, 127, 130, 132, 137–141, 143, 145, 146, 148, 149, 151, 403, 405, 407
IAO 62
Iblis 387
Icarus 207
Idealism 158
Idra Rabba 46, 58, 71, 129, 138
Idra Zuta 46, 71, 138
Idrot 46, 56, 57, 71–72, 73
Ignorance 434
ilah 262
Iliad 410
Imma 43, 47, 47–48, 51, 188, 208, 266, 275
Indra 259
Inferior Mother 200
Initiation 279, 433
Inner-Plane Adepti 418
Innocent VIII 146
Intelligence 329, 351, 365–369
Ipsissimus 123, 125
Irrigation 15
Isaac 255
Isaac the Blind - see R. Isaac the Blind
Isaiah
    Book of 31, 45, 65, 90
    Prophet 66
Ishim 200, 208
Isis 134, 275
Isis Unveiled 220

Jachin 187
Jacob's Ladder 127
Jah 32, 267
Jahoel 288
Janus 292, 299
Jaynes, Julian 410
Jeremiah
    Book of 50
Jesus 57, 69, 70, 113, 119, 211, 235, 245, 298, 392, 394, 422, 424
Jeu 62, 66
Job
    Book of 85, 278, 340
John

Book of 279, 421, 422
John Barleycorn 423
Joyce, James 178
jubilee 275, 276
Judas Thomas 110
Judge Death 257
Judge Dredd 257
Jung, C.G. 43, 112, 381, 384, 385, 386, 403, 404, 414, 415, 416, 418, 419, 420
Jupiter 123, 144, 253, 258, 299
Justice 263
Justinian, Emperor 134, 160

Kabbalah Denudata 58
Kafka, Franz 75, 256
Kallah 54, 55, 200, 208
Kamael 252, 263
Kant, Immanuel 75, 91, 102, 213, 307, 394
Kaplan, Aryeh 310
kav 72
kavod 45, 50, 51, 65
Keats, John 388
Kelly, Edward 100, 150, 301, 401
kerux 234
Keter 25, 28, 30, 32, 47, 54, 64, 73, 76, 81, 82, 91, 95, 99, 123, 126, 151, 165, 172, 173, 175, 176, 185, 187, 192, 195, 201, 208, 212, 213, 268, 269, 274, 280, 281–290, 292, 299, 322, 324, 330, 332, 333, 395, 425, 426, 427, 430
Key of Solomon 120, 302
Khorsia 208, 266
Kiddush Levanah 54
King 16, 49, 50, 51, 81, 111, 191, 222, 230, 240, 245, 254, 382, 424, 425, 426
King, Martin Luther 329
Kingdom of Heaven 133
Kings of Edom 48, 88, 96, 305
Kingsford, Anna 423, 424
Kircher, Athanasius 22, 23, 318
Kirk, James T. 192
klippah 86

klippot 78, 89, 92, 95, 96, 97, 99, 101, 152, 185, 247, 256, 299, 305, 339, 430, 436
Knight, Gareth 39, 125, 196, 309
Koestler, Arthur 35
Kokab 228
Koran 387
Korzybski, Arthur 325
kosher 256
Kramer, Heinrich 146
Kronos 277
Kundalini Yoga 72

La Belle Dame Sans Merci 388
La Nausée 324
Laban 57, 208
laban 218
Lamed Vav 87
lapis 385, 423
Laplace, Pierre-Simon 286
Lawrence, D.H. 283, 287
Lazarus 422
Lead (Metal) 326
Leah 57, 208
Left Side 99, 102, 123, 203, 257, 263
legomena 124
Leibniz, Gottfried Wilhelm 161
Lekha Dodi 55
Lenin, Vladimir 205
Lesser Assembly 71
Lesser Banishing Ritual 405
Lesser Mother 268, 275
Letters (Hebrew Alphabet) 310–320
Levanah 216
Levi, Eliphas 220
Leviathon 259
Leviticus 394
Liber 231 304
Liber 418, The Vision and the Voice 301
Liber 777 196
Liber AL vel Legis 414, 415
Liber Novus (Red Book) 416
Lightning Flash 122, 176, 184, 186, 187–192, 300, 327
Lilith 53, 54, 89, 113, 203

Long Face 46
Lovecraft, H.P. 89, 306
Lower Sea 15
Lucifer 306
Luria, R. Isaac 18, 35, 43, 56, 58, 71, 72, 85, 88, 92, 94, 101, 112, 195, 203, 318, 320, 338, 339, 435
Luzzatto, R. Moses 17, 24, 49, 59

ma'lak 248
Maccabees 393
Macrocosm 82, 109, 177, 270, 337, 338, 405
Macroprosopus 46, 282
Mad Tom O'Bedlam 302
Madim 252
maggid 406
Magus 123
Maimonides 6, 48, 67, 71, 263
Malakim 240, 248
Malkah 54, 55, 200, 208
Malkhut 28, 29, 30, 32, 39, 40, 44, 51, 52, 52–54, 56, 64, 73, 76, 81, 82, 86, 91, 95, 107, 122, 137, 151, 165, 173, 176, 178, 185, 187, 191, 192, 195, 199–213, 217, 219, 222, 223, 224, 225, 233, 244, 255, 258, 260, 268, 269, 274, 275, 276, 284, 285, 286, 287, 288, 290, 299, 305, 306, 322, 324, 325, 326, 330, 332, 395, 425, 426, 427, 428
Malleus Maleficarum 146
Mandala 211
Mandeans 63, 73
Mandela, Nelson 329
Mandlebrot Set 286
Mani 111
Marah 266
Marcos, Imelda 261
Marduk 159, 259, 306, 427
Marpa 378
Mars 89, 123, 252, 261, 263
Marx, Karl 205
Masorites 311
Master of the Temple 123, 125

Materialism 158
Mathers, S.L. 39, 58, 96, 100, 413, 414, 424
Matronita 52
Matt, Daniel 89
Matter 15, 30, 76, 84, 139, 145, 158, 161, 163, 164, 165, 172, 200, 279, 286, 349, 386
Matthew
  Book of 392
Maxwell, James Clerk 157
Mazlot 267, 280
Mead, G.R.S. 149
Medici
  Cosimo 142, 143
  Lorenzo 143
  Piero 143
melekh 240
Melqart 187
Mercury 123, 222, 228, 230, 233, 234
Mercy 13, 31, 186, 188, 189, 253, 255
Merkavah
  Mystics 75, 78, 125
  Period 208, 284
  Texts 125, 289, 412
  Throne Chariot 65, 78, 284, 288, 289, 405
Merlin 141
Messiah 62
Metatron 45, 66, 67, 78, 288
Metropolis (Film) 368
Michael 66, 236, 240, 248, 300, 345, 388
Microcosm 82, 109, 177, 269, 337, 338, 405
Microprosopus 46, 240, 241, 242, 294
Middle Pillar 35, 73, 95, 219, 244
Midgard Serpent 259
Milarepa 378
Mildness 186
Milton, John 306, 383
Mind 145, 158, 416
Minsky, Marvin 372, 385, 386
Mishnah 32, 56
Mishneh Torah 263
Mithras Liturgy 420

mitosis 298
mitzvot 78, 92, 93, 255, 256, 322
Moon 54, 122, 216, 222, 223, 245, 246, 293, 296, 382, 383, 384, 385
Moore, Alan 304
Morlocks 205
Morris, William 40
Moses 8, 50, 66, 84, 96, 143, 255, 275, 276, 287, 435
Moses of Leon - see R. Moses of Leon
Most High 100
Mother 16, 44, 47, 48, 50–56, 72, 165, 280, 293, 332
Mother Earth 200
Mother Letters 316
Mother of Form 188, 190, 266, 279, 322, 331
Mother Zion 50
Mount Sinai 275
mushin 370
musica universalis 144

Nathan of Gaza 93
Nature 434, 436
Necessity 294, 296, 297, 298, 327, 339, 376, 379
Nefesh 107, 108, 112, 426
Negative Evil 98
Neopagan 211
Neoplatonism 29, 76, 165, 172, 173, 176, 219, 221, 230, 286, 338, 365, 379, 386
Nephesh 78
Neshamah 78, 107, 108, 111, 112, 426
neti neti 283
Netzach 28, 32, 39, 48, 51, 64, 73, 81, 82, 95, 123, 151, 152, 187, 190, 191, 192, 209, 210, 217, 223, 224, 227–237, 241, 269, 270, 274, 322, 326, 327, 328, 395
Neuburg, Victor 301, 302, 428
New Age iii, iv, 165, 220, 342, 348
Newton, Isaac 157, 161
Nicomachean Ethics 94
niddah 54

Nietzsche, Friedrich 247, 331
Nightside of Eden 304, 305, 306
Nihilism 247, 430
nitzotzot 92
Nogah
noosphere 326
Nothingness 11
Noumena 213, 223, 306
nous 329
Nukva 43, 49, 51, 54–55, 56, 57, 218, 222, 275, 293, 407
Nukva Ze'ir - see *Nukva*

Odin 159
Odysseus 372
Oedipus Aegyptiacus 22, 23
olam ha-ba 274
Old Father Time 278
Old Ones 306
Olympus 383
Omer 276
On the Origin of the Species 221
Ophanim 267
Origen 67, 69
Orpheus 121, 145, 377, 435
Orphic
  Mysteries 377, 423, 424
  Singing 144
  Tradition 121
Orwell, George 256
Osiris 134

Pachad 28, 252, 257
Pankhurst, Emmeline 329
Paradise Lost 383
Pardes 201, 268
Pardes Rimonim 22, 27, 28
Partzuf 34, 188, 241, 244
Partzufim 5, 16, 43–59, 71, 72, 112, 155, 196
Pascal, Blaise 411
Passover 275
Patai, Raphael 411
Paths 320–333
Paths to Wisdom 196

Penis 268
Persephone 121, 423
Peter of Abano 146
Phaedo 362
Phenomena 223, 306
Philae 134
Philemon (Jung) 415, 418
Philo 65
Philosopher's Stone 240, 372
Philosophus 123
Phoenicia 262
Picatrix 146, 408
Pico, Giovanni 109, 143, 146, 147, 148
Pillar of Mercy 268
Pillar of Severity 268
Pillars (of the Tree) 13, 22, 31, 126, 149, 165, 172, 184, 186–187, 285, 309, 347, 436
Pillars of Hercules 187
Pirkei d'Rabbi Eliezar 405
Pistis Sophia 119, 120, 127, 211, 246, 298
Pistoia, Leonardo de' 143
Plato 15, 106, 110, 121, 133, 142, 143, 145, 146, 160, 161, 162, 163, 166, 271, 293, 296, 346, 362, 372, 391, 393, 435
Platonic Academy 134, 160
Plenitude 15, 287
Pleroma 338
Pletho - see Gemistus, George
Plotinus 9, 15, 76, 78, 127, 138, 139, 142, 145, 160, 161, 163, 164, 165, 241, 242, 243, 244, 296, 337, 338
Poimandres 105, 110, 434
Poison 299
Pole (celestial) 293
Porphyry 138, 139, 146
Portae Lucis 22
Positive Evil 98, 99
Practical Wisdom 200, 394
Practicus 123
Primordial Adam 5, 16, 45, 61–74, 138, 230
Princess 16

prisca theologia 8, 148
Procession and Reversion 7, 17, 221
Proclus 127, 143, 144, 146, 148, 160, 212, 386
Prospero 141, 433
Provençal Kabbalists 5
Proverbs 270, 330
Psalms 259
pseudo-Dionysus 120, 124
psyche 106, 197
Ptolomy, astronomer 120
Pullman, Philip 406
Pythagoras 8, 121, 133, 144, 159, 435

qarin 406
qualia 145
Queen 16, 49, 50–56, 111, 165, 191, 208, 222, 382
Quintessence 209, 221

R. Abbahu of Caesarea 87
R. Akiva 70, 290
R. Isaac of Acre 135
R. Isaac the Blind 6
R. Moses of Leon 108, 109, 135
r'tzon 174, 273, 284
Ra (sun god) 255
Rachamim 28, 240
Rachel 50, 57, 208
Ramak - see Cordovero, R. Moses
Ramban - see ben Nachman, R. Moses
Randi, James 400
Raphael 228, 236, 248, 388
rasha 78
Ratziel 267
Reason 372, 373, 383
Receptacle of the Emanations 216, 217
Reconciliation 13
Redeemer 62, 249, 385
Regardie, Israel 125
Reuchlin, Johann 147, 148
Revelation of St. John 45, 289, 290, 383, 422, 427

Rhineland 413
Riccio, Paolo 22, 30, 196
Ripley, Ellen 192, 261
Rosencreutz, Christian 423
Rosenroth, Knorr von 58
Rosicrucian Manifestos 423
Rossetti, Dante Gabriel 111
Rowling J.K. 132
Ruach 78, 107, 108, 112, 426
Rum Maalah 282
Run and Return 17, 72, 332

Sabbatai Zevi - see Zevi, Sabbatai
Sabbath 55
Sabbath Queen 55
Sacrificed God 81, 240, 245, 246, 424, 425, 426
Safed 71, 91
Safed Tree 22
Saklas 373, 376
Samael 54, 89, 252, 257, 263, 299, 301, 373, 376, 428
Sandalphon 200, 207, 208, 284, 288
Sartre, Jean-Paul 324
Satan 113, 387
Satanism 132
Saturday 275
Saturn 123, 144, 275, 277
Scale-Independence 18
Scale-Invariance 196
Scholem, Gershom 4, 70, 73, 101, 111, 186, 408
Scrooge 427
Scrying 401
sechel 269
Second Temple 50, 84
Secret Book of John 376
Sefer Chasidim 137, 413
Sefer de-Tzeniuta 46, 47, 48, 58, 71, 96
Sefer Raziel 131
Sefer Yetzirah 17, 25, 29, 30, 38, 39, 45, 67, 161, 187, 208, 212, 276, 284, 289, 293, 294, 304, 309, 310, 312, 313, 318
Self 240, 322

Self-Similarity 18
Semen 218, 268
Separation 31, 90, 164, 192, 201, 232, 235, 261, 272, 322, 324, 331, 346, 347, 434
Serafim 252, 263
Seven 275
Seven Days of Creation 40, 159, 188, 274, 275, 276
Severity 13, 31, 186, 188, 189, 252, 255
sh'va 275
shabbat 55, 275, 276
Shabtai 266, 275, 277
Shaddai 32
Shakespeare, William 91, 302, 399
Shavuot 275, 276
Shekhinah 45, 50–56, 57, 137, 203, 208, 275, 435
Shema 24, 213, 284, 324, 405
Shemesh 240
shevirah 35
shevirat ha-kelim 88, 92
Shi'ur Komah 45, 48, 66–67, 70, 71, 108
shmita 276
Shokek, Simon 93
Short Face 46
Shushan Sodot 408
Simeon Stylites 392
Sirius 292
Sister 50–56
sitra achra 92, 93, 299, 305
Smith, Morton 119
Societas Rosicruciana in Anglia 122
Society for Psychical Research 399
Society of Mind 376, 378, 381, 385–389
Socrates 353, 362, 363
Sodom 87, 263
Solar Plexus 240
Solomon 68, 270, 422
Son 16, 44, 47, 57, 72, 240, 292, 295
Son of God 240
Song of Songs 48, 51, 52, 54, 67–71, 111, 218

Sophia 57, 338
Sothis 292
Soul
   Administering Intelligence 344, 349
   Aesthesis 107
   Animal 107, 355–358
   Archetypes 112
   As the image of God 108
   Ascent 109
   Awakening 109
   Composite 351, 354
   Corruption 132
   Descent 140
   Dianoia 107
   Dignity 108
   Divine 362–363
   Ego 112, 192
   Fall 108
   Fragility 344
   Harmony of the Body 362
   Higher Self 111, 347
   Id 112
   Imprisoned 197
   Intellectual 107
   Neoplatonism 145, 163, 164
   Nutritive 107, 354–355
   Platonism 348
   Rational 107, 358–362
   Rectification 152, 244, 246, 337–349, 354, 433
   Simulacrum 352
   Structure 106
   Superego 112
   Synonyms 347
Spanish Inquisition 84, 146
Spermatozoa 268
Spiritualism 220, 342
Spock 191, 327, 390
Sponheim 148
Sprenger, James 146
SRIA - see *Societas Rosicruciana in Anglia*
St. Anthony 428
St. Bernard of Clairvaux 69
St. Paul 63, 65, 69, 345
Stanford Prison Experiment 436

Star Trek (TV) 377
Star Trek Voyager (TV) 371
Steinsaltz, R. Adin 92, 93
Stolistes 123
Summis Desiderantes Affectibus 146
Sun 123, 144, 145, 222, 240, 245, 246, 293, 296, 382, 385, 401, 408
sunthemata 140, 145, 151, 152, 405, 419
Superior Mother 266, 275
Surround Inhibition 371
Symmetry Breaking 286
Synchronicity 404
Syzygy 51, 56

T4 Bacteriophage 367, 368
Talmud 6, 49, 66, 69, 87, 90, 124, 218, 276, 401
Tanya 78, 92
Taoism 13, 332
Tarot 401
Tartarus 258
Tebunah 47, 266
Tectatrys 161, 162
Telesterion 122
Teli 294, 297
temenos 211, 405
Ten Commandments 255
terma 142
terton 142
teshuvah 19, 332, 337, 338
Tetragrammaton 12, 16, 32, 44, 46, 47, 48, 54, 62, 71, 135, 136, 190, 207, 208, 230, 236, 240, 241, 244, 255, 262, 288
Tetramorph 293
The Book of Lies 303
The Book of Sacred Magic of Abramelin the Mage 411
The Brethren of Purity 6
The Celestial Hierarchies 120, 124
The Cosmic Doctrine 279, 416, 417
The Divine Comedy 111
The Exegesis on the Soul 407
The Godfather 157

The Golden Bough 245, 423
The Good 15, 30, 161, 163, 165
The Inner Light 424
The Intelligible 161, 162
The Lady of Shalott 427
The Many 140, 224
The Matrix 111
The Mystical Qabalah 196, 221, 404
The One 15, 17, 30, 76, 138, 140, 145, 161, 163, 164, 192, 386
The One and the Many 7, 12, 160, 164, 172, 178, 193, 212, 244, 245, 322, 324, 330
The Origin of Consciousness in the Breakdown of the Bicameral Mind 410
The Perfect Sermon - see Asclepius
The Republic 163, 393
The Simpsons 353
The Society of Mind (Book) 385
The Theology of Aristotle 243
Theoricus 122
Theosophical Society 417, 423, 424
Theosophy 221, 342
theourgia 134
Theurgy 109, 129–153, 197, 397, 404, 419
Thirty-Two Paths 101, 276, 309
Thor 259, 260, 427
Thoth/Hermes 8
Three Books of Occult Philosophy 135, 147, 148, 196, 198
Three Pillars - see Pillars (of the Tree)
Throne of Glory 65, 66, 67, 70, 78, 412
Tiamat 159, 259
Tiferet 28, 32, 39, 44, 48, 51, 57, 64, 69, 73, 81, 82, 95, 99, 107, 123, 151, 165, 177, 178, 187, 189, 190, 191, 192, 210, 219, 222, 223, 224, 230, 234, 239–249, 255, 269, 293, 295, 322, 327, 328, 329, 330, 363, 395, 406, 408, 418, 419, 424, 425, 426, 427, 428, 430
tikkun 129, 305, 337

tikkun olam 19, 94, 102, 337
Tilopa 378
Timaeus 166, 293
Tishby, Isaiah 22, 285
Titans 258, 259, 306
tohu va-bohu 259
Tolkien, J.R.R. 403
Torah 6, 55, 84, 275, 311, 394, 404
Torequemada, Tomas de 146
Treasure House of Images 216
Tree of Emanation 26, 100, 319
Tree of Knowledge 203, 339, 346, 434
Tree of Life 4, 21–41
Triads 309
Trithemius 147, 148
tselem 111
Tselem, the Concept of the Astral Body 408
Tunnels of Set 305
Two Faces 309
tympanum 133
Tyson, Donald 147
tzabaot 230, 236
tzadik 49, 88, 216, 218
Tzadikim 108
Tzadikim Nistarim 87
Tzadkiel 253, 262
Tzedek 253
tzeruf 137, 405, 409, 411
tzimtzum 72, 92

Unconsciousness 370
Underwood, Frank 396
Ungrund 221, 368
Unmanifest 169, 322
Upper Sea 15
Uriel 388
Uterus 268

Valentinus 407
Valhalla 204, 383
Vedanta 283
Venice Ghetto 84
Venus 123, 144, 222, 230, 232, 233,

234, 383
Via Dolorosa 423
Viaticum 121
Vices 95
Vices (on the Tree) 395
Vilna Gaon 92
Virgil 419
Virtues 95, 390–396
Virtues (on the Tree) 395
Vita Pythagorae 146
Vital, R. Hayyim 58, 94
Vrita 259

Waite, Arthur Edward 136
Water (element) 229, 230, 233, 234
Webb, Philip 40
Weiner, Norbert 329
Westcott, Wynn 424
Western Esoteric Tradition 127, 433
Wilber, Ken 37, 78
Will 175, 273, 284, 285, 286, 287
Winograd, Terry 366
Womb 332
World Soul 15, 76, 143, 161

Yahoel 66
Yahweh 259, 262, 427
Yahweh Tzabaot 32, 230
Yam 259
Yang 86, 87, 332
Yechidah 108
yesh 12
Yesod 28, 32, 39, 48, 49, 51, 64, 73, 81, 82, 95, 107, 122, 151, 178, 187, 191, 192, 209, 210, 212, 215–225, 233, 244, 245, 269, 270, 275, 276, 293, 294, 299, 324, 325, 326, 327, 395, 427, 428
Yetzirah 16, 75, 77, 78, 81, 147, 269, 271, 425, 426
yichudim 212
yidam 406
Yin 86, 87, 332
Yin-Yang Symbol 13, 86, 332
Ymir 159

yotzer bereshit 66

Zalman, R. Shneur 78
Zanoni 300
Ze'ir Anpin 34, 39, 43, 46, 47, 48, 48–50, 51, 56, 57, 66, 69, 138, 203, 218, 222, 240, 241, 242, 244, 255, 268, 274, 275, 287, 293, 295, 407
Zelator 122
Zen 429
Zeus 121, 258, 259
Zevi, Sabbatai 93, 222
Zoas (Blake) 292, 297
Zodiac 280
Zohar 6, 12, 16, 21, 22, 25, 35, 39, 46, 48, 51, 55, 56, 57, 58, 66, 70, 71, 72, 85, 88, 89, 92, 94, 101, 102, 112, 135, 160, 188, 195, 285, 311, 407, 412
Zoroaster 435

Printed in Great Britain
by Amazon